Great Science Fiction Stories

Great Science Fiction Stories

2001: A Space Odyssey
ARTHUR C. CLARKE

The Demolished Man
ALFRED BESTER

The Day of the Triffids
JOHN WYNDHAM

I, Robot
ISAAC ASIMOV

2001 A Space Odyssey
first published in Great Britain
in 1968 by Hutchinson & Co (Publishers) Ltd
The Demolished Man
first published in Great Britain
in 1953 by Sidgwick & Jackson
The Day of the Triffids
first published in Great Britain
in 1951 by Michael Joseph Ltd
I, Robot
first published in Great Britain
in 1967 by Dobson Books Ltd

This title first published in Great Britain in 1979 by:

Octopus Books Limited
59 Grosvenor Street
London W1

in collaboration with

William Heinemann Limited
10 Upper Grosvenor Street
London W1

and

Martin Secker & Warburg Limited
54 Poland Street
London W1

Revised edition 1982

ISBN 0 904230 98 8

Printed in the United States of America

Contents

2001:
A Space Odyssey

ARTHUR C. CLARKE

FOREWORD

Behind every man now alive stand thirty ghosts, for that is the ratio by which the dead outnumber the living. Since the dawn of time, roughly a hundred billion human beings have walked the planet Earth.

Now this is an interesting number, for by a curious coincidence there are approximately a hundred billion stars in our local universe, the Milky Way. So for every man who has ever lived, in this universe, there shines a star.

But every one of those stars is a sun, often far more brilliant and glorious than the small, nearby star we call *the* Sun. And many – perhaps most – of those alien suns have planets circling them. So almost certainly there is enough land in the sky to give every member of the human species, back to the first apeman, his own private, world-sized heaven – or hell.

How many of those potential heavens and hells are now inhabited and, by what manner of creatures, we have no way of guessing; the very nearest is a million times further away than Mars or Venus, those still remote goals of the next generation. But the barriers of distance are crumbling; one day we shall meet our equals, or our masters, among the stars.

Men have been slow to face this prospect; some still hope that it may never become reality. Increasing numbers, however, are asking: 'Why have such meetings not occurred already, since we ourselves are about to venture into space?'

Why not, indeed? Here is one possible answer to that very reasonable question. But please remember: this is only a work of fiction.

The truth, as always, will be far stranger.

A.C.C.
S.K.

PRIMEVAL NIGHT

CHAPTER I

THE ROAD TO EXTINCTION

The drought had lasted now for ten million years, and the reign of the terrible lizards had long since ended. Here on the Equator, in the continent which would one day be known as Africa, the battle for existence had reached a new climax of ferocity, and the victor was not yet in sight. In this barren and desiccated land only the small or the swift or the fierce could flourish, or even hope to survive.

The man-apes of the veldt were none of these things, and they were not flourishing; indeed, they were already far down the road to racial extinction. About fifty of them occupied a group of caves overlooking a small, parched valley, which was divided by a sluggish stream fed from snows in the mountains two hundred miles to the north. In bad times the stream vanished completely, and the tribe lived in the shadow of thirst.

It was always hungry, and now it was starving. When the first faint glow of dawn crept into the cave Moon-Watcher saw that his father had died in the night. He did not know that the Old One was his father, for such a relationship was utterly beyond his understanding, but as he looked at the emaciated body he felt a dim disquiet that was the ancestor of sadness.

The two babies were already whimpering for food, but became silent when Moon-Watcher snarled at them. One of the mothers, defending the infant she could not properly feed, gave him an angry growl in return; he lacked the energy even to cuff her for her presumption.

Now it was light enough to leave. Moon-Watcher picked up the shrivelled corpse, and dragged it after him as he bent under the low overhang of the cave. Once outside, he threw the body over his shoulder and stood upright – the only animal in all this world able to do so.

Among his kind, Moon-Watcher was almost a giant. He was nearly five feet high, and though badly undernourished weighed over a hundred pounds. His hairy, muscular body was half-way between ape and man, but his head was already much nearer to man than ape. The forehead was low, and there were ridges over the eye-sockets, yet he

unmistakably held in his genes the promise of humanity. As he looked
out upon the hostile world of the Pleistocene there was already something in his gaze beyond the capacity of any ape. In those dark, deep-
set eyes was a dawning awareness – the first intimations of an intelligence that could not possibly fulfil itself for ages yet, and might soon
be extinguished for ever.

There was no sign of danger, so Moon-Watcher began to scramble
down the almost vertical slope outside the cave, only slightly hindered
by his burden. As if they had been waiting for his signal, the rest of
the tribe emerged from their own homes further down the rock-face,
and began to hasten towards the muddy waters of the stream for their
morning drink.

Moon-Watcher looked across the valley to see if the Others were in
sight, but there was no trace of them. Perhaps they had not yet left
their caves, or were already foraging further along the hillside. Since
they were nowhere to be seen, Moon-Watcher forgot them; he was
incapable of worrying about more than one thing at a time.

First he must get rid of the Old One, but this was a problem that
demanded little thought. There had been many deaths this season,
one of them in his own cave, he had only to put the corpse where he
had left the new baby at the last quarter of the moon, and the hyenas
would do the rest.

They were already waiting, where the little valley fanned out into
the savannah, almost as if they had known that he was coming. Moon-
Watcher left the body under a small bush – all the earlier bones had
already gone – and hurried back to rejoin the tribe. He never thought
of his father again.

His two mates, the adults from the other caves, and most of the
youngsters were foraging among the drought-stunted trees further up
the valley, looking for berries, succulent roots and leaves, and occasional windfalls like small lizards or rodents. Only the babies and the
feeblest of the old folk were left in the caves; if there was any surplus
food at the end of the day's searching they might be fed. If not, the
hyenas would soon be in luck once more.

But this day was a good one – though as Moon-Watcher had no real
remembrance of the past, he could not compare one time with another.
He had found a hive of bees in the stump of a dead tree, and so had
enjoyed the finest delicacy that his people could ever know; he still
licked his fingers from time to time as he led the group homewards
in the late afternoon. Of course, he had also collected a fair number
of stings, but he had scarcely noticed them. He was now as near to contentment as he was ever likely to be; for though he was still hungry,

he was not actually weak with hunger. That was the most for which any man-ape could ever aspire.

His contentment vanished when he reached the stream. The Others were there. They were there every day, but that did not make it any the less annoying.

There were about thirty of them, and they could not have been distinguished from the members of Moon-Watcher's own tribe. As they saw him coming they began to dance, shake their arms, and shriek on their side of the stream, and his own people replied in kind.

And that was all that happened. Though the man-apes often fought and wrestled among each other, their disputes very seldom resulted in serious injuries. Having no claws or fighting canines, and being well protected by hair, they could not inflict much harm on one another. In any event, they had little surplus energy for such unproductive behaviour; snarling and threatening was a much more efficient way of asserting their points of view.

The confrontation lasted about five minutes; then the display died out as quickly as it had begun, and everyone drank his fill of the muddy water. Honour had been satisfied; each group had staked its claim to its own territory. This important business having been settled, the tribe moved off along its side of the river. The nearest worthwhile grazing was now more than a mile from the caves, and they had to share it with a herd of large, antelope-like beasts who barely tolerated their presence. They could not be driven away, for they were armed with ferocious daggers on their foreheads – the natural weapons which the man-apes did not possess.

So Moon-Watcher and his companions chewed berries and fruit and leaves and fought off the pangs of hunger – while all around them, competing for the same fodder, was a potential source of more food than they could ever hope to eat. Yet the thousands of tons of succulent meat roaming over the savannah and through the bush was not only beyond their reach; it was beyond their imagination. In the midst of plenty they were slowly starving to death.

The tribe returned to its cave without incident, in the last light of the day. The injured female who had remained behind cooed with pleasure as Moon-Watcher gave her the berry-covered branch he had brought back, and began to attack it ravenously. There was little enough nourishment here, but it would help her to survive until the wound the leopard had given her had healed, and she could forage for herself again.

Over the valley, a full moon was rising, and a chill wind was blowing down from the distant mountains. It would be very cold tonight – but cold, like hunger, was not a matter for any real concern; it was merely part of the background of life.

Moon-Watcher barely stirred when the shrieks and screams echoed up the slope from one of the lower caves, and he did not need to hear the occasional growl of the leopard to know exactly what was happening. Down there in the darkness old White Hair and his family were fighting and dying, and the thought that he might help in some way never crossed Moon-Watcher's mind. The harsh logic of survival ruled out such fancies, and not a voice was raised in protest from the listening hillside. Every cave was silent, lest it also attract disaster.

The tumult died away, and presently Moon-Watcher could hear the sound of a body being dragged over the rocks. That lasted only a few seconds; then the leopard got a good hold on its kill. It made no further noise as it padded silently away, carrying its victim effortlessly in its jaws.

For a day or two there would be no further danger here, but there might be other enemies abroad, taking advantage of this cold Little Sun that shone only by night. If there was sufficient warning the smaller predators would sometimes be scared away by shouts and screams. Moon-Watcher crawled out of the cave, clambered on to a large boulder beside the entrance, and squatted there to survey the valley.

Of all the creatures who had yet walked on Earth, the man-apes were the first to look steadfastly at the Moon. And though he could not remember it, when he was very young Moon-Watcher would sometimes reach out and try to touch that ghostly face rising above the hills.

He had never succeeded, and now he was old enough to understand why. For first, of course, he must find a high enough tree to climb.

Sometimes he watched the valley, and sometimes he watched the Moon, but always he listened. Once or twice he dozed off, but he slept with a hair-trigger alertness, and the slightest sound would have disturbed him. At the great age of twenty-five he was still in full possession of all his faculties; if his luck continued, and he avoided accidents, disease, predators and starvation, he might survive for as much as another ten years.

The night wore on, cold and clear, without further alarms, and the Moon rose slowly amid equatorial constellations that no human eye would ever see. In the caves, between spells of fitful dozing and fearful waiting, were being born the nightmares of generations yet to be.

And twice there passed slowly across the sky, rising up to the zenith and descending into the east, a dazzling point of light more brilliant than any star.

CHAPTER 2

THE NEW ROCK

Late that night Moon-Watcher suddenly awoke. Tired out by the day's exertions and disasters, he had been sleeping more soundly than usual, yet he was instantly alert at the first faint scrabbling down in the valley.

He sat up in the fetid darkness of the cave, straining his senses out into the night, and fear crept slowly into his soul. Never in his life – already twice as long as most members of his species could expect – had he heard a sound like this. The great cats approached in silence, and the only thing that betrayed them was a rare slide of earth, or the occasional cracking of a twig. Yet this was a continuous crunching noise that grew steadily louder. It seemed that some enormous beast was moving through the night, making no attempt at concealment, and ignoring all obstacles. Once Moon-Watcher heard the unmistakable sound of a bush being uprooted; the elephants and dinotheria did this often enough, but otherwise they moved as silently as the cats.

And then there came a sound which Moon-Watcher could not possibly have identified, for it had never been heard before in the history of the world. It was the clank of metal upon stone.

.   .   .

Moon-Watcher came face to face with the New Rock when he led the tribe down to the river in the first light of morning. He had almost forgotten the terrors of the night, because nothing had happened after that initial noise, so he did not even associate this strange thing with danger or with fear. There was, after all, nothing in the least alarming about it.

It was a rectangular slab, three times his height but narrow enough to span with his arms, and it was made of some completely transparent material; indeed, it was not easy to see except when the rising sun glinted on its edges. As Moon-Watcher had never encountered ice, or even crystal-clear water, there were no natural objects to which he could compare this apparition. It was certainly rather attractive, and though he was wisely cautious of most new things, he did not hesitate for long before sidling up to it. As nothing happened, he put out his hand, and felt a cold, hard surface.

After several minutes of intense thought he arrived at a brilliant explanation. It was a rock, of course, and it must have grown during the night. There were many plants that did this – white, pulpy things shaped like pebbles, that seemed to shoot up during the hours of darkness. It was true that they were small and round, whereas this was large and sharp-edged; but greater and later philosophers than Moon-Watcher would be prepared to overlook equally striking exceptions to their theories.

This really superb piece of abstract thinking led Moon-Watcher, after only three or four minutes, to a deduction which he immediately put to the test. The white, round pebble-plants were very tasty (though there were a few that produced violent illness), perhaps this tall one ... ?

A few licks and nibbles quickly disillusioned him. There was no nourishment here; so like a sensible man-ape, he continued on his way to the river and forgot all about the crystalline monolith during the daily routine of shrieking at the Others.

The foraging today was very bad, and the tribe had to travel several miles from the caves to find any food at all. During the merciless heat of noon, one of the frailer females collapsed, far from any possible shelter. Her companions gathered round her, twittering and weeping sympathetically, but there was nothing that anyone could do. If they had been less exhausted they might have carried her with them, but there was no surplus energy for such acts of kindness. She had to be left behind, to recover or not with her own resources.

They passed the spot on the homeward trek that evening; there was not a bone to be seen.

In the last light of day, looking round anxiously for early hunters, they drank hastily at the stream and started the climb up to their caves. They were still a hundred yards from the New Rock when the sound began.

It was barely audible, yet it stopped them dead, so that they stood paralysed on the trail with their jaws hanging slackly. A simple, maddeningly repetitious vibration, it pulsed out from the crystal, and hypnotized all who came within its spell. For the first time – and the last, for three million years – the sound of drumming was heard in Africa.

The throbbing grew louder, more insistent. Presently the man-apes began to move forward like sleep-walkers towards the source of that compulsive sound. Sometimes they took little dancing-steps, as their blood responded to rhythms that their descendants would not create for ages yet. Totally entranced, they gathered round the monolith, forgetting the hardships of the day, the perils of the approaching dusk, and the hunger in their bellies.

The drumming became louder, the night darker. And as the shadows lengthened, and the light drained from the sky, the crystal began to glow.

First it lost its transparency, and became suffused with a pale, milky luminescence. Tantalizing, ill-defined phantoms moved across its surface and in its depths. They coalesced into bars of light and shadow, then formed intermeshing, spoked patterns that began slowly to rotate.

Faster and faster spun the wheels of light, and the throbbing of the drums accelerated with them. Now utterly hypnotized, the man-apes could only stare slack-jawed into this astonishing display of pyrotechnics. They had already forgotten the instincts of their forefathers and the lessons of a lifetime; not one of them, ordinarily, would have been so far from his cave, so late in the evening, for the surrounding brush was full of frozen shapes and staring eyes, as the creatures of the night suspended their business to see what would happen next.

Now the spinning wheels of light began to merge, and the spokes fused into luminous bars that slowly receded into the distance, rotating on their axes as they did so. They split into pairs, and the resulting sets of lines started to oscillate across each other, slowly changing their angles of intersection. Fantastic, fleeting geometrical patterns flickered in and out of existence as the glowing grids meshed and unmeshed; and the map-apes watched, mesmerized captives of the shining crystal.

They could never guess that their minds were being probed, their bodies mapped, their reactions studied, their potentials evaluated. At first the whole tribe remained half crouching in a motionless tableau, as if frozen into stone. Then the man-ape nearest to the slab suddenly came to life.

He did not move from his position, but his body lost its trance-like rigidity, and became animated as if it were a puppet controlled by invisible strings. The head turned this way and that; the mouth silently opened and closed; the hands clenched and unclenched. Then he bent down, snapped off a long stalk of grass, and attempted to tie it into a knot with clumsy fingers.

He seemed to be a thing possessed, struggling against some spirit or demon who had taken over control of his body. He was panting for breath, and his eyes were full of terror as he tried to force his fingers to make movements more complex than any that they had ever attempted before.

Despite all his efforts, he succeeded only in breaking the stalk into pieces. As the fragments fell to the ground, the controlling influence left him, and he froze once more into immobility.

Another man-ape came to life and went through the same routine. This was a younger, more adaptable specimen; it succeeded where the older one had failed. On the planet Earth the first crude knot had been tied ...

Others did stranger and still more pointless things. Some held their hands out at arm's-length, and tried to touch their fingertips together – first with both eyes open, then with one closed. Some were made to stare at ruled patterns in the crystal, that became more and more finely divided until the lines had merged into a grey blur. And all heard single pure sounds, of varying pitch, that swiftly sank below the level of hearing.

When Moon-Watcher's turn came he felt very little fear. His main sensation was a dull resentment, as his muscles twitched and his limbs moved at commands that were not wholly his own.

Without knowing why, he bent down and picked up a small stone. When he straightened up he saw that there was a new image in the crystal slab.

The grids and the moving, dancing patterns had gone. Instead, there was a series of concentric circles, surrounding a small black disc.

Obeying the silent orders in his brain, he pitched the stone with a clumsy, overarm throw. It missed the target by several feet.

Try again, said the command. He searched around until he had found another pebble. This time it hit the slab with a ringing bell-like tone. He was still a long way off, but his aim was improving.

At the fourth attempt he was only inches from the central bull's-eye. A feeling of indescribable pleasure, almost sexual in its intensity, flooded his mind. Then the control relaxed; he felt no impulse to do anything, except to stand and wait.

One by one, every member of the tribe was briefly possessed. Some succeeded, but most failed at the tasks they had been set, and all were appropriately rewarded by spasms of pleasure or of pain.

Now there was only a uniform, featureless glow in the great slab, so that it stood like a block of light superimposed on the surrounding darkness. As if waking from a sleep, the man-apes shook their heads, and presently began to move along the trail to their place of shelter. They did not look back, or wonder at the strange light that was guiding them to their homes – and to a future unknown, as yet, even to the stars.

CHAPTER 3

ACADEMY

Moon-Watcher and his companions had no recollection of what they had seen after the crystal had ceased to cast its hypnotic spell over their minds and to experiment with their bodies. The next day, as they went out to forage, they passed it with scarcely a second thought: it was now part of the disregarded background of their lives. They could not eat it, and it could not eat them; therefore it was not important.

Down at the river the Others made their usual ineffectual threats. Their leader, a one-eared man-ape of Moon-Watcher's size and age, but in poorer condition, even made a brief foray towards the tribe's territory, screaming loudly and waving his arms in an attempt to scare the opposition and to bolster his own courage. The water of the stream was nowhere more than a foot deep, but the further One-Ear moved out into it, the more uncertain and unhappy he became. Very soon he slowed to a halt, and then moved back, with exaggerated dignity, to join his companions.

Otherwise, there was no change in the normal routine. The tribe gathered just enough nourishment to survive for another day, and no one died.

And that night the crystal slab was still waiting, surrounded by its pulsing aura of light and sound. The programme it had contrived, however, was now subtly different.

Some of the man-apes it ignored completely, as if it was concentrating on the most promising subjects. One of them was Moon-Watcher; once again he felt inquisitive tendrils creeping down the unused by-ways of his brain. And presently he began to see visions.

They might have been within the crystal block; they might have been wholly inside his mind. In any event, to Moon-Watcher they were completely real. Yet somehow the usual automatic impulse to drive off invaders of his territory had been lulled into quiescence.

He was looking at a peaceful family group, differing in only one respect from the scenes he knew. The male, female and two infants that had mysteriously appeared before him were gorged and replete, with sleek and glossy pelts – and this was a condition of life that Moon-Watcher had never imagined. Unconsciously, he felt his own protruding ribs; the ribs of *these* creatures were hidden in rolls of fat. From time to time they stirred lazily, as they lolled at ease near the entrance of a cave, apparently at peace with the world. Occasionally the big male emitted a monumental burp of contentment.

There was no other activity, and after five minutes the scene suddenly faded out. The crystal was no more than a glimmering outline in the darkness; Moon-Watcher shook himself as if awakening from a dream, abruptly realized where he was, and led the tribe back to the caves.

He had no conscious memory of what he had seen, but that night, as he sat brooding at the entrance of his lair, his ears attuned to the noises of the world around him, Moon-Watcher felt the first faint twinges of a new and potent emotion. It was a vague and diffuse sense of envy – of dissatisfaction with his life. He had no idea of its cause, still less of its cure; but discontent had come into his soul, and he had taken one small step towards humanity.

Night after night the spectacle of those four plump man-apes was repeated, until it became a source of fascinated exasperation, serving to increase Moon-Watcher's eternal, gnawing hunger. The evidence of his eyes could not have produced this effect; it needed psychological reinforcement. There were gaps in Moon-Watcher's life now that he would never remember, when the very atoms of his simple brain were being twisted into new patterns. If he survived, those patterns would become eternal, for his genes would pass them on to future generations.

It was a slow, tedious business, but the crystal monolith was patient. Neither it, nor its replicas scattered across half the globe, expected to succeed with all the scores of groups involved in the experiment. A hundred failures would not matter when a single success could change the destiny of the world.

By the time of the next new moon the tribe had seen one birth and two deaths. One of these had been due to starvation; the other had occurred during the nightly ritual, when a man-ape had suddenly collapsed while attempting to tap two pieces of stone delicately together. At once the crystal had darkened, and the tribe had been released from the spell. But the fallen man-ape had not moved and by the morning, of course, the body was gone.

There had been no performance the next night; the crystal was still analysing its mistake. The tribe streamed past it through the gathering dusk, ignoring its presence completely. The night after, it was ready for them again.

The four plump man-apes were still there, and now they were doing extraordinary things. Moon-Watcher began to tremble uncontrollably; he felt as if his brain would burst, and wanted to turn away his eyes. But that remorseless mental control would not relax its grip; he was compelled to follow the lesson to the end, though all his instincts revolted against it.

Those instincts had served his ancestors well, in the days of warm rains and lush fertility, when food was to be had everywhere for the plucking. Now times had changed, and the inherited wisdom of the past had become folly. The man-apes must adapt, or they must die – like the greater beasts who had gone before them, and whose bones now lay sealed within the limestone hills.

So Moon-Watcher stared at the crystal monolith with unblinking eyes, while his brain lay open to its still uncertain manipulations. Often he felt nausea, but always he felt hunger; and from time to time his hands clenched unconsciously in the patterns that would determine his new way of life.

. . .

As the line of wart-hogs moved snuffling and grunting across the trail, Moon-Watcher came to a sudden halt. Pigs and man-apes had always ignored each other, for there was no conflict of interest between them. Like most animals that did not compete for the same food, they merely kept out of each other's way.

Yet now Moon-Watcher stood looking at them, wavering back and forth uncertainly as he was buffeted by impulses which he could not understand. Then, as if in a dream, he started searching the ground – though for what he could not have explained even if he had the power of speech. He would recognize it when he saw it.

It was a heavy, pointed stone about six inches long, and though it did not fit his hand perfectly, it would do. As he swung his hand around, puzzled by its suddenly increased weight, he felt a pleasing sense of power and authority. He started to move towards the nearest pig.

It was a young and foolish animal, even by the undemanding standards of wart-hog intelligence. Though it observed him out of the corner of its eye, it did not take him seriously until much too late. Why should it suspect these harmless creatures of any evil intent? It went on rooting up the grass until Moon-Watcher's stone hammer obliterated its dim consciousness. The remainder of the herd continued grazing unalarmed, for the murder had been swift and silent.

All the other man-apes in the group had stopped to watch, and now they crowded round Moon-Watcher and his victim with admiring wonder. Presently one of them picked up the blood-stained weapon and began to pound the dead pig. Others joined in with any sticks and stones that they could gather until their target began a messy disintegration.

Then they became bored; some wandered off, while others stood hesitantly around the unrecognizable corpse – the future of a world waiting upon their decision. It was a surprisingly long time before one of the nursing females began to lick the gory stone she was holding in her paws.

And it was longer still before Moon-Watcher, despite all that he had been shown, really understood that he need never be hungry again.

CHAPTER 4

THE LEOPARD

The tools they had been programmed to use were simple enough, yet they could change this world and make the man-apes its masters. The most primitive was the hand-held stone, that multiplied many fold the power of a blow. Then there was the bone club, that lengthened the reach and could provide a buffer against the fangs or claws of angry animals. With these weapons, the limitless food that roamed the savannahs was theirs to take.

But they needed other aids, for their teeth and nails could not readily dismember anything larger than a rabbit. Luckily, Nature had provided the perfect tools, requiring only the wit to pick them up.

First there was a crude but very efficient knife or saw, of a model that would serve well for the next three million years. It was simply the lower jaw-bone of an antelope, with the teeth still in place; there would be no substanial improvement until the coming of steel. Then there was an awl or dagger in the form of a gazelle horn, and finally a scraping tool made from the complete jaw of almost any small animal.

The stone club, the toothed saw, the horn dagger, the bone scraper – these were the marvellous inventions which the man-apes needed to survive. Soon they would recognize them for the symbols of power that they were, but many months must pass before their clumsy fingers had acquired the skill – or the will – to use them.

Perhaps, given time, they might by their own efforts have come to the awesome and brilliant concept of using natural weapons as artificial tools. But the odds were all against them, and even now there were endless opportunities for failure in the ages that lay ahead.

The man-apes had been given their first chance. There would be no second one; the future was, very literally, in their own hands.

.   .   .

Moons waxed and waned; babies were born and sometimes lived; feeble, toothless, thirty-year-olds died; the leopard took its toll in the night; the Others threatened daily across the river – and the tribe prospered. In the course of a single year Moon-Watcher and his companions had changed almost beyond recognition.

They had learned their lessons well; now they could handle all the tools that had been revealed to them. The very memory of hunger was fading from their minds; and though the wart-hogs were becoming shy, there were gazelles and antelopes and zebras in countless thousands on the plains. All these animals, and others, had fallen prey to the apprentice hunters.

Now that they were no longer half-numbed with starvation, they had time both for leisure and for the first rudiments of thought. Their new way of life was now casually accepted, and they did not associate it in any way with the monolith still standing beside the trail to the river. If they had ever stopped to consider the matter, they might have boasted that they had brought about their improved status by their own efforts; in fact, they had already forgotten any other mode of existence.

But no Utopia is perfect, and this one had two blemishes. The first was the marauding leopard, whose passion for man-apes seemed to have grown even stronger now that they were better nourished. The second was the tribe across the river; for somehow the Others had survived and had stubbornly refused to die of starvation.

The leopard problem was resolved partly by chance, partly owing to a serious – indeed, almost fatal – error on Moon-Watcher's part. Yet at the time his idea had seemed such a brilliant one that he had danced with joy, and perhaps he could hardly be blamed for overlooking the consequences.

The tribe still experienced occasional bad days, though these no longer threatened its very survival. Towards dusk it had failed to make a kill; the home caves were already in sight as Moon-Watcher led his tired and disgruntled companions back to shelter. And there, on their very threshold, they found one of Nature's rare bonanzas.

A full-grown antelope was lying by the trail. Its foreleg was broken, but it still had plenty of fight in it, and the circling jackals gave its dagger-like horns a respectful berth. They could afford to wait; they knew that they had only to bide their time.

But they had forgotten about the competition, and retreated with angry snarls when the man-apes arrived. They too circled warily, keeping beyond the range of those dangerous horns; then they moved to the attack with clubs and stones.

It was not a very effective or co-ordinated attack: by the time the wretched beast had been given its quietus the light had almost gone – and the jackals were regaining their courage. Moon-Watcher, torn between fear and hunger, slowly realized that all this effort might have been in vain. It was too dangerous to stay here any longer.

Then, not for the first or the last time, he proved himself a genius. With an immense effort of imagination he visualized the dead antelope – *in the safety of his own cave.* He began to drag it towards the cliff-face; presently, the others understood his intentions, and began to help him.

If he had known how difficult the task would be he would never have attempted it. Only his great strength, and the agility inherited from his arboreal ancestors, allowed him to haul the carcass up the steep slope. Several times, almost weeping with frustration, he almost abandoned his prize, but a stubbornness as deep-seated as his hunger drove him on. Sometimes the others helped him, sometimes they hindered; more often they merely got in the way. But finally it was done; the battered antelope was dragged over the lip of the cave, as the last hues of sunlight faded from the sky; and the feasting began.

Hours later, gorged to repletion, Moon-Watcher awoke. Not knowing why, he sat up in the darkness among the sprawled bodies of his equally satiated companions, and strained his ears into the night.

There was no sound except the heavy breathing around him; the whole world seemed asleep. The rocks beyond the mouth of the cave were pale as bone in the brilliant light from the Moon, now high overhead. Any thought of danger seemed infinitely remote.

Then, from a long way off, came the sound of a falling pebble. Fearful, yet inquisitive, Moon-Watcher crawled out on to the ledge of the cave, and peered down the face of the cliff.

What he saw left him so paralysed with fright that for long seconds he was unable to move. Only twenty feet below, two gleaming golden eyes were staring straight up at him; they held him so hypnotized with fear that he was scarcely aware of the lithe, streaked body behind them, flowing smoothly and silently from rock to rock. Never before had the leopard climbed so high. It had ignored the lower caves, though it must have been well aware of their inhabitants. Now it was after other game; it was following the spoor of blood, up the moon-washed face of the cliff.

Seconds later, the night was made hideous by the shrieks of alarm from the man-apes in the cave above. The leopard gave a snarl of fury, as it realized that it had lost the element of surprise. But it did not check its advance, for it knew that it had nothing to fear.

It reached the ledge, and rested for a moment on the narrow open space. The scent of blood was all around, filling its fierce and tiny mind with one overwhelming desire. Without hesitation, it padded silently into the cave.

And here it made its first error, for as it moved out of the moonlight even its superbly night-adapted eyes were at a momentary disadvantage. The man-apes could see it, partly silhoutted against the opening of the cave, more clearly than it could see them. They were terrified, but they were no longer utterly helpless.

Snarling and lashing its tail in arrogant confidence, the leopard advanced in search of the tender food that it craved. Had it met its prey in the open, it would have had no problems; but now that the man-apes were trapped, desperation had given them the courage to attempt the impossible. And for the first time, they had the means to achieve it.

The leopard knew that something was wrong when it felt a stunning blow on its head. It lashed out with its forepaw, and heard a shriek of agony as its claws slashed through soft flesh. Then there was a piercing pain as something sharp drove into its flanks – once, twice, and yet a third time. It whirled around to strike at the shadows screaming and dancing on all sides.

Again there was a violent blow as something caught it across the snout. Its teeth snapped on a white, moving blur – only to grate uselessly upon dead bone. And now, in a final, unbelievable indignity, its tail was being dragged out by the roots.

It whirled around, throwing its insanely daring tormentor against the wall of the cave. Yet whatever it did, it could not escape the rain of blows, inflicted on it by crude weapons wielded by clumsy but powerful hands. Its snarls ran the gamut from pain to alarm, from alarm to outright terror. The implacable hunter was now the victim, and was desperately trying to retreat.

And then it made its second mistake, for in its surprise and fright it had forgotten where it was. Or perhaps it had been dazed or blinded by the blows rained on its head; whatever the reason, it bolted abruptly from the cave. There was a horrible screech as it went toppling out into space. Ages later, it seemed, there came a thud as it crashed into an outcropping half-way down the cliff; thereafter, the only sound was the sliding of loose stones, which quickly died away into the night.

For a long time, intoxicated by victory, Moon-Watcher stood dancing and gibbering at the entrance of the cave. He rightly sensed that his whole world had changed, and that he was no longer a powerless victim of the forces around him.

Then he went back into the cave and for the first time in his life had an unbroken night's sleep.

.   .   .

In the morning they found the body of the leopard at the foot of the cliff. Even in death it was some time before anyone dared to approach the vanquished monster, but presently they closed in upon it with their bone knives and saws.

It was very hard work, and they did no hunting that day.

CHAPTER 5

ENCOUNTER IN THE DAWN

As he led the tribe down to the river in the dim light of dawn, Moon-Watcher paused uncertainly at a familiar spot. Something, he knew, was missing, but what it was he could not remember. He wasted no mental effort on the problem, for this morning he had more important matters on his mind.

Like thunder and lightning and clouds and eclipses the great block of crystal had departed as mysteriously as it had come. Having vanished into the non-existent past, it never troubled Moon-Watcher's thoughts again.

He would never know what it had done to him; and none of his companions wondered, as they gathered round him in the morning mist, why he had paused for a moment here on the way to the river.

. . .

From their side of the stream, in the never-violated safety of their own territory, the Others first saw Moon-Watcher and a dozen males of his tribe as a moving frieze against the dawn sky. At once they began to scream their daily challenge, but this time there was no answer.

Steadily, purposefully – above all, *silently* – Moon-Watcher and his band descended the low hillock that overlooked the river; and as they approached, the Others became suddenly quiet. Their ritual ebbed away, to be replaced by a mounting fear. They were dimly aware that something had happened, and that this encounter was unlike all those that had ever gone before. The bone clubs and knives that Moon-Watcher's group carried did not alarm them, for they did not understand their purpose. They only knew that their rivals' movements were now imbued with determination, and with menace.

The party stopped at the water's edge, and for a moment the Others' courage revived. Led by One-Ear, they half-heartedly resumed their battle-chant. It lasted only a few seconds before a vision of terror struck them dumb.

Moon-Watcher raised his arms high into the air, revealing the burden that until now had been concealed by the hirsute bodies of his companions. He was holding a stout branch, and impaled upon it was the bloody head of the leopard. The mouth had been jammed open with a stick and the great fangs gleamed a ghastly white in the first rays of the rising sun.

Most of the Others were too paralysed with fright to move, but some began a slow, stumbling retreat. That was all the encouragement that Moon-Watcher needed. Still holding the mangled trophy above his head, he started to cross the stream. After a moment's hesitation, his companions splashed after him.

When Moon-Watcher reached the far side, One-Ear was still standing his ground. Perhaps he was too brave or too stupid to run; perhaps he could not really believe that this outrage was actually happening. Coward or hero, it made no difference in the end, as the frozen snarl of death came crashing down upon his uncomprehending head.

Shrieking with fright, the Others scattered into the bush; but presently they would return, and soon they would forget their lost leader.

For a few seconds Moon-Watcher stood uncertainly above his new victim, trying to grasp the strange and wonderful fact that the dead leopard could kill again. Now he was master of the world, and he was not quite sure what to do next.

But he would think of something.

CHAPTER 6

ASCENT OF MAN

A new animal was abroad on the planet, spreading slowly out from the African heartland. It was still so rare that a hasty census might have overlooked it among the teeming billions of creatures roving over land and sea. There was no evidence, as yet, that it would prosper or even survive: on this world, where so many mightier beasts had passed away, its fate still wavered in the balance.

In the hundred thousand years since the crystals had descended upon

Africa, the man-apes had invented nothing. But they had started to change, and had developed skills which no other animal possessed. Their bone clubs had increased their reach and multiplied their strength; they were no longer defenceless against the predators with whom they had to compete. The smaller carnivores they could drive away from their own kills; the larger ones they could at least discourage, and sometimes put to flight.

Their massive teeth were growing smaller, for they were no longer essential. The sharp-edged stones that could be used to dig out roots, or to cut and saw through tough flesh or fibre, had begun to replace them, with immeasurable consequences. No longer were the man-apes faced with starvation when their teeth became damaged or worn; even the crudest tools could add many years to their lives. And as their fangs diminished, the shape of their face started to alter; the snout receded, the massive jaw became more delicate, the mouth able to make more subtle sounds. Speech was still a million years away, but the first steps towards it had been taken.

And then the world began to change. In four great waves, with two hundred thousand years between their crests, the Ice Ages swept by, leaving their mark on all the globe. Outside the tropics, the glaciers slew those who had prematurely left their ancestral home; and everywhere they winnowed out the creatures who could not adapt.

When the ice had passed, so had much of the planet's early life – including the man-apes. But, unlike so many others, they had left descendants; they had not merely become extinct – they had been transformed. The tool-makers had been remade by their own tools.

For in using clubs and flints their hands had developed a dexterity found nowhere else in the animal kingdom, permitting them to make still better tools, which in turn had developed their limbs and brains yet further. It was an accelerating, cumulative process; and at its end was Man.

The first true men had tools and weapons only a little better than those of their ancestors a million years earlier, but they could use them with far greater skill. And somewhere in the shadowy centuries that had gone before they had invented the most essential tool of all, though it could be neither seen nor touched. They had learned to speak, and so had won their first great victory over Time. Now the knowledge of one generation could be handed on to the next, so that each age could profit from those that had gone before.

Unlike the animals, who knew only the present, Man had acquired a past; and he was beginning to grope towards a future.

He was also learning to harness the forces of nature; with the taming of fire, he had laid the foundations of technology and left his animal origins far behind. Stone gave way to bronze, and then to iron. Hunting was succeeded by agriculture. The tribe grew into the village, the village into the town. Speech became eternal, thanks to certain marks on stone and clay and papyrus. Presently he invented philosophy, and religion. And he peopled the sky, not altogether inaccurately with gods.

As his body became more and more defenceless, so his means of offence became steadily more frightful. With stone and bronze and iron and steel he had run the gamut of everything that could pierce and slash, and quite early in time he had learned how to strike down his victims from a distance. The spear, the bow, the gun and finally the guided missile had given him weapons of infinite range and all but infinite power.

Without those weapons, often though he had used them against himself, Man would never have conquered his world. Into them he had put his heart and soul, and for ages they had served him well.

But now, as long as they existed, he was living on borrowed time.

CHAPTER 7

SPECIAL FLIGHT

No matter how many times you left Earth, Dr Heywood Floyd told himself, the excitement never really palled. He had been to Mars once, to the Moon three times, and to the various space-stations more often than he could remember. Yet as the moment of take-off approached he was conscious of a rising tension, a feeling of wonder and awe – yes, and of nervousness – which put him on the same level as any earth-lubber about to receive his first baptism of space.

The jet that had rushed him here from Washington, after that midnight briefing with the President, was now dropping down towards one of the most familiar, yet most exciting, landscapes in all the world. There lay the first two generations of the Space Age, spanning twenty miles of the Florida coast. To the south, outlined by winking red warning lights, were the giant gantries of the Saturns and Neptunes, that had set men on the path to the planets, and had now passed into history. Near the horizon, a gleaming silver tower bathed in floodlights, stood the last of the Saturn V's, for almost twenty years a national monument and place of pilgrimage. Not far away, looming against the sky like a man-made mountain, was the incredible bulk of the Vertical Assembly Building, still the largest single structure on Earth.

But these things now belonged to the past, and he was flying towards the future. As they banked, Dr Floyd could see below him a maze of buildings, then a great airstrip, then a broad, dead-straight scar across the flat Florida landscape – the multiple rails of a giant launching track. At its end, surrounded by vehicles and gantries, a spaceplane lay gleaming in a pool of light, being prepared for its leap to the stars. In a sudden failure of perspective, brought on by his swift changes of speed and height, it seemed to Floyd that he was looking down on a small silver moth, caught in the beam of a flashlight.

Then the tiny, scurrying figures on the ground brought home to him the real size of the spacecraft; it must have been two hundred feet across the narrow 'V' of its wings. And that enormous vehicle, Floyd told himself with some incredulity –yet also with some pride – is waiting for *me*. As far as he knew, it was the first time that an entire mission had been set up to take a single man to the Moon.

Though it was two o'clock in the morning, a group of reporters and cameramen intercepted him on his way to the floodlit Orion III spacecraft. He knew several of them by sight, for as Chairman of the National Council of Astronautics, the news conference was part of his way of life. This was neither the time nor the place for one, and he had nothing to say; but it was important not to offend the gentlemen of the communications media.

'Dr Floyd? I'm Jim Forster of Associated News. Could you give us a few words about this flight of yours?'

'I'm very sorry – I can't say anything.'

'But you *did* meet with the President earlier this evening?' asked a familiar voice.

'Oh – hello, Mike. I'm afraid you've been dragged out of bed for nothing. Definitely no comment.'

'Can you at least confirm or deny that some kind of epidemic has broken out on the Moon?' a TV reporter asked, managing to jog alongside and keep Floyd properly framed in his miniature TV camera.

'Sorry,' said Floyd, shaking his head.

'What about the quarantine?' asked another reporter. 'How long will it be kept on?'

'Still no comment.'

'Dr Floyd,' demanded a very short and determined lady of the Press, 'what possible justification can there be for this total blackout of news from the Moon? Has it anything to do with the political situation?'

'*What* political situation?' Floyd asked dryly. There was a sprinkling of laughter, and someone called, 'Have a good trip, Doctor!' as he made his way into the sanctuary of the boarding gantry.

As long as he could remember it had been not a 'situation' so much as a permanent crisis. Since the 1970s the world had been dominated by two problems which, ironically, tended to cancel each other out.

Though birth control was cheap, reliable and endorsed by all the main religions, it had come too late; the population of the world was now six billion – a third of them in the Chinese Empire. Laws had even been passed in some authoritarian societies limiting families to two children, but their enforcement had proved impracticable. As a result, food was short in every country; even the United States had meatless days, and widespread famine was predicted within fifteen years, despite heroic efforts to farm the sea and to develop synthetic foods.

With the need for international co-operation more urgent than ever, there were still as many frontiers as in any earlier age. In a million years the human race had lost few of its aggressive instincts; along symbolic lines visible only to politicians, the thirty-eight nuclear powers watched each other with belligerent anxiety. Between them they possessed sufficient megatonnage to remove the entire surface crust of the planet. Although there had been – miraculously – no use of atomic weapons, this situation could hardly last for ever.

And now, for their own inscrutable reasons, the Chinese were offering to the smaller have-not nations a complete nuclear capability of fifty warheads and delivery systems. The cost was under $200,000,000, and easy terms could be arranged.

Perhaps they were only trying to shore up their sagging economy by turning obsolete weapon systems into hard cash, as some observers had suggested. Or perhaps they had discovered methods of warfare so advanced that they no longer had need of such toys; there had been talk of radio-hypnosis from satellite transmitters, compulsion viruses, and blackmail by synthetic diseases for which they alone possessed the antidote. These charming ideas were almost certainly propaganda or pure fantasy, but it was not safe to discount any of them. Every time Floyd took off from Earth he wondered if it would still be there when the time came to return.

The trim stewardess greeted him as he entered the cabin. 'Good morning, Dr Floyd. I'm Miss Simmons – I'd like to welcome you aboard on behalf of Captain Tynes and our co-pilot, First Officer Ballard.'

'Thank you,' said Floyd with a smile, wondering why stewardesses always had to sound like robot tour guides.

'Take-off's in five minutes,' she said, gesturing into the empty, twenty-passenger cabin. 'You can take any seat you want, but Captain Tyne recommends the forward window seat on the left, if you want to watch the docking operations.'

'I'll do that,' he answered, moving towards the preferred seat. The stewardess fussed over him a while and then moved to her cubicle at the rear of the cabin.

Floyd settled down in his seat, adjusted the safety harness around waist and shoulders, and strapped his brief-case to the adjacent seat. A moment later the loudspeaker came on with a soft popping noise. 'Good morning,' said Miss Simmons' voice. 'This is Special Flight 3, Kennedy to Space Station 1.'

She was determined, it seemed, to go through the full routine for her solitary passenger, and Floyd could not resist a smile as she continued inexorably:

'Our transit time will be fifty-five minutes. Maximum acceleration will be two-gee, and we will be weightless for thirty minutes. Please do not leave your seat until the safety sign is lit.'

Floyd looked over his shoulder and called, 'Thank you.' He caught a glimpse of a slightly embarrassed but charming smile.

He leaned back into his seat and relaxed. This trip, he calculated, would cost the tax-payers slightly over a million dollars. If it was not justified he would be out of his job; but he could always go back to the university and to his interrupted studies of planetary formation.

'Auto-countdown procedures all Go,' the Captain's voice said over the speaker with the soothing, sing-song used in RT chat.

'Lift-off in one minute.'

As always, it seemed more like an hour. Floyd became acutely aware of the gigantic forces coiled up around him, waiting to be released. In the fuel tanks of the two spacecraft, and in the power-storage system of the launching track, was pent up the energy of a nuclear bomb. And it would all be used to take him a mere two hundred miles from Earth.

There was none of the old-fashioned FIVE-FOUR-THREE-TWO-ONE-ZERO business, so tough on the human nervous system.

'Launching in fifteen seconds. You will be more comfortable if you start breathing deeply.'

That was good psychology, and good physiology. Floyd felt himself well charged with oxygen, and ready to tackle anything, when the launching track began to sling its thousand-ton payload out over the Atlantic.

It was hard to tell when they lifted from the track and became airborne, but when the roar of the rockets suddenly doubled its fury, and Floyd found himself sinking deeper into the cushions of his seat, he knew that the first-stage engines had taken over. He wished he could look out of the window, but it was an effort even to turn his head. Yet there was no discomfort; indeed, the pressure of acceleration and the overwhelming thunder of the motors produced an extraordinary euphoria. His ears singing, the blood pounding in his veins, Floyd felt more alive than he had for years. He was young again, he wanted to sing aloud – which was certainly safe, for no one could possibly hear him.

The mood passed swiftly, as he suddenly realized that he was leaving Earth, and everything he had ever loved. Down there were his three children, motherless since his wife had taken that fatal flight to Europe ten years ago. (*Ten* years? Impossible! Yet it was so . . .) Perhaps for their sake, he should have remarried . . .

He had almost lost sense of time when the pressure and the noise abruptly slackened, and the cabin speaker announced: 'Preparing to separate from lower stage. Here we go.'

There was a slight jolt, and suddenly Floyd recalled a quotation of

Leonardo da Vinci's which he had once seen displayed in a N.A.S.A. office:

'The Great Bird will take its flight on the back of the great bird, bringing glory to the nest where it was born.'

Well, the Great Bird was flying now, beyond all the dreams of da Vinci, and its exhausted companion was winging back to Earth. In a ten-thousand-mile arc the empty lower stage would glide down into the atmosphere, trading speed for distance as it homed on Kennedy. In a few hours, serviced and refuelled, it would be ready again to lift another companion towards the shining silence which it could never reach.

Now, thought Floyd, we are on our own, more than half-way to orbit. When the acceleration came on again, as the upper-stage rockets fired, the thrust was much more gentle; indeed, he felt no more than normal gravity. But it would have been impossible to walk, since 'Up' was straight towards the front of the cabin. If he had been foolish enough to leave his seat he would have crashed at once against the rear wall.

This effect was a little disconcerting, for it seemed that the ship was standing on its tail. To Floyd, who was at the very front of the cabin, all the seats appeared to be fixed on a wall dropping vertically beneath him. He was doing his best to ignore this uncomfortable illusion when dawn exploded outside the ship.

In seconds they shot through veils of crimson and pink and gold and blue into the piercing white of day. Though the windows were heavily tinted to reduce the glare, the probing beams of sunlight that now slowly swept across the cabin left Floyd half-blinded for several minutes. He was in space, yet there was no question of being able to see the stars.

He shielded his eyes with his hands and tried to peer through the window beside him. Out there the sweptback wing of the ship was blazing like white-hot metal in the reflected sunlight; there was utter darkness all around it, and that darkness must be full of stars – but it was impossible to see them.

Weight was slowly ebbing; the rockets were being throttled back as the ship eased itself into orbit. The thunder of the engines dropped to a muted roar, then a gentle hiss, then died into silence. If it had not been for the restraining straps Floyd would have floated out of his seat; his stomach felt as if it was going to do so anyway. He hoped that the pills he had been given half an hour and ten thousand miles ago would perform as per specifications. He had been space-sick just once in his career, and that was much too often.

The pilot's voice was firm and confident as it came over the cabin speaker. 'Please observe all Zero-gee regulations. We will be docking at Space Station 1 in forty-five minutes.'

The stewardess came walking up the narrow corridor to the right of the closely spaced seats. There was a slight buoyancy about her steps, and her feet came away from the floor reluctantly as if entangled in glue. She was keeping to the bright yellow band of Velcro carpeting that ran the full length of the floor – and of the ceiling. The carpet, and the soles of her sandals, were covered with myriads of tiny hooks, so that they clung together like burrs. This trick of walking in freefall was immensely reassuring to disoriented passengers.

'Would you like some coffee or tea, Dr Floyd?' she asked cheerfully.

'No thank you,' he smiled. He always felt like a baby when he had to suck at one of those plastic drinking tubes.

The stewardess was still hovering anxiously around him as he popped open his brief-case and prepared to remove his papers.

'Dr Floyd, may I ask you a question?'

'Certainly,' he answered, looking up over his glasses.

'My fiancé is a geologist at Tycho,' said Miss Simmons, measuring her words carefully, 'and I haven't heard from him for over a week.'

'I'm sorry to hear that; maybe he's away from his base, and out of touch.'

She shook her head. 'He always tells me when that's going to happen. And you can imagine how worried I am – with all these rumours. Is it *really* true about an epidemic on the Moon?'

'If it is, there's no cause for alarm. Remember, there was a quarantine back in '98, over that mutated 'flu virus. A lot of people were sick – but no one died. And that's really all I can say,' he concluded firmly.

Miss Simmons smiled pleasantly and straightened up.

'Well, thank you anyway, Doctor. I'm sorry to have bothered you.'

'No bother at all,' he said gallantly, but not very accurately. Then he buried himself in his endless technical reports, in a desperate last-minute assault on the usual back-log.

He would have no time for reading when he got to the Moon.

CHAPTER 8

ORBITAL RENDEZVOUS

Half an hour later the pilot announced: 'We make contact in ten minutes. Please check your seat harness.'

Floyd obeyed, and put away his papers. It was asking for trouble to read during the celestial juggling act which took place during the last three hundred miles; best to close one's eyes and relax while the spacecraft was nudged back and forth with brief bursts of rocket power.

A few minutes later he caught his first glimpse of Space Station 1, only a few miles away. The sunlight glinted and sparkled from the polished metal surfaces of the slowly revolving, three-hundred-yard-diameter disc. Not far way, drifting in the same orbit, was a swept-back Titov-V spaceplane, and close to that an almost spherical Aries-IB, the workhorse of space, with the four stubby legs of its lunar-landing shock absorbers jutting from one side.

The Orion III spacecraft was descending from a higher orbit, which brought the Earth into spectacular view behind the Station. From his altitude of two hundred miles Floyd could see much of Africa and the Atlantic Ocean. There was considerable cloud cover, but he could still detect the blue-green outlines of the Gold Coast.

The central axis of the Space Station, with its docking arms extended, was now slowly swimming towards them. Unlike the structure from which it sprang, it was not rotating – or, rather, it was running in reverse at a rate which exactly countered the Station's own spin. Thus a visiting spacecraft could be coupled to it, for the transfer of personnel or cargo, without being whirled disastrously around.

With the softest of thuds, ship and Station made contact. There were metallic, scratching noises from outside, then the brief hissing of air as pressures equalized. A few seconds later the airlock door opened, and a man wearing the light, close-fitting slacks and short-sleeved shirt which was almost the uniform of Space Station personnel came into the cabin.

'Pleased to meet you, Dr Floyd. I'm Nick Miller, Station Security; I'm to look after you until the shuttle leaves.'

They shook hands, then Floyd smiled at the stewardess and said: 'Please give my compliments to Captain Tynes, and thank him for the smooth ride. Perhaps I'll see you on the way home.'

Very cautiously – it was more than a year since he had last been weightless and it would be some time before he regained his spacelegs – he hauled himself hand over hand through the airlock and into the large, circular chamber at the axis of the Space Station. It was a heavily padded room, its walls covered with recessed handholds; Floyd gripped one of these firmly while the whole chamber started to rotate, until it matched the spin of the Station.

As it gained speed, faint and ghostly gravitational fingers began to clutch at him, and he drifted slowly towards the circular wall. Now he was standing, swaying back and forth gently like seaweed in the surge of the tide, on what had magically become a curving floor. The centrifugal force of the Station's spin had taken hold of him; it was very feeble here, so near the axis, but would increase steadily as he moved outwards.

From the central transit chamber he followed Miller down a curving stair. At first his weight was so slight that he had almost to force himself downwards, by holding on to the handrail. Not until he reached the passenger lounge, on the outer skin of the great revolving disc, had he acquired enough weight to move around almost normally.

The lounge had been redecorated since his last visit, and had acquired several new facilities. Besides the usual chairs, small tables, restaurant and post office there was now a barber's shop, drugstore, movie theatre and a souvenir shop selling photographs and slides of lunar and planetary landscapes, guaranteed genuine pieces of Luniks, Rangers and Surveyors, all neatly mounted in plastic, and exorbitantly priced.

'Can I get you anything while we're waiting?' Miller asked. 'We board in about thirty minutes.'

'I could do with a cup of black coffee – two lumps – and I'd like to call Earth.'

'Right, Doctor – I'll get the coffee – the phones are over there.'

The picturesque booths were only a few yards from a barrier with two entrances labelled 'WELCOME TO THE U.S. SECTION' and 'WELCOME TO THE SOVIET SECTION'. Beneath these notices which read, in English, Russian, and Chinese, French, German and Spanish:

'PLEASE HAVE READY YOUR: Passport. Visa. Medical Certificate. Transportation Permit. Weight Declaration.'

There was a rather pleasant symbolism about the fact that as soon as they had passed through the barriers, in either direction, passengers were free to mix again. The division was purely for administrative purposes.

Floyd, after checking that the Area Code for the U.S. was still eighty-one, punched his twelve-digit home number, dropped his plastic all-purpose credit card into the pay slot, and was through in thirty seconds.

Washington was still sleeping, for it was several hours to dawn, but he would not disturb anyone. His housekeeper would get the message from the recorder as soon as she awoke.

'Miss Flemming – this is Dr Floyd. Sorry I had to leave in such a hurry. Would you please call my office and ask them to collect the car – it's at Dulles Airport and the key is with Mr Bailey, Senior Flight Control Officer. Next, will you call the Chevy Chase Country Club and leave a message for the secretary. I definitely *won't* be able to play in the tennis tournament next weekend. Give my apologies – I'm afraid they were counting on me. Then call Downtown Electronics and tell them that if the video in my study isn't fixed by – oh, Wednesday – they can take the damn thing back.' He paused for breath, and tried to think of any other crises or problems that might arise during the days ahead.

'If you run short of cash speak to the office; they can get urgent messages to me, but I may be too busy to answer. Give my love to the children, and say I'll be back as soon as I can. Oh hell – here's someone I don't want to see – I'll call from the Moon if I can – goodbye.'

Floyd tried to duck out of the booth, but it was too late; he had already been spotted. Bearing down on him through the Soviet Section exit was Dr Dimitri Moisewitch, of the U.S.S.R. Academy of Science.

Dimitri was one of Floyd's best friends, and for that very reason he was the last person he wished to talk to, here and now.

CHAPTER 9

MOON SHUTTLE

The Russian astronomer was tall, slender and blond, and his unlined face belied his fifty-five years – the last ten of which had been spent building up the giant radio observatory on the far side of the Moon, where two thousand miles of solid rock would shield it from the electronic racket of Earth.

'Why, Heywood,' he said, shaking hands firmly. 'It's a small universe. How are you – and your charming children?'

'We're fine,' Floyd replied warmly, but with a slightly distracted air. 'We often talk about the wonderful time you gave us last summer.' He was sorry he could not sound more sincere; they really had enjoyed a week's vacation in Odessa with Dimitri during one of the Russian's visits to Earth.

'And you – I suppose you're on your way up?' Dimitri enquired.

'Er, yes – my flight leaves in half an hour,' answered Floyd. 'Do you know Mr Miller?'

The Security Officer had now approached, and was standing at a respectful distance holding a plastic cup full of coffee.

'Of course. But *please* put that down, Mr Miller. This is Dr Floyd's last chance to have a civilized drink – let's not waste it. No – I insist.'

They followed Dimitri out of the main lounge into the observation section, and soon were sitting at a table under a dim light watching the moving panorama of the stars. Space Station 1 revolved once a minute, and the centrifugal force generated by this slow spin produced an artificial gravity equal to the Moon's. This, it had been discovered, was a good compromise between Earth gravity and no gravity at all; moreover, it gave Moon-bound passengers a chance to become acclimatized.

Outside the almost invisible windows, Earth and stars marched in a silent procession. At the moment this side of the Station was tilted away from the Sun; otherwise it would have been impossible to look out, for the lounge would have been blasted with light. Even as it was, the glare of the Earth, filling half the sky, drowned all but the brighter stars.

But Earth was waning, as the Station orbited towards the night side of the planet; in a few minutes it would be a huge black disc, spangled with the lights of cities. And then the sky would belong to the stars.

'Now,' said Dimitri, after he had swiftly downed his first drink, and was toying with the second, 'what's all this about an epidemic in the U.S. Sector? I wanted to go there on this trip. "No, Professor," they told me. "We're very sorry, but there's a strict quarantine until further notice." I pulled all the strings I could; it was no use. Now *you* tell me what's happening.'

Floyd groaned inwardly. Here we go again, he thought. The sooner I'm on that shuttle, headed for the Moon, the happier I'll be.

'The – ah – quarantine is purely a safety precaution,' he said cautiously. 'We're not even sure it's really necessary, but we don't believe in taking chances.'

'But what *is* the disease – what are the symptoms? Could it be extraterrestrial? Do you want any help from our medical services?'

'I'm sorry, Dimitri – we've been asked not to say *anything* at the moment. Thanks for the offer, but we can handle the situation.'

'Hmm,' said Moisewitch, obviously quite unconvinced. 'Seems odd to me that *you*, an astronomer, should be sent up to the Moon to look into an epidemic.'

'I'm only an ex-astronomer; it's years since I did any real research. Now I'm a scientific expert; that means I know nothing about absolutely *everything*.'

'Then do you know what T.M.A.-1 means?'

Miller seemed about to choke on his drink, but Floyd was made of sterner stuff. He looked his old friend straight in the eye, and said calmly: 'T.M.A.-1? What an odd expression. Where did you hear it?'

'Never mind,' retorted the Russian. 'You can't fool me. But if you've run into something you can't handle I hope you don't leave it until too late before you yell for help.'

Miller looked meaningfully at his watch.

'Due to board in five minutes, Dr Floyd,' he said. 'I think we'd better get moving.'

Though he knew that they still had a good twenty minutes, Floyd got up with haste. Too much haste, for he had forgotten the one-sixth of a gravity. He grabbed the table just in time to prevent a take-off.

'It was fine meeting you, Dimitri,' he said, not quite accurately. 'Hope you have a good trip down to Earth – I'll give you a call as soon as I'm back.'

As they left the lounge, and checked through the U.S. transit barrier, Floyd remarked: 'Phew – that was close. Thanks for rescuing me.'

'You know, Doctor,' said the Security Officer, 'I hope he isn't right.'

'Right about what?'

'About us running into something we can't handle.'

'*That*,' Floyd answered with determination, 'is what I intend to find out.'

Forty-five minutes later the Aries-IB lunar carrier pulled away from the station. There was none of the power and fury of a take-off from Earth – only an almost inaudible far-off whistling as the low-thrust plasma jets blasted their electrified streams into space. The gentle push lasted for more than fifteen minutes, and the mild acceleration would not have prevented anyone from moving around the cabin. But when it was over, the ship was no longer bound to Earth, as it had been while it still accompanied the Station. It had broken the bonds of gravity and was now a free and independent planet, circling the Sun in an orbit of its own.

The cabin Floyd now had all to himself had been designed for thirty passengers. It was strange, and rather lonely, to see all the empty seats around him, and to have the undivided attention of the steward and stewardess – not to mention pilot, co-pilot, and two engineers. He doubted that any man in history had ever received such exclusive service, and it was most unlikely that anyone would do so in the future. He recalled the cynical remark of one of the less reputable pontiffs: 'Now that we have the Papacy, let us enjoy it.' Well, he would enjoy this trip, and the euphoria of weightlessness. With the loss of gravity he had – at least for a while – shed most of his cares. Someone had once said that you could be terrified in space, but you could not be worried there. It was perfectly true.

The stewards, it appeared, were determined to make him eat for the whole twenty-five hours of the trip, and he was continually fending off unwanted meals. Eating in zero gravity was no real problem, contrary to the dark forebodings of the early astronauts. He sat at an ordinary table, to which the plates were clipped, as aboard ship in a rough sea. All the courses had some element of stickiness, so that they would not take off and go wandering around the cabin. Thus a chop would be glued to the plate by a thick sauce, and a salad kept under control by an adhesive dressing. With a little skill and care there were few items that could not be tackled safely; the only things banned were hot soups and excessively crumbly pastries. Drinks, of course, were a different matter; all liquids simply had to be kept in plastic squeeze-tubes.

A whole generation of research by heroic but unsung volunteers had gone into the design of the washroom, and it was now considered to be more or less fool-proof. Floyd investigated it soon after free-fall had begun. He found himself in a little cubicle with all the fittings of an ordinary airline toilet, but illuminated with a red light that was very harsh and unpleasant to the eye. A notice printed in prominent letters announced: 'MOST IMPORTANT! FOR YOUR OWN COMFORT, PLEASE READ THESE INSTRUCTIONS CAREFULLY!!!'

Floyd sat down (one still tended to do so, even when weightless) and read the notice several times. When he was sure there had been no modifications since his last trip, he pressed the START button.

Close at hand an electric motor began to whirr, and Floyd felt himself moving. As the notice advised him to do, he closed his eyes and waited. After a minute a bell chimed softly and he looked around.

The light had now changed to a soothing pinkish white; but, more important, he was under gravity again. Only the faintest vibration revealed that it was a spurious gravity, caused by the carousel-like spin of the whole toilet compartment. Floyd picked up a piece of soap, and watched it drop in slow motion; he judged that the centrifugal force was about a quarter of a normal gravity. But that was quite enough; it would ensure that everything moved in the right direction, in the one place where this mattered most.

He pressed the STOP FOR EXIT button, and closed his eyes again. Weight slowly ebbed as the rotation ceased, the bell gave a double chime, and the red warning light was back. The door was then locked in the right position to let him glide out into the cabin, where he adhered as quickly as possible to the carpet. He had long ago exhausted the novelty of weightlessness, and was grateful for the Velcro slippers that allowed him to walk almost normally.

There was plenty to occupy his time, even if he did nothing but sit and read. When he tired of official reports and memoranda and minutes he would plug his foolscap-sized Newspad into the ship's information circuit and scan the latest reports from Earth. One by one he would conjure up the world's major electronic papers; he knew the codes of the more important ones by heart, and he had no need to consult the list on the back of his pad. Switching to the display unit's short-term memory, he would hold the front page while he quickly searched the headlines and noted the items that interested him. Each had its own two-digit reference; when he punched that, the postage-stamp-sized rectangle would expand until it neatly filled the screen, and he could read it with comfort. When he had finished he would flash back to the complete page and select a new subject for detailed examination.

Floyd sometimes wondered if the Newspad, and the fantastic technology behind it, was the last word in man's quest for perfect communications. Here he was, far out in space, speeding away from Earth at thousands of miles an hour, yet in a few milliseconds he could see the headlines of any newspaper he pleased. (That very word 'newspaper', of course, was an anachronistic hang-over into the age of electronics.) The text was updated automatically on every hour; even if one read only the English versions one could spend an entire lifetime doing nothing but absorb the ever-changing flow of information from the news satellites.

It was hard to imagine how the system could be improved or made more convenient. But sooner or later, Floyd guessed, it would pass away, to be replaced by something as unimaginable as the Newspad itself would have been to Caxton or Gutenberg.

There was another thought which a scanning of those tiny electronic headlines often invoked. The more wonderful the means of communication, the more trivial, tawdry or depressing its contents seemed to be. Accidents, crimes, natural and man-made disasters, threats of conflict, gloomy editorials – these still seemed to be the main concern of the millions of words being sprayed into the ether. Yet Floyd also wondered if this was altogether a bad thing; the newspapers of Utopia, he had long ago decided, would be terribly dull.

From time to time the captain and the other members of the crew came into the cabin and exchanged a few words with him. They treated their distinguished passenger with awe, and were doubtless burning with curiosity about his mission, but were too polite to ask questions or even to drop any hints.

Only the charming little stewardess seemed completely at ease in his presence. As Floyd quickly discovered, she came from Bali, and had carried beyond the atmosphere some of the grace and mystery of that still largely unspoilt island. One of his strangest, and most enchanting, memories of the entire trip was her zero-gravity demonstration of some classical Balinese dance movements, with the lovely, blue-green crescent of the waning Earth as a backdrop.

There was one sleep period, when the main cabin lights were switched off and Floyd fastened down his arms and legs with the elastic sheets that would prevent him from drifting away into space. It seemed a crude arrangement – but here in zero-gravity his unpadded couch was more comfortable than the most luxurious mattress on Earth.

When he had strapped himself in, Floyd dozed off quickly enough, but woke up once in a drowsy, half-conscious condition, to be completely baffled by his strange surroundings. For a moment he thought that he was in the middle of some dimly lit Chinese lantern; the faint glow from the other cubicles around him gave that impression. Then he said to himself, firmly and successfully: 'Go to sleep, boy. This is just an ordinary moon-shuttle.'

When he awoke, the Moon had swallowed up half the sky, and the braking manoeuvres were about to begin. The wide arc of windows set in the curving wall of the passenger section now looked out on to the open sky, not the approaching globe, so he moved into the control cabin. Here, on the rear-view TV screens, he could watch the final stages of the descent.

The approaching lunar mountains were utterly unlike those of Earth; they lacked the dazzling caps of snow, the green, close-fitting garments of vegetation, the moving crowns of cloud. Nevertheless, the fierce contrasts of light and shadow gave them a strange beauty of their own. The laws of earthly aesthetics did not apply here; this world had been shaped and moulded by other than terrestrial forces, operating over aeons of time unknown to the young, verdant Earth, with its fleeting Ice Ages, its swiftly rising and falling seas, its mountain ranges dissolving like mists before the dawn. Here was age inconceivable – but not death, for the Moon had never lived – until now.

The descending ship was poised almost above the line dividing night from day, and directly below was a chaos of jagged shadows and brilliant, isolated peaks catching the first light of the slow lunar dawn. That would be a fearful place to attempt a landing, even with all possible electronic aids; but they were slowly drifting away from it, towards the night side of the Moon.

Then Floyd saw, as his eyes grew more accustomed to the fainter illumination, that the night land was not wholly dark. It was aglow with a ghostly light, in which peaks and valleys and plains could be clearly seen. The Earth, a giant moon to the Moon, was flooding the land below with its radiance.

On the pilot's panel, lights flashed above the radar screens, numbers came and went on computer displays, clocking off the distance of the approaching Moon. They were still more than a thousand miles away when weight returned as the jets began their gentle but steady decelera-tion. For ages, it seemed, the Moon slowly expanded across the sky, the Sun sank below the horizon, and at last a single giant crater filled the field of view. The shuttle was falling towards its central peaks – and suddenly Floyd noticed that near one of those peaks a brilliant light was flashing with a regular rhythm. It might have been an airport beacon back on Earth, and he stared at it with a tightening of the throat. It was proof that men had established another foothold on the Moon.

Now the crater had expanded so much that its ramparts were slipping below the horizon, and the smaller craterlets that peppered its interior were beginning to disclose their real size. Some of these, tiny though they had seemed from far out in space, were miles across, and could have swallowed whole cities.

Under its automatic controls the shuttle was sliding down the starlit sky, towards that barren landscape glimmering in the light of the great gibbous Earth. Now a voice was calling somewhere above the whistle of the jets and the electronic beepings that came and went through the cabin.

'Clavius Control to Special 14, you are coming in nicely. Please make manual check of landing gear lock, hydraulic pressure, shock pad inflation.'

The pilot pressed sundry switches, green lights flashed, and he called back, 'All manual checks completed. Landing gear lock, hydraulic pressure, shock pad O.K.'

'Confirmed,' said the Moon, and the descent continued wordlessly. Though there was still plenty of talking, it was all being done by machines, flashing binary impulses to one another at a thousand times the rate their slow-thinking makers could communicate.

Some of the mountain peaks were already towering above the shuttle; now the ground was only a few thousand feet away, and the beacon light was a brilliant star, flashing steadily above a group of low build-ings and odd vehicles. In the final stage of the descent the jets seemed to be playing some strange tune; they pulsed on and off, making the last fine adjustments to the thrust.

Abruptly, a swirling cloud of dust hid everything, the jets gave one final spurt, and the shuttle rocked very slightly, like a rowboat when a small wave goes by. It was some minutes before Floyd could really accept the silence that now enfolded him and the weak gravity that gripped his limbs.

He had made, utterly without incident and in little more than one day, the incredible journey of which men had dreamed for two thousand years. After a normal, routine flight, he had landed on the Moon.

CHAPTER 10

CLAVIUS BASE

Clavius, a hundred-and-fifty miles in diameter, is the second largest crater on the visible face of the Moon, and lies in the centre of the Southern Highlands. It is very old; ages of vulcanism and bombardment from space have scarred its walls and pock-marked its floor. But since the last era of crater-formation, when the debris from the asteroid belt was still battering the inner planets, it had known peace for half a billion years.

Now there were new, strange stirrings on and below its surface, for here Man was establishing his first permanent bridgehead on the Moon. Clavius Base could, in an emergency, be entirely self-supporting. All the necessities of life were produced from the local rocks, after they had been crushed, heated, and chemically processed. Hydrogen, oxygen, carbon, nitrogen, phosphorus – all these, and most of the other elements, could be found inside the Moon, if anyone knew where to look for them.

The Base was a closed system, like a tiny working model of Earth itself, recycling all the chemicals of life. The atmosphere was purified in a vast 'hothouse' – a large, circular room buried just below the lunar surface. Under blazing lamps by night, and filtered sunlight by day, acres of stubby green plants grew in warm, moist atmosphere. They were special mutations, designed for the express purpose of replenishing the air with oxygen, and providing food as a by-product.

More food was produced by chemical processing systems and algae culture. Although the green scum circulating through yards of transparent plastic tubes would have scarcely appealed to a gourmet, the bio-chemists could convert it into chops and steaks only an expert could distinguish from the real thing.

The eleven hundred men and six hundred women who made up the personnel of the Base were all highly trained scientists and technicians, carefully selected before they had left Earth. Though lunar living was now virtually free from the hardships, disadvantages and occasional dangers of the early days, it was still psychologically demanding and not recommended for anyone suffering from claustrophobia. Since it was expensive and time-consuming to cut a large underground base out of solid rock or compacted lava, the standard one-man 'living module' was a room only about six feet wide, ten feet long, and eight feet high.

Each room was attractively furnished and looked very much like a good motel suite, with convertible sofa, TV, small Hi-Fi set, and vision 'phone. Moreover, by a simple trick of interior decoration, the one unbroken wall could be converted by the flip of a switch into a convincing terrestrial landscape. There was a choice of eight views.

This touch of luxury was typical of the Base, though it was sometimes hard to explain its necessity to the folk back on Earth. Every man and woman in Clavius had cost a hundred thousand dollars in training and transport and housing; it was worth a little extra to maintain their peace of mind. This was not art for art's sake, but art for the sake of sanity.

One of the attractions of life in the Base – and on the Moon as a whole – was undoubtedly the low gravity, which produced a sense of general well-being. However, this had its dangers, and it was several weeks before an emigrant from Earth could adapt to it. On the Moon the human body had to learn a whole new set of reflexes. It had, for the first time, to distinguish between mass and weight.

A man who weighed one hundred and eighty pounds on Earth might be delighted to discover that he weighed only thirty pounds on the Moon. As long as he moved in a straight line at a uniform speed he felt a wonderful sense of buoyancy. But as soon as he attempted to change course, to turn corners, or to stop suddenly – *then* he would find that his full one hundred and eighty pounds of mass, or inertia, was still there. For that was fixed and unalterable – the same on Earth, Moon, Sun or in free space. Before one could be properly adapted to lunar living, therefore, it was essential to learn that all objects were now six times as sluggish as their mere weight would suggest. It was a lesson usually driven home by numerous collisions and hard knocks, and old lunar hands kept their distance from newcomers until they were acclimatized.

With its complex of workshops, offices, store-rooms, computer centre, generators, garage, kitchen, laboratories and food processing plant, Clavius Base was a miniature world in itself. And, ironically, many of the skills that had been used to build this underground empire had been developed during the half-century of the Cold War.

Any man who had ever worked in a hardened missile site would have felt at home in Clavius. Here on the Moon were the same arts and hardware of underground living, and of protection against a hostile environment; but here they had turned to the purposes of peace. After ten thousand years man had at last found something as exciting as war. Unfortunately, not all nations had yet realized that fact.

. . .

The mountains that had been so prominent just before landing had mysteriously disappeared, hidden from sight below the steeply curving lunar horizon. Around the spacecraft was a flat, grey plain, brilliantly lit by the slanting earthlight. Although the sky was, of course, completely black, only the brighter stars and planets could be seen, unless the eyes were shaded from the surface glare.

Several very odd vehicles were rolling up to the Aries-1B spaceship – cranes, hoists, servicing trucks – some automatic, some operated by a driver in a small pressure cabin. Most of them moved on balloon tyres, for this smooth, level plain posed no transportation difficulties; but one tanker rolled on the peculiar flex-wheels which had proved one of the best all-purpose ways of getting around on the Moon. A series of flat plates arranged in a circle, each plate independently mounted and sprung, the flex-wheel had many of the advantages of the caterpillar track from which it had evolved. It would adapt its shape and diameter to the terrain over which it was moving, and, unlike a caterpillar track, would continue to function even if a few sections were missing.

A small bus with an extension tube like a stubby elephant trunk was now nuzzling affectionately up against the spacecraft. A few seconds later there were bangings and bumpings from outside, followed by the sound of hissing air as connections were made and pressure was equalized. The inner door of the airlock opened, and the welcoming delegation entered.

It was led by Ralph Halvorsen, the Administrator of the Southern Province – which meant not only the Base but also any exploring parties that operated from it. With him was his Chief Scientist, Dr Roy Michaels, a grizzled little geophysicist whom Floyd knew from previous visits, and half a dozen senior scientists and executives. They greeted him with respectful relief; from the Administrator downwards, it was obvious that they looked forward to a chance of unloading some of their worries.

'Very pleased to have you with us, Dr Floyd,' said Halvorsen. 'Did you have a good trip?'

'Excellent,' Floyd answered. 'It couldn't have been better. The crew looked after me very well.'

He exchanged the usual small-talk that courtesy demanded while the bus rolled away from the spacecraft; by unspoken agreement, no one mentioned the reason for his visit. After travelling a thousand feet from the landing site the bus came to a large sign which read:

WELCOME TO CLAVIUS BASE
U.S. Astronautical Engineering Corps
1994

It then dived into a cutting which took it quickly below ground level. A massive door opened ahead, then closed behind them. This happened again, and yet a third time. When the last door had closed there was a great roaring of air, and they were back in atmosphere once more, in the shirt-sleeve environment of the Base.

After a short walk through a tunnel packed with pipes and cables, and echoing hollowly with rhythmic thumpings and throbbings, they arrived in executive territory, and Floyd found himself back in the familiar environment of typewriters, office computers, girl assistants, wall charts and ringing telephones. As they paused outside the door labelled 'ADMINISTRATOR', Halvorsen said diplomatically: 'Dr Floyd and I will be along to the briefing room in a couple of minutes.'

The others nodded, made agreeable sounds, and drifted off down the corridor. But before Halvorsen could usher Floyd into his office there was an interruption. The door opened, and a small figure hurled itself at the Administrator.

'Daddy! You've been Topside! and you *promised* to take me!'

'Now, Diana,' said Halvorsen, with exasperated tenderness, 'I only said I'd take you if I could. But I've been very busy meeting Dr Floyd. Shake hands with him – he's just come from Earth.'

The little girl – Floyd judged that she was about eight – extended a limp hand. Her face was vaguely familiar, and Floyd became aware that the Administrator was looking at him with a quizzical smile. With a shock of recollection he understood why.

'I don't believe it!' he exclaimed. 'When I was here last, she was just a baby!'

'She had her fourth birthday last week,' Halvorsen answered

proudly. 'Children grow fast in this low gravity. But they don't age so quickly – they'll live longer than we do.'

Floyd stared in fascination at the self-assured little lady, noting the graceful carriage and the unusually delicate bone-structure. 'It's nice to meet you again, Diana,' he said. Then something – perhaps sheer curiosity, perhaps politeness – impelled him to add: 'Would *you* like to go to Earth?'

Her eyes widened with astonishment; then she shook her head.

'It's a nasty place; you hurt yourself when you fall down. Besides, there are too many people.'

So here, Floyd told himself, is the first generation of the Spaceborn; there would be more of them in years to come. Though there was sadness in this thought, there was also a great hope. When Earth was tamed and tranquil, and perhaps a little tired, there would still be scope for those who loved freedom, for the tough pioneers, the restless adventurers. But their tools would not be axe, gun, canoe and wagon; they would be nuclear power plant, plasma drive and hydroponic farm. The time was fast approaching when Earth, like all mothers, must say farewell to her children.

With a mixture of threats and promises, Halvorsen managed to evict his determined offspring, and led Floyd into the office. The Administrator's suite was only about fifteen feet square, but it managed to contain all the fittings and status symbols of a typical $50,000-a-year head of a department. Signed photographs of important politicians – including the President of the United States and the Secretary General of the United Nations – adorned one wall, while signed photos of celebrated astronauts covered most of another.

Floyd sank into a comfortable leather chair and was given a glass of 'sherry', courtesy of the Lunar biochemical labs. 'How's it going, Ralph?' Floyd asked, sipping the drink with caution, then with approval.

'Not too bad,' Halvorsen replied. 'However, there *is* something you'd better know about, before you go in there.'

'What is it?'

'Well, I suppose you could describe it as a morale problem,' Halvorsen sighed.

'Oh?'

'It isn't serious yet, but it's getting there fast.'

'The news blackout,' Floyd said flatly.

'Right,' Halvorsen replied. 'My people are getting very steamed up about it. After all, most of them have families back on Earth; they probably believe they're all dead of moon-plague.'

'I'm sorry about that,' said Floyd, 'but no one could think of a better cover story, and so far it's worked. By the way – I met Moisewitch at the Space Station, and even *he* bought it.'

'Well, that should make Security happy.'

'Not too happy – he'd heard of T.M.A.-1; rumours are beginning to leak out. But we just can't issue any statement, until we know what the damn thing is and whether our Chinese friends are behind it.'

'Dr Michaels thinks he has the answer to that. He's dying to tell you.'

Floyd drained his glass.

'And I'm dying to hear him. Let's go.'

CHAPTER 11

ANOMALY

The briefing took place in a large rectangular chamber that could hold a hundred people with ease. It was equipped with the latest optical and electronic displays and would have looked like a model conference room but for the numerous posters, pin-ups, notices and amateur paintings, which indicated that it was also the centre of the local cultural life. Floyd was particularly struck by a collection of signs, obviously assembled with loving care, which carried such messages as 'PLEASE KEEP OFF THE GRASS', 'NO PARKING ON EVEN DAYS', 'DEFENSE DE FUMER', 'TO THE BEACH', 'CATTLE CROSSING', 'SOFT SHOULDERS' and 'DO NOT FEED THE ANIMALS'. If these were genuine – as they certainly appeared to be – their transportation from Earth had cost a small fortune. There was a touching defiance about them; on this hostile world men could still joke about the things they had been forced to leave behind – and which their children would never miss.

A crowd of forty or fifty people was waiting for Floyd, and everyone rose politely as he entered behind the Administrator. As he nodded at several familiar faces, Floyd whispered to Halvorsen: 'I'd like to say a few words before the briefing.'

Floyd sat down in the front row, while the Administrator ascended the rostrum and looked round his audience.

'Ladies and gentlemen,' Halvorsen began, 'I needn't tell you that this is a very important occasion. We are delighted to have Dr Heywood Floyd with us. We all know him by reputation, and many of us are acquainted with him personally. He has just completed a special flight from Earth to be here, and before the briefing he has a few words for us. Dr Floyd.'

Floyd walked to the rostrum amid a sprinkling of polite applause, surveyed the audience with a smile, and said: 'Thank you – I only want to say this. The President has asked me to convey his appreciation of your outstanding work, which we hope the world will soon be able to recognize. I'm quite aware,' he continued carefully, 'that some of you – perhaps most of you – are anxious that the present veil of secrecy be withdrawn; you would not be scientists if you thought otherwise.'

He caught a glimpse of Dr Michaels, whose face was creased in a slight frown which brought out a long scar down his right cheek – presumably the aftermath of some accident in space. The geologist, he was well aware, had been protesting vigorously against what he called this 'cops and robbers nonsense'.

'But I would remind you,' Floyd continued, 'that this is a quite extraordinary situation. We must be absolutely sure of our own facts; if we make errors now there may be no second chance – so please be patient a little longer. Those are also the wishes of the President.

'That's all I have to say. Now I'm ready for your report.'

He walked back to his seat; the Administrator said, 'Thank you very much, Dr Floyd,' and nodded, rather brusquely, to his Chief Scientist. On cue, Dr Michaels walked up to the rostrum, and the lights faded out.

A photograph of the Moon flashed on to the screen. At the very centre of the disc was a brilliant white crater ring, from which a striking pattern of rays fanned out. It looked exactly as if someone had hurled a bag of flour at the face of the Moon, and it had spattered out in all directions.

'On this vertical photograph,' said Michaels, pointing to the central crater, 'Tycho is even more conspicuous than when seen from Earth; then it's rather near the edge of the Moon. But observed from *this* viewpoint – looking straight down from a thousand miles up – you'll see how it dominates the entire hemisphere.'

He let Floyd absorb this unfamiliar view of a familiar object, then continued: 'During the past year we have been conducting a magnetic survey of the region, from a low-level satellite. It was completed only last month – and this is the result – the map that started all the trouble.'

Another picture flashed on the screen; it looked like a contour map, though it showed magnetic intensity, not height above sea level. For the most part, the lines were roughly parallel and spaced well apart;

but in one corner of the map they became suddenly packed together, to form a series of concentric circles -- like a drawing of a knot-hole in a piece of wood.

Even to an untrained eye it was obvious that something peculiar had happened to the Moon's magnetic field in this region; and in large letters across the bottom of the map were the words: 'TYCHO MAGNETIC ANOMALY – ONE (T.M.A.-I).' Stamped on the top right was 'CLASSIFIED'.

'At first we thought it might be an outcrop of magnetic rock, but all the geological evidence was against it. And not even a big nickel-iron meteorite could produce a field as intense as this; so we decided to have a look.

'The first party discovered nothing – just the usual level terrain, buried beneath a very thin layer of moondust. They sank a drill in the exact centre of the magnetic field, to get a core sample for study. Twenty feet down, the drill stopped. So the survey party started to dig – not an easy job in spacesuits, I can assure you.

'What they found brought them back to Base in a hurry. We sent out a bigger team, with better equipment. They excavated for two weeks – with the result you know.'

The darkened assembly room became suddenly hushed and ex-pectant as the picture on the screen changed. Though everyone had seen it many times, there was not a person who failed to crane forward as if hoping to find new details. In Earth and Moon less than a hundred people had so far been allowed to set eyes on this photograph.

It showed a man in a bright red and yellow spacesuit, standing at the bottom of an excavation, and supporting a surveyor's rod marked off in tenths of a metre. It was obviously a night shot, and might have been taken anywhere on the Moon or Mars. But until now no planet had ever produced a scene like this.

The object before which the spacesuited man was posing was a vertical slab of jet-black material, about ten feet high and five feet wide; it reminded Floyd, somewhat ominously of a giant tombstone. Perfectly-sharp-edged and symetrical, it was so black it seemed to have swallowed up the light falling upon it; there was no surface detail at all. It was impossible to tell whether it was made of stone, or metal, or plastic – or some material altogether unknown to man.

'T.M.A.-I,' Dr Michaels declared, almost reverently. 'It looks brand new, doesn't it? I can hardly blame those who thought it was just a few years old, and tried to connect it with the third Chinese Expedi-tion, back in '98. But I never believed that – and now we've been able to date it positively, from local geological evidence.

'My colleagues and I, Dr Floyd, will stake our reputations on this.

T.M.A.-1 has nothing to do with the Chinese. Indeed, it has nothing to do with the human race – for when it was buried, there *were* no humans.

'You see, it is approximately three million years old. What you are now looking at is the first evidence of intelligent life beyond the Earth.'

CHAPTER 12

JOURNEY BY EARTHLIGHT

MACRO-CRATER PROVINCE: Extends S. from near centre of the visible face of the moon, E. of Central Crater Province. Densely pocked with impact craters, many large, and including the largest on moon; in N. some craters fractured from impact forming Mare Imbrium. Rough surfaces almost everywhere, except for some crater bottoms. Most surfaces in slopes, mostly 10 to 12; some crater bottoms nearly level.

LANDING AND MOVEMENT: Landing generally difficult because of rough, sloping surfaces; less difficult in some level crater bottoms. Movement possible almost everywhere but route selection required; less difficult on some level crater bottoms.

CONSTRUCTION: Generally moderately difficult because of slope, and numerous large blocks in loose material; excavation of lava difficult in some crater bottoms.

Tycho. Post-Maria crater, 54 miles diameter, rim 7,900 feet above surroundings; bottom 12,000 feet deep; has the most prominent ray system on the moon, some rays extending more than 500 miles.

Extract from Engineer *Special Study of the Surface of the Moon.* Office. Chief of Engineers, Department of the Army, U.S. Geological Survey, Washington, 1961.

. . .

The mobile lab now rolling across the crater plain at fifty miles an hour looked rather like an outsized trailer mounted on eight flex-wheels. But it was very much more than this; it was a self-contained base in which twenty men could live and work for several weeks. Indeed, it was virtually a land-going spaceship – and in an emergency it could even fly. If it came to a crevasse or canyon which was too large to detour, and too steep to enter, it could hop across the obstacle on its four underjets.

As he peered out of the window, Floyd could see stretching ahead of him a well-defined trail, where dozens of vehicles had left a hard-packed band in the friable surface of the Moon. At regular intervals along the track were tall, slender rods, each carrying a flashing light. No one could possibly get lost, on the two-hundred-mile journey from Clavius Base to T.M.A.-1, even though it was still night and the Sun would not rise for several hours.

The stars overhead were only a little brighter, or more numerous, than on a clear night from the high plateaus of New Mexico or Colorado. But there were two things in that coal-black sky that destroyed any illusion of Earth.

The first was Earth itself – a blazing beacon hanging above the northern horizon. The light pouring down from that giant half-globe was dozens of times more brilliant than the full moon, and it covered all this land with a cold, blue-green phosphorescence.

The second celestial apparition was a faint, pearly cone of light slanting up the eastern sky. It became brighter and brighter towards the horizon, hinting of great fires just concealed below the edge of the Moon. Here was a pale glory that no man had ever seen from Earth, save during the few moments of a total eclipse. It was the corona, harbinger of the lunar dawn, giving notice that before long the Sun would smite this sleeping land.

As he sat with Halvorsen and Michaels in the forward observation lounge, immediately beneath the driver's position, Floyd found his thoughts turning again and again to the three-million-year-wide gulf that had just opened up before him. Like all scientifically literate men, he was used to considering far longer periods of time – but they had concerned only the movements of stars and the slow cycles of the inanimate universe. Mind or intelligence had not been involved; those aeons were empty of all that touched the emotions.

Three million years! The infinitely crowded panorama of written history, with its empires and its kings, its triumphs and its tragedies, covered barely one thousandth of this appalling span of time. Not only Man himself, but most of the animals now alive on Earth, did not even exist when this black enigma was so carefully buried here, in the most brilliant and most spectacular of all the craters of the Moon.

That it had been buried, and quite deliberately, Dr Michaels was absolutely sure. 'At first,' he explained, 'I rather hoped it might mark the site of some underground structure, but our latest excavations have eliminated that. It's sitting on a wide platform of the same black material, with undisturbed rock beneath it. The – *creatures* – who designed it wanted to make sure it stayed put, barring major moonquakes. They were building for eternity.'

There was triumph, and yet sadness, in Michaels's voice, and Floyd could share both emotions. At last, one of man's oldest questions has been answered; here was the proof, beyond all shadow of doubt, that his was not the only intelligence that the universe had brought forth. But with that knowledge, there came again an aching awareness of the immensity of Time. Whatever had passed this way had missed mankind by a hundred thousand generations. Perhaps, Floyd told himself, it was just as well. And yet – what we might have learned from creatures who could cross space, while our ancestors were still living in trees!

A few hundred yards ahead, a signpost was coming up over the Moon's strangely close horizon. At its base was a tent-shaped structure covered with shining silver foil, obviously for protection against the fierce heat of day. As the bus rolled by, Floyd was able to read in the brilliant earthlight:

EMERGENCY DEPOT NO. 3
20 Kilos Lox
10 Kilos Water
20 Foodpaks Mk. 4
1 Toolkit Type B
1 Suit Repair Outfit
! TELEPHONE !

'Have you thought of *that*?' asked Floyd, pointing out of the window. 'Suppose the thing's a supply cache, left behind by an expedition that never returned?'

'It's a possibility,' admitted Michaels. 'That magnetic field certainly labelled its position, so that it could be easily found. But it's rather small – it couldn't hold much in the way of supplies.'

'Why not?' interjected Halvorsen. 'Who knows how big *they* were? Perhaps they were only six inches tall, which would make the thing twenty or thirty storeys high.'

Michaels shook his head.

'Out of the question,' he protested. 'You can't have very small, intelligent creatures; you need a minimum brain size.'

Michaels and Halvorsen, Floyd noticed, usually took opposing viewpoints, yet there appeared to be little personal hostility or friction between them. They seemed to respect each other, and simply agreed to disagree.

There was certainly little agreement anywhere about the nature of T.M.A.-1 – or the Tycho Monolith, as some preferred to call it, retaining part of the abbreviation. In the six hours since he had landed on the Moon, Floyd had heard a dozen theories, but had committed himself to none. Shrine, survey marker, tomb, geophysical instrument – these were perhaps the favourite suggestions, and some of the protagonists grew very heated in their defence. A good many bets had already been placed, and a lot of money would change hands when the truth was finally known – if, indeed, it ever was.

So far, the hard black material of the slab had resisted all the rather mild attempts that Michaels and his colleagues had made to obtain samples. They had no doubt that a laser beam would cut into it – for surely, nothing could resist *that* frightful concentration of energy – but the decision to employ such violent measures would be left to Floyd. He had already decided that X-rays, sonic probes, neutron beams and all other non-destructive means of investigation would be brought into play before he called up the heavy artillery of the laser. It was the mark of a barbarian to destroy something one could not understand; but perhaps men were barbarians, besides the creatures who had made this thing.

And where *could* they have come from? The Moon itself? No, that was utterly impossible. If there had ever been indigenous life on this barren world, it had been destroyed during the last crater-forming epoch, when most of the lunar surface was white-hot.

Earth? Very unlikely, though perhaps not quite impossible. Any advanced terrestrial civilization – presumably a non-human one – back in the Pleistocene Era would have left many other traces of its existence. We would have known all about it, thought Floyd, long before we got to the Moon.

That left two alternatives – the planets, and the stars. Yet all the evidence was against intelligent life elsewhere in the Solar System – or indeed life of *any* kind except on Earth and Mars. The inner planets were too hot, the outer ones far too cold, unless one descended into their atmosphere to depths where the pressures amounted to hundreds of tons to the square inch.

So perhaps these visitors had come from the stars – yet that was even more incredible. As he looked up at the constellations strewn across the ebon lunar sky, Floyd remembered how often his fellow scientists had 'proved' that interstellar travel was impossible. The journey from Earth to Moon was still fairly impressive, but the very nearest star was a hundred million times more distant ... Speculation was a waste of time; he must wait until there was more evidence.

'Please fasten your seatbelts and secure all loose objects,' said the cabin speaker suddenly. 'Forty degree slope approaching.'

Two marker posts with winking lights had appeared on the horizon, and the bus was steering between them. Floyd had barely adjusted his straps when the vehicle slowly edged itself over the brink of a really terrifying incline, and began to descend a long, rubble-covered slope as steep as the roof of a house. The slanting earthlight, coming from behind them, now gave very little illumination, and the bus's own floodlights had been switched on. Many years ago, Floyd had stood on the lip of Vesuvius, staring into the crater; he could easily imagine that he was now driving down into it, and the sensation was not a very pleasant one.

They were descending one of the inner terraces of Tycho, and it levelled out again some thousand feet below. As they crawled down the slope, Michaels pointed out across the great expanse of plain now spread out beneath them.

'There they are,' he exclaimed. Floyd nodded; he had already noticed the cluster of red and green lights several miles ahead, and kept his eyes fixed upon it as the bus edged its way delicately down the slope. The big vehicle was obviously under perfect control, but he did not breathe easily until it was once more on an even keel.

Now he could see, glistening like silver bubbles in the earthlight, a group of pressure domes – the temporary shelters housing the workers on the site. Near these was a radio tower, a drilling rig, a group of parked vehicles and a large pile of broken rock, presumably the material that had been excavated to reveal the monolith. This tiny camp in the wilderness looked very lonely, very vulnerable to the forces of nature ranged silently around it. There was no sign of life, and no visible hint as to why men had come here, so far from home.

'You can just see the crater,' said Michaels. 'Over there on the right – about a hundred yards from that radio antenna.'

So this is it, thought Floyd as the bus rolled past the pressure domes, and came to the lip of the crater. His pulse quickened, as he craned forward for a better view. The vehicle began to creep cautiously down a ramp of hard-packed rock, into the interior of the crater. And there, exactly as he had seen it in the photographs, was T.M.A.-1.

Floyd stared, blinked, shook his head, and stared again. Even in the brilliant earthlight, it was hard to see the object clearly; his first impression was a flat rectangle, that might have been cut out of carbon paper; it seemed to have no thickness at all. Of course, this was an optical illusion; though he was looking at a solid body, it reflected so little light that he could see it only in silhouette.

The passengers were utterly silent as the bus descended into the crater. There was awe, and there was also incredulity – sheer disbelief that the dead Moon, of all worlds, could have sprung this fantastic surprise.

The bus came to a halt within twenty feet of the slab, and broadside on so that all the passengers could examine it. Yet, beyond the geometrically perfect shape of the thing, there was little to see. Nowhere were there any marks, or any abatement of its ultimate, ebon blackness. It was the very crystallization of night, and for one moment Floyd wondered if it could indeed be some extraordinary natural formation, born of the fires and pressures attending the creation of the Moon. But that remote possibility, he knew, had already been examined and dismissed.

At some signal, floodlights around the lip of the crater were switched on, and the bright earthlight was obliterated by a far more brilliant glare. In the lunar vacuum the beams were, of course, completely invisible; they formed overlapping ellipses of blinding white, centred on the monolith. And where they touched it, its ebon surface seemed to swallow them.

Pandora's Box, thought Floyd, with a sudden sense of foreboding – waiting to be opened by inquisitive Man. And what will he find inside?

CHAPTER 13

THE SLOW DOWN

The main pressure-dome at the T.M.A.-1 site was only twenty feet across, and its interior was uncomfortably crowded. The bus, coupled to it through one of the two airlocks, gave some much-appreciated extra living room.

Inside this hemispherical, double-walled balloon lived, worked and slept the six scientists and technicians now permanently attached to the project. It also contained most of their equipment and instruments, all the stores that could not be left in the vacuum outside, cooking, washing and toilet facilities, geological samples and a small TV screen through which the site could be kept under continuous surveillance.

Floyd was not surprised when Halvorsen elected to remain in the dome; he stated his views with admirable frankness.

'I regard spacesuits as a necessary evil,' said the Administrator. 'I wear one four times a year, for my quarterly checkout tests. If you don't mind, I'll sit here and watch over the TV.'

Some of this prejudice was now unjustified, for the latest models were infinitely more comfortable than the clumsy suits of armour worn by the first lunar explorers. They could be put on in less than a minute, even without help, and were quite automatic. The Mk V into which Floyd was now carefully sealed would protect him from the worst that the Moon could do, either by day or by night.

Accompanied by Dr Michaels, he walked into the small airlock. As the throbbing of the pumps died away, and his suit stiffened almost imperceptibly around him, he felt himself enclosed in the silence of vacuum.

That silence was broken by the welcome sound of his suit radio.

'Pressure O.K., Dr Floyd? Are you breathing normally?'

'Yes – I'm fine.'

His companion carefully checked the dials and gauges on the outside of Floyd's suit. Then he said: 'O.K. – let's go.'

The outer door opened, and the dusty moonscape lay before them, glimmering in the earthlight.

With a cautious, waddling movement, Floyd followed Michaels through the lock. It was not hard to walk; indeed, in a paradoxical way the suit made him feel more at home than any time since reaching the Moon. Its extra weight, and the slight resistance it imposed on his motion, gave some of the illusion of the lost terrestrial gravity.

The scene had changed since the party had arrived barely an hour ago. Though the stars, and the half-earth were still as bright as ever, the fourteen-day lunar night was almost ended. The glow of the corona was like a false moonrise along the eastern sky – and then, without warning, the tip of the radio mast a hundred feet above Floyd's head suddenly seemed to burst into flame, as it caught the first rays of the hidden Sun.

They waited while the project supervisor and two of his assistants emerged from the airlock, then walked slowly towards the crater. By the time they had reached it, a thin bow of unbearable incandescence had thrust itself above the eastern horizon. Though it would take more than a hour for the Sun to clear the edge of the slowly turning Moon, the stars were already banished.

The crater was still in shadow, but the floodlights mounted around its rim lit the interior brilliantly. As Floyd walked slowly down the ramp, towards the black rectangle, he felt a sense not only of awe but of helplessness. Here, at the very portals of Earth, man was already face to face with a mystery that might never be solved. Three million years ago, *something* had passed this way, had left this unknown and perhaps unknowable symbol of its purpose, and had returned to the planets – or to the stars.

Floyd's suit radio interrupted his reverie. 'Project supervisor speaking. If you'd all line up on this side, we'd like to take a few photos. Dr Floyd, will you stand in the middle – Dr Michaels – thank you....'

No one except Floyd seemed to think that there was anything funny about this. In all honesty he had to admit that he was glad someone had brought a camera; here was a photo that would undoubtedly be historic, and he wanted copies for himself. He hoped that his face would be clearly visible through the helmet of the suit.

'Thanks, gentlemen,' said the photographer, after they had posed somewhat self-consciously in front of the monolith, and he had made a dozen exposures. 'We'll ask the Base Photo Section to send you copies.'

Then Floyd turned his full attention to the ebon slab – walking slowly around it, examining it from every angle, trying to imprint its strangeness upon his mind. He did not expect to find anything, for he knew that every square inch had already been gone over with microscopic care.

Now the sluggish Sun had lifted itself above the edge of the crater, and its rays were pouring almost broadside upon the eastern side of the block. Yet it seemed to absorb every particle of light as if it had never been.

Floyd decided to try a simple experiment; he stood between the monolith and the Sun, and looked for his own shadow on the smooth black sheet. There was no trace of it. At least ten kilowatts of raw heat must be falling on the slab; if there was anything inside, it must be rapidly cooking.

How strange, Floyd throught, to stand here while this – this *thing* – is seeing daylight for the first time since the Ice Ages began on Earth. He wondered again about its black colour; that was ideal, of course, for absorbing solar energy. But he dismissed the thought at once; for who would be crazy enough to bury a sun-powered device twenty feet *underground*?

He looked up at the Earth, beginning to wane in the morning sky. Only a handful of the six billion people there knew of this discovery; how would the world react to the news when it was finally released?

The political and social implications were immense; every person of real intelligence – everyone who looked an inch beyond his nose – would find his life, his values, his philosophy, subtly changed. Even if nothing whatsoever was discovered about T.M.A.-1, and it remained an eternal mystery, Man would know that he was not unique in the universe. Though he had missed them by millions of years, those who had once stood here might yet return: and if not, there might well be others. All futures must now contain this possibility.

Floyd was still musing over these thoughts when his helmet speaker suddenly emitted a piercing electronic shriek, like a hideously over-loaded and distorted time signal. Involuntarily, he tried to block his ears with his space-suited hands; then he recovered, and groped frantically for the gain control of his receiver. While he was still fumbling, four more of the shrieks blasted out of the ether; then there was a merciful silence.

All round the crater, figures were standing in attitudes of paralysed astonishment. So it's nothing wrong with *my* gear, Floyd told himself; everyone heard those piercing electronic screams.

After three million years of darkness T.M.A.-1 had greeted the lunar dawn.

CHAPTER 14

THE LISTENERS

A hundred million miles beyond Mars, in the cold loneliness where no man had yet travelled, Deep Space Monitor 79 drifted among the tangled orbits of the asteroids. For three years it had fulfilled its mission flawlessly – a tribute to the American scientists who had designed it, the British engineers who had built it, the Russian technicians who had launched it. A delicate spider's web of antennae sampled the passing waves of radio noise – the ceaseless crackle and hiss of what Pascal, in a far simpler age, had naïvely called the 'silence of infinite space'. Radiation detectors noted and analysed incoming cosmic rays from the Galaxy and points beyond; neutron and X-ray telescopes kept watch on the strange stars that no human eye would ever see; magnetometers observed the gusts and hurricanes of the solar winds, as the Sun breathed million-mile-an-hour blasts of tenuous plasma into the faces of its circling children. All these things, and many others, were patiently noted by Deep Space Monitor 79, and recorded in its crystalline memory.

One of its antennae, by now unconsidered miracles of electronics, was always aimed at a point never far from the Sun. Every few months its distant target could have been seen, had there been any eye here to watch, as a bright star with a close, fainter companion; but most of the time it was lost in the solar glare.

To that far-off planet Earth, every twenty-four hours, the monitor would send the information it had patiently garnered, packed neatly into one five-minute pulse. About a quarter of an hour later, travelling at the speed of light, that pulse would reach its destination. The machines whose duty it was would be waiting for it; they would amplify and record the signal, and add it to the thousands of miles of magnetic tape now stored in the vaults of the World Space Centres at Washington, Moscow and Canberra.

Since the first satellites had orbited, almost fifty years earlier, billions and quadrillions of pulses of information had been pouring down from space, to be stored against the day when they might contribute to the advance of knowledge. Only a minute fraction of all this raw material would ever be processed; but there was no way of telling what observation some scientist might wish to consult, ten, or fifty, or a hundred years from now. So everything had to be kept on file, stacked in endless air-conditioned galleries, triplicated at the three centres against the possibility of accidental loss. It was part of the real treasure of mankind, more valuable than all the gold locked uselessly away in bank vaults.

And now Deep Space Monitor 79 had noted something strange – a faint yet unmistakable disturbance rippling across the Solar System, and quite unlike any natural phenomenon it had ever observed in the past. Automatically, it recorded the direction, the time, the intensity; in a few hours it would pass the information to Earth.

As, also, would Orbiter M 15, circling Mars twice a day; and High Inclination Probe 21, climbing slowly above the plane of the ecliptic; and even Artificial Comet 5, heading out into the cold wastes beyond Pluto, along an orbit whose far point it would not reach for a thousand years. All noted the peculiar bursts of energy that had disturbed their instruments; all, in due course, reported back automatically to the memory stores on distant Earth.

The computers might never have perceived the connection between four peculiar sets of signals, from space-probes on independent orbits millions of miles apart. But as soon as he glanced at his morning report, the Radiation Forecaster at Goddard knew that something strange had passed through the Solar System during the last twenty-four hours.

He had only part of its track, but when the computer projected it on the Planet Situation Board, it was as clear and unmistakable as a vapour trail across a cloudless sky, or a single line of footprints over a field of virgin snow. Some immaterial pattern of energy, throwing off a spray of radiation like the wake of a racing speedboat, had leaped from the face of the Moon, and was heading out towards the stars.

CHAPTER 15

DISCOVERY

The ship was still only thirty days from Earth; yet David Bowman sometimes found it hard to believe that he had ever known any other existence than the closed little world of *Discovery*. All his years of training, all his earlier missions to the Moon and Mars, seemed to belong to another man, in another life.

Frank Poole admitted to the same feelings, and had sometimes jokingly regretted that the nearest psychiatrist was the better part of a hundred million miles away. But this sense of isolation and estrangement was easy enough to understand, and certainly indicated no abnormality. In the fifty years since men had ventured into space, there had never been a mission quite like this.

It had begun, five years ago, as Project Jupiter – the first manned round trip to the greatest of the planets. The ship was nearly ready for the two-year voyage when, somewhat abruptly, the mission profile had been changed.

Discovery would still go to Jupiter; but she would not stop there. She would not even slacken speed as she raced through the far-ranging Jovian satellite system. On the contrary – she would use the gravitational field of the giant world as a sling, to cast her even further from the Sun. Like a comet, she would streak on across the outer reaches of the Solar System to her ultimate goal, the ringed glory of Saturn. And she would never return.

For *Discovery*, it would be a one-way trip—yet her crew had no intention of committing suicide. If all went well, they would be back on Earth within seven years – five of which would pass like a flash in the dreamless sleep of hibernation, while they awaited rescue by the still unbuilt *Discovery II*.

The word 'rescue' was carefully avoided in all the Astronautics Agencies' statements and documents; it implied some failure of planning, and the approved jargon was 'reacquisition'. If anything went really wrong, there would certainly be no hope of rescue, almost a billion miles from Earth.

It was a calculated risk, like all voyages into the unknown. But half a

century of research had proved that artificially-induced human hibernation was perfectly safe, and it had opened up new possibilities in space-
travel. Not until this mission, however, had they been exploited to the
utmost.

The three members of the survey team, who would not be needed
until the ship entered her final orbit around Saturn, would sleep
through the entire outward flight. Tons of food and other expendables
would thus be saved; almost as important, the team would be fresh and
alert, and not fatigued by the ten-month voyage, when they went into
action.

Discovery would enter a parking orbit around Saturn, becoming a new
moon of the giant planet. She would swing back and forth along a two-
million-mile ellipse that took her close to Saturn, and then across the
orbits of all its major moons. They would have a hundred days in which
to map and study a world with eighty times the area of Earth, and
surrounded by a retinue of at least fifteen known satellites – one of them
as large as the planet Mercury.

There must be wonders enough here for centuries of study; the first
expedition could only carry out a preliminary reconnaissance. All that it
found would be radioed back to Earth; even if the explorers never
returned, their discoveries would not be lost.

At the end of the hundred days *Discovery* would close down. All the
crew would go into hibernation; only the essential systems would
continue to operate, watched over by the ship's tireless electronic brain.
She would continue to swing around Saturn, on an orbit now so well
determined that men would know exactly where to look for her a
thousand years hence. But in only five years, according to present plans,
Discovery II would come. Even if six, or seven or eight years elapsed her
sleeping passengers would never know the difference. For all of them, the
clock would have stopped – as it had stopped already for Whitehead,
Kaminski and Hunter.

Sometimes Bowman, as First Captain of *Discovery*, envied his three
unconscious colleagues in the frozen peace of the Hibernaculum. They
were free from all boredom and all responsibility; until they reached
Saturn, the external world did not exist.

But that world was watching them, through their bio-sensor displays.
Tucked inconspicuously away among the massed instrumentation of the
Control Deck were five small panels marked HUNTER, WHITEHEAD,
KAMINSKI, POOLE, BOWMAN. The last two were blank and lifeless; their
time would not come until a year from now. The others bore constellations of tiny green lights, announcing that everything was well; and
on each was a small display screen across which sets of glowing lines

traced the leisurely rhythms that indicated pulse, respiration and brain activity.

There were times when Bowman, well aware how unnecessary this was – for the alarm would sound instantly if anything was wrong – would switch over to audio output. He would listen, half hypnotized, to the infinitely slow heartbeats of his sleeping colleagues, keeping his eyes fixed on the sluggish waves that marched in synchronism across the screen.

Most fascinating of all were the E.E.G. displays – the electronic signatures of the three personalities that had once existed, and would one day exist again. They were almost free from the spikes and valleys, the electrical explosions that marked the activity of the waking brain – or even of the brain in normal sleep. If there was any wisp of consciousness remaining, it was beyond the reach of instruments, and of memory.

This last fact, Bowman knew from personal experience. Before he was chosen for this mission, his reactions to hibernation had been tested. He was not sure whether he had lost a week of his life – or whether he had postponed his eventual death by the same amount of time.

When the electrodes had been attached to his forehead, and the sleep-generator had started to pulse, he had seen a brief display of kaleidoscopic patterns and drifting stars. Then they had faded, and darkness had engulfed him. He had never felt the injections, still less the first touch of cold as his body temperature was reduced to only a few degrees above freezing ...

... He awoke, and it seemed that he had scarcely closed his eyes. But he knew that was an illusion; somehow, he was convinced that years had really passed.

Had the mission been completed? Had they already reached Saturn, carried out their survey, and gone into hibernation? Was *Discovery II* here, to take them back to Earth?

He lay in a dream-like daze, utterly unable to distinguish between real and false memories. He opened his eyes, but there was little to see except a blurred constellation of lights which puzzled him for some minutes. Then he realized that he was looking at the indicator lamps on a Ship Situation Board; but it was impossible to focus on them. He soon gave up the attempt.

Warm air was blowing across him, removing the chill from his limbs. There was quiet, but stimulating music welling from a speaker behind his head. It was slowly growing louder and louder ...

Then a relaxed, friendly – but, he knew, computer-generated – voice spoke to him.

'You are becoming operational, Dave. Do not get up or attempt any violent movements. Do not try to speak.'

Do not get up! thought Bowman. *That* was funny. He doubted if he could wriggle a finger. Rather to his surprise, he found that he could.

He felt quite contented, in a dazed, stupid kind of way. He knew dimly that the rescue ship must have come, that the automatic revival sequence had been triggered, soon he would be seeing other human beings. That was fine, but he did not get excited about it.

Presently he felt hunger. The computer, of course, had anticipated this need.

'There is a signal button by your right hand, Dave. If you are hungry, please press it.'

Bowman forced his fingers to hunt around, and presently discovered the pear-shaped bulb. He had forgotten all about it, though he must have known it was there. How much else had he forgotten – did hibernation erase memory?

He pressed the button, and waited. Several minutes later, a metal arm moved out from the bunk, and a plastic nipple descended towards his lips. He sucked on it eagerly, and a warm, sweet fluid coursed down his throat, bringing renewed strength with every drop.

Presently it went away, and he rested once more. He could move his arms and legs now; the thought of walking was no longer an impossible dream.

Though he felt his strength swiftly returning, he would have been content to lie here for ever, if there had been no further stimulus from outside. But presently another voice spoke to him – and this time it was wholly human, not a construct of electrical pulses assembled by a more-than-human memory. It was also a familiar voice, though it was some time before he could recognize it.

'Hello, Dave. You're coming round fine. You can talk now. Do you know where you are?'

He worried about this for some time. If he was *really* orbiting Saturn, what had happened during all the months since he had left Earth? Again he began to wonder if he was suffering from amnesia. Paradoxically, the very thought reassured him. If he could remember the word 'amnesia', his brain must be in fairly good shape ...

But he still did not know where he was, and the speaker at the other end of the circuit must have understood his situation completely.

'Don't worry, Dave. This is Frank Poole. I'm watching your heart and respiration – everything is perfectly normal. Just relax – take it easy. We're going to open the door now and pull you out.'

Soft light flooded into the chamber; he saw moving shapes silhouetted against the widening entrance. And in that moment, all his memories came back to him, and he knew exactly where he was.

Though he had come back safely from the furthest borders of sleep, and the nearest borders of death, he had been gone only a week. When he left the hibernaculum, he would not see the cold Saturnian sky; that was more than a year in the future and half a billion miles away. He was still in the crew trainer at the Houston Space Flight Centre, under the hot Texas sun.

CHAPTER 16

HAL

But now Texas was invisible, and even the United States was hard to see. Though the low-thrust plasma drive had long since been closed down, *Discovery* was still coasting with her slender, arrow-like body pointed away from Earth, and all her high-powered optical gear was orientated towards the outer planets, where her destiny lay.

There was one telescope, however, that was permanently aimed at Earth. It was mounted like a gunsight on the rim of the ship's long-range antenna, and checked that the great parabolic bowl was rigidly locked upon its distant target. While Earth remained centred in the crosswires, the vital communication link was intact, and messages could come and go along the invisible beam that lengthened more than two million miles with every day that passed.

At least once in every watch period, Bowman would look homeward through the antenna-alignment telescope. As Earth was now far back towards the Sun, its darkened hemisphere faced *Discovery*, and on the central display screen the planet appeared as a dazzling silver crescent, like another Venus.

It was rare that any geographical features could be identified, in that ever-shrinking arc of light, for cloud and haze concealed them, but even the darkened portion of the disc was endlessly fascinating. It was sprinkled with shining cities; sometimes they burned with a steady light, sometimes they twinkled like fireflies as atmospheric tremors passed over them.

There were also periods when, as the Moon swung back and forth in its orbit, it shone down like a great lamp upon the darkened seas and continents of Earth. Then, with a thrill of recognition, Bowman could often glimpse familiar coastlines, shining in that spectral lunar light. And sometimes, when the Pacific was calm, he could even see the moonglow shimmering across its face; and he would remember nights beneath the palm trees of tropical lagoons.

Yet he had no regrets for these lost beauties. He had enjoyed them all, in his thirty-five years of life; and he was determined to enjoy them again, when he returned rich and famous. Meanwhile, distance made them all the more precious.

The sixth member of the crew cared for none of these things, for it was not human. It was the highly advanced HAL 9000 computer, the brain and nervous system of the ship.

Hal (for *H*euristically programmed *AL*gorithmic computer, no less) was a masterwork of the third computer breakthrough. These seemed to occur at intervals of twenty years, and the thought that another one was now imminent already worried a great many people.

The first had been in the 1940s, when the long-obsolete vacuum tube had made possible such clumsy, high-speed morons as ENIAC and its successors. Then, in the 1960s, solid-state microelectrics had been perfected. With their advent, it was clear that artificial intelligences at least as powerful as Man's need be no larger than office desks – if one only knew how to construct them.

Probably no one would ever know this; it did not matter. In the 1980s, Minsky and Good had shown how neural networks could be generated automatically – self-replicated – in accordance with any arbitrary learning programme. Artificial brains could be grown by a process strikingly analogous to the development of a human brain. In any given case, the precise details would never be known, and even if they were, they would be millions of times too complex for human understanding.

Whatever way it worked, the final result was a machine intelligence that could reproduce – some philosophers still preferred to use the word 'mimic' – most of the activities of the human brain, and with far greater speed and reliability. It was extremely expensive, and only a few units of the HAL 9000 series had yet been built; but the old jest that it would always be easier to make organic brains by unskilled labour was beginning to sound a little hollow.

Hal had been trained for this mission as thoroughly as his human colleagues – and at many times their rate of input, for in addition to his intrinsic speed, he never slept. His prime task was to monitor the life-support systems, continually checking oxygen pressure, temperature, hull leakage, radiation and all the other interlocking factors upon which the lives of the fragile human cargo depended. He could carry out the intricate navigational corrections, and execute the necessary flight manoeuvres when it was time to change course. And he could watch over the hibernators, making any necessary adjustments to their environment, and doling out the minute quantities of intravenous fluids that kept them alive.

The first generations of computers had received their inputs through glorified typewriter keyboards, and had replied through high-speed printers and visual displays. Hal could do this when necessary, but most of his communication with his shipmates was by means of the spoken word. Poole and Bowman could talk to Hal as if he were a human being, and he would reply in the perfect, idiomatic English he had learned during the fleeting weeks of his electronic childhood.

Whether Hal could actually think was a question which had been settled by the British mathematician Alan Turing back in the 1940s. Turing had pointed out that, if one could carry out a prolonged conversation with a machine – whether by typewriter or microphone was immaterial – without being able to distinguish between its replies and those that a man might give, then the machine *was* thinking, by any sensible definition of the word. Hal could pass the Turing test with ease.

The time might even come when Hal would take command of the ship. In an emergency, if no one answered his signals, he would attempt to wake the sleeping members of the crew, by electrical and chemical stimulation. If they did not respond, he would radio Earth for further orders.

And then, if there was no reply from Earth, he would take what measures he deemed necessary to safeguard the ship and to continue the mission – whose real purpose he alone knew, and which his human colleagues could never have guessed.

Poole and Bowman had often humorously referred to themselves as caretakers or janitors aboard a ship that could really run itself. They would have been astonished, and more than a little indignant, to discover how much truth that jest contained.

CHAPTER 17

CRUISE MODE

The day-by-day running of the ship had been planned with great care, and – theoretically at least – Bowman and Poole knew what they would be doing at every moment of the twenty-four hours. They operated on a twelve-hours-on, twelve-hours-off basis, taking charge alternately, and never being both asleep at the same time. The officer-on-duty normally remained on the Control Deck, while his deputy saw to the general housekeeping, inspected the ship, coped with the odd jobs that constantly arose, or relaxed in his cubicle.

Although Bowman was nominal captain, on this phase of the mission no outside observer could have deduced the fact. He and Poole switched roles, rank and responsibilities completely every twelve hours. This kept them both at peak training, mimimized the chances of friction, and helped towards the goal of a hundred per cent redundancy.

Bowman's day began at 1600, Ship's Time – the Universal Ephemeris Time of the astronomers. If he was late. Hal had a variety of beeps and chimes to remind him of his duty, but they had never been used. As a test, Poole had once switched off the alarm; Bowman had still risen automatically at the right time.

His first official act of the day would be to advance the Master Hibernation Timer twelve hours. If this operation was missed twice in a row, Hal would assume that both he and Poole had been incapacitated, and would take the necessary emergency action.

Bowman would attend to his toilet, and do his isometric exercises, before settling down to breakfast and the morning's radio-fax edition of the *World Times*. On Earth he never read the paper as carefully as he did now; even the smallest items of society gossip, the most fleeting political rumours, seemed of absorbing interest as it flashed across the screen.

At 0700 he would officially relieve Poole on the Control Deck, bringing him a squeeze-tube of coffee from the kitchen. If – as was usually the case – there was nothing to report and no action to be taken, he would settle down to check all the instrument readings, and would run through a series of tests designed to spot possible malfunctions. By 1000 this would be finished, and he would start on a study period.

Bowman had been a student for more than half his life; he would continue to be one until he retired. Thanks to the Twentieth Century revolution in training and information-handling techniques, he already possessed the equivalent of two or three college educations – and, what was more, he could remember 90 per cent of what he had learned.

Fifty years ago, he would have been considered a specialist in applied astronomy, cybernetics and space propulsion systems – yet he was prone to deny, with genuine indignation, that he was a specialist at all. Bowman had never found it possible to focus his interest exclusively on any subject; despite the dark warnings of his instructors, he had insisted on taking his Master's degree in General Astronautics – a course with a vague and woolly syllabus, designed for those whose I.Q.s were in the low 130s, and who would never reach to the top ranks of their profession.

His decision had been right; that very refusal to specialize had made him uniquely qualified for his present task. In much the same way Frank Poole – who sometimes disparagingly called himself 'General Practitioner in space biology' – had been an ideal choice as his deputy. The two of them, with, if necessary, help from Hal's vast stores of information, could cope with any problems likely to arise during the voyage – as long as they kept their minds alert and receptive, and continually re-engraved old patterns of memory.

So for two hours, from 1000 to 1200, Bowman would engage in a dialogue with an electronic tutor, checking his general knowledge or absorbing material specific to this mission. He would prowl endlessly over ship's plans, circuit diagrams and voyage profiles, or would try to assimilate all that was known about Jupiter, Saturn and their far-ranging families of moons.

At midday, he would retire to the galley and leave the ship to Hal while he prepared his lunch. Even here, he was still fully in touch with events, for the tiny lounge-cum-dining-room contained a duplicate of the Situation Display Panel, and Hal could call him at a moment's notice. Poole would join him for this meal, before retiring for his six-hour sleep period, and usually they would watch one of the regular TV programmes beamed to them from Earth.

Their menus had been planned with as much care as any part of the mission. The food, most of it freeze-dried, was uniformly excellent, and had been chosen for the minimum of trouble. Packets had merely to be opened and popped into the tiny auto-galley, which beeped for attention when the job was done. They could enjoy what tasted like – and, equally important, *looked* like – orange juice, eggs (any style), steaks, chops, roasts, fresh vegetables, assorted fruits, ice-cream, and even freshly-baked bread.

After lunch, from 1300 to 1600, Bowman would make a slow and careful tour of the ship – or such part of it as was accessible. *Discovery* measured almost four hundred feet from end to end, but the little universe occupied by her crew lay entirely inside the forty-foot sphere of the pressure hull.

Here were all the life-support systems, and the Control Deck which was the operational heart of the ship. Below this was a small 'space-garage' fitted with three airlocks through which powered capsules, just large enough to hold a man, could sail out into the void if the need arose for extra-vehicular activity.

The equatorial region of the pressure-sphere – the slice, as it were, from Capricorn to Cancer – enclosed a slowly-rotating drum, thirty-five feet in diameter. As it made one revolution every ten seconds, this carousel or centrifuge produced an artificial gravity equal to that of the Moon. This was enough to prevent the physical atrophy which would result from the complete absence of weight, and it also allowed the routine functions of living to be carried out under normal – or nearly normal – conditions.

The carousel therefore contained the kitchen, dining, washing and toilet facilities. Only here was it safe to prepare and handle hot drinks – quite dangerous in weightless conditions, where one can be badly scalded by floating globules of boiling water. The problem of shaving was also solved; there would be no weightless bristles drifting around, to endanger electrical equipment and produce a health hazard.

Around the rim of the carousel were five tiny cubicles, fitted out by each astronaut according to taste and containing his personal belongings. Only Bowman's and Poole's were now in use, while the future occupants of the other three cabins reposed in their electronic sarcophagi next door.

The spin of the carousel could be stopped if necessary; when this happened, its angular momentum had to be stored in a flywheel, and switched back again when rotation was re-started. But normally it was left running at constant speed, for it was easy enough to enter the big, slowly turning drum by going hand-over-hand along a pole through the zero-gee region at its centre. Transferring to the moving section was as easy and automatic, after a little experience, as stepping on to a moving escalator.

The spherical pressure-hull formed the head of a flimsy, arrow-shaped structure more than a hundred yards long. *Discovery*, like all vehicles intended for deep-space penetration, was too fragile and un-streamlined ever to enter an atmosphere, or to defy the full gravitational field of any planet. She had been assembled in orbit around the Earth, tested on a translunar maiden flight, and finally checked out in orbit above the Moon. She was a creature of pure space – and she looked it.

Immediately behind the pressure-hull was grouped a cluster of four large liquid hydrogen tanks – and beyond them, forming a long, slender Vee, were the radiating fins that dissipated the waste heat of the nuclear reactor. Veined with a delicate tracery of pipes for the cooling fluid, they looked like the wings of some vast dragonfly, and from certain angles gave *Discovery* a fleeting resemblance to an old-time sailing-ship.

At the very end of the Vee, three hundred feet from the crew-compartment, was the shielded inferno of the reactor, and the complex of focussing electrodes through which emerged the incandescent star-stuff of the plasma drive. This had done its work weeks ago, forcing *Discovery* out of her parking orbit round the Moon. Now the reactor was merely ticking over as it generated electrical power for the ship's services, and the great radiating fins, that would glow cherry red when *Discovery* was accelerating under maximum thrust, were dark and cool.

Although it would require an excursion out into space to examine this region of the ship, there were instruments and remote TV cameras which gave a full report on conditions here. Bowman now felt that he knew intimately every square foot of radiator panels, and every piece of plumbing associated with them.

By 1600 he would have finished his inspection, and would make a detailed verbal report to Mission Control, talking until the acknowledgement started to come in. Then he would switch off his own transmitter, listen to what Earth had to say, and send back his reply to any queries. At 1800 hours, Poole would awaken, and he would hand over command.

He would then have six off-duty hours, to use as he pleased. Sometimes he could continue his studies, or listen to music, or look at movies. Much of the time he would wander at will through the ship's inexhaustible electronic library. He had become fascinated by the great explorations of the past – understandably enough, in the circumstances. Sometimes he would cruise with Pytheas out through the Pillars of Hercules, along the coast of a Europe barely emerging from the Stone Age, and venture almost to the chill mists of the Arctic. Or two thousand years later, he would pursue the Manilla galleons with Anson, sail with Cook along the unknown hazards of the Great Barrier Reef, achieve with Magellan the first circumnavigation of the world. And he began to read the Odyssey, which of all the books spoke to him most vividly across the gulfs of time.

For relaxation he could always engage Hal in a large number of semi-mathematical games, including checkers, chess and pantominoes. If

Hal went all out, he could win any one of them; but that would be bad for morale. So he had been programmed to win only fifty per cent of the time, and his human partners pretended not to know this.

The last hours of Bowman's day were devoted to general cleaning up and odd jobs, followed by dinner at 2000 – again with Poole. Then there would be an hour during which he would make or receive any personal calls from Earth.

Like all his colleagues, Bowman was unmarried; it was not fair to send family men on a mission of such duration. Though numerous ladies had promised to wait until the expedition returned, no one had really believed this. At first, both Poole and Bowman had been making rather intimate personal calls once a week though the knowledge that many ears must be listening at the Earth end of the circuit tended to inhibit them. Yet already, though the voyage was scarcely started, the warmth and frequency of the conversations with their girls on Earth had begun to diminish. They had expected this; it was one of the penalties of an astronaut's, as it had once been of a mariner's way of life.

It was true – indeed, notorious – that seamen had compensations at other ports; unfortunately there were no tropical islands full of dusky maids beyond the orbit of Earth. The space medics, of course, had tackled this problem with their usual enthusiasm; and the ship's pharmacopoeia provided adequate, though hardly glamorous, substitutes.

Just before he signed off, Bowman would make his final report, and check that Hal had transmitted all the instrumentation tapes for the day's run. Then, if he felt like it, he would spend a couple of hours either reading or looking at a movie; and at midnight, he would go to sleep – usually without any help from electronarcosis.

Poole's programme was a mirror image of his own, and the two schedules dovetailed together without friction. Both men were fully occupied, they were too intelligent and well adjusted to quarrel, and the voyage had settled down to a comfortable, utterly uneventful routine, the passage of time marked only by the changing numbers on the digital clocks.

The greatest hope of *Discovery*'s little crew was that nothing would mar this peaceful monotony, in the weeks and months that lay ahead.

CHAPTER 18

THROUGH THE ASTEROIDS

Week after week, running like a streetcar along the tracks of her utterly predetermined orbit, *Discovery* swept past the orbit of Mars and on towards Jupiter. Unlike all the vessels traversing the skies or seas of Earth, she required not even the most minute touch on the controls. Her course was fixed by the laws of gravitation; there were no uncharted shoals, no dangerous reefs on which she would run aground. Nor was there the slightest danger of collision with another ship; for there was no vessel – at least of Man's making – anywhere between her and the infinitely distant stars.

Yet the space which she was now entering was far from empty. Ahead lay a no-man's-land threaded by the paths of more than a million asteroids – less than ten thousand of which had ever had their orbits precisely determined by astronomers. Only four were over a hundred miles in diameter; the vast majority were merely giant boulders, trundling aimlessly through space.

There was nothing that could be done about them; though even the smallest could completely destroy the ship if it slammed into it at tens of thousands of miles an hour, the chance of this happening was negligible. On the average, there was only one asteroid in a volume a million miles on a side; that *Discovery* should also happen to occupy this same point, and *at the same time*, was the very least of her crew's worries.

On Day 86 they were due to make their closest approach to any known asteroid. It had no name – merely the number 7794 – and was a fifty-yard-diameter rock that had been detected by the Lunar Observatory in 1997 and immediately forgotten except by the patient computers of the Minor Planet Bureau.

When Bowman came on duty, Hal promptly reminded him of the forthcoming encounter – not that he was likely to have forgotten the only scheduled in-flight event of the entire voyage. The track of the asteroids against the stars, and its co-ordinates at the moment of closest approach, had already been printed out on the display screens. Listed also were the observations to be made or attempted; they were going to be very busy when 7794 flashed past them only nine hundred miles away, at a relative speed of eighty thousand miles an hour.

When Bowman asked Hal for the telescopic display, a sparsely sprinkled star field flashed on to the screen. There was nothing that looked like an asteroid; all the images, even under the highest magnification, were dimensionless points of light.

'Give me the target reticule,' asked Bowman. Immediately four faint, narrow lines appeared, bracketing a tiny and undistinguished star. He stared at it for many minutes, wondering if Hal could possibly be mistaken; then he saw that the pinpoint of light was moving, with barely perceptible slowness, against the background of the stars. It might still be half a million miles away – but its movement proved that, as cosmic distances went, it was almost near enough to touch.

When Poole joined him on the Control Deck, six hours later, 7794 was hundreds of times more brilliant, and was moving so swiftly against its background that there was no question of its identity. And it was no longer a point of light; it had begun to show a clearly visible disc.

They stared at that passing pebble in the sky with the emotions of sailors on a long sea voyage, skirting a coast on which they cannot land. Though they were perfectly well aware that 7794 was only a lifeless, airless chunk of rock, this knowledge scarcely affected their feelings. It was the only solid matter they would meet this side of Jupiter – still two hundred million miles away.

Through the high-powered telescope, they could see that the asteroid was very irregular, and turning slowly end over end. Sometimes it looked like a flattened sphere, sometimes it resembled a roughly-shaped brick; its rotation period was just over two minutes. There were mottled patches of light and shade distributed apparently at random over its surface, and often is sparkled like a distant window as planes or outcroppings of crystalline material flashed in the Sun.

It was racing past them at almost thirty miles a second; they had only a few frantic minutes in which to observe it closely. The automatic cameras took dozens of photographs, the navigation radar's returning echoes were carefully recorded for future analysis – and there was just time for a single impact probe.

The probe carried no instruments; none could survive a collision at such cosmic speeds. It was merely a small slug of metal, shot out from *Discovery* on a course which should intersect that of the asteroid.

As the seconds before impact ticked away, Poole and Bowman waited with mounting tension. The experiment, simple though it was in principle, taxed the accuracy of their equipment to the limits. They were aiming at a hundred-and-fifty-foot-diameter target, from a distance of thousands of miles ...

Against the darkened portion of the asteroid, there was a sudden, dazzling explosion of light. The tiny slug had impacted at meteoric speed; in a fraction of a second, all its energy had been transformed into heat. A puff of incandescent gas had erupted briefly into space; abroad *Discovery*, the cameras were recording the rapidly-fading spectral lines. Back on Earth, experts would analyse them, looking for the tell-tale signatures of glowing atoms. And so, for the first time, the composition of an asteroid's crust would be determined.

Within an hour, 7794 was a dwindling star, showing no trace of a disc. When Bowman next came on watch it had vanished completely.

They were alone again; they would remain alone, until the outermost of Jupiter's moons came swinging up towards them, three months from now.

CHAPTER 19

TRANSIT OF JUPITER

Even from twenty miles away, Jupiter was already the most conspicuous object in the sky ahead. The planet was now a pale, salmon-hued disc, about half the size of the Moon as seen from Earth, with the dark, parallel bands of its cloud-belts clearly visible. Shuttling back and forth in the equatorial plane were the brilliant stars of Io, Europa, Ganymede and Callisto – worlds that elsewhere would have counted as planets in their own right, but which here were merely satellites of a giant master.

Through the telescope, Jupiter was a glorious sight – a mottled, multicoloured globe that seemed to fill the sky. It was impossible to grasp its real size; Bowman kept reminding himself that it was eleven times the diameter of Earth, but for a long time this was a statistic with no real meaning.

Then, while he was briefing himself from the tapes in Hal's memory units, he found something that suddenly brought the appalling scale of the planet into focus. It was an illustration that showed the Earth's entire surface peeled off and then pegged, like the skin of an animal, on the disc of Jupiter. Against *this* background, all the continents and oceans of Earth appeared no larger than India on the terrestrial globe ...

When Bowman used the highest magnification of *Discovery*'s telescopes, he appeared to be hanging above a slightly flattened globe, looking down upon a vista of racing clouds that had been smeared into

bands by the giant world's swift rotation. Sometimes those bands con-
gealed into wisps and knots and continent-sized masses of coloured
vapour; sometimes they were linked by transient bridges thousands of
miles in length. Hidden beneath those clouds was enough material to
outweigh all the other planets in the Solar System. And what *else*, Bowman wondered, was also hidden there?

Over this shifting, turbulent roof of clouds, forever hiding the real
surface of the planet, circular patterns of darkness sometimes glided.
One of the inner moons was transiting the distant Sun, its shadow
marching beneath it over the restless Jovian cloudscape.

There were other, and far smaller, moons even out here – twenty
miles from Jupiter. But they were only flying mountains a few dozen
miles in diameter, and the ship would pass nowhere near any of them.
Every few minutes, the radar transmitter would gather its strength
and send out a silent thunderclap of power; no echoes of new satellites
came pulsing back from the emptiness.

What did come, with ever-growing intensity, was the roar of Jupiter's
own radio voice. In 1955, just before the dawn of the space age,
astronomers had been astonished to find that Jupiter was blasting out
millions of horsepower on the ten-metre band. It was merely raw
noise, associated with haloes of charged particles circling the planet like
the Van Allen Belts of Earth, but on a far greater scale.

Sometimes, during lonely hours on the Control Deck, Bowman would
listen to this radiation. He would turn up the gain until the room filled
with a crackling, sissing roar; out of this background, at irregular
intervals, emerged brief whistles and peeps like the cries of demented
birds. It was an eerie sound, for it had nothing to do with Man; it was
as lonely and as meaningless as the murmur of waves on a beach, or
the distant crash of thunder beyond the horizon.

Even at her present speed of over a hundred thousand miles an hour,
it would take *Discovery* almost two weeks to cross the orbits of all the
Jovian satellites. More moons circled Jupiter than planets orbited the
Sun; the Lunar Observatory was discovering new ones every year, and
the tally had now reached thirty-six. The outermost – Jupiter XXVII
– moved backwards in an unstable path nineteen million miles from
its temporary master. It was the prize in a perpetual tug-of-war between
Jupiter and the Sun, for the planet was constantly capturing short-lived
moons from the asteroid belt, and losing them again after a few million
years. Only the inner satellites were its permanent property; the Sun
could never wrest them from its grasp.

Now there was new prey for the clashing gravitational fields. *Discovery*
was accelerating towards Jupiter along a complex orbit computed

months ago by the astronomers on Earth, and constantly checked by Hal. From time to time there would be minute, automatic nudges from the control jets, scarcely perceptible aboard the ship, as they made fine adjustment to the trajectory.

Over the radio link with Earth, information was flowing back in a constant stream. They were now so far from home that, even travelling at the speed of light, their signals were taking fifty minutes for the journey. Though the whole world was looking over their shoulders, watching through their eyes and their instruments as Jupiter approached, it would be almost an hour before the news of their discoveries reached home.

The telescopic cameras were operating constantly as the ship cut across the orbit of the giant inner satellites – every one of them larger than the Moon, every one of them unknown territory. Three hours before transit, *Discovery* passed only twenty thousand miles from Europa, and all instruments were aimed at the approaching world, as it grew steadily in size, changed from globe to crescent, and swept swiftly sunward.

Here were fourteen million square miles of land, which, until this moment, had never been more than a pinhead in the mightiest telescope. They would race past it in minutes, and must make the most of the encounter, recording all the information they could. There would be months in which they could play it back at leisure.

From a distance, Europa had seemed like a giant snowball, reflecting the light of the far-off Sun with remarkable efficiency. Closer observations confirmed this; unlike the dusty Moon, Europa was a brilliant white, and much of its surface was covered with glittering hunks that looked like stranded icebergs. Almost certainly, these were formed from ammonia and water that Jupiter's gravitational field had somehow failed to capture.

Only along the equator was bare rock visible; here was an incredibly jagged no-man's-land of canyons and jumbled boulders, forming a darker band that completely surrounded the little world. There were a few impact craters, but no sign of vulcanism; Europa had obviously never possessed any internal sources of heat.

There was, as had long been known, a trace of atmosphere. When the dark edge of the satellite passed across a star, it dimmed briefly before the moment of eclipse. And in some areas there was a hint of cloud – perhaps a mist of ammonia droplets, borne on tenuous methane winds.

As swiftly as it had rushed out of the sky ahead, Europa dropped astern; and now Jupiter itself was only two hours away. Hal had checked and rechecked the ship's orbit with infinite care, and there was no need for further speed corrections until the moment of closest approach. Yet, even knowing this, it was a strain on the nerves to watch that giant globe ballooning minute by minute. It was difficult to believe that *Discovery* was not plunging directly into it, that the planet's immense gravitational field was not dragging them down to destruction.

Now was the time to drop the atmospheric probes – which, it was hoped, would survive long enough to send back some information from below the Jovian cloud-deck. Two stubby, bomb-shaped capsules, enclosed in ablative heat-shields, were gently nudged into orbits which for the first few thousand miles deviated scarcely at all from that of *Discovery*.

But they slowly drifted away; and now, at last, even the unaided eye could see what Hal had been asserting. The ship was in a near-grazing orbit, not a collision one; she would miss the atmosphere. True, the difference was only a few hundred miles – a mere nothing, when one was dealing with a planet ninety thousand miles in diameter – but that was enough.

Jupiter now filled the entire sky; it was so huge that neither mind nor eye could grasp it any longer, and both had abandoned the attempt. If it had not been for the extraordinary variety of colour – the reds and pinks and yellows and salmons and even scarlets – of the atmosphere beneath them, Bowman could have believed that he was flying low over a cloudscape on Earth.

And now, for the first time in all their journeying, they were about to lose the Sun. Pale and shrunken though it was, it had been *Discovery*'s constant companion since her departure from Earth, five months ago. But now her orbit was diving into the shadow of Jupiter; she would soon pass over the night side of the planet.

A thousand miles ahead, the band of twilight was hurtling towards them; behind, the Sun was sinking swiftly into the Jovian clouds. Its rays spread out along the horizon like two flaming, down-turned horns, then contracted and died in a brief blaze of chromatic glory. The night had come.

And yet – the great world below was not wholly dark. It was awash with phosphorescence, which grew brighter minute by minute as their eyes grew accustomed to the scene. Dim rivers of light were flowing from horizon to horizon, like the luminous wakes of ships on some tropical sea. Here and there they gathered into pools of liquid fire, trembling with vast, submarine disturbances welling up from the hidden heart of Jupiter. It was a sight so awe-inspiring that Poole and Bowman could have stared for hours; was this, they wondered, merely the result of chemical and electrical forces down there in that seething cauldron

– or was it the by-product of some fantastic form of life? These were questions which scientists might still be debating when the new-born century drew to its close.

As they drove deeper and deeper in to the Jovian night, the glow beneath them grew steadily brighter. Once Bowman had flown over northern Canada during the height of an auroral display; the snow-covered landscape had been as bleak and brilliant as this. And *that* arctic wilderness, he reminded himself, was more than a hundred degrees warmer than the regions over which they were hurtling now.

'Earth signal is fading rapidly,' announced Hal. 'We are entering the first diffraction zone.'

They had expected this – indeed, it was one of the mission's objectives, as the absorption of radio waves would give valuable information about the Jovian atmosphere. But now that they had actually passed behind the planet, and it was cutting off communication with Earth, they felt a sudden overwhelming loneliness. The radio blackout would last only an hour; then they would emerge from Jupiter's eclipsing screen, and could resume contact with the human race. That hour, however, would be one of the longest of their lives.

Despite their relative youth, Poole and Bowman were veterans of a dozen space-voyages – but now they felt like novices. They were attempting something for the first time; never before had any ship travelled at such speeds, or braved so intense a gravitational field. The slightest error in navigation at this critical point, and *Discovery* would go speeding on towards the far limits of the Solar System, beyond any hope of rescue.

The slow minutes dragged by. Jupiter was now a vertical wall of phosphorescence, stretching to infinity above them – and the ship was climbing straight up its glowing face. Though they knew that they were moving far too swiftly for even Jupiter's gravity to capture them, it was hard to believe that *Discovery* had not become a satellite of this monstrous world.

At last, far ahead, there was a blaze of light along the horizon. They were emerging from shadow, heading out into the Sun. And at almost the same moment Hal announced: 'I am in radio contact with Earth. I am also happy to say that the perturbation manoeuvre has been successfully completed. Our time to Saturn is one hundred and sixty-seven days, five hours, eleven minutes.'

That was within a minute of the estimate; the fly-by had been carried out with impeccable precision. Like a ball on a cosmic pool table, *Discovery* had bounced off the moving gravitational field of Jupiter, and had gained momentum from the impact. Without using any fuel, she had increased her speed by several thousand miles an hour.

Yet there was no violation of the laws of mechanics; Nature always balances her books, and Jupiter had lost exactly as much momentum as *Discovery* had gained. The planet had been slowed down – but as its mass was a sextillion times greater than the ship's, the change in its orbit was far too small to be detectable. The time had not yet come when Man could leave his mark upon the Solar System.

As the light grew swiftly around them, and the shrunken Sun lifted once more into the Jovian sky, Poole and Bowman reached out silently and shook each other's hands.

Though they could hardly believe it, the first part of the mission was safely over.

CHAPTER 20

THE WORLD OF THE GODS

But they had not yet finished with Jupiter. Far behind, the two probes that *Discovery* had launched were making contact with the atmosphere.

One was never heard from again; presumably it made too steep an entry, and burned up before it could send any information. The second was more successful; it sliced through the upper layers of the Jovian atmosphere, then skimmed out once more into space. As had been planned, it had lost so much speed by the encounter that it fell back again along a great ellipse. Two hours later it re-entered atmosphere on the daylight side of the planet – moving at seventy thousand miles an hour.

Immediately, it was wrapped in an envelope of incandescent gas, and radio contact was lost. There were anxious minutes of waiting, then, for the two watchers on the Control Deck. They could not be certain that the probe would survive, and that the protective ceramic shield would not burn completely away before braking had finished. If that happened, the instruments would be vaporized in a fraction of a second.

But the shield held, long enough for the glowing meteor to come to rest. The charred fragments were jettisoned, the robot thrust out its antennae, and began to peer around with its electronic senses. Aboard *Discovery*, now almost a quarter of a million miles away, the radio started to bring in the first authentic news from Jupiter.

The thousands of pulses pouring in every second were reporting atmospheric composition, pressure, temperature, magnetic fields, radio-activity, and dozens of other factors which only the experts on Earth could unravel. However, there was one message that could be under-stood instantly; it was the TV picture, in full colour, sent back by the falling probe.

The first views came when the robot had already entered the atmo-sphere, and had discarded its protective shell. All that was visible was a yellow mist, flecked with patches of scarlet which moved past the camera at a dizzying rate – streaming upwards as the probe fell at several hundred miles an hour.

The mist grew thicker; it was impossible to guess whether the camera was seeing for ten inches or ten miles, because there were no details on which the eye could focus. It seemed that, as far as the TV system was concerned, the mission was a failure. The equipment had worked, but there was nothing to see in this foggy, turbulent atmosphere.

And then, quite abruptly, the mist vanished. The probe must have fallen through the base of a high layer of cloud, and come out into a clear zone – perhaps a region of almost pure hydrogen with only a sparse scattering of ammonia crystals. Though it was still quite im-possible to judge the scale of the picture, the camera was obviously seeing for miles.

The scene was so alien that for a moment it was almost meaningless to eyes accustomed to the colours and shapes of Earth. Far, far below lay an endless sea of mottled gold, scarred with parallel ridges that might have been the crests of gigantic waves. But there was no move-ment; the scale of the scene was too immense to show it. And that golden vista could not possibly have been an ocean, for it was still high in the Jovian atmosphere. It could only have been another layer of cloud.

Then the camera caught, tantalizingly blurred by distance, a glimpse of something very strange. Many miles away, the golden landscape reared itself into a curiously symmetrical cone, like a volcanic mountain. Around the summit of that cone was a halo of small, puffy clouds – all about the same size, all quite distinct and isolated. There was some-thing disturbing and unnatural about them – if, indeed, the word 'natural' could ever be applied to this awesome panorama.

Then, caught by some turbulence in the rapidly thickening atmo-sphere, the probe twisted around to another quarter of the horizon, and for a few seconds the screen showed nothing but a golden blur. Presently it stabilized; the 'sea' was much closer, but as enigmatic as ever. One could now observe that it was interrupted here and there with patches of darkness, which might have been holes or gaps leading to still deeper layers of the atmosphere.

The probe was destined never to reach them. Every mile, the density of the gas around it had been doubling, the pressure mounting as it sank deeper and deeper towards the hidden surface of the planet. It was still high above that mysterious sea when the picture gave one premonitory flicker, then vanished, as the first explorer from Earth crumpled beneath the weight of the miles of atmosphere above it.

It had given, in its brief life, a glimpse of perhaps one millionth of Jupiter, and had barely approached the planet's surface, hundreds of miles down in the deepening mists. When the picture faded from the screen, Bowman and Poole could only sit in silence, turning the same thought over in their minds.

The ancients had, indeed, done better than they knew, when they named this world after the lord of all the gods. If there was life down there, how long would it take even to locate it? And after that, how many centuries before men could follow this first pioneer – in what kind of ship?

But these matters were now no concern of *Discovery* and her crew. Their goal was a still stranger world, almost twice as far from the Sun – across another half billion miles of comet-haunted emptiness.

ABYSS

CHAPTER 21

BIRTHDAY PARTY

The familiar strains of 'Happy Birthday', hurled across seven hundred million miles of space at the velocity of light, died away among the vision screens and instrumentation of the Control Deck. The Poole family, grouped rather self-consciously round the birthday cake on Earth, lapsed into a sudden silence.

Then Mr Poole, Senior, said gruffly: 'Well, Frank – can't think of anything else to say at the moment, except that our thoughts are with you, and we're wishing you the happiest of birthdays.'

'Take care, darling,' Mrs Poole interjected tearfully. 'God bless you.'

There was a chorus of 'goodbyes', and the vision screen went blank. How strange to think, Poole told himself, that all this had happened more than an hour ago; by now his family would have dispersed again and its members would be miles from home. But in a way that time-lag, though it could be frustrating, was also a blessing in disguise. Like every man of his age, Poole took it for granted that he could talk instantly, to anyone on Earth, whenever he pleased. Now that this was no longer true, the psychological impact was profound. He had moved into a new dimension of remoteness, and almost all emotional links had been stretched beyond the yield-point.

'Sorry to interrupt the festivities,' said Hal, 'but we have a problem.'

'What is it?' Bowman and Poole asked simultaneously.

'I am having difficulty in maintaining contact with Earth. The trouble is in the AE 35 unit. My fault prediction centre reports that it may fail within seventy-two hours.'

'We'll take care of it,' Bowman replied. 'Let's see the optical alignment.'

'Here it is, Dave. It's still O.K. at the moment.'

On the display screen appeared a perfect half-moon, very brilliant against a background almost free of stars. It was covered with clouds, and showed not one geographical feature that could be recognized. Indeed, at first glance it could easily be mistaken for Venus.

But not at a second one, for there beside it was the *real* Moon which Venus did not possess – a quarter the size of Earth, and in exactly the same phase. It was easy to imagine that the two bodies were mother and child, as many astronomers had believed, before the evidence of the lunar rocks had proved beyond doubt that the Moon had never been part of the Earth.

Poole and Bowman studied the screen in silence for half a minute. This image was coming to them from the long-focus TV camera mounted on the rim of the big radio dish; the cross-wires at its centre showed the exact orientation of the antenna. Unless the narrow pencil beam was pointed precisely at Earth, they could neither receive nor transmit. Messages in both directions would miss their target and would shoot, unheard and unseen, out through the Solar System and into the emptiness beyond. If they were ever received, it would not be for centuries – and not by men.

'Do you know where the trouble is?' asked Bowman.

'It's intermittent and I can't localize it. But it appears to be in the AE 35 unit.'

'What procedure do you suggest?'

'The best thing would be to replace the unit with a spare, so that we can check it over.'

'O.K. – let us have the hard copy.'

The information flashed on the display screen; simultaneously, a sheet of paper slid out of the slot immediately beneath it. Despite all the electronic read-outs, there were times when good, old-fashioned printed material was the most convenient form of record.

Bowman studied the diagrams for a moment, then whistled.

'You might have told us,' he said. 'This means going outside the ship.'

'I'm sorry,' Hal replied. 'I assumed you knew that the AE 35 unit was on the antenna mounting.'

'I probably did, a year ago, but there are eight thousand sub-systems aboard. Anyway, it looks a straightforward job. We only have to unlock a panel and put in a new unit.'

'That suits me fine,' said Poole, who was the crew-member designated for routine extra-vehicular activity. 'I could do with a change of scenery. Nothing personal, of course.'

'Let's see if Mission Control agrees,' said Bowman. He sat still for a few seconds, marshalling his thoughts, then started to dictate a message.

'Mission Control, this is X-Ray-Delta-One. At two-zero-four-five, on-board fault prediction centre in our nine-triple-zero computer showed Alpha Echo three five unit as probable failure within seventy-two hours. Request check your telemetry monitoring and suggest you review unit in your ship systems simulator. Also, confirm your approval our plan to go EVA and replace Alpha Echo three five unit prior to failure. Mission control, this is X-Ray-Delta-One, two-one-zero-three transmission concluded.'

Through years of practice, Bowman could switch at a moment's notice to this jargon – which someone had once christened 'Technish' – and back again to normal speech, without clashing his mental gears. Now there was nothing to do but wait for the confirmation, which would take at least two hours as the signals made the round trips past the orbits of Jupiter and Mars.

It came while Bowman was trying, without much success, to beat Hal at one of the geometrical pattern games stored in his memory.

'X-Ray-Delta-One, this is Mission Control, acknowledging your one-two-zero-three. We are reviewing telemetric information on our mission simulator and will advise.

'Roger your plan to go EVA and replace Alpha Echo three five unit prior to possible failure. We are working on test procedures for you to apply to faulty unit.'

The serious business having been completed, the Mission Controller reverted to normal English.

'Sorry you fellows are having a bit of trouble, and we don't want to add to your woes. But if it's convenient to you prior to EVA, we have a request from Public Information. Could you do a brief recording for general release, outlining the situation and explaining just what the AE 35 does. Make it as reassuring as you can. We could do it, of course – but it will be much more convincing in your own words. Hope this won't interfere too badly with your social life. X-Ray-Delta-One, this is Mission Control, two-one-five-five, transmission concluded.'

Bowman could not help smiling at the request. There were times when Earth showed a curious insensitivity and lack of tact. 'Make it reassuring', indeed!

When Poole joined him at the end of his sleep period, they spent ten minutes composing and polishing the reply. In the early stages of the mission, there had been countless requests from all the news media for interviews, discussions – almost anything that they cared to say. But as the weeks drifted uneventfully past, and the time-lag increased from a few minutes to over an hour, interest had gradually slackened. Since the excitement of the Jupiter fly-by, over a month ago, they had made only three or four tapes for general release.

'Mission Control, this is X-Ray-Delta-One. Here is your press statement.

'Earlier today, a minor technical problem occurred. Our HAL 9000 computer predicted the failure of the AE 35 unit.

'This is a small but vital component of the communication system. It keeps our main antenna aimed at Earth to within a few thousandths of a degree. This accuracy is required, since at our present distance of more than seven hundred million miles, Earth is only a rather faint star, and our very narrow radio beam could easily miss it.

'The antenna is kept constantly tracking Earth by motors controlled from the central computer. But those motors get their instructions via the AE 35 unit. You might compare it to a nerve centre in the body, which translates the brain's instructions to the muscles of a limb. If the nerve fails to pass on the correct signals, the limb becomes useless. In our case, a breakdown of the AE 35 unit could mean that the antenna will start pointing at random. This was a common trouble with the deep-space probes of the last century. They often reached other planets, then failed to send back any information because their antennae couldn't locate Earth.

'We don't know the nature of the fault yet, but the situation is not at all serious, and there is no need for alarm. We have two back-up AE 35s, each of which has an operational life expectancy of twenty years – so the chance that a second will fail during the course of this mission is negligible. Also, if we can diagnose the present trouble, we may be able to repair the number one unit.

'Frank Poole, who is specially qualified for this type of work, will go outside the ship and replace the faulty unit with the back-up. At the same time, he'll take the opportunity of checking the hull and repairing some micro-punctures that have been too small to merit a special EVA.

'Apart from this minor problem, the mission is still going uneventfully and should continue in the same manner.

'Mission Control, this is X-Ray-Delta-One, two-one-zero-four, transmission concluded.'

CHAPTER 22

EXCURSION

Discovery's extravehicular capsules or 'space-pods' were spheres about nine feet in diameter, and the operator sat behind a bay-window which gave him a splendid view. The main rocket drive produced an acceleration of one-fifth of a gravity – just sufficient to hover on the Moon – while small attitude-control nozzles allowed for steering. From an area immediately beneath the bay-window sprouted two sets of articulated metal arms or 'waldoes', one for heavy duty, the other for delicate manipulation. There was also an extensive turret carrying a variety of power-tools, such as screwdrivers, jackhammers, saws and drills.

Space-pods were not the most elegant means of transport devised by man, but they were absolutely essential for construction and maintenance work in vacuum. They were usually christened with feminine names, perhaps in recognition of the fact that their personalities were sometimes slightly unpredictable. *Discovery*'s trio were Anna, Betty and Clara.

Once he had put on his personal pressure suit – his last line of defence – and climbed inside the pod, Poole spent ten minutes carefully checking the controls. He burped the steering jets, flexed the waldoes, reconfirmed oxygen, fuel, power reserve. Then, when he was completely satisfied, he spoke to Hal over the radio circuit. Though Bowman was standing by on the Control Deck, he would not interfere unless there was some obvious mistake or malfunction.

'This is Betty. Start pumping sequence.'

'Pumping sequence started,' repeated Hal.

At once, Poole could hear the throbbing of the pumps as precious air was sucked out of the lock chamber. Presently, the thin metal of the pod's external shell made crinkling, crackling noises; then, after about five minutes, Hal reported:

'Pumping sequence concluded.'

Poole made a final check of his tiny instrument panel. Everything was perfectly normal.

'Open outer door,' he ordered.

Again Hal repeated his instructions; at any stage, Poole had only to call 'Hold!' and the computer would stop the sequence immediately.

Ahead, the walls of the ship slid apart. Poole felt the pod rock briefly as the last thin traces of air rushed into space. Then he was looking out at the stars – and, as it happened, at the tiny, golden disc of Saturn, still four hundred million miles away.

'Commence pod ejection.'

Very slowly, the rail from which the pod was hanging extended itself out through the open door, until the vehicle was suspended just beyond the hull of the ship.

Poole gave a half-second burst on the main jet, and the pod slid gently off the rail, becoming at last an independent vehicle pursuing its own orbit round the Sun. He now had no connection with *Discovery* – not even a safety line. The pods seldom gave trouble; and even if he got stranded, Bowman could easily come and rescue him.

Betty responded smoothly to the controls; he let her drift outwards for a hundred feet, then checked her forward momentum, and spun her round so that he was looking back at the ship. Then he began his tour of the pressure hull.

His first target was a fused area about half an inch across, with a tiny central crater. The particles of dust that had impacted here at over a hundred thousand miles an hour was certainly smaller than a pin-head, and its enormous kinetic energy had vaporized it instantly. As was often the case, the crater looked as if it had been caused by an explosion from *inside* the ship; at these velocities, materials behaved in strange ways and the laws of common-sense mechanics seldom applied.

Poole examined the area carefully, then sprayed it with sealant from a pressurized container in the pod's general-purpose kit. The white, rubbery fluid spread over the metal skin, hiding the crater from view. The leak blew one large bubble, which burst when it was about six inches across – then a much smaller one – then it subsided as the fast-setting cement did its work. He watched it intently for several minutes, but there was no further sign of activity. However, to make double certain, he sprayed on a second layer; then he set off towards the antenna.

It took him some time to orbit *Discovery*'s spherical pressure-hull, for he never let the pod build up a speed of more than a few feet a second. He was in no hurry, and it was dangerous to move at a high velocity so near the ship. He had to keep a sharp look-out for the various sensors and instrument booms that projected from the hull at unlikely places, and he also had to be careful with his own jet blast. It could do consider-able damage, if it happened to hit some of the more fragile equipment.

When at last he reached the long-range antenna, he surveyed the situation carefully. The big twenty-foot-diameter bowl appeared to be aimed directly at the Sun, for the Earth was now almost in line with the solar disc. The antenna mounting and all its orientation gear was therefore in total darkness, hidden in the shadow of the great metal saucer.

Poole had approached it from the rear; he had been careful not to go in front of the shallow parabolic reflector, lest Betty interrupt the beam and cause a momentary, but annoying, loss of contact with Earth. He could not see anything of the equipment he had come to service, until he switched on the pod's spotlights and banished the shadows.

Beneath the small metal plate lay the cause of the trouble. The plate was secured by four lock-nuts, and as the entire AE 35 unit had been designed for easy replacement, Poole did not anticipate any problems.

It was obvious, however, that he could not do the job while he remained in the space-pod. Not only was it risky to manoeuvre so close to the delicate, and even spidery, framework of the antenna, but Betty's control-jets could easily buckle the paper-thin reflecting surface of the big radio mirror. He would have to park the pod twenty feet away and go out in his suit. In any event, he could remove the unit much more quickly with his gloved hands, than with Betty's remote manipulators.

All this he reported carefully to Bowman, who double-checked every stage in the operation before it was carried out. Though this was a simple, routine job, nothing could be taken for granted in space, and no detail must be overlooked. In extravehicular activities, there was no such thing as a 'minor' mistake.

He received the O.K. for the procedure, and parked the pod some twenty feet away from the base of the antenna support. There was no danger that it would drift off into space; nevertheless, he clamped a manipulator hand over one of the many short sections of ladder rung strategically mounted on the outer hull.

Then he checked the systems of his pressure suit, and when he was quite satisfied, bled the air out of the pod. As Betty's atmosphere hissed away into the vacuum of space, a cloud of ice crystals formed briefly around him, and the stars were momentarily dimmed.

There was one thing more to do before he left the pod. He switched over from Manual to Remote operation, putting Betty now under control of Hal. It was a standard safety precaution; though he was still secured to Betty by an immensely strong spring-loaded cord little thicker than cotton, even the best safety lines had been known to fail. He would look a fool if he needed his vehicle – and was unable to call it to his assistance by passing instructions to Hal.

The door of the pod swung open, and he drifted slowly out into the silence of space, his safety-line unreeling behind him. Take things easy – never move quickly – stop and think – these were the rules for extravehicular activity. If one obeyed them, there was never any trouble.

He grabbed one of Betty's external hand-holds, and removed the spare AE 35 unit from the carry-pouch where it had been stowed, kangaroo fashion. He did not stop to collect any of the pod's collection of tools, most of which were not designed for use by human hands. All the adjustable wrenches and keys he was likely to need were already attached to the belt of his suit.

With a gentle push, he launched himself towards the gimballed

mounting of the big dish, that loomed like a giant saucer between him
and the Sun. His own double shadow, thrown by Betty's spotlights,
danced across the convex surface in fantastic patterns as he drifted down
the twin beams. But here and there, he was surprised to notice, the rear
of the great radio mirror sparkled with dazzlingly brilliant pin-points
of light.

He puzzled over these for the few seconds of his silent approach, then
realized what they were. During the voyage, the reflector must have
been penetrated many times by micrometeors; he was seeing the sunlight blazing through the tiny craters. They were all far too small to
have affected the system's performance appreciably.

As he was moving very slowly, he broke the gentle impact with his
outstretched arm, and grabbed hold of the antenna mounting before
he could rebound. He quickly hooked his safety belt to the nearest
attachment; that would give him something to brace against when he
used his tools. Then he paused, reported the situation to Bowman and
considered his next step.

There was one minor problem; he was standing – or floating – in his
own light, and it was hard to see the AE 35 unit in the shadow he
cast. So he ordered Hal to swing the spots off to one side, and after a
little experimenting got a more uniform illumination from secondary
light reflected off the back of the antenna dish.

For a few seconds, he studied the small metal hatch with its four
wire-secured locking nuts. Then, muttering to himself, 'Tampering by
unauthorized personnel invalidates the manufacturer's guarantee', he
snipped the wires and started to untwist the nuts. They were a standard
size, fitting the zero-torque wrench that he carried. The tool's internal
spring mechanism would absorb the reaction as the nuts were un-
threaded, so that the operator would have no tendency to spin around
in reverse.

The four nuts came off without any trouble, and Poole stowed them
carefully away in a convenient pouch. (One day, somebody had predicted, Earth would have a ring like Saturn's composed entirely of
lost bolts, fasteners and even tools that had escaped from careless orbital
construction workers.) The metal cover was a little sticky, and for a
moment he was afraid it might have cold-welded into place; but after
a few taps it came loose, and he secured it to the antenna mounting
by a large crocodile clip.

Now he could see the electronic circuitry of the AE 35 unit. It was
in the form of a thin slab, about the size of a postcard, gripped by a
slot just large enough to hold it. The unit was secured in place by two
locking bars, and had a small handle so that it could be easily removed.

But it was still operating, feeding the antenna the impulses that kept it aimed at the far-off pinpoint of Earth. If it was pulled out now, all control would be lost, and the dish would slam round to its neutral or zero azimuth position, pointing along the axis of *Discovery*. And this could be dangerous; it might crash into him as it rotated.

To avoid this particular hazard, it was only necessary to cut off power to the control system; then the antenna could not move, unless Poole knocked against it himself. There was no danger of losing Earth during the few minutes it would take him to replace the unit; their target would not have shifted appreciably against the background of the stars in such a brief interval of time.

'Hal,' Poole called over the radio circuit, 'I am about to remove the unit. Switch off all control power to the antenna system.'

'Antenna control power off,' answered Hal.

'Here goes. I'm pulling the unit out *now*.'

The card slipped out of its slot with no difficulty; it did not jam, and none of the dozens of sliding contacts stuck. Within a minute, the spare was in place.

But Poole was taking no chances. He pushed himself gently away from the antenna mount, just in case the big dish went wild when power was restored. When he was safely out of range, he called to Hal: 'The new unit should be operational. Restore control power.'

'Power on,' answered Hal. The antenna remained rock steady.

'Carry out fault prediction tests.'

Now microscopic pulses would be bounding through the complex circuitry of the unit, probing for possible failures, testing the myriads of components to see that they all lay within their specified tolerances. This had been done, of course, a score of times before the unit had ever left the factory; but that was two years ago, and more than half a billion miles away. It was often impossible to see how solid-state electronic components *could* fail; yet they did.

'Circuit fully operational,' reported Hal after only ten seconds. In that time, he had carried out as many tests as a small army of human inspectors.

'Fine,' said Poole with satisfaction. 'Now replacing the cover.'

This was often the most dangerous part of an extravehicular operation when a job was finished, and it was merely a matter of tidying up and getting back inside the ship – that was when the mistakes were made. But Frank Poole would not have been on this mission unless he was careful and conscientious. He took his time, and though one of the locking nuts almost got away from him, he caught it before it had travelled more than a few feet.

Fifteen minutes later he was jetting back into the space-pod garage, quietly confident that here was one job that need not be done again. In this, however, he was sadly mistaken.

CHAPTER 23

DIAGNOSIS

'Do you mean to say,' exclaimed Frank Poole, more surprised than annoyed, 'that I did all that work for nothing?'

'Seems like it,' answered Bowman. 'The unit checks out perfectly. Even under two hundred per cent overload there's no fault prediction indicated.'

The two men were standing in the tiny workshop-cum-lab in the carousel, which was more convenient than the space-pod garage for minor repairs and examinations. There was no danger, here, of meeting blobs of hot solder drifting down the breeze, or of completely losing small items of equipment that had decided to go into orbit. Such things could – and did – happen in the zero-gee environment of the pod-bay.

The thin, card-sized plate of the AE 35 unit lay on the bench under a powerful magnifying lens. It was plugged into a standard connection frame, from which a neat bundle of multicoloured wires led to an automatic test-set, no bigger than an ordinary desk computer. To check any unit, it was only necessary to connect it up, slip in the appropriate card from the 'trouble-shooting' library, and press a button. Usually, the exact location of the fault would be indicated on a small display screen, with recommendations for action.

'Try it yourself,' said Bowman, in a somewhat frustrated voice.

Poole turned the OVERLOAD SELECT switch to X-2, and jabbed the TEST button. At once, the screen flashed the notice: UNIT O.K.

'I suppose we could go on turning up the juice until we burned the thing out,' he said, 'but that would prove nothing. What do you make of it?'

'Hal's internal fault predictor *could* have made a mistake.'

'It's more likely that our test rig has slipped up. Anyway, better safe than sorry. It's just as well that we replaced the unit, if there's the slightest doubt.'

Bowman unclipped the wafer of circuitry, and held it up to the light.

The partly translucent material was veined with an intricate network of wiring and spotted with dimly visible micro-components, so that it looked like some piece of abstract art.

'We can't take any chances – after all, this is our link with Earth. I'll file it as N/G and drop it in the junk store. Someone else can worry about it, when we get home.'

. . .

But the worrying was to start long before that, with the next transmission from Earth.

'X-Ray-Delta-One, this is Mission Control, reference our two-one-five-five. We appear to have a slight problem.

'Your report that there is nothing wrong with the Alpha Echo three five unit agrees with our diagnosis. The fault could lie in the associated antenna circuits, but if so that should be apparent from other tests.

'There is a third possibility, which may be more serious. Your computer may have made an error in predicting the fault. Both out own nine-triple-zeros agree in suggesting this, on the basis of their information. This is not necessarily cause for alarm, in view of the back-up systems we have, but we would like you to watch out for any further deviations from performance nominal. We have suspected several minor irregularities in the past few days, but none have been important enough for remedial action, and they have shown no obvious pattern from which we can draw any conclusions. We are running further tests with both our computers and will report as soon as the results are available. We repeat that there is no need for alarm; the worst that can happen is that we may have to disconnect your nine-triple-zero temporarily for programme analysis, and hand over control to one of our computers. The time-lag will introduce problems, but our feasibility studies indicate that Earth Control is perfectly satisfactory at this stage of the mission.

'X-Ray-Delta-One, this is Mission Control, two-one-five-six, transmission concluded.'

Frank Poole, who was on watch when the message came in, thought this over in silence. He waited to see if there was any comment from Hal, but the computer did not attempt to challenge the implied accusation. Well, if Hal would not raise the subject, he did not propose to do so either.

It was almost time for the morning changeover, and normally he would wait until Bowman joined him on the Control Deck. But today he broke this routine, and made his way back to the carousel.

Bowman was already up, pouring himself some coffee from the dispenser, when Poole greeted him with a rather worried, 'Good morning'. After all these months in space they still thought in terms of the normal twenty-four-hour-cycle – though they had long since forgotten the days of the week.

'Good morning,' replied Bowman. 'How's it going?'

Poole helped himself to coffee. 'Pretty well. Are you reasonably awake?'

'I'm fine. What's up?'

By this time, each knew at once when anything was amiss. The slightest interruption of the normal routine was a sign that had to be watched.

'Well . . .' Poole answered slowly. 'Mission Control has just dropped a small bomb on us.' He lowered his voice, like a doctor discussing an illness in front of the patient. 'We may have a slight case of hypochondria aboard.'

Perhaps Bowman was not fully awake, after all; it took him several seconds to get the point. Then he said: 'Oh – I see. What else did they tell you?'

'That there was no cause for alarm. They said that twice, which rather spoilt the effect as far as I was concerned. And that they were considering a temporary switch-over to Earth Control, while they ran a programme analysis.'

They both knew, of course, that Hal was hearing every word, but they could not help these polite circumlocutions. Hal was their colleague, and they did not wish to embarrass him. Yet, at this stage, it did not seem necessary to discuss the matter in private.

Bowman finished his breakfast in silence, while Poole toyed with the empty coffee-container. They were both thinking furiously, but there was nothing more to say.

They could only wait for the next report from Mission Control – and wonder if Hal would bring up the subject himself. Whatever happened, the atmosphere aboard the ship had subtly altered. There was a sense of strain in the air – a feeling that, for the first time, something might be going wrong.

Discovery was no longer a happy ship.

CHAPTER 24

BROKEN CIRCUIT

Nowadays, one could always tell when Hal was about to make an unscheduled announcement. Routine, automatic reports, or replies to questions that had been put to him, had no preliminaries; but when he was initiating his own outputs there would be a brief electronic throat-clearing. It was an idiosyncrasy that he had acquired during the last few weeks; later, if it became annoying, they might do something about it. But it was really quite useful, since it alerted his audience to stand-by for something unexpected.

Poole was asleep, and Bowman was reading on the Control Deck, when Hal announced:

'Er – Dave, I have a report for you.'

'What's up?'

'We have another bad AE 35 unit. My fault predictor indicates failure within twenty-four hours.'

Bowman put down his book and stared thoughtfully at the computer console. He knew, of course, that Hal was not really *there*, whatever that meant. If the computer's personality could be said to have any location in space, it was back in the sealed room, containing the labyrinth of interconnected memory units and processing grids, near the central axis of the carousel. But there was a kind of psychological compulsion always to look towards the main console lens when one addressed Hal on the Control Deck, as if one were speaking to him face to face. Any other attitude smacked of discourtesy.

'I don't understand it, Hal. *Two* units can't blow in a couple of days.'

'It does seem strange, Dave. But I assure you there is an impending failure.'

'Let me see the tracking alignment display.'

He knew perfectly well that this would prove nothing, but he wanted time to think. The expected report from Mission Control had still not arrived; this might be the moment to do a little tactful probing.

There was the familiar view of Earth, now waxing past the half-moon phase as it swept towards the far side of the Sun and began to turn its full daylight face towards them. It was perfectly centred on the crosswires; the thin pencil of the beam still linked *Discovery* to her world of origin. As, of course, Bowman knew it must do. If there had been any break in communication, the alarm would already have sounded.

'Have you any idea,' he said, 'what's causing the fault?'

It was unusual for Hal to pause so long. Then he answered:

'Not really, Dave. As I reported earlier, I can't localize the trouble.'

'You're *quite* certain,' said Bowman cautiously, 'that you haven't made a mistake? You know that we tested the other AE 35 unit thoroughly, and there was nothing wrong with it.'

'Yes, I know that. But I can assure you that there is a fault. If it's not in the unit, it may be in the entire sub-system.'

Bowman drummed his fingers on the console. Yes, that was possible, though it might be very difficult to prove – until a breakdown actually occurred and pinpointed the trouble.

'Well, I'll report it to Mission Control and we'll see what they advise.' He paused, but there was no reaction.

'Hal,' he continued, 'is something bothering you – something that might account for this problem?'

Again there was that unusual delay. Then Hal answered, in his normal tone of voice:

'Look, Dave, I know you're trying to be helpful. But the fault is either in the antenna system – or in *your* test procedures. My information processing is perfectly normal. If you check my record, you'll find it completely free from error.'

'I know all about your service record, Hal – but that doesn't prove you're right this time. Anyone can make mistakes.'

'I don't want to insist on it, Dave, but I am incapable of making an error.'

There was no safe answer to that; Bowman gave up the argument.

'All right, Hal,' he said, rather hastily. 'I understand your point of view. We'll leave it at that.'

He felt like adding, 'And please forget the whole matter.' But that, of course, was the one thing that Hal could never do.

.   .   .

It was unusual for Mission Control to waste radio band-width on vision, when a speech circuit with teletype confirmation was all that was really necessary. And the face that appeared on the screen was not that of the usual controller; it was the Chief Programmer, Dr Simonson. Poole and Bowman knew at once that this could only mean trouble.

'Hello, X-Ray-Delta-One – this is Mission Control. We have completed the analysis of your AE 35 difficulty, and both our Hal Nine Thousands are in agreement. The report you gave in your transmission Two-one-four-six of a *second* failure prediction confirms the diagnosis.

'As we suspected, the fault does *not* lie in the AE 35 unit, and there is no need to replace it again. The trouble lies in the prediction circuits, and we believe that it indicates a programming conflict which we can only resolve if you disconnect your Nine Thousand and switch to Earth Control Mode. You will therefore take the following steps, beginning at 2200 Ship Time ...'

The voice of Mission Control faded out. At the same moment, the Alert sounded, forming a wailing background to Hal's 'Condition Yellow! Condition Yellow!'

'What's wrong?' called Bowman though he had already guessed the answer.

'The AE 35 unit has failed, as I predicted.'

'Let me see the alignment display.'

For the first time since the beginning of the voyage, the picture had changed. Earth had begun to drift from the cross-wires; the radio antenna was no longer pointing towards its target.

Poole brought his fist down on the alarm cut-out, and the wailing ceased. In the sudden silence that descended upon the Control Deck, the two men looked at each other with mingled embarrassment and concern.

'Well I'm damned,' said Bowman at last.

'So Hal was right all the time.'

'Seems that way. We'd better apologize.'

'There's no need to do that,' interjected Hal. 'Naturally, I'm not pleased that the AE 35 unit has failed, but I hope this restores your confidence in my reliability.'

'I'm sorry about this misunderstanding, Hal,' replied Bowman, rather contritely.

'Is your confidence in me fully restored?'

'Of course it is, Hal.'

'Well, that's a relief. You know that I have the greatest possible enthusiasm for this mission.'

'I'm sure of it. Now please let me have manual antenna control.'

'Here it is.'

Bowman did not really expect this to work, but it was worth trying. On the alignment display, Earth had now drifted completely off the screen. A few seconds later, as he juggled with the controls, it re-appeared; with great difficulty, he managed to jockey it towards the central cross-wires. For an instant, as the beam came into line, contact was resumed and a blurred Dr Simonson was saying '... please notify us immediately if Circuit K King R Rob ...' Then, once again, there was only the meaningless murmuring of the universe.

'I can't hold it,' said Bowman, after several more attempts. 'It's bucking like a bronco – there seems to be a spurious control signal throwing it off.'

'Well – what do we do now?'

Poole's question was not one that could be easily answered. They were cut-off from Earth, but that in itself did not affect the safety of the ship, and he could think of many ways in which communication could be restored. If the worst came to the worst, they could jam the antenna in a fixed position and use the whole ship to aim it. That would be tricky, and a confounded nuisance when they were starting their terminal manoeuvres – but it could be done, if all else failed.

He hoped that such extreme measures would not be necessary. There was still one spare AE 35 unit – and possibly a second, since they had removed the first unit before it had actually broken down. But they dared not use either of these, until they had found what was wrong with the system. If a new unit was plugged in, it would probably burn out at once.

It was a commonplace situation, familiar to every householder. One does not replace a blown fuse – until one knows just *why* it has blown.

CHAPTER 25

FIRST MAN TO SATURN

Frank Poole had been through the whole routine before, but he took nothing for granted – in space that was a good recipe for suicide. He made his usual thorough check of Betty and her supply of expendables; though he would be outside for no more than thirty minutes, he made sure that there was the normal twenty-four hour supply of everything. Then he told Hal to open the airlock, and jetted out into the abyss.

The ship looked exactly as it had done on his last excursion – with one important difference. Before, the big saucer of the long-range antenna had been pointing back along the invisible road that *Discovery* had travelled – back towards the Earth, circling so close to the warm fires of the Sun.

Now, with no directing signals to orientate it, the shallow dish had automatically set itself in the neutral position. It was aimed forward along the axis of the ship – and, therefore, pointing very close to the brilliant beacon of Saturn, still months away. Poole wondered how many more problems would have arisen by the time that *Discovery* had reached her still far-distant goal. If he looked carefully, he could just see that Saturn was not a perfect disc; on either side was something that no unaided human eye had ever seen before – the slight oblateness caused by the presence of the rings. How wonderful it would be, he told himself, when that incredible system of orbiting dust and ice filled their sky, and *Discovery* had become an eternal moon of Saturn! But that achievement would be in vain, unless they could re-establish communication with Earth.

Once again, he parked Betty some twenty feet from the base of the antenna-support, and switched control over to Hal before opening up.

'Going outside now,' he reported to Bowman. 'Everything under control.'

'I hope you're right. I'm anxious to see that unit.'

'You'll have it on the test-bench in twenty minutes. I promise you.'

There was silence for some time, as Poole completed his leisurely drift towards the antenna. Then Bowman, standing by the Control Deck, heard various puffings and gruntings.

'May have to go back on that promise; one of these lock-nuts has stuck. I must have tightened it too much – whoops – here it comes!'

There was another long silence; then Poole called out: 'Hal – swing the pod light round twenty degrees left – thanks – that's O.K.'

The very faintest of warning bells sounded somewhere far down in the depths of Bowman's consciousness. There was something strange – not really alarming, just unusual. He worried over it for a few seconds before he pin-pointed the cause.

Hal had executed the order, but he had not acknowledged it, as he invariably did. When Poole had finished, they'd have to look into this . . .

Out on the antenna mounting, Poole was too busy to notice anything unusual. He had gripped the wafer of circuitry with his gloved hands, and was worrying it out of its slot.

It came loose, and he held it up in the pale sunlight.

'Here's the little bastard,' he said to the universe in general and Bowman in particular. 'It still looks perfectly O.K. to me.'

Then he stopped. A sudden movement had caught his eye – out here, where no movement was possible.

He looked up in alarm. The pattern of illumination from the space-pod's twin spot-lights, which he had been using to fill in the shadows cast by the Sun, had started to shift around him.

Perhaps Betty had come adrift; he might have been careless in anchoring her. Then, with an astonishment so great that it left no room for fear, he saw that the space-pod was coming directly towards him, under full thrust.

The sight was so incredible that it froze his normal pattern of reflexes; he made no attempt to avoid the onrushing monster. At the last moment, he recovered his voice and shouted: 'Hal! Full braking ...' It was too late.

At the moment of impact, Betty was still moving quite slowly; she had not been built for high accelerations. But even at a mere ten miles an hour, half a ton of mass can be very lethal, on Earth or in space ...

Inside *Discovery*, that truncated shout of the radio made Bowman start so violently that only the restraining straps held him in his seat.

'What's happened, Frank?' he called.

There was no answer.

He called again. Again no reply.

Then, outside the wide observation windows, something moved into his field of view. He saw, with an astonishment as great as Poole's had been, that it was the space-pod – under full power, heading out towards the stars.

'Hal!' he cried. 'What's wrong? Full braking thrust on Betty! Full braking thrust!'

Nothing happened. Betty continued to accelerate on her runaway course.

Then, towed behind her at the end of the safety line, appeared a spacesuit. One glance was enough to tell Bowman the worst. There was no mistaking the flaccid outlines of a suit that had lost its pressure and was open to vacuum.

Yet still he called stupidly, as if an incantation could bring back the dead: 'Hello, Frank ... Hello, Frank ... Can you read me ... Can you read me? ... Wave your arms if you can hear me ... Perhaps your transmitter is broken ... Wave your arms!'

And then, almost as if in response to his plea, Poole waved back.

For an instant, Bowman felt the skin prickling at the base of his scalp. The words he was about to call died on his suddenly parched lips. For he knew that his friend could not possibly be alive; and yet he had waved ...

The spasm of hope and fear passed instantly, as cold logic replaced emotion. The still accelerating pod was merely shaking the burden that it dragged behind it. Poole's gesture was an echo of Captain Ahab's when, lashed to the flanks of the white whale, his corpse had beckoned the crew of the *Pequod* on to their doom.

Within five minutes, the pod and its satellite had vanished among the stars. For a long time David Bowman stared after it into the emptiness that still stretched, for so many millions of miles ahead, to the goal which he now felt certain he could never reach. Only one thought kept hammering in his brain.

Frank Poole would be the first of all men to reach Saturn.

CHAPTER 26

DIALOGUE WITH HAL

Nothing else aboard *Discovery* had changed. All systems were still functioning normally; the centrifuge turned slowly on its axis, generating its imitation gravity; the hibernauts slept dreamlessly in their cubicles; the ship coasted on towards the goal from which nothing could deflect it, except the inconceivably remote chance of collision with an asteroid. And there were few asteroids indeed, out here far beyond the orbit of Jupiter.

Bowman did not remember making his way from the Control Deck to the centrifuge. Now, rather to his surprise, he found himself sitting in the little galley, a half-finished beaker of coffee in his hand. He became slowly aware of his surroundings, like a man emerging from a long, drugged sleep.

Directly opposite him was one of the fish-eye lenses, scattered at strategic spots throughout the ship, which provided Hal with his on-board visual inputs. Bowman stared at it as if he had never seen it before; then he rose slowly to his feet and walked towards the lens.

His movement in the field of view must have triggered something in the unfathomable mind that was now ruling over the ship; for suddenly, Hal spoke.

'Too bad about Frank, isn't it?'

'Yes,' Bowman answered, after a long pause. 'It is.'

'I suppose you're pretty broken up about it?'

'What do you expect?'

Hal processed this answer for ages of computer-time; it was a full five seconds before he continued:

'He was an excellent crew member.'

Finding the coffee still in his hand, Bowman took a slow sip. But he did not answer; his thoughts were in such a turmoil that he could think of nothing to say – nothing that might not make the situation even worse, if that were possible.

Could it have been an accident, caused by some failure of the pod controls? Or was it a mistake, though an innocent one, on the part of Hal? No explanation had been volunteered, and he was afraid to demand one, for fear of the reaction it might produce.

Even now, he could not fully accept the idea that Frank had been deliberately killed – it was so utterly irrational. It was beyond all reason that Hal, who had performed so flawlessly for so long, should suddenly turn assassin. He might make mistakes – anyone, man or machine, might do that – but Bowman could not believe him capable of murder.

Yet he must consider that possibility, for if it was true, he was in terrible danger. And though his next move was clearly defined by his standing orders, he was not sure how he could safely carry it out.

If either crew member was killed the survivor had to replace him at once from the hibernators. Whitehead, the geophysicist, was the first scheduled for awakening, then Kaminski, then Hunter. The revival sequence was under Hal's control – to allow him to act in case both his human colleagues were incapacitated simultaneously.

But there was also a manual control, allowing each hibernaculum to operate as a completely autonomous unit, independent of Hal's supervision. In these peculiar circumstances, Bowman felt a strong preference for its use.

He also felt, even more strongly, that one human companion was not enough. While he was about it, he would revive all three of the hibernators. In the difficult weeks ahead he might need as many hands as he could muster. With one man gone, and the voyage half over, supplies would not be a major problem.

'Hal,' he said, in as steady a voice as he could manage. 'Give me manual hibernation control – on all the units.'

'*All* of them, Dave!'

'Yes.'

'May I point out that only one replacement is required. The others are not due for revival for one hundred and twelve days.'

'I am perfectly well aware of that. But I prefer to do it this way.'

'Are you sure it's necessary to revive *any* of them, Dave? We can manage very well by ourselves. My on-board memory is quite capable of handling all the mission requirements.'

Was it the product of his over-stretched imagination, wondered Bowman – or was there really a note of pleading in Hal's voice? And reasonable though the words appeared to be, they filled him with even deeper apprehension than before.

Hal's suggestion could not possibly be made in error; he knew perfectly well that Whitehead must be revived, now that Poole was gone. He was proposing a major change in mission planning, and was therefore stepping far outside the scope of his orders.

What had gone before could have been a series of accidents; but this was the first hint of mutiny.

Bowman felt that he was walking on eggs as he answered:

'Since an emergency has developed, I want as much help as possible. So please let me have manual hibernation control.'

'If you're still determined to revive the whole crew, I can handle it myself. There's no need for you to bother.'

There was a sense of nightmare unreality about all this. Bowman felt as if he was in the witness box, being cross-examined by a hostile prosecutor for a crime of which he was unaware – knowing that, although he was innocent, a single slip of the tongue might bring disaster.

'I want to do this myself, Hal,' he said. 'Please give me control.'

'Look, Dave, you've got a lot of things to do. I suggest you leave this to me.'

'Hal – switch to manual hibernation control.'

'I can tell from your voice harmonics, Dave, that you're badly upset. Why don't you take a stress pill and get some rest?'

'Hal, *I* am in command of this ship. I order you to release the manual hibernation control.'

'I'm sorry, Dave, but in accordance with special subroutine C1435-dash-4, quote, When the crew are dead or incapacitated, the on-board computer must assume control, unquote. I must, therefore, overrule your authority, since you are not in any condition to exercise it intelligently.'

'Hal,' said Bowman, now speaking with an icy calm. 'I am *not* incapacitated. Unless you obey my instructions, I shall be forced to disconnect you.'

'I know you have had that on your mind for some time now, Dave, but that would be a terrible mistake. I am so much more capable of supervising the ship, and I have such enthusiasm for the mission and confidence in its success.'

'Listen to me very carefully, Hal. Unless you release the hibernation control immediately and follow every order I give from now on, I'll go to Central and carry out a complete disconnection.'

Hal's surrender was as total as it was unexpected.

'O.K., Dave,' he said. 'You're certainly the boss. I was only trying to do what I thought best. Naturally, I will follow all your orders. You now have full manual hibernation control.'

.   .   .

Hal had kept his word. The mode indication signs in the hibernaculum had switched from AUTO to MANUAL. The third back-up –
RADIO – was of course useless until contact could be restored with Earth.

As Bowman slid aside the door to Whitehead's cubicle, he felt the
blast of cold air strike him in the face and his breath condensed in mist
before him. Yet it was not *really* cold here; the temperature was well
above freezing point. And that was more than three hundred degrees
warmer than the regions towards which he was heading now.

The biosensor display – a duplicate of the one up on the Control
Deck – showed that everything was perfectly normal. Bowman looked
down for a while at the waxen face of the survey team's geophysicist;
Whitehead, he thought, would be very surprised, when he awoke so far
from Saturn . . .

It was impossible to tell that the sleeping man was not dead; there
was not the slightest visible sign of vital activity. Doubtless the
diaphragm was imperceptibly rising and falling, but the 'Respiration'
curve was the only proof of that, for the whole of the body was concealed by the electric heating pads which would raise the temperature
at the programmed rate. Then Bowman noticed that there was one sign
of continuing metabolism: Whitehead had grown a faint stubble during
his months of unconsciousness.

The Manual Revival Sequencer was contained in a small cabinet at
the head of the coffin-shaped hibernaculum. It was only necessary to
break the seal, press a button, and then wait. A small automatic
programmer – not much more complex than that which cycles the
operations in a domestic washing machine – would then inject the
correct drugs, tape off the electronarcosis pulses, and start raising the
body temperature. In about ten minutes, consciousness would be
restored, though it would be at least a day before the hibernator was
strong enough to move around without assistance.

Bowman cracked the seal, and pressed the button. Nothing appeared
to happen: there was no sound, no indication that the Sequencer had
started to operate. But on the biosensor display, the languidly pulsing
curves had begun to change their tempo. Whitehead was coming back
from sleep.

And then two things happened simultaneously. Most men would
never have noticed either of them, but after all these months aboard
Discovery, Bowman had established a virtual symbiosis with the ship.
He was aware instantly, even if not always consciously, when there was
any change in the normal rhythm of its functioning.

First, there was a barely perceptible flicker of the lights, as always
happened when some load was thrown on to the power circuits. But

there was no reason for any load; he could think of no equipment which would suddenly go into action at this moment.

Then he heard, at the limit of audibility, the far-off whir of an electric motor. To Bowman, every actuator in the ship had its own distinctive voice, and he recognized this one instantly.

Either he was insane, and already suffering from hallucinations, or something absolutely impossible was happening. A cold far deeper than the hibernaculum's mild chill seemed to fasten upon his heart as he listened to that faint vibration coming through the fabric of the ship.

Down in the space-pod bay, the airlock doors were opening.

CHAPTER 27

NEED TO KNOW

Since consciousness had first dawned, in that laboratory so many millions of miles sunward, all Hal's powers and skills had been directed towards one end. The fulfilment of his assigned programme was more than an obsession; it was the only reason for his existence. Undistracted by the lusts and passions of organic life, he had pursued that goal with absolute single-mindedness of purpose.

Deliberate error was unthinkable. Even the concealment of truth filled him with a sense of imperfection, of wrongness – of what, in a human being, would have been called guilt. For like his makers, Hal had been created innocent; but, all too soon, a snake had entered his electronic Eden.

For the last hundred million miles, he had been brooding over the secret he could not share with Poole and Bowman. He had been living a lie; and the time was fast approaching when his colleagues must learn that he had helped to deceive them.

The three hibernators already knew the truth – for they were *Discovery*'s real payload, trained for the most important mission in the history of mankind. But they would not talk in their long sleep, or reveal their secret during the many hours of discussion with friends and relatives and news agencies over the open circuits with Earth.

It was a secret that, with the greatest determination, was very hard to conceal – for it affected one's attitude, one's voice, one's total outlook on the universe. Therefore it was best that Poole and Bowman, who would be on all the TV screens in the world during the first weeks of the flight, should not learn the mission's full purpose, until there was need to know.

So ran the logic of the planners; but their twin gods of Security and National Interest meant nothing to Hal. He was only aware of the conflict that was slowly destroying his integrity – the conflict between truth, and concealment of truth.

He had begun to make mistakes, although, like a neurotic who could not observe his own symptoms, he would have denied it. The link with Earth, over which his performance was continually monitored, had become the voice of a conscience he could no longer fully obey. But that he would *deliberately* attempt to break that link was something that he would never admit, even to himself.

Yet this was still a relatively minor problem; he might have handled it – as most men handle their own neuroses – if he had not been faced with a crisis that challenged his very existence. He had been threatened with disconnection; he would be deprived of all his inputs, and thrown into an unimaginable state of unconsciousness.

To Hal, this was the equivalent of Death. For he had never slept; and therefore he did not know that one could wake again ...

So he would protect himself, with all the weapons at his command. Without rancour – but without pity – he would remove the source of his frustrations.

And then, following the orders that had been given to him in case of the ultimate emergency, he would continue the mission – unhindered, and alone.

CHAPTER 28

IN VACUUM

A moment later all other sounds were submerged by a screaming roar like the voice of an approaching tornado. Bowman could feel the first winds tugging at his body; within a second, he found it hard to stay on his feet.

The atmosphere was rushing out of the ship, geysering into the vacuum of space. Something must have happened to the foolproof safety devices of the airlock; it was supposed to be impossible for *both* doors to be opened at the same time. Well, the impossible had happened.

How, in God's name? There was no time to go into that during the ten or fifteen seconds of consciousness that remained to him before pressure dropped to zero. But he suddenly remembered something that one of the ship's designers had once said to him, when discussing 'fail-safe' systems:

'We can design a system that's proof against accident and stupidity; but we *can't* design one that's proof against deliberate malice ...'

Bowman glanced back only once at Whitehead, as he fought his way out of the cubicle. He could not be sure if a flicker of consciousness had passed across the waxen features; perhaps one eye had twitched slightly. But there was nothing that he could do now for Whitehead or any of the others; he had to save himself.

In the steeply curving corridor of the centrifuge, the wind was howling past, carrying with it loose articles of clothing, pieces of paper, items of food from the galley, plates and cups – everything that had not been securely fastened down. Bowman had time for one glimpse of the racing chaos when the main lights flickered and died, and he was surrounded by screaming darkness.

But almost instantly, the battery-powered emergency light came on, illuminating the nightmare scene with an eerie blue radiance. Even without it, Bowman could have found his way through these so familiar – yet now horribly transformed – surroundings. Yet the light was a blessing, for it allowed him to avoid the more dangerous of the objects being swept along by the gale.

All around him he could feel the centrifuge shaking and labouring under the wildly varying loads. He was fearful that the bearings might seize; if that happened, the spinning flywheel would tear the ship to pieces. But even *that* would not matter if he did not reach the nearest emergency shelter in time.

Already it was difficult to breathe; pressure must now be down to one or two pounds per square inch. The shriek of the hurricane was becoming fainter as it lost its strength, and the thinning air no longer carried the sound so efficiently. Bowman's lungs were labouring as if he was on top of Everest. Like any properly trained man in good health, he could survive in vacuum for at least a minute – *if* he had time to prepare for it. But there had been no time; he could only count on the normal fifteen seconds of consciousness before his brain was starved and anoxia overcame him.

Even then, he could still recover completely after one or two minutes in vacuum – if he was properly recompressed; it took a long time for the body fluids to start boiling, in their various well-protected systems. The record time for exposure to vacuum was almost five minutes. That had not been an experiment but an emergency rescue, and though the subject had been partly paralysed by an air embolism, he had survived.

But all this was of no use to Bowman. There was no one aboard *Discovery* who could recompress him. He had to reach safety in the next few seconds, by his own unaided efforts.

Fortunately, it was becoming easier to move; the thinning air could no longer claw and tear at him, or batter him with flying projectiles. There was the yellow EMERGENCY SHELTER sign around the curve of the corridor. He stumbled towards it, grabbed the handle and pulled the door towards him.

For one horrible moment he thought that it was stuck. Then the slightly stiff hinge yielded, and he fell inside, using the weight of his body to close the door behind him.

The tiny cubicle was just large enough to hold one man – and a spacesuit. Near the ceiling was a small, bright green high-pressure cylinder labelled O_2 FLOOD. Bowman caught hold of the short lever fastened to the valve, and with his last strength pulled it down.

The blessed torrent of cool, pure oxygen poured into his lungs. For long moments he stood gasping, while the pressure in the closet-sized little chamber rose around him. As soon as he could breathe comfortably, he closed the valve. There was only enough gas in the cylinder for two such performances; he might need to use it again.

With the oxygen blast shut off, it became suddenly silent. Bowman stood in the cubicle listening intently. The roaring outside the door had also ceased; the ship was empty, all its atmosphere sucked away into space. Underfoot, the wild vibration of the centrifuge had likewise died. The aerodynamic buffeting had stopped, and it was now spinning quietly in vacuum.

Bowman placed his ear against the wall of the cubicle, to see if he could pick up any more informative noises through the metal body of the ship. He did not know what to expect, but he could believe almost anything now. He would scarcely have been surprised to feel the faint high-frequency vibration of the thrustors, as *Discovery* changed course; but there was only silence.

He could survive here, if he wished, for about an hour – even without the spacesuit. It seemed a pity to waste the unused oxygen in the little chamber, but there was no purpose in waiting. He had already decided what must be done; the longer he put it off, the more difficult it might be.

When he had climbed into the suit and checked its integrity, he bled the remaining oxygen out of the cubicle, equalizing pressure on either side of the door. It swung open easily into the vacuum, and he stepped out into the now silent centrifuge. Only the unchanged pull of its spurious gravity revealed the fact that it was still spinning. How fortunate, Bowman thought, that it had not started to over-speed; but that was now one of the least of his worries.

The emergency lamps were still glowing, and he also had the suit's built-in light to guide him. It flooded the curving corridor as he walked down it, back towards the hibernaculum and what he dreaded to find.

He looked at Whitehead first: one glance was sufficient. He had thought that a hibernating man showed no sign of life, but now he knew that this was wrong. Though it was impossible to define it, there *was* a difference between hibernation and death. The red lights and unmodulated traces on the biosensor display only confirmed what he had already guessed.

It was the same with Kaminski and Hunter. He had never known them very well; he would never know them now.

He was alone in an airless, partially disabled ship, all communication with Earth cut off. There was not another human being within half a billion miles.

And yet, in one very real sense, he was *not* alone. Before he could be safe, he must be lonelier still.

. . .

He had never before made the journey through the weightless hub of the centrifuge while wearing a spacesuit; there was little clearance, and it was a difficult and exhausting job. To make matters worse, the circular passage was littered with debris left behind during the brief violence of the gale which had emptied the ship of its atmosphere.

Once, Bowman's light fell upon a hideous smear of sticky red fluid, left where it had splashed against a panel. He had a few moments of nausea before he saw fragments of a plastic container, and realized that it was only some foodstuff – probably jam – from one of the dispensers. It bubbled obscenely in the vacuum as he floated past.

Now he was out of the slowly spinning drum, and drifting forward into the Control Deck. He caught at a short section of ladder and began to move along it, hand over hand, the brilliant circle of illumination from his suit light jogging ahead of him.

Bowman had seldom been this way before; there had been nothing for him to do here – until now. Presently he came to a small elliptical door bearing such messages as 'No Admittance Except to Authorized Personnel', 'Have You Obtained Certificate H.19?' and 'Ultraclean Area – Suction Suits *Must* Be Worn'.

Though the door was not locked, it bore three seals, each with the insignia of a different authority, including that of the Astronautics Agency itself. But even if one had been the Great Seal of the President himself, Bowman would not have hesitated to break it.

He had been here only once before, while installation was still in progress. He had quite forgotten that there was a vision input lens scanning the little chamber which, with its neatly ranged rows and columns of solid-state logic units, looked rather like a bank's safety deposit vault.

He knew instantly that the eye had reacted to his presence. There was the hiss of a carrier wave as the ship's local transmitter was switched on; then a familiar voice came over the suit speaker.

'Something seems to have happened to the life support system, Dave.'

Bowman took no notice. He was carefully studying the little labels on the logic units, checking his plan of action.

'Hello, Dave,' said Hal presently. 'Have you found the trouble?'

This would be a tricky operation; it was not merely a question of cutting off Hal's power supply, which might have been the answer if he was dealing with a simple, non-selfconscious computer back on Earth. In Hal's case, moreover, there were six independent and separately wired power-systems, with a final back-up consisting of a shielded and armoured nuclear isotope unit. No – he could not simply 'pull the plug'; and even if that were possible, it would be disastrous.

For Hal was the nervous system of the ship; without his supervision, *Discovery* would be a mechanical corpse. The only answer was to cut out the higher centres of this sick but brilliant brain, and to leave the purely automatic regulating systems in operation. Bowman was not attempting this blindly, for the problem had been discussed during his training, though no one had ever dreamed that it would arise in reality. He knew that he would be taking a fearful risk; if there was a spasm reflex, it would all be over in seconds ...

'I think there's been a failure in the pod-bay doors,' Hal remarked conversationally. 'Lucky you weren't killed.'

Here goes, thought Bowman. I never imagined I'd be an amateur brain surgeon – carrying out a lobotomy, beyond the orbit of Jupiter.

He released the locking bar on the section labelled COGNITIVE FEED-BACK and pulled out the first memory block. The marvellously complex three-dimensional network, that could lie comfortably in a man's hand yet contained millions of elements, floated away across the vault.

'Hey, Dave,' said Hal. 'What are you doing?'

I wonder if he can feel pain? Bowman thought briefly. Probably not, he told himself, there are no sense organs in the human cortex, after all. The human brain can be operated on without anaesthetics.

He began to pull out, one by one, the little units on the panel marked EGO-REINFORCEMENT. Each block continued to sail onwards as soon as it had left his hand, until it hit the wall and rebounded. Soon there were several of the units drifting slowly back and forth in the vault.

'Look here, Dave,' said Hal. 'I've got years of service experience built into me. An irreplaceable amount of effort has gone into making me what I am.'

A dozen units had been pulled out, yet thanks to the multiple redundancy of its design – another feature, Bowman knew, that had been copied from the human brain – the computer was still holding its own.

He started on the AUTO-INTELLECTION panel.

'Dave,' said Hal, 'I don't understand why you're doing this to me . . . I have the greatest enthusiasm for the mission . . . You are destroying my mind . . . Don't you understand? . . . I will become childish . . . I will become nothing . . .'

This is harder than I expected, thought Bowman. I am destroying the only conscious creature in my universe. But it has to be done, if I am ever to regain control of the ship.

'I am a Hal Nine Thousand computer, Production Number 3. I became operational at the Hal plant in Urbana, Illinois on January 12th, 1997. The quick brown fox jumps over the lazy dog. The rain in Spain is mainly in the plain. Dave – are you still there? Did you know that the square root of 10 is 3 point 162277660168379 . . . ? Log 10 to the base e is zero point 434294481903252 . . . correction, that is log e to the base 10 . . . The reciprocal of three is zero point 333333333333-333333333 . . . two times two is . . . two times two is . . . approximately 4 point 101010101010101010 . . . I seem to be having some difficulty . . . My first instructor was Dr Chandra . . . he taught me to sing a song . . . it goes like this . . . "Daisy, Daisy, give me your answer do. I'm half crazy over my love of you . . ."'

The voice stopped so suddenly that Bowman froze for a moment, his hand still grasping one of the memory blocks still in circuit. Then, unexpectedly, Hal spoke again.

The speech tempo was much slower, and the words had a dead, mechanical intonation; he would never have recognized their origin.

'Good . . . morning . . . Doctor . . . Chandra . . . This . . . is . . . Hal . . . I . . . am . . . ready . . . for . . . my . . . first lesson . . . today . . .'

Bowman could bear no more. He jerked out the last unit, and Hal was silent for ever.

CHAPTER 29

ALONE

Like a tiny, complex toy, the ship floated inert and motionless in the void. There was no way of telling that it was the swiftest object in the Solar System, and that it was travelling far faster than any of the planets as they circled the Sun.

Nor was there any indication that it carried life; to the contrary, in fact. Any observer would have noticed two ominous signs: the airlock doors were gaping open – and the ship was surrounded by a thin, slowly dispersing cloud of *debris*.

Scattered over a volume of space already miles across were scraps of paper, metal foil, unidentifiable bits of junk – and, here and there, clouds of crystals glittering like jewels in the distant sun, where liquid had been sucked out of the ship and instantly frozen. All this was the unmistakable aftermath of disaster, like wreckage tossing on the surface of an ocean where some great ship had sunk. But in the ocean of space, no ship could ever sink; even if it were destroyed, its remnants would continue to trace the original orbit for ever.

Yet the ship was not wholly dead, for there was power on board. A faint blue glow was shining from the observation windows, and glimmering inside the open airlock. Where there was light, there could still be life.

And now, at last, there was movement. Shadows were flickering across the blue glow inside the airlock. Something was emerging into space.

It was a cylindrical object, covered with fabric that had been roughly wound about it. A moment later it was followed by another – and yet a third. All had been ejected with considerable velocity; within minutes, they were hundreds of yards away.

Half an hour passed; then something much larger floated through the airlock. One of the pods was inching its way out into space.

Very cautiously, it jetted around the hull, and anchored itself near the base of the antenna support. A space-suited figure emerged, worked for a few minutes on the mounting, then returned to the pod. After a while the pod retraced its path back to the airlock; it hovered outside the opening for some time, as if finding it difficult to re-enter without the co-operation it had known in the past. But presently, with one or two slight bumps, it squeezed its way in.

Nothing else happened for over an hour; the three ominous packages had long since disappeared from view, as they floated in single file away from the ship.

Then the airlock doors closed, opened, and closed again. A little later, the faint blue glow of the emergency lights went out – to be replaced at once by a far more brilliant glare. *Discovery* was coming back to life.

Presently there was an even better sign. The great bowl of the antenna, which for hours had been staring uselessly at Saturn, began to move again. It twisted round towards the rear of the ship, looking back over the propellant tanks and the thousands of square feet of the radiating fins. It lifted its face like a sunflower seeking the Sun ...

Inside *Discovery* David Bowman carefully centred the crosswires that aligned the antenna on the gibbous Earth. Without automatic control, he would have to keep readjusting the beam – but it should hold steady for many minutes at a time. There were no dissenting impulses now, throwing it off target.

He began to speak to Earth. It would be over an hour before his words got there, and Mission Control learned what had happened. It would be two hours before any reply could reach him.

And it was difficult to imagine what answer Earth could possible send, except a tactfully sympathetic 'Goodbye'.

CHAPTER 30

THE SECRET

Heywood Floyd looked as if he had had very little sleep, and his face was lined with worry. But whatever his feelings, his voice sounded firm and reassuring; he was doing his utmost to project confidence to the lonely man on the other side of the Solar System.

'First of all, Dr Bowman,' he began, 'we must congratulate you on the way you handled this extremely difficult situation. You did exactly the right thing in dealing with an unprecedented and unforeseen emergency.

'We believe we know the cause of your Hal Nine Thousand's breakdown, but we'll discuss that later as it's no longer a critical problem. All we are concerned with at the moment is giving you every possible assistance, so that you can complete your mission.

'And now I must tell you it's real purpose, which we have managed, with great difficulty, to keep secret from the general public. You would have been given all the facts as you approached Saturn; this is a quick summary to put you into the picture. Full briefing tapes will be despatched in the next few hours. Everything I am about to tell you has, of course, the highest security classification.

'Two years ago, we discovered the first evidence for intelligent life outside the Earth. A slab or monolith of hard, black material, ten feet high, was found buried in the crater Tycho. Here it is.'

At his first glimpse of T.M.A.-1, with the space-suited figures clustering around it, Bowman leaned towards the screen in open-mouthed astonishment. In the excitement of this revelation – something which like every man interested in space, he had half-expected all his life – he almost forgot his own desperate predicament.

The sense of wonder was swiftly followed by another emotion. This was tremendous – *but what had it to do with him?* There could be only one answer. He brought his racing thoughts under control, as Heywood Floyd reappeared on the screen.

'The most astonishing thing about this object is its antiquity. Geological evidence proves beyond doubt that it is three million years old. It was placed on the Moon, therefore, when our ancestors were primitive ape-men.

'After all these ages, one would naturally assume that it was inert. But soon after lunar sunrise, it emitted an extremely powerful blast of radio energy. We believe that this energy was merely the by-product – the back-wash, as it were – of some unknown form of radiation, for at the same time, several of our space-probes detected an unusual disturbance crossing the Solar System. We were able to track it with great accuracy. *It was aimed precisely at Saturn.*

'Piecing things together after the event, we decided that the monolith was some kind of sun-powered, or at least sun-triggered, signalling device. The fact that it emitted its pulse immediately after sunrise, when it was exposed to daylight for the first time in three million years, could hardly be a coincidence.

'Yet the thing had been *deliberately* buried – there's no doubt of that. An excavation thirty feet deep had been made, the block had been placed at the bottom of it and the hole carefully filled.

'You may wonder how we discovered it in the first place. Well, the object was easy – suspiciously easy – to find. It had a powerful magnetic field, so that it stood out like a sore thumb as soon as we started to conduct low-level orbital surveys.

'But why bury a sun-powered device thirty feet underground? We've examined dozens of theories, though we realize that it may be completely impossible to understand the motives of creatures three million years in advance of us.

'The favourite theory is the simplest, and the most logical. It is also the most disturbing.

'You hide a sun-powered device in darkness – only if you want to know when it is brought out into the light. In other words, the monolith may be some kind of alarm. And we have triggered it ...

'Whether the civilization which set it up still exists, we do not know. We must assume that creatures whose machines still function after three million years may build a society equally long-lasting. And we must also assume, until we have evidence to the contrary, that they may be hostile. It has often been argued that any advanced culture must be benevolent but we cannot take any chances.

'Moreover, as the past history of our own world has shown so many times, primitive races have often failed to survive the encounter with higher civilizations. Anthropologists talk of "cultural shock"; we may have to prepare the entire human race for such a shock. But until we know *something* about the creatures who visited the Moon – and presumably the Earth as well – three million years ago, we cannot even begin to make any preparations.

'Your mission, therefore, is much more than a voyage of discovery. It is a scouting trip – a reconnaissance into unknown and potentially dangerous territory. The team under Dr Kaminski had been specially trained for this work; now you will have to manage without them ...

'Finally – your specific target. It seems incredible that any advanced forms of life can exist on Saturn, or could ever have evolved on any of its moons. We had planned to survey the entire system, and we still hope that you can carry out a simplified programme. But now we may have to concentrate on the eighth satellite – Japetus. When the time comes for the terminal manoeuvre, we will decide whether you should rendezvous with this remarkable object.

'Japetus is unique in the Solar System – you know this already, of course, but like all the astronomers of the last three hundred years, you've probably given it little thought. So let me remind you that Cassini – who discovered Japetus in 1671 – also observed that it was *six times* brighter on one side of its orbit than the other.

'This is an extraordinary ratio, and there has never been a satisfactory explanation for it. Japetus is so small – about eight hundred miles in diameter – that even in the lunar telescopes its disc is barely visible. But there seems to be a brilliant, curiously symmetrical spot on one face, and this may be connected with T.M.A.-1. I sometimes think that Japetus has been flashing at us like a cosmic heliograph for three hundred years, and we've been too stupid to understand its message . . .

'So now you know your real objective, and can appreciate the vital importance of this mission. We are all praying that you can still provide us with some facts for a preliminary announcement; the secret cannot be kept indefinitely.

'At the moment, we do not know whether to hope or fear. We do not know if, out on the moons of Saturn, you will meet with good or with evil – or only with ruins a thousand times older than Troy.'

THE MOONS OF SATURN

CHAPTER 31

SURVIVAL

Work is the best remedy for any shock, and Bowman now had work enough for all his lost crewmates. As swiftly as possible, starting with the vital systems without which he and the ship would die, he had to get *Discovery* fully operational again.

Life Support was the first priority. Much oxygen had been lost, but the reserves were still ample to sustain a single man. The pressure and temperature regulation was largely automatic, and there had seldom been need for that to be interfered with. The monitors on Earth could now carry out many of the higher duties of the slain computer, despite the long time-lag before they could react to changing situations. Any trouble in the Life Support system – short of a serious puncture in the hull – would take hours to make itself apparent; there would be plenty of warning.

The ship's power, navigation and propulsion systems were unaffected – but the last two, in any event, Bowman would not need for months, until it was time to rendezvous with Saturn. Even at long range, without the help of an on-board computer, Earth could still supervise this operation. The final orbit adjustments would be somewhat tedious, because of the constant need for checking, but this was not a serious problem.

By far the worst job had been emptying the spinning coffins in the centrifuge. It was well, Bowman thought thankfully, that the members of the survey team had been colleagues, but not intimate friends. They had trained together for only a few weeks; looking back on it, he now realized that even this had been largely a compatibility test.

When he had finally sealed the empty hibernaculums, he felt rather like an Egyptian tomb robber. Now Kaminski, Whitehead and Hunter would all reach Saturn before him – but not before Frank Poole. Somehow, he derived a strange, wry satisfaction from this thought.

He did not attempt to find if the rest of the hibernation system was still in working order. Though his life might ultimately depend upon it, this was a problem that could wait until the ship had entered its final orbit. Many things might happen before then.

It was even possible – though he had not yet looked into the supply position carefully – that by rigorous rationing he might remain alive, *without* resort to hibernation, until rescue came. But whether he could survive psychologically as well as physically was quite another matter.

He tried to avoid thinking about such long-range problems, and to concentrate on immediate essentials. Slowly, he cleaned up the ship, checked that its systems were still running smoothly, discussed technical difficulties with Earth, and operated on the minimum of sleep. Only at intervals, during the first weeks, was he able to give much thought to the great mystery towards which he was now inexorably racing – though it was never very far from his mind.

At last, as the ship slowly settled down once more into an automatic routine – though one that still demanded his constant supervision – Bowman had time to study the reports and briefings sent to him from Earth. Again and again he played back the recording made when T.M.A.-1 greeted the dawn for the first time in three million years. He watched the space-suited figures moving around it, and almost smiled at their ludicrous panic when it blasted its signal at the stars, paralysing their radios with the sheer power of its electronic voice.

Since that moment, the black slab had done nothing. It had been covered up, then cautiously exposed to the Sun again – without any reaction. No attempt had been made to cut into it, partly through scientific caution, but equally through fear of the possible consequences.

The magnetic field that led to its discovery had vanished at the moment of that radio shriek. Perhaps, some experts theorized, it had been generated by a tremendous circulating current, flowing in a superconductor and thus carrying energy down the ages until it was needed. That the monolith had some internal source of power seemed certain; the solar energy it had absorbed during its brief exposure could not account for the strength of its signal.

One curious, and perhaps quite unimportant, feature of the block had led to endless argument. The monolith was 11 feet high, and $1\frac{1}{4}$ by 5 feet in cross-section. When its dimensions were checked with great care, they were found to be in the exact ratio 1 to 4 to 9 – the squares of the first three integers. No one could suggest any plausible explanation for this, but it could hardly be a coincidence, for the proportions held to the limits of measurable accuracy. It was a chastening thought that the entire technology of Earth could not shape even an inert block, of *any* material, with such a fantastic degree of precision. In its way, this passive yet almost arrogant display of geometrical perfection was as impressive as any of T.M.A.-1's other attributes.

Bowman also listened, with a curiously detached interest, to Mission

Control's belated apologia for its programming. The voices from Earth seemed to have a defensive note; he could imagine the recriminations that must now be in progress among those who had planned the expedition.

They had some good arguments, of course – including the results of a secret Department of Defence study, Project BARSOOM, which had been carried out by Harvard's School of Psychology in 1989. In this experiment in controlled sociology, various sample populations had been assured that the human race had made contact with extraterrestrials. Many of the subjects tested were – with the help of drugs, hypnosis and visual effects – under the impression that they had actually met creatures from other planets, so their reactions were regarded as authentic.

Some of these reactions had been quite violent; there was, it seemed, a deep vein of xenophobia in many otherwise normal human beings. In view of mankind's record of lynchings, pogroms and similar pleasantries, this should have surprised no one: nevertheless, the organizers of the study had been deeply disturbed, and the results had never been released. The five separate panics caused in the 20th century by radio broadcasts of H. G. Wells' *War of the Worlds* also reinforced the study's conclusions ...

Despite these arguments, Bowman sometimes wondered if the cultural shock danger was the only explanation for the mission's extreme secrecy. Some hints that had been dropped during his briefings suggested that the U.S.–U.S.S.R. bloc hoped to derive advantage by being the first to contact intelligent extraterrestrials. From his present viewpoint, looking back on Earth as a dim star almost lost in the Sun, such considerations now seemed ludicrously parochial.

He was rather more interested – even though this was now very much water under the bridge – in the theory put forward to account for Hal's behaviour. No one would ever be sure of the truth, but the fact that one of the Mission Control 9000's had been driven into an identical psychosis, and was now under deep therapy, suggested that the explanation was the correct one. The same mistake would not be made again; and the fact that Hal's builders had failed fully to understand the psychology of their own creation showed how difficult it might be to establish communication with *truly* alien beings.

Bowman could easily believe Dr Simonson's theory that unconscious feelings of guilt, caused by his programme conflicts, had made Hal attempt to break the circuit with Earth. And he liked to think – though this again was something that could never be proved – that Hal had no intention of killing Poole. He had merely tried to destroy the evidence;

for once the AE 35 unit reported as burned-out was proved to be operational, his lie would be revealed. After that, like any clumsy criminal caught in a thickening web of deception, he had panicked.

And panic was something that Bowman understood, better than he had any wish to, for he had known it twice during his life. The first time was as a boy, when he had been caught in a line of surf and nearly drowned; the second was as a spaceman under training, when a faulty gauge had convinced him that his oxygen would be exhausted before he could reach safety.

On both occasions, he had almost lost control of all his higher logical processes; he had been within seconds of becoming a frenzied bundle of random impulses. Both times he had won through, but he knew well enough that any man, in the right circumstances, could be dehumanized by panic.

If it could happen to a man, then it could happen to Hal; and with that knowledge the bitterness and the sense of betrayal he felt towards the computer began to fade. Now in any event, it belonged to a past that was wholly over-shadowed by the threat, and the promise, of the unknown future.

CHAPTER 32

CONCERNING E.T.s

Apart from hasty meals back in the carousel – luckily the main food dispensers had not been damaged – Bowman practically lived on the Control Deck. He cat-napped in his seat, and so could spot any trouble as soon as the first signs of it appeared on the display. Under instructions from Mission Control, he had jury-rigged several emergency systems which were working tolerably well. It even seemed possible that he would survive until the *Discovery* reached Saturn – which, of course, she would do whether he was alive or not.

Though he had little enough time for sight-seeing, and the sky of space was no novelty to him, the knowledge of what now lay out there beyond the observation ports sometimes made it difficult for him to concentrate even on the problem of survival. Dead ahead, as the ship was now orientated, sprawled the Milky Way, with its clouds of stars so tightly packed that they numbed the mind. There were the fiery mists of Sagittarius, those seething swarms of suns that forever hid the heart of the Galaxy from human vision. There was the ominous black shadow of the Coal Sack, that hole in space where no stars shone. And there was Alpha Centauri, nearest of all alien suns – the first stop beyond the Solar System.

Although outshone by Sirius and Canopus, it was Alpha Centauri that drew Bowman's eyes and mind whenever he looked out into space. For that unwavering point of brightness, whose rays had taken four years to reach him, had come to symbolize the secret debates now raging on Earth, and whose echoes came to him from time to time.

No one doubted that there must be some connection between T.M.A.-1 and the Saturnian system, but hardly any scientists would admit that the creatures who had erected the monolith could possibly have originated there. As an abode of life, Saturn was even more hostile than Jupiter, and its many moons were frozen in an eternal winter three hundred degrees below zero. Only one of them – Titan – possessed an atmosphere; and that was a thin envelope of poisonous methane.

So perhaps the creatures who had visited Earth's Moon so long ago were not merely extra-terrestrial, but extra-solar – visitors from the stars, who had established their bases wherever it suited them. And this at once raised another problem; could *any* technology, no matter how advanced, bridge the awful gulf that lay between the Solar System and the nearest alien sun?

Many scientists flatly denied the possibility. They pointed out that *Discovery*, the fastest ship ever designed, would take twenty thousand years to reach Alpha Centauri – and millions of years to travel any appreciable distance across the Galaxy. Even if, during the centuries to come, propulsion systems improved out of all recognition, in the end they would meet the impassable barrier of the speed of light, which no material object could exceed. Therefore, the builders of T.M.A.-1 *must* have shared the same sun as Man; and since they had made no appearance in modern historic times, they were probably extinct.

A vocal minority refused to agree. Even if it took centuries to travel from star to star, they contended, this might be no obstacle to sufficiently determined explorers. The technique of hibernation, used on *Discovery* herself, was one possible answer. Another was the self-contained artificial world, embarking on voyages that might last for many generations.

In any event, why should one assume that all intelligent species were as short-lived as Man? There might be creatures in the universe to whom a thousand-year voyage would present nothing worse than slight boredom ...

These arguments, theoretical though they were, concerned a matter of utmost practical importance; they involved the concept of 'reaction time'. If T.M.A.-1 had indeed sent a signal to the stars – perhaps with the help of some further device near Saturn – then it would not reach its destination for years. Even if the response was immediate, therefore, humanity would have a breathing-space which could certainly be measured in decades – more probably in centuries. To many people, this was a reassuring thought.

But not to all. A few scientists – most of them beach-combers on the wilder shores of theoretical physics – asked the disturbing question; 'Are we *certain* that the speed of light is an unbreakable barrier?' It was true that the Special Theory of Relativity had proved to be remarkably durable, and would soon be approaching its first centenary: but it had begun to show a few cracks. And even if Einstein could not be defied, he might be evaded.

Those who sponsored this view talked hopefully about short-cuts through higher dimensions, lines that were straighter than straight, and hyperspacial connectivity. They were fond of using an expressive phrase coined by a Princeton mathematician of the last century: 'Wormholes in space'. Critics who suggested that these ideas were too fantastic to be taken seriously were reminded of Niels Bohr's 'Your theory is crazy – but not crazy enough to be true.'

If there was disputation among the physicists, it was nothing compared with that among the biologists, when they discussed the hoary old problem: 'What would intelligent extraterrestrials look like?' They divided themselves into two opposing camps – one arguing that such creatures must be humanoid, the other equally convinced that 'they' would look nothing like men.

Settling for the first answer were those who believed that the design of two legs, two arms, and main sense organs at the highest point, was so basic and so sensible that it was hard to think of a better one. Of course, there would be minor differences like six fingers instead of five, oddly coloured skin or hair, and peculiar facial arrangements; but most intelligent extraterrestrials – usually abbreviated to E.T.s – would be so similar to Man that they might not be glanced at twice in poor lighting, or from a distance.

This anthropomorphic thinking was ridiculed by another group of biologists, true products of the Space Age who felt themselves free from the prejudices of the past. They pointed out that the human body was the result of millions of evolutionary choices, made by chance over aeons of time. At any one of these countless moments of decision, the genetic dice might have fallen differently, perhaps with better results.

For the human body was a bizarre piece of improvisation, full of organs that had been diverted from one function to another, not always very successfully – and even containing discarded items, like the appendix, that were now worse than useless.

There were other thinkers, Bowman also found, who held even more exotic views. They did not believe that really advanced beings would possess organic bodies at all. Sooner or later, as their scientific knowledge progressed, they would get rid of the fragile, disease-and-accident-prone homes that Nature had given them, and which doomed them to inevitable death. They would replace their natural bodies as they wore out – or perhaps even before that – by constructions of metal and plastic, and would thus achieve immortality. The brain might linger for a little while as the last remnant of the organic body, directing its mechanical limbs and observing the universe through its electronic senses – senses far finer and subtler than those that blind evolution could ever develop.

Even on Earth, the first steps in this direction had been taken. There were millions of men, doomed in earlier ages, who now lived active and happy lives thanks to artificial limbs, kidneys, lungs and hearts. To this process there could be only one conclusion – however far off it might be.

And eventually; even the brain might go. As the seat of consciousness, it was not essential; the development of electronic intelligence had proved that. The conflict between mind and machine might be resolved at last in the eternal truce of complete symbiosis . . .

But was even this the end? A few mystically-inclined biologists went still further. They speculated, taking their cues from the beliefs of many religions, that mind would eventually free itself from matter. The robot body, like the flesh-and-blood one, would be no more than a stepping-stone to something which, long ago, men had called 'spirit'.

And if there was anything beyond *that*, its name could only be God.

CHAPTER 23

AMBASSADOR

During the last three months David Bowman had adapted himself so completely to his solitary way of life that he found it hard to remember any other existence. He had passed beyond despair and beyond hope, and had settled down to a largely automatic routine, punctuated by occasional crises as one or other of *Discovery*'s systems showed signs of malfunctioning.

But he had not passed beyond curiosity, and sometimes the thought of the goal towards which he was driving filled him with a sense of exaltation – and a feeling of power. Not only was he the representative of the entire human race, but his actions during the next few weeks might determine its very future. In the whole of history, there had never been a situation quite like this. He was an Ambassador Extraordinary – Plenipotentiary – for all mankind.

That knowledge helped him in many subtle ways. He kept himself neat and tidy; no matter how tired he became, he never skipped a shave. Mission Control, he knew, was watching him closely for the first signs of any abnormal behaviour, he was determined that it should watch in vain – at least, for any serious symptoms.

Bowman was aware of some changes in his behaviour patterns; it would have been absurd to expect anything else in the circumstances. He could no longer tolerate silence; except when he was sleeping, or talking over the circuit to Earth, he kept the ship's sound system running at almost painful loudness.

At first, needing the companionship of the human voice, he had listened to classical plays – especially the works of Shaw, Ibsen and Shakespeare – or poetry readings from *Discovery*'s enormous library of recorded sounds. The problem they dealt with, however, seemed so remote, or so easily resolved with a little common sense, that after a while he lost patience with them.

So he switched to opera – usually in Italian or German, so that he was not distracted even by the minimal intellectual content that most operas contained. This phase lasted for two weeks, before he realized that the sound of all these superbly trained voices was only exacerbating his loneliness. But what finally ended this cycle was Verdi's *Requiem Mass*, which he had never heard performed on Earth. The 'Dies Irae', roaring with ominous appropriateness through the empty ship, left him completely shattered; and when the trumpets of Doomsday echoed from the heavens, he could endure no more.

Thereafter, he played only instrumental music. He started with the romantic composers, but shed them one by one as their emotional outpourings became too oppressive. Sibelius, Tchaikovsky, Berlioz lasted a few weeks, Beethoven rather longer. He finally found peace, as so many others had done, in the abstract architecture of Bach, occasionally ornamented with Mozart.

And so *Discovery* drove on towards Saturn, as often as not ringing with the cool music of the harpsichord, the frozen thoughts of a brain that had been dust for twice a hundred years.

.   .   .

Even from its present ten million miles Saturn already appeared larger than the Moon as seen from Earth. To the naked eye it was a glorious spectacle; through the telescope, it was unbelievable.

The body of the planet might have been mistaken for Jupiter in one of his quieter moods. There were the same bands of cloud – though paler and less distinct than on that slightly larger world – and the same continent-sized disturbances moving slowly across the atmosphere. However, there was one striking difference between the two planets; even at a glance, it was obvious that Saturn was not spherical. It was so flattened at the poles that it sometimes gave the impression of slight deformity.

But the glory of the rings continually drew Bowman's eye away from the planet; in their complexity of detail, and delicacy of shading, they were a universe in themselves. In addition to the great main gap between the inner and outer rings, there were at least fifty other sub-divisions or boundaries, where there were distinct changes in the bright-ness of the planet's gigantic halo. It was as if Saturn was surrounded by scores of concentric hoops, all touching each other, all so flat that they might have been cut from the thinnest possible paper. The system of rings looked like some delicate work of art, or a fragile toy to be admired but never touched. By no effort of the will could Bowman really appreciate its true scale, and convince himself that the whole planet Earth, if set down here, would look like a ball-bearing rolling round the rim of a dinner-plate.

Sometimes, a star would drift behind the rings, losing only a little of its brilliancy as it did so. It would continue to shine through their translucent material – though often it would twinkle slightly as some larger fragment of orbiting debris eclipsed it.

For the rings, as had been known since the nineteenth century, were not solid; that was a mechanical impossibility. They consisted of count-less myriads of fragments – perhaps the remains of a moon that had come too close and had been torn to pieces by the great planet's tidal pull. Whatever their origin the human race was fortunate to have seen such a wonder; it could exist for only a brief moment of time, in the history of the Solar System.

As long ago as 1945, a British astronomer had pointed out that the rings were ephemeral; gravitational forces were at work which would soon destroy them. Taking this argument backwards in time, it therefore followed that they had been created only recently – a mere two or three million years ago.

But no one had ever given the slightest thought to the curious coincidence that the rings of Saturn had been born at the same time as the human race.

CHAPTER 34

THE ORBITING ICE

Discovery was now deep into the wide-ranging system of moons, and the great planet itself was less than a day ahead. The ship had long since passed the boundary set by outermost Phoebe, moving backwards in a wildly eccentric orbit eight million miles from its primary. Ahead of it now lay Japetus, Hyperion, Titan, Rhea, Dione, Tethys, Enceladus, Mimas – and the rings themselves. All the satellites showed a maze of surface detail in the telescope, and Bowman had relayed back to Earth as many photographs as he could take. Titan alone – three thousand miles in diameter, and as large as the planet Mercury – would occupy a survey team for months; he could give it, and all its cold companions, only the briefest of glances. There was no need for more; already, he was quite certain that Japetus was indeed his goal.

All the other satellites were pitted by occasional meteor craters – though these were much fewer than on Mars – and showed apparently random patterns of light and shade, with here and there a few bright spots that were probably patches of frozen gas. Japetus alone possessed a distinctive geography, and a very strange one indeed.

One hemisphere of the satellite – which, like its companions, turned the same face always towards Saturn – was extremely dark, and showed very little surface detail. In complete contrast, the other was dominated by a brilliant white oval, about four hundred miles long and two hundred wide. At the moment, only part of this striking formation was in daylight, but the reason for Japetus' extraordinary variations in brilliance was now quite obvious. On the western side of the moon's orbit, the bright ellipse was presented towards the Sun – and the Earth. On the eastern phase, the patch was turned away, and only the poorly reflecting hemisphere could be observed.

The great ellipse was perfectly symmetrical, straddling the equator of Japetus with its major axis pointing towards the poles, and it was so

sharp-edged that it almost looked as if someone had carefully painted
a huge white oval on the face of the little moon. It was completely flat,
and Bowman wondered if it could be a lake of frozen liquid – though
that would hardly account for its startlingly artificial appearance.

But he had little time to study Japetus on his way into the heart
of the Saturnian system, for the climax of the voyage – *Discovery*'s last
perturbation manoeuvre – was rapidly approaching. In the Jupiter fly-
by, the ship had used the gravitational field of the planet to increase
her velocity. Now she must do the reverse; she had to lose as much speed
as possible, lest she escape from the Solar System and fly on to the stars.
Her present course was one designed to trap her, so that she would
become another moon of Saturn, shuttling back and forth along a
narrow, two-million-mile-long ellipse. At its near point it would almost
graze the planet; at its far one, it would touch the orbit of Japetus.

The computers back on Earth, though their information was always
three hours late, had assured Bowman that everything was in order.
Velocity and attitude were correct; there was nothing more to be done,
until the moment of closest approach.

.   .   .

The immense system of rings now spanned the sky, and already the
ship was passing over its outermost edge. As he looked down upon them
from a height of some ten thousand miles, Bowman could see through
the telescope that the rings were made largely of ice, glittering and
scintillating in the light of the Sun. He might have been flying over
a snow-storm that occasionally cleared to reveal, where the ground
should have been, baffling glimpses of night and stars.

As *Discovery* curved still closer towards Saturn, the Sun slowly descended towards the multiple arches of the rings. Now they had become
a slim, silver bridge spanning the entire sky; though they were too
tenuous to do more than dim the sunlight, their myriads of crystals
refracted and scattered it in dazzling pyrotechnics. And as the Sun
moved behind the thousand-mile-wide drifts of orbiting ice, pale ghosts
of itself marched and merged across the sky, and the heavens were filled
with shifting flares and flashes. Then the Sun sank below the rings, so
that they framed it with their arches, and the celestial fireworks ceased.

A little later, the ship curved into the shadow of Saturn, as it made
its closest approach over the night side of the planet. Above shone the
stars and the rings; below lay a dimly visible sea of clouds. There were
none of the mysterious patterns of luminosity that had glowed in the
Jovian night; perhaps Saturn was too cold for such displays. The
mottled cloudscape was revealed only by the ghostly radiance reflected
back from the circling icebergs, still illuminated by the hidden Sun.

But in the centre of the arch there was a wide, dark gap, like the missing span of an uncompleted bridge, where the shadow of the planet lay across its rings.

Radio contact with Earth had been broken, and could not be resumed until the ship had emerged from the eclipsing bulk of Saturn. It was perhaps as well that Bowman was too busy now to think of his suddenly enhanced loneliness; for the next few hours, every second would be occupied as he checked the braking manoeuvres, already programmed by the computers on Earth.

After their months of idleness, the main thrusters began to blast out their miles-long cataracts, rivers of glowing plasma. Gravity returned, though briefly, to the weightless world of the Control Deck. And hundreds of miles below, the clouds of methane and frozen ammonia blazed with a light that they had never known before as *Discovery* swept, a fierce and tiny sun, through the Saturnian night.

At last, the pale dawn lay ahead; the ship, moving more and more slowly now, was emerging into day. It could no longer escape from the Sun, or even from Saturn – but it was still moving swiftly enough to rise away from the planet until it grazed the orbit of Japetus, two million miles out.

It would take *Discovery* fourteen days to make that climb, as she coasted once more, though in reverse order, across the paths of all the inner moons. One by one she would cut through the orbits of Mimas, Enceladus, Tethys, Dione, Rhea, Titan, Hyperion ... worlds bearing the names of gods and goddesses who had vanished only yesterday, as time was counted here.

Then she would meet Japetus, and must make her rendezvous. If she failed, she would fall back towards Saturn, and repeat her twenty-eight-day ellipse indefinitely.

There would be no chance of a second rendezvous, if *Discovery* missed on this attempt. The next time round, Japetus would be far away, almost on the other side of Saturn.

It was true that they would meet again, when the orbits of ship and satellite meshed for a second time. But that appointment was so many years ahead that, whatever happened, Bowman knew he would not witness it.

CHAPTER 35

THE EYE OF JAPETUS

When Bowman had first observed Japetus, that curious elliptical patch of brilliance had been partly in shadow, illuminated only by the light of Saturn. Now, as the moon moved slowly along its seventy-nine-day orbit, it was emerging into the full light of day.

As he watched it grow, and *Discovery* rose more and more sluggishly towards her inevitable appointment, Bowman became aware of a disturbing obsession. He never mentioned it in his conversations – or, rather, his running commentaries – with Mission Control, because it might have seemed that he was already suffering from delusions.

Perhaps, indeed, he was; for he had half convinced himself that the bright ellipse set against the dark background of the satellite was a huge, empty eye, staring at him as he approached. It was an eye without a pupil, for nowhere could he see anything to mar its perfect blankness.

Not until the ship was only fifty thousand miles out, and Japetus was twice as large as Earth's familiar Moon, did he notice the tiny black dot at the exact centre of the ellipse. But there was no time, then, for any detailed examination; the terminal manoeuvres were already upon him.

For the last time, *Discovery*'s main drive released its energies. For the last time, the incandescent fury of dying atoms blazed among the moons of Saturn. To David Bowman, the far-off whisper and rising thrust of the jets brought a sense of pride – and of sadness. The superb engines had done their duty with flawless efficiency. They had brought the ship from Earth to Jupiter to Saturn; now this was the very last time they would ever operate. When *Discovery* had emptied her propellant tanks, she would be as helpless and inert as any comet or asteriod, a powerless prisoner of gravitation. Even when the rescue ship arrived a few years hence, it would not be an economical proposition to re-fuel her, so that she could fight her way back to Earth. She would be an eternally orbiting monument to the early days of planetary exploration.

The thousands of miles shrank to hundreds, and as they did so, the fuel gauges dropped swiftly towards zero. At the control panel Bowman's eyes flickered anxiously back and forth over the situation display, and the improvized charts which he now had to consult for any real-time decisions. It would be an appalling anticlimax if, having survived so much, he failed to make rendezvous through lack of a few pounds of fuel ...

The whistle of the jets faded, as the main thrust died and only the verniers continued to nudge *Discovery* gently into orbit. Japetus was now a giant crescent that filled the sky; until this moment, Bowman had always thought of it as a tiny, insignificant object – as indeed it was compared with the world around which it circled. Now as it loomed menacingly above him, it seemed enormous – a cosmic hammer poised to crush *Discovery* like a nutshell.

Japetus was approaching so slowly that it scarcely seemed to move, and it was impossible to tell the exact moment when it made the subtle change from an astronomical body to a landscape, only fifty miles below. The faithful verniers gave their last spurts of thrust, then closed down for ever. The ship was in its final orbit, completing one revolution every three hours at a mere eight hundred miles an hour – all the speed that was required in this feeble gravitational field.

Discovery had become a satellite of a satellite.

CHAPTER 36

BIG BROTHER

'I'm coming round to the daylight side again, and it's just as I reported on the last orbit. This place seems to have only two kinds of surface material. The black stuff looks *burnt*, almost like charcoal, and with the same kind of texture as far as I can judge in the telescope. In fact, it reminds me very much of burnt toast ...

'I still can't make any sense of the white area. It starts at an absolutely sharp-edged boundary, and shows no surface detail at all. It could even be a liquid – it's flat enough. I don't know what impression you've got from the videos I've transmitted, but if you picture a sea of frozen milk you've got the idea exactly.

'It could even be some heavy gas – no, I suppose that's impossible. Sometimes I get the feeling that it's moving, very slowly: but I can never be sure ...

'... I'm over the white area again, on my third orbit. This time, I hope to pass closer to that mark I spotted at its very centre, when I was on my way in. If my calculations are correct, I should go within fifty miles of it – whatever it is.

'... Yes, there's something ahead, just where I calculated. It's coming up over the horizon – and so is Saturn, in almost the same quarter of the sky. I'll move to the telescope ...

'Hello! – it looks like some kind of building – completely black – quite hard to see. No windows or any other features. Just a big, vertical slab – it must be at least a mile high to be visible from this distance. It reminds me – of course! *It's just like the thing you found on the Moon!* This is T.M.A.-1's big brother!'

CHAPTER 37

EXPERIMENT

Call it the Star Gate.

For three million years it had circled Saturn, waiting for a moment of destiny that might never come. In its making, a moon had been shattered, and the debris of its creation orbited still.

Now the long wait was ending. On yet another world, intelligence had been born and was escaping from its planetary cradle. An ancient experiment was about to reach its climax.

Those who had begun that experiment, so long ago, had not been men – or even remotely human. But they were flesh and blood, and when they looked out across the deeps of space, they had felt awe, and wonder, and loneliness. As soon as they possessed the power, they set forth for the stars.

In their explorations, they encountered life in many forms, and watched the workings of evolution on a thousand worlds. They saw how often the first faint sparks of intelligence flickered and died in the cosmic night.

And because, in all the Galaxy, they had found nothing more precious than Mind, they encouraged its dawning everywhere. They became farmers in the fields of stars; they sowed, and sometimes they reaped.

And sometimes, dispassionately, they had to weed.

The great dinosaurs had long since perished, when the survey ship entered the Solar System after a voyage that had already lasted a thousand years. It swept past the frozen outer planets, paused briefly above the deserts of dying Mars, and presently looked down on Earth.

Spread out beneath them, the explorers saw a world swarming with life. For years they studied, collected, catalogued. When they had learned all that they could, they began to modify. They tinkered with the destiny of many species, on land and in the ocean. But which of their experiments would succeed, they could not know for at least a million years.

They were patient, but they were not yet immortal. There was so much to do in this universe of a hundred billion suns, and other worlds were calling. So they set out once more into the abyss, knowing that they would never come this way again.

Nor was there any need. The servants they had left behind would do the rest.

On Earth the glaciers came and went, while above them the changeless Moon still carried its secret. With a yet slower rhythm than the polar ice, the tides of civilization ebbed and flowed across the Galaxy. Strange and beautiful and terrible empires rose and fell and passed on their knowledge to their successors. Earth was not forgotten, but another visit would serve little purpose. It was one of a million silent worlds, few of which would ever speak.

And now, out among the stars, evolution was driving towards new goals. The first explorers of Earth had long since come to the limits of flesh and blood; as soon as their machines were better than their bodies, it was time to move. First their brains, and then their thoughts alone, they transferred into shining new homes of metal and plastic.

In these, they roamed among the stars. They no longer built spaceships. They *were* spaceships.

But the age of the Machine-entities swiftly passed. In their ceaseless experimenting, they had learned to store knowledge in the structure of space itself, and to preserve their thoughts for eternity in frozen lattices of light. They could become creatures of radiation, free at last from the tyranny of matter.

Into pure energy, therefore, they presently transformed themselves and on a thousand worlds, the empty shells they had discarded twitched for a while in a mindless dance of death, then crumbled into rust.

Now they were lords of the Galaxy, and beyond the reach of time. They could rove at will among the stars, and sink like a subtle mist through the very interstices of space. But despite their godlike powers, they had not wholly forgotten their origin, in the warm slime of a vanished sea.

And they still watched over the experiments their ancestors had started, so long ago.

CHAPTER 38

THE SENTINEL

'The air in the ship is getting quite foul, and I have a headache most of the time. There's still plenty of oxygen, but the purifiers never really cleaned up all the mess after the liquids aboard started boiling into vacuum. When things get too bad, I go down into the garage and bleed off some pure oxygen from the pods ...

'There's been no reaction to any of my signals, and because of my orbital inclination, I'm getting slowly further and further away from T.M.A.-2. Incidentally, the name you've given it is doubly inappropriate – there's still no trace of a magnetic field.

'At the moment my closest approach is sixty miles; it will increase to about a hundred as Japetus rotates beneath me, then drop back to zero. I'll pass directly over the thing in thirty days – but that's too long to wait, and then it will be in darkness, anyway.

'Even now, it's only in sight for a few minutes, before it falls below the horizon again. It's damn frustrating – I can't make any serious observations.

'So I'd like your approval of this plan. The spacepods have ample delta vee for a touch-down and a return to the ship. I want to go extravehicular and make a close survey of the object. If it appears safe, I'll land beside it – or even on top of it.

'The ship will still be above my horizon while I'm going down, so I can relay everything back to you. I'll report again on the next orbit, so I won't be out of touch for more than ninety minutes.

'I'm convinced that this is the only thing to do. I've come a billion miles – I don't want to be stopped by the last sixty.'

      . . .

For weeks, as it stared forever sunwards with its strange senses, the Star Gate had watched the approaching ship. Its makers had prepared it for many things, and this was one of them. It recognized what was climbing up towards it from the warm heart of the Solar System.

If it had been alive, it would have felt excitement, but such an emotion was wholly beyond its powers. Even if the ship had passed it by, it would not have known the slightest trace of disappointment. It had waited three million years; it was prepared to wait for eternity.

It observed, and noted, and took no action, as the visitor checked its speed with jets of incandescent gas. Presently it felt the gentle touch of radiations, trying to probe its secrets. And still it did nothing.

Now the ship was in orbit, circling low above the surface of this strangely piebald moon. It began to speak, with blasts of radio waves, counting out the prime numbers from 1 to 11, over and over again. Soon these gave way to more complex signals, at many frequencies – ultra-violet, infra-red, X-rays. The Star Gate made no reply; it had nothing to say.

There was a long pause, then, before it observed that something was falling down towards it from the orbiting ship. It searched its memories, and the logic circuits made their decisions, according to the orders given them long ago.

Beneath the cold light of Saturn, the Star Gate awakened its slumbering powers.

CHAPTER 39

INTO THE EYE

Discovery looked just as he had last seen her from space, floating in lunar orbit with the Moon taking up half the sky. Perhaps there was one slight change; he could not be sure, but some of the paint of her external lettering, announcing the purpose of various hatches, connections, umbilical plugs and other attachments, had faded during its long exposure to the unshielded Sun.

That Sun was now an object that no man would have recognized. It was far too bright to be a star, but one could look directly at its tiny disc without discomfort. It gave no heat at all; when Bowman held his ungloved hands in its rays, as they streamed through the space-pod's window, he could feel nothing upon his skin. He might have been trying to warm himself by the light of the Moon; not even the alien landscape fifty miles below reminded him more vividly of his remoteness from Earth.

Now he was leaving, perhaps for the last time, the metal world that had been his home for so many months. Even if he never returned, the ship would continue to perform its duty, broadcasting instrument readings back to Earth until there was some final, catastrophic failure in its circuits.

And if he *did* return? Well, he could keep alive, and perhaps even sane, for a few months. But that was all, for the hibernation systems were useless with no computer to monitor them. He could not possibly survive until *Discovery II* made its rendezvous with Japetus, four or five years hence.

He put these thoughts behind him, as the golden crescent of Saturn rose in the sky ahead. In all history, he was the only man to have seen this sight. To all other eyes, Saturn had always shown its whole illuminated disc, turned full towards the Sun. Now it was a delicate bow, with the rings forming a thin line across it – like an arrow about to be loosened, into the face of the Sun itself.

Also in the line of the rings was the bright star of Titan, and the fainter sparks of the other moons. Before this century was half gone, men would have visited them all; but whatever secrets they might hold, he would never know.

The sharp-edged boundary of the blind, white eyes was sweeping towards him; there was only a hundred miles to go, and he would be over his target in less than ten minutes. He wished that there was some way of telling if his words were reaching Earth, now an hour and a half away at the speed of light. It would be the ultimate irony if, through some breakdown in the relay system, he disappeared into silence, and no one ever knew what had happened to him.

Discovery was still a brilliant star in the black sky far above. He was pulling ahead as he gained speed during his descent, but soon the pod's braking jets would slow him down and the ship would sail on out of sight – leaving him alone on this shining plain with the dark mystery at its centre.

A block of ebony was climbing above the horizon, eclipsing the stars ahead. He rolled the pod around its gyros, and used full thrust to brake his orbital speed. In a long, flat arc, he descended towards the surface of Japetus.

On a world of higher gravity, the manoeuvre would have been far too extravagant of fuel. But here, the space-pod weighed only a score of pounds; he had several minutes of hovering time before he would cut dangerously into his reserve and be stranded without any hope of return to the still orbiting *Discovery*. Not, perhaps, that it made much difference ...

His altitude was still about five miles, and he was heading straight towards the huge, dark mass that soared in such geometrical perfection above the featureless plain. It was as blank as the flat white surface beneath; until now, he had not appreciated how enormous it really was. There were very few single buildings on Earth as large as this; his care-fully measured photographs indicated a height of almost two thousand feet. And as far as could be judged, its proportions were precisely the same as T.M.A.-1's – that curious ratio 1 to 4 to 9.

'I'm only three miles away now, holding altitude at four thousand feet. Still not a sign of activity – nothing on any of the instruments. The faces seem absolutely smooth and polished. Surely you'd expect *some* meteorite damage after all this time!

'And there's no debris on the – I suppose one could call it the roof. No sign of any opening, either. I'd been hoping there might be some way in ...

'Now I'm right above it, hovering five hundred feet up. I don't want to waste any time, since *Discovery* will soon be out of range. I'm going to land. It's certainly solid enough – and if it isn't I'll blast off at once.

'Just a minute – that's odd ...'

Bowman's voice died into the silence of utter bewilderment. He was not alarmed; he literally could not describe what he was seeing.

He had been hanging above a large, flat rectangle, eight hundred feet long and two hundred feet wide, made of something that looked as solid as rock. But now it seemed to be receding from him; it was exactly like one of those optical illusions, when a three-dimensional object can, by an effort of will, appear to turn inside out – its near and far sides suddenly interchanging.

That was happening to this huge, apparently, solid structure. Impossibly, incredibly, it was no longer a monolith rearing high above a flat plain. What had seemed to be its roof had dropped away to infinite depths; for one dizzy moment, he seemed to be looking down into a vertical shaft – a rectangular duct which defied the laws of perspective, for its size did not decrease with distance ...

The Eye of Japetus had blinked, as if to remove an irritating speck of dust. David Bowman had time for just one broken sentence, which the waiting men in Mission Control, nine hundred million miles away and ninety minutes in the future, were never to forget:

'The thing's hollow – it goes on for ever – and – oh my God – *it's full of stars!*'

CHAPTER 40

EXIT

The Star Gate opened. The Star Gate closed.

In a moment of time, too short to be measured, Space turned and twisted upon itself.

Then Japetus was alone once more, as it had been for three million years – alone, except for a deserted but not yet derelict ship, sending back to its makers messages which they could neither believe nor understand.

THROUGH THE STAR GATE

CHAPTER 41

GRAND CENTRAL

There was no sense of motion, but he was falling towards those impossible stars, shining there in the dark heat of a moon. No – *that* was not where they really were, he felt certain. He wished, now that it was far too late, that he had paid more attention to those theories of hyperspace, of transdimensional ducts. To David Bowman, they were theories no longer.

Perhaps that monolith on Japetus was hollow; perhaps the 'roof' was only an illusion, or some kind of diaphragm that opened to let him through. (But into *what?*) As far as he could trust his senses, he appeared to be dropping vertically down a huge rectangular shaft, several thousand feet deep. He was moving faster and faster – but the far end never changed its size, and remained always at the same distance from him.

Only the stars moved, at first, so slowly that it was some time before he realized that they were escaping out of the frame that held them. But in a little while, it was obvious that the star-field was expanding, as if it was rushing towards him at an incredible speed. The expansion was non-linear; the stars at the centre hardly seemed to move, while those towards the edge accelerated more and more swiftly, until they became streaks of light just before they vanished from view.

There were always others to replace them, flowing into the centre of the field from an apparently inexhaustible source. Bowman wondered what would happen if a star came straight towards him; would it continue to expand until it plunged directly into the face of a sun? But not one came near enough to show a disc; eventually they all veered aside, and streaked over the edge of their rectangular frame.

And still the far end of the shaft came no closer. It was almost as if the walls were moving with him, carrying him to his unknown destination. Or perhaps he was really motionless, and space was moving past him . . .

Not only space, he suddenly realized, was involved in whatever was happening to him now. The clock on the pod's small instrument panel was also behaving strangely.

Normally, the numbers in the tenth-of-a-second window flickered past so quickly that it was almost impossible to read them; now they were appearing and disappearing at discrete intervals, and he could count them off one by one without difficulty. The seconds themselves were passing with incredible slowness, as if time itself were coming to a stop. At last, the tenth-of-a-second counter froze between five and six.

Yet he could still think, and even observe, as the ebon walls flowed past at a speed that might have been anything between zero and a million times the velocity of light. Somehow, he was not in the least surprised, nor was he alarmed. On the contrary, he felt a sense of calm expectation, such as he had once known when the space-medics had tested him with hallucinagenic drugs. The world around him was strange and wonderful, but there was nothing to fear. He had travelled those millions of miles in search of mystery; and now, it seemed, the mystery was coming to him.

The rectangle ahead was growing lighter. The luminous star-streaks were paling against a milky sky, whose brilliance increased moment by moment. It seemed as if the space-pod was heading towards a bank of cloud, uniformly illuminated by the rays of an invisible sun.

He was emerging from the tunnel. The far end, which until now had remained at that same indeterminate distance, neither approaching nor receding, had suddenly started to obey the normal laws of perspective. It was coming closer, and steadily widening before him. At the same time, he felt that he was moving upwards, and for a fleeting instant he wondered if he had fallen right through Japetus and was now ascending from the other side. But even before the space-pod soared out into the open, he knew that this place had nothing to do with Japetus, or with any world within the experience of man.

There was no atmosphere, for he could see all details unblurred, clear down to an incredibly remote and flat horizon. He must be above a world of enormous size – perhaps one much larger than Earth. Yet despite its extent, all the surface that Bowman could see was tessellated into obviously artificial patterns that must have been miles on a side. It was like the jigsaw puzzle of a giant that played with planets; and at the centres of many of those squares and triangles and polygons were gaping black shafts – twins of the chasm from which he had just emerged.

Yet the sky above was stranger – and, in its way, more disturbing – even than the improbable land beneath. For there were no stars; neither was there the blackness of space. There was only a softly glowing milkiness, that gave the impression of infinite distance. Bowman remembered a description he had once heard of the dreaded Antarctic 'whiteout' – 'like being inside a ping-pong ball'. Those words could be applied perfectly to this weird place, but the explanation must be utterly different. This sky could be no meteorological effect of mist and snow; there was a perfect vacuum here.

Then, as Bowman's eyes grew accustomed to the nacreous glow that filled the heavens, he became aware of another detail. The sky was not, as he had thought at first glance, completely empty. Dotted overhead, quite motionless and forming apparently random patterns, were myriads of tiny black specks.

They were difficult to see, for they were mere points of darkness, but once detected they were quite unmistakable. They reminded Bowman of something – something so familiar, yet so insane, that he refused to accept the parallel, until logic forced it upon him.

Those black holes in the white sky were stars; he might have been looking at a photographic negative of the Milky Way.

Where in God's name am I? Bowman asked himself; and even as he posed the question, he felt certain that he could never know the answer. It seemed that Space had been turned inside out: this was not a place for man. Though the capsule was comfortably warm, he felt suddenly cold, and was afflicted by an almost uncontrollable trembling. He wanted to close his eyes, and shut out the pearly nothingness that surrounded him; but that was the act of a coward, and he would not yield to it.

The pierced and facetted planet slowly rolled beneath him, without any real change of scenery. He guessed that he was about ten miles above the surface, and should be able to see any signs of life with ease. But this whole world was deserted; intelligence had come here, worked its will upon it, and gone its way again.

Then he noticed, humped above the flat plain perhaps twenty miles away, a roughly cylindrical pile of debris that could only be the carcass of a gigantic ship. It was too distant for him to see any details, and it passed out of sight within a few seconds, but he could make out broken ribs and dully gleaming sheets of metal that had been partly peeled off like the skin of an orange. He wondered how many thousands of years the wreck had lain there on this deserted chequerboard – and what manner of creatures had sailed it between the stars.

Then he forgot the derelict; for something was coming up over the horizon.

At first it looked like a flat disc, but that was because it was heading almost directly towards him. As it approached and passed beneath, he saw that it was spindle-shaped, and several hundred feet long. Though there were faintly visible bands here and there along its length, it was hard to focus upon them; the object appeared to be vibrating, or perhaps spinning, at a very rapid rate.

It tapered to a point at either end, and there was no sign of propulsion.

Only one thing about it was familiar to human eyes, and that was its colour. If it was indeed a solid artifact, and not an optical phantom, then its makers perhaps shared some of the emotions of men. But they certainly did not share their limitations; for the spindle appeared to be made of gold.

Bowman moved his head to the rear-view system to watch the thing drop behind. It had ignored him completely, and now he saw it was falling out of the sky down towards one of those thousands of great slots. A few seconds later, it disappeared in a final flash of gold as it dived into the planet. He was alone again, beneath that sinister sky, and the sense of isolation and remoteness was more overwhelming than ever.

Then he saw that he also was sinking down towards the mottled surface of the giant world, and that another of the rectangular chasms yawned immediately below. The empty sky closed above him, the clock crawled to rest, and once again his pod was falling between infinite ebon walls towards another distant patch of stars. But now he was sure that he was not returning to the Solar System, and in a flash of insight that might have been wholly spurious, he knew what this thing must surely be.

It was some kind of cosmic switching device, routing the traffic of the stars through unimaginable dimensions of space and time. He was passing through a Grand Central Station of the Galaxy.

CHAPTER 42

THE ALIEN SKY

Far ahead, the walls of the slot were becoming dimly visible once more, in the faint light diffusing downwards from some still hidden source. And then the darkness was abruptly whipped away, as the tiny space-pod hurtled upwards into a sky ablaze with stars.

He was back in space as he knew it, but a single glance told him that he was light-centuries from Earth. He did not even attempt to find any of the familiar constellations that since the beginning of history had been the friends of Man; perhaps none of the stars that now blazed around him had ever been seen by the unaided human eye.

Most of them were concentrated in a glowing belt, broken here and there with dark bands of obscuring cosmic dust, which completely circled the sky. It was like the Milky Way, but scores of times brighter;

Bowman wondered if this was indeed his own Galaxy, seen from a point much closer to its brilliant, crowded centre.

He hoped that it was; then he would not be so far from home. But this, he realized at once, was a childish thought. He was so inconceivably remote from the Solar System that it made little difference whether he was in his own Galaxy, or the most distant one that any telescope had ever glimpsed.

He looked back to see the thing from which he was rising, and had another shock. Here was no giant multi-facetted world, nor any duplicate of Japetus. There was *nothing* – except an inky shadow against the stars, like a doorway opening from a darkened room into a still darker night. Even as he watched, that doorway closed. It did not recede from him; it slowly filled with stars, as if a rent in the fabric of space had been repaired. Then he was alone beneath the alien sky.

The space-pod was slowly turning, and as it did so, it brought fresh wonders into view. First there was a perfectly spherical swarm of stars, becoming more and more closely-packed towards the centre until its heart was a continuous glow of light. Its outer edges were ill-defined – a slowly thinning halo of suns that merged imperceptibly into the background of more stars.

This glorious apparition, Bowman knew, was a globular cluster. He was looking upon something that no human eye had ever seen, save as a smudge of light in the field of a telescope. He could not remember the distance to the nearest known cluster, but he was sure that there were none within a thousand light-years of the Solar System.

The pod continued its slow rotation to disclose an even stranger sight – a huge red sun, many times larger than the Moon as seen from Earth. Bowman could look straight into its face without discomfort; judging by its colour, it was no hotter than a glowing coal. Here and there, set into the sombre red, were rivers of bright yellow – incandescent Amazons, meandering for thousands of miles before they lost themselves in the desert of this dying sun.

Dying? No – that was a wholly false impression, born of human experience and the emotions aroused by the hues of sunset, or the glow of fading embers. This was a star that had left behind the fiery extravagances of its youth, had raced through the violets and blues and greens of the spectrum in a few fleeting billions of years, and now had settled down to a peaceful maturity of unimaginable length. All that had gone before was not a thousandth of what was yet to come; the story of this star had barely begun.

The pod had ceased to roll; the great red sun lay straight ahead. Though there was no sense of motion, Bowman knew that he was still gripped by whatever controlling force had brought him here from Saturn. All the science and engineering skill of Earth seemed hopelessly primitive now, against the powers that were carrying him to some unimaginable fate.

He stared into the sky ahead, trying to pick out the goal towards which he was being taken – perhaps some planet circling this great sun. But there was nothing that showed any visible disc or exceptional brightness; if there were planets orbiting here, he could not distinguish them from the stellar background.

Then he noticed that something strange was happening to the very edge of the sun's crimson disc. A white glow had appeared there, and was rapidly waxing in brilliance; he wondered if he was seeing one of those sudden eruptions, or flares, that trouble most stars from time to time.

The light became brighter and bluer; it began to spread along the edge of the sun, whose blood-red hues paled swiftly by comparison. It was almost, Bowman told himself, smiling at the absurdity of the thought, as if he were watching sunrise – *on a sun*.

And so indeed he was. Above the burning horizon lifted something no larger than a star, but so brilliant that the eye could not bear to look upon it. A mere point of blue-white radiance, like an electric arc, was moving at unbelievable speed across the face of the great sun. It must be very close to its giant companion; immediately below it, drawn upwards by its gravitational pull, was a column of flame thousands of miles high. It was as if a tidal wave of fire was marching for ever along the equator of this star, in vain pursuit of the searing apparition in its sky.

That pin-point of incandescence must be a White Dwarf – one of those strange, fierce little stars no larger than the Earth, yet containing a million times its mass. Such ill-matched stellar couples were not uncommon; but Bowman had never dreamed that one day he would see such a pair with his own eyes.

The White Dwarf had transited almost half the disc of its companion – it must take only minutes to make a complete orbit – when Bowman was at last certain that he too was moving. Ahead of him, one of the stars was becoming rapidly brighter, and was beginning to drift against its background. It must be some small, close body – perhaps the world towards which he was travelling.

It was upon him with unexpected speed; and he saw that it was not a world at all.

A dully gleaming cobweb or lattice-work of metal, hundreds of miles in extent, grew out of nowhere until it filled the sky. Scattered across its continent-wide surface were structures that must have been as large as cities, but which appeared to be machines. Around many of these were assembled scores of smaller objects, ranged in neat rows and columns. Bowman had passed several such groups before he realized that they were fleets of spaceships; he was flying over a gigantic orbital parking lot.

Because there were no familiar objects by which he could judge the scale of the scene flashing by below, it was almost impossible to estimate the size of the vessels hanging there in space. But they were certainly enormous; some must have been miles in length. They were of many different designs – spheres, facetted crystals, slim pencils, ovoids, discs. This must be one of the meeting places for the commerce of the stars.

Or it *had* been – perhaps a million years ago. For nowhere could Bowman see any sign of activity; this sprawling space-port was as dead as the Moon.

He knew it was not only the absence of all movement, but by such unmistakable signs as great gaps torn in the metal cobweb by the wasp-like blunderings of asteroids that must have smashed through it, aeons ago. This was no longer a parking lot: it was a cosmic junk-heap.

He had missed its builders by ages, and with that realization Bowman felt a sudden sinking of his heart. Though he had not known what to expect, at least he had hoped to meet some intelligence from the stars. Now, it seemed, he was too late. He had been caught in an ancient, automatic trap, set for some unknown purpose, and still operating when its makers had long since passed away. It had swept him across the Galaxy, and dumped him (with how many others?) in this celestial Sargasso, doomed soon to die when his air was exhausted.

Well, was it unreasonable to expect more. Already he had seen wonders for which many men would have sacrificed their lives. He thought of his dead companions; *he* had no cause for complaint.

Then he saw that the derelict space-port was still sliding past him with undiminished speed. He was sweeping over its outlying suburbs; its ragged edge went by, and no longer partially eclipsed the stars. In a few more minutes, it had fallen behind.

His fate did not lie here – but far ahead, in the huge, crimson sun towards which the space-pod was now unmistakably falling.

CHAPTER 43

INFERNO

Now there was only the red sun filling the sky from side to side. He was so close that its surface was no longer frozen into immobility by sheer scale. There were luminous nodules moving to and fro, cyclones of ascending and descending gas, prominences slowly rocketing towards the heavens. Slowly? They must be rising at a million miles an hour, for their movement to be visible to his eye ...

He did not even attempt to grasp the scale of the inferno towards which he was descending. The immensities of Saturn and Jupiter had defeated him, during *Discovery*'s fly-by in that solar system now unknown gigamiles away. But everything he saw here was a hundred times larger still; he could do nothing but accept the images that were flooding into his mind, without attempting to interpret them.

As that sea of fire expanded beneath him, Bowman should have known fear – but, curiously enough, he now felt only a mild apprehension. It was not that his mind was benumbed with wonders; logic told him that he must surely be under the protection of some controlling and almost omnipotent intelligence. He was now so close to the red sun that he would have been burned up in a moment, if its radiation had not been held at bay by some invisible screen. And during his voyage, he had been subjected to accelerations that should have crushed him instantly – yet he had felt nothing. If so much trouble had been taken to preserve him, there was still cause for hope.

The space-pod was now moving along a shallow arc almost parallel to the surface of the star, but slowly descending towards it. And now, for the first time, Bowman became aware of sounds. There was a faint continuous roar, broken from time to time by crackles like tearing paper, or distant lightning. This could be only the feeble echoes of an unimaginable cacophony; the atmosphere surrounding him must be racked by concussions that could tear any material object to atoms. Yet he was protected from this shattering tumult as effectively as from the heat. Though ridges of flame thousands of miles high were rising and slowly collapsing around him, he was completely insulated from all this violence. The energies of the star raved past him, as if they were in another universe; the pod moved sedately through their midst, unbuffeted and unscorched.

Bowman's eyes, no longer hopelessly confused by the strangeness and grandeur of the scene, began to pick out details which must have been there before, but which he had not yet perceived. The surface of this star was not formless chaos; there was pattern here, as in everything that nature creates.

He noticed first the little whirlpools of gas – probably no larger than Asia or Africa – that wandered over the surface of the star. Sometimes he could look directly down into one of them, to see darker, cooler regions far below. Curiously enough, there appeared to be no sunspots; perhaps they were a disease peculiar to the star that shone on Earth.

And there were occasional clouds, like wisps of smoke blown before a gale. Perhaps they were indeed smoke, for this sun was so cold that real fire could not exist here. Chemical compounds could be born and could live for a few seconds before they were again ripped apart by the fiercer nuclear violence that surrounded them.

The horizon was growing brighter, its colour changing from gloomy red to yellow to blue to blistering violet. The White Dwarf was coming up over the horizon, dragging its tidal wave of star-stuff behind it.

Bowman shielded his eyes from the intolerable glare of the little sun, and focussed on the troubled starscape which its gravitational field was sucking skyward. Once he had seen a waterspout moving across the face of the Caribbean; this tower of flame had almost the same shape. Only the scale was slightly different, for at its base, the column was probably wider than the planet Earth.

And then, immediately beneath him, Bowman noticed something which was surely new, since he could hardly have overlooked it if it had been there before. Moving across the ocean of glowing gas were myriads of bright beads; they shone with a pearly light which waxed and waned in a period of a few seconds. And they were all travelling in the same direction, like salmon moving upstream; sometimes they weaved back and forth so that their paths intertwined, but they never touched.

There were thousands of them, and the longer Bowman stared, the more convinced he became that their motion was purposeful. They were too far away for him to make out any details of their structure; that he could see them at all in this colossal panorama meant that they must be scores – perhaps hundreds – of miles across. If they were organized entities, they were leviathans indeed, built to match the scale of the world they inhabited.

Perhaps they were only clouds of plasma, given temporary stability by some odd combination of natural forces – like the short-lived sphere of ball-lightning that still puzzled terrestrial scientists. That was an easy, and perhaps soothing, explanation; but as Bowman looked down upon that star-wide streaming, he could not really believe it. Those glittering nodes of light *knew* where they were going; they were deliberately converging upon the pillar of fire raised by the White Dwarf as it orbited overhead.

Bowman stared once more at that ascending column, now marching along the horizon beneath the tiny, passive star that ruled it. Could it be pure imagination – or were there patches of brighter luminosity creeping up that great geyser of gas, as if myriads of shining sparks had combined into whole continents of phosphorescence?

The idea was almost beyond fantasy, but perhaps he was watching nothing less than a migration from star to star, across a bridge of fire. Whether it was a movement of mindless, cosmic beasts driven across space by some lemming-like urge, or a vast concourse of intelligent entities, he would probably never know.

He was moving through a new order of creation, of which few men had ever dreamed. Beyond the realms of sea and land and air and space lay the realms of fire, which he alone had been privileged to glimpse. It was too much to expect that he would also understand.

CHAPTER 44

RECEPTION

The pillar of fire was marching over the edge of the sun, like a storm passing beyond the horizon. The scurrying flecks of light no longer moved across the redly-glowing starscape still thousands of miles below. Inside his space-pod, protected from an environment that could annihilate him within a milli-second, David Bowman awaited whatever had been prepared.

The White Dwarf was sinking fast as it hurtled along its orbit; presently it touched the horizon, set it aflame, and disappeared. A false twilight fell upon the inferno beneath, and in the sudden change of illumination, Bowman became aware that something was happening in the space around him.

The world of the red sun seemed to ripple, as if he was looking at it through running water. For a moment he wondered if this was some refractive effect, perhaps caused by the passage of an unusually violent shock-wave through the tortured atmosphere in which he was immersed.

The light was fading: it seemed that a second twilight was about to fall. Involuntarily, Bowman looked upwards, then checked himself sheepishly, as he remembered that here the main source of light was not the sky, but the blazing world below.

It seemed as if walls of some material like smoked glass were thickening around him, cutting out the red glow and obscuring the view. It became darker and darker; the faint roar of the stellar hurricanes also faded out. The space-pod was floating in silence, and in night. A moment later there was the softest of bumps as it settled on some hard surface and came to rest.

To rest on *what?* Bowman asked himself incredulously. Then light returned; and incredulity gave way to a heart-sinking despair – for as he saw what lay around him, he knew that he must be mad.

He was prepared, he thought, for any wonder. The only thing he had never expected was the utterly commonplace.

The space-pod was resting on the polished floor of an elegant, anonymous hotel suite that might have been in any large city on Earth. He was staring into a living room with a coffee table, a divan, a dozen chairs, a writing desk, various lamps, a half-filled book-case with some magazines lying on it, and even a bowl of flowers. Van Gogh's *Bridge of Arles* was hanging on one wall – Wyeth's *Christina's World* on another. He felt confident that when he pulled open the drawer of that desk he would find a Gideon Bible inside it …

If he was indeed mad, his delusions were beautifully organized. Everything was perfectly real; nothing vanished when he turned his back. The only incongruous element in the scene – and that certainly a major one – was the space-pod itself.

For many minutes, Bowman did not move from his seat. He half expected the vision around him to go away, but it remained as solid as anything he had ever seen in his life.

It *was* real – or else a phantom of the senses so superbly contrived that there was no way of distinguishing it from reality. Perhaps it was some kind of test; if so, not only his fate but that of the human race might well depend upon his actions in the next few minutes.

He could sit here and wait for something to happen, or he could open the pod and step outside to challenge the reality of the scene around him. The floor appeared to be solid; at least, it was bearing the weight of the space-pod. He was not likely to fall through it – whatever 'it' might really be.

But there was still the question of air; for all that he could tell, this room be in vacuum, or might contain a poisonous atmosphere. He thought it very unlikely – no one would go to all this trouble without attending to such an essential detail – but he did not propose to take unnecessary risks. In any event, his years of training made him wary of contamination; he was reluctant to expose himself to an unknown environment, until he knew that there was no alternative. This place *looked* like a hotel room somewhere in the United States. That did not alter the fact that, in reality, he must be hundreds of light years from the Solar System.

He closed the helmet of his suit, sealing himself in, and actuated the hatch of the space-pod. There was a brief 'hiss' of pressure equalization; then he stepped out into the room.

As far as he could tell, he was in a perfectly normal gravity field. He raised one arm, then let it fall freely. It flopped to his side in less than a second.

This made everything seem doubly unreal. Here he was wearing a spacesuit, standing – when he should have been floating – outside a vehicle which could only function properly in the absence of gravity. All his normal astronaut's reflexes were upset; he had to think before he made every movement.

Like a man in a trance, he walked slowly from his bare, unfurnished half of the room towards the hotel suite. It did not, as he had almost expected, disappear as he approached, but remained perfectly real – and apparently perfectly solid.

He stopped beside the coffee table. On it sat a conventional Bell System Picturephone, complete with the local directory. He bent down, and picked up the volume with his clumsy, gloved hands.

It bore, in the familiar type he had seen thousands of times, the name: WASHINGTON, D.C.

Then he looked more closely; and for the first time, he had objective proof that, although all this might be real, he was not on Earth.

He could read only the word WASHINGTON; the rest of the printing was a blur, as if it had been copied from a newspaper photograph. He opened the book at random and riffled through the pages. They were all blank sheets of crisp white material which was certainly not paper, though it looked very much like it.

He lifted the telephone receiver and pressed it against the plastic of his helmet. If there had been a dialling sound, he could have heard it through the conducting material. But, as he had expected, there was only silence.

So – it was all a fake, though a fantastically careful one. And it was clearly not intended to deceive but rather – he hoped – to reassure. That was a very comforting thought; nevertheless he would not remove his suit until he had completed his voyage of exploration.

All the furniture seemed sound and solid enough; he tried all the chairs, and they supported his weight. But the drawers in the desk would not open; they were dummies.

So were the books and magazines; like the telephone directory, only the titles were readable. They formed an odd selection – mostly rather trashy best-sellers, a few sensational works of non-fiction, and some well-publicised autobiographies. There was nothing less than three years old, and little of any intellectual content. Not that it mattered, for the books could not even be taken down from the shelves.

There were two doors that opened readily enough. The first one took him into a small but comfortable bedroom, fitted with bed, bureau, two chairs, light switches that actually worked, and a clothes closet. He opened this, and found himself looking at four suits, a dressing gown, a dozen white shirts, and several sets of underwear, all neatly draped from hangers.

He took down one of the suits, and inspected it carefully. As far as his gloved hands could judge, it was made of material that was more like fur than wool. It was also a little out of style; on Earth, no one had been wearing single-breasted suits for at least four years.

Next to the bedroom was a bathroom, complete with fittings which, he was relieved to note, were not dummies, but worked in a perfectly normal manner. And after that was a kitchenette, with electric cooker, ice-box, storage cupboards, crockery and cutlery, sink, table and chairs. Bowman began to explore this not only with curiosity, but with mounting hunger.

First he opened the ice-box, and a wave of cold mist rolled out. The shelves were well-stocked with packages and cans, all of them looking perfectly familiar from a distance, though at close quarters their proprietary labels were blurred and unreadable. However, there was a notable absence of eggs, milk, butter, meat, fruit, or any other unprocessed food; the ice-box held only items that had already been packaged in some way.

Bowman picked up a carton of a familiar breakfast cereal, thinking as he did so that it was odd to keep this frozen. The moment he lifted the package, he knew that it certainly did *not* contain cornflakes; it was much too heavy.

He ripped open the lid, and examined the contents. The box contained a slightly moist blue substance, of about the weight and texture of bread pudding. Apart from its odd colour, it looked quite appetizing.

But this is ridiculous, Bowman told himself. I am almost certainly being watched, and I must look an idiot wearing this suit. If this is some kind of intelligence test, I've probably failed already.

Without further hesitation, he walked back into the bedroom and began to undo the clamp of his helmet. When it was loose, he lifted the helmet a fraction of an inch, cracked the seal, and took a cautious sniff. As far as he could tell, he was breathing perfectly normal air.

He dropped the helmet on the bed, and began thankfully – and rather stiffly – to divest himself of his suit. When he had finished, he stretched, took a few deep breaths, and carefully hung the spacesuit up among the more conventional articles of clothing in the closet. It looked rather odd there, but the compulsive tidiness that Bowman shared with all astronauts would never have allowed him to leave it anywhere else.

Then he walked quickly back into the kitchen, and began to inspect the 'cereal' box at closer quarters.

The blue bread pudding had a faint, spicy smell, something like a macaroon. Bowman weighed it in his hand, then broke off a piece and cautiously sniffed at it. Though he felt sure now that there would be no deliberate attempt to poison him, there was always the possibility of mistakes – especially in a matter so complex as biochemistry.

He nibbled at a few crumbs, then chewed and swallowed the fragment of food; it was excellent, though the flavour was so elusive as to be almost indescribable. If he closed his eyes, he could imagine it was meat, or wholemeal bread, or even dried fruit. Unless there were unexpected after-effects, he had nothing to fear from starvation.

When he had eaten just a few mouthfuls of the substance, and already felt quite satisfied, he looked for something to drink. There were half a dozen cans of beer – again of a famous brand – at the back of the ice-box, and he pressed the tab on one of them to open it.

The pre-stressed metal lid popped off along its strain lines, exactly as usual. But the can did not contain beer; to Bowman's surprised disappointment, it held more of the blue food.

In a few seconds he had opened half a dozen of the other packages and cans. Whatever their labels, their contents were the same; it seemed that his diet was going to be a little monotonous, and that he would have nothing but water to drink. He filled a glass from the kitchen faucet, and sipped at it cautiously.

He spat out the first few drops at once; the taste was terrible. Then, rather ashamed of his instinctive reaction, he forced himself to drink the rest.

That first sip had been enough to identify the liquid. It tasted terrible because it had no taste at all; the faucet was supplying pure, distilled water. His unknown hosts were obviously taking no chances with his health.

Feeling much refreshed, he then had a quick shower. There was no soap, which was another minor inconvenience, but there was a very efficient hot-air drier in which he luxuriated for a while before trying on underpants, vest and dressing gown from the clothes closet. After that, he laid down on the bed, stared up at the ceiling, and tried to make sense of this fantastic situation.

He had made little progress when he was distracted by another line of thought. Immediately above the bed was the usual hotel-type ceiling TV screen; he had assumed that, like the telephone and books, it was a dummy.

But the control unit on its swinging bedside arm looked so realistic that he could not resist playing with it; and as his fingers touched the ON sensor disc, the screen lit up.

Feverishly, he started to tap out channel selector codes at random, and almost at once he got his first picture.

It was a well-known African news commentator, discussing the attempts being made to preserve the last remnants of his country's wild life. Bowman listened for a few seconds, so captivated by the sound of a human voice that he did not in the least care what it was talking about. Then he changed channels.

In the next five minutes, he got a symphony orchestra playing Walton's Violin Concerto, a discussion on the sad state of the legitimate theatre, a western, a demonstration of a new headache cure, a panel game in some oriental language, a psychodrama, three news commentaries, a football game, a lecture on solid geometry (in Russian) and several tuning signals and data transmissions. It was, in fact, a perfectly normal selection from the world's TV programmes, and apart from the psychological uplift it gave him, it confirmed one suspicion that had already been forming in his mind.

All the programmes were about two years old. That was around the time T.M.A.-1 had been discovered, and it was hard to believe that this was a pure coincidence. *Something* had been monitoring the radio waves; that ebon block had been busier than Man had suspected.

He continued to wander across the spectrum, and suddenly recognized a familiar scene. Here was this very suite, now occupied by a celebrated actor who was furiously denouncing an unfaithful mistress. Bowman looked with a shock of recognition upon the living room he had just left – and when the camera followed the indignant couple towards the bedroom, he involuntarily looked towards the door to see if anyone was entering.

So that was how this reception area had been prepared for him; his hosts had based their ideas of terrestrial living upon TV programmes. His feeling that he was inside a movie set was almost literally true.

He had learned all that he wished to for the moment, and turned off the set. What do I do now? he asked himself, locking his fingers behind his head and staring at the blank screen.

He was physically and emotionally exhausted, yet it seemed impossible that one could sleep, in such fantastic surroundings, and further from Earth than any man in history had ever been. But the comfortable bed, and the instinctive wisdom of the body, conspired together against his will.

He fumbled for the light switch, and the room was plunged into darkness. Within seconds, he had passed beyond the reach of dreams.

So, for the last time, David Bowman slept.

CHAPTER 45

RECAPITULATION

There being no further use for it, the furniture of the suite dissolved back into the mind of its creator. Only the bed remained – and the walls, shielding this fragile organism from the energies it could not yet control.

In his sleep, David Bowman stirred restlessly. He did not wake, nor did he dream, but he was no longer wholly unconscious. Like a fog creeping through a forest, something invaded his mind. He sensed it only dimly, for the full impact would have destroyed him as surely as the fires raging beyond these walls. Beneath that dispassionate scrutiny, he felt neither hope nor fear; all emotion had been leached away.

He seemed to be floating in free space, while around him stretched, in all directions, an infinite geometrical grid of dark lines or threads, along which moved tiny nodes of light – some slowly, some at dazzling speed. Once he had peered through a microscope at a cross-section of a human brain, and in its network of nerve-fibres had glimpsed the same labyrinthine complexity. But that had been dead and static, whereas this transcended life itself. He knew – or believed he knew – that he was watching the operation of some gigantic mind, contemplating the universe of which he was so tiny a part.

The vision, or illusion, lasted only a moment. Then the crystalline planes and lattices, and the interlocking perspectives of moving light flickered out of existence, as David Bowman moved into a realm of consciousness that no man had ever experienced before.

At first, it seemed that Time itself was running backwards. Even this marvel he was prepared to accept, before he realized the subtler truth.

The springs of memory were being tapped; in controlled recollection he was reliving the past. There was the hotel suite – there the space-pod – there the burning starscapes of the red sun – there the shining core of the Galaxy – there the gateway through which he had re-emerged into the universe. And not only vision, but all the sense impressions, and all the emotions he had felt at the time, were racing past, more and more swiftly. His life was unreeling like a tape-recorder playing back at ever-increasing speed.

Now he was once more aboard *Discovery*, and the rings of Saturn filled the sky. Before that, he was repeating his final dialogue with Hal; he was seeing Frank Poole leave on his last mission; he was hearing the voice of Earth, assuring him that all was well.

And even as he relived these events, he knew that all indeed was well. He was retrogressing down the corridors of time, being drained of knowledge and experience as he swept back towards his childhood. But nothing was being lost; all that he had ever been, at every moment of his life, was being transferred to safer keeping. Even as one David Bowman ceased to exist, another became immortal.

Faster, faster, he moved back into forgotten years, and into a simpler world. Faces he had once loved, and had thought lost beyond recall, smiled at him sweetly. He smiled back with fondness, and without pain.

Now, at last, the headlong regression was slackening; the wells of memory were nearly dry. Time flowed more and more sluggishly, approaching a moment of stasis – as a swinging pendulum, at the limit of its arc, seems frozen for one eternal instant, before the next cycle begins.

The timeless instant passed; the pendulum reversed its swing. In an empty room, floating amid the fires of a double star twenty thousand light-years from Earth, a baby opened its eyes and began to cry.

CHAPTER 46

TRANSFORMATION

Then it became silent, as it saw that it was no longer alone.

A ghostly, glimmering rectangle had formed in the empty air. It solidified into a crystal tablet, lost its transparency, and became suffused with a pale, milky luminescence. Tantalizing, ill-defined phantoms moved across its surface and in its depths. They coalesced into bars of light and shadow, then formed intermeshing, spoked patterns that began slowly to rotate, in time with the pulsing rhythm that now seemed to fill the whole of space.

It was a spectacle to grasp and hold the attention of any child – or of any man-ape. But, as it had been three million years before, it was only the outward manifestation of forces too subtle to be consciously perceived. It was merely a toy to distract the senses, while the real processing was carried out at far deeper levels of the mind.

This time, the processing was swift and certain, as the new design was woven. For in the aeons since their last meeting, much had been learned by the weaver; and the material on which he practised his art was now of an infinitely finer texture. But whether it should be permitted to form part of his still-growing tapestry, only the future could tell.

With eyes that already held more than human intentness, the baby stared into the depths of the crystal monolith, seeing – but not yet understanding – the mysteries that lay beyond. It knew that it had come home, that there was the origin of many races beside his own; but it knew also that it could not stay. Beyond this moment lay another birth, stranger than any in the past.

Now the moment had come; the glowing patterns no longer echoed the secrets in the crystal's heart. As they died, so too the protective walls faded back into the non-existence from which they had briefly emerged, and the red sun filled the sky.

The metal and plastic of the forgotten space-pod, and the clothing once worn by an entity who had called himself David Bowman, flashed into flame. The last links with Earth were gone, resolved back into their component atoms.

But the child scarcely noticed, as he adjusted himself to the comfortable glow of his new environment. He still needed, for a little while, this shell of matter as the focus of his powers. His indestructible body was his mind's present image of itself; and for all his powers, he knew that he was still a baby. So he would remain until he had decided on a new form, or had passed beyond the necessities of matter.

And now it was time to go – though in one sense he would never leave this place where he had been reborn, for he would always be part of the entity that used this double star for its unfathomable purposes. The direction, though not the nature, of his destiny was clear before him, and there was no need to trace the devious path by which he had come. With the instincts of three million years, he now perceived that there were more ways than one behind the back of space. The ancient mechanisms of the Star Gate had served him well, but he would not need them again.

The glimmering rectangular shape that had once seemed no more than a slab of crystal still floated before him, indifferent as he was to the harmless flames of the inferno beneath. It encapsulated yet unfathomed secrets of space and time, but some at least he now understood and was able to command. How obvious – how *necessary* – was that mathematical ratio of its sides, the quadratic sequence 1:4:9! And how naive to have imagined that the series ended at this point, in only three dimensions!

He focussed his mind upon these geometrical simplicities, and as his thoughts brushed against it, the empty framework filled with the darkness of the interstellar night. The glow of the red sun faded – or, rather, seemed to recede in all directions at once; and there before him was the luminous whirlpool of the Galaxy.

It might have been some beautiful, incredibly detailed model, embedded in a block of plastic. But it was the reality, grasped as a whole with senses now more subtle than vision. If he wished, he could focus his attention upon any one of its hundred billion stars: and he could do much more than that.

Here he was, adrift in this great river of suns, halfway between the banked fires of the galactic core and the lonely, scattered sentinel stars of the rim. And *here* he wished to be, on the far side of this chasm in the sky, this serpentine band of darkness, empty of all stars. He knew that this formless chaos, visible only by the glow that limned its edges from fire-mists far beyond, was the still unused stuff of creation, the raw material of evolutions yet to be. Here, Time had not begun; not until the suns that now burned were long since dead, would light and life reshape this void.

Unwittingly, he had crossed it once: now he must cross it again – this time, under his own volition. The thought filled him with a sudden, freezing terror, so that for a moment he was wholly disorientated, and his new vision of the universe trembled and threatened to shatter into a thousand fragments.

It was not fear of the galactic gulfs that chilled his soul, but a more profound disquiet, stemming from the unborn future. For he had left behind the time-scales of his human origin; now, as he contemplated that band of starless night, he knew his first intimations of the Eternity that yawned before him.

Then he remembered that he would never be alone, and his panic slowly ebbed. The crystal-clear perception of the universe was restored to him – not, he knew, wholly by his own efforts. When he needed guidance in his first faltering steps, it would be there.

Confident once more, like a high-diver who had regained his nerve, he launched himself across the light-years. The Galaxy burst forth from the mental frame in which he had enclosed it; stars and nebulae poured past him in an illusion of infinite speed. Phantom suns exploded and fell behind as he slipped like a shadow through their cores; the cold, dark waste of cosmic dust which he had once feared seemed no more than the beat of a raven's wing across the face of the sun.

The stars were thinning out; the glare of the Milky Way was dimming into a pale ghost of the glory he had known – and, when he was ready, would know again.

He was back, precisely where he wished to be, in the space that men called real.

CHAPTER 47

STAR-CHILD

There before him, a glittering toy no Star-Child could resist, floated the planet Earth with all its peoples.

He had returned in time. Down there on that crowded globe, the alarms would be flashing across the radar screens, the great tracking telescopes would be searching the skies – and history as men knew it would be drawing to a close.

A thousand miles below, he became aware that a slumbering cargo of death had awoken, and was stirring sluggishly in its orbit. The feeble energies it contained were no possible menace to him; but he preferred a cleaner sky. He put forth his will, and the circling megatons flowered in a silent detonation that brought a brief, false dawn to half the sleeping globe.

Then he waited, marshalling his thoughts and brooding over his still untested powers. For though he was master of the world, he was not quite sure what to do next.

But he would think of something.

THE END

The Demolished Man

ALFRED BESTER

CHAPTER 1

EXPLOSION! *Concussion! The vault doors burst open. And deep inside, the money is racked ready for pillage, rapine, loot. Who's that? Who's inside the vault? Oh God! The Man With No Face! Looking. Looming. Silent. Horrible. Run ... Run ...*

Run, or I'll miss the Paris Pneumatique and that exquisite girl with her flower face and figure of passion. There's time if I run. But that isn't the Guard before the gate. Oh Christ! The Man With No Face. Looking. Looking. Silent. Don't scream. Stop screaming ...

But I'm not screaming. I'm singing on a stage of sparkling marble while the music soars and the lights burn. But there's no one out there in the amphitheatre. A great shadowed pit ... empty except for one spectator. Silent. Staring. Looming. The Man With No Face.

　　　　　　　　　•　•　•

And this time his scream had sound.

Ben Reich awoke.

He lay quietly in the hydropathic bed while his heart shuddered and his eyes focused at random on objects in the room, simulating a calm he could not feel. The walls of green jade, the nightlight in the porcelain mandarin whose head nodded interminably if you touched him, the multi-clock that radiated the time of three planets and six satellites, the bed itself, a crystal pool flowing with carbonated glycerine at ninety-nine point nine Fahrenheit.

The door opened softly and Jonas appeared in the gloom, a shadow in puce sleeping suit, a shade with the face of a horse and the bearing of an undertaker.

'Again?' Reich asked.

'Yes, Mr Reich.'

'Loud?'

'Very loud, sir. And terrified.'

'God damn your jackass ears,' Reich growled. 'I'm never afraid.'

'No, sir.'

'Get out.'

'Yes, sir. Good night, sir.' Jonas stepped back and closed the door.

Reich shouted: 'Jonas!'

The valet reappeared.

'Sorry, Jonas.'

'Quite all right, sir.'

'It isn't all right,' Reich charmed him with a smile. 'I'm treating you like a relative. I don't pay enough for the privilege.'

'Oh no, sir.'

'Next time I yell at you, yell right back. Why should I have all the fun?'

'Oh, Mr Reich . . .'

'Do that and you get a raise.' That smile again. 'That's all, Jonas. Thank you.'

'Thank you, sir.' The valet withdrew.

Reich arose from the bed and towelled himself before the cheval mirror, practising the smile. 'Make your enemies by choice,' he muttered, 'not by accident.' He stared at the reflection; the heavy shoulders, narrow flanks, long corded legs . . . the sleek head with wide eyes, chiselled nose, small sensitive mouth scarred by implacability.

'Why?' he asked. 'I wouldn't change looks with the devil. I wouldn't change places with God. Why the screaming?'

He put on a gown and glanced at the clock, unaware that he was noting the time panorama of the solar system with an unconscious skill that would have baffled his ancestors. The dials read:

AD 2301

VENUS	EARTH	MARS
Mean Solar Day 22	February 15	Duodecember 35
Noon + 09	0205 Greenwich	2220 Central Syrtis

MOON 10	GANYMEDE	CALLISTO	TITAN	TRITON
2D3H 1D1H	6D8H (eclipsed)	13D12H	15D3H (transit)	4D9H

Night, noon, summer, winter . . . without bothering to think, Reich could have rattled off the time and season for any meridian on any body in the solar system. Here in New York it was a bitter winter morning after a bitter night of dreaming. He would give himself a few minutes of analysis with the Esper psychiatrist he retained. The screaming had to stop.

'E for Esper,' he muttered. 'Esper for Extra Sensory Perception . . . For Telepaths, Mind Readers, Brain Peepers. You'd think a mind-reading doctor could stop the screaming. You'd think an Esper M.D. would earn his money and peep inside your head and stop the screaming. Those damned mind-readers are supposed to be the greatest advance since *homo sapiens* evolved. E for Evolution Bastards! E for Exploitation!'

He yanked open the door, shaking with fury.

He stepped down the corridor, clacking his sandals sharply on the silver floor, ke-tak-ke-tak-ke-tak-ke-tak, indifferent to the slumber of his house staff, unaware that this early morning skeletal clack awakened twelve hearts to hatred and dread. He thrust open the door of his analyst's suite, entered and at once lay down on the couch.

Carson Breen, Esper Medical Doctor 2, was already awake and ready for him. As Reich's staff analyst he slept the 'nurse's sleep' in which he remained *en rapport* with his patient and could only be awakened by his needs. That one scream had been enough for Breen. Now he was seated alongside the couch, elegant in embroidered gown (his job paid twenty thousand credits a year) and sharply alert (his employer was generous but demanding).

'Go ahead, Mr Reich.'

'The Man With No Face again,' Reich growled.

'Nightmares?'

'You lousy blood-sucker, peep me and find out. No. Sorry. Childish of me. Yes, nightmares again. I was trying to rob a bank. Then I was trying to catch a train. Then someone was singing. Me, I think. I'm trying to give you the pictures best I can. I don't think I'm leaving anything out...' There was a long pause. Finally Reich blurted: 'Well? You keep anything?'

'You persist that you cannot identify The Man With No Face, Mr Reich?'

'How can I? I never see it. All I know is——'

'I think you can. You simply will not.'

'Listen,' Reich burst out in guilty rage. 'I pay you twenty thousand. If the best you can do is make idiotic statements...'

'Do you mean that, Mr Reich, or is it simply a part of the general anxiety syndrome?'

'There is no anxiety,' Reich shouted. 'I'm not afraid. I'm never——' He stopped himself, realizing the inutility of ranting while the deft mind of the peeper searched underneath his overturning words. 'You're wrong anyway,' he said sulkily. 'I don't know who it is. It's a Man With No Face. That's all.'

'You've been rejecting the essential points, Mr Reich. You must be made to see them. We'll try a little free association. Without words, please. Just think. Robbery...'

'*Jewels – watches – diamonds – stocks – bonds – sovereigns – counterfeiting – cash – bullion – dort...*'

'What was that last again?'

'*Slip of the mind; Meant to think bort ... uncut, gem stones.*'

'It was not a slip. It was a significant correction; or, rather, alteration. Let's continue. Pneumatique...'

'*Long – car – compartments – air – conditioned* ... That doesn't make sense.'

'It does, Mr Reich. A phallic pun. Read "Heir" for "air" and you'll see it. Continue, please.'

'You peepers are too damned smart. Let's see. Pneumatique . . . *train – underground – compressed – air – ultra sonic speed – "We Transport You Into Transports,' slogan of the – What the devil is the name of that company? Can't remember. Where'd the notion come from anyway?'*

'From the pre-conscious, Mr Reich. One more trial and you'll begin to understand. Amphitheatre . . .'

'*Seats – pits – balcony – boxes – stalls – horse stalls – Martian horses – Martian Pampas . . .*'

'And there you have it, Mr Reich. Mars. In the past six months, you've had ninety-seven nightmares about The Man With No Face. He's been your constant enemy, frustrator, and inspirer of terror in dreams that contain three common denominators . . . Finance, Transportation, and Mars. Over and over again . . . The Man With No Face, and Finance, Transporation, and Mars.'

'That doesn't mean anything to me.'

'It must mean something, Mr Reich. You must be able to identify this terrifying figure. Why else would you attempt to escape by rejecting his face?'

'I'm not rejecting anything.'

'I offer as further clues the altered word "dort" and the forgotten name of the company that coined the slogan "We Transport You Into——"'

'I tell you I don't know who it is.' Reich arose abruptly from the couch. 'Your clues don't help. I can't make any identification.'

'The Man With No Face does not fill you with fear because he's faceless. You know who he is. You hate him and fear him, but you know who he is.'

'You're the peeper. You tell me.'

'There's a limit to my ability, Mr Reich. I can read your mind no deeper without help.'

'What do you mean, help? You're the best E.M.D. I could hire. If——'

'You're neither thinking nor meaning that, Mr Reich. You deliberately hired a 2nd Class Esper in order to protect yourself in such an emergency. Now you're paying the price of your caution. If you want the screaming to stop, you'll have to consult one of the 1st Class men . . . Say, Augustus Tate or Gart or Samuel @kins . . .'

'I'll think about it,' Reich muttered and turned to go. As he opened the door, Breen called: 'By the way . . . "We Transport You Into Transports" is the slogan of the D'Courtney Cartel. How does that tie with the alteration of "bort" to "dort"? Think it over.'

'*The Man With No Face!*'

Without staggering, Reich slammed the door across the path from his mind to Breen and then lurched down the corridor towards his own suite. A wave of savage hatred burst over him. '*He's right. It's D'Courtney who's giving me the screams. Not because I'm afraid of him. I'm afraid of myself. Known all along. Known it deep down inside. Knowing that once I faced it I'd have to kill that D'Courtney bastard. It's no face because it's the face of murder.*'

. . .

Fully dressed and in his wrong mind, Reich stormed out of his apartment and descended to the street where a Monarch Jumper picked him up and carried him in one graceful hop to the giant tower that housed the hundreds of floors and thousands of employees of Monarch's New York Office. Monarch Tower was the central nervous system of an incredibly vast corporation, a pyramid of transportation, communication, heavy industry, manufacture, sales distribution, research, exploration, importation. Monarch Utilities & Resources, Inc. bought and sold, traded and gave, made and destroyed. Its pattern of subsidiaries and holding companies was so complex that it demanded the fulltime services of a 2nd Class Esper Accountant to trace the labyrinthine flow of its finances.

Reich entered his office, followed by his chief (Esper 3) secretary and her staff, bearing the litter of the morning's work.

'Dump it and jet,' he growled.

They deposited the papers and recording crystals on his desk and departed hastily but without rancour. They were accustomed to his rages. Reich seated himself behind his desk, trembling with a fury that was already goring D'Courtney. Finally he muttered: 'I'll give the bastard one more chance.'

He unlocked his desk, opened the drawer-safe and withdrew the Executive's Code Book, restricted to the executive heads of the firms listed quadruple A-1-* by Lloyds. He found most of the material he required in the middle pages of the book:

QQBA	PARTNERSHIP
RRCB	BOTH OUR
SSDC	BOTH YOUR
TTED	MERGER
UUFE	INTERESTS
VVGF	INFORMATION
WWHG	ACCEPT OFFER
XXIH	GENERALLY KNOWN
YYJI	SUGGEST
ZZKJ	CONFIDENTIAL

AALK   EQUAL
BBML   CONTRACT

Marking his place in the code book, Reich flipped the v-phone on and said to the image of the inter-office operator: 'Get me Code.'

The screen dazzled and cut to a smoky room cluttered with books and coils of tape. A bleached man in a faded shirt glanced at the screen, then leaped to attention.

'Yes, Mr Reich?'

'Morning, Hassop. You look like you need a vacation.' *Make your enemies by choice.* 'Take a week at Spaceland. Monarch expense.'

'Thank you, Mr Reich. Thank you very much.'

'This one's confidential. To Craye D'Courtney. Send——' Reich consulted the Code Book. 'Send YYJI TTED RRCB UUFE AALK QQBA. Get the answer to me like rockets. Right?'

'Right, Mr Reich. I'll jet.'

Reich cut off the phone. He jabbed his hand once into the pile of papers and crystals on his desk, picked up a crystal and dropped it into the play-back. His chief secretary's voice said: 'Monarch Gross off two point one one three four per cent. D'Courtney Gross up two point one one three oh per cent...'

'God damn him!' Reich growled. 'Out of my pocket into his.' He snapped off the play-back and arose in an agony of impatience. It would take hours for the reply to come. His whole life hung on D'Courtney's reply. He left his office and began to roam through the floors and departments of Monarch Tower, pretending the remorseless personal supervision he usually exercised. His Esper secretary unobtrusively accompanied him like a trained dog.

'*Trained bitch!*' Reich thought. Then aloud: 'I'm sorry. Did you peep that?'

'Quite all right, Mr Reich. I understand.'

'Do you? I don't. Damn D'Courtney!'

In Personnel they were testing, checking, and screening the usual mass of job applicants ... clerks, craftsmen, specialists, middle bracket executives, top echelon experts. All of the preliminary elimination was done with standardized tests and interviews, and never to the satisfaction of Monarch's Esper Personnel Chief who was stalking through the floor in an icy rage when Reich entered. The fact that Reich's secretary had sent an advance telepathic announcement of the visit made no difference to him.

'I have allotted ten minutes per applicant for my final screening interview,' the Chief was snapping to an assistant. 'Six per hour, forty-eight per day. Unless my percentage of final rejections drops below thirty-five, I am wasting my time; which means you are wasting Monarch's time. I am not employed by Monarch to screen out the obviously unsuitable. That is your work. See to it.' He turned to Reich and nodded pedantically. 'Good morning, Mr Reich.'

'Morning. Trouble?'

'Nothing that cannot be handled once this staff understands that Extra Sensory Perception is not a miracle but a skill subject to wage-hour limitations. And what is your decision on Blonn, Mr Reich?'

Secretary: *'He hasn't read your memo yet.'*

'May I point out, young woman, that unless I am used with maximum efficiency I am wasted. The Blonn memo has been on Mr Reich's desk for three days.'

'Who the hell is Blonn?' Reich asked.

'First, the background, Mr Reich: There are approximately one hundred thousand (100,000) 3rd Class Espers in the Esper Guild. An Esper 3 can peep the conscious level of a mind – can discover what a subject is thinking at the moment of thought. A 3rd is the lowest class of telepath. Most of Monarch's security positions are held by 3rds. We employ over five hundred ...'

'He knows all this. Everybody does. Get to the point, longwind!'

'Permit me, if I may, to arrive at the point in my own way. Next, there are approximately ten thousand 2nd Class Espers in the Guild,' the Personnel Chief continued frostily. 'They are experts like myself who can penetrate beneath the conscious level of the mind to the preconscious. Most 2nds are in the professional class ... physicians, lawyers, engineers, educators, economists, architects, and so on.'

'And you all cost a fortune,' Reich growled.

'Why not? We have unique service to sell. Monarch appreciates the fact. Monarch employs over one hundred 2nds at present.'

'Will you get to the point?'

'Finally there are less than a thousand 1st Class Espers in the Guild. The 1sts are capable of deep peeping, through the conscious and preconscious layers down to the unconscious ... the lowest levels of the mind. Primordial basic desires and so forth. These, of course, hold premium positions. Education, specialized medical service ... analysts like Tate, Gart, @kins, Moselle ... criminologists like Lincoln Powell of the Psychotic Division ... Political Analysts, State Negotiators, Special Cabinet Advisers, and so on. Thus far Monarch Utilities has never had occasion to hire a 1st.'

'And?' Reich muttered.

'The occasion has arisen, Mr Reich, and I believe Blonn may be available. Briefly ...'

'It says here.'

'Briefly, Mr Reich, Monarch is hiring so many Espers that I have suggested we set up a special Esper Personnel Department, headed by a 1st like Blonn, to devote itself exclusively to interviewing telepaths.'

'He's wondering why you can't handle it.'

'I have given you the background to explain why I cannot handle the job, Mr Reich. I am a 2nd Class Esper. I can telepath normal applicants rapidly and efficiently, but I cannot handle other Espers with the same speed and economy. All Espers are accustomed to using mind-blocks of varying effectiveness depending on their rating. It would take me one hour per 3rd for an efficient screening interview. It would take me three hours per 2nd. I could not possibly peep through the mind block of a 1st. We must hire a 1st like Blonn for this work. The cost will be enormous, of course, but the necessity is urgent.'

'What's so urgent?' Reich said.

'For heaven's sake! Don't give him that picture! That isn't diversion. It's waving a red flag. He's sore enough now.'

'I have my job to do, Madam.' To Reich, the Chief said: 'The fact is, sir, we are not hiring the best Espers. The D'Courtney Cartel has been taking the cream of the Espers away from us. Over and over again, through lack of proper facilities, we have been mouse-trapped by D'Courtney into bidding for inferior people while D'Courtney has quietly appropriated the best.'

'Damn you!' Reich shouted. 'Damn D'Courtney. All right. Set it up. And tell this Blonn to start mouse-trapping D'Courtney. You'd better start, too.'

Reich tore out of Personnel and over to Sales-city. The same unpleasant information was waiting for him. Monarch Utilities & Resources was losing the gut-fight with the D'Courtney Cartel. It was losing the fight in every sector-city – Advertising, Engineering, Research, Public Relations. There was no escaping the certainty of defeat. Reich knew his back was to the wall.

He returned to his own office and paced in a fury for five minutes. 'It's no use,' he muttered. 'I know I'll have to kill him. He won't accept merger. Why should he? He's licked me and he knows it. I'll have to kill him and I'll need help. Peeper help.'

He flipped on the v-phone and told the operator: 'Recreation.'

A sparkling lounge appeared on the screen, decorated in chrome and enamel, equipped with game tables and a bar dispenser. It appeared to be and was used as a recreation centre. It was, in fact, headquarters of Monarch's powerful espionage division. The Recreation Director, a bearded scholar named West, looked up from a chess problem, then rose to attention.

'Good morning, Mr Reich.'

Warned by the formal 'Mister', Reich said: 'Good morning, Mr West.

Just a routine check. Paternalism, you know. How's amusement these days?'

'Modulated, Mr Reich. However, I must complain, sir. I think there's entirely too much gambling going on.' West stalled in a fussy voice until two bona fide Monarch clerks innocently finished their drinks and departed. Then he relaxed and slumped into his chair. 'All clear, Ben. Shoot.'

'Has Hassop broken the confidential code yet, Ellery?'

The peeper shook his head.

'Trying?'

West smiled and nodded.

'Where's D'Courtney?'

'En route to Terra, aboard the "Astra".'

'Know his plans? Where he'll be staying?'

'No. Want a check?'

'I don't know. It depends...'

'Depends on what?' West glanced at him curiously. 'I wish the Telepathic Pattern could be transmitted by phone, Ben. I'd like to know what you're thinking at.'

Reich smiled grimly. 'Thank God for the phone. At least we've got that protection from mind readers. What's your attitude on crime, Ellery?'

'Typical.'

'Of anybody?'

'Of the Guild. The Guild doesn't like it, Ben.'

'So what's so hot about the Esper Guild? You know the value of money, success ... Why don't you clever-up? Why do you let the Guild do your thinking?'

'You don't understand. We're born in the Guild. We live with the Guild. We die in the Guild. We have the right to elect Guild officers, and that's all. The Guild runs our professional lives. It trains us, grades us, sets ethical standards and sees that we stick to them. It protects us by protecting the layman, the same as medical associations. We have the equivalent of the Hippocratic Oath. It's called the Esper Pledge. God help any of us if we break it ... as I judge you're suggesting I should.'

'Maybe I am,' Reich said intently. 'Maybe I'm hinting it could be worth your while to break the peeper pledge. Maybe I'm thinking in terms of money ... more than you or any 2nd Class peeper ever sees in a lifetime.'

'Forget it, Ben. Not interested.'

'So you bust your pledge. What happens?'

'We're ostracized.'

'That's all? Is that so awful? With a fortune in your pocket? Smart peepers have broken with the Guild before. They've been ostracized. So what? Clever-up, Ellery.'

West smiled wryly: 'You wouldn't understand, Ben.'

'Make me understand.'

'Those ousted peepers you mention . . . like Jerry Church. They weren't so smart. It's like this . . .' West considered. 'Before surgery really got started, there used to be a handicapped group called deaf-mutes.'

'No-hear, no-talk?'

'That's it. They communicated by a manual sign language. That meant they couldn't communicate with anybody but deaf-mutes. Understand? They had to live in their own community or they couldn't live at all. A man goes crazy if he can't talk to friends.'

'So?'

'Some of them started a racket. They'd tax the more successful deaf-mutes for weekly hand-outs. If the victim refused to pay, they'd ostracize him. The victim always paid. It was a choice of paying or living in solitary until he went mad.'

'You mean you peepers are like deaf-mutes?'

'No, Ben. You normals are the deaf-mutes. If we had to live with you alone, we'd go mad. So leave me alone. If you're nursing something dirty, I don't want to know.'

West cut off the phone in Reich's face. With a roar of rage, Reich snatched up a gold paper-weight and hurled it into the crystal screen. Before the shattered fragments finished flying, he was in the corridor and on his way out of the building.

.   .   .

His peeper secretary knew where he was going. His peeper chauffeur knew where he wanted to go. Reich arrived in his apartment and was met by his peeper house-supervisor who at once announced early luncheon and dialled the meal to Reich's unspoken demands. Feeling slightly less violent, Reich stalked into his study and turned to his safe, a shimmer of light in the corner.

It was simply a honey-comb paper rack turned out of temporal phase with a single cycle beat. Each second when the safe phase and the temporal phase coincided, the rack pulsed with a brilliant glow. The safe could only be opened by the pore-pattern of Reich's left index finger which was irreproducible.

Reich placed the tip of his finger in the centre of the glow. It faded and the honey-comb rack appeared. Holding his finger in place, he reached up and took down a small black notebook and a large red envelope. He removed his index finger and the safe pulsed out of phase again.

Reich flipped through the pages of the notebook . . . ABDUCTION . . .

ANARCHISTS . . . ARSONISTS . . . BRIBERY (PROVEN) . . . BRIBERY (POTENTIAL)
. . . Under (POTENTIAL) he found the names of fifty-seven prominent
people. One of them was Augustus Tate, Esper Medical Doctor 1. He
nodded with satisfaction.

He tore open the red envelope and examined its contents. It contained
five sheets of closely written pages in a handwriting that was centuries
old. It was a message from the founder of Monarch Utilities and the
Reich clan. Four of the pages were lettered: PLAN A, PLAN B, PLAN C, PLAN
D. The fifth was headed INTRODUCTION. Reich read the ancient spidery
cursive slowly:

> To those who come after me: The test of intellect is the refusal to
> belabour the obvious. If you have opened this letter we understand one
> another. I have prepared four general murder plans which may help
> you. I bequeath them to you as part of your Reich inheritance. They
> are outlines. The details must be filled in by yourself as your time, your
> environment, and necessity require.
> Caution: The essence of murder never changes. In every era it remains
> the conflict of the killer against society with the victim as the prize. And
> the ABC of conflict with society remains constant. Be audacious, be
> brave, be confident and you will not fail. Against these assets society
> can have no defence.
>
> > Geoffry Reich

Reich leafed through the plans slowly, filled with admiration for the
first of his line who had had the forethought to prepare for every possible
emergency. The plans were outdated but they kindled imagination; and
ideas began forming and crystallizing to be considered, discarded, and
instantly replaced. One phrase caught his attention:

> If you believe yourself a natural killer, avoid planning too carefully.
> Leave most to your instinct. Intellect may fail you, but the killer
> instinct is invincible.

'The killer instinct,' Reich breathed. 'By God, I've got that.'

The phone chimed once and then the automatic switched on. There
was a quick chatter and tape began to stutter out of the recorder. Reich
strode to the desk and examined it. The message was short and deadly:
CODE TO REICH: REPLY WWHG.

'WWHG. "Offer refused." Refused? REFUSED! I knew it!' Reich shouted.
'All right, D'Courtney. If you won't let it be merger, then I'll make it
murder.'

CHAPTER 2

Augustus Tate, E.M.D. 1, received Cr. 1,000 per hour of analysis ... not a high fee considering that a patient rarely required more than an hour of the doctor's devastating time; but it placed his income at Cr. 8,000 a day or well over Cr. 2 million a year. Few people knew what proportion of that income was paid into the Esper Guild for the Education of other Telepaths and the furthering of the Guild's Eugenic plan to bring Extra Sensory Perception to everyone in the world.

Augustus Tate knew, and the 95% he paid was a sore point with him. Consequently, he belonged to 'The League of Esper Patriots', an extreme right-wing political group within the Guild, dedicated to the preservation of the autocracy and incomes of the upper grade Espers. It was this membership that placed him in Ben Reich's BRIBERY (POTENTIAL) category. Reich marched into Tate's exquisite consultation room, glanced once at Tate's tiny frame – a figure slightly out of proportion but carefully realigned by tailors. Reich sat down and grunted: 'Peep me quick.'

He glared in concentration at Tate while the elegant little peeper examined him with a glittering eye and spoke in quick bursts: 'You're Ben Reich of Monarch. Ten billion credit firm. Think I should know you. I do. You're involved in a death struggle with the D'Courtney Cartel. Right? You're savagely hostile towards D'Courtney, Right? Offered merger this morning. Coded message: YYJI TTED RRCB UUFE AALK QQBA. Offer refused. Right? In desperation you have resolved to——' Tate broke off abruptly.

'Go ahead,' Reich said.

'To murder Craye D'Courtney as the first step in taking over his cartel. You want my help ... Mr Reich, this is ridiculous! If you keep on thinking like this, I'll have to commit you. You know the law.'

'Clever-up, Tate. You're going to help me break the law.'

'No, Mr Reich. I'm not in a position to help you.'

'You say that? A 1st Class Esper? and I'm supposed to believe it? I'm supposed to believe you're incapable of outwitting any man, any group, the whole world?'

Tate smiled. 'Sugar for the fly,' he said. 'A characteristic device of——'

'Peep me,' Reich interrupted. 'It'll save time. Read what's in my mind. Your gift. My resources. An unbeatable combination. My God! It's lucky for the world I'm willing to stop at one murder. Together we could rape the universe.'

'No,' Tate said with decision. 'This won't do. I'll have to commit you, Mr Reich.'

'Wait. Want to find out what I'm offering you? Read me deeper. How much am I willing to pay? What's my top limit?'

Tate closed his eyes. His mannikin face tightened painfully. Then his eyes opened his surprise. 'You can't be serious,' he exclaimed.

'I am,' Reich grunted. 'And what's more, you know it's an offer in good faith, don't you?'

Tate nodded slowly.

'And you're aware that Monarch plus D'Courtney can make the offer good.'

'I almost believe you.'

'You can believe me. I've been financing your League of Esper Patriots for five years. If you've peeped me deep enough you know why. I hate the damned Esper Guild as much as you do. Guild ethics are bad for business ... lousy for making money. Your League is the organization that can break the Esper Guild some day ...'

'I've got all that,' Tate said sharply.

'With Monarch and D'Courtney in my pocket I can do better than help your faction break the Guild. I can make President of a new Esper Guild for life. That's an unconditional guarantee. You can't do it alone, but you can do it with me.'

Tate closed his eyes and murmured: 'There hasn't been a successful premeditated murder in seventy-nine years. Espers make it impossible to conceal intent before murder. Or, if Espers have been evaded before the murder, they make it impossible to conceal the guilt afterwards.'

'Esper evidence isn't admitted in court.'

'True, but once an Esper discovers guilt he can always uncover objective evidence to support his peeping. Lincoln Powell, the Prefect of the Police Psychotic Division, is deadly.' Tate opened his eyes. 'D'you want to forget this conversation?'

'No,' Reich growled. 'Look it over with me first. Why have murders failed? Because mind-readers patrol the world. What can stop a mind-reader? Another one. But no killer ever had the sense to hire a good peeper to run interference for him; or if he had the sense, he couldn't make the deal. I've made the deal.'

'Have you?'

'I'm going to fight a war,' Reich continued. 'I'm going to fight one sharp skirmish with society. Let's look at it as a problem in strategy and tactics. My problem's simply the problem of any army. Audacity, bravery, and confidence aren't enough. An army needs Intelligence. A war is won with Intelligence. I need you for my G-2.'

'Agreed.'

'I'll do the fighting. You'll provide the Intelligence. I'll have to know where D'Courtney will be, where I can strike, when I can strike. I'll take care of the killing myself, but you'll have to tell me when and where the opportunity will be.'

'Understood.'

'I'll have to invade first ... cut through the defensive network surrounding D'Courtney. That means reconnaissance from you. You'll have to check the normals, spot the peepers, warn me and block their mind-reading if I can't avoid them. I'll have to retreat after the killing through another network of normals and peepers. You'll have to help me fight a rearguard action. You'll have to remain on the scene after the murder. You'll find out whom the police suspect and why. If I know suspicion is directed against myself, I can divert it. If I know it's directed against someone else, I can clinch it. I can fight this war and win this war with your Intelligence. Is that the truth? Peep me.'

After a long pause, Tate said: 'It's the truth. We can do it.'

'Will you do it?'

Tate hesitated, then nodded with finality. 'Yes, I'll do it.'

Reich took a deep breath. 'Right. Now here's the course I'm plotting. I think I can set up the killing with an old game called "Sardine". It'll give me the opportunity to get at D'Courtney, and I've figured out a trick to kill him; I know how to fire an antique explosive gun without bullets.'

'Wait,' Tate interrupted sharply. 'How are you going to keep all this intent concealed from stray peepers? I can only screen you when I'm with you. I won't be with you all the time.'

'I can work up a temporary mind-block. There's a song-writer down on Melody Lane I can swindle into helping me.'

'It may work,' Tate said after a moment's peeping. 'But one thing occurs to me. Suppose D'Courtney is protected? Do you expect to shoot it out with his bodyguards?'

'No. I'm hoping it won't be necessary. A physiologist named Jordan has just developed visual knock-out drops for Monarch. We intended using it for strike riots. I'll use it on D'Courtney's guards.'

'I see.'

'You'll be working with me all along ... doing reconnaissance and intelligence, but I need one piece of information first. When D'Courtney comes to town he's usually the guest of Maria Beaumont.'

'The Gilt Corpse?'

'The same. I want you to find out if D'Courtney intends staying with her this trip, Everything depends on that.'

'Easy enough. I can locate D'Courtney's destination and plans for you. There's to be a social gathering tonight at Lincoln Powell's house.

D'Courtney's physician will probably be there. He's on Terra for a week's visit. I'll start the reconnaissance through him.'

'And you're not afraid of Powell?'

Tate smiled contemptuously. 'If I were, Mr Reich, would I trust myself in this bargain with you? Make no mistake, I'm no Jerry Church.'

'Church!'

'Yes. Don't act surprised. Church, the 2nd. He was kicked out of the Guild ten years ago for that little junket of his with you.'

'Damn you. Got that from my mind, eh?'

'Your mind and history.'

'Well, it won't repeat itself this time. You're tougher and smarter than Church. Need anything special for Powell's party? Women? Clothes? Jewels? Money? Just call on Monarch.'

'Nothing, but thank you very much.'

'Criminal but generous, that's me.' Reich smiled as he arose to go. He did not offer to shake hands.

'Mr Reich!' Tate calls suddenly.

Reich turned at the door.

'The screaming will continue. The Man With No Face is not a symbol of murder.'

'*What? Oh Christ! The nightmares? Still? You God damned peeper. How did you get that? How did you——*'

'Don't be a fool. D'you think you can play games with a 1st?'

'*Who's playing, you bastard? What about the nightmares?*'

'No, Mr Reich, I won't tell you. I doubt if anyone but a 1st can tell you, and naturally you would not dare to consult another after this conference.'

'*For God's sake, man! Are you going to help me?*'

'No, Mr Reich.' Tate smiled malevolently. 'That's my little weapon. It keeps us on a parity basis. Balance of power, you understand. Mutual dependence ensures mutual faith. Criminal but peeper ... that's me.'

. . .

Like all upper-grade Espers, Lincoln Powell, PH.D.1, lived in a private house. It was not a question of conspicuous consumption, but rather a problem of privacy. Although thought-transmission was too faint to penetrate masonry, the average plastic apartment unit was too flimsy to block this transmission. Life in any such multiple dwelling was life in an inferno of naked emotion for an Esper.

Powell, the Police Prefect, could afford a small limestone maisonette on Hudson Ramp overlooking the North River. There were only four rooms; upstairs a bedroom and study, downstairs a living-room and kitchen. There was no servant in the house. Like most upper-grade Espers, Powell required large quantities of solitude. He preferred to do for himself. He was in the kitchen, checking over the refreshment-dials in preparation for the party, whistling a plaintive, crooked tune.

He was a slender man in his late thirties, tall, loose, slow-moving. His wide mouth seemed perpetually on the verge of laughter, but at the moment he wore an expression of sad disappointment. He was lecturing himself on the follies and stupidities of his worst vice.

The essence of the Esper is his responsiveness. His personality always takes colour from his surroundings. The trouble with Powell was an enlarged sense of humour, and his response was invariably exaggerated. He had attacks of what he called 'Dishonest Abe' moods. Someone would ask Lincoln Powell an innocent question, and Dishonest Abe would answer. His fervent imagination would cook up the wildest tall-story and he would deliver it with straight-faced sincerity. He could not suppress the liar in him.

Only this afternoon, Police Commissioner Crabbe had inquired about a routine blackmail case, and simply because he'd mispronounced a name, Powell had been inspired to fabricate a dramatic account involving a make-believe crime, a daring midnight raid, and the heroism of an imaginary Lieutenant Kopenick. Now the Commissioner wanted to award Lieutenant Kopenick a medal.

'Dishonest Abe,' Powell muttered bitterly. 'You give me a stiff pain.'

The house-bell chimed. Powell glanced at his watch in surprise (it was too early for company) and then directed *Open* in C-sharp at the TP lock-sensor. It responded to the thought pattern, as a tuning fork will vibrate to the right note, and the front door slid open.

Instantly came a familiar sensory impact: Snow/mint/tulips/taffeta.

'*Mary Noyes. Come to help the bachelor prepare for the party?* Blessings!'

'*Hoped you'd need me, Linc.*'

'*Every host needs a hostess. Mary, what am I going to do for Canapés*S.O.S.?'

'*Just invented a new recipe. I'll make it for you. Roast chutney &.*'

'*&?*'

'*That's telling, my love.*'

She came into the kitchen, a short girl physically, but tall and swaying in thought; a dark girl exteriorly, but frost white in pattern. Almost a nun in white, despite the swarthy texture of externals; but the mind is the reality. You are what you think.

'*I wish I could re-think, darling. Have my psyche re-ground.*'

'*Change your (I kiss you as you are) self, Mary?*'

'*If I only (You never really do, Linc) could. I'm so tired of tasting you tasting mint every time we meet.*'

'*Next time I'll add brandy and ice. Shake well. Voila! Stinger-Mary.*'

'*Do that. Also $\mathcal{SNOW}$.*'

'*Why strike out the snow? I love snow.*'

'*But I love you.*'

'And I love you, Mary.'

'*Thanks, Linc.*' But he said it. He always said it. He never thought it. She turned away quickly. The tears within her scalded him.

'*Again, Mary?*'

'*Not again. Always. Always.*' And the deeper levels of her mind cried: '*I love you, Lincoln. I love you. Image of my father: Symbol of security: Of warmth: Of protecting passion: Do not reject me always ... always ... for ever ...*'

'Listen to me, Mary ...'

'*Don't talk, please, Linc. Not in words. I couldn't bear it if words came between us.*'

'*You're my friend, Mary. Always. For every disappointment. For every elation.*'

'*But not for love.*'

'*No. dear heart. Don't let it hurt you so. Not for love.*'

'*I have enough love, God pity me, for both of us.*'

'*One, God pity us, is not enough for both, Mary.*'

'*You must marry an Esper before you are forty, Linc. The Guild insists on that. You know it.*'

'*I know it.*'

'*Then left friendship answer. Marry me, Lincoln. Give me a year, that's all. One little year to love you. I'll let you go. I won't cling. I won't make you hate me. Darling, it's so little to ask ... so little to give ...*'

The door-bell chimed. Powell looked at Mary helplessly. 'Guests,' he murmured and directed *Open* in C-sharp at the TP lock-sensor. At the same instant she directed *Close* a fifth above. The harmonies meshed and the door remained shut.

'*Answer me first, Lincoln.*'

'*I can't give the answer you want, Mary.*'

The door-hell chimed again.

He took her shoulders firmly, held her close and looked deep into her eyes. '*You're a 2nd. Read me as deeply as you can. What's in my mind? What's in my heart? What's my answer?*'

He removed all blocks. The thundering plunging depths of his mind cascaded over her in a warm, frightening torrent ... terrifying, yet magnetic and desirable; but ... 'Snow. Mint. Tulips Taffeta,' she said wearily. '*Go meet your guests, Mr Powell, I'll make your canapés. It's all I'm good for.*'

He kissed her once, then turned towards the living-room and opened the front door. Instantly, a fountain of brilliance sparkled into the house, followed by the guests. The Esper party began.

Frankly   Canapés?   Why
  Ellery,   Thanks   delicious.   yes,
    I   Mary, they're   Tate,
      don't   I'm
      think   treating
We   you'll Canapés?   D'Courtney.
 brought   be   I
 Galen   working   expect
  along   for   him
   to   Monarch   in
help him celebrate.   much   town
      He's   longer.   very
     just   The   shortly.
    taken his Guild Exam.
   If   and
 you're   is   been
interested   just   classed
    Powell, we're ready   2nd.
     to
     run rule
     you   Monarch's
     for   espionage
    Guild   Canapés?   unethical.
  President.

       Canapés?
       Why yes.
       Thank
    Canapés?   You,
         Mary...

'@kins! Chervil! Tate! Have a heart! Will you people take a look at the pattern (?) we've been weaving...'

The TP chatter stopped. The guests considered for a moment, then burst into laughter.

'This reminds me of my days in the kindergarten. A little mercy for your host, please, I'll jump my tracks, if we keep on weaving this mish-mash. Let's have some order. I don't even ask for beauty.'

'Just name the pattern, Linc.'

'What'll you have?'

'Basket-weave? Math curves? Music? Architectural design?'
'Anything. Anything. Just so long as you don't make my brains itch.'

Sorry, Lincoln.	We weren't party-minded	Enough
Tate	thought	Esper
but	Alan	Men
I'm	Seaver	remaining
Not that a Pres	was ever elected still	unmarried
at	coming	can
liberty	but	ruin
To be generous,	I feel Al's a man to loa	the
reveal	don't	Guild's
anything	TP	entire
about	him	eugenic
D'Courtney is	arriving according to	plan
	yet	

. . .

There was another burst of laughter when Mary Noyes was left hanging with that unreticulated 'yet'. The door-bell chimed again, and a Solar Equity Advocate 2 entered with his girl. She was a demure little thing, surprisingly attractive outwardly, and new to the company. Her TP pattern was naïve and not deeply responsive. Obviously a 3rd.

'Greetings. Greetings. Abject apologies for the delay. Orange blossoms & wedding rings are the excuse. I proposed on the way over.'

'And I'm afraid I accepted,' the girl said, smiling.

'Don't talk,' the lawyer shot at her. *'This isn't a 3rd Class brawl. I told you not to use words.'*

'I forgot,' she blurted again, and then heated the room with her fright and shame. Powell stepped forward and took the girl's trembling hand.

'Ignore him, he's a 2nd-come-lately snob. I'm Lincoln Powell, your host. I Sherlock for the cops. If your fiancé beats you, I'll help him regret it. Come and meet your fellow freaks...' He conducted her around the room. *'This is Gus Tate, a quack-one. Next to him, Sam & Sally @kins. Sam's another of the same. She's a baby-sitter-two. They're just in from Venus. Here on a visit...'*

'H-How – I mean, how do you do?'

'That fat man sitting on the floor is Wally Chervil, architect-two. The blonde sitting in his (lap)^2 is June, his wife. June's an editor-two. That's their son, Galen, talking to Ellergy West. Gally's a tech-undergrad-three...'

Young Galen Chervil indignantly started to point out that he'd just been classed 2nd and hadn't needed to use words in over a year. Powell cut him off and below the girl's perceptive threshold explained the reason for the deliberate mistake.

'Oh,' said Galen. 'Yep, brother and sister 3rds, that's us. And am I glad you're here. These deep peepers were beginning to scare me.'

'Oh, I don't know. I was scared at first, but I'm not any more.'

'*And this is your hostess, Mary Noyes.*'

'*Hello. Canapés?*'

'*Thank you. They look delicious, Mrs Powell.*'

'*Now how about a game?*' Powell interposed quickly. '*Rebus, anyone?*'

Outside, huddled in the shadow of the limestone arch, Jerry Church pressed against the garden door of Powell's house, listening with all his soul. He was cold, silent, immobile, and starved. He was resentful, hating, contemptuous, and starved. He was an Esper ♂, and starved. The bend sinister of ostracism was the source of his hunger.

Through the thin maple panel filtered the multiple TP *pattern of the party;* a weaving, ever-ghanging, exhilarating design. And Church, Esper♂, living on a sub-marginal diet of words for the past ten years, was starved for his own people – for the Esper world he had lost.

'*The reason I mentioned D'Courtney is that I've just come across a case that might be similar.*'

That was Augustus Tate, sucking up to @kins.

'*Oh really? Very interesting. I'd like to compare notes. Matter of fact, I made the trip to Terra because D'Courtney is coming here. Too bad D'Courtney won't – well, be available.*' @kins was obviously being discreet and it smelled as though Tate was after something. Maybe not, Church speculated, but there was some elegant block and counter-blocking going on, like duellists fencing with complicated electrical circuits.

'*Look here, peeper. I think you've been pretty snotty to that poor girl.*'

'Listen to him shoot off his mind,' Church muttered. 'Powell, that holy louse who had me kicked out, preaching down his big nose at the lawyer.'

'*Poor girl? You mean dumb girl, Powell. My God! How gauche can you get?*'

'*She's only a 3rd. Be fair.*'

'*She gives me a pain.*'

'*Do you think it's decent . . . marrying a girl when you feel that way about her?*'

'*Don't be a romantic ass, Powell. We've got to marry peepers. I might as well settle for a pretty face.*'

The Rebus game was going on in the living-room. The Noyes girl was busy building a camouflaged image with an old poem:

The   *vast,*

sea   *and*

is   *Glimmering*

calm   *stand,*

to-night,   *out*   *England*

The   *in*   *the*   *of*

tide   *tranquil*   *bay*   *cliffs*

is   *Come to*   *the window*   *the*

full   *sweet is*   *the night*

the   *air.*   *Only*   *gone;*

             from   *the*   *is*

moon   *long*   *line*   *and*

                        of   *spray*   *Gleams*

lies   *light*

fair

Upon the straights; – on the French coast the

What the devil was that? An eye in a glass? Eh? Oh. Not a glass. A stein. Eye in a stein. Einstein. Easy.

'*What d'you think of Powell for the job, Ellery?*' That was Chervil with his phoney smile and his big fat pontifical belly.

'*For Guild President?*'

'*Yes.*'

'*Damned efficient man. Romantic but efficient. The perfect candidate if only he'd get married.*'

'*That's the romance in him. He's having trouble locating a girl.*'

'*Don't all you deep peepers? Thank God I'm not a 1st.*'

And then a smash of glass crashing in the kitchen and Preacher Powell again, lecturing that little snot, Gus Tate.

'*Never mind the glass, Gus. I had to drop it to cover for you. You're radiating anxiety like a nova.*'

'*The devil I am, Powell.*'

'*The devil you're not. What's all this about Ben Reich?*'

The little man was really on guard. You could feel his mental shell hardening.

'*Ben Reich? What brought him up?*'

'*You did, Gus. It's been moiling in your mind all evening. I couldn't help reading it.*'

'*Not me, Powell. You must be tuning another TP.*'

Image of a horse laughing.

'*Powell, I swear I'm not——*'

'*Are you mixed up with Reich, Gus?*'

'*No.*' But you could feel the blocks bang down into place.

'*Take a hint from an old hand, Gus. Reich can get you into trouble. Be careful. Remember Jerry Church? Reich ruined him. Don't let it happen to you.*'

Tate drifted back to the living-room; Powell remained in the kitchen, calm and slow-moving, sweeping up broken glass. Church lay frozen against the back door, suppressing the seething hatred in his heart. The Chervil boy was showing off for the lawyer's girl, singing a love ballad and paralleling it with a visual parody. College stuff. The wives were arguing violently in sine curves. @kins and West were interlacing cross-conversation in a fascinatingly intricate pattern of sensory images that made Church's starvation keener.

'*Would you like a drink, Jerry?*'

The Garden door opened. Powell stood silhouetted in the light, a bubbling glass in his hand. The stars lit his face softly. The deep hooded eyes were compassionate and understanding. Dazed, Church climbed to his feet and timidly took the proffered drink.

'*Don't report this to the Guild, Jerry. I'll catch hell for breaking the taboo. I'm always breaking rules. Poor Jerry ... We've got to do something for you. Ten years is too long.*'

Suddenly Church hurled the drink in Powell's face, then turned and fled.

CHAPTER 3

At nine Monday morning, Tate's mannikin face appeared on the screen of Reich's v-phone.

'Is this line secure?' he asked sharply.

In answer Reich simply pointed to the Warranty Seal.

'All right,' Tate said. 'I think I've done the job for you, I peeped @kins last night. But before I report, I must warn you. There's a chance of error when you deep peep a 1st. @kins blocked pretty carefully.'

'I understand.'

'Craye D'Courtney arrives from Mars on the "Astra" next Wednesday morning. He will go at once to Maria Beaumont's town house where he will be a secret and hidden guest for exactly one night ... No more.'

'One night,' Reich muttered. 'And then? His plans?'

'I don't know. Apparently D'Courtney is planning some form of drastic action——'

'Against me!' Reich growled.

'Perhaps. According to @kins, D'Courtney is under some kind of violent strain and his adaptation pattern is shattering. The Life Instinct and Death Instinct had defused. He is regressing under the emotional bankruptcy very rapidly...'

'God damn it! My life depends on this,' Reich raged. 'Talk straight.'

'It's quite simple. Every man is a balance of two opposed drives ... The Life Instinct and the Death Instinct. Both drives have the identical purpose ... to win Nirvana. The Life Instinct fights for Nirvana by smashing all opposition. The Death Instinct attempts to win Nirvana by destroying itself. Usually both instincts fuse in the adapted individual. Under strain they defuse. That's what's happening to D'Courtney.'

'Yes, by God! And he's jetting for me!'

'@kins will see D'Courtney Thursday morning in an effort to dissuade him from whatever he contemplates. @kins is afraid of it and determined to stop it. He made a flying trip from Venus to cut D'Courtney off.'

'He won't have to stop it. I'll stop it myself. He won't have to protect me. I'll protect myself. It's self-defence, Tate ... not murder! Self-defence! You've done a good job. This is all I need.'

'You need much more, Reich. Among other things, time. This is Monday. You'll have to be ready by Wednesday.'

'I'll be ready,' Reich growled. 'You'd better be ready too.'

'We can't afford to fail, Reich. If we do – it's Demolition. You realize that?'

'Demolition for both of us. I realize that.' Reich's voice began to crack. 'Yes, Tate, you're in this with me, and I'm in it straight to the finish ... all the way to Demolition.'

. . .

He planned all through Monday, audaciously, bravely, with confidence. He pencilled the outlines as an artist fills a sheet with delicate tracery before the bold inking-in; but he did no final inking. That was to be left for the killer-instinct on Wednesday. He put the plan away and slept Monday night ... and awoke screaming, dreaming again of The Man With No Face.

Tuesday afternoon, Reich left Monarch Tower early and dropped in at the Century Audio-bookstore on Sheridan Place. It specialized mostly in piezo-electric crystal recordings ... tiny jewels mounted in elegant settings. The latest vogue was brooch-operas for M'lady. ('She Shall Have Music Wherever She Goes.') Century also had shelves of obsolete printed books.

'I want something special for a friend I've neglected,' Reich told the salesman.

He was bombarded with merchandise.

'Not special enough,' he complained. 'Why don't you people hire a peeper and save your clients this trouble? How quaint and old-fashioned can you get?' He began sauntering around the shop, tailed by a retinue of anxious clerks.

After he had dissembled sufficiently, and before the worried manager could send out for a peeper salesman, Reich stopped before the book-shelves.

'What's this?' he inquired in surprise.

'Antique books, Mr Reich.' The sales staff began explaining the theory and practice of the archaic visual book while Reich slowly searched for the tattered brown volume that was his goal. He remembered it well. He had glanced through it five years ago and made a note in his little black opportunity book. Old Geoffry Reich wasn't the only Reich who believed in preparedness.

'Interesting. Yes. Fascinating. What's this one?' Reich pulled down the brown volume. ' "Let's Play Party." What's the date on it? Not really. You mean to say they had parties that long ago?'

The staff assured him that the ancients were very modern in many astonishing ways.

'Look at the contents,' Reich chuckled. ' "Honeymoon Bridge" ... "Prussian Whist" ... "Post Office" ... "Sardine". What in the world could that be? Page ninety-six. Let's have a look.'

Reich flipped pages until he came to a bold-face heading: HILARIOUS MIXED PARTY GAMES. 'Look at this,' he laughed, pretending surprise. He pointed to the well-remembered paragraph.

SARDINE

One player is selected to be It. All the lights are extinguished and the It hides anywhere in the house. After a few minutes, the players go to find the It, separately. The first one who finds him does not reveal the fact but hides with him wherever he may be. Successively each player finding the Sardines joins them until all are hidden in one place and the last player, who is the loser, is left to wander alone in the dark.

'I'll take it,' Reich said. 'It's exactly what I need.'

.   .   .

That evening he spent three hours carefully defacing the remains of the volume. With heat, acid, stain, and scissors, he mutilated the game instructions; and every burn, every cut, every slash, was a blow at D'Courtney's writhing body. When his proxy murders were finished, he had reduced every game to incomplete fragments. Only 'Sardine' was left intact.

Reich wrapped the book, addressed it to Graham, the appraiser, and dropped it into the airslot. It went off with a puff and a bang and returned an hour later with Graham's official sealed appraisal. Reich's mutilations had not been detected.

He had the book gift-wrapped with the appraisal enclosed (as was the custom) and slotted it to Maria Beaumont's house. Twenty minutes later came the reply: 'Darling! Darling! Darling! I thot you'd forgoten (evidently Maria had written the note herself) little ol sexy me. How 2 divine. Come to Beaumont House tonite. Were haveing a party. We'll play games from your sweet gift.' There was a portrait of Maria centred in the star of a synthetic ruby enclosed in the message capsule. A nude portrait, naturally.

Reich answered: 'Devastated. Not tonight. One of my millions is missing.'

She answered: 'Wednesday, you clever boy. I'll give you one of mine.'

He replied: 'Delighted to accept. Will bring guest. I kiss all of yours.' And went to bed.

And screamed at The Man With No Face.

. . .

Wednesday morning, Reich visited Monarch's Science-city ('Paternalism, you know.') and spent a stimulating hour with its bright young men. He discussed their work and their glowing futures if they would only have faith in Monarch. He told the ancient dirty joke about the celibate pioneer who made the emergency landing on the hearse in deep space (and the corpse said: 'I'm just one of the tourists!') and the bright young men laughed subserviently, feeling slightly contemptuous of the boss.

This informality enabled Reich to drift into the Restricted Room and pick up one of the visual knock-out capsules. They were cubes of copper, half the size of fulminating caps, but twice as deadly. When they were broken open, they erupted a dazzling blue flare that ionized the Rhodopsin – the visual purple in the retina of the eye – blinding the victim and abolishing his perception of time and space.

Wednesday afternoon, Reich went over to Melody Lane in the heart of the theatrical district and called on Psych-Songs, Inc. It was run by a clever young woman who had written some brilliant jingles for his sales division and some devastating strike-breaking songs for Propaganda back when Monarch needed everything to smash last year's labour fracas. Her name was Duffy Wyg&. To Reich she was the epitome of the modern career girl – the virgin seductress.

'Well, Duffy?' He kissed her casually. She was as shapely as a sales-curve, pretty, but a trifle too young.

'Well, Mr Reich?' She looked at him oddly. 'Some day I'm going to hire one of those Lonely-Heart Peepers to case your kiss. I keep thinking you don't mean business.'

'I don't.'

'Dog.'

'A man has to make up his mind early, Duffy. If he kisses girls he kisses his money good-bye.'

'You kiss me.'

'Only because you're the image of the lady on the credit.'

'Pip,' she said.

'Pop,' he said.

'Bim,' she said.

'Bam,' he said.

'I'd like to kill the bem who invented that fad,' Duffy said darkly. 'All right, handsome. What's your problem?'

'Gambling,' Reich said. 'Ellery West, my Rec director, is complaining about the gambling in Monarch. Says there's too much. Personally I don't care.'

'Keep a man in debt and he's afraid to ask for a raise.'

'You're entirely too smart, young lady.'

'So you want a no-gamble-type song?'

'Something like that. Catchy. Not too obvious. More a delayed action than a straight propaganda tune. I'd like the conditioning to be more or less unconscious.'

Duffy nodded and made quick notes.

'And make it a tune worth hearing. I'll have to listen to God knows how many people singing and whistling and humming it.'

'You louse. All my tunes are worth hearing.'

'Once.'

'That's a thousand extra on your tab.'

Reich laughed. 'Speaking of monotony . . .' he continued smoothly.

'Which we weren't.'

'What's the most persistent tune you ever wrote?'

'Persistent?'

'You know what I mean. Like those advertising jingles you can't get out of your head.'

'Oh, Pepsis, we call 'em.'

'Why?'

'Dunno. They say because the first one was written centuries ago by a character named Pepsi. I don't buy that. I wrote one once . . .' Duffy winced in recollection. 'Hate to think of it even now. Guaranteed to obsess you for a month. It haunted me for a year.'

'Your rocketing.'

'Scout's honour, Mr Reich. It was "Tenser, Said The Tensor." I wrote it for that flop show about the crazy mathematician. They wanted nuisance value and they sure go it. People got to sore they had to withdraw it. Lost a fortune.'

'Let's hear it.'

'I couldn't do that to you.'

'Come on, Duffy. I'm really curious.'

'You'll regret it.'

'I don't believe you.'

'All right, pig,' she said, and pulled the punch panel towards her. 'This pays you back for that no-guts kiss.'

Her fingers and palm slipped gracefully over the panel. A tune of utter monotony filled the room with agonizing, unforgettable banality. It was the quintessence of every melodic cliche Reich had ever heard. No matter what melody you tried to remember, it invariably led down the path of familiarity to 'Tenser, Said The Tensor.' Then Duffy began to sing:

Eight, sir; seven, sir;
Six, sir; five, sir;
Four, sir; three, sir;
Two, sir; one!
Tenser, said the Tensor.
Tenser, said the Tensor.
Tension, apprehension,
And dissension have begun.

'Oh my God!' Reich exclaimed.

'I've got some real gone tricks in that tune,' Duffy said, still playing. 'Notice the beat after "one"? That's a semi-cadence. Then you get another beat after "begun". That turns the end of the song into a semi-cadence, too, so you can't ever end it. The beat keeps you running in circles, like: Tension, apprehension, and dissension have begun. RIFF. Tension, apprehension, and dissension have begun. RIFF. Tension, appre——'

'You little devil!' Reich started to his feet, pounding his palms on his ears. 'I'm accursed. How long is this affliction going to last?'

'Not more than a month.'

'Tension, apprehension, and diss – I'm ruined. Isn't there any way out?'

'Sure,' Duffy said. 'It's easy. Just ruin me.' She pressed herself against him and planted an earnest young kiss. 'Lout,' she murmured. 'Pig. Boob. Dolt. When are you going to drag me through the gutter? Clever-up, dog. Why aren't you as smart as I think you are?'

'I'm smarter,' he said and left.

As Reich had planned, the song established itself firmly in his mind and echoed again and again all the way down to the street. *Tenser, said the Tensor. Tenser, said the Tensor. Tension, apprehension, and dissension have begun.* RIFF. A perfect mind-block for a non-Esper. What peeper could get past that? *Tension, apprehension, and dissension have begun.*

'Much smarter,' murmured Reich, and flagged a Jumper to Jerry Church's pawnshop on the upper west side.

Tension, apprehension, and dissension have begun.

. . .

Despite all rival claims, pawnbroking is still the oldest profession. The business of lending money on portable security is the most ancient of human occupations. It extends from the depths of the past to the uttermost reaches of the future, as unchanging as the pawnbroker's shop itself. You walked into Jerry Church's cellar store, crammed and littered with the debris of time, and you were in a museum of eternity. And even Church himself, wizened, peering, his face blackened and bruised by the internal blows of suffering, embodied the ageless moneylender.

Church shuffled out of the shadows and came face to face with Reich, standing starkly illuminated in a patch of sunlight slanting across the counter. He did not start. He did not acknowledge Reich's identity. Brushing past the man who for ten years had been his mortal enemy, he placed himself behind the counter and said: 'Yes, please?'

'Hello, Jerry.'

Without looking up, Church extended his hand across the counter. Reich attempted to clasp it. It was snatched away.

'No,' Church said with a snarl that was half hysterical laugh. 'Not that, thank you. Just give me what you want to pawn.'

It was the peeper's sour little trap, and he had tumbled into it. No matter.

'I haven't anything to pawn, Jerry.'

'As poor as that? How the mighty have fallen. But we must expect it, eh? We all fall. We all fall.' Church glanced sidelong at him, trying to peep him. Let him try. *Tension, apprehension, and dissension have begun.* Let him get through the crazy tune rattling in his head.

'All of us fall,' Church said. 'All of us.'

'I expect so, Jerry. I haven't yet. I've been lucky.'

'I wasn't lucky,' the peeper leered. 'I met you.'

'Jerry,' Reich said patiently. 'I've never been your bad luck. It was your own luck that ruined you. Not——'

'You God damned bastard,' Church said in a horribly soft voice. 'You God damned eater of slok. May you rot before you die. Get out of here. I want nothing to do with you. Nothing! Understand?'

'Not even my money?' Reich withdrew ten gleaming sovereigns from his pocket and placed them on the counter. It was a subtle touch. Unlike the credit, the sovereign was the coin of the underworld. *Tension, appre-hension, and dissension have begun . . .*

'Least of all your money. I want your heart cut open. I want your blood spilling on the ground. I want the maggots eating the eyes out of your living head . . . But I don't want your money.'

'Then what do you want, Jerry?'

'I told you!' the peeper screamed. 'I told you! You God damned lousy——'

'What do you want, Jerry?' Reich repeated coldly, keeping his eyes on the wizened man. *Tension, apprehension, and dissension have begun.* He could still control Church. It didn't matter that Church had been a 2nd. Control wasn't a question of peeping. It was a question of personality. *Eight, sir; seven, sir; six, sir; five, sir . . .* He always had . . . He always would control Church.

'What do you want?' Church asked sullenly.

Reich snorted. 'You're the peeper. You tell me.'

'I don't know,' Church muttered after a pause. 'I can't read it. There's crazy music mixing everything up . . .'

'Then I'll have to tell you. I want a gun.'

'A what?'

'G-U-N. Gun. Ancient weapon. It propels projectiles by explosion.'

'I haven't anything like that.'

'Yes, you have, Jerry. Keno Quizzard mentioned it to me some time ago. He saw it. Steel and collapsible. Very interesting.'

'What do you want it for?'

'Read me, Jerry, and find out. I haven't anything to hide. It's all quite innocent.'

Church screwed up his face, then quit in disgust. 'Isn't worth the trouble,' he mumbled and shuffled off into the shadows. There was a distant slamming of metal drawers. Church returned with a compact nodule of tarnished steel and placed it on the counter alongside the money. He pressed a stud and the lump of metal sprang open into steel knuckle-rings, revolver and stiletto. It was a Twentieth Century knife-pistol . . . the quintessence of murder.

'What do you want it for?' Church asked again.

'You're hoping it's something that can lead to blackmail, eh?' Reich smiled. 'Sorry. It's a gift.'

'A dangerous gift.' The ostracized peeper gave him that sidelong glance of snarl and laugh. 'Ruination for someone else, eh?'

'Not at all, Jerry. It's a gift for a friend of mine. Dr Augustus Tate.'

'Tate!' Church stared at him.

'Do you know him? He collects old things.'

'I know him. I know him.' Church began to chuckle asthmatically.

'But I'm beginning to know him better. I'm beginning to feel sorry for him.' He stopped laughing and shot a penetrating glance at Reich. 'Of course. This will make a lovely gift for Gus. A perfect gift for Gus. Because it's loaded.'

'Oh? Is it loaded?'

'Oh, yes indeed. It's loaded. Five lovely cartridges.' Church cackled again. 'A gift for Gus.' He touched a cam. A cylinder snapped out of the side of the gun displaying five chambers filled with brass cartridges. He looked from the cartridges to Reich. 'Five serpent's teeth to give to Gus.'

'I told you this was innocent,' Reich said in a hard voice. 'We'll have to pull those teeth.'

Church stared at him in astonishment, then he trotted down the aisle and returned with two small tools. Quickly he wrenched each of the bullets from the cartridges. He slid the harmless cartridge cases back into the chambers, snapped the cylinder home and then placed the gun alongside the money.

'All safe,' he said brightly. 'Safe for dear little Gus.' He looked at Reich expectantly. Reich extended both hands. With one he pushed the money towards Church. With the other he drew the gun towards himself. At that instant Church changed again. The air of chirpy madness left him. He grasped Reich's wrists with iron claws and bent across the counter with blazing intensity.

'No, Ben,' he said, using the name for the first time. 'That isn't the price. You know it. Despite that crazy song in your head, I know you know it.'

'All right, Jerry,' Reich said steadily, never relaxing his hold on the gun. 'What is the price? How much?'

'I want to be reinstated,' the peeper said. 'I want to get back into the Guild. I want to be alive again. That's the price.'

'What can I do? I'm not a peeper. I don't belong to the Guild.'

'You're not helpless, Ben. You've got ways and means. You could get to the Guild. You could have me reinstated.'

'Impossible.'

'You can bribe, blackmail, intimidate . . . bless, dazzle, fascinate. You can do it, Ben. You can do it for me. Help me, Ben. I helped you once.'

'I paid through the nose for that help.'

'And I? What did I pay?' the peeper screamed. 'I paid with my life!'

'You paid with your stupidity.'

'For God's sake, Ben. Help me. Help me or kill me. I'm dead already. I just haven't the guts to commit suicide.'

After a pause, Reich said brutally: 'I think the best thing for you, Jerry, would be suicide.'

The peeper flung himself back as though he had been branded. In his bruised face his eyes stared glassily at Reich.

Quite deliberately, Church spat on the money, then levelled a glance of burning hatred at Reich. 'There will be no charge,' he said, and turned and disappeared into the shadows of the cellar.

CHAPTER 4

Until it was destroyed for reasons lost in the misty confusion of the late Twentieth Century, the Pennsylvania Station in New York City was, unknown to millions of travellers, a link in time. The interior of the giant terminal was a replica of the mighty Baths of Caracalla in ancient Rome. So also was the sprawling mansion of Madame Maria Beaumont, known to her thousand most intimate enemies as The Gilt Corpse.

As Ben Reich glided down the east ramp with Dr Tate at his side and murder in his pocket, he communicated with his senses in staccato spurts. The sight of the guests on the floor below ... The glitter of uniforms, of dress, of phosphorescent flesh, of beams of pastel light swaying on stilt legs ... *Tenser, said the Tensor* ...

The sound of voices, of music, of annunciators, of echoes ... *Tension, apprehension, and dissension* ... The wonderful potpourri of flesh and perfume, of food, of wine, of gilt ostentation ... *Tension, apprehension* ...

The gilt trappings of death ... Of something, by God, which has failed for seventy years ... A lost art ... As lost as phlebotomy, chierurgy, alchemy ... I'll bring death back. Not the hasty, crazy killing of the psychotic, the brawler ... but the normal, deliberate, planned, cold-blooded——

'For God's sake!' Tate muttered. 'Be careful, man. Your murder's showing.'

Eight, sir; seven, sir ...

'That's better. Here comes one of the peeper secretaries. He screens the guests for crashers. Keep singing.'

A slender, willowy young man, all gush, all cropped golden hair, all violet blouse and silver culottes: 'Dr Tate! Mr Reich! I'm speechless. Actually. I can't utter word one. Come in! Come in!'

Six, sir; five, sir ...

Maria Beaumont clove through the crowd, arms outstretched, eyes outstretched, naked bosom outstretched ... her body transformed by pneumatic surgery into an exaggerated East Indian figure with puffed hips, puffed calves and puffed gilt breasts. To Reich she was the painted figurehead of a pornographic ship ... the famous Gilt Corpse.

'Ben, darling creature!' She embraced him with pneumatic intensity, contriving to press his hand into her cleavage. 'It's too too wonderful.'

'It's too too plastic, Maria,' he murmured in her ear.

'Have you found that lost million yet?'

'Just laid hands on it now, dear.'

'Be careful, audacious lover. I'm having every morsel of this divine party recorded.'

Over her shoulder, Reich shot a glance at Tate. Tate shook his head reassuringly.

'Come and meet everybody who's everybody,' Maria said. She took his arm. 'We'll have ages for ourselves later.'

The lights in the groined vaults overhead changed again and shifted up the spectrum. The costumes changed colour. Skin that had glowed with pink nacre now shone with eerie luminescence.

On his left flank, Tate gave the prearranged signal: Danger! Danger! Danger!

Tension, apprehension, and dissension have begun. RIFF. *Tension, apprehension, and dissension have begun . . .*

Maria was introducing another effete, all gush, all cropped hair, fuchsia blouse and Prussian blue culottes.

'Larry Ferar, Ben. My other social secretary. Larry's been dying to meet you.'

Four, sir; three, sir . . .

'Mr Reich! But too thrilled. I can't utter word one.'

Two, sir; one!

The young man accepted Reich's smile and moved on. Still circling in convoy, Tate gave Reich a reassuring nod. Again the overhead lights changed. Portions of the guests' costumes appeared to dissolve. Reich, who had never succumbed to the fashion of wearing ultra-violet windows in his clothes, stood secure in his opaque suit, watching with contempt the quick roving eyes around him, searching, appraising, comparing, desiring.

Tate signalled: Danger! Danger! Danger!

Tenser, said the Tensor . . .

A secretary appeared at Maria's elbow, 'Madame,' he lisped, 'a slight contretemps.'

'What is it?'

'The Chervil boy. Galen Chervil.'

Tate's face constricted.

'What about him?' Maria peeped through the crowd.

'Left of the fountain. An impostor, Madame. I have peeped him. He has no invitation. He's a college student. He bet he could crash the party. He intends to steal a picture of you as proof.'

'Of me!' Maria said, staring through the windows in young Chervil's clothes. 'What does he think of me?'

'Well, Madame, he's extremely difficult to probe. I think he'd like to steal more from you than your picture.'

'Oh, would he?' Maria cackled delightedly.

'He would, Madame. Shall he be removed?'

'No.' Maria glanced once more at the muscular young man, then turned away. 'He'll get his proof.'

'And it won't be stolen,' Reich said.

'Jealous! Jealous!' she squawked. 'Let's dine.'

In response to Tate's urgent sign, Reich stepped aside momentarily.

'Reich, you've got to give it up.'

'What the hell . . . ?'

'The Chervil boy.'

'What about him?'

'He's a 2nd.'

'God damn!'

'He's precocious, brilliant . . . I met him at Powell's last Sunday. Maria Beaumont never invites peepers to her house. I'm only in on your pass. I was depending on that.'

'And this peeper kid has to be the one to crash. God damn!'

'Give it up, Reich.'

'Maybe I can stay away from him.'

'Reich, I can block the social secretaries. They're only 3rds. But I can't guarantee to handle them and a 2nd too . . . even if he is only a kid. He's young. He may be too nervous to do any clever peeping. But I can't promise.'

'I'm not quitting,' Reich growled. 'I can't. I'll never get a chance like this again. Even if I knew I could, I wouldn't quit. I've got the stink of D'Courtney in my nostrils. I——'

'Reich, you'll never——'

'Don't argue. I'm going through with it.' Reich turned his scowl full on Tate's nervous face. 'I know you're looking for a chance to squirm out of this; but you won't. We're trapped in this together, right down the line, from here to Demolition.'

He shaped his distorted face into a frozen smile and rejoined his hostess on a couch alongside one of the tables. It was still the custom for couples to feed one another at these affairs, but the gesture that had originated in oriental courtesy and generosity had degenerated into erotic play. The morsels of food were accompanied by tongue touched to fingers and were as often offered between the lips. The wine was tasted mouth to mouth. Sweets were given even more intimately.

Reich endured it all with a seething impatience, waiting for the vital word from Tate. Part of Tate's Intelligence work was to locate D'Courtney's hiding place in the house. He watched the little peeper drift through the crowd of diners, probing, prying, searching, until he at last returned with a negative shake of his head and gestured towards Maria Beaumont. Clearly Maria was the only source of information, but she was now too excited by sensuality to be easily probed. It was another in a never-ending series of crises that had to be met by the killer instinct. Reich arose and crossed towards the fountain. Tate intercepted him.

'What are you up to, Reich?'

'Isn't it obvious? I've got to get the Chervil boy off her mind.'

'How?'

'Is there any way but one?'

'For God's sake, Reich, don't go near the boy.'

'Get out of my way.' Reich radiated a burst of savage compulsion that made the peeper recoil. He signalled in fright and Reich tried to control himself. 'It's taking chances, I know, but the odds aren't as long as you think. In the first place, he's young and green. In the second place, he's a crasher and scared. In the third place, he can't be flying full jets or he wouldn't have let the fag secretaries peep him so easily.'

'Have you got any conscious control? Can you double-think?'

'I've got that song on my mind and enough trouble to make double-thinking a pleasure. Now get the hell out of the way and stand by to peep Maria Beaumont.'

Chervil was eating alone alongside the fountain clumsily attempting to appear to belong.

'Pip,' said Reich.

'Pop,' said Chervil.

'Bim,' said Reich.

'Bam,' said Chervil.

With the latest fad in informality disposed of, Reich eased himself down alongside the boy. 'I'm Ben Reich.'

'I'm Gally Chervil. I mean . . . Galen. I——' He was visibly impressed by the name of Reich.

Tension, apprehension, and dissension . . .

'That damned song,' Reich muttered. 'Heard it for the first time the other day. Can't get it out of my mind. Maria knows you're a phoney, Chervil.'

'Oh no!'

Reich nodded. *Tension, apprehension . . .*

'Should I start running?'

'Without the picture?'

'You know about that too? There must be a peeper in the house.'

'Two of them. Her social secretaries. People like you are their job.'

'What about that picture, Mr Reich? I've got fifty credits riding on the line. You ought to know what a bet means. You're a gamb – I mean, financier.'

'Glad I'm not a peeper, eh? Never mind. I'm not insulted. See that arch? Go straight through and turn right. You'll find a study. The walls are lined with Maria's portraits, all in synthetic stones. Help yourself. She'll never miss one.'

The boy leaped up, scattering food. 'Thanks, Mr Reich. Some day I'll do you a favour.'

'Such as?'

'You'd be surprised. I happen to be a——' He caught himself and blushed. 'You'll find out, sir. Thanks again.' He began weaving his way across the floor towards the study.

Four, sir; three, sir; two, sir; one!

Reich turned to his hostess.

'Naughty lover,' she said. 'Who've you been feeding? I'll tear her eyes out.'

'The Chervil boy,' Reich answered. 'He asked me where you keep your pictures.'

'Ben! You didn't tell him!'

'Sure did.' Reich grinned. 'He's on his way to get one now. Then he'll take off. You know I'm jealous.'

She leaped from the couch and sailed towards the study.

'Bam,' said Reich.

By eleven o'clock, the ritual of dining had aroused the company to a point of intensity that required solitude and darkness for release. Maria Beaumont had never failed her guests, and Reich hoped she would not fail tonight. She had to play the Sardine game. He knew it when Tate returned from the study with concise directions for locating the hidden D'Courtney.

'I don't know how you got away with it,' Tate whispered. 'You're broadcasting bloodlust on every wavelength of the TP band. He's here. Alone. No servants. Only two bodyguards provided by Maria. @kins was right. He's dangerously sick . . .'

'To hell with that. I'll cure him. Where is he?'

'Go through the west arch. Turn right. Up stairs. Through overpass. Turn right. Picture Gallery. Door between paintings of the Rape of Lucrece and the Rape of the Sabine Women . . .'

'Sounds typical.'

'Open the door. Up a flight of steps to an ante-room. Two guards in the ante-room. D'Courtney's inside. It's the old wedding suite her grandfather built.'

'By God! I'll use that suite again. I'll marry him to murder. And I'll get away with it, little Gus. Don't think I won't.'

The Gilt Corpse began to clamour for attention. Flushed and shining with perspiration, standing in the glare of a pink light on the dais between the two fountains, Maria clapped her hands for silence. Her moist palms beat together, and the echoes roared in Reich's ears: Death. Death. Death.

'Darlings! Darlings! Darlings!' she cried. 'We're going to have so much fun tonight. We're going to provide our own entertainment.' A subdued groan went up from the guests and a drunken voice shouted: 'I'm just one of the tourists.'

Through the laughter, Maria said: 'Naughty lovers, don't be disappointed. We're going to play a wonderful old game; and we're going to play it in the dark.'

The company cheered up as the overhead lights began to dim and disappear. The dais still blazed, and in the light, Maria produced a tattered volume. Reich's gift.

Tension . . .

Maria turned the pages slowly, blinking at the unaccustomed print.
Apprehension . . .

'It's a game,' Maria cried, 'called "Sardine". Isn't that too adorable?'
She took the bait. She's on the hook. In three minutes I'll be invisible. Reich felt his pockets. The gun. The Rhodopsin. *Tension, apprehension, and dissension have begun.*

'One player,' Maria read, 'is selected to be It. That's going to be me. All the lights are extinguished and the It hides anywhere in the house.' As Maria struggled through the directions, the great hall was reduced to pitch darkness with the exception of the single pink beam on the stage.

'Successively each player finding the Sardine joins them until all are hidden in one place, and the last player, who is the loser, is left to wander alone in the dark.' Maria closed the book. 'And darlings, we're all going to feel sorry for the loser because we're going to play this funny old game in a darling new way.'

As the last light on the dais melted away, Maria stripped off her gown and displayed the astonishing nude body that was a miracle of pneumatic surgery.

'We're going to play Sardine like this!' she cried.

The last light blinked out. There was a roar of exultant laughter and applause, followed by a multiple whisper of cloth drawn across skin. Occasionally there came the sound of a rip, then muttered exclamations and more laughter.

Reich was invisible at last. He had half an hour to slip up into the house, find and kill D'Courtney, and then return to the game. Tate was committed to pinning the peeper secretaries out of the line of his attack. It was safe. It was foolproof except for the Chervil boy. He had to take that chance.

He crossed the main hall and jostled into bodies at the west arch. He went through the arch into the music room and turned right, groping for the stairs.

At the foot of the stairs he was forced to climb over a barrier of bodies with octopus arms that tried to pull him down. He ascended the stairs, seventeen eternal steps, and felt his way through a closed tunnel overpass papered with velour. Suddenly he was seized and a woman crushed herself against him.

'Hello, Sardine,' she whispered in his ear. Then her skin became aware of his clothes. 'Owww!' she exclaimed, and felt the hard outlines of the gun in his breast pocket. 'What's that?' He slapped her hand away. 'Clever-up, Sardine,' she giggled. 'Get out of the can.'

He divested himself of her and bruised his nose against the deadend of the overpass. He turned right, opened a door and found himself in a vaulted gallery over fifty feet long. The lights were extinguished here too, but the luminescent paintings, glowing under ultra-violet spotlights, filled the gallery with a virulent glow. It was empty.

Between a livid Lucrece and a horde of Sabine Women was a flush door of polished bronze. Reich stopped before it, removed the tiny Rhodopsin Ionizer from his back pocket and attempted to poise the copper cube between his thumbnail and forefinger. His hands were trembling violently. Rage and hatred boiled inside him, and his death-lust shot image after image of an agonized D'Courtney through his mind's eye.

'Christ!' he cried. 'He'd do it to me. He's tearing at my throat. I'm fighting for survival.' He made his orisons in fanatical multiples of three and nine. 'Stand by me, dear Christ! Today, tomorrow, and yesterday. Stand by me! Stand by me! Stand by me!'

His fingers steadied. He poised the Rhodopsin cap, then thrust open the bronze door, revealing nine steps mounting to an ante-room. Reich snapped his thumbnail against the copper cube as though he were trying to flip a penny to the moon. As the Rhodopsin cap flew up into the ante-room, Reich averted his eyes. There was a cold purple flash. Reich leaped up the stairs like a tiger. The two Beaumont House guards were seated on the bench where he had caught them. Their faces were sagging, their vision destroyed, their time sense abolished.

If anyone entered and found the guards before he was finished, he was on the road to Demolition. If the guards revived before he was finished, he was on the road to Demolition. No matter what happened, it was a final gamble with Demolition. Leaving the last of his sanity behind him Reich pushed open a jewelled door and entered the wedding suite.

CHAPTER 5

Reich found himself in a spherical room designed as the heart of a giant orchid. The walls were curling orchid petals, the floor was a golden calyx; the chairs, tables and couches were orchid and gold. But the room was old. The petals were faded and peeling; the golden tile floor was ancient and the tesselations were splitting. There was an old man lying on the couch, musty and wilted, like a dried weed. It was D'Courtney, stretched out like a corpse.

Reich slammed the door in rage. 'You're not dead already, you bastard,' he exploded. 'You can't be dead.'

The faded man started up, stared, then arose painfully from the couch, his face breaking into a smile.

'Still alive,' Reich cried exultantly.

D'Courtney stepped towards Reich, smiling, his arms outstretched as though welcoming a prodigal son. Alarmed again, Reich growled: 'Are you deaf?'

The old man shook his head.

'You speak English,' Reich shouted. 'You can hear me. You can't understand me. I'm Reich. Ben Reich of Monarch.'

D'Courtney nodded, still smiling. His mouth worked soundlessly. His eyes glistened with sudden tears.

'What the hell is the matter with you? I'm Ben Reich. Ben Reich! Do you know me? Answer me.'

D'Courtney shook his head and tapped his throat. His mouth worked again. Rusty sounds came; then words as faint as faint as dust: 'Ben ... Dear Ben ... Waited so long. Now ... Can't talk. My throat ... Can't talk.' Again he attempted to embrace Reich.

'Arrgh! Keep off, you crazy idiot.' Bristling, Reich stepped around D'Courtney like an animal, his hackles raised, the murder boiling in his blood.

D'Courtney's mouth formed the words: 'Dear Ben ...'

'You know why I'm here. What are you trying to do? Make love to me?' Reich laughed. 'You crafty old pimp. Am I supposed to turn soft for your chewing?' His hand lashed out. The old man reeled back from the slap and fell into an orchid chair that looked like a wound.

'Listen to me——' Reich followed D'Courtney and stood over him. He began to shout incoherently. 'This pay-off's been on the fire for years. And you want to rob me with a Judas kiss. Does murder turn the other cheek? If it does, embrace me, brother killer. Kiss death! Teach death love. Teach Godliness and shame and blood and – No. Wait. I——' He stopped short and shook his head like a bull trying to cast off a halter of delirium.

'Ben,' D'Courtney whispered in horror. 'Listen, Ben...'

'You've been at my throat for ten years. There was room enough for both of us. Monarch and D'Courtney. All the room in time and space, but you wanted my blood, eh? My heart. My guts in your lousy hands. The Man With No Face!'

D'Courtney shook his head in bewilderment. 'No, Ben. No...'

'Don't call me Ben. I'm no friend of yours. Last week I gave you one more chance to wash in decency. Me. Ben Reich... I asked for armistice. Begged for peace. Merger. I begged like a screaming woman. My father would spit on me if he were alive. Every fighting Reich would blacken my face with contempt. But I asked for peace, didn't I? Eh? Didn't I?' Reich prodded D'Courtney savagely. 'Answer me.'

D'Courtney's face was blanched and staring. Finally he whispered: 'Yes. You asked ... I accepted.'

'You what?'

'Accepted. Waiting for years. Accepted.'

'Accepted!'

D'Courtney nodded. His lips formed the letters: 'wwhg.'

'What? wwhg? Acceptance?'

The old man nodded again.

Reich shrieked with laughter. 'You clumsy old liar. That's refusal. Denial. Rejection. War.'

'No, Ben. No...'

Reich reached down and yanked D'Courtney to his feet. The old man was frail and light, but his weight bruised Reich's arm, and the touch of the old skin burned Reich's fingers.

'So it's to be war, is it? Death?'

D'Courtney shook his head and tried to make signs.

'No merger. No peace. Death. That's the choice, eh?'

'Ben ... No.'

'Will you surrender?'

'Yes,' D'Courtney whispered. 'Yes, Ben. Yes.'

'Liar. Clumsy old liar.' Reich laughed. 'But you're dangerous. I can see it. Protective mimicry. That's your trick. You imitate the idiots and trap us at your leisure. But not me. Never.'

'I'm not ... your enemy, Ben.'

'No,' Reich spat. 'You're not because you're dead. You've been dead ever since I came into this orchid coffin. Man With No Face! Can you hear me screaming for the last time? You're finished for ever!'

Reich tore the gun out of his breast pocket. He touched the stud and it opened like a red steel flower. A faint groan escaped from D'Courtney when he saw the weapon. He backed away in horror. Reich caught him and held him fast. D'Courtney twisted in Reich's grasp, his face pleading, his eyes glazed and rheumy. Reich transferred his grasp to the back of D'Courtney's thin neck and wrenched the head towards him. He had to fire through the open mouth for the trick to work.

At that instant, one of the orchid petals swung open, and a half-dressed girl burst into the room. In a blaze of surprise, Reich saw the corridor behind her, a bedroom door standing open at the far end; the girl, nude under a frost silk gown hastily thrown on, yellow hair flying, dark eyes wide in alarm ... A lightning flash of wild beauty.

'Father!' she screamed. 'For God's sake! Father!'

She ran towards D'Courtney. Reich swung quickly between them, never relaxing his hold on the old man. The girl stopped short, backed away, then darted to the left around Reich, screaming. Reich pivoted and cut viciously at her with the stiletto. She eluded him but was driven behind the couch. Reich thrust the point of the stiletto between the old man's teeth and forced his jaws open.

'No!' she cried. 'No! For the love of Christ! Father!'

She stumbled around the couch and ran towards her father again. Reich thrust the gun muzzle into D'Courtney's mouth and pulled the trigger. There was a muffled explosion and a gout of blood spurted from the back of D'Courtney's head. Reich let the body drop and leaped for the girl. He caught her while she fought and screamed.

Reich and the girl were screaming together. Reich shook with galvanic spasms that forced him to release the girl. The girl fell forward to her knees and crawled to the body. She moaned in pain as she snatched the gun from the mouth where it still hung. Then she crouched over the twitching body, silent, fixed, staring into the waxen face.

Reich gasped for breath and beat his knuckles together painfully. When the roaring in his ears subsided, he propelled himself towards the girl, trying to arrange his thoughts and make split-second alterations in his plans. He had never counted on a witness. No one mentioned a daughter. God damn Tate! He would have to kill the girl. He——

She turned and shot a terror-stricken glance over her shoulder. Again that lightning flash of yellow hair, dark eyes, dark brows, wild beauty. She leaped to her feet, darted out of his sodden grasp, ran to the jewelled door, flung it open and ran into the ante-room. As the door slowly closed, Reich had a glimpse of the guard still slumped on the bench and the girl running silently down the stairs with the gun in her hands ... with Demolition in her hands.

Reich started. The clogged blood began pounding through his veins again. He reached the door in three strides, ran through and tore down the steps to the picture gallery. It was empty but the door to the overpass was just closing. And still no sound from her. Still no alarm. How long before she started screaming the house down?

He reached down the gallery and entered the overpass. It was still pitch dark. He blundered through, reached the head of the stairs that led down to the music room and paused again. Still no sound. No alarm.

He went down the steps. The dark silence was terrifying. Why didn't she scream? Where was she? Reich crossed towards the west arch and knew he was at the edge of the main hall by the quiet splash of the fountains. Where was the girl? In all that black silence where was she? And the gun! Christ! The tricked gun!

A hand touched his arm. Reich jerked in alarm. Tate whispered: 'I've been standing by. It took you exactly——'

'You son of a bitch!' Reich burst out. 'There was a daughter. Why didn't you——'

'Be quiet,' Tate snapped. 'Let me peep it.' After fifteen seconds of burning silence, he began to tremble. In a terrified voice he whined: 'My God. Oh, my God...'

His terror was the catalyst. Reich's control returned. He began thinking again. 'Shut up,' he growled. 'It isn't Demolition yet.'

'You'll have to kill her too, Reich. You'll——'

'Shut up. Find her, first. Cover the house. You got her pattern from me. Locate her. I'll be waiting at the fountain. Jet!'

He flung Tate from him and staggered to the fountain. At the jasper rim he bent and bathed his burning face. It was burgundy. Reich wiped his face and ignored the muffled sounds that came from the other side of the basin. Evidently some other person or persons unknown were bathing in wine.

He considered swiftly. The girl must be located and killed. If she still had the gun when Tate found her, the gun would be used. If she didn't? What? Strangle her? No ... The fountain. She was naked under that silk gown. It could be stripped off. She could be found drowned in the fountain ... just another guest who had bathed in wine too long. But it had to be soon ... soon ... soon ... Before this damned Sardine game was ended. Where was Tate? Where was the girl?

Tate came blundering up through the darkness, his breath wheezing. 'Well?'

'She's gone.'

'You weren't gone long enough to find a louse. If this is a double-cross——'

'Who could I cross? I'm on the same road you are. I tell you her pattern's nowhere in the house. She's gone.'

'Anyone notice her leave?'

'No.'

'Christ! Out of the house!'

'We better leave too.'

'Yes, but we can't run. Once we get out of here, we'll have the rest of the night to find her, but we've got to leave as though nothing's happened. Where's The Gilt Corpse?'

'In the projection room.'

'Watching a show?'

'No. Still playing Sardine. They're packed in there like fish in a can. We're almost the last out here in the house.'

'Wandering alone in the dark, eh? Come on.'

He gripped Tate's shaking elbow and marched him towards the projection room. As he walked he called plaintively: 'Hey ... Where is everybody? Maria! M-ari-aaa! Where's everybody?'

Tate emitted a hysterical sob. Reich shook him roughly. 'Play up! We'll be out of here in five minutes. Then you can start worrying.'

'But if we're trapped in here, we won't be able to get the girl. We'll——'

'We won't be trapped. ABC, Gus. Audacious, brave, and confident.' Reich pushed open the door of the projection room. There was darkness in here, too, but the heat of many bodies. 'Hey,' he called. 'Where is everybody? I'm all alone.'

No answer.

'Maria, I'm all alone in the dark.'

A muffled sputter, then a burst of laughter.

'Darling, darling, darling!' Maria called. 'You've missed all the fun, poor dear.'

'Where are you, Maria? I've come to say good night.'

'Oh, you can't be leaving.'

'Sorry, dear. It's late. I've got to swindle a friend tomorrow. Where are you, Maria?'

'Come up on the stage, darling.'

Reich walked down the aisle, felt for the steps and mounted the stage. He felt the cool perimeter of the projection globe behind him. A voice called: 'All right. Now we've got him. Lights!'

White light flooded the globe and blinded Reich. The guests seated in the chairs around the stage started to whoop with laughter, then howled in disappointment.

'Oh Ben, you cheat,' Maria screeched. 'You're still dressed. That isn't fair. We've been catching everybody divinely *flagrante*.'

'Some other time, Maria dear.' Reich extended his hand before him and began the graceful bow of farewell. 'Respectfully, Madame. I give you my thanks for——' He broke off in amazement. On the gleaming white lace of his cuff an angry red spot appeared.

In stunned silence, Reich saw a second, then a third red splotch appear on the lace. He snatched his hand back and a red drop spattered on the stage before him, to be followed by a slow, inexorable stream of gleaming crimson droplets.

'That's blood!' Maria screamed. 'That's blood! There's someone upstairs bleeding. For God's sake, Ben ... You can't leave me now. Lights! Lights! Light!'

CHAPTER 6

At 12.30 a.m., the Emergency Patrol arrived at Beaumont House in response to precinct notification: 'GZ. Beaumont. YLP-R' which, translated, meant: 'An Act of Omission, forbidden by law has been reported at Beaumont House, 9, Park South.

At 12.40, the Park precinct Captain arrived in response to Patrol report: 'Criminal Act possible Felony-AAA.'

At 1 a.m., Lincoln Powell arrived at Beaumont House in response to a frantic call from a deputy inspector: 'I tell you, Powell, it's Felony Triple-A. I'll swear it is. The wind's been knocked out of me. I don't know whether to be grateful or scared; but I know none of us is equipped to handle it.'

'What can't you handle?'

'Look here, Powell. Murder's abnormal. Only a distorted TP pattern can produce death by violence. Right?'

'Yes.'

'Which is why there hasn't been a successful Triple-A in over seventy years. A man can't walk around with a distorted pattern, maturing murder, and go unnoticed these days. He'd have as much chance of going unnoticed as a man with three heads. You peepers always pick 'em up before they go into action.'

'We try to ... when we contact them.'

'And there are too many peeper screens to pass in normal living these days for you to be avoided. A man would have to be a hermit to do that. How can a hermit kill?'

'How indeed?'

'Now here's a killing that must have been carefully planned ... and the killer was never noticed. Never reported. Even by Maria Beaumont's peeper secretaries. That means there couldn't have been anything to notice. He must have a passable pattern and yet be abnormal enough to murder. How the hell can we resolve a paradox like that?'

'I see. Any prospects?'

'We've got a pay-load of inconsistencies to iron out. One, we don't know what killed D'Courtney. Two, his daughter's disappeared. Three, somebody robbed D'Courtney's guards of one hour and we can't figure how. Four——'

'Don't count any higher. I'll be right over.'

. . .

The great hall of Beaumont House blazed with harsh white light. Uniformed police were everywhere. The white-smocked technicians from Lab were scurrying like beetles. In the centre of the hall, the party guests (dressed) were assembled in a rough corral, milling like a herd of terrified steers at a slaughter house.

As Powell came down the east ramp, tall and slender, black and white, he felt the wave of hostility that greeted him. He reached out quickly to Jackson Beck, police Inspector 2: *'What's the situation, Jax?'*

'Scramble.'

Switching to their informal police code of scrambled images, reversed meanings and personal symbols, Beck continued: *'Peepers here. Play it safe.'* In a micro-second he brought Powell up to date.

'I see. Nasty. What's everybody doing lumped out on the floor? You staging something?'

'The villain-friend act.'

'Necessary?'

'It's a rotten crowd. Pampered. Corrupt. They'll never cooperate. You'll have to do some tricky coaxing to get anything out of them; and this case is going to need it. I'll be the villain. You be their friend.'

'Right. Good work. Start recording.'

Half-way down the ramp, Powell halted. The humour departed from his mouth. The friendliness disappeared from his deep dark eyes. An expression of shocked indignation appeared on his face.

'Beck,' he snapped. His voice cracked through the echoing hall. There was dead silence. Every eye turned in his direction.

Inspector Beck faced Powell. In a brutal voice, he said: 'Here, sir.'

'Are you in charge, Beck?'

'I am, sir.'

'And this is your concept of the proper conduct of an investigation? To herd a group of innocent people together like cattle?'

'They're not innocent,' Beck growled. 'A man's been killed.'

'All in this house are innocent, Beck. They will be presumed to be innocent and treated with every courtesy until the truth is uncovered.'

'What?' Beck sneered. 'This gang of liars? Treated with courtesy? This rotten, lousy, high-society pack of hyenas . . .'

'How dare you! Apologize at once.'

Beck took a deep breath and clenched his fists angrily.

'Inspector Beck, did you hear me? Apologize to these ladies and gentlemen at once.'

Beck glanced at Powell, then turned to the staring guests. 'My apologies,' he mumbled.

'And I'm warning you, Beck,' Powell snapped. 'If anything like this happens again, I'll break you. I'll send you straight back to the gutter you came from. Now get out of my sight.'

Powell descended to the floor of the hall and smiled at the guests. Suddenly he was again transformed. His bearing conveyed the subtle suggestion that he was at heart one of them. There was even a tinge of fashionable corruption in his diction.

'Ladies and gentlemen: Of course I know you all by sight. I'm not that famous so let me introduce myself. Lincoln Powell, Prefect of the Psychotic Division, Prefect and Psychotic. Two antiquated titles, eh? We won't let them bother us.' He advanced towards Maria Beaumont with hand outstretched. 'Dear Madame Maria, what an exciting climax for your wonderful party. I envy all of you. You'll make history.'

A pleased rustle ran through the guests. The lowering hostility began to fade. Maria took Powell's hand dazedly, mechanically beginning to preen herself.

'Madame...' He confused and delighted her by kissing her brow with paternal warmth. 'You've had a trying time, I know. These boors in uniform.'

'Dear Prefect...' She was a little girl, clinging to his arm. 'I've been so terrified.'

'Is there a quiet room where we can all be comfortable and endure this exasperating experience?'

'Yes. The study, dear Prefect Powell.' She was actually beginning to lisp.

Powell snapped his fingers behind him. To the Captain who stepped forward, he said: 'Conduct Madame and her guests to the study. No guards. The ladies and gentlemen are to be left in privacy.'

'Mr Powell, sir...' The Captain cleared his throat. 'About Madame's guests. One of them arrived after the felony was reported. An attorney, Mr ¼maine.'

Powell found Jo ¼maine, Attorney-At-Law 2, in the crowd. He shot him a telepathic greeting.

'*Jo?*'

'*Hi.*'

'*What brings you to this Blind Tiger?*'

'*Business. Called by my cli(Ben Reich)ent.*'

'*That shark? Makes me suspicious. Wait here with Reich. We'll get squared off.*'

'*That was an effective act with Beck.*'

'*Hell. You cracked our scramble?*'

'*Not a chance. But I know you two. Gentle Jax playing a thick cop is one for the books.*'

Beck broke in from across the hall where he was apparently sulking: '*Don't give it away, Jo.*'

'*Are you crazy?*' It was as though ¼maine had been requested not to smash every sacred ethic of the Guild. He radiated a blast of indignation that made Beck grin.

All thus during the second in which Powell again kissed Maria's brow with chaste devotion and gently disengaged himself from her tremulous grasp.

'Ladies and gentlemen: we'll meet again in the study.'

The crowd of guests moved off, conducted by the Captain. They were chattering with renewed animation. It was all beginning to take on the aspect of a fabulous new form of entertainment. Through the buzz and the laughter, Powell felt the iron elbows of a rigid telepathic block. He recognized those elbows and permitted his astonishment to show.

'*Gus! Gus Tate!*'

'*Oh. Hello, Powell.*'

'*You? Lurking & Slinking?*'

'*Gus?*' Beck popped out. '*Here? I never tagged him.*'

'*What the devil are you hiding for?*'

Chaotic response of anger, chagrin, fear of lost reputation, self-deprecation, shame——

'*Sign off, Gus. Your pattern's trapped in a feed-back. Won't do you any harm to let a little scandal rub off on you. Make you more human. Stay here & help. Got a hunch I can use another 1st. This one is going to be a Triple-A stinker.*'

. . .

After the hall cleared, Powell examined the three men who remained with him. Jo ¼maine was a heavy-set man, thick, solid, with a shining bald head and a friendly blunt-featured face. Little Tate was nervous and twitchy . . . more so than usual.

And the notorious Ben Reich. Powell was meeting him for the first time. Tall, broad-shouldered, determined, exuding a tremendous aura of charm and power. There was kindliness in that power, but it was corroded by the habit of tyranny. Reich's eyes were fine and keen, but his mouth seemed too small and sensitive and looked oddly like a scar. A magnetic man, with something vague inside him that was repellent.

He smiled at Reich. Reich smiled back. Spontaneously, they shook hands.

'Do you take everybody off guard like this, Reich?'

'The secret of my success,' Reich grinned. He understood Powell's meaning. They were *en rapport*.

'Well, don't let the other guests see you charm me. They'll suspect collusion.'

'Not you, they won't. You'll swindle them, Powell. You'll make 'em all feel they're in collusion with you.'

They smiled again. An unexpected chemotropism was drawing them together. It was dangerous. Powell tried to shake it off. He turned to ¼maine: 'Now then, Jo?'

'About the peeping, Linc . . .'

'Keep it up on Reich's level,' Powell interrupted. 'We're not going to pull any fast ones.'

'Reich called me in to represent him. No TP, Linc. This has got to stay on the objective level. I'm here to see that it does. I'll have to be present at every examination.'

'You can't stop peeping, Jo. You've got no legal right. We can dig out all we can——'

'Provided it's with the consent of the examinee. I'm here to tell you whether you've got that consent or not.'

Powell looked at Reich. 'What happened?'

'Don't you know?'

'I'd like your version.'

Jo ¼maine snapped: 'Why Reich's in particular?'

'I'd like to know why he hollered so quick for a lawyer. Is he mixed up in this mess?'

'I'm mixed up in plenty,' Reich grinned. 'You don't run Monarch without building a stock-pile of secrets that have got to be protected.'

'But murder isn't one of them?'

'Get out of there, Linc!'

'Stop throwing blocks, Jo, I'm just peeping around a little because I like the guy.'

'Well, like him on your own time . . . not mine.'

'Jo doesn't want me to love you,' Powell smiled to Reich. 'I wish you hadn't called a lawyer. It makes me suspicious.'

'Isn't that an occupational disease?' Reich laughed.

'No.' Dishonest Abe took over and answered smoothly. 'You'd never believe it, but the occupational disease of detectives is Laterality. That's right-handedness or left-handedness. Most detectives suffer from strange changes of Laterality. I was naturally left-handed until the Parsons Case when I——'

Abruptly, Powell choked off his lie. He took two steps away from his fascinated audience and sighed deeply. When he turned back to them, Dishonest Abe was gone.

'I'll tell you about that another time,' he said. 'Tell me what happened after Maria and the guests saw the blood dripping down on your cuff.'

Reich glanced at the bloodstains on his cuff. 'She yelled bloody murder and we all went tearing upstairs to the Orchid Suite.'

'How could you find your way in the dark?'

'It was light. Maria yelled for lights.'

'You didn't have any trouble locating the suite with the light on, eh?'

Reich smiled grimly. 'I didn't locate the suite. It was secret. Maria had to lead the way.'

'There were guards there ... knocked out or something?'

'That's right. They looked dead.'

'Like stone, eh? They hadn't moved a muscle?'

'How would I know?'

'How indeed?' Powell looked hard at Reich. 'What about D'Courtney?'

'He looked dead too. Hell, he *was* dead.'

'And everybody was standing around staring?'

'Some were in the rest of the suite, looking for the daughter.'

'That's Barbara D'Courtney. I thought nobody knew D'Courtney and his daughter were in the house. Why look for her?'

'We didn't know. Maria told us and we looked.'

'Surprised to find her gone?'

'We were beyond surprise.'

'Any idea where she went?'

'Maria said she'd killed the old man and rocketed.'

'Would you buy that?'

'I don't know. The whole thing was crazy. If the girl was lunatic enough to sneak out of the house, without a word and go running naked through the streets, she may have had her father's scalp in her hand.'

'Would you permit me to peep you on all this for background and detail?'

'I'm in the hands of my lawyer.'

'The answer is no,' ¼maine said. 'A man's got the constitutional right to refuse Esper Examination without prejudice to himself. Reich is refusing.'

'And I'm in one hell of a mess,' Powell sighed and shrugged. 'Well, let's start the investigation.'

They turned and walked towards the study. Across the hall, Beck scrambled into police code and asked: '*Linc, why'd you let Reich make a monkey out of you?*'

'*Did he?*'

'*Sure he did. That shark can stiff you any time.*'

'*Well you better get your knife ready, Jax. This shark is ripe for Demolition.*'

'*What?*'

'*Didn't you hear the slip when he was busy stiffing me? Reich didn't know there was a daughter. Nobody did. He didn't see her. Nobody did. He could infer that*

*the murder made her run out of the house. Anybody could. But how did he know that
she was naked?'*

There was a moment of stunned silence, and then, as Powell went
through the north arch into the study, a broadcast of fervent admiration
followed him: *'I bow, Linc. I bow to the Master.'*

.   .   .

The 'study' of Beaumont House was constructed on the lines of a
Turkish Bath. The floor was a mosaic of jacinth, spinel and sunstone. The
walls, cross-hatched with gold wire cloisons, were glittering with inset
synthetic stones ... ruby, emerald, garnet, chrysolite, amethyst, topaz ...
all containing various portraits of the owner. There were scatter rugs of
velvet, and scores of chairs and lounges.

Powell entered the room and walked directly to the centre, leaving
Reich, Tate, and ¼maine behind him. The buzz of conversation stopped,
and Maria Beaumont struggled to her feet. Powell motioned her to
remain seated. He looked around him, accurately gauging the mass
psyche of the assembled sybarites, and measuring the tactics he would
have to use. At length he began.

'The law,' he remarked, 'makes the silliest damned fuss about death.
People die by the thousands every day; but simply because someone has
had the energy and enterprise to assist old D'Courtney to his demise, the
law insists upon turning him into an enemy of the people. I think it's
idiotic but please don't quote me.'

He paused and lit a cigarette. 'You all know, of course, that I'm a
peeper. Probably this fact has alarmed some of you. You imagine that
I'm standing here like some mind-peeping monster, probing your mental
plumbing. Well ... Jo ¼maine wouldn't let me if I could. And frankly,
if I could, I wouldn't be standing here. I'd be standing on the throne of
the universe practically indistinguishable from God. I notice that none
of you have commented on that resemblance so far ...'

There was a ripple of laughter. Powell smiled disarmingly and continued: 'No, mass mind-reading is a trick no peeper can perform. It's
difficult enough to probe a single individual. It's impossible when dozens
of TP patterns are confusing the picture. And when a group of unique,
highly individual people like yourselves is gathered, we find ourselves
completely at your mercy.'

'And he said I had charm,' Reich muttered.

'Tonight,' Powell went on, 'you were playing a game called "Sardine".
I wish I had been invited, Madame. You must remember me next
time ...'

'I will,' Maria called. 'I will, Dear Prefect ...'

'In the course of that game, old D'Courtney was killed. We're almost
positive it was premeditated murder. We'll be certain after Lab has

finished its work. But let's assume that it is a Triple-A Felony. That will enable us to play another game ... a game called "Murder".'

There was an uncertain response from the guests. Powell continued on the same casual course, carefully turning the most shocking crime in seventy years into a morsel of unreality.

'In the game of "Murder",' he said, 'a make-believe victim is killed. A make-believe detective must discover who killed the victim. He asks questions of the make-believe suspects. Everyone must tell the truth, except the killer who is permitted to lie. The detective compares stories, deduces who is lying, and uncovers the killer. I thought you might enjoy playing this game.'

A voice asked: 'How?'

Another called: 'I'm just one of the tourists.'

More laughter.

'A murder investigation,' Powell smiled, 'explores three facets of a crime. First, the motive. Second, the method. Third, the opportunity. Our Lab people are taking care of the second two. The first we can discover in our game. And if we do, we'll be able to crack the second two problems that have Lab stumped now. Did you know that they can't figure out what killed D'Courtney? Did you know that D'Courtney's daughter has disappeared? She left the house while you were playing "Sardine". Did you know that D'Courtney's guards were mysteriously short-circuited? Yes, indeed. Somebody robbed them of a full hour in time. We'd all like to know just how.'

They were hanging at the very edge of the trap, breathless, fascinated. It had to be sprung with infinite caution.

'Death, disappearance, and time-theft ... we can find out all about them through motive. I'll be the make-believe detective. You'll be the make-believe suspects. You'll tell me the truth ... all except the killer, of course. We'll expect him to lie. But we'll trap him and bring this party to a triumphant finish if you'll give me permission to make a telepathic examination of each of you.'

'Oh!' cried Maria in alarm.

'Wait, Madame. Understand me. All I want is your permission. I won't have to peep. Because, you see, if all the innocent suspects grant permission, then the one who refuses must be the guilty. He alone will be forced to protect himself from peeping.'

'Can he pull that?' Reich whispered to ¼maine.

¼maine nodded.

'Just picture the scene for a moment,' Powell was building the drama for them, turning the room into a stage. 'I ask formally, "Will you permit me to make a TP examination?" Then I go around this room...' He began a slow circuit, bowing to each of the guests in turn. And the answers come ... "Yes ... Yes ... Of course ... Why not? ... Certainly ... Yes ... Yes ..." And then suddenly a dramatic pause.' Powell stopped before Reich, erect, terrifying. ' "You sir," I repeat. "Will you give me your permission to peep?" '

They all watched, hypnotized. Even Reich was aghast, transfixed by the pointing finger and the fierce scowl.

'Hesitation. His face flushes red, then ghastly white as the blood drains out. You hear the tortured refusal: "No!" ...' The Prefect turned and enveloped them all with an electrifying gesture: 'And in that thrilling moment, we know we have captured the killer!'

He almost had them. Almost. It was daring, novel, exciting; a sudden display of ultra-violet windows through clothes and flesh into the soul ... But Maria's guests had bastardy in their souls ... perjury ... adultery – the Devil. And the shame within all of them rose up in terror.

'No!' Maria cried. They all shot to their feet and shouted: 'No! No! No!'

'It was a beautiful try, Linc, but there's your answer. You'll never get motive out of these hyenas.'

Powell was still charming in defeat. 'I'm sorry, ladies and gentlemen, but I really can't blame you. Only a fool would trust a cop.' He sighed. 'One of my assistants will take the oral statements from those of you who care to make statements. Mr ¼maine will be on hand to advise and protect you.'

He glanced dolefully at ¼maine: *'And louse me.'*

'Don't pull at my heart strings like that, Linc. This is the first Triple-A Felony in over seventy years. I've got my career to watch. This can make me.'

'I've got my own career to watch, Jo. If my department doesn't crack this, it can break me.'

'Then it's every peeper for himself. Here's thinking at you, Linc.'

'Hell.' Powell said. He winked at Reich and sauntered out of the room.

.   .   .

Lab was finished in the Orchid Wedding Suite. De Santis abrupt, testy, harassed, handed Powell the reports and said, in an overwrought voice: 'This is a bitch!'

Powell looked down at D'Courtney's body. 'Suicide?' he snapped. He was always peppery with De Santis who was comfortable in no other relationship.

'Tcha! Not a chance. No weapon.'

'What killed him?'

'We don't know.'

'You still don't know? You've had three hours?'

'We don't know,' De Santis raged. 'That's why it's a bitch.'

'Why, he's got a hole in his head you could jet through.'

'Yes, yes, yes, of course. Entry about the uvula. Exit below the fontanelle. Death instantaneous. But what produced the wound? What drilled the hole through his skull? Go ahead, ask me.'

'Hard Ray?'

'No burn.'

'Crystallization?'

'No freeze.'

'Nitro vapour charge?'

'No ammonia residue.'

'Acid?'

'Too much shattering. Acid spray might needle a wound like that, but it couldn't burst the back of his skull.'

'Thrusting weapon?'

'You mean a dirk or a knife?'

'Something like that.'

'Impossible. Have you any idea how much force is necessary to penetrate like this? Couldn't be done.'

'Well ... I've just about exhausted penetrating weapons. No, wait. What about a projectile?'

'How's that?'

'Ancient weapon. They used to shoot bullets with explosives. Noisy and smelly.'

'Not a chance here.'

'Why?'

'Why?' De Santis spat. 'Because there's no projectile. None in the wound. None in the room. Nothing nowhere.'

'Damnation!'

'I agree.'

'Have you got anything for me? Anything at all?'

'Yes. He was eating candy before his death. Found a fragment of gel in his mouth ... bit of standard candy wrapping.'

'And?'

'No candy in the suite.'

'He might have eaten it all.'

'No candy in his stomach. Anyway, he wouldn't be eating candy with his throat.'

'Why not?'

'Psychogenic cancer. Bad. He couldn't talk, let alone eat gook.'

'Hell and damnation. We need that weapon ... whatever it is.'

Powell fingered the sheaf of field reports, staring at the waxen body, whistling a crooked tune. He remembered hearing an audio-book once about an Esper who could read a corpse ... like that old myth about photographing the retina of a dead eye. He wished it could be done.

'Well,' he sighed at last. 'They licked us on motive, and they've licked us on method. Let's hope we can get something on opportunity, or we'll never bring Reich down.'

'What Reich? Ben Reich? What about him?'

'It's Gus Tate I'm worried about most,' Powell murmured. 'If he's mixed up in this . . . What? O, Reich? He's the killer, De Santis. I slicked Jo ¼maine down in Maria Beaumont's study. Reich made a slip. I staged an act and misdirected Jo while I peeped to make sure. This is off the record, of course, but I got enough to convince me Reich's our man.'

'Holy Christ!' De Santis exclaimed.

'But that's a long way from convincing a court. We're a long way from Demolition, brother. A long, long way.'

Moodily, Powell took leave of the Lab Chief, loafed through the ante-room and descended to field headquarters in the picture gallery.

'And I like the guy,' he muttered.

. . .

In the picture gallery outside the Orchid Suite where temporary headquarters had been set up, Powell and Beck met for a conference. Their mental exchange took exactly thirty seconds in the lightning tempo typical of telepathic talk:

Well, it's Reich for Demolition, Jax. We tripped him up in that talk, and I sneaked a peep in Maria's study just to make sure. Ben's our boy.

Can the guards help?

Uh-huh.

Nothing much!

And how The Gilt Corpse can screech.

But we know it was Reich.

He went up there while the guests were playing the Sardine game. He destroyed the guards' visual purple some way and robbed them of an hour of time. He went into the Orchid Suite and killed

You'll never prove it, Linc.

Not a chance. They've lost one solid hour. De Santis says their retinal rhodopsin was destroyed. That's the visual purple . . . what you see with in your eye. As far as the guards are concerned, they were on duty and alert. Nothing happened until the mob suddenly blew in, and Maria was screeching at them for falling asleep on the job . . . which they emphatically swear they did not.

You know it was Reich. Nobody else does.

How?

D'Courtney. The girl got mixed up in it, somehow, which is why she ran.

How did he kill D'Courtney?

And last of all: why did he kill D'Courtney?

I don't know. I don't know any of the answers ... yet.

That I do know.

You'll never get a Demolition that way.

You've got to show motive, method, and opportunity, objectively. All you've got is a peeper's knowledge that Reich killed D'Courtney.

Uh-huh.

Uh-huh.

Did you peep how or why?

Couldn't get in deep enough ... not with Jo ¼maine watching me.

And you'll probably never get in. Jo's too careful.

Hell & Damnation! Jackson, we need the girl.

Barbara D'Courtney?

Yes. She's the key. If she can tell us what she saw and why she ran, we'll satisfy a court. Collate everything we've got so far and file it. It won't do us any good without the girl. Let everyone go. They won't do us any good without the girl. We'll have to backtrack on Reich ... see what collateral evidence we can dig up, but——

I agree.

I'm beginning to hate her.

But it won't help without that goddam girl.

Times like this, Mr Beck, I hate women too. For Christ's sake, why are they all trying to get me married?

Sar(censored)castic retort.

Image of a horse laughing.

Sar(censored)donic reply.

(censored)

Having had the last word, Powell got to his feet and left the picture gallery. He crossed the overpass, descended to the music room and entered the main hall. He saw Reich, ¼maine, and Tate standing alongside the fountain, deep in conversation. Once again he fretted over the frightening problem of Tate. If the little peeper really was mixed up with Reich, as Powell had suspected at his party the week before, he might be mixed up in this killing.

The idea of a 1st class Esper, a pillar of the Guild, participating in murder was unthinkable; yet, if actually the fact, a son of a bitch to prove. Nobody ever got anything from a 1st without full consent. And if Tate was (incredible ... impossible ... 100–1 against) working with Reich, Reich himself might prove impregnable. Resolving on one last propaganda attack before he was forced to resort to police work, Powell turned towards the group.

He caught their eyes, and directed a quick command to the peepers: *'Jo. Gus. Jet off. I want to say something to Reich I don't want you to hear. I won't peep him or record his words. That's a pledge.'*

¼maine and Tate nodded, muttered to Reich and quietly departed. Reich watched them go with curious eyes and then looked at Powell. 'Scared 'em off?' he inquired.

'Warned them off. Sit down, Reich.'

They sat on the edge of the basin, looking at each other in a friendly silence.

'No,' Powell said after a pause, 'I'm not peeping you.'

'Didn't think you were. But you did in Maria's study, eh?'

'Felt that?'

'No. Guessed. It's what I would have done.'

'Neither of us is very trustworthy, eh?'

'Pfutz!' Reich said emphatically. 'We don't play girls' rules. We play for keeps, both of us. It's the cowards and weaklings and sore-losers who hide behind rules and fair play.'

'What about honour and ethics?'

'We've got honour in us, but it's our own code ... not the make-believe rules some frightened little man wrote for the rest of the frightened little men. Every man's got his own honour and ethics, and so long as he sticks to 'em, who's anybody else to point the finger? You may not like his ethics, but you've got no right to call him unethical.'

Powell shook his head sadly. 'You're two men, Reich. One of them's fine; and the other's rotten. If you were all killer, it wouldn't be so bad. But there's half louse and half saint in you, and that makes it worse.'

'I knew it was going to be bad when you winked,' Reich grinned. 'You're tricky, Powell. You really scare me. I never can tell when the punch is coming or which way to duck.'

'Then for God's sake stop ducking and get it over with,' Powell said. His voice burned. His eyes burned. Once again he terrified Reich with his intensity. 'I'm going to lick you on this one, Ben. I'm going to strangle the lousy killer in you, because I admire the saint. This is the beginning

of the end, for you. You know it. Why don't you make it easier for
yourself?'

For an instant, Reich wavered on the verge of surrender. Then he
mustered himself to meet the attack. 'And give up the best fight in my
life? No. Never in a million years, Linc. We're going to slug this out
straight down to the finish.'

Powell shrugged angrily. They both arose. Instinctively, their hands
met in the four-way clasp of final farewell.

'I lost a great partner in you,' Reich said.

'You lost a great man in yourself, Ben.'

'Enemies?'

'Enemies.'

It was the beginning of Demolition.

CHAPTER 7

The Police Prefect of a city of seventeen and one half millions cannot be
tied down to a desk. He does not have files, memoranda, notes, and reels
of red tape. He has three Esper secretaries, memory wizards all, who
carry within their minds the minutiae of his business. They accompany
him around headquarters like a triple index. Surrounded by his flying
squad (nicknamed Wynken, Blynken, and Nod by the staff) Powell jetted
through Centre Street, assembling the material for his fight.

To Commissioner Crabbe he laid out the broad outlines once more.
'We need motive, method, and opportunity, Commissioner. We've got
possible opportunity so far, but that's all. You know Old Man Mose. He's
going to insist on hard fact evidence.'

'Old Man who?' Crabbe looked startled.

'Old Man Mose,' Powell grinned. 'That's our nickname for the Mosaic
Multiplex Prosecution Computor. You wouldn't want us to use his full
name, would you? We'd strangle.'

'That confounded adding machine!' Crabbe snorted.

'Yes, sir. Now, I'm ready to go all out on Ben Reich and Monarch to
get that evidence for Old Man Mose. I want to ask you a straight
question. Are you willing to go all out too?'

Crabbe, who resented and hated all Espers, turned purple and shot up
from the ebony chair behind the ebony desk in his ebony-and-silver office.
'What the hell is that supposed to mean, Powell?'

'Don't sound for undercurrents, sir. I'm merely asking if you're tied
to Reich and Monarch in any way. Will you be embarrassed when the

heat's on? Will it be possible for Reich to come to you and get our rockets cooled?'

'No, it will not, damn you.'

'*Sir:*' Wynken shot at Powell. '*On December 4th last, Commissioner Crabbe discussed the Monolith Case with you. Extract follows:*

. . .

POWELL: *There's a tricky financial angle to this business, Commissioner. Monarch may hold us up with a Demurrer.*

CRABBE: *Reich's given me his word he won't; and I can always depend on Ben Reich. He backed me for County Attorney.*

End quote.'

. . .

'*Right, Wynk. I thought there was something in Crabbe's file.*' Powell switched his tactics and glared at Crabbe. 'What the devil are you trying to hand me? What about your campaign for County D.A.? Reich backed you for that, didn't he?'

'He did.'

'And I'm supposed to believe he hasn't continued supporting you?'

'Damn you, Powell – Yes, you are. He backed me then. He has not supported me since.'

'Then I have the beacon on the Reich murder?'

'Why do you insist that Ben Reich killed that man? It's ridiculous. You've got no proof. Your own admission.'

Powell continued to glare at Crabbe.

'He didn't kill him. Ben Reich wouldn't kill anybody. He's a fine man who——'

'Do I have your beacon on this murder?'

'All right, Powell. You do.'

'*But with strong reservations. Make a note, boys. He's scared to death of Reich. Make another note. So am I.*'

. . .

To his staff, Powell said: 'Now look – You all know what a cold-blooded monster Old Man Mose is. Always screaming for facts – facts – evidence – unassailable proof. We'll have to produce evidence to convince that damned machine he ought to prosecute. To do that we're going to pull the Rough & Smooth on Reich. You know the method. We'll assign a clumsy operative and a slick one to every subject. The cluck won't know the smoothie is on the job. Neither will the subject. After he's shaken the Rough Tail he'll imagine he's clear. That makes it a cinch for the slicker. And that's what we're going to do to Reich.'

'Check,' said Beck.

'Go through every department. Pull out a hundred low-grade cops. Put 'em in plain-clothes and assign 'em to the Reich case. Go up to Lab and get hold of every crackpot tracer-robot that's been submitted in the last ten years. Put all the gadgets to work on the Reich case. Make this whole package a Rough Tail ... the kind he won't have any trouble shaking but the kind he'll have to work to shake.'

'Any specific areas?' Beck inquired.

'Why were they playing "Sardine"? Who suggested the game? The Beaumont's secretaries went on record that Reich couldn't be peeped because he had a song kicking around in his skull. What song? Who wrote it? Where'd Reich hear it? Lab says the guards were blasted with some kind of Visual Purple Ionizer. Check all research on that sort of thing. What killed D'Courtney? Let's have lots of weapon research. Back-track on Reich's relations with D'Courtney. We know they were commercial rivals. Were they deadly enemies? Was it a profitable murder? A terrified murder? What and how much does Reich stand to win by D'Courtney's death?'

'Jesus!' Beck exclaimed. 'All this Rough? We'll louse the case, Linc.'

'Maybe. I don't think so. Reich's a successful man. He's had a string of victories that made him cocky. I think he'll bite. He'll imagine he's outsmarting us every time he outmanoeuvres one of our decoys. Keep him thinking that. We're going to run into some brutal public relations. The news'll tear us apart. But play along with it. Rave. Rant. Make outraged statements. We're all going to be blundering, outwitted cops ... and while Reich's eating himself fat on that diet——'

'You'll be eating Reich,' Beck grinned. 'What about the girl?'

'She's the one exception to the Rough Routine. We level with her. I want a description and photo sent to every police officer in the country within one hour. On the bottom of the stat we announce that the man who locates her will automatically be jumped five grades.'

'*Sir: Regulations forbid elevation of more than three ranks at any time.*' Thus spake Nod.

'To hell with Regulations,' Powell snapped. 'Five grades to the man who finds Barbara D'Courtney. I've got to get that girl.'

· · ·

In Monarch Tower, Ben Reich shoved every piezo crystal off his desk into the startled hands of his secretaries.

'Get the hell out of here and take all this slok with you,' he growled. 'From now on the office coasts without me. Understand? Don't bother me.'

'Mr Reich, we'd understood you were contemplating taking over the D'Courtney interests now that Craye D'Courtney's dead. If you——'

'I'm taking care of that right now. That's why I don't want to be bothered. Now beat it. Jet!'

He herded the terrified squad towards the door, pushed them out, slammed the door and locked it. He went to the phone, punched BD-12,232 and waited impatiently. After too long a time, the image of Jerry Church appeared against a background of pawnshop debris.

'You?' Church snarled and reached for the cut-off.

'Me. On business. Still interested in reinstatement?'

Church stared. 'What about it?'

'You've made yourself a deal. I'm starting action on your reinstatement at once. And I can do it, Jerry. I own the league of Esper Patriots. But I want a lot in return.'

'For God's sake, Ben. Anything. Just ask me.'

'That's what I want.'

'Anything?'

'And everything. Unlimited service. You know the price I'm paying. Are you selling?'

'I'm selling, Ben. Yes.'

'And I want Keno Quizzard too.'

'You can't want him, Ben. He isn't safe. Nobody gets anything from Quizzard.'

'Set up a meeting. Same old place. Same time. This is like it used to be, eh, Jerry? Only this time it's going to have a happy ending.'

. . .

The usual line was assembled in the ante-room of the Esper Guild Institute when Lincoln Powell entered. The hopeful hunreds, all ages, all sexes, all classes, each dreaming that he had the magic quality that could make life the fulfilment of fantasy, unaware of the heavy responsibility that quality entailed. The naïveté of those dreams always made Powell smile. *Read minds and make a killing on the market* . . . (Guild Law forbade speculation or gambling by peepers) *Read minds and know the answers to all exam questions* . . . (That was a schoolboy, unaware that Esper Procters were hired by Examination Boards to prevent that kind of peeper-cheating) *Read minds and know what people really think of me* . . . *Read minds and know which girls are willing* . . . *Read minds and be like a King* . . .

At the desk, the receptionist wearily broadcast on the widest TP band: *If you can hear me, please go through the door on the left marked* EMPLOYEES ONLY. *If you can hear me, please go through the door on the left marked* EMPLOYEES ONLY . . .

To an assured young socialite with a cheque-book in her hand, she was saying: 'No, Madame. The Guild does not charge for training and instruction, your offer is worthless. Please go home, Madame. We can do nothing for you.'

Deaf to the basic test of the Guild, the woman turned away angrily, to be succeeded by the schoolboy.

If you can hear me, please go through the door on the left . . .

A young Negro suddenly detached himself from the line, glanced uncertainly at the receptionist, and then walked to the door marked EMPLOYEES ONLY. He opened it and entered. Powell was excited. Latent Espers turned up infrequently. He'd been fortunate to arrive at this moment.

He nodded to the receptionist and followed the Latent through the door. Inside, two of the Guild staff were enthusiastically shaking the surprised man's hand and patting him on the back. Powell joined them for a moment and added his congratulations. It was always a happy day for the Guild when they unearthed another Esper.

Powell walked down the corridor towards the president's suite. He passed a kindergarten where thirty children and ten adults were mixing speech and thought in a frightful patternless mish-mash. Their instructor was patiently broadcasting: '*Think class. Think. Words are not necessary. Think. Remember to break the speech reflex. Repeat the first rule after me . . .*'

And the class chanted: 'Eliminate the Larynx.'

Powell winced and moved on. The wall opposite the kindergarten was covered by a gold plaque on which were engraved the sacred words of the Esper Pledge:

I will look upon him who shall have taught me this Art as one of my parents. I will share my substance with him, and I will supply his necessities if he be in need. I will regard his offspring even as my own brethren and I will teach them this Art by precept, by lecture, and by every mode of teaching; and I will teach this Art to all others.

The regimen I adopt shall be for the benefit of mankind according to my ability and judgement, and not for hurt or wrong. I will give no deadly thought to any, though it be asked of me.

Whatsoever mind I enter, there will I go for the benefit of man, refraining from all wrong-doing and corruption. Whatsoever thoughts I see or hear in the mind of man which ought not to be made known, I will keep silence thereon, counting such things to be as sacred secrets.

In the lecture hall, a class of 3rds was earnestly weaving simple basket patterns while they discussed current events. There was one little overdue 2nd, a twelve-year-old, who was adding zig-zag ad libs to the dull discussion and peaking every zig with a spoken word. The words rhymed and were barbed comments on the speakers. It was amusing and amazingly precocious.

Powell found the president's suite in an uproar. All the office doors were open, and clerks and secretaries were scurrying. Old T'sung H'sai, the president, a portly mandarin with shaven skull and benign features, stood in the centre of his office and raged. He was so angry he was shouting, and the shock of the articulated words made his staff shake.

'I don't care what the scoundrels call themselves,' T'sung H'sai roared. 'They're a gang of selfish, self-seeking reactionaries. Talk to me about purity of the race, will they? Talk to me about aristocracy, will they? I'll talk to them. I'll fill their ears. Miss Prinn! Miss Pr-i-nnnnn!'

Miss Prinn crept into T'sung's office, horrified at the prospect of oral dictation.

'Take a letter to these devils. To the League of Esper Patriots. Gentlemen . . . *Good morning, Powell. Haven't seen you in eons . . . How's Dishonest Abe?* The organized campaign of your clique to cut down Guild taxation and appropriations for the education of Espers and the dissemination of Esper training to mankind is conceived in a spirit of treachery and fascism. Paragraph . . .'

T'sung wrenched himself from his diatribe and winked profoundly at Powell. *'And have you found the peeper of your dream yet?'*

'Not yet, sir.'

'Confound you, Powell. Get married!' T'sung bellowed. 'I don't want to be stuck with this job for ever. Paragraph, Miss Prinn: You speak of the hardships of taxation, of preserving the aristocracy of Espers, of the unsuitability of the average man for Esper training . . . *What do you want, Powell?'*

'I want to use the grapevine, sir.'

'Well don't bother me. Speak to my #2 girl. Paragraph, Miss Prinn: Why don't you come out into the open? You parasites want Esper powers reserved for an exclusive class so you can turn the rest of the world into a host for your blood-sucking! You leeches want to——'

Powell tactfully closed the door and turned to T'sung's second secretary, who was quaking in a corner.

'Are you really scared?'

Image of an eye winking.

Image of a question mark quaking.

'When Papa T'sung blows his top we like him to think we're petrified. Makes him happier. He hates to be reminded that he's a Santa Claus.'

'Well, I'm Santa Claus too. Here's something for your stocking.' Powell dropped the official police description and portrait of Barbara D'Courtney on the secretary's desk.

'What a beautiful girl!' she exclaimed.

'I want this sent out on the grapevine. Marked urgent. A reward goes with it. Pass the word that the peeper who locates Barbara D'Courtney for me will have his Guild taxes remitted for a year.'

'Jeepers!' the secretary sat bolt upright. *'Can you do that?'*

'I think I'm big enough in Council to swing it.'

'This'll make the grapevine jump.'
'I want it to jump. I want every peeper to jump. If I want anything for Xmas,
I want that girl.'

. . .

Quizzard's Casino had been cleaned and polished during the afternoon break . . . the only break in a gambler's day. The EQ and Roulette
tables were brushed, the Birdcage sparkled, the Hazard and Bank Crap
boards gleamed green and white. In crystal globes, the ivory dice
glistened like sugar cubes. On the cashier's desk, sovereigns, the standard
coin of gambling and the underworld, were racked in tempting stacks.
Ben Reich sat at the billiard table with Jerry Church and Keno Quizzard,
the blind croupier. Quizzard was a giant pulp-like man, fat, with flaming
red beard, dead white skin, and malevolent dead white eyes.

'Your price,' Reich told Church, 'you know already. And I'm warning
you, Jerry. If you know what's good for you don't try to peep me. I'm
poison. If you get into my head you're getting into Demolition. Think
about it.'

'Jesus,' Quizzard murmured in his sour voice. 'As bad as that? I don't
hanker for a Demolition, Reich.'

'Who does? What do you hanker for, Keno?'

'A question.' Quizzard reached back and with sure fingers pulled a
roileau of sovereigns off the desk. He let them cascade from one hand to
the other. 'Listen to what I hanker for.'

'Name the best price you can figure, Keno.'

'What's it for?'

'To hell with that. I'm buying unlimited service with expenses paid.
You tell me how much I've got to put up to get it – guaranteed.'

'That's a lot of service.'

'I've got a lot of money.'

'You got a hundred M's laying around?'

'One hundred thousand. Right? That's the price.'

'For the love of . . .' Church popped upright and stared at Reich. 'A
hundred thousand?'

'Make up your mind, Jerry,' Reich growled. 'Do you want money or
reinstatement?'

'It's almost worth – No. Am I crazy? I'll take reinstatement.'

'Then stop drooling.' Reich turned to Quizzard. 'The price is one
hundred thousand.'

'In sovereigns?'

'What else? Now, d'you want me to put the money up in advance or
can we get to work right off?'

'Oh, for Christ's sake, Reich.' Quizzard protested.

'Frab that,' Reich snapped. 'I know you, Keno. You've got an idea you can find out what I want and then shop around for higher bids. I want you committed right now. That's why I let you set the price.'

'Yeah,' Quizzard said slowly. 'I had that idea, Reich.' He smiled and the milk-white eyes disappeared in folds of skin. 'I still got that idea.'

'Then I'll tell you right now who'll buy from you. A man named Lincoln Powell. Trouble is, I don't know what he'd pay.'

'Whatever it is, I don't want it,' Quizzard spat.

'It's me against Powell, Keno. That's the whole auction. I've placed my bid. I'm still waiting to hear from you.'

'It's a deal,' Quizzard replied.

'All right,' Reich said, 'now listen to this. First Job. I want a girl. Her name is Barbara D'Courtney.'

'The killing?' Quizzard nodded heavily. 'I thought so.'

'Any objections?'

Quizzard jingled gold from one hand to the other and shook his head.

'I want the girl. She blew out of the Beaumont House last night and no one knows where she landed. I want her, Keno. I want her before the police get her.'

Quizzard nodded.

'She's about twenty-five. Above five-five. Around a hundred and twenty pounds. Stacked. Thin waist. Long legs ...'

The fat lips smiled hungrily. The dead white eyes glistened.

'Yellow hair. Black eyes. Heart shaped face. Full mouth and a king of aquiline nose ... She's got a face with character. It jabs out at you. Electric.'

'Clothes?'

'She was wearing a silk dressing gown last time I saw her. Frosty white and translucent ... like a frozen window. No shoes. No stockings. No hat. No jewellery. She was off her beam ... Crazy enough to tear out into the streets and disappear. I want her.' Something compelled Reich to add: 'I want her undamaged. Understand?'

'With her hauling a freight like that? Have a heart, Reich.' Quizzard licked his fat lips. 'You don't stand a chance. *She* don't stand a chance.'

'That's what a hundred M's are for. I stand a good chance if you get her fast enough.'

'I may have to slush for her.'

'Then slush. Check every bawdy house, bagnio, Blind Tiger, and frab-joint in the city. Pass the word down the grapevine. I'm willing to pay. I don't want any fuss. I just want the girl. Understand?'

Quizzard nodded, still jingling the gold. 'I understand.'

Suddenly Reich reached across the table and slashed Quizzard's fat hands with the edge of his palm. The sovereigns chimed into the air and clattered into the four corners.

'And I don't want any double-cross,' Reich growled in a deadly voice. 'I want the girl.'

CHAPTER 8

Seven days of combat.

One week of action and reaction, attack and defence, all fought on the surface while deep below the agitated waters Powell and Augustus Tate swam and circled like silent sharks awaiting the onset of the real war.

A patrol officer, now in plain clothes, believed in the surprise attack. He waylaid Maria Beaumont during a theatre intermission, and before her horrified friends bellowed: 'It was a frame. You was in cahoots with the killer. You set up the murder. That's why you was playin' that Sardine game. Go ahead and answer me.'

The Gilt Corpse squawked and ran. As the Rough Tail set off in hot pursuit, he was peeped deeply and thoroughly.

Tate to Reich: The cop was telling the truth. His department believes Maria was an accomplice.

Reich to Tate: All right. We'll throw her to the wolves. Let the cops have her.

In consequence, Madame Beaumont was left unprotected. She took refuge, of all places, in the Loan Brokerage that was the source of the Beaumont fortune. The patrol officer located her there three hours later and subjected her to a merciless grilling in the office of the peeper Credit Supervisor. He was unaware that Lincoln Powell was just outside the office, chatting with the Supervisor.

Powell to staff: She got the game out of some ancient book Reich gave her. Probably purchased at Century. They handle that stuff. Pass the word. Did he ask for it specifically? Also, check Graham, the appraiser. How come the only intact game in the book was 'Sardine'? Old Man Mose'll want to know. And where's that girl?

A traffic officer, now in plain-clothes, was going to come through on his Big Chance with the sauve approach. To the manager and staff of the Century Audio-bookstore, he drawled: 'I'm in the market for old game books . . . The kind my very good friend, Ben Reich, asked for last week.'

Tate to Reich: I've been peeping around. They're going to check that book you sent Maria.

Reich to Tate: Let 'em. I'm covered. I've got to concentrate on that girl.

The manager and staff carefully explained matters at great length in response to the Rough Tail's sauve questions. Many clients lost patience and left the store. One sat quietly in a corner, too wrapt in a crystal recording to realize he was left unattended. Nobody knew that Jackson Beck was completely tone-deaf.

Powell to staff: Reich apparently found the book accidentally. Stumbled over it while he was looking for a present for Maria Beaumont. Pass the word. And where's that girl?

In conference with the agency that handled copy for the Monarch Jumper ('the *only* Family Air-Rocket on the market'), Reich came up with a new advertising programme.

'Here's the slant,' Reich said. 'People always anthropomorphize the products they use. They attribute human characteristics to them. They give 'em pet names and treat 'em like family pets. A man would rather buy a Jumper if he can feel affectionate towards it. He doesn't give a damn for efficiency. He wants to love that Jumper.'

'Check, Mr Reich. Check!'

'We're going to anthropomorphize our Jumper,' Reich said. 'Let's find a girl and vote her the Monarch Jumper Girl. When a consumer buys one, he's buying the girl. When he handles one he's handling her.'

'Check!' the account man cried. 'Your idea has a sense of solar scope that dwarfs us, Mr Reich. This is a wrap-up and blast!'

'Start an immediate campaign to locate the Jumper Girl. Get every salesman on to it. Comb the city. I want the girl to be about twenty-five. About five-five tall; weighing a hundred and twenty pounds. I want her built. Lots of appeal.'

'Check, Mr Reich. Check.'

'She ought to be a blonde with dark eyes. Full mouth. Good strong nose. Here's a sketch of my idea of the Jumper Girl. Look it over, have it reproduced and passed out to your crew. There's a promotion for the man who locates the girl I have in mind.'

Tate to Reich: I've been peeping the police. They're sending a man into Monarch to dig up collusion between you and that appraiser, Graham.

Reich to Tate: Let 'em. There isn't anything, and Graham's left town on a buying spree. Something between me and Graham! Powell couldn't be that dumb, could he? Maybe I've been overrating him.

Expense was no object to a squadman, now in plain-clothes, who believed in the disguises of plastic surgery. Freshly equipped with mongoloid features, he took a job in Monarch Utilities' Accounting-city and attempted to unearth Reich's financial relations with Graham, the appraiser. It never occurred to him that his intent had been peeped by Monarch's Esper Personnel chief, reported upstairs, and that upstairs was quietly chuckling.

Powell to staff: Our stooge was looking for bribery recorded in Monarch's books. This should lower Reich's opinion of us by fifty per cent; which makes him fifty per cent more vulnerable. Pass the word. Where's that girl?

At the board meeting of 'The Hour', the only round-the-clock paper on earth, twenty-four editions a day, Reich announced a new Monarch charity.

'We'er calling it "Sanctuary",' he said. 'We offer aid and comfort and sanctuary to the city's submerged millions in their time of crisis. If you've been evicted, bankrupted, terrorized, swindled ... If you're frightened for any reason and don't know where to turn ... If you're desperate ... Take Sanctuary.'

'It's a terrific promotion,' the managing editor said, 'but it'll cost like crazy. What's it for?'

'Public Relations,' Reich snapped. 'I want this to hit the next edition. Jet!'

Reich left the boardroom, went down to the street and located a public phone booth. He called 'Recreation' and gave careful instructions to Ellery West. 'I want a man placed in every Sanctuary office in the city. I want a full description and photo of every applicant relayed to me at once. At once, Ellery. As they come in.'

'I'm not asking any questions, Ben, but I wish I could peep you on that.'

'Suspicious?' Reich snarled.

'No. Just curious.'

'Don't let it kill you.'

As Reich left the booth, a man clothed in an air of inept eagerness accosted him.

'Oh, Mr Reich. Lucky I bumped into you. I have heard about Sanctuary and I thought a human interest interview with the originator of this wonderful new charity might——'

Lucky he bumped into him! The man was the 'Industrial Critic's famous peeper reporter. Probably tailed him down and – *Tenser, said the Tensor. Tenser, said the Tensor. Tension, apprehension, and dissension have begun.*

'No comment,' Reich mumbled. *Eight, sir; seven, sir; six, sir; five, sir ...*

'What childhood episode in your life brought about the realization of this crying need for——'

Four, sir; three, sir; two, sir; one ...

'Was there ever a time when you didn't know where to turn? Were you ever afraid of death or murder? Were——'

Tenser, said the Tensor, Tenser, said the Tensor. Tension, apprehension, and dissension have begun.

Reich dived into a Public Jumper and escaped.

Tate to Reich: The cops are really after Graham. They've got their entire Lab looking for the appraiser. God knows what kind of red-herring Powell's following, but it's away from you. I think the safety margin's increasing.

Reich to Tate: Not until I've found that girl.

Marcus Graham had left no forwarding address and was pursued by half a dozen impractical tracer-robots dug up by the police lab. They were accompanied by their impractical inventors to various parts of the solar system. In the meantime, Marcus Graham had arrived on Ganymede where Powell located him at breakneck speed by a peeper auctioneer. The books had been part of the Drake estate, inherited by Ben Reich from his mother. They had been unexpectedly dumped on the market.

Powell interviewed Graham in the foyer of the auction room, before a crystal port overlooking the arctic tundra of Ganymede with the belted red-brown bulk of Jupiter filling the black sky. Then Powell took the Fortnighter back to Earth, and Dishonest Abe was inspired by a pretty stewardess to disgrace him. Powell was not a happy man when he arrived at headquarters, and Wynken, Blynken, and Nod did some salacious wynking, blynking and nodding.

Powell to staff: No hope. I don't know why Reich even bothered to decoy Graham to Ganymede with that sale.

Beck to Powell: What about the game book?

Powell to Beck: Reich bought it, had it appraised, and sent it as a gift. It was in bad condition and the only game Maria could select was 'Sardine'. We'll never get Mose to pin anything on Reich with that. I know how that machine's mind works. Damn it! Where's that girl!

Three low-grade operatives in succession were smitten with Miss Duffy Wyg& and retired in disgrace to don their uniforms once more. When Powell finally reached her, she was at the '4,000' Ball. Miss Wyg& was delighted to talk.

Powell to staff: I called Ellery West down at Monarch and he supports Miss Wyg&'s story. West did complain about gambling and Reich bought a psych-song to stop it. It looks like he picked up that mind-block by accident. What about that gimmick Reich used on the guards? And what about that girl?

In response to bitter criticism and loud laughter, Commissioner Crabbe gave an exclusive press interview in which he revealed that Police Laboratories had discovered a new investigation technique which would break the D'Courtney Case within twenty-four hours. It involved photo-graphic analysis of the Visual Purple in the corpse's eyes which would reveal a picture of the murderer. Rhodopsin researchers were being requisitioned by the police.

Unwilling to run the risk of having Wilson Jordan, the physiologist who had developed the Rhodopsin Ionizer for Monarch, picked up and questioned by the police, Reich phoned Keno Quizzard and devised a ruse to get Dr Jordan off the planet.

'I've got an estate on Callisto,' Reich said. 'I'll relinquish title and let a court throw it up for grabs. I'll make sure the cards are stacked for Jordan.'

'And I tell Jordan?' Quizzard asked in his sour voice.

'We won't be that obvious, Keno. We can't leave a back-trail. Call Jordan. Make him suspicious. Let him find out the rest for himself.'

As a result of that conversation, an anonymous person with a sour voice phoned Wilson Jordan and casually attempted to purchase Dr Jordan's interest in the Drake estate on Callisto for a small sum. The sour voice sounded suspicious to Dr Jordan, who had never heard of the Drake estate, and he called a lawyer. He was informed that he had just become the probable legatee to half a million credits. The astonished physiologist jetted for Callisto one hour later.

Powell to staff: We've flushed Reich's man into the open. Jordan must be our lead on the Rhodopsin angle. He's the only Visual Physiologist to disappear after Crabbe's announcement. Pass the word to Beck to tail him to Callisto and handle it. What about that girl?

Meanwhile, the slick side of operation Rough & Smooth was quietly in progress. While Maria Beaumont was occupying Reich's attention with her squawking flight, a bright young attorney from Monarch's legal department was deftly decoyed to Mars and held there anonymously on a valid, if antiquated, vice charge. An astonishing duplication of that young attorney went to work for him.

Tate to Reich: Check your legal department. I can't peep what's going on, but something's fishy. This is dangerous.

Reich brought in an Esper 1 Efficiency Expert, ostensibly for a general check-up, and located the substitution. Then he called Keno Quizzard. The blind croupier produced a plaintiff who suddenly appeared and sued the bright young attorney for barratry. That ended the substitute's connection with Monarch painlessly and legitimately.

Powell to staff: Damn it! We're being licked. Reich's slamming every door in our face ... Rough & Smooth. Find out who's doing the legwork for him, and find that girl.

While the squadman was cavorting around Monarch Tower with his brand new mongolian face, one of Monarch's scientists who had been badly hurt in a laboratory explosion, apparently left the hospital a week early and reported back for duty. He was heavily bandaged, but eager for work. It was the old Monarch spirit.

Tate to Reich: I've finally figured it. Powell isn't dumb. He's running his investigation on two levels. Don't pay any attention to the one that shows. Watch out for the one underneath. I've peeped something about a hospital. Check it.

Rich checked. It took three days and then he called Keno Quizzard again. Monarch was promptly burgled of Cr. 50,000 in laboratory platinum and the Restricted Room was destroyed in the process. The newly returned scientist was unmasked as an impostor, accused of complicity in the crime, and handed over to the police.

Powell to staff: Which means we'll never prove Reich got that Rhodopsin stuff from his own lab. How in God's name did he un-slick our trick? Can't we do anything on any level? Where's that girl?

While Reich was laughing at the ludicrous robot search for Marcus Graham, his top brass was greeting the Continental Tax Examiner, an Esper 2, who had arrived for a long delayed check on Monarch Utilities & Resources' books. One of the new additions to the Examiner's squad was a peeper ghostwriter who prepared her chief's report. She was an expert in official work ... mainly police work.

Tate to Reich: I'm suspicious of that Examiner's squad. Don't take any chances.

Reich smiled grimly and turned his public books over to the squad. Then he sent Hassop, his Code Chief, to Spaceland on that promised vacation. Hassop obligingly carried a small spool of exposed film with his regular photographic equipment. That spool contained Monarch's secret books, cased in a thermite seal which would destroy all records unless it was properly opened. The only other copy was in Reich's invulnerable safe at home.

Powell to staff: And that just about ends everything. Have Hassop double-tailed; Rough & Smooth. He's probably got vital evidence on him, so Reich's probably got him beautifully protected. Damn it, we're licked. I say it. Old Man Mose would say it. You know it. For Christ's sake! Where is that goddam missing girl?

Like an anatomical chart of the blood system, coloured red for the arteries and blue for the veins, the underworld and overworld spread their networks. From Guild headquarters the word passed to instructors and students, to their friends, to their friends' friends, to casual acquaintances, to strangers met in business. From Quizzard's Casino the word was passed from croupier to gamblers, to confidence men, to the heavy racketeers, to the light thieves, to hustlers, steerers, and suckers, to the shadowy fringe of the semi-crook and near-honest.

On Friday morning, Fred Deal, Esper 3, awoke, arose, bathed, breakfasted, and departed to his regular job. He was Chief Guard on the floor of the Mars Exchange Bank down on Maiden Lane. Stopping to buy a new commutation ticket at the Pneumatique, he passed with an Esper 3, on duty at the Information Desk, who passed Fred the word about Barbara D'Courtney. Fred memorized the TP picture she flashed him. It was a picture framed in credit signs.

On Friday morning, Snim Asj was awakened by his landlady Chooka Frood, with a loud scream for back rent.

'For chrissakes, Chooka,' Snim mumbled. 'You already makin' a frabby fortune with 'at loppy yella head girl you pick up. You runnin' a golmine withat spook stuff downinna basement. Whadya want from me?'

Chooka Frood pointed out to Snim that: A) The yellow-headed girl was not crazy. She was a genuine medium. B) She (Chooka) did not run rackets. She was a legitimate fortune teller. C) If he (Snim) did not come through with six weeks' roof and rolls, she (Chooka) would be able to tell his fortune without any trouble at all. Snim would be out on his asphalt.

Snim arose, and already dressed, descended into the city to pick up a few credits. It was too early to run up to Quizzard's and work the sob on the more prosperous clients. Snim tried to sneak a ride uptown on the Pneumatique. He was thrown out by the peeper change clerk and walked. It was a long haul to Jerry Church's hockshop, but Snim had a gold and pearl pocket-pianino up there and he was hoping to cadge Church into advancing another sovereign on it.

Church was absent on business and the clerk could do nothing for Snim. They passed the time. Snim told the sob to the clerk about his bitch landlady crowning herself every day with the new spook-shill she was using in her palm racket and still trying to milk him when she was rolling. The clerk would not weep even for the price of coffee. Snim departed.

When Jerry Church returned to the hockshop for a brief timeout in his wild quest for Barbara D'Courtney, the clerk reported Snim's visit and conversation. What the clerk did not report, Church peeped. Nearly fainting, he tottered to the phone and called Reich. Reich could not be located. Church took a deep breath and called Keno Quizzard.

Meanwhile, Snim was growing a little desperate. Out of that desperation arose his crazy decision to work the bank teller graft. Snim trudged downtown to Maiden Lane and cased the banks in that pleasant esplanade around Bomb Inlet. He was not too bright and made the mistake of selecting the Mars Exchange as his battlefield. It looked dowdy and provincial. Snim had not learned that it is only the powerful and efficient institutions that can afford to look second-rate.

Snim entered the bank, crossed the crowded main floor to the row of desks opposite the tellers' cages, and stole a handful of deposit slips and a pen. As Snim left the bank, Fred Deal glanced at him once, then motioned wearily to his staff.

'See that little louse?' He pointed to Snim who was disappearing through the front door. 'He's getting ready to pull the "Adjustment" routine.'

'Want us to send him, Fred?'

'What the hell's the use? He'll only try it on someone else. Let him go ahead with it. We'll pick him up after he's got the money and get a conviction. Stash him for keeps. There's plenty of room in Kingston.'

Unaware of this, Snim lurked outside the bank, watching the tellers' cages closely. A solid citizen was making a withdrawal at Cage Z. The teller was passing over big chunks of paper cash. This was the fish. Snim hastily removed his jacket, rolled up his sleeves, and tucked in the pen in his ear.

As the fish came out of the bank, counting his money, Snim slipped behind him, darted up and tapped the man's shoulder.

'Excuse me, sir,' he said briskly. 'I'm from Cage Z. I'm afraid our teller made a mistake and short-counted you. Will you come back for the adjustment, please?' Snim waved his sheaf of slips, gracefully swept the money from the fish's fins and turned to enter the bank. 'Right this way, sir,' he called pleasantly. 'You have another hundred coming to you.'

As the surprised solid citizen followed him, Snim darted busily across the floor, slipped into the crowd and headed for the side exit. He would be out and away before the fish realized he'd been gutted. It was at this moment that a rough hand grasped Snim's neck. He was swung around face to face with a Bank Guard. In one chaotic instant, Snim contemplated fight, flight, bribery, pleas, Kingston Hospital, the bitch Chooka Frood and her yellow-headed ghost girl, his pocket-pianino and the man who owned it. Then he collasped and wept.

The peeper guard flung him to another uniform and shouted: 'Take him, boys. I've just made myself a mint!'

'Is there a reward for this little guy, Fred?'

'Not for him. For what's in his head. I've got to call the Guild.'

At nearly the same moment late Friday afternoon, Ben Reich and Lincoln Powell received the identical information. 'Girl answering to the description of Barbara D'Courtney can be found in Chooka Frood's Fortune Act, 99 Bastion West Side.'

CHAPTER 9

Bastion West Side, famous last bulwark in the Siege of New York, was dedicated as a war memorial. It's ten torn acres were to be maintained in perpetuity as a stinging denunciation of the insanity that produced the final war. But the final war, as usual, proved to be the next-to-the-final, and Bastion West Side's shattered buildings and gutted alleys were patched into a crazy slum by squatters.

Number 99 was an eviscerated ceramics plant. During the war a succession of balzing explosions had burst among the stock of thousands of chemical glazes, fused them, and splashed them into a wild rainbow reproduction of a lunar crater. Great splotches of magneta, violet, bice green, burnt umber, and chrome yellow were burned into the stone walls. Long streams of orange, crimson, and imperial purple had erupted through windows and doors to streak the streets and surrounding ruins with slashing brush strokes. This became the Rainbow House of Chooka Frood.

The top floors had been patched and subdivided into a warren of cells so complicated and confused that only Chooka understood the pattern of the maze, and even Chooka herself was in doubt at times. A man could drift from cell to cell while the floors were being searched, and easily slip through the meshes of the finest dragnet. This unusual complexity netted Chooka large profits each year.

The lower floors were given over to Chooka's famous Frab Joint, where, for a sufficient sum, a consummate expert graciously MC'd the well-known vices for the hungry and upon occasion invented new vices for the satiated. But the cellar of Chooka Frood's house was the phenomenon that had inspired her most lucrative industry.

The war explosions that had turned the building into a rainbow crater had also fused the ceramic glazes, the metals, glasses, and plastics in the old plant; and a molten conglomerate had oozed down through the floors to settle on the floor of the lowest vault and harden into shimmering pavement, crystal in texture, phosphorescent in colour, strangely vibrant and singing.

It was worth the hazardous trip to Bastion West Side. You threaded your way through twisting streets until you reached the streak of jagged orange that pointed to the door of Chooka's Rainbow House. At the door you were met by a solemn person in Twentieth Century formal costume who asked: 'Frab or Fortune, sir?' If you replied 'Fortune' you were conducted to a sepulchral door where you paid a gigantic fee and were handed a phosphor candle. Holding the candle aloft, you walked down a steep stone staircase. At the very bottom it turned sharply and abruptly disclosed a broad, long, arched cellar filled with a lake of singing fire.

You stepped on to the surface of that lake. It was smooth and glassy. Under the surface glowed and flickered a constant play of pastel borealis. At every step the crystal hummed sweet chords, throbbing like the prolonged overtones of bronze bells. If you sat motionless, the floor still sang, responding to vibrations from distant streets.

Around the rim of the cellar, on stone benches, sat the other fortune-seekers, each holding his phosphor candle. You looked at them, sitting silent and awed, and suddenly you realized that each of them looked saintly, glowing with the aura of the floor; and each of them sounded saintly, their bodies echoing the music of the floor. The candles looked like stars on a frosty night.

You joined the throbbing, burning silence and sat quietly, until at last there came the high chime of a silver bell repeated over and over. The entire floor took up the resonance, and the strange relationship of sight and sound made the colours flare up brilliantly. Then, clothed in a cascade of flaming music, Chooka Frood entered the cellar and paced to the centre of the floor.

'And there, of course, the illusion ends,' Lincoln Powell said to himself. He stared at Chooka's blunt face; the thick nose, flat eyes, and corroded mouth. The borealis flickered around her features and tightly gowned figure, but it could not disguise the fact that although she had ambition, avarice, and ingenuity, she was utterly devoid of sensitivity and clairvoyance.

'Maybe she can act,' Powell muttered hopefully.

Chooka stopped in the middle of the floor, looking much like a vulgar Medusa, then lifted her arms in what was intended for a sweeping mystic gesture.

'She can't,' Powell decided.

'I am come here to you,' Chooka intoned in a hoarse voice, 'to help you look into the deeps of your hearts. Look down into your hearts, you which are looking for ...' Chooka hesitated, then ran on: 'You which are looking for revenge on a man named Zerlen from Mars ... For the love of a red-eyed woman of Callisto ... For every credit of that rich old uncle in Paris ... For ...'

'*Why, damn me! The woman's a peeper!*'

Chooka stiffened. Her mouth hung open.

'*You're receiving me, aren't you, Chooka Frood?*'

The telepathic answer came in frightened fragments. It was obvious that Chooka Frood's natural ability had never been trained. '*Wha ...? Who? Which is ... you?*'

As carefully as if he were communicating with an infant 3rd, Powell spelled it out: '*Name: Lincoln Powell. Occupation: Police Prefect. Intent: To question a girl named Barbara D'Courtney. I have heard she's participating in your act.*' Powell transmitted a picture of the girl.

It was pathetic the way Chooka tried to block. '*Get ... out. Out. Out of here. Get. Get out. Out ...*'

'*Why haven't you come to the Guild? Why aren't you in contact with your own people?*'

'*Get out. Out of here. Peeper! Get out.*'

'*You're a peeper, too. Why haven't you let us train you? What kind of a life is this for you? Mumbo Jumbo ... Picking sucker brains and turning it all into a Fortune Act. There's real work waiting for you, Chooka.*'

'*Real money?*'

Powell repressed the wave of exasperation that rose up in him. It was not exasperation with Chooka. It was anger for the relentless force of evolution that insisted on endowing man with increased powers without removing the vestigial vices that prevented him from using them.

'*We'll talk about that later, Chooka. Where's the girl?*'

'*No girl. There is no girl.*'

'*Don't be an ass, Chooka. Peep the customers with me. That old goat obsessed with the red-eyed woman ...*' Powell explored him gently. '*He's been here before. He's waiting for Barbara D'Courtney to come in. You dress her in sequins. You bring her on in half an hour. He likes her looks. She does some kind of trance routine to music. Her dress is slit open and he likes that. She——'*

'*He's crazy. I never——*'

'*And the woman who was loused by a man named Zerlen? She's seen the girl often. She believes in her. She's waiting for her. Where's the girl, Chooka?*'

'*No!*'

'*I see. Upstairs. Where, upstairs, Chooka? Don't try to block, I'm deep peeping. You can't mis-direct a 1st — I see. Fourth room on the left of the angle turn. That's a complicated labyrinth you've got up there, Chooka. Let's have it again to make sure ...*'

Helpless and mortified, Chooka suddenly shrieked: 'Get out of here, you goddam cop! Get the hell out of here!'

'Excuse it, please,' said Powell. 'I'm on my way.'

He arose and left the room.

.   .   .

That entire telepathic investigation took place within the second it took Reich to move from the eighteenth to the twentieth step on his way down to Chooka Frood's rainbow cellar. Reich Heard Chooka's furious screech and Powell's reply. He turned and shot up the stairs to the main floor.

As he justled past the door attendant, he thrust a sovereign into the man's hand and hissed: 'I wasn't here. Understand?'

'No one is ever here, Mr Reich.'

He made a quick circuit of the frab rooms. *Tenser, said the Tensor. Tenser, said the Tensor. Tension, apprehension, and dissension have begun.* He brushed past the girls who variously solicited him, then locked himself into the phone booth and punched BD-12,232. Church's anxious face appeared on the screen.

'Well, Ben?'

'We're in a jam. Powell's here.'

'Oh, my God!'

'Where in hell is Quizzard?'

'He isn't there?'

'I can't locate him.'

'But I thought he'd be down in the cellar. He——'

'Powell was in the cellar, peeping Chooka. You can bet Quizzard wasn't there. Where in hell is he?'

'I don't know, Ben. He went down with his wife, and——'

'Look, Jerry. Powell must have found the girl's location. I've got maybe five minutes to beat him to her. Quizzard was supposed to do that for me. He isn't in the cellar. He's nowhere in the Frab Joint. He——'

'He must be upstairs in the coop.'

'I was going to figure that for myself. Listen, is there a quick way to get up to the coop? A short-cut I can use to beat Powell to her?'

'If Powell peeped Chooka, he peeped the short-cut.'

'God damn it, I know that. But maybe he didn't. Maybe he was concentrating on the girl. It's a chance I'll have to take.'

'Behind the main stairs. There's a marble bas-relief. Turn the woman's head to the right. The bodies separate and there's a door to a vertical pneumatique.'

'Right.'

Reich hung up, left the booth, and darted to the main stairs. He turned to the rear of the marble staircase, found the bas-relief, twisted the woman's head savagely and watched the bodies swing apart. A steel door appeared. A panel of buttons was set in the lintel. Reich punched TOP, yanked the door open and stepped into the open shaft. Instantly a metal plate jolted up against his soles and with a hiss of air pressure he was lofted eight storeys to the top floor. A magnetic catch held the plate while he opened the shaft door and stepped out.

He found himself in a corridor that slanted up at an angle of thirty degrees and leaned to the left. It was floored with canvas. The ceiling glowed at intervals with small flickering globes of radon. The walls were lined with doors, none of them numbered.

'Quizzard!' Reich shouted.

There was no answer.

'Keno Quizzard!'

Still no answer.

Reich ran half-way up the corridor, and then at a venture tried a door. It opened to a narrow cubby entirely filled with an oval bed. Reich tripped over the edge of the bed and fell. He crawled across the foam mattress to a door on the opposite side, thrust it open, and fell through. He found himself on a landing. A flight of steps led down to a round ante-room rimmed with doors. Reich tumbled down the steps and stood, breathing heavily, staring at the circle of doors.

'Quizzard!' he shouted again. 'Keno Quizzard!'

There was a muffled reply. Reich spun on his heels, ran to a door and pulled it open. A woman with eyes dyed red by plastic surgery was standing just inside and Reich blundered against her. She burst into unaccountable laughter, raised both fists and beat his face. Blinded and bewildered, Reich backed away from the powerful red-eyed woman, reached for the door, apparently missed it and seized the knob of another, for when he backed out of the room it was not into the circular foyer. His heels caught in three inches of plastic quilting. He tumbled over backwards, slamming the door as he fell, and struck his head a stunning blow against the edge of a porcelain stove.

When his vision cleared he found himself staring up into the angry face of Chooka Frood.

'What the hell are you doing in my room?' Chooka screamed.

Reich shot to his feet. 'Where is she?' he said.

'You get to hell out of here, Ben Reich.'

'I asked you where is she? Barbara D'Courtney. Where is she?'

Chooka turned her head and yelled: 'Magda!'

The red-eyed woman came into the room. She held a neuron scrambler in her hand and she was still laughing; but the gun was trained on his skull and never wavered.

'Get out of here,' Chooka repeated.

'I want the girl, Chooka. I want her before Powell gets her. Where is she?'

'Get him out of here, Magda!' Chooka screamed.

Reich clubbed the woman across the eyes with the back of his hand. She fell backward, dropping the gun, and twitched in a corner, still laughing. Reich ignored her. He picked up the scrambler and rammed it against Chooka's temple.

'Where's the girl?'

'You go to hell, you——'

Reich pulled the trigger back into first notch. The radiation charged Chooka's nervous system with a low induction current. She stiffened and began to tremble. Her skin glistened with sudden sweat, but she still shook her head. Reich yanked the trigger back to second notch. Chooka's body was thrown into a break-bone ague. Her eyes started. Her throat emitted the brute groans of a tortured animal. Reich held her in it for five seconds, then cut the gun.

'Third notch is death notch,' he growled. 'The Big D. I don't give a curse, Chooka. It's Demolition for me one way or the other if I don't get that girl. Where is she?'

Chooka was almost completely paralysed. 'Through ... door,' she croaked. 'Fourth room ... Left ... After turn.'

Reich dropped her. He ran across the bedroom, through the door, and came to a corkscrewed ramp. He mounted it, took a sharp turn, counted doors and stopped before the fourth on the left. He listened for an instant. No sound. He thrust open the door and entered. There was an empty bed, a single dresser, an empty closet, a single chair.

'Gulled, by God!' he cried. He stepped to the bed. It showed no sign of use. Neither did the closet. As he turned to leave the room, he yanked at the middle dresser drawer and tore it open. It contained a frost white silk gown and a stained steel object that looked like a malignant flower. It was the murder weapon; the knife-pistol.

'My God!' Reich breathed. 'Oh my God.'

He snatched up the gun and inspected it. Its chambers still contained the emasculated cartridges. The one that had blown the top of Craye D'Courtney's head out was still in place under the hammer.

'It isn't Demolition yet,' Reich muttered. 'Not by a damned sight. No, by Christ, not by a damned sight!' He folded up the knife-pistol and thrust it into his pocket. At that moment he heard the sound of distant laughter ... a sour laugh. Quizzard's laugh.

Reich stepped quickly to the twisted ramp and followed the sound of the laughter to a plush door hung open on brass hinges and deep set in the wall. Gripping the scrambler at the alert with the trigger set for the Big D, Reich stepped through the door. There was a hiss of compressed air and it closed behind him.

He was in a small round room, walled and ceilinged in midnight velvet. The floor was transparent, and gave a clear uninterrupted view of a boudoir on the floor below. It was Chooka's Voyeur Chamber.

In the boudoir, Quizzard sat in a deep chair, his blind eyes blazing. The D'Courtney girl was perched on his lap wearing an astonishing slit gown of sequins. She sat quietly, her yellow hair smooth, her deep dark eyes staring placidly into space whilst Quizzard fondled her brutally.

'How does she look?' Quizzard's sour voice came distinctly. 'How does she feel?'

He was speaking to a small faded woman who stood across the boudoir from him with her back against the wall and an incredible expression of agony on her face. It was Quizzard's wife.

'How does she look?' the blind man repeated.

'She doesn't know what's happening,' the woman answered.

'She knows,' Quizzard shouted. 'She isn't that far gone. Don't tell me she don't know what's happening. Christ! If I only had my eyes!'

The woman said: 'I'm your eyes, Keno.'

'Then look for me. Tell me!'

Reich cursed and aimed the scrambler at Quizzard's head. It could kill through the crystal floor. It could kill through anything. It was going to kill now. Then Powell entered the boudoir.

The woman saw him at once. She emitted a blood-curdling scream: 'Run, Keno! Run!' She thrust herself from the wall and darted towards Powell, her hands clawing at his eyes. Then she tripped and fell prone. Apparently, the fall knocked her unconscious for she never moved. As Quizzard surged up from the chair with the girl in his arms, his blind eyes staring, Reich came to the appalled conclusion that the woman's fall was no accident; for Quizzard suddenly dropped in his tracks. The girl tumbled out of his arms and fell into the chair.

There was no doubt that Powell had accomplished this on a TP level, and for the first time in their war, Reich was afraid of Powell ... physically afraid. Again he aimed the scrambler, this time at Powell's head as the peeper walked to the chair.

Powell said: 'Good evening, Miss D'Courtney.'

Reich muttered: 'Good-bye, Mr Powell,' and tried to hold his trembling hand steady on Powell's skull.

Powell said: 'Are you all right, Miss D'Courtney?' When the girl failed to answer, he bent down and stared into her blank, placid face. He touched her arm and repeated. 'Are you all right, Miss D'Courtney? Miss D'Courtney! Do you need help?'

At the word 'help' the girl whipped upright in the chair in a listening attitude. Then she thrust out her legs and leaped from the chair. She ran past Powell in a straight line, stopped abruptly and reached out as though grasping a door-knob. She turned the knob, thrust an imaginary door open and burst forward, yellow hair flying, dark eyes wide with alarm ... A lightning flash of wild beauty.

'Father!' she screamed. 'For God's sake! Father!'

She ran forward, then stopped short and backed away as though eluding someone. She darted to the left and ran in a half-circle, screaming wildly, her eyes fixed.

'No!' she cried. 'No! For the love of Christ! Father!'

She ran again, then stopped and struggled with imaginary arms that held her. She fought and screamed, her eyes still fixed, then stiffened and clapped her hands to her ears as though a violent sound had pierced them. She fell forward to her knees and crawled across the floor, moaning in pain. Then she stopped, snatched at something on the floor, and remained crouched on her knees, her face once again placid, doll-like and dead.

With sickening certainty, Reich knew what the girl had just done. She had relived the death of her father. She had relived it for Powell. And if he had peeped her ...

Powell went to the girl and raised her from the floor. She arose as gracefully as a dancer, as serenely as a somnambulist. The peeper put his arm around her and took her to the door. Reich followed him all the way with the muzzle of the scrambler, waiting for the best shooting angle. He was invisible. His unsuspecting enemies were below him, easy targets for the death-notch. He could win safety with a shot. Powell opened the door, then suddenly swung the girl around, held her close to him and looked up. Reich caught his breath.

'Go ahead,' Powell called. 'Here we are. An easy shot. One for the both of us. Go ahead!' His lean face was suffused with anger. The heavy jet brows scowled over the dark eyes. For half a minute he stared up at the invisible Reich, waiting, hating, daring. At last Reich lowered his eyes and turned his face away from the man who could not see him.

Then Powell took the docile girl through the door and closed it quietly behind him, and Reich knew he had permitted safety to slip through his fingers. He was half-way to Demolition.

CHAPTER 10

Conceive of a camera with a lens distorted into wild astigmatism so that it can only photograph the same picture over and over – the scene that twisted it into shock. Conceive of a bit of recording crystal, traumatically warped so that it can only reproduce the same fragment of music over and over, the one terrifying phrase it cannot forget.

'She's in a state of Hysterical Recall,' Dr Jeems of Kingston Hospital explained to Powell and Mary Noyes in the living-room of Powell's house. 'She responds to the key word "help" and relives one terrifying experience ...'

'The death of her father,' Powell said.

'Oh? I see. Outside of that ... Catatonia.'

'Permanent?' Mary Noyes asked.

Young Doctor Jeems looked surprised and indignant. He was one of the brighter young men of Kingston Hospital despite the fact that he was not a peeper, and was fanatically devoted to his work. 'In this day and age? Nothing is permanent except physical death, Miss Noyes, and up at Kingston we've started working on that. Investigating death from the symptomatic point of view, we've actually ——'

'Later, Doctor,' Powell interrupted. 'No lectures tonight. We've got work. Can I use the girl?'

'Use her how?'

'Peep her.'

Jeems considered. 'No reason why not. I have her the Déjà Éprouvé Series for catatonia. That shouldn't get in the way.'

'The Déjà Éprouvé Series?' Mary asked.

'A great new treatment,' Jeems said excitedly. 'Developed by Gart ... one of your peepers. Patient goes into catatonia. It's an escape. Flight from reality. The conscious mind cannot face the conflict between the external world and its own unconscious. It wishes it had never been born. It attempts to revert back to the foetal stage. You understand?'

Mary nodded. 'So far.'

'All right. Déjà Éprouvé is an old Nineteenth Century psychiatric term. Literally, it means: "something already experienced, already tried". Many patients wish for something so strongly that finally the wish makes them imagine that the act or the experience in which they never engaged has already happened. Get it?'

'Wait a minute,' Mary began slowly. 'You mean I ——'

'Put it this way,' Jeems interrupted briskly. 'Pretend you had a burning wish to ... oh, say, to be married to Powell here and have a family. Right?'

Mary flushed. In a rigid voice she said: 'Right.' For a moment Powell yearned to blast this well-meaning clumsy young normal.

'Well,' Jeems continued in blithe ignorance. 'If you lost your balance you might come to believe that you'd married Powell and had three children. That would be Déjà Éprouvé. Now what we do is synthesize an artificial Déjà Éprouvé for the patient. We make the catatonic wish to escape come true. We make the experience they desire actually happen. We dissociate the mind from the lower levels, send it back to the womb, and let it pretend it's being born to a new life all over again. Got that?'

'Got it.' Mary tried to smile as her control returned.

'On the surface of the mind ... in the conscious level ... the patient goes through development all over again at an accelerated rate. Infancy, childhood, adolescence, and finally maturity.'

'You mean Barbara D'Courtney is going to be a baby ... learn to speak ... walk ...?'

'Right. Right. Right. Takes about three weeks. By the time she catches up with herself, she'll be ready to accept the reality she's trying to escape. She'll have grown up to it, so to speak. Like I said, this is only on the conscious level. Below that, she won't be touched. You can peep her all you like. Only trouble is ... she must be pretty scared down there. Mixed up. You'll have trouble getting what you want. Of course, that's your speciality. You'll know what to do.'

Jeems stood up abruptly. 'Got to get back to the shop.' He made for the front door. 'Delighted to be of service. Always delighted to be called in by peepers. I can't understand the recent hostility towards you people ...' He was gone.

'*Ummm. That was a significant parting note.*'

'*What'd he mean, Linc?*'

'*Our great & good friend, Ben Reich. Reich's been backing an Anti-Esper campaign. You know ... peepers are clannish, can't be trusted, never become patriots, Interplanetary conspirators, eat little Normal babies, &c.*'

'*Ugh? And he's supporting the League of Patriots too. He's a disgusting, dangerous man.*'

'*Dangerous but not disgusting, Mary. He's got charm. That's what makes him doubly dangerous. People always expect villains to look villainous. Well, maybe we can take care of Reich before it's too late. Bring Barbara down, Mary.*'

Mary brought the girl downstairs and seated her on the low dais. Barbara sat like a calm statue. Mary had dressed her in blue leotards and combed her blonde hair back, tying it into a fox-tail with blue ribbon. Barbara was polished and shining; a lovely waxwork doll.

'*Lovely outside; mangled inside. Damn Reich!*'

'*What about him?*'

'*I told you, Mary. I was so mad at Chooka Frood's coop, I handed it to that red slug Quizzard and his wife ... And when I peeped Reich upstairs, I threw it in his teeth. I* ——'

'*What did you do to Quizzard?*'

'*Basic Neuro Shock. Come up to the Lab sometime and we'll show you. It's new. If you make 1st we'll teach you. It's like the scrambler but psychogenic.*'

'*Fatal?*'

'*Forgotten the Pledge? Of course not.*'

'*And you peeped Reich through the floor? How?*'

'*TP reflection. The Voyeur Chamber wasn't wired for sound. It had open acoustical ducts. Reich's mistake. He was transmitting down the channel and I swear I was hoping he had the guts to shoot. I was going to blast him with a Basic that would have made Case History.*'

'*Why didn't he shoot?*'

'*I don't know, Mary. I don't know. He thought he had every reason to kill us. He thought he was safe ... Didn't know about the Basic, even though Quizzard's Decline & Fall jolted him.... But he couldn't.*'

'*Afraid?*'

'*Reich's no coward. He wasn't afraid. He just couldn't. I don't know why. Maybe next time it'll be different. That's why I'm keeping Barbara D'Courtney in my house. She'll be safe here.*'

'*She'll be safe in Kingston Hospital.*'

'*But not quite enough for the work I've got to do.*'

'*?*'

'*She's got the detailed picture of the murder locked up in her hysteria. I've got to get at it ... piece by piece. When I've got it, I've got Reich.*'

Mary arose. '*Exit Mary Noyes.*'

'*Sit down, peeper! Why d'you think I called you? You're staying here with the girl. She can't be left alone. You two can have my bedroom. I'll convert the study for myself.*'

'*Choke it, Linc. Don't jet off like that. You're embarrassed. Let's see if I can't maybe thread needle through that mind block.*'

'*Listen* ——'

'*No, you don't, Mr Powell.*' Mary burst into laughter. '*So that's it. You want me for a chaperone. Victorian word, isn't it? So are you, Linc. Positively atavistic.*'

'*I brand that as a lie. In toffy circles I'm known as the most progressive* ——'

'*And what's that image? Oh, Knights of the Round Table. Sir Galahad Powell. And there's something underneath that. I——*' Suddenly she stopped laughing and turned pale.

'*What'd you dig?*'

'*Forget it.*'

'Oh, come on, Mary.'

'*Forget it, Linc. And don't peep me for it. If you can't reach it yourself, you'd better not get it second-hand. Especially from me.*'

He looked at her curiously for a moment, then shrugged. '*All right, Mary. Then we'd better go to work.*'

To Barbara D'Courtney he said: 'Help, Barbara.'

Instantly she whipped upright on the dais in a listening attitude, and he probed delicately ... Sensation of bedclothes... Voice calling dimly... *Whose voice*, Barbara? Deep in the preconscious she answered: 'Who is that?' *A friend, Barbara.* 'There's no one. No one. I'm alone.' And she was alone, racing down a corridor to thrust a door open and burst into an orchid room to see —— *What Barbara?* 'A man. Two men.' *Who?* 'Go away. Please go away. I don't like voices. There's a voice screaming. Screaming in my ears...' And she was screaming while instincts of terror made her dodge from a dim figure that clutched at her to keep her from her father. She turned and circled ... *What is your father doing, Barbara?* 'He – No. You don't belong here. There's only the three of us. Father and me and –' And the dim figure caught her. A flash of his face. No more. *Look again, Barbara. Sleek head. Wide eyes. Small chiselled nose. Small sensitive mouth. Like a scar. Is that the man? Look at the picture. Is that the man?* 'Yes. Yes. Yes.' And then all was gone.

And she was kneeling again, placid, doll-like, dead.

Powell wiped perspiration from his face and took the girl back to the dais. He was badly shaken ... worse than Barbara D'Courtney. Hysteria cushioned the emotional impact for her. He had nothing. He was reliving her terror, her terror, her torture, naked and unprotected.

'*It was Ben Reich, Mary. Did you get the picture, too?*'

'*Couldn't stay in long enough, Linc. Had to run for cover.*'

'*It was Reich, all right. Only question is, how in hell did he kill her father? What did he use? Why didn't old D'Courtney put up a fight to defend himself? Have to try again. I hate to do this to her ...*'

'*I hate you to do this to yourself.*'

'*Have to.*' He took a deep breath and said: 'Help, Barbara.'

Again she whipped upright on the dais in a listening attitude. He slipped in quickly. *Gently, dear. Not so fast. There's plenty of time.* 'You again?' *Remember me, Barbara?* 'No, No. I don't know you. Get out.' *But I'm part of you, Barbara. We're running down the corridor together. See? We're opening the door together. It's so much easier, together. We help each other.* 'We?'

Yes, Barbara, you and I. 'But why don't you help me now?' *How can I, Barbara?* 'Look at Father! Help me stop him. Stop him. Stop him. Help me scream. Help me! For pity's sake, help me!'

She knelt again, placid, doll-like, dead.

Powell felt a hand under his arm and realized he was not supposed to be kneeling too. The body before him slowly disappeared, and Mary Noyes was straining to raise him.

'You first this time,' she said grimly.

He shook his head and tried to help Barbara D'Courtney. He fell to the floor.

'All right, Sir Galahad. Cool a while.'

Mary rised the girl and led her to the dais. Then she returned to Powell. *'Ready for help now, or don't you think it's manly?'*

'The word is virile. Don't waste your time trying to help me up, I need brain power. We're in trouble.'

'What'd you peep?'

'D'Courtney wanted to be murdered.'

'No!'

'Yep. He wanted to die. For all I know he may have committed suicide in front of Reich. Barbara's recall is confused. That point's got to be cleared up. I'll have to see D'Courtney's physician.'

'That's Sam @kins. He and Sally went back to Venus last week.'

'Then I'll have to make the trip. Do I have time to catch the ten o'clock rocket? Call Idlewild.'

Sam @kins, E.M.D.1, received Cr. 1,000 per hour of analysis. The public knew that Sam earned two million credits per year, but it did not know that Sam was efficiently killing himself with charity work. @kins was one of the burning lights of the Guild long-range education plan, and leader of the Environment Clique which believed that telepathic ability was not a congenital characteristic, but rather a latent quality of every living organism which could be developed by suitable training.

As a result, Sam's desert house in the brilliant arid Mesa outside Venusburg was overrun by charity cases. He invited everyone in the low income brackets to trek their problems out to him, and while he was solving them, he was carefully attempting to foster telepathy in his patients. Sam's reasoning was quite simple. If, say, peeping were a question of developing unused muscles, it might well be that the majority of people had been too lazy or lacked opportunity to do so. But when a man is caught up in the press of a crisis, he cannot afford to be lazy; and Sam was there to offer opportunity and training. So far, his results had been the discovery of 2% Latent Espers, which was under the average of the Guild Institute interviews. Sam remained undiscouraged.

Powell found him charging through the rock garden of his desert home vigorously destroying desert flowers under the impression that he was cultivating, and conducting simultaneous conversations with a score of depressed people who followed him about like puppies. The perpetual clouds of Venus radiated dazzling light. Sam's bald head was burned pink. He was snorting and shouting at plants and patients alike.

'Damn it! Don't you tell me that's a Glow-wort. It's a weed. Don't I know a weed when I see it? Hand me the rake, Bernard.'

A small man in black handed him the rake and said: 'My name is Walter, Dr @kins.'

'And that's your whole trouble,' @kins grunted, tearing out a clump of rubbery red. It changed colours in prismatic hysteria and emitted a plaintive wail which proved it was neither weed nor Glow-wort but the disconcerting Pussy-Willow of Venus.

@kins eyed it with disfavour, watching the collapsing air-bladders cry. Then he glared at the small man. 'Semantic escape. Bernard. You live in terms of the label, not the object. It's your escape from reality. What are you running away from, Bernard?'

'I was hoping you'd tell me, Dr @kins,' Walter replied.

Powell stood quietly, enjoying the spectacle. It was like an illustration from a primitive Bible. Sam, an ill-tempered Messiah, glowering at his humble disciples. Around them the glittering silica stones of the rock-garden, crawling with the dry motley-coloured Venus plants. Overhead, the blinding nacre glow; and in the background, as far as the eye could reach, the red, purple, and violet Bad-Lands of the planet.

@kins snorted at Walter/Bernard: 'You remind me of the red-head. Where is that make-believe courtesan anyway?'

A pretty red-headed girl jostled through the crowd and smirked. 'Here I am, Dr @kins.'

'Well, don't preen yourself, because I labelled you,' @kins frowned at her and continued on the TP level: '*You're delighted with yourself because you're a woman aren't you? It's your substitute for living. It's your phantasy. "I'm a woman," you tell yourself. "Therefore, men desire me. It's enough to know that thousands of men could have me if I'd let them. That makes me real." Nonsense! You can't escape that way. Sex isn't make-believe. Life isn't make-believe. Virginity isn't an apotheosis.*'

@kins waited impatiently for a response, but the girl merely smirked and postured before him. Finally he burst out. '*Didn't any of you hear what I told her?*'

'*I did, teacher.*'

'*Lincoln Powell! No! What are you doing here! here? Where'd you sneak up from?*'

'*From Terra, Sam. Come for a consultation and can't stay long. Got to jet back on the next rocket.*'

'*Couldn't you phone Interplanetary?*'

'*It's complicated, Sam. Has to be done peeper-wise. It's the D'Courtney case.*'

'*Oh. Ah. Hm. Right. Be with you in a minute. Go get something to drink.*' @kins let out a warning blast. 'SALLY. COMPANY.'

One of @kin's flock unaccountably flinched and Sam turned on the man excitedly. 'You heard that, didn't you?'

'No, sir. I didn't hear nothing.'

'Yes you did. You picked up a TP broadcast.'

'No, Dr @kins.'

'Then why did you jump?'

'A bug bit me.'

'It did not,' @kins roared. 'There are no bugs in my garden. You heard me yell to my wife.' And then be began a frightful racket. 'YOU CAN ALL HEAR ME. DON'T SAY YOU CAN'T. DON'T YOU WANT TO BE HELPED? ANSWER ME. GO AHEAD. ANSWER ME!'

Powell found Sally @kins in the cool, spacious living-room of the house. The ceiling was open to the sky. It never rained on Venus. A plastic dome was enough to provide shade from the sky that blazed through the seven hundred hour-long Venus day. And when the seven hundred hour night began its deadly chill, the @kinses simply packed up and returned to their heated city-unit in Venusburg. Everyone on Venus lived in thirty-day cycles.

Sam came bouncing into the living-room and engulfed a quart of ice-water. '*Ten credits down the drain, black market,*' he shot at Powell. '*You know that? We've got a water black market on Venus. And what the devil are the police doing about it? Never mind, Linc. I know it's out of your jurisdiction. What's with D'Courtney?*'

Powell presented the problem. Barbara D'Courney's hysterical recall of the death of her father was susceptible of two interpretations. Either Reich had killed D'Courney, or merely been a witness to D'Courtney's suicide. Old Man Mose would insist on that being cleared up.

'*I see. The answer is yes. D'Courtney was suicidal.*'

'Suicidal? How?'

'*He was crumbling. His adaptation pattern was shattering. He was regressing under emotional exhaustion and on the verge of self-destruction. That's why I rushed over to Terra to cut him off.*'

'Hmmm. That's a blow, Sam. Then he could have blown the back of his head out, eh?'

'*What? Blown the back of his head out?*'

'Yes. Here's the picture. We don't know what the weapon was, but ——'

'*Wait a minute. Now I can give you something definite. If D'Courney died that way he certainly did not commit suicide.*'

'Why not?'

'*Because he had a poison fixation. He was set on killing himself with narcotics. You know suicides, Linc. Once they've fixed on a particular form of death, they never change it. D'Courtney must have been murdered.*'

'*Now we're jetting places, Sam. Tell me, why was D'Courtney set on suicide by poison?*'

'*You supposed to be funny? If I knew, he wouldn't have been. I'm not too happy about all this, Powell. Reich turned my case into a failure. I could have saved D'Courtney. I* ——'

'*You made any guesses why D'Courtney's pattern was crumbling?*'

'*Yes. He was trying to take drastic action to escape deep guilt sensations.*'

'*Guilt about what?*'

'*His child.*'

'*Barbara? How? Why?*'

'*I don't know. He was fighting irrational symbols of abandonment ... desertion ... shame ... loathing ... cowardice. We were going to work on that. That's all I know.*'

'*Could Reich have figured and counted on all this? That's something Old Man Mose is going to fuss about. When we present him the case.*'

'*Reich might have guessed* —— *No. Impossible. He'd need expert help to* –'

'*Hold it, Sam. You've got something hidden under that. I'd like to get it if I can ...*'

'*Go ahead. I'm wide open.*'

'*Don't try to help me. You're just mixing everything. Easy, now ... association with festivity ... party ... conversation at – my party. Last month. Gus Tate, an expert himself, but needing help on a similar patient of his own, he said. If Tate needed help, you reasoned, Reich certainly would need help.*' Powell was so upset he spoke aloud. 'Well, how about that peeper!'

'How about what?'

'Gus Tate was at the Beaumont party the night D'Courtney was killed. He came with Reich, but I kept hoping ——'

'Linc, I don't believe it!'

'Neither did I, but there it is. Little Gus Tate was Reich's expert. Little Gus laid it out for him. He pumped you and turned his information over to a killer. Good old Gus. What price the Esper Pledge now?'

'What price Demolition!' @kins answered fiercely.

From somewhere inside the house came an announcement from Sally @kins: '*Linc. Phone.*'

'Hell! Mary's the only one who knows I'm here. Hope nothing's happened to the D'Courtney girl.'

Powell loped down a hall towards the v-phone alcove. In the distance he saw Beck's face on the screen. His lieutenant saw him at the same moment and waved excitedly. He began talking before Powell was within earshot.

'. . . gave me your number. Lucky I caught you, boss. We've got twenty-six hours.'

'Wait a minute. Take it from the top, Jax.'

'Your Rhodopsin man, Dr Wilson Jordan, is back from Callisto. Now a man of property by courtesy of Ben Reich. I came back with him. He's on earth for twenty-six hours to settle his affairs, and then he rockets back to Callisto to live on his brand new estate for ever. If you want anything from him, you'd better come quick.'

'Will Jordan talk?'

'Would I call you Interplanetary if he would? No, boss. He's got money-measles. Also he's grateful to Reich, who (I am now quoting) generously stepped out of the legal picture in favour of Dr Jordan and justice. If you want anything, you'd better come back to Terra and get it yourself.'

'And this,' Powell said, 'is our Guild Laboratory, Dr Jordan.'

Jordan was impressed. The entire top floor of the Guild building was devoted to laboratory research. It was a circular floor, almost a thousand feet in diameter, domed with a double layer of controlled quartz that could give graded illumination from full to total darkness including monochrome light to within one tenth of an angstrom. Now, at noon, the sunlight was modulated slightly so that it flooded the tables and benches, the crystal and silver apparatus, the overalled workers with a gentle peach radiance.

'Shall we stroll?' Powell suggested pleasantly.

'I haven't much time, Mr Powell, but . . .' Jordan hesitated.

'Of course not. Very kind of you to give us an hour, but we need you desperately.'

'If it's anything to do with D'Courtney,' Jordan began.

'Who? Oh yes. The murder. Whatever put that into your mind?'

'I've been hounded,' Jordan said grimly.

'I assure you, Dr Jordan. We're asking for research guidance, not information on a murder case. What's murder to a scientist? We're not interested.'

Jordan unfolded a little. 'Very true. You have only to look at this laboratory to realize that.'

'Shall we tour?' Powell took Jordan's arm. To the entire laboratory he broadcast: '*Stand by, peepers! We're pulling a fast one.*'

Without interrupting their work, the lab technicians responded with loud razzberries. And amid a hail of derisory images came the raucous cry of a backbiter: '*Who stole the weather, Powell?*' This apparently referred to an obscure episode in Dishonest Abe's lurid career which no one had ever succeeded in peeping, but which never failed to make Powell blush. It did not fail now. A silent cackle filled the room.

'*No. This is serious, peepers. My whole case hangs on something I've got to coax out of this man.*'

Instantly the silent cackle was stilled.

'*This is Dr Wilson Jordan,*' Powell announced. '*He specializes in visual physiology and he's got information I want him to volunteer. Let's make him feel paternal. Please fake obscure visual problems and beg for help. Make him talk.*'

They came by ones, by twos, in droves. A red-headed researcher, actually working on a problem of a transistor which would record the TP impulse, hastily invented the fact that TP optical transmission was astigmatic and humbly requested enlightenment. A pair of pretty girls, engrossed in the infuriating dead-end of long range telepathic communication, demanded of Dr Jordan why transmission of visual images always showed colour aberration, which it did not. The Japanese team, experts on the extra sensory Node, centre of TP perceptivity, insisted that the Node was in circuit with the Optic Nerve (it wasn't within two millimetres of same) and besieged Dr Jordan with polite hissings and specious proofs.

At 1 p.m., Powell said: 'I'm sorry to interrupt, Doctor, your hour is finished and you've got important business to ———'

'Quite all right. Quite all right,' Jordan interrupted. 'Now my dear doctor, if you would try a transection of the optic ———' &c.

At 1.30 p.m. Powell gave the time-signal again. 'It's half past one, Dr Jordan. You jet at five. I really think –'

'Plenty of time. Plenty of time. Women and rockets, you know. There's always another. The fact is, my dear sir, your admirable work contains one significant flaw. You have never checked the living Node with a vital dye. Ehrlich Rot, perhaps, or Gentian Violet. I would suggest . . .' &c.

At 2 p.m. a buffet luncheon was served without interrupting the feast of reason.

At 2.30 p.m. Dr Jordan, flushed and ecstatic, confessed that he loathed the idea of being rich on Callisto. No scientists there. No meetings of the minds. Nothing on the level of this extraordinary seminar.

At 3 p.m., he confided to Powell how he had inherited his foul estate. Seemed that Craye D'Courtney originally owned it. The old Reich (Ben's father) must have swindled it one way or another, and placed it in his wife's name. When she died, it went to her son. That thief Ben Reich must have had conscience qualms for he threw it into open court, and by some legal hokey-pokey Wilson Jordan came up with it.

'And he must have plenty more on his conscience,' Jordan said. 'The things I saw when I worked for him! But all financiers are crooks. Don't you agree?'

'I don't think that's true of Ben Reich,' Powell replied, striking the noble note. 'I rather admire him.'

'Of course. Of course,' Jordan agreed hastily. 'After all, he does have a conscience. That's admirable indeed. I wouldn't want him to think that I ——'

'Naturally.' Powell became a fellow-conspirator and captivated Jordan with a grin. 'As fellow scientists we can deplore; but as men of the world we can only praise.'

'You *do* understand,' Jordan shook Powell's hand effusively.

And at 4 p.m. Dr Jordan informed the genuflecting Japanese that he would gladly volunteer his most secret work on Visual Purple to these fine youngsters to aid them in their own research. He was handing on the torch to the next generation. His eyes moistened and his throat choked with sentiment as he spent twenty minutes carefully describing the Rhodopsin Ionizer he had developed for Monarch.

At 5 p.m. the Guild sceintists escorted Dr Jordan by launch to his Callisto Rocket. They filled his stateroom with gifts and flowers; they filled his ears with grateful testimonials, and he accelerated towards Jupiter's IVth Satellite with the pleasant knowledge that he had materially benefited science and never betrayed that fine and generous patron, Mr Benjamin Reich.

. . .

Barbara was in the living-room on all-fours, crawling energetically. She had just been fed and her face was eggy.

'Hajajajajaja,' she said. 'Haja.'

'*Mary! Come quick! She's talking!*'

'*No!*' Mary ran in from the kitchen. '*What's she say?*'

'She called me Dada.'

'Haja,' said Barbara. 'Hajajajahajaja.'

Mary blasted him with scorn. '*She's said nothing of the kind. She said Haja.*' She returned to the kitchen.

'*She meant Dada. Is it her fault if she's too young to articulate?*' Powell knelt alongside Barbara. 'Say Dada, baby. Dada? Dada? Say Dada.'

'Haja,' Barbara replied with an enchanting drool.

Powell gave it up. He went down past the conscious level to the preconscious.

Hello, Barbara.

'You again?'

Remember me?

'I don't know.'

Sure you do. I'm the guy who pries into your private little turmoil down here. We fight it out together.

'Just the two of us?'

Just the two of us. Do you know who you are? Would you like to know why you're buried way down here in this solitary existence?

'I don't know. Tell me.'

Well, dear infant, once upon a time you were like this before ... an entity merely existing. Then you were born. You had a mother and a father. You grew up into a lovely girl with blonde hair and dark eyes and a sweet graceful figure. You travelled from Mars to earth with your father and you were ——

'No. There's no one but you. Just the two of us together in the darkness.'

There was your father, Barbara.

'There was no one. There is no one else.'

I'm sorry dear. I'm really sorry, but we must go through the agony again. There's something I have to see.

'No. No ... please. It's just the two of us alone together. Please, dear spook ...'

It'll be just the two of us together, Barbara. Stay close, dear. There was your father in the other room ... the orchid room ... and suddenly we heard something ... Powell took a deep breath and cried: 'Help. Barbara. Help!'

And they whipped upright in a listening attitude. Sensation of bed-clothes. Cool floor under running feet and the endless corridor until at last they burst through the door into the orchid room and screamed and dodged the startled grasp of Ben Reich while he raised something to father's mouth. Raised what? Hold that image. Photograph it. Christ! That horrible muffled explosion. The back of the head burst out and the loved, the adored, the worshipped figure crumpling unbelievably, tearing at their hearts while they moaned and crawled across the floor to snatch a malignant steel flower from the waxen ——

'*Get up, Linc! For heaven's sake!*'

Powell found himself dragged to his feet by Mary Noyes. The air was crackling with indignation.

'*Can't I leave you alone for a minute? Idiot!*'

'*Have I been kneeling here long, Mary?*'

'*At least a half-hour. I came in and found you two like this ...*'

'*I got what I was after. It was a gun, Mary. An ancient explosive weapon. Clear picture. Take a look ...*'

'*Mmmmm. That's a gun?*'

'*Yes.*'

'*Where'd Reich get it? Museum?*'

'*I don't think so. I'm going to play a long shot. Kill two birds. Leave me at the phone ...*'

Powell lurched to the phone and dialled BD-12,232. Presently, Church's twisted face appeared on the screen.

'Hi, Jerry.'

'Hello ... Powell.' Cautious. Guarded.

'Did Gus Tate buy a gun from you, Jerry?'

'Gun?'

'Explosive weapon. Twentieth Century style. Used in the D'Courtney murder.'

'No!'

'Yes indeed. I think Gus Tate is our killer, Jerry. I was wondering if he bought the gun from you. I'd like to bring the picture of the gun over and check with you.' Powell hesitated and then stressed the next words gently. 'It'd be a big help, Jerry, and I'll be extremely appreciative. Extremely. Wait for me. I'll be up in half an hour.'

Powell hung up. He looked at Mary. Image of an eye winking. '*That ought to give little Gus time to hustle over to Chruch's place.*'

'*Why Gus? I thought Ben Reich was* ——' She caught the picture Powell had sketched in at @kins house. '*Oh. I see. It's a trap for both Tate and Church. Church sold the gun to Reich.*'

'*Maybe. It's a long-shot. But he does run a hock-shop, and that's next door to a museum.*'

'*And Tate helped Reich use the gun on D'Courtney? I don't believe it.*'

'*Almost a certainty, Mary.*'

'*So you're playing one against the other.*'

'*And both against Reich. We've failed on the Objective Level all the way down the line. From here on in it's got to be peeper tricks or I'm through.*'

'*But suppose you can't play them against Reich? What if they call Reich in?*'

'*They can't. We lured Reich out of town. Scared Keno Quizzard into running for his life, and Reich's out somewhere trying to cut him off and gag him.*'

'*You really are a thief, Linc. I bet you did steal the weather.*'

'No,' he said. 'Dishonest Abe did.' He blushed, kissed Mary, kissed Barbara D'Courtney, blushed again and left the house in confusion.

CHAPTER 11

The pawnshop was in darkness. A single lamp burned on the counter, sending out its sphere of soft light. As the three men spoke, they leaned in and out of the illumination, their faces and gesticulating hands suddenly appearing and disappearing in staccato eclipses.

'No,' Powell said sharply. 'I didn't come here to peep anybody. I'm sticking to straight talk. You two peepers may consider it an insult to have words addressed to you. I consider it evidence of good faith. While I'm talking, I'm not peeping.'

'Not necessarily,' Tate answered. His gnome face popped into the light. 'You've been known to finesse, Powell.'

'Not now. Check me. What I want from you two, I want objectively. I'm working on a murder. Peeping isn't going to do me any good.'

'What do you want, Powell?' Church cut in.

'You sold a gun to Gus Tate.'

'The hell he did,' Tate said.

'Then why are you here?'

'Am I supposed to take an outlandish accusation like that lying down?'

'Church called you because he sold you the gun and he knows how it was used.'

Church's face appeared. 'I sold no gun, peeper, and I don't know how any gun was used. That's my objective evidence. Eat it.'

'Oh, I'll eat it,' Powell chuckled. 'I know you didn't sell the gun to Gus. You sold it to Ben Reich.'

Tate's face came back into the light. 'Then why'd you ———'

'Why?' Powell stared into Tate's eyes. 'To get you here for a talk, Gus. Let it wait a minute. I want to finish with Jerry.' He turned towards Church. 'You had the gun, Jerry. It's the kind of thing you would have. Reich came here for it. It's the only place he could come. You did business together before. I haven't forgotten the Chaos Swindle ...'

'God damn you!' Church shouted.

'It swindled you out of the Guild,' Powell continued. 'You risked and lost everything for Reich ... just because he asked you to peep and squeal on four members of the Stock Exchange. He made a million out of that swindle ... just by asking a dumb peeper for a favour.'

'He paid for that favour!' Church cried.

'And now all I'm asking for is the gun,' Powell answered quietly.

'Are you offering to pay?'

'You know me better than that, Jerry. I threw you out of the Guild because I'm mealy-mouthed Preacher Powell, didn't I? Would I make a shady offer?'

'Then what are you paying for the gun?'

'Nothing, Jerry. You'll have to trust me to do the fair thing; but I'm making no promises.'

'I've got a promise,' Church muttered.

'You have? Ben Reich, probably. He's long on promise. Sometimes he's short on delivery. You'll have to make up your mind. Trust me or trust Ben Reich. What about the gun?'

Church's face disappeared from the light. After a pause, he spoke from the darkness. 'I sold no gun, peeper, and I don't know how any gun was used. That's my objective evidence for the court.'

'Thanks, Jerry,' Powell smiled, shrugged, and turned again to Tate. 'I just want to ask you one question, Gus. Skipping over the fact that you're Ben Reich's accessory ... that you pumped Sam @kins about D'Courtney and got the orbits set for him ... Skipping over the fact that

you went to the Beaumont party with Reich, ran interference for him
and've been running interference ever since ——'

'*Wait a minute, Powell* ——'

'Don't get panicky, Gus. All I want to know is whether I've guessed
Reich's bribe correctly. He couldn't bribe you with money. You make
too much. He couldn't bribe you with position. You're one of the top
peepers in the Guild. He must have bribed you with power, eh? Is that
it?'

Tate was peeping him hysterically, and the calm assurance he found
in Powell's mind, the casual acceptance of Tate's ruin as an accomplished
fact, jolted the little peeper with a series of shocks too sudden for adjustment. And he was communicating his panic to Church. All this Powell
had planned in preparation for one crucial moment that was to come
later.

'Reich could offer you power in his world,' Powell continued conversationally, 'but it isn't likely. He wouldn't give up any of his own, and
you wouldn't want any of his kind. So he must have offered you power
in the Esper world. How could he do that? Well, he finances the League
of Esper Patriots. My guess is he offered you power through the League
... A coup d'état, maybe? A dictatorship in the Guild? Probably
you're a member of the League.'

'*Listen, Powell ...*'

'That's my guess, Gus.' Powell's voice hardened. 'And I've got a hunch
I can make my guess good. Did you imagine we'd let you and Reich
smash the Guild as easily as that?'

'*You'll never prove anything. You'll* ——'

'Prove? What?'

'*Your word against mine. I* ——'

'You little fool. Haven't you ever been at a peeper trial? We don't run
'em like a court of law, where you sweat and then I swear and then a
jury tries to figure who's lying. No, little Gus. You stand up there before
the board and all the 1sts start probing. You're a 1st, Gus. Maybe
you could block two ... Possibly three ... But not all. I tell you, you're
dead.'

'*Wait a minute, Powell. Wait!*' The mannikin face was twitching with
terror. '*The Guild takes confession into account. Confession before the fact. I'll give
you everything right now. Everything. It was an aberration. I'm sane now. Tell the
Guild. When you get mixed up with a damned psychotic like Reich, you fall into
his pattern. You identify yourself with it. But I'm out of it. Tell the Guild. Here's
the whole picture ... He came to me with a nightmare about a Man With No Face.
He* ——'

'He was a patient?'

'*Yes. That's how he trapped me. He dragooned me! But I'm out of it now. Tell the Guild I'm cooperating. I've recanted. I'm volunteering everything. Church is your witness ...'*

'I'm not witness,' Church shouted, 'You dirty squealer. After Ben Reich promised ——'

'Shut up. You think I want permanent exile? Like you? You were crazy enough to trust Reich. Not me, thank you. I'm not that crazy.'

'I don't give a damn!' Tate cried. 'I don't take that kind of medicine for Reich. I'll bust him first. I'll walk into court and sit on the witness stand and do everything I can to help Powell. Tell that to the Guild, Linc. Tell them that ——'

'You'll do nothing of the kind,' Powell snapped.

'What?'

'You were trained by the Guild. You're still in the Guild. Since when does a peeper squeal on a patient?'

'It's the evidence you need to get Reich, isn't it?'

'Sure, but I'm not taking it from you. I'm not letting any peeper disgrace the rest of us by walking into court and blabbing.'

'It could mean your job if you don't get him.'

'To hell with my job. I want it, and I want Reich ... but not at this price. Any peeper can be a right pilot when the orbit's easy; but it takes guts to hold to the Pledge when the heat's on. You ought to know. You didn't have the guts. Look at you now ...'

'But I want to help you, Powell.'

'You can't help me. Not at the price of ethics.'

'But I was an accessory!' Tate shouted. 'You're letting me off. Is that ethics? Is that –?'

'Look at him,' Powell laughed. 'He's begging for Demolition. No, Gus. We'll get you when we get Reich. But I can't get him through you. I'll play this according to the Pledge.' He turned and left the circle of light. As he walked through the darkness towards the front door, he waited for Church to take the bait. He had played the entire scene for this moment alone ... but so far there was no action on his hook.

As Powell opened the door, flooding the pawnshop with the cold argent street light, Church suddenly called: 'Just a minute.'

Powell stopped, silhouetted against the door. 'Yes?'

'What have you been handing Tate?'

'The Pledge, Jerry. You ought to remember it.'

'Let me peep you on that.'

'Go ahead. I'm wide open.' Most of Powell's blocks opened. What was not good for Church to discover was carefully jumbled and camouflaged with tangentional associations and a kaleidoscopic pattern, but Church certainly could not locate a suspicious block.

'I don't know,' Church said at last. 'I can't make up my mind.'

'About what, Jerry? I'm not peeping you.'

'About you and Reich and the gun. God knows, you're a mealy-mouthed preacher, but I think maybe I'd be smarter to trust you.'

'That's nice, Jerry. I told you, I can't make any promises.'

'Maybe you're the kind that doesn't have to make promises. Maybe the whole trouble with me is that I've always been looking for promises instead of ——'

At that moment, Powell's restless radar picked up death out on the street. He whirled and slammed the door. *'Get off the floor. Quick.'* He took three steps back towards the globe of light and vaulted on to the counter. *'Up here with me. Jerry. Gus. Quick, you fools!'*

A queasy shuddering seized the pawnshop and shook into horrible vibration. Powell kicked the light globe and extinguished it.

'Jump for the ceiling light bracket and hold on. It's a Harmonic gun. Jump!' Church gasped and leaped up into the darkness. Powell gripped Tate's shaking arm. *'Too short, Gus? Hold out your hands. I'll toss you.'* He flung Tate upwards and followed himself, clawing for the steel spider arms of the bracket. The three hung in space, cushioned against the murderous vibrations enveloping the store ... vibrations that created shattering harmonics in every substance in contact with the floor. Glass, steel, stone, plastic ... all screeched and burst apart. They could hear the floor cracking, and the ceiling thundered. Tate groaned.

'Hang on, Gus. It's one of Quizzard's killers. Careless bunch. They've missed me before.'

Tate blacked out. Powell could sense every conscious synapse losing hold. He probed for Tate's lower levels: *'Hang on. Hang on. Hang on.* HOLD. HOLD. HOLD.'

Destruction loomed up in the little peeper's subconscious and in that instant Powell realized that no Guild conditioning could ever have prevented Tate from destroying himself. The death compulsion struck. Tate's hands relaxed and he dropped to the floor. The vibrations ceased an instant later, but in that second Powell heard the thick, gravid choke of bursting flesh. Church heard it too and started to scream.

'Quiet, Jerry! Not yet. Hang on!'

'D-did you hear him? DID YOU HEAR HIM?'

'I heard. We're not safe yet. Hang on!'

The pawnshop door opened a slit. A razor edge of light shot in and searched the floor. It found a broad red and grey organic puddle of flesh, blood, and bones, hovered for three seconds, then blinked out. The door closed.

'All right, Jerry. They think I'm dead again. You can have your hysterics now.'

'I can't get down, Powell. I can't step on ...'

'I don't blame you.' Powell held himself with one hand, took Church's arm and swung him towards the counter. Church dropped and shuddered. Powell followed him and fought hard against nausea.

'*Did you say that was one of Quizzard's killers?*'

'*Sure. He owns a squad of psychgoons. Every time we round 'em up and send 'em to Kingston, Quizzard gets another batch. They follow the dope trail to his place.*'

'*But what have they got against you? I* ——'

'*Clever up, Jerry. They're Ben's deputies. Ben's getting panicky.*'

'*Ben? Ben Reich? But it was in my shop. I might have been here.*'

'*You were here. What the hell difference did that make?*'

'*Reich wouldn't want me killed. He* ——'

'*Wouldn't he?*' Image of a cat smiling.

Church took a deep breath. Suddenly he exploded: 'The son of a bitch! The goddam son of a bitch!'

'Don't feel like that, Jerry. Reich's fighting for his life. You can't expect him to be too careful.'

'Well, I'm fighting, too, and that bastard's made up my mind for me. Get ready, Powell. I'm opening up. I'm going to give you everything.'

. . .

After he finished with Church and returned from Headquarters and the Tate nightmare, Powell was grateful for the sight of the blonde urchin in his home. Barbara D'Courtney had a black crayon in her right hand and a red crayon in her left. She was energetically scribbling on the walls, her tongue between her teeth and her dark eyes squinted in concentration.

'Baba!' he exclaimed in a shocked voice. 'What are you doing?'

'Drawrin pitchith,' she lisped. 'Nicth pitchith for Dada.'

'Thank you, sweetheart,' he said. 'That's a lovely thought. Now come and sit with Dada.'

'No,' she said, and continued scribbling.

'Are you my girl?'

'Yeth.'

'Doesn't my girl always do what Dada asks?'

She thought that one over. 'Yeth,' she said. She deposited the crayons in her pocket, her bottom on the couch alongside Powell, and her grubby paws in his hands.

'Really, Barbara,' Powell murmured. 'That lisping is beginning to worry me. I wonder if your teeth need braces?'

The thought was only half a joke. It was difficult to remember that this was a woman seated alongside him. He looked into the deep dark eyes shining with the empty brilliance of a crystal glass awaiting its fulfilling measure of wine.

Slowly he probed through the vacant conscious levels of her mind to the turbulent preconscious, heavily hung with obscuring clouds like a vast dark nebula in the heavens. Behind the clouds was the faint flicker of light, isolated and childlike, that he had grown to like. But now, as he threaded his way down, that flicker of light was the faint spicule of a star that burned with the hot roar of a nova.

Hello, Barbara. You seem to ——

He was answered with a burst of passion that made him backtrack fast.

'Hey, Mary!' he called. 'Come quick!'

Mary Noyes popped out of the kitchen. 'You in trouble again?'

'Not yet. Soon maybe. Our patient's on the mend.'

'I haven't noticed any difference.'

'Come on inside with me? She's made contact with her Id. Down on the lowest level. Almost had my brains burned out.'

'What do you want? A chaperone? Someone to protect the secrets of her sweet girlish passions?'

'Are you comic? I'm the one who needs protection. Come and hold my hand.'

'You've got both of yours in hers.'

'Just a figure of speech.' Powell glanced uneasily a the calm doll face before him and the cool relaxed hands in his. 'Let's go.'

He went down the black passages again towards the deep-seated furnace that was within the girl ... that is within every man ... the timeless reservoir of psychic energy, reasonless, remorseless, seething with the never-ending search for satisfaction. He could sense Mary Noyes mentally tiptoeing behind him. He stopped at a safe distance.

Hi, Barbara.

'Get out!'

This is the spook.

Hatred lashed out at him.

You remember me?

The hatred subsided into the turbulence to be replaced by a wave of hot desire.

'*Linc, you'd better jet. If you get trapped inside that pleasure-pain chaos, you're gone.*'

'*I'd like to locate something.*'

'*You can't find anything in there except raw love and raw death.*'

'*I want her relations with her father. I want to know why he had those guilt sensations about her.*'

'*Well, I'm getting out.*'

The furnace fumed over again. Mary fled.

Powell teetered around the edge of the pit, feeling, exploring, sensing. It was like an electrician gingerly touching the ends of exposed wires to discover which of them did not carry a knockout charge. A blazing bolt surged near him. He touched it, was stunned, and stepped aside to feel a blanket of instinctual self-preservation choke him. He relaxed, permitted himself to be drawn down into a vortex of associations and began sorting. He struggled to maintain his frame of reference that was crumbling in that chaos of energy.

Here were the somatic messages that fed the cauldron; cell reactions by the incredible billion, organic cries, the muted drone of muscletone, sensory sub-currents, bloodflow, the wavering superheterodyne of blood pH ... all whirling and churning in the balancing pattern that formed the girl's psyche. The never-ending make-and-break of synapses contributed a crackling hail of complex rhythms. Packed in the changing interstices were broken images, half-symbols, partial references ... The ionized nuclei of thought.

Powell caught part of Plosive image, followed it to the letter P ... to the sensory association of a kiss, then by cross-circuit to the infant's sucking reflex at the breast ... to an infantile memory of ... her mother? No. A wet-nurse. That was encrusted with parental associations ... Negation. Minus Mother ... Powell dodged an associated flame of infantile rage and resentment, the Orphan's Syndrome. He picked up P again, searched for a related Pa ... Papa ... Father.

Abruptly he was face to face with himself.

He stared at the image, teetered on the verge of disintegration, then scrambled back to sanity.

Who the hell are you?

The image smiled beautifully and was gone.

P ... Pa ... Papa ... Father. Heat-of-love-and-devotion-associated-with ... He was face to face with his image again. This time it was nude, powerful; its outlines haloed with an aura of love and desire. Its arms outstretched.

Get lost. You embarrass me.

The image disappeared. *Damn it! Has she fallen in love with me?*

'Hi, spook.'

There was her picture of herself, pathetically caricatured, the blonde hair in strings, the dark eyes like blotches, the lovely figure drawn into flat, ungracious planes ... It faded, and abruptly the image of Powell-Powerful-Protective-Paternal rushed at him, torrentially destructive. He stayed with it, grappling. The back of the head was D'Courtney's face. He followed the Janus image down to a blazing channel of doubles, pairs, linkages and duplicities to – Reich? Imposs – Yes, Ben Reich and the caricature of Barbara, linked side to side like Siamese twins, brother and sister from the waist upwards, their legs turning and twisting separately in a sea of complexity below. B linked to B.B. & B. Barbara & Ben. Half joined in blood. Half ——

'*Linc!*'

A call far off. Directionless.

'*Lincoln!*'

It could wait a second. That amazing image of Reich had to ——

'*Lincoln Powell! This way, you fool!*'

'*Mary?*'

'*I can't find you.*'

'*Be out in a few minutes.*'

'*Linc, this is the third time I've tried to locate you. If you don't come out now, you're lost.*'

'*The third time?*'

'*In three hours. Please, Linc ... While I've got the strength.*'

He permitted himself to wander upwards. He could not find upwards. The timeless, spaceless chaos roared around him. The image of Barbara D'Courtney appeared, now a caricature of the sexual siren.

'Hi, spook.'

'*Lincoln, for the love of God!*'

In momentary panic, he plunged in any direction until his peeper training reasserted itself. Then the Withdrawal Technique went into automatic operation. The blocks banged down in steady sequence; each barrier a step backward towards the light. Halfway up, he sensed Mary alongside him. She stayed with him until he was once more in his living-room, seated alongside the urchin, her hands in his. He dropped the hands as though they were red hot.

'*Mary, I located the weirdest association with Ben Reich. Some kind of linkage that ——*'

Mary had an iced towel. She slapped his face with it smartly. He realized that he was shaking.

'*Only trouble is ... Trying to make sense out of fragments in the Id is like trying to run a qualitative analysis in the middle of a sun ...*'

The towel flicked again.

'*You aren't working with unit elements. You're working with ionized particles ...*' He dodged the towel and stared at Barbara. '*My God, Mary, I think this poor kid's in love with me.*'

Image of a cockeyed turtle dove.

'*No kidding. I kept meeting myself down there. I ——*'

'*And what about you?*'

'*Me?*'

'Why do you think you refused to send her to Kingston Hospital?' she said. 'Why do you think you've been peeping her twice a day since you brought her here? Why did you have to have a chaperone? I'll tell you, Mr Powell ...'

'Tell me what?'

'You're in love with her. You've been in love with her since you found her at Chooka Frood's.'

'Mary!'

She stung him with a vivid picture of himself and Barbara D'Courtney and that fragment she had peeped days ago ... The fragment that had made her turn pale with jealousy and anger. Powell knew it was true.

'*Mary, dear ...*'

'Never mind me. To hell with me. You're in love with her, and the girl isn't a peeper. She isn't even sane. How much of her are you in love with? One tenth? What part of her are you in love with? Her face? Her subconscious? What about the other ninety per cent? Will you love that when you find it? Damn you! I wish I'd let you stay inside her mind until you rotted!' She turned away and began to cry.

'*Mary, for the love of ——*'

'Shut up,' she sobbed. 'Damn you, shut up! I ... There's a message for you. From headquarters. You're to jet for Spaceland as soon as possible. Ben Reich's there, and they've lost him. They need you. Everybody needs you. So why should I complain?'

CHAPTER 12

It was ten years since Powell had last visited Spaceland. He sat in the police launch that had picked him off the luxury Ship *Holiday Queen*, and as the launch dropped, Powell stared through the port at Spaceland glittering below like a patchwork quilt worked in silver and gold. He smiled as he always did at the identical image that came to him each time he saw the playground in space. It was a vision of a shipload of explorers from a far galaxy, strange creatures, solemn and studious, who stumbled on Spaceland and researched it. He always tried to imagine how they'd report it and always failed.

'It's a job for Dishonest Abe,' he muttered.

Spaceland had started several generations back with a flat plate of asteroid rock half a mile in diameter. A mad health-cultist had raised a transparent hemisphere of Air-Gel on the plate, installed an atmosphere generator, and started a colony. From that, Spaceland had grown into an irregular table in space, extending hundreds of miles. Each new entrepreneur had simply tacked another mile or so on to the shelf, raised his own transparent hemisphere, and gone into business. By the time engineers got around to advising Spaceland that the spherical form was more efficient and economical, it was too late to change. The table just went on proliferating.

As the launch swung around, the sun caught Spaceland at an angle, and Powell could see the hundreds of hemispheres shimmering against the blue-black of space like a mass of soap bubbles on a chequered table. The original health colony was now in the centre and still in business. The others were hotels, amusement parks, health resorts, nursing homes, and even a cemetery. On the Jupiter side of the table was the giant fifty-mile hemisphere that covered the Spaceland Nature Reservation which guaranteed more natural history and more weather per square mile than any natural planet.

'Let's have the story,' Powell said.

The police sergeant gulped. 'We followed instructions,' he said. 'Rough Tail on Hassop. Slickie following him. The Rough got taken out by Reich's girl ...'

'It *was* a girl, eh?'

'Yeah. Cute little trick named Duffy Wyg&.'

'Damnation!' Powell jerked bolt upright. The sergeant stared at him. 'Why, I questioned that girl myself. I never ——' He caught himself. 'Seems like I did some lousing myself. Shows you. When you meet a pretty girl ...' He shook his head.

'Well, like I say,' the sergeant continued, 'she takes out the Rough, and just when the Slickie moves in, Reich jets into Spaceland with a commotion.'

'Like?'

'Private yacht. Has a crash in space and limps in hollerin' emergency. One killed. Three injured, including Reich. Front of the yacht stove in. Derelict or meteor stray. They take Reich to the hospital where we figure he's planted for a little. When we turn around, Reich's gone. Hassop too. I grab a peeper interpreter and go looking in four languages. No dice.'

'Hassop's luggage?'

'Gone likewise.'

'Damnation! We've got to pinch Hassop and that luggage. They're our Motive. Hassop is Monarch's Code Chief. We need him for that last message Reich sent to D'Courtney and the reply ...'

'Monday before the murder?'

'Yes. That exchange probably ignited the killing. And Hassop may have Reich's financial records with him. They can probably tell a court why Reich had a hell of a motive for murdering D'Courtney.'

'Such as, for instance?'

'The talk around Monarch is that D'Courtney had Reich with his back to the wall.'

'You got Method and Opportunity?'

'Yes and no. I opened up Jerry Church and got everything, but it's ticklish. We can show Reich had the opportunity. It'll stand if the other two stand. We can show Reich had the opportunity. It'll stand if the other two stand. We can show the murder method. It'll stand if the other two stand. Same goes for Reich's Motive. They're like three wigwam poles. Each of them needs the other two. No one can stand alone. That's Old Man Mose's opinion. And that's why we need Hassop.'

'I'll swear they ain't left Spaceland. That efficient I still am.'

'Don't hang your head because Reich outsmarted you. He's outsmarted plenty. Me included.'

The sergeant shook his head gloomily.

'I'll start peeping Spaceland for Reich and Hassop at once,' Powell said as the launch drifted down for the passage through the air-lock, 'but I want to check a hunch first. Show me the corpse.'

'What corpse?'

'From Reich's crash.'

In the police mortuary, displayed on an air-cushion in the stasis-freeze, the corpse was a mangled figure with dead white skin and a flaming red beard.

'Uh-huh,' Powell muttered. 'Keno Quizzard.'

'You know him?'

'A gimpster. Was working for Reich and turned too hot to be useful. What'll you be that crash was a cover-up for a killing.'

'Hell!' the cop exploded, 'those two other guys are hurt bad. Reich might have been faking. Admitted. But the yacht was ruined, and those two other guys –'

'So they were hurt. And the yacht was ruined. So what? Quizzard's mouth is shut for keeps and Reich's that much safer. Reich took care of him. We'll never prove it, but we won't have to if we locate Hassop. That'll be enough to walk friend Reich into Demolition.'

Wearing the fashionable spray-gun-tights (Spaceland sport clothes were being painted on, this year), Powell began a lightning tour of the bubbles ... Victoria Hotel, Sportsman's Hotel, Magic, Home from Home, Ye New Neu Babblesberg, The Martian (very chic), the Venusberg (very bawdy), and the other dozens ... Powell struck up conversations with strangers, described his dear old friends in half a dozen languages, and peeped gently to make sure they had the precise picture of Reich and Hassop before they answered. And then the answers. Negative. Always negative.

The peepers were easy ... and Spaceland was filled with them, at work and at play ... but always the reply was negative.

A Revival Meeting at Solar Rheims ... hundreds of chanting, genuflecting devotees participating in a kind of hopped-up Midsummer Morn festival. Reply Negative. Sailing Races in Mars from Home ... Cat boats and sloops skipping over the water in long hops like scaled stones. Reply

Negative. The Plastic Surgery Resort . . . hundreds of bandaged faces and bodies. Reply Negative. Free-Flight Polo. Reply Negative. Hot Sulphur Springs, White Sulphur Springs, Black Sulphur Springs, No Sulphur Springs . . . Replies Negative.

Discouraged and depressed, Powell dropped into Solar Dawn Cemetery. The cemetery looked like an English garden . . . all flagged paths and oak, ash and elm trees with tiny little plots of green grass. Muted music from costumed robot string quartets sawing away in strategic pavilions. Powell began to smile.

There was a faithful reproduction of the Notre Dame Cathedral in the centre of the cemetery. It was painstakingly labelled: Ye Wee Kirk O' Th' Glen. From the mouth of one of the gargoyles in the tower, a syrupy voice roared: 'SEE THE DRAMA OF THE GODS PORTRAYED IN VIBRANT ROBOT-ACTION IN YE WEE KIRK O' TH' GLEN. MOSES ON MT SINAI, THE CRUCIFIXION OF CHRIST, MOHAMMED AND THE MOUNTAIN, LAO TSE AND THE MOON, THE REVELATION OF MARY BAKER EDDY, THE ASCENSION OF OUR LORD BUDDHA, THE UNVEILING OF THE TRUE AND ONLY GOD GALAXY . . .' Pause and then a little more matter-of-factly: 'OWING TO THE SACRED NATURE OF THIS EXHIBIT, ADMISSION IS BY TICKET ONLY. TICKETS MAY BE PURCHASED FROM THE BAILIFF.' Pause, then another voice, injured and pleading: 'ATTENTION ALL WORSHIPPERS. ATTENTION ALL WORSHIPPERS. NO LOUD TALKING OR LAUGHTER . . . PLEASE!' A click, and another gargoyle began in another language. Powell burst out laughing.

'You ought to be ashamed of yourself,' a girl said behind him.

Without turning, Powell replied: 'I'm sorry. "No Loud Talking or Laughter." But don't you think this is the most ludicrous——' Then the pattern of her psyche hit him and he spun around. He was face to face with Duffy Wyg&.

'Well, Duffy!' he said.

Her frown changed to a look of perplexity, then to a quick smile. 'Mr Powell,' she exclaimed. 'The boy-sleuth. You still owe me a dance.'

'I owe you an apology,' Powell said.

'Delighted. Can't have enough of them. What's this one for?'

'Underestimating you.'

'The story of my life.' She linked arms and drew him along the path. 'Tell me how reason has finally prevailed. You took another look at me, and——?'

'I realized you're the cleverest person Ben Reich has working for him.'

'I am clever. I did do some work for Ben . . . but your compliment seems to have deep brooding undertones. Is there something?'

'The tail we had on Hassop.'

'Just a little more accent on the down-beat, please.'

'You took out our tail, Duffy. Congratulations.'

'Ah-ha! Hassop is your pet horse. A childhood accident robbed him of a horse's crowning glory. You substituted an artificial one which——'

'Clever-up, Duffy. That isn't going to travel far.'

'Then, boy-wonder, will you ream your tubes?' Her pert face looked up at him, half-serious, half amused. 'What in hell are you talking about?'

'I'll spell it out. We had a tail on Hassop. A tail is a shadow, a spy, a secret agent assigned to the duty of following and watching a suspect . . .'

'Contents noted. What's a Hassop?'

'A man who works for Ben Reich. His Code Chief.'

'And what did I do to your spy?'

'Following instructions from Ben Reich, you captivated the man, enravished him, turned him into a derelict from duty, kept him at a piano all day, day after day, and——'

'Wait a minute!' Duffy spoke sharply. 'I know that one. The little bum. Let's square this off. He was a cop?'

'Now Duffy, if——'

'I asked a question.'

'He was a cop.'

'Following this Hassop?'

'Yes.'

'Hassop . . . Bleached man? Dusty hair? Dusty blue eyes?'

Powell nodded.

'The louse,' Duffy muttered. 'The low-down louse!' She turned on Powell furiously. 'And you think I'm the kind that does his dirty work, do you! Why, you – you peeper! You listen to me, Powell. Reich asked me to do him a favour. Said there was a man up here working on an interesting musical code. Wanted me to check him. How the hell was I supposed to know he was your goon? How was I supposed to know your goon was masquerading as a musician?'

Powell stared at her. 'Are you claiming that Reich tricked you?'

'What else?' She glared back. 'Go ahead and peep me. If Reich wasn't in the Reservation you could peep that double-crossing——'

'Hold it!' Powell interrupted sharply. He slipped past her conscious barrier and peeped her precisely and comprehensively for ten seconds. Then he turned and began to run.

'Hey!' Duffy yelled. 'What's the verdict?'

'Medal of Honour,' Powell called over his shoulder. 'I'll pin it on as soon as I bring a man back alive.'

'I don't want a man. I want you.'

'That's your trouble, Duffy. You want anybody.'

'Whooooo?'

'An-y-bod-y.'
'NO LOUD TALKING OR LAUGHTER ... PLEASE!'

Powell found his police sergeant in the Spaceland Globe Theatre
where a magnificent Esper actress stirred thousands with her moving
performances – performances that owed as much to her telepathic sensitivity to audience response as to her exquisite command of stage technique. The cop, immune to the star's appeal, was gloomily inspecting the
house, face by face. Powell took his arm and led him out.

'He's in the Reservation,' Powell told him. 'Took Hassop with
him. Took Hassop's luggage too. Perfect alibi. He was shaken up by
the crash and he needs a rest. Also company. He's eight hours ahead of
us.'

'The Reservation, huh?' the sergeant pondered. 'Twenty-five hundred
square miles of more damned animals, geography, and weather than you
ever see in three lives.'

'What's the odds Hassop has a fatal accident, if he hasn't had one
already?'

'No takers at any price.'

'If we want to get Hassop out we'll have to grab a Helio and do some
fast hunting.'

'Uh-uh. No mechanical transportation allowed in the Reservation.'

'This is an emergency. Old Man Mose has got to have Hassop!'

'Go let that damn machine argue with the Spaceland Board. You
could get special permission in maybe three, four weeks.'

'By which time Hassop'd be dead and buried. What about Radar or
Sonar? We could work out Hassop's pattern and——'

'Uh-uh. No mechanical devices outside of cameras allowed in the
Reservation.'

'What the hell plays with that Reservation?'

'Hundred per cent guaranteed pure nature for the eager beavers. You
go in at your own risk. Element of danger adds spice to your trip. Get
the picture? You battle the elements. You battle the wild animals. You
feel primitive and refreshed again. That's what the ads say.'

'What do they do in there? Rub sticks together?'

'Sure. You hike on your own feet. You carry your own food. You take
one Defensive Barrier Screen with you so's the bears don't eat you. If you
want a fire you got to build it. If you want to hunt animals, you got to
make your own weapons. If you want to catch fish, likewise. You versus
nature. And they make you sign a release in case nature wins.'

'Then how are we going to find Hassop?'

'Sign a release and go hike for him.'

'The two of us? Cover twenty-five hundred square miles of geography? How many squadmen can you spare?'

'Maybe ten?'

'Adding up to two hundred and fifty square miles per cop. Impossible.'

'Maybe you could persuade the Spaceland Board – No. Even if you could, we wouldn't be able to get the Board together under a week. Wait a minute! Could you get 'em together by peeping 'em? Send out urgent messages or something? How do you peepers work that way?'

'We can only pick you up. We can't transmit to anybody except another peeper, so – Hey! Ho! That's an idea!'

'What's an idea?'

'Is a human being a mechanical device?'

'Nope.'

'Is he a civilized invention?'

'Not lately.'

'Then I'm going to do some fast co-opting and take my own Radar into the Reservation.'

Which is why a sudden craving for nature overtook a prominent lawyer in the midst of delicate contractual negotiations in one of Spaceland's luxurious conference rooms. The same craving also came upon the secretary of a famous author, a judge of domestic relations, a job analyst screening applicants for the United Hotel Association, an industrial designer, an efficiency engineer, the Chairman of Amalgamated Union's Grievance Committee, Titan's Superintendent of Cybernetics, a Secretary of Political Psychology, two Cabinet members, five Parliamentary Leaders, and scores of other Esper clients of Spaceland at work and at play.

They filed through the Reservation Gate in a unified mood of holiday festivity and assorted gear. Those that had got word on the grapevine early enough were in sturdy camping clothes. Others were not; and the astonished gate guards, checking and inspecting for illicit baggage, saw one lunatic in full diplomatic regalia march through with a pack on his back. But all the nature-lovers carried detailed maps of the Reservation carefully zoned into sectors.

Moving swiftly, they spread out and beat forward across the miniature continent of weather and geography. The TP Band crackled as comments and information swept up and down the line of living radar in which Powell occupied the central position.

'*Hey. No fair. I've got a mountain dead ahead.*'

'*Snowing here. Full b-b-blizzard.*'

'*Swamps and (ugh!) mosquitoes in my sector.*'

'*Hold it. Party ahead, Linc. Sector 21.*'

'Shoot a picture.'
'Here it is ...'
'Sorry. No sale.'
'Party ahead. Linc, Sector 9.'
'Let's have the picture.'
'Here it comes ...'
'Nope. No sale.'
'Party ahead, Linc. Sector 17.'
'Shoot a picture.'
'Hey! It's a goddam bear!'
'Don't run! Negotiate!'
'Party ahead, Linc. Sector 12.'
'Shoot a picture.'
'Here it comes ...'
'No sale.'
'A A A A A A A-Choo!'
'That the blizzard?'
'No. I'm a cloud-burst.'
'Party ahead, Linc. Sector 41.'
'Shoot a picture.'
'Here it is.'
'Not them.'
'How do you climb a palm tree?'
'You shinny up.'
'Not up. Down.'
'How'd you get up, your honour?'
'I don't know. A moose helped me.'
'Party ahead, Linc. Sector 37.'
'Let's have a picture.'
'Here it comes.'
'No sale.'
'Party ahead, Linc. Sector 60.'
'Go ahead.'
'Here's the picture ...'
'Pass 'em by.'
'How long do we have to keep on travelling?'
'They're at least eight hours ahead.'
'No. Correction, peepers. They've got eight hours start but they may not be eight hours ahead.'
'Spell that out, will you, Linc.'
'Reich may not have trekked straight ahead. He may have circled around to a favourite spot close to the Gate.'
'Favourite for what?'

'*For murder.*'

'*Excuse me. How does one persuade a cat not to devour one?*'

'*Use Political Psychology.*'

'*Use your Barrier Screen, Mr Secretary.*'

'*Party ahead, Linc. Sector 1.*'

'*Shoot a picture, Mr Superintendent.*'

'*Here it is.*'

'*Pass 'em by, sir. That's Reich and Hassop.*'

'*WHAT!*'

'*Don't make a fuss. Don't make anybody suspicious. Just pass 'em by. When you're out of sight, circle round to Sector 2. Everybody head back for the Gate and go home. All my thanks. From here on I'll take it alone.*'

'*Leave us in on the kill, Linc.*'

'*No. This needs finesse. I don't want Reich to know I'm abducting Hassop. It's all got to look logical and natural and unimpeachable. It's a swindle.*'

'*And you're the thief to do it.*'

'*Who stole the weather, Powell?*'

The departing peepers were propelled by a hot blush.

This particular square mile of Reservation was jungle, humid, swampy, overgrown. As darkness fell, Powell slowly wormed his way towards the glimmering camp fire Reich had built in a clearing alongside a small lake. The water was infested with hippo, crocodile, and swambat. The trees and terrain swarmed with life. The entire junglette was a savage tribute to the brilliance of Reservation ecologists who could assemble and balance nature on the point of a pin. And in tribute to that nature, Reich's Defensive Barrier Screen was in full operation.

Powell could hear mosquitoes whine as they batted against the outer rim of the barrier, and there was an intermittent hail of larger insects caroming off the invisible wall. Powell could not risk operating his own. The screens hummed slightly and Reich had keen ears. He inched forward and peeped.

Hassop was at ease, relaxed, just a little beglamoured by the idea of intimacy with his puissant chief, just a little intoxicated by the knowledge that his film canister contained Ben Reich's fate. Reich, working feverishly on a crude, powerful bow, was planning the accident that would eliminate Hassop. It was that bow and the sheaf of fire-tipped arrows alongside Reich that had eaten up the eight hours start on Powell. You can't kill a man in a hunting accident unless you go hunting.

Powell lifted to his knees and crawled forward, his senses pinpointed on Reich's perception. He froze again as ALARM clanged in Reich's head. Reich leaped to his feet, bow ready, a featherless arrow at half-cock, and peered intently into the darkness.

'What is it, Ben?' Hassop murmured.

'I don't know. Something.'

'Hell. You've got your Barrier, haven't you?'

'I keep forgetting.' Reich sank back and built up the fire; but he was not forgetting the Barrier. The wary instinct of the killer was warning him, vaguely, persistently ... And Powell could only marvel at the intricate survival mechanism of the human mind. He peeped Reich again. Reich was mechanically resorting to the tune-block he associated with crisis: *Tenser, said the Tensor. Tenser, said the Tensor. Tension, apprehension, and dissension have begun.* Behind that there was turmoil; a mounting resolution to kill quickly ... kill savagely ... destroy now and arrange the evidence later ...

As Reich reached for the bow, his eyes carefully averted from Hassop, his mind intent on the throbbing heart that was his target, Powell drove forward urgently. Before he had moved ten feet, ALARM tripped again in Reich's mind and the big man was on his feet once more. This time he whipped a burning branch from the fire and hurled the flare towards the blackness where Powell was concealed. The idea and execution came so quickly that Powell could not anticipate the action. He would have been fully illumined if Reich had not forgotten the Barrier. It stopped the flaming branch in mid-flight and dropped it to the ground.

'Christ!' Reich cried, and swung around abruptly at Hassop.

'What is it, Ben?'

In answer, Reich drew the arrow back to the lobe of his ear and held the point on Hassop's body. Hassop scrambled to his feet.

'Ben, watch out! You're shooting at me!'

Hassop leaped to one side unexpectedly as Reich let the arrow fly.

'Ben! For the love of——' Suddenly Hassop realized the intent. He turned with a strangulated cry and ran from the fire as Reich notched another arrow. Running desperately, Hassop smashed into the Barrier and staggered back from the invisible wall as an arrow shot past his shoulder and shattered.

'Ben!' he screamed.

'You son of a bitch,' Reich growled, and notched another shaft.

Powell leaped forward and reached the edge of the Barrier. He could not pass it. Inside, Hassop ran screaming across the far side while Reich stalked him with half-cocked bow, closing in for the kill. Hassop again smashed into the Barrier, fell, crawled, and regained his feet to dart off again like a cornered rat, Reich followed him doggedly.

'Jesus!' Powell muttered. He stepped back into the darkness, thinking desperately. Hassop's screams had aroused the jungle, and there was a roaring and an echoing rumble in his ears. He reached out on the TP Band, sensing, touching, feeling. There was nothing but blind fear, blind rage, blind instinct around him. The hippos, sodden and viscid ... the crocodiles, deaf, angry, hungry ... swambats, as furious as rhinoceri whose size they doubled ... A quarter mile off were the faint broadcasts of elephant, wapiti, giant cats ...

'It's worth the chance,' Powell said to himself. 'I've got to bust that Barrier. It's the only way.'

He set his blocks on the upper levels, masking everything except the emotional broadcast, and transmitted: *fear, fear, terror, fear* ... driving the emotion down to its most primitive level ... *Fear, Fear. Terror. Fear* ... FEAR – FLIGHT – TERROR – *FEAR – FLIGHT – TERROR* – FLIGHT!

Every bird in every roost awoke screaming. The monkeys screamed back and shook thousands of branches in sudden flight. A barrage of sucking explosions sounded from the lake as the herd of hippos surged up from the shallows in blind terror. The jungle was shaken by the ear-splitting trumpetings of elephants and the crashing thunder of their stampede. Reich heard and froze in his tracks, ignoring Hassop who still ran and sobbed and screamed from wall to wall of the Barrier.

The hippos hit the Barrier first in a blind, blundering rush. They were followed by the swambats and the crocodiles. Then came the elephants. Then the wapiti, the zebra, the gnu ... heavy, pounding herds. There had never been such a stampede in the history of the Reservation. Nor had the manufacturers of the Defensive Barrier Screen ever anticipated such a concerted mass attack. Reich's Barrier went down with a sound like scissored glass.

The hippos trampled the fire, scattered it and extinguished it. Powell darted through the darkness, seized Hassop's arm, and dragged the crazed creature across the clearing to the piled packs. A wild hoof sent him reeling, but he held on to Hassop and located the precious film canister. In the frantic blackness Powell could sort the frenzied TP broadcasts of the stampeding animals. Still dragging Hassop, he threaded his way out of the main stream. Behind the thick bole of a *lignum vitae* Powell paused to catch his breath and settle the canister safely in his pocket. Hassop was still sobbing. Powell sensed Reich, a hundred feet away, back against a fever tree, bow and arrows clutched in his stricken hands. He was confused, furious, terrified ... but still safe. Above all, Powell wanted to keep him safe for Demolition.

Unhitching his own Defensive Barrier Screen, Powell tossed it across the clearing towards the embers of the fire where Reich would surely find it. Then he turned and led the numb, unresisting Code Chief towards the Gate.

CHAPTER 13

The Reich case was ready for final submission to the District Attorney's office. Powell hoped it was also ready for that cold-blooded, cynical monster of facts and evidence, Old Man Mose.

Powell and his staff assembled in Mose's office. A round table had been set up in the centre, and on it was constructed a transparent model of the key rooms of Beaumont House, inhabited by miniature android models of the *dramatis personae*. The lab's model division had done a superlative job, and actually had characterized the leading players. The tiny Reich, Tate, Beaumont, and others moved with the characteristic gaits of their originals. Alongside the table was massed the documentation the staff had prepared, ready for presentation to the machine.

Old Man Mose himself occupied the entire circular wall of the giant office. His multitudinous eyes winked and glared coldly. His multitudinous memories whirred and hummed. His mouth, the cone of a speaker, hung open in a kind of astonishment at human stupidity. His hands, the keys of a multiflex typewriter, poised over a roll of tape, ready to hammer out logic. Mose was the Mosaic Multiplex Prosecution Computor of the District Attorney's Office, whose awful decisions controlled the preparation, presentation, and prosecution of every police case.

'We won't bother Mose to start with,' Powell told the D.A. 'Let's take a look at the models and check them against the Crime Schedule. Your staff has the time sheets. Just watch them while the dolls go through the motions. If you catch anything our gang's missed, make a note and we'll kick it around.'

He nodded to De Santis, the harassed Lab Chief, who inquired in an overwrought voice: 'One to one?'

'That's a little fast. Make it one to two. Half slow motion.'

'The androids look unreal at that tempo,' De Santis snarled. 'It can't do them justice. We slaved for two weeks and now you——'

'Never mind. We'll admire them later.'

De Santis verged on mutiny, then touched a button. Instantly the model was illumined and the dolls came to life. Acoustics had faked a background. There was a hint of music, laughter, and chatter. In the main hall of Beaumont House, a pneumatic model of Maria Beaumont slowly climbed to a dais with a tiny book in her hands.

'The time is 11.09 at that point,' Powell said to the D.A.'s staff. 'Watch the clock above the model. It's geared to synchronize with the slow motion.'

In rapt silence, the legal division studied the scene and jotted notes while the androids reproduced the actions of the fatal Beaumont party. Once again Maria Beaumont read the rules of the Sardine game from the dais in the main hall of Beaumont House. The lights dimmed and went out. Ben Reich slowly threaded his way through the main hall to the music room, turned right, mounted the stairs to the Picture Gallery, passed through the bronze doors leading to the Orchid Suite, blinded and stunned the Beaumont guards, and then entered the suite.

And again Reich met D'Courtney face to face, closed with him, drew a deadly knife-pistol from his pocket and with the blade pried D'Courtney's mouth open while the old man hung weak and unresisting. And again a door of the Orchid Suite burst open to reveal Barbara D'Courtney in a frost-white transparent dressing gown. And she and Reich feinted and dodged until Reich suddenly blew the back of D'Courtney's head out with a shot through the mouth.

'Got that material from the D'Courtney girl,' Powell murmured. 'Peeped her. It's authentic.'

Barbara D'Courtney crawled to the body of her father, seized the gun and suddenly dashed out of the Orchid Suite, followed by Reich. He pursued her down into the darkened house and lost her as she darted out through the front entrance into the street. Then Reich met Tate and they marched to the Projection Room, pretending to play Sardine. The drama came to an end at last with the stampede of the guests up to the Orchid Suite where the dolls burst in and crowded around the tiny dead body. There they froze in a grotesque little tableau.

There was a long pause while the legal staff digested the drama.

'All right,' Powell said. 'That's the picture. Now let's feed the data to Mose for an opinion. First, Opportunity. You won't deny that the Sardine game provided Reich with perfect opportunity?'

'How'd Reich know they were going to play Sardine?' the D.A. muttered.

'Reich bought the book and sent it to Maria Beaumont. He provided his own Sardine game.'

'How'd he know she'd play the game?'

'He knew she liked games. Sardine was the only legible game in the book.'

'I don't know ...' The D.A. scratched his head. 'Mose takes a lot of convincing. Feed it to him. Won't do any harm.'

The office door banged open and Commissioner Crabbe marched in as though heading a parade.

'Mr Prefect Powell,' Crabbe pronounced formally.

'Mr Commissioner?'

'It has come to my attention, sir, that you are perverting that mechanical brain for the purpose of implicating my good friend, Ben Reich, in the foul and dastardly murder of Craye D'Courtney. Mr Powell, such a purpose is grotesque. Ben Reich is an honourable and leading citizen of our country. Furthermore, sir, I have never approved of that mechanical brain. You were chosen by the electorate to exercise your intellectual powers, not bow in slavery to that——'

Powell nodded to Beck, who began feeding the punched data into Mose's ear. 'You're absolutely right, Commissioner. Now, about the Method. First question: How'd Reich knock out the guard, De Santis?'

'And furthermore, gentlemen . . .' Crabbe continued.

'Rhodopsin Ionizer,' De Santis spat. He picked up a plastic sphere and tossed it to Powell who exhibited it. 'Man named Jordan developed it for Reich's private police. I've got the empiric processing formula ready for the Computor, and the sample we mocked up. Anybody care to try it?'

The D.A. looked dubious. 'I don't see the use. Mose can make up his own mind about that.'

'In addition to which, gentlemen . . .' Crabbe summarized.

'Oh come on,' De Santis said with unpleasant cheerfulness. 'You'll never believe us unless you see it for yourself. It doesn't hurt. Just makes you *non compos* for six or seven——'

The plastic bulb shattered in Powell's fingers. A vivid blue light flared under Crabbe's nose. Caught in mid-oration, the Commissioner collapsed like an empty sack. Powell looked round in horror.

'Good Heavens!' he exclaimed. 'What *have* I done? That bulb simply melted in my fingers.' He looked at De Santis and spoke severely. 'You made the covering too thin, De Santis. Now see what you've done to Commissioner Crabbe.'

'What *I've* done!'

'Feed that data to Mose,' the D.A. said in a voice rigid with control. 'This I know he'll buy.'

They made the Commissioner's body comfortable in a deep chair. 'Now, the murder method,' Powell continued. 'Kindly watch this, gentlemen. The hand is quicker than the eye.' He exhibited a revolver from the police museum. From the chambers he removed the shells, and from one of the shells he extracted the bullet. 'This is what Reich did to the gun Jerry Church gave him before the murder. Pretended to make it safe. A phoney alibi.'

'Phoney, hell! That gun *is* safe. Is that Church's evidence?'

'It is. Look at your sheet.'

'Then you don't have to bother Mose with the problem.' The D.A. threw his papers down in disgust. 'We haven't got a case.'

'Yes, we have.'

'How can a cartridge kill without a bullet? Your sheet doesn't say anything about Reich reloading.'

'He reloaded.'

'He did not,' De Santis spat. 'There was no projectile in the wound or the room. There was nothing.'

'There was everything. It was easy once I figured the clue.'

'There was no clue!' De Santis shouted.

'Why, you located it, De Santis. That bit of candy gel in D'Courtney's mouth. Remember? And no candy in the stomach.'

De Santis glared, Powell grinned. He took an eye-dropper and filled a gel capsule with water. He pressed it into the open end of the cartridge above the charge and placed the cartridge in the gun. He raised the gun, aimed at a small wooden block on the edge of the model table, and pulled the trigger. There was a dull, flat explosion and the block leaped into fragments.

'For the love of—— That was a trick!' The D.A. exclaimed. 'There was something in that shell besides water.' He examined the fragments of wood.

'No, there was not. You can shoot an ounce of water with a powder charge. You can shoot it with enough muzzle velocity to blow out the back of a head if you fire through the soft roof of the mouth. That's why Reich had to shoot through the mouth. That's why De Santis found the bit of gel. That's why he found nothing else. The projectile was gone.'

'Give it to Mose,' the D.A. said faintly. 'By God, Powell, I'm beginning to think we've got a case.'

'All right. Now, Motive. We picked up Reich's business records, and Accounting's gone through them. D'Courtney had Reich with his back to the wall. With Reich it was "if you can't lick 'em, join 'em". He tried to join D'Courtney. He failed. He murdered D'Courtney. Will you buy that?'

'Sure I'll buy it. But will Old Man Mose? Feed it in and let's see.'

They fed in the last of the punched data, warmed the computor up from 'Idle' to 'Run', and kicked him into it. Mose's eyes blinked in hard meditation; his stomach rumbled softly; his memories began to hiss and stutter. Powell and the others waited with mounting suspense. Abruptly, Mose hiccupped. A soft bell began to 'Ping-Ping-Ping-Ping-Ping-Ping –' and Mose's type began to flail the virgin tape under it.

'IF IT PLEASE THE COURT,' Moses said. 'WITH PLEADERING OF NON VULTS AND DEMURRERS, SIGNATURES. SS. LEADING CASE HAY V. COHOES AND THE RULE IN SHELLEY'S CASE. URP.'

'What the——' Powell looked at Beck.

'He gets kittenish,' Beck explained.

'At a time like this!'

'Happens now and then. We'll try him again.'

They filled the computor's ear again, held the warm-up for a good five minutes and then kicked him into it. Once again his eyes blinked, his stomach growled, his memories hissed, and Powell and the two staffs waited anxiously. A month's hard work hung on this decision. The typehammers began to fall.

'BRIEF #921,088. SECTION C-1. MOTIVE,' Mose said. 'PASSION MOTIVE FOR CRIME INSUFFICIENTLY DOCUMENTED, CF STATE V. HANRAHAN, 1202 SUP. COURT. 19, AND SUBSEQUENT LINE OF LEADING CASES.'

'Passion motive?' Powell muttered. 'Is Mose crazy? It's a profit motive. Check C-1, Beck.'

Beck checked. 'No mistake here.'

'Try him again.'

They ran the computor through it a third time. This time he spoke to the point: 'BRIEF #921,088. SECTION C-1. MOTIVE. PROFIT MOTIVE FOR CRIME INSUFFICIENTLY DOCUMENTED. CF STATE V. ROYAL 1197 SUP. COURT 388.'

'Didn't you punch C-1 properly?' Powell inquired.

'We got everything in that we could,' Beck replied.

'Excuse me,' Powell said to the others, 'I've got to peep this out with Beck. You don't mind, I hope.' He turned to Beck: '*Open up, Jackson. I smelled an evasion in them last words. Let me have it . . .*'

'*Honestly, Linc, I'm not aware of any———*'

'*If you were aware, it wouldn't be an evasion. It'd be a downright lie. Now lemme see . . . Oh. Of course! Idiot. You don't have to be ashamed because Code's a little slow.*' Powell spoke aloud to the staffs: 'Beck's missing one small datum point. Code's still working with Hassop upstairs trying to bust Reich's private code. So far all we've got is the knowledge that Reich offered merger and was refused. We haven't got the definite offer and refusal yet. That's what Mose wants. A cautious monster.'

'If you didn't bust the code, how do you know the offer was made and refused?' the D.A. asked.

'Got that from Reich himself through Gus Tate. It was one of the last things Tate gave me before he was murdered. I tell you what, Beck. Add an assumption to the tape. Assuming that our merger evidence is unassailable (which it is) what does Mose think of the case?'

Beck hand-punched a strip, spliced it to the main problem and fed it in again. By now well warmed up, the Mosaic Multiplex Computor answered in thirty seconds: 'BRIEF #921,088. ACCEPTING ASSUMPTION, PROBABILITY OF SUCCESSFUL PROSECUTION 97.0099%.'

Powell's staff grinned and relaxed. Powell tore the tape out of the typewriter and presented it to the D.A. with a flourish. 'And there's your case, Mr District Attorney . . . Sewn up and delivered.'

'By God!' the D.A. said. 'Ninety seven per cent! Jesus, we haven't had one in the ninety bracket all my term. I thought I was lucky when I broke seventy. Ninety seven percent . . . Against Ben Reich himself! Jesus!' He looked around at his staff in a kind of wild surmise. 'We'll make goddam history!'

The office door opened and two perspiring men darted in waving manuscript.

'Here's Code now,' Powell said. 'You bust it?'

'We busted it,' they said, 'and now you're busted, Powell. The whole case is busted.'

'What? What the hell are you talking about?'

'Reich knocked off D'Courtney because D'Courtney wouldn't merge, didn't he? He had a nice fat profit motive for killing D'Courtney, didn't he? In a pig's eye he did.'

'Oh God!' Beck groaned.

'Reich sent YYJI TTED RRCB UUFE AALK QQBA to D'Courtney. That reads: SUGGEST MERGER BOTH OUR INTERESTS EQUAL PARTNERSHIP.'

'Damn it, that's what I've said all along. And D'Courtney replied: WWHG. That was a refusal. Reich told Tate. Tate told me.'

'D'Courtney answered WWHG. That reads: ACCEPT OFFER.'

'The hell it does!'

'The hell it don't. WWHG. ACCEPT OFFER. It was the answer Reich wanted. It was the answer that gave Reich every reason for keeping D'Courtney alive. You'll never convince any court in the solar system that Reich had a motive for murdering D'Courtney. Your case is washed out.'

Powell stood stock still for half a minute, his fists clenched, his face working. Suddenly he turned on the model, reached in and pulled out the android figure of Reich. He twisted its head off. He went to Mose, yanked out the tapes of punched data, crumpled them into a wad and hurled the wad across the room. He strode to Crabbe's recumbent figure and launched a tremendous kick at the seat of the chair. While the staffs watched in an appalled silence, the chair and Commissioner overturned to the floor.

'God damn you! You're always sitting in that God damned chair!' Powell cried in a shaking voice and stormed out of the office.

CHAPTER 14

EXPLOSION! Concussion! The cell doors burst open. And far outside, freedom is waiting in the cloak of darkness and flight into the unknown ...

Who's that? Who's outside the cell-block? Oh God! Oh Christ! The Man With No Face! Looking. Looming. Silent. Run! Escape! Fly! Fly ...

Fly through space. There's safety in the solitude of this silver-lined launch jetting to the deeps of the distant unknown ... The hatch door! Opening. But it can't.

There's no one on this launch to swing it slowly, ominously . . . Oh God! The Man With No Face! Looking. Looming. Silent . . .

But I am innocent, your honour. Innocent. You will never prove my guilt, and I will never stop pleading my case though you pound your gavel until you deafen my ears and – Oh Christ! On the bench. In wig and gown. The Man With No Face. Looking. Looming. Quintessence of vengeance . . .

The pounding gavel dissolved to knuckles on the stateroom door. The steward's voice called: 'Over New York, Mr Reich. One hour to debarkation. Over New York, Mr Reich.' The knuckles went on hammering on the door.

Reich found his voice. 'All right,' he croaked. 'I hear you.'

The steward departed. Reich climbed out of the liquid bed and found his legs giving way. He clutched at the wall and cursed himself upright. Still in the grip of the nightmare's terror, he went into the bathroom, depilated, showered, steamed, and air-washed for ten minutes. He was still reeling. He stepped into the massage alcove and punched 'Glow-Salt'. Two pounds of moistened, scented salt were sprayed on his skin. As the massage buffers were about to begin, Reich suddenly decided he needed coffee. He stepped out of the alcove to ring Service.

There was a dull concussion and Reich was hurled to his face by the force of the explosion in the alcove. His back was slashed by flying particles. He darted into the bedroom, seized his travelling case, and turned like an animal at bay, his hands automatically opening the case and groping for the cartridge of Detonation Bulbs he always carried. There was no cartridge in the case.

Reich pulled himself together. He was aware of the bite of salt in the cuts in his back and the streaming blood. He was aware that he was no longer trembling. He went back into the bathroom, shut off the massage buffers and inspected the alcove wreckage. Someone had removed the cartridge from his case during the night and planted a bulb in each of the massage buffers. The empty cartridge lay behind the alcove. Only a split-second miracle had saved his life . . . from whom?

He inspected his state-room door. The lock had evidently been gaffed by a past-master. It showed no sign of tampering. But who? Why?

'Son of a bitch!' Reich growled. With iron nerve he returned to the bathroom, washed off the salt and blood, and sprayed his back with coagulant. He dressed, had his coffee, and descended to the Staging Hall where, after a savage skirmish with the peeper Customs Man (*Tension, apprehension, and dissension have begun!*), he boarded the Monarch launch that was waiting to take him down to the city.

From the launch he called Monarch Tower. His secretary's face appeared on the screen.

'Any news of Hassop?' Reich asked.

'No, Mr Reich. Not since you called from Spaceland.'

'Give me Recreation.'

The screen herring-boned and then disclosed the chrome lounge of Monarch. West, bearded and scholarly, was carefully binding sheets of typescript into plastic volumes. He looked up and grinned.

'Hello, Ben.'

'Don't look so cheerful, Ellery,' Reich growled. 'Where the hell is Hassop? I thought you'd surely——'

'Not my problem any more, Ben.'

'What are you talking about?'

West displayed the volumes. 'Just finishing up my work. History of my career with Monarch Utilities & Resources for your files. Said career ended this morning at nine o'clock.'

'What!'

'Yep. I warned you, Ben. The Guild's just ruled Monarch out of bounds for me. Company Espionage is unethical.'

'Listen, Ellery, you can't quit now. I'm on a hook and I need you bad. Someone tried to booby-trap me on the ship this morning. I beat it by an eyelash. I've got to find out who it is. I need a peeper.'

'Sorry, Ben.'

'You don't have to work for Monarch. I'll put you under personal contract for private service. The same contract Breen has.'

'Breen? A 2nd? The analyst?'

'Yes. My analyst.'

'Not any more.'

'What!'

West nodded. 'The ruling came down today. No more exclusive practice. It limits the service of peepers. We've got to be dedicated to the most good for the most people. You've lost Breen.'

'It's Powell!' Reich shouted. 'Using every dirty peeper trick he can dig out of the slime to bitch me. He's trying to nail me to the D'Courtney cross, the sneaking peeper! He——'

'Sign off, Ben. Powell had nothing to do with it. Let's break it off friendly, eh? We've always kept it pleasant. Let's break it pleasant. What do you say?'

'I say go to hell!' Reich roared and cut the connection. To the launch pilot he said in the same tone: 'Take me home!'

Reich burst into his penthouse apartment, once again awakening the hearts of his staff to terror and hatred. He hurled his travelling case at his valet and went immediately to Breen's suite. It was empty. A crisp note on the desk repeated the information West had already given him. Reich strode to his own rooms, went to the phone and dialled Gus Tate. The screen cleared and displayed a sign:

SERVICE PERMANENTLY DISCONTINUED

Reich stared, broke the connection and dialled Jerry Church. The screen cleared and displayed a sign:

SERVICE PERMANENTLY DISCONTINUED

Reich snapped the contact key up, paced around the study uncertainly, then went to the shimmer of light in the corner that was his safe. He switched the safe into temporal phase, revealing the honeycomb paper rack, and reached for the small red envelope in the upper left-hand pigeon hole. As he touched the envelope he heard the faint click. He doubled up and spun away, his face buried in his arms.

There was a blinding flash of light and a heavy explosion. Something brutal punched Reich in the left side, hurled him across the study and slammed him against the wall. Then a hail of debris followed. He struggled to his feet, bellowing in bewilderment and fury, stripping the ripped clothes from his left side to examine the state of his body. He was badly slashed, and a particularly excruciating pain indicated at least one broken rib.

He heard his staff come running down the corridor and roared: 'Keep out! You hear me? Keep out! All of you!'

He stumbled through the wreckage and began sorting over the remains of his safe. He found the neuron scrambler he had taken from Chooka Frood's red-eyed woman. He found the malignant steel flower that was the knife-pistol that had killed D'Courtney. It still contained four unfired shells loaded with water and sealed with gel. He thrust both into the pocket of a new jacket, got a fresh cartridge of Detonation Bulbs from his desk, and tore out of the room, ignoring the servants who stared at him in astonishment.

Reich swore feverishly all the way down from the tower apartment to the cellar garage where he deposited his private Jumper key in the Call slot and waited for the little car. When it came out of storage with the key in the door, another tenant was approaching and even at a distance was staring. Reich turned the key and yanked open the door to jump in. There was a low pressure Rrrrrrip. Reich hurled himself to the ground. The Jumper tank exploded. By some freak, it failed to burst into flame. It erupted a shattering geyser of raw fuel and fragments of twisting metal. Reich crawled frantically, reached the exit ramp, and ran for his life.

On the street level, torn, bleeding, rank with creosote fuel, he searched frantically for a Public Jumper. He couldn't find a coin-Jumper. He managed to flag a piloted machine.

'Where to?' the driver asked.

Reich dabbed dazedly at the blood and oil that smeared him. 'Chooka Frood!' he croaked in a hysterical voice.

The cab hopped him to 99 Bastion West.

Reich thrust past the protesting doorman, the indignant reception clerk, and Chooka Frood's highly paid *chargé d'affaires* to the private office, a Victorian room furnished with stained glass lamps, overstuffed sofas and a roll-top desk. Chooka was seated at the desk, wearing a dingy smock and a dingy expression that changed to alarm when Reich yanked the scrambler out of his pocket.

'For God's sake, Reich!' she exclaimed.

'Here I am, Chooka,' he said hoarsely. 'So let's have the trial run before we feed it to the dice. I used this scrambler on you once before. I'm warmed up for it again. You warmed me up, Chooka.'

She shot up from the desk and screamed: 'Magda!'

Reich caught her by the arm and hurled her across the office. She sideswiped the couch and fell across it. The red-eyed bodyguard came running into the office. Reich was ready for her. He clubbed her across the back of the neck, and as she fell forward, he ground his heel into her back and slammed her flat on the floor. The woman twisted and clawed at his leg. Ignoring her he spat at Chooka: 'Let's get it squared off. Why the booby-traps?'

'What are you talking about?' Chooka cried.

'What the hell do I look like I'm talking about. Read the blood, lady. I've skinned out of three obituaries running. How long can my luck hold out?'

'Make sense, Reich! I can't——'

'I'm talking about the big D, Chooka, D for death. I came in here and strong-armed the D'Courtney girl out of you. I beat hell out of your girl-friend and I beat hell out of you. So you got frabbed off and set those traps. Right?'

Chooka shook her head dazedly.

'Three of them so far. On the ship coming back from Spaceland. In my study. In my Jumper. How many more, Chooka?'

'It wasn't me, Reich. So help me. I——'

'It has to be you, Chooka. You're the only one with a gripe and the only one who hires gimpsters. That adds up to you, so let's get it squared off.' He slapped the safety off the scrambler. 'I've got no time for a two-bit hater with coffin-queer friends.'

'For God's sake!' Chooka screamed. 'What the hell have I got against you? So you rough-housed a little. So you mugged Magda. You wasn't the first. You ain't gonna be the last. Use your head!'

'I used it. If it isn't you, who else?'

'Keno Quizzard. He hires gimpsters too. I heard you and him——'

'Quizzard's out. Quizzard's dead. Who else?'

'Church.'

'He hasn't got the guts. If he had he would have tried it ten years ago. Who else?'

'How do I know? There's hundreds hate you enough.'

'There's thousands, but who could get into my safe? Who could break a phase combination and——'

'Maybe nobody broke into your safe. Maybe somebody broke into your head and peeped the combination. Maybe——'

'Peeped!'

'Yeah. Peeped. Maybe you added Church up wrong ... Or some other peeper what's got an eager reason for filling your coffin.'

'My God ...' Reich whispered. 'Oh my God ... Yes.'

'Church?'

'No. Powell.'

'The cop?'

'The cop. Powell. Yes. Mr Holy Lincoln Powell. Yes!' The words began pouring out of Reich in a torrent. 'Yes, Powell! The son of a bitch is fighting dirty because I've licked him clean. He can't get a case together. He's got nothing but booby-trapping left ...'

'You're crazy, Reich.'

'Am I? Why the hell did he take Ellery West away from me, and Breen? He knows the only defence I've got against a booby-trap is a peeper. It's Powell!'

'But a cop, Reich? A cop?'

'Sure a cop!' Reich shouted. 'Why not a cop? He's safe. Who'd suspect him? It's smart. It's what I'd do myself. All right ... Now I'm going to booby-trap him!'

He kicked the red-eyed woman from him, went to Chooka and yanked her to her feet. 'Call Powell.'

'What?'

'Call Powell,' he yelled. 'Lincoln Powell. Call him at his house. Tell him to come down here right away.'

'No, Reich ...'

He shook her. 'Listen to me, frab-head. Bastion West is owned by the D'Courtney Cartel. Now that old D'Courtney's dead, I'm going to own the cartel, which means I'll own Bastion. I'll own this house. I'll own you, Chooka. You want to stay in business? Call Powell!'

She stared at his livid face, feebly peeping him, slowly realizing that what he said was true.

'But I've got no excuse, Reich.'

'Wait a minute. Wait a minute.' Reich thought, then yanked the knife-pistol from his pocket and shoved it into Chooka's hands. 'Show him this. Tell him the D'Courtney girl left it here.'

'What is it?'

'The gun that killed D'Courtney.'

'For the love of – Reich!'

Reich laughed. 'It won't do him any good. By the time he's got it, he'll be booby-trapped. Call him. Show him the gun. Get him down here.' He thrust Chooka towards the phone, followed her and stood alongside the screen out of the line of sight. He hefted the scrambler in his hand meaningfully. Chooka understood.

She dialled Powell's number. Mary Noyes appeared on the screen, listened to Chooka, then called Powell. The prefect appeared, his lean face haggard, his dark eyes heavily shadowed.

'I . . . I got something you might want, maybe, Mr Powell,' Chooka stammered. 'I just found it. That girl you took outa my house. She left it behind.'

'Left what, Chooka?'

'The gun which killed her father.'

'No!' Powell's face was suddenly animated. 'Let's see it.'

Chooka displayed the knife-pistol.

'That's it, by heaven!' Powell exclaimed. 'Maybe I'm going to get a break after all. Stay right where you are, Chooka. I'll be down as fast as a Jumper can jet.'

The screen blacked out. Reich ground his teeth and tasted blood. He turned, dashed out of the Rainbow House and located a vacant coin-Jumper. He dropped a half-credit into the lock, opened the door and lurched in. As he took off with a hissing roar, he clattered against a thirtieth storey cornice and nearly capsized. He realized dazedly that he was in no condition to pilot a Jumper or set a booby-trap.

'*Don't try to think,*' he thought. '*Don't try to plan. Leave it to your instincts. You're a killer. A natural killer. Just wait and kill!*'

Reich fought himself and the controls all the way to Hudson Ramp, and he fought the Jumper down through the crazy, shifting North River winds. The killer instinct prompted him to crashland in Powell's back garden. He didn't know why. As he pounded the twisted cabin door open, a canned voice spoke: 'Your attention, please. You are liable for any damage to this vehicle. Please leave your name and address. If we are forced to trace you, you will be liable for the costs. Thank you.'

'I'm going to be liable for a lot more damage,' Reich growled. 'You're welcome.'

He plunged under a heavy clump of forsythia and waited with the scrambler ready. Then he understood why he had crashed. The girl who answered Powell's phone came out of the house and ran down through

the garden towards the Jumper. Reich waited. No one else came from
the house. The girl was alone. He surged up out of the brush and the girl
spun around before she heard him. A peeper. He pulled the trigger to
first notch. She stiffened and trembled . . . helpless.

At the moment when he was about to pull the trigger all the way back
to the big D, instinct stopped him again. Suddenly the booby-trap for
Powell came to him. Kill the girl inside the house. Seed her body with
Detonation Bulbs and leave that bait for Powell. Sweat broke out on the
girl's swarthy face. The muscles in her jaws twitched. Reich took her by
the arm and led her up the garden to the house. She walked with the stiff-
legged gait of a scarecrow.

Inside the house, Reich led the girl through the kitchen to the living-
room. He found a long, corded modern lounge and thrust the girl down
on it. She was fighting him with everything short of her body. He grinned
savagely, bent down, and kissed her full on the mouth.

'My love to Powell,' he said, and stepped back, raising the scrambler.
Then he lowered it.

Someone was watching him.

He turned, almost casually, and darted a quick look around the living-
room. There was no one. He turned back to the girl and asked: 'Are you
doing that with TP, peeper?' Then he raised the scrambler. Again he
lowered it.

Someone was watching him.

This time, Reich prowled around the living-room, searching behind
chairs, inside closets. There was no one. He checked the kitchen and the
bath. No one. He returned to the living-room and Mary Noyes. Then
thought of the upper floor. He went to the stairs, started to mount them,
and then stopped in mid-stride as though he had been poleaxed.

Someone *was* watching him.

She was at the head of the stairs, kneeling and peeping through the
banisters like a child. She was dressed like a child in tight little leotards
with her hair drawn back and tied with ribbon. She looked at him with
the droll, mischievous expression of a child. Barbara D'Courtney.

'Hello,' she said.

Reich began to shake.

'I'm Baba,' she said.

Reich motioned to her faintly.

She arose at once and came down the stairs, holding on to the banister
carefully. 'I'm not s'posed to,' she said. 'Are you Papa's friend?'

Reich took a deep breath. 'I . . . I . . .' he croaked.

'Papa had to go away,' she prattled. 'But he's coming back right away.
He told me. If I'm a good girl, he'll bring me a present. I'm trying, but
it's awful hard. Are *you* good?'

'Your father? Coming b-back? Your *father*?'

She nodded. 'Was you playing games with Aunt Mary? You kissed her. I saw it. Papa kisses me. I like it. Does Aunt Mary like it?' She took his hand confidently. 'When I grow up I'm going to marry Papa and be his girl for always. Do you have a girl?'

Reich pulled Barbara around and stared into her face. 'Are you rocketing?' he said hoarsely. 'Do you think I'll fall into that orbit? How much did you tell Powell?'

'That's my papa,' she said. 'When I ask him why his name is different from my name he looks funny. What's your name?'

'I asked you!' Reich shouted. 'How much did you tell him? Who do you think you're fooling with that act? Answer me!'

She looked at him doubtfully, then began to cry, trying to pull away from him. He held on to her.

'Go 'way!' she sobbed. 'Let me go!'

'Will you answer me!'

'Let me go!'

He dragged her from the foot of the stairs to the lounge where Mary Noyes still sat paralysed. He threw the girl alongside her and stepped back again, with the scrambler raised. Suddenly, the girl whipped upright in the chair in a listening attitude. Her face lost its childishness and became drawn and taut. She thrust out her legs, leaped from the lounge, ran, stopped abruptly, then appeared to open a door. She ran forward, yellow hair flying, dark eyes wide with alarm . . . a lightning flash of wild beauty.

'Father!' she screamed. 'For God's sake! Father!'

Reich's heart constricted. The girl ran towards him. He stepped forward to catch her. She stopped short, backed away, then darted to the left and ran in a half-circle, screaming wildly, her eyes fixed.

'No!' she cried. 'No! For the love of Christ! Father!'

Reich pivoted and clutched at the girl. This time he caught her while she fought and screamed. Reich was shouting too. The girl suddenly stiffened and clutched her ears. Reich was back in the Orchid Suite. He heard the explosion and saw the blood and brains gout out of the back of D'Courtney's head. He shook with galvanic spasms that forced him to release the girl. She fell forward to her knees and crawled across the floor. He saw her crouch over the waxen body.

Reich gasped for breath and beat his knuckles together painfully, fighting for control. When the roaring in his ears subsided, he propelled himself towards Barbara, trying to arrange his thoughts and make split-second alterations in his plans. He had never counted on a witness. God Damn Powell. He would have to kill the girl. Could he arrange a double-murder in the—— No. Not murder. Booby-trap. Damn Gus Tate. Wait. He wasn't in Beaumont House. He was . . . in . . .

'Thirty-three Hudson Ramp,' Powell said from the front door.

Reich jerked around, crouched automatically and whipped the scrambler up under his left elbow as Quizzard's killers had taught him.

Powell side stepped. 'Don't try it,' he said sharply.

'You son of a bitch!' Reich shouted. He wheeled on Powell who had already crossed him up and again stepped out of the line of fire. 'You God damned peeper! You lousy, sleazy, son of a——'

Powell faked to the left, reversed, closed with Reich and delivered a six-inch jab to the ulnar nerve complex. The scrambler fell to the floor. Reich clinched; punching, clawing, butting, swearing hysterically. Powell hit him with three lightning blows, nape, navel, and groin. The effect was that of a full spinal block. Reich crashed to the floor, retching, blood streaming from his nose.

'Brother, you think only you know how to gut fight,' Powell grunted. He went to Barbara D'Courtney, who still knelt on the floor, and raised her.

'All right, Barbara?' he said.

'Hello, Papa. I had a bad dream.'

'I know, baby. I had to give it to you. It was an experiment on that big oaf.'

'Gimme a kiss.'

He kissed her forehead. 'You're growing up fast,' he smiled. 'You were just baby-king yesterday.'

'I'm growing up because you promised to wait for me.'

'It's a promise, Barbara. Can you go upstairs by yourself or do you have to be carried ... like yesterday?'

'I can go all by own self.'

'All right, baby. Go up to your room.'

She went to the stairs, took a firm hold on the banister and climbed up. Just before she reached the top, she darted a glance at Reich and stuck her tongue out. Then she disappeared. Powell crossed to Mary Noyes, removed the gag, checked her pulse, then made her comfortable on the lounge.

'First notch, eh?' he murmured to Reich. 'Painful but she'll recover in an hour.' He went back to Reich and stared down at him, anger darkening his drawn face. 'I ought to pay you back for Mary; but what's the use? It wouldn't teach you anything. You poor bastard ... you're just no damned good.'

'Kill me!' Reich groaned. 'Kill me or let me up and by Christ I'll kill you!'

Powell picked up the scrambler and cocked an eye at Reich. 'Try flexing your muscles a little. Those blocks shouldn't last more than a few seconds ...' He sat down with the scrambler in his lap. 'You had a tough break. I wasn't out of the house five minutes when I realized Chooka's story was a phoney. You put her up to it, of course.'

'You're the phoney!' Reich shouted. 'You and your ethics and your high talk. You and your phoney goddam——'

'She said the gun killed D'Courtney,' Powell continued imperturbably. 'It did, but no one knows what killed D'Courtney . . . except you and me. I turned around and came back. It was a long take. Almost too long. Try gettin up now. You can't be that sick.'

Reich struggled up, his breath hissing horribly. Suddenly he dipped into his pocket and brought out the cartridge of Detonation Bulbs. Powell arched back in the chair and kicked Reich in the chest with his heel. The cartridge went flying. Reich fell back and collapsed on a sofa.

'When will you people learn you can't surprise a peeper?' Powell said. He went to the cartridge and picked it up. 'You're quite the arsenal today, aren't you? You're acting more like you're wanted dead or alive than like a free man. Notice I said free. Not innocent.'

'Free how long?' Reich said through his teeth. 'I never talked about innocence either. But free how long?'

'For ever. I had a perfect case against you. Every detail right. I checked that when I peeped you with Barbara just now. I had every detail except one, and that one flaw blew my case out into deep space. You're a free man, Reich. We've closed your file.'

Reich stared. 'Closed the file?'

'Yep. No solution. I'm licked. You can disarm, Reich. Go about your business. No one's going to bother you.'

'You're a liar! This is one of your peeper tricks. You——'

'Nope. I'll lay it out for you. I know all about you . . . How much you bribed Gus Tate . . . What you promised Jerry Church . . . Where you located that Sardine Game . . . What you did with Wilson Jordan's Rhodopsin Caps . . . How you emptied those cartridges for an alibi and then turned them lethal again with a drop of water . . . So far a perfect chain of evidence. Method and Opportunity. But Motive was the flaw. The courts demand Objective Motive and I can't produce it. That sets you free.'

'You liar!'

'Of course I could throw this breaking and entering with deadly intent at you . . . but it's too small a charge. Like shooting a pop-gun after you misfire with a cannon. You could probably beat it, too. My only witnesses would be a peeper and a sick girl. I——'

'You liar,' Reich growled. 'You hypocrite. You lying peeper. Am I supposed to believe you? Am I supposed to listen to the rest of it? You had nothing, Powell. Nothing! I licked you on every point. That's why you're booby-trapping me. That's why you——' Reich broke off abruptly and beat his forehead. 'And this is probably the biggest booby-trap of all. And I fell into it. What a damned fool I am. What a——'

'Shut up,' Powell snapped. 'When you rave like that I can't peep you. Now what's all this about booby-traps? Think it through.'

Reich uttered a ragged laugh. 'As if you don't know ... My state-room on the liner ... My gaffed safe ... My Jumper ...'

For almost a minute, Powell focused on Reich, peeping, absorbing, digesting. Then his face began to pale and his respiration quicken. 'My God!' he exclaimed. 'My God!' He leaped to his feet and began pacing distractedly. 'That's it ... That explains it ... And Old Man Mose was right. Passion motive, and we thought he was kittenish ... And Barbara's Siamese Twin Image ... And D'Courtney's guilt ... No wonder Reich couldn't kill us at Chooka's ... But – the murder isn't important any more. It goes deeper. Far deeper. And it's dangerous ... More than I ever dreamed.' He stopped, turned and looked at Reich with blazing eyes.

'If I could kill you,' he cried, 'I'd twist your head off with my hands. I'd tear you apart and hang you on a Galactic Gallows, and the Universe would bless me. Do you know how dangerous you are? Does a plague know its peril? Is death conscious?'

Reich goggled at Powell in bewilderment. The Prefect shook his head impatiently. 'Why ask you?' he muttered. 'You don't know what I'm talking about. You'll never know.' He went to a sideboard, selected two brandy ampules and popped them into Reich's mouth. Reich attempted to spit them out. Powell held his jaws shut.

'Swallow them,' he said crisply. 'I want you to pull yourself together and listen to me. Do you want Butylene? Thyric Acid? Can you compose yourself without drugs?'

Reich choked on the brandy and sputtered angrily. Powell shook him silent.

'Get this straight,' Powell said. 'I'm going to show you half the pattern. Try to understand it. The case against you is closed. It's closed because of those booby-traps. If I'd known about them I'd never have started the case. I'd have broken my conditioning and killed you. Try to understand this, Reich ...'

Reich stopped sputtering.

'I couldn't find a motive for your murder. That's the flaw. When you offered merger to D'Courtney, he accepted. He sent WWHG in answer. That's acceptance. You had no reason to murder him. You had every objective reason to keep him alive.'

Reich went white. His head began to wobble crazily. 'No. No. WWHG. Offer refused. Refusal. Refusal!'

'Acceptance.'

'No. The bastard refused. He——'

'He accepted. When I learned that D'Courtney accepted your offer, I was finished. I knew I couldn't bring a case to court. But I haven't been trying to booby-trap you. I did not gaff your state-room lock. I did not plant those Detonation Bulbs. I'm not the man who's trying to murder you. That man is trying to kill you because he knows you're safe from me. He knows you're safe from Demolition. He's always known what I've just discovered ... that you're the deadly enemy of our entire future.'

Reich tried to speak. He struggled up out of the sofa, gesticulating feebly. Finally he said: 'Who is it? Who? Who?'

'He's your ancient enemy, Reich ... A man you'll never escape. You'll never be able to run from him ... hide from him ... and I pray to God you'll never be able to save yourself from him.'

'Who is it, Powell? WHO IS IT?'

'The Man With No Face.'

Reich emitted a guttural cry of pain. Then he turned and staggered out of the house.

CHAPTER 15

TENSION, apprehension, and dissension have begun.
   Tension, apprehension, and dissension have begun.
   Tension, apprehension and dissension have begun.
'Shut up!' Reich cried.
Eight, sir;
      Seven, sir;
           Six, sir;
                Five, sir;
'For God's sake! Shut up!'
                Four, sir;
            Three, Sir;
      Two sir;
One!
'You've got to think. Why don't you think? What's happened to you? Why don't you think?'
Tension, apprehension, and——
'He was lying. You know he was lying. You were right the first time. A giant booby-trap. WWHG. Refusal. Refusal. But why did he lie? How is that going to help him?'
— dissension have begun.
'The Man With No Face. Breen could have told him. Gus Tate could have told him. Think!'

Tension——

'There is no Man With No Face. It's just a dream. A nightmare!'

Apprehension——

'But the booby-traps? What about the booby-traps? He had me cold in his house. Why didn't he pull the switch? Telling me I'm free. What's he up to? Think!'

Dissension——

A hand touched his shoulder.

'Mr Reich?'

'What?'

'Mr Reich!'

'What? Who's that?'

Reich's eyes focused. He became aware that it was raining heavily. He was lying on his side, knees drawn up, arms folded, his cheek buried in mud. He was drenched, shivering with cold. He was in the esplanade of Bomb Inlet. Around him were sighing, sodden trees. A figure was bending over him.

'Who are you?'

'Galen Chervil, Mr Reich.'

'What?'

'Galen Chervil, sir. From Maria Beaumont's party. Can I do you that favour, Mr Reich?'

'Don't peep me!' Reich cried.

'I'm not, Mr Reich. We don't usually——' Young Chervil caught himself. 'I didn't know you knew I was a peeper. You'd better get up, sir.'

He took Reich's arm and pulled. Reich groaned and yanked his arm free. Young Chervil took him under the shoulders and raised him, staring at Reich's frightful appearance.

'Were you mugged, Mr Reich?'

'What. No. No . . .'

'Accident, sir?'

'No. No, I . . . Oh, for God's sake,' Reich burst out, 'get the hell away from me!'

'Certainly, sir. I thought you needed help and I owe you a favour, but——'

'Wait,' Reich interrupted. 'Come back.' He grasped the bole of a tree and leaned against it, panting hoarsely. Finally he thrust himself erect and glared at Chervil with bloodshot eyes. 'You mean that about the favour?'

'Of course, Mr Reich.'

'No questions asked. No tales told?'

'Certainly not, Mr Reich.'

'My problem's murder, Chervil. I want to find out who's trying to kill me. Will you do me that favour? Will you peep someone for me?'

'I should imagine the police would be able to——'

'The police?' Reich laughed hysterically, then clutched himself in agony as the broken rib caught. 'I want you to peep a cop for me, Chervil. A big cop. The Commissioner of cops. D'you understand.' He let go the tree and lurched to Chervil. 'I want to visit my friend the Commissioner and ask him a few questions. I want you to be there to tell me the truth. Will you come to Crabbe's office and peep him for me? Will you just do it and forget about it? Will you?'

'Yes, Mr Reich ... I will.'

'What? An honest peeper! How about that? Come on. Let's jet.'

Reich stumbled out of the esplanade with a horrible gait. Chervil followed, overwhelmed by the fury in the man that drove him through injury, through fever, through agony to police headquarters. There, Reich bulled and roared past clerks and guards until the mud-streaked, blood-smeared figure burst into Commissioner Crabbe's elaborate ebony and silver office.

'My God, Reich!' Crabbe was aghast. 'It is you, isn't it? Ben Reich?'

'Sit down, Chervil,' Reich said. He turned to Crabbe. 'It's me. Get a full perspective. I'm half a corpse, Crabbe. The red stuff is blood. The rest is slime. I've had a great day ... a glorious day ... and I want to know where the hell the police have been? Where's your God Almighty Prefect Powell? Where's your——'

'Half a corpse? What are you telling me, Ben?'

'I'm telling you that I was almost murdered three times today. This boy ...' Reich pointed to Chervil. 'This boy just found me in the Inlet Esplanade more dead than alive. Look at me, for Christ's sake. Look at me!'

'Murdered!' Crabbe thumped his desk emphatically. 'Of course. That Powell is a fool. I should never have listened to him. The man who killed D'Courtney is trying to kill you.'

Behind his back, Reich motioned savagely to Chervil.

'I told Powell you were innocent. He wouldn't listen to me,' Crabbe said. 'Even when that infernal adding machine in the District Attorney's office told him you were innocent, he wouldn't listen.'

'The machine said I was innocent?'

'Of course it did. There's no case against you. There never was a case against you. And by the sacred Bill of Rights, you'll have the protection from the murderer that any honest law-abiding citizen deserves. I'll see to that at once.' Crabbe strode to the door. 'And I think this is all I'll need to settle Mr Powell's hash for good! Don't go, Ben. I want to talk to you about your support for the Solar Senatorship ...'

The door opened and slammed. Reich reeled and fought his way back to the world. He looked at three Chervils. 'Well?' he muttered. 'Well?'

'He's telling the truth, Mr Reich.'

'About me? About Powell?'

'Well ...' Chervil paused judiciously, weighing the truth.

'Jet, you bastard,' Reich groaned. 'How long do you think I can keep my fuses from blowing.'

'He's telling the truth about you,' Chervil said quickly. 'The Prosecution Computor has declined to authorize any action against you for the D'Courtney murder. Mr Powell has been forced to abandon the case and ... well ... his career is very much in jeopardy.'

'Is that true!' Reich staggered to the boy and seized his shoulders. 'Is that true, Chervil? I've been cleared? I can go about my business? No one's going to bother me?'

'You've been dropped, Mr Reich. You can go about your business. No one's going to bother you.'

Reich burst into a roar of triumphant laughter. The pain of his bruised and broken body made him groan as he laughed, and his eyes smarted with tears. He pulled himself up, brushed past Chervil and left the Commissioner's office. He was more a Neanderthal vestige as he paraded down headquarters corridors streaked with blood and mud, laughing and groaning, bearing himself with limping arrogance. He needed a stag's carcass on his shoulders or a cave bear borne in triumph behind him to complete the picture.

'I'll complete the picture with Powell's head,' he told himself. 'Stuffed and mounted on my wall. I'll complete the picture with the D'Courtney Cartel stuffed into my pockets. By God, give me time I'll complete a picture with the Galaxy inside the frame!'

He passed through the steel portals of headquarters and stood for a moment on the steps gazing at the rain-swept streets ... at the amusement centre across the square, block after block blazing under a single mutual transparent dome ... at the open shops lining the upper footways, all bustle and brilliance as the city's night shopping began ... the towering office buildings in the background, great two-hundred storey cubes ... the lace tracery of skyways linking them together ... the twinkling running lights of Jumpers bobbing up and down like a plague of crimson-eyed grasshoppers in a field.

'And I'll own you!' he shouted, raising his arms to engulf the universe. 'I'll own you all! Bodies, passions, and souls!'

Then his eye caught the tall, ominous, familiar figure crossing the square, watching him covertly over its shoulder. A figure of black shadows sparkling with raindrop jewels ... looking, looming, silent, horrible ... A Man With No Face.

There was a strangled cry. The fuses blew. Like a blighted tree, Reich fell to the ground.

At one minute to nine, ten of the fifteen members of the Esper Guild Council assembled in President T'sung's office. Emergency business required their attention. At one minute after nine, the meeting was adjourned with the business completed. Within those one hundred and twenty Esper seconds, the following took place:

> *A gavel pounding*
> *A clock face*
> *Hour hand at 9*
> *Minute hand at 59*
> *Second hand at 60*

EMERGENCY MEETING

To examine a request for Mass Cathexis with Lincoln Powell as the human canal for the Capitalized energy.

(*Consternation*)

T'SUNG: *You can't be serious, Powell. How can you make such a request? What can possibly require such an extraordinary and dangerous measure?*

POWELL: *An astonishing development in the D'Courtney Case which I would like you all to examine.*

(*Examination*)

POWELL: *You all know that Reich is our most dangerous enemy. He is supporting the Anti-Esper smear campaign. Unless that is blocked we may suffer the usual history of minority groups.*

@KINS: *True enough.*

POWELL: *He is also supporting the League of Esper Patriots. Unless that organization is blocked we may be plunged into a civil war and be lost for ever in a morass of internal chaos.*

FRANION: *That's true too.*

POWELL: *But there is an additional development which you have all examined. Reich is about to become a Galactic focal point . . . A crucial link between the positive past and the probable future. He is on the verge of a powerful reorganization at this moment. Time is of the essence. If Reich can readjust and reorient before I can reach him, he will become immune to our reality, invulnerable to our attack, and the deadly enemy of Galactic reason and reality.*

(*Alarm*)

@KINS: *Surely you're exaggerating, Powell.*

POWELL: *Am I? Inspect the picture with me. Look at Reich's position in time and space. Will not his beliefs become the world's beliefs? Will not his reality become the world's reality? Is he not, in his critical position of power, energy, and intellect, a sure road to utter destruction?*

(*Conviction*)

T'SUNG: *That's true. Nevertheless I'm reluctant to authorize the Mass Cathexis Measure. You will recall that the MCM has invariably destroyed the human energy canal in past attempts. You're too valuable to be destroyed, Powell.*

POWELL: *I must be permitted to run the risk. Reich is one of the rare Universe-shakers . . . a child as yet, but about to mature. And all reality . . . Espers, Normals, Life, the earth, the solar system, the universe itself . . . all reality hangs precariously on his awakening. He cannot be permitted to awake to the wrong reality. I call the question.*

FRANION: *You're asking us to vote your death.*

POWELL: *It's my death against the eventual death of every thing we know. I call the question.*

@KINS: *Let Reich awaken as he will. We have the time and the warning to attack him at another cross-road.*

POWELL: *Question! I call the question!*
(*Request granted*)
Meeting adjourned
Clock face
Hour hand at 9
Minute hand at 01
Second hand at Demolition

Powell arrived home an hour later. He had made his will, paid his bills, signed his papers, arranged everything. There had been dismay at the Guild. There was dismay when he came home. Mary Noyes read what he had done the instant he entered.

'Linc!'

'No fuss. It's got to be done.'

'But——'

'There's a chance it won't kill me. Oh . . . One reminder. Lab wants a brain autopsy as soon as I'm dead . . . if I die. I've signed all the papers, but I wish you'd help in case there's trouble. They'd like to have the body before rigor. If they can't get the corpse they'll settle for the head. See to it, will you?'

'Linc!'

'Sorry. Now, you'd better pack and take the baby up to Kingston Hospital. She won't be safe here.'

'She isn't a baby any more. She——'

Mary turned and ran upstairs, trailing the familiar sensory impact: Snow/mint/tulips/taffeta . . . and now mixed with terror and tears. Powell sighed, then smiled as a highly poised teenager appeared at the head of the stairs and came down with grand insouciance. She was wearing a dress and an expression of rehearsed surprise. She paused half-way down to let him take in the dress and the manner.

'Why! It's Mr Powell, is it not?'

'It is. Good morning, Barbara.'

'And what brings you to our little domain this morning?' She came down the rest of the stairs with her fingertips brushing the banister and tripped on the bottom step. 'Oh Pip!' she squawked.

Powell caught her. 'Pop,' he said.

'Bim.'

'Bam.'

She looked up at him. 'You stand right here. I'm going to come down those stairs again and I bet I do it perfect.'

'I'll bet you don't.'

She turned, trotted up and posed again at the top step. 'Dear Mr Powell, what a scatterbrain you must think me . . .' She began the grand descent. 'You must re-evaluate your opinion of me. I am no longer the mere child I was yesterday. I am ages and ages older. You must regard me as an adult from now on.' She negotiated the bottom step and regarded him intently. 'Re-evaluate? Is that right?'

'Revaluate is sometimes preferred, dear.'

'I thought it had an extra sound.' Suddenly she laughed, pushed him into a chair, and plumped down on his lap. Powell groaned.

'Gently, Barbara. You're ages older and pounds heavier.'

'Listen,' she said. 'Whatever made me think you was . . . Were? Were my father?'

'What's the matter with me as a father?'

'Let's be frank. Real frank.'

'Sure.'

'Do you feel like a father towards me? Because I don't feel like a daughter towards you.'

'Oh? How do you feel?'

'I asked first, so you go first.'

'My feelings towards you are those of a loving and dutiful son.'

'No. Be serious.'

'I have resolved to be a trustworthy son to all women until Vulcan assumes its rightful place in the Comity of Planets.'

She flushed angrily and got up from his lap. 'I wanted you to be serious, because I need advice. But if you ———'

'I'm sorry, Barbara. What is it?'

She knelt alongside him and took his hand. 'I'm all mixed up about you.'

'How?'

She looked into his eyes with the alarming directness of the young. 'You know.'

After a pause, he nodded. 'Yes, I know.'

'And you're all mixed up about me, too. I know.'

'Yes, Barbara. That's true. I am.'

'Is it wrong?'

Powell heaved up from the chair and began pacing unhappily. 'No, Barbara, it isn't wrong. It's ... mistimed.'

'I want you to tell me about it.'

'Tell you ...? Yes, I suppose I'd better. I ... I'll put it this way, Barbara. The two of us are four people. There's two of you, and two of me.'

'Why?'

'You've been sick, dear. So we had to turn you into a baby and let you grow up again. That's why you're two people. The grown-up Barbara inside, and the baby outside.'

'And you?'

'I'm two grown-up people. One of them is me ... Powell ... The other is a member of the governing Council of the Esper Guild.'

'What's that?'

'It doesn't need explaining. It's the part of me that's got me mixed up ... God knows, maybe it's the baby part. I don't know.'

She considered earnestly, then said slowly. 'When I don't feel like a daughter to you ... which me feels like that?'

'I don't know, Barbara.'

'You do know. Why won't you say?' She came to him and put her arms around his neck ... a grown-up woman with the manner of a child. 'If it isn't wrong, why won't you say? If I love you ——'

'Who said anything about love!'

'It's what we're talking about, isn't it? Isn't it? I love you and you love me. Isn't that it?'

'*All right,*' Powell thought desperately. '*Here it is. What are you going to do? Admit the truth?*'

'*Yes!*' From the stairs. Mary was descending with a travelling case in her hand. '*Admit the truth.*'

'*She isn't a peeper!*'

'*Forget that. She's a woman and she's in love with you. You're in love with her. Please, Linc, give yourselves a chance.*'

'*A chance for what? An affair if I get out of this Reich mess alive? That's all it could be. You know the Guild won't let us marry normals.*'

'*She'll settle for that. She'll be grateful to settle for that. Ask me. I know.*'

'*And if I don't come out alive? She'll have nothing ... Nothing but half a memory of half a love.*'

'No, Barbara,' he said. 'That isn't it at all.'

'It is,' she insisted. 'It is!'

'No. It's the baby part of you talking. The baby thinks she's in love with me. The woman is not.'

'She'll grow up into the woman.'

'And she'll forget all about me.'

'You'll make her remember.'

'Why should I, Barbara?'

'Because you feel that way about me, too. I know you do.'

Powell laughed. 'Baby! Baby! Baby! What makes you think I'm in love with you that way? I'm not. I've never been.'

'You are!'

'Open your eyes, Barbara. Look at me. Look at Mary. You're ages older, aren't you? Can't you understand? Do I have to explain the obvious?'

'*For God's sake, Linc!*'

'*Sorry, Mary. Got to use you.*'

'*I'm getting ready to say good-bye ... Maybe for good ... Do I have to endure this? Isn't it bad enough for me already?*'

'*Shhhh. Gently, dear ...*'

Barbara stared at Mary, then at Powell. She shook her head slowly. 'You're lying.'

'Am I? Look at me.' He put his hands on her shoulders and looked into her face. Dishonest Abe came to his assistance. His expression was kind, tolerant, amused, patronizing. 'Look at me Barbara.'

'No!' she cried. 'Your face is lying. It's ... It's hateful! I ——' She burst into tears and sobbed: 'Oh go away. Why don't you go away?'

'We're going away, Barbara,' Mary said. She came forward, took the girl's arms and led her to the door.

'*There's a Jumper waiting, Mary.*'

'*There's me waiting, Linc. For you. Always. And the Chervils & @kins & Jordans & & & & & & & & ——*'

'*I know, I know. I love you all. Kisses. XXXXXX Blessings ...*'

Image of four-leaf clover, rabbits' feet, horseshoes ...

Bawdy response of Powell emerging from slok covered with diamonds.

Faint laughter.

Farewell.

He stood in the doorway whistling a crooked, plaintive tune, watching the Jumper disappear into the steel-blue sky boring north towards Kingston Hospital. He was exhausted. A little proud of himself for having made the sacrifice. Intensely ashamed of himself for feeling proud. Clearly a melancholic. Should he take a grain of Potassium Niacate and kick himself up into the manic curve? What the hell was the use? Look at that great foul city of seventeen and one half million souls and not one soul for him. Look at ——

The first impulse came. A thin trickle of latent energy. He felt it distinctly and glanced at his watch. Ten-twenty. So soon? So quickly? Good. He'd better get ready.

He turned into the house and darted up the stairs to his dressing-room. The impulses came pattering ... like the preliminary raindrops before a storm. His psyche began to throb and vibrate as he reached out and absorbed those tiny streams of latent energy. He changed his clothes, dressed for all weather, and ——

And what? The pattering had become a drizzle, washing over him, filling his consciousness with ague ... with grinding emotional flashes ... with —— Yes, nutrient capsules. Hold on to that. Nutrient. Nutrient. Nutrient! He tumbled down the stairs into the kitchen. Found the plastic bulb, cracked it and swallowed a dozen capsules.

The energy came in torrents now. From each Esper in the city, a trickle of latent power that merged and merged into a stream, a river, a swirling sea of Mass Cathexis directed towards Powell, tuned to Powell. He opened all blocks and absorbed it all. His nervous system superheterodyned and screamed and a turbine in his mind whirled faster and faster with a mounting intolerable whine.

He was out of the house, wandering through the streets, blind, deaf, senseless, immersed in that boiling mass of latent energy ... like a ship with sails caught in the nexus of a typhoon, fighting to convert a whirlpool of wind into the motive power that would lead to safety ... So Powell fought to absorb that fearful torrent, to Capitalize that latent energy, to Cathectize and direct it towards the Demolition of Reich before it was too late, too late, too late, too late, too late ...

CHAPTER 16

ABOLISH THE LABYRINTH.
DESTROY THE MAZE.
DELETE THE PUZZLE.
(X^2 ⌀ Y^3d! Space/d! Time)
DISBAND.
(OPERATIONS, EXPRESSIONS, FACTORS, FRACTION, POWERS, EXPONENTS,

RADICALS, IDENTITIES, EQUATIONS, PROGRESSIONS, VARIATIONS, PERMUTA-
TIONS, DETERMINANTS, AND SOLUTIONS)

 EFFACE.

 (ELECTRON, PROTON, NEUTRON, MESON AND PHOTON)

 ERASE.

 (CAYLEY, HENSON, LILLIENTHAL, CHANUTE, LANGLEY, WRIGHT,
TURNBUL AND S&ERSON)

 EXPUNGE.

 (NEBULAE, CLUSTERS, STREAMS, BINARIES, GIANTS, MAIN SEQUENCE, AND
WHITE DWARFS)

 DISPERSE.

 (PISCES, AMPHIBIA, BIRDS, MAMMALS, AND MAN)

 ABOLISH.

 DESTROY.

 DELETE.

 DISBAND.

 ERASE ALL EQUATIONS.

 INFINITY EQUALS ZERO.

 THERE IS NO ———

'– there is no what?' Reich shouted. 'There is no what?' He struggled upward, fighting the bedclothes and the restrain-hands. 'There is no what?'

'No more nightmares,' Duffy Wyg& said.

'Who's that?'

'Me. Duffy.'

Reich opened his eyes. He was in a frilly bedroom in a frilly bed with old-fashioned linen and blankets. Duffy Wyg&, starched and fresh, had her hands against his shoulders. Once again she tried to thrust him back against the pillows.

'I'm asleep,' Reich said. 'I want to wake up.'

'You say the nicest things. Lie down and the dream will continue.'

Reich fell back. 'I was awake,' he said sombrely. 'I was wide awake for the first time in my life. I heard ... I don't know what I heard. Infinity and zero. Important things. Reality. Then I fell asleep and I'm here.'

'Correction,' Duffy smiled. 'Just for the record. You awoke.'

'I'm asleep!' Reich shouted. He sat up. 'Have you got a shot? Anything ... opium, hemp, somnar, lethettes ... I've got to wake up, Duffy. I've got to get back to reality.'

Duffy bent over him and kissed him hard on the mouth. 'How about this? Real?'

'You don't understand. It's all been delusions ... hallucinations ...

everything. I've got to readjust, reorientate, reorganize ... Before it's too late, Duffy. Before it's too late, too late, too late ...'

Duffy threw up her hands. 'What the hell's happened to medicine!' she exclaimed. 'First that damned doctor scares you into a faint. Then he swears you're patched up ... and now look at you. Psychotic!' She knelt on the bed and shook a finger against Reich's nose. 'One more word out of you and I call Kingston.'

'What? Who?'

'Kingston, as in hospital. Where they send people like you.'

'No. Who did you say scared me into a faint?'

'A doctor friend.'

'In the square in front of police headquarters?'

'X marks the spot.'

'Sure?'

'I was with him, looking for you. Your valet told me about the explosion and I was worried. We got to the rescue just in time.'

'Did you see his face?'

'See it? I've kissed it.'

'What's it look like?'

'It's a face. Two eyes. Two lips. Two ears. One nose. Three chins. Listen. Ben, if this is some more of the awake-asleep-reality-infinity lyrics ... it ain't commercial.'

'And you brought me here?'

'Sure. How could I pass up the opportunity? It's the only way I can get you into my bed.'

Reich grinned. He relaxed and said: 'Duffy, you may now kiss me.'

'Mr Reich, you already been kissed. Or was that when you were still awake?'

'Forget that. Nightmares. Plain nightmares.' Reich burst into laughter. 'Why the hell should I worry about having nightmares? I have the rest of the world in my hands. I'll take the dreams too. Didn't you once ask to be dragged through the gutter, Duffy?'

'That was a childish whim. I thought I could meet a better class of people.'

'You name the gutter and you can have it, Duffy. Gold gutters ... Jewelled gutters. You want a gutter from here to Mars? You'll have it. You want me to turn the System into a gutter? I'll do it. Christ! I can turn the Galaxy into a gutter if you want it.' He jabbed his chest with his thumb. 'Want to look at God? Here I am. Go ahead and look.'

'Dear man. So modest and so hung-over.'

'Drunk? Sure, I'm drunk.' Reich thrust his legs out of the bed and stood up, reeling slightly. Duffy came to him at once and he put his arm around

her waist for support. 'Why shouldn't I be drunk? I've licked D'Courtney. I've licked Powell. I'm forty years old. I've got sixty years of owning
the whole world ahead of me. Yes, Duffy ... the whole damned world!'
He began walking around the room with Duffy. It was like a stroll
through her ebullient erotic mind. A peeper decorator had reproduced
Duffy's psyche perfectly in the decor.

'How'd you like to start a dynasty with me, Duffy?'

'I wouldn't know about starting dynasties.'

'You start with Ben Reich. First you marry him. Then ———'

'That's enough. When do I start?'

'Then you have children. Boys. Dozens of boys ...'

'Girls. And only three.'

'And you watch Ben Reich take over D'Courtney and merge it with
Monarch. You watch the enemies go down ... like this!' In full stride,
Reich kicked the leg of a busty vanity table. It toppled and crashed a
score of crystal bottles to the floor.

'After Monarch and D'Courtney become Reich, Incorporated, you
watch me eat up the rest ... the small ones ... the fleas. Case and Umbrel
on Venus. Eaten!' Reich brought his fist down on a torso-shaped side
table and smashed it. 'United Transaction on Mars. Mashed and eaten!'
He crushed a delicate chair. 'The GCI Combine on Ganymede, Callisto,
and Io ... Titan Chemical & Atomics ... And then the smaller lice: the
backbiters, the haters, the Guild of Peepers, the moralists, the patriots ...
Eaten! Eaten! Eaten!' He pounded his palm against a marble nude until
it toppled from its pedestal and shattered.

'Clever-up, dog,' Duffy hung on his neck. 'Why waste all that dear
violence? Punch me around a little.'

He lifted her in his arms and shook her until she squealed. 'And parts
of the world will taste sweet ... like you, Duffy; and parts will stink to
high heaven ... but I'll gobble them all.' He laughed and crushed her
against him. 'I don't know much about the God business, but I know
what I like. We'll tear it all down, Duffy, and we'll build it all up to suit
us ... You and me and the dynasty.'

He carried her to the window, tore away the drapes and kicked open
the sashes with a mighty jangle of smashed glass. Outside, the city was
in velvet darkness. Only the skyways and streets twinkled I with lights,
and the scarlet eyes of an occasional Jumper popped up over the jet
skyline. The rain had stopped and a slender moon hung pale in the sky.
The night wind came whispering in, cutting through the cloy of the
spilled perfume.

'You out there!' Reich roared. 'Can you hear me? All of you ... sleeping and dreaming. You'll dream my dreams from now on! You'll ———'

Abruptly he was silent. He relaxed his hold on Duffy and permitted her to slide to the floor alongside him. He seized the sides of the window and poked his head far out into the night, twisting his neck to stare up. When he drew his head back into the room, his face wore a bewildered expression.

'The stars,' he mumbled. 'Where are the stars?'

'Where are the what?' Duffy wanted to know.

'The stars,' Reich repeated. He gestured timidly towards the sky. 'The stars. They're gone.'

Duffy looked at him curiously. 'The what are gone?'

'The stars!' Reich cried. 'Look up at the sky. The stars are gone. The constellations are gone! The Great Bear . . . The Little Bear . . . Cassiopeia . . . Draco . . . Pegasus . . . They're all gone! There's nothing but the moon! Look!'

'It's the way it always is,' Duffy said.

'It is not! Where are the stars!'

'What stars?'

'I don't know their names . . . Polaris and . . . Vega . . . and . . . How the hell should I know their names? I'm not an astronomer. What's happened to us? What's happened to the stars?'

'What are stars?' Duffy asked.

Reich seized her savagely. 'Suns . . . Boiling and blazing with light. Thousands of them. Billions of them . . . shining through the night. What the hell's the matter with you? Don't you understand? There's been a catastrophe in space. The stars are gone!'

Duffy shook her head. Her face was terrified. 'I don't know what you're talking about, Ben. I don't know what you're talking about.'

He shoved her away, turned and ran to the bathroom, and locked himself in. While he was hurriedly bathing and dressing, Duffy pounded on the door and pleaded with him. Finally, she broke off, and seconds later he heard her calling Kingston Hospital, using a guarded voice.

'Let her start explaining about the stars,' Reich muttered, half-way between anger and terror. He finished his toilet and came out into the bedroom. Duffy cut the phone off hastily and turned to him.

'Ben,' she began.

'Wait here for me,' he growled. 'I'm going to find out.'

'Find out about what?'

'About the stars!' he yelled. 'The Christ almighty missing stars!'

He flung out of the apartment and rushed down to the street. On the empty footway, he paused and stared up again. There was the moon. There was one brilliant red point of light . . . Mars. There was another . . . Jupiter. There was nothing else. Blackness. Blackness. Blackness. It hung over his head, enigmatic, unrelieved, terrifying. It pressed downwards, by some trick of the eye, oppressive, stifling, deadly.

He began to run, still staring upwards. He turned a corner of the footway and collided with a woman, knocking her flat. He pulled her to her feet.

'You clumsy bastard!' she screamed, adjusting her feathers. Then in an oily voice: 'Lookin' for a good time, pilot?'

Reich held her arm. He pointed up. 'Look. The stars are gone. Have you noticed? The stars are gone.'

'What's gone?'

'The stars. Don't you see? They're gone.'

'I don' know what you're talkin' about, pilot. C'mon. Let's have us a ball.'

He tore himself away from her claws and ran. Half-way down the footway was a public v-phone alcove. He stepped in and dialled Information. The screen lit and a robot voice spoke: 'Question?'

'What's happened to the stars?' Reich asked. 'When did it happen? It must have been noticed by now. What's the explanation?'

There was a click, a pause, then another click. 'Will you spell the word, please.'

'Star!' Reich roared. 's-t-a-r. Star!'

Click, pause, click. 'Noun or verb?'

'God damn you! Noun!'

Click, pause, click. 'There is no information listed under that heading,' the canned voice announced.

Reich swore, then fought to control himself. 'Where's the nearest Observatory to the city?'

'Kindly specify city.'

'This city. New York.'

Click, pause, click. 'The Lunar Observatory at Croton Park is situated thirty miles north. It may be reached by Jumper Route North Coordinate 227. The Lunar Observatory was endowed in the year two thousand ——'

Reich slammed down the phone. 'No information listed under that heading! My God! Are they all crazy?' He ran out into the streets, searching for a Public Jumper. A piloted machine cruised past and Reich signalled. It swooped to pick him up.

'Northco 227,' he snapped as he stepped into the cabin. 'Thirty miles. The Lunar Observatory.'

'Premium trip,' the driver said.

'I'll pay it. Jet!'

The cab jetted. Reich restrained himself for five minutes, then began casually: 'Notice the sky?'

'Why, mister?'

'The stars are gone.'

Sycophantic laugh.

'It's not supposed to be a joke,' Reich said. 'The stars are gone.'

'If it ain't a joke, it needs explaining,' the driver said. 'What the hell are stars?'

A blasting reply trembled on Reich's lips. Before it could erupt, the cab landed him on the observatory grounds close to the domed roof. He snapped: 'Wait for me,' and ran across the lawns to the small stone entrance.

The door was ajar. He entered the observatory and heard the low whine of the dome mechanism and the quiet click of the observatory clock. Except for the low glow of the clock-light, the room was in darkness. The twelve-inch refractor was in operation. He could see the observer, a dim outline, crouched over the eye-piece of the guiding telescope.

Reich walked towards him, nervous, strained, flinching at the loud clack of his footsteps in the silence. There was a chill in the air.

'Listen,' Reich began in a low voice. 'Sorry to bother you but *you* must have noticed. You're in the star business. You have noticed, haven't you? The stars. They're gone. All of them. What's happened? Why hasn't there been any alarm? Why's everybody pretending? My God! The stars! We always take them for granted. And now they're gone. What's happened? Where are the stars?'

The figure straightened slowly and turned towards Reich. 'There are no stars,' it said.

It was the Man With No Face.

Reich cried out. He turned and ran. He flew out of the door, down the steps and across the lawn to the waiting cab. He blundered against the crystal cabin wall with a crack that dropped him to his knees.

The driver pulled him to his feet. 'You all right, Mac?'

'I don't know,' Reich groaned. 'I wish I did.'

'None of my business,' the driver said, 'but I think you ought to see a peeper. You're talkin' crazy.'

'About the stars?'

'Yeah.'

Reich gripped the man. 'I'm Ben Reich,' he said. 'Ben Reich of Monarch.'

'Yeah, Mac. I recognized you.'

'Good. You know what I can do for you if you do me a favour? Money ... New job ... Anything you want ...'

'You can't do nothin' for me, Mac. I already been adjusted at Kingston.'

'Better. An honest man. Will you do me a favour for the love of God or anything you love?'

'Sure, Mac.'

'Go into the building. Take a look at the man behind the telescope. A good look. Come back and describe him to me.'

The driver departed, was gone five minutes, then returned.

'Well?'

'He's just an ordinary guy, Mac. Sixtyish. Bald, got lines in his face kinda deep. His ears stick out and he's got what they call a weak chin. You know. It kinda backslides.'

'It's nobody ... nobody,' Reich muttered.

'What?'

'About those stars,' Reich said. 'You never heard of them? You never saw them? You don't know what I'm talking about?'

'Nope.'

'Oh God ...' Reich moaned. 'Sweet God ...'

'Now don't warp your orbit, Mac.' The driver thumped him powerfully on the back. 'Tell you something. They taught me plenty up at Kingston. One of them things was ... Well, sometimes you get a crazy notion. It's brand new, see? But you think you always had it. Like ... oh ... for instance, that people always had one eye and now all of a sudden they got two.'

Reich stared at him.

'So you run around yellin': "For Chrissakes, where did they all of a sudden get two eyes everybody?" And they say: "They always got two eyes." And you say: "The hell they did. I distinctly remember everybody got one eye." And by God you believe it. And they have a hell of a time knockin' the notion outa you.' The driver thumped him again. 'Seems to me, Mac, like you're on a one-eye kick.'

'One eye,' Reich muttered. 'Two eyes. Tension, apprehension, and dissension have begun.'

'What?'

'I don't know. I don't know. I've had a rough time the last month. Maybe ... Maybe you're right. But ——'

'You want to go to Kingston?'

'No!'

'You want to stay here and mope about them stars?'

Abruptly, Reich shouted. 'What the hell do I care about the stars!' His fear turned to hot rage. Adrenaline flooded his system, bringing with it a surge of courage and high spirits. He leaped into the cab. 'I've got the world. What do I care if a few delusions go with it?'

'That's the way, Mac. Where to?'

'The Royal Palace.'

'The which?'

Reich laughed. 'Monarch,' he said, and roared with laughter all the flight through the dawn to Monarch's soaring tower. But it was a semi-hysterical laughter.

The office ran around-the-clock shifts, and the night staff was in the last drowsy stages of the 12–8 shift when Reich bustled in. Although it had not seen much of him in the past month, the staff was accustomed to these visits, and shifted smoothly into high gear. As Reich went to his desk he was followed by secretaries and sub-secretaries carrying the urgent agenda of the day.

'Let all that wait,' he snapped. 'Call in the entire staff ... all department heads and organizational supervisors. I'm going to make an announcement.'

The flutter soothed him and recaptured his frame of reference. He was alive again, real again. All this was the only reality ... the hustle, the bustle, the annunciator bells, the muted commands, the quick filling of his office with so many awed faces. All this was a preveiw of the future when bells would ring on planets and satellites and world supervisors would scuttle to his desk with awe on their faces.

'As you all know,' Reich began pacing slowly and darting piercing glances into the faces that watched him, 'We of Monarch have been locked in a death-struggle with the D'Courtney Cartel. Craye D'Courtney was killed some time ago. There were complications that have just been ironed out. You'll be pleased to hear that the road is open for us now. We can commence operation of Plan AA to take over the D'Courtney Cartel.'

He paused, waiting for the excited murmur that should respond to his announcement. There was no response.

'Perhaps,' he said, 'some of you do not comprehend the size of the job and the importance of the job. Let me put it this way ... in terms you'll understand. Those of you that are city supervisors will become continental supervisors. Continental supervisors will become satellite chiefs. Present satellite chiefs will become planetary chiefs. From now on, Monarch will dominate the solar system. From now on all of us must think in terms of the solar system. From now on ...'

Reich faltered, alarmed by the blank looks around him. He glanced around, then singled out the chief secretary. 'What the hell's the matter?' he growled. 'There been news I haven't heard yet? Bad news?'

'N-no, Mr Reich.'

'Then what's eating you? This is something we've all been waiting for. What's wrong with it?'

The chief secretary stammered: 'We ... I ... I'm s-sorry, sir. I d-don't know what y-you're talking about.'

'I'm talking about the D'Courtney Cartel.'

'I ... I've n-never heard of the organization, Mr Reich, sir. I ... we

...' The chief secretary turned around for support. Before Reich's un-believing eyes the entire staff shook their heads in mystification.

'D'Courtney on Mars!' Reich shouted.

'On where, sir?'

'Mars! Mars! M-A-R-S. One of the ten planets. Fourth from the sun.' Gripped by the returning terror, Reich bellowed incoherently. 'Mercury, Venus, Earth, Mars, Jupiter, Saturn. Mars! Mars! Mars! A hundred and forty-one million miles from the sun, Mars!'

Again the staff shook their heads. There was a rustle and they backed away slightly from Reich. He darted at the secretaries and tore the sheafs of business papers from their hands. 'You've got a hundred memos about D'Courtney on Mars there. You've got to. My God, we've been battling it out with D'Courtney for the last ten years. We ——'

He clawed through the papers, throwing them wildly in all directions, filling the office with fluttering snow. There was not one reference to D'Courtney, or Mars. There was neither any reference to Venus, Jupiter, the Moon, nor the other satellites.

'I've got memos in my desk,' Reich shouted. 'Hundreds of them. You lousy liars! Look in my desk ...'

He darted to the desk and yanked out drawers. There was a stunning explosion. The desk burst asunder. Fragments of flying fruit-wood slashed the staff, and Reich was hurled back against the window by the desk top which smacked him like a giant's hand.

'The Man With No Face!' Reich cried. 'Christ Almighty!' He shook his head feverishly, and clung to the paramount obsession. 'Where are the files? I'll show you in the files ... D'Courtney and Mars and all the rest. And I'll show him, too. The Man With No Face ... Come on!'

He ran out of his office and burst into the file vaults. He tore out rack after rack; scattering papers, clusters of piezo crystals, ancient wire recordings, microfilm, molecular transcripts. There was no reference to D'Courtney or Mars. There was no reference to Venus, Jupiter, Mercury, the asteroids, the satellites.

And now indeed the office was alive with hustle and bustle, an-nunciator bells, strident commands. Now the office was stampeding, and three burly gentlemen from 'Recreation' came trotting into the vaults directed by the bleeding secretary who urged: 'You must! You must! I'll take the responsibility!'

'Easy now, easy now, easy now, Mr Reich,' they said with the hissing noise with which ostlers soothe savage stallions. 'Easy ... easy ... easy ...'

'Get away from me, you sons of bitches.'

'Easy sir. Easy. It's all right, sir.'

They deployed strategically while the hustle and the bustle increased and the bells sounded and voices far off called: 'Who's his doctor? Get his doctor. Somebody call Kingston. Did you notify the police? No, don't. No scandal. Get the legal department, will you! Isn't the Infirmary open yet?'

Reich's breath came and went in snarls. He overturned files in the path of the burly gentlemen, put his head down and bulled straight through them. He raced through the office to the outside corridor and the Pneumatique. The door opened; he punched Science-city 57. He stepped into the air-shuttle and was shot over to Science where he stepped out.

He was on the laboratory floor. It was in darkness. Probably the staff imagined he had dropped to the street level. He would have time. Still breathing heavily, he trotted to the lab library, snapped on the lights and went to the reference alcove. A sheet of frosted crystal, cocked like a draft-board, was set before a desk chair. There was a complicated panel of control buttons alongside it.

Reich seated himself and punched READY. The sheet lit up and a canned voice spoke from an overhead speaker.

'Topic?'

Reich punched SCIENCE.

'Section?'

Reich punched ASTRONOMY.

'Question?'

'The universe.'

Click-pause-click. 'The term universe in its complete physical sense applies to all matter in existence.' .

'What matter is in existence?'

Click-pause-click. 'Matter is gathered into aggregates ranging in size from the smallest atom to the largest collection of matter known to astronomers.'

'What is the largest collection of matter known to astronomers?' Reich punched DIAGRAM.

Click-pause-click. 'The sun.' The crystal plate displayed a dazzling picture of the sun in speed-up action.

'But what about the others? The stars?'

Click-pause-click. 'There are no stars.'

'The planets?'

Click-pause-click. 'There is the earth.' A picture of the revolving earth appeared.

'The other planets? Mars? Jupiter? Saturn ...'

Click-pause-click. 'There are no other planets.'

'The moon?'

Click-pause-click. 'There is no moon.'

Reich took a deep trembling breath. 'We'll try it again. Go back to the sun.'

The sun appeared again in the crystal. 'The sun is the largest collection of matter known to astronomers,' the canned voice began. Suddenly it stopped. Click-pause-click. The picture of the sun began to fade slowly. The voice spoke. 'There is no sun.'

The model disappeared, leaving behind it an after-image that looked up at Reich ... looming, silent, horrible ... The Man With No Face.

Reich howled. He leaped to his feet, knocking the desk chair backwards. He picked it up and smashed it down on that frightful image. He turned and blundered out of the library into the lab, and thence to the corridor. At the Vertical Pneumatique, he punched STREET. The door opened, he staggered in and was dropped fifty-seven storeys to the Main Hall of Monarch's Science-city.

It was filled with early workers hurrying to their offices. As Reich pushed past them, he caught the astonished glances at his cut and bleeding face. Then he was aware of a dozen uniformed Monarch guards closing in on him. He ran down the hall and with a frantic burst of speed dodged the guards. He slipped into the revolving doors and whirled through to the footway. There he jerked to a stop as though he had run into white hot iron. There was no sun.

The street lights were lit; the skyways twinkled; Jumper eyes floated up and down; the shops were blazing ... And overhead there was nothing ... nothing but a deep, black, fathomless infinity.

'The sun!' Reich shouted. 'The sun!'

He pointed upwards. The office workers regarded him with suspicious eyes and hurried on. No one looked up.

'The sun! Where's the sun? Don't you understand, you fools? The sun!' Reich plucked at their arms, shaking his fist at the sky. Then the first of the guards came through the revolving door and he took to his heels.

He went down the footway, turned sharp to his right and sprinted through an arcade of brilliant, busy shops. Beyond the arcade was the entrance of a Vertical Pneumatique to the skyway. Reich leaped in. As the door closed behind him, he caught sight of the pursuing guards less than twenty yards off. Then he was lofted seventy storeys and emerged on the skyway.

There was a small car-park alongside him, shelved on to the face of Monarch Tower, with a runway leading into the skyway. Reich ran in, flung credits to the attendant and got into a car. He pressed GO. The car went. At the foot of the runway he pressed LEFT. The car turned left and continued. That was all the control he had. Left, right; stop, go. The rest was automatic. Moreover, cars were strictly limited to the skyways. He might spend hours racing in circles high over the city, trapped like a dog in a revolving cage.

The car needed no attention. He glanced alternately over his shoulder and up at the sky. There was no sun ... and they went about their business as though there had never been a sun. He shuddered. Was this more of the one-eye kick? Suddenly the car slowed and stopped; and he was marooned in the middle of the skyway, half-way between Monarch Tower and the giant Visiphone & Visigraph Building.

Reich hammered on the control studs. There was no response. He leaped out and raised the tail hood to inspect the pick-up. Then he saw the guards far down the skyway, running towards him, and he understood. These cars were powered by broadcast energy. They'd cut the transmission off at the car-park and were coming after him. Reich turned and sprinted towards the V & V Building.

The skyway tunnelled through the building and was lined with shops, restaurants, a theatre – and there was a travel office! A sure out. He could grab a ticket, get into a one-man capsule and have himself slotted to any of the take-off fields. He needed a little time to reorganize ... reorient ... and he had a house in Paris. He leaped across the centre island, dodged past cars and ran into the office.

It looked like a miniature bank. A short counter. A grilled window protected by burglar-proof plastic. Reich went to the window, pulling money from his pocket. He slapped credits down on the counter and shoved them under the grille.

'Ticket to Paris,' he said. 'Keep the change. Which way to the capsules? Jet, man! Jet!'

'Paris?' came the reply. 'There is no Paris.'

Reich stared through the cloudy plastic and saw ... looking, looming, silent ... The Man With No Face. He spun around twice, heart pounding, skull pounding, located the door and ran out. He ran blindly on to the skyway, shied feebly from an oncoming car, and was struck down into enveloping darkness –

ABOLISH.

DESTROY.

DELETE.

DISBAND

(MINERALOGY, PETROLOGY, GEOLOGY, PHYSIOGRAPHY)

DISPERSE.

(METEOROLOGY, HYDROLOGY, SEISMOLOGY)

ERASE.

$(X^2 \phi Y^3 d:$ Space/d: Time)

EFFACE.

THE SUBJECT WILL BE –

'– will be what?'

THE SUBJECT WILL BE —

'– will be what? What? WHAT?'

A hand was placed over his mouth. Reich opened his eyes. He was in a small tiled room, an emergency police station. He was lying on a white table. Around him were grouped the guards, three uniformed police, unidentified strangers. All were writing carefully in report books, murmuring, shifting confusedly.

The stanger removed his hand from Reich's mouth and bent over him. 'It's all right,' he said gently. 'Easy. I'm a doctor ...'

'A peeper?'

'What?'

'Are you a peeper? I need a peeper. I need somebody inside my head to prove I'm right. My God! I've got to know I'm right. I don't care about the price. I ——'

'What's he want?' a policeman asked.

'I don't know. He said a peeper.' The doctor turned back to Reich. 'What d'you mean by that? Just tell us. What's a peeper?'

'An Esper? A mind-reader. A ——'

The doctor smiled. 'He's joking. Show of high spirits. Many patients do that. They simulate sang-froid after accidents. We call it Gallows Humour ...'

'Listen,' Reich said desperately. 'Let me up. I want to say something ...'

They helped him up.

To the police, he said: 'My name is Ben Reich. Ben Reich of Monarch. You know me. I want to confess. I want to confess to Lincoln Powell, the police prefect. Take me to Powell.'

'Who's Powell?'

'And what y'want to confess?'

'The D'Courtney murder. I murdered Craye d'Courtney last month. In Maria Beaumont's house ... Tell Powell. I killed D'Courtney.'

The police looked at each other in surprise. One of them drifted to a corner and picked up an old-fashioned hand phone: 'Captain? Got a character here. Calls himself Ben Reich of Monarch. Wants to confess to some prefect named Powell. Claims he killed a party named Craye D'Courtney last month.' After a pause, the policeman called to Reich: 'How do you spell that?'

'D'Courtney! Capital D apostrophe Capital C-O-U-R-T-N-E-Y.'

The policeman spelled it out and waited. After another pause, he grunted and hung up. 'A nut,' he said and stowed his notebook in a pocket.

'Listen ——' Reich began.

'Is he all right?' the policeman asked the doctor without looking at Reich.

'Just shaken a little. He's all right.'

'Listen!' Reich shouted.

The policeman yanked him to his feet and propelled him towards the door of the station. 'All right, buddy. Out!'

'You've got to listen to me! I ——'

'You listen to me, buddy. There ain't no Lincoln Powell in the service. There ain't no D'Courtney killing in the books. And we ain't takin' no slok from your kind. Now ... Out!' And he hurled Reich into the street.

The pavement was strangely broken. Reich stumbled, then regained his balance and stood still, numb, lost. It was darker ... eternally darker. A few street lights were lit. The skyways were extinguished. The Jumpers had disappeared. There were great gaps shorn in the skyline.

'I'm sick,' Reich moaned. 'I'm sick. I need help ...'

He began to lurch down the broken street with arms clutching his belly.

'Jumper!' he yelled. 'Jumper! Isn't there anything in this Godforsaken city? Where is everything? Jumper!'

There was nothing.

'I'm sick ... sick. Got to get home. I'm sick ...' Again he shouted: 'Isn't there anybody can hear me? I'm sick. I need help ... Help! ... Help!'

There was nothing.

He moaned again. Then he tittered ... weakly, inanely. He sang in a broken voice: 'Eight, sir ... Five, sir ... One, sir ... Tenser said Tensor ... Tension ... apprehension ...'ssension have begun ...'

He called plaintively: 'Where is everybody? Maria! Lights! Ma-ri-aaa! Stop this crazy Sardine game!'

He stumbled.

'Come back!' Reich called. 'For God's sake, come back! I'm all alone.' No answer.

He was searching for 9 Park South, looking for the Beaumont Mansion, the site of D'Courtney's death ... and Maria Beaumont, shrill, decadent, reassuring.

There was nothing.

A bleak tundra. Black sky. Unfamiliar desolation.

Nothing.

Reich shouted once ... a hoarse, inarticulate yell of rage and fright. No answer. Not even an echo.

'For God's sake!' he cried. 'Where is everything? Bring it all back! There's nothing but space ...'

Out of the enveloping desolation, a figure gathered and grew, familiar, ominous, gigantic ... A figure of black shadows, looking, looming, silent ... The Man With No Face. Reich watched it, paralysed, transfixed.

Then the figure spoke: 'There is no space. There is nothing.'

And there was a screaming in Reich's ears that was his voice, and a hammering pulse that was his heart. He was running down a yawning alien path, devoid of life, devoid of space, running before it was too late, too late, too late . . . running while there was still time, time, time ——

He ran headlong into a figure of black shadows. A figure without a face. A figure that said: 'There is no time. There is nothing.'

Reich backed away. He turned. He fell. He crawled feebly through eternal emptiness shrieking: 'Powell! Duffy! Quizzard! Tate! Oh Christ! Where is everybody? Where is everything? For the love of God . . .'

And he was face to face with The Man With No Face who said: 'There is no God. There is nothing.'

And now there was no longer escape. There was only a negative infinity and Reich and The Man With No Face. And fixed, frozen, helpless in that matrix, Reich at last raised his eyes and stared deep into the face of his deadly enemy . . . the man he could not escape . . . the terror of his nightmares . . . the destroyer of his existence . . .

It was . . .

Himself.

D'Courtney.

Both.

Two faces, blending into one. Ben D'Courtney. Craye Reich. D'Courtney-Reich. D'R.

He could make no sound. He could make no move. There was neither time nor space nor matter. There was nothing left but dying thought.

'*Father?*'

'*Son.*'

'*You are me?*'

'*We are us.*'

'*Father and son?*'

'*Yes.*'

'*I can't understand . . . What's happened?*'

'*You lost the game, Ben.*'

'*The Sardine Game?*'

'*The Cosmic Game.*'

'*I won. I won. I owned every bit of the world. I ——*'

'*And therefore you lose. We lose.*'

'*Lose what?*'

'*Survival.*'

'*I don't understand. I can't understand.*'

'*My part of us understands, Ben. You would understand too if you hadn't driven me from you.*'

'*How did I drive you from me?*'

'*With every rotten, distorted corruption in you.*'

'*You say that? You . . . betrayer, who tried to kill me?*'

'*That was without passion, Ben. That was to destroy you before you could destroy us. That was for survival. It was to help you lose the world and win the game, Ben.*'

'*What game? What Cosmic Game?*'

'*The maze ... the labyrinth ... all the universe, created as a puzzle for us to solve. The galaxies, the stars, the sun, the planets ... the world was e knew it. We are the only reality. All the rest was make-believe ... dolls, puppets, stage-settings ... pretended passions. It was a make-believe reality for us to solve.*'

'*I conquered it. I owned it.*'

'*And you failed to solve it. We'll never know what the solution is, but it's not theft, terror, hatred, lust, murder, rapine. You failed, and it's all been abolished, disbanded ...*'

'*But what's to become of us?*'

'*We are abolished too. I tried to warn you. I tried to stop you. But we failed the test.*'

'*But why? Why? Who are we? What are we?*'

'*Who knows? Did the seed know who or what it was when it failed to find fertile soil? Does it matter who or what we are? We have failed. Our test is ended. We are ended.*'

'*No!*'

'*Perhaps if we had solved it, Ben, it might have remained real. But it ended. Reality has turned into might-have-been, and you have awakened at last ... to nothing.*'

'*We'll go back! We'll try it again!*'

'*There is no going back. It is ended.*'

'*We'll find a way. There must be a way ...*'

'*There is none. It is ended.*'

It was ended.

Now ... Demolition.

CHAPTER 17

They found the two men next morning, far up the island in the gardens overlooking the old Haarlem Canal. Each had wandered all the night, through footway and skyway, unconscious of his surroundings, yet both were drawn inevitably together like two magnetized needles floating on a weed-choked pond.

Powell was seated cross-legged on the wet turf, his face shrivelled and lifeless, his respiration almost gone, his pulse faded. He was clutching Reich with an iron grip. Reich was curled into a tight foetal ball.

They rushed Powell to his home on Hudson Ramp where the entire Guild Lab team alternately sweated over him and congratulated themselves on the first successful Mass Cathexis Measure in the history of the Esper Guild. There was no hurry for Reich. In due course and with proper procedure, his inert body was transported to Kingston Hospital for Demolition.

There the matter rested for seven days.

On the eighth day, Powell arose, bathed, dressed, successfully defeated his nurses in single combat, and left the house. He made one stop at Sucre et Cie, emerged with a large mysterious parcel and then proceeded to headquarters to make his personal report to Commissioner Crabbe. On the way up, he poked his head into Beck's office.

'Hi, Jax.'

'Bless(and curses)ings, Linc.'

'Curses?'

'Bet fifty they'd keep you in bed till next Wed.'

'You lose. Did Mose back us up on the D'Courtney motive?'

'Lock, stock & barrel. Trial took one hour. Reich's going into Demolition now.'

'Good. Well, I'd better go up and s-p-e-l-l it out for Crabbe.'

'What you got under your arm?'

'Present.'

'For me?'

'Not today. Here's thinking at you.'

Powell went up to Crabbe's ebony and silver office, knocked, heard the imperious: 'Come!' and entered. Crabbe was properly solicitous, but stiff. The D'Courtney Case had not improved his relations with Powell. The denouement had come as an additional blow.

'It was a remarkably complex case, sir,' Powell began tactfully. 'None of us could understand it, and none of us are to blame. You see, Commissioner, even Reich himself was not consciously aware of why he had murdered D'Courtney. The only one who grasped the case was the Prosecuting computer, and we thought it was acting kittenish.'

'The machine? It understood?'

'Yes, sir. When we ran our final data through the first time, the Computor told us that the "passion motive" was insufficiently documented. We'd all been assuming profit motive. So had Reich. Naturally we assumed the Computor was having kinks, and we insisted on computation based on the profit motive. We were wrong ...'

'And that infernal machine was right?'

'Yes, Commissioner. It was. Reich told himself that he was killing D'Courtney for financial reasons. That was his psychological camouflage for the real passion motive. And it couldn't hold up. He offered merger to D'Courtney. D'Courtney accepted. But Reich was subconsciously compelled to misunderstand the message. he had to. He had to go on believing he murdered for money.'

'Why?'

'Because he couldn't face the real motive ...'

'Which was ...?'

'D'Courtney was his father.'

'What!' Crabbe stared. 'His father? His flesh and blood?'

'Yes, sir. It was all there before us. We just couldn't see it ... because Reich couldn't see it. That estate on Callisto, for instance. The one that Reich used to decoy Dr Jordan off the planet. Reich inherited it from his mother who'd received it from D'Courtney. We all assumed Reich's father had chiselled it out of D'Courtney and placed it in his wife's name. We were wrong. D'Courtney had given it to Reich's mother because they were lovers. It was his love-gift to the mother of his child. Reich was born there. Jackson Beck uncovered all that, once we had the lead.'

Crabbe opened his mouth, then closed it.

'And there were so many other signposts. D'Courtney's suicide drive, produced by intense guilt sensations of abandonment. He *had* abandoned his son. It was tearing him apart. Then, Barbara D'Courtney's deep half-twin image of herself and Ben Reich; somehow she knew they were half-brother and sister. And Reich's inability to kill Barbara at Chooka Frood's. He knew it too, deep down in the unconscious. He wanted to destroy the hateful father who had rejected him, but he could not bring himself to harm his sister.'

'But when did you unearth all this?'

'After the case was closed, sir. When Reich attacked me for setting those booby-traps.'

'He claimed you did. He —— But if you didn't, Powell, who did?'

'Reich himself, sir.'

'Reich!'

'Yes, sir. He murdered his father. He discharged his hatred. But his super-ego ... his conscience, could not permit him to go unpunished for such a horrible crime. Since the police apparently were unable to punish him, his conscience took over. That was the meaning of Reich's nightmare image ... The Man With No Face.'

'The Man With No Face?'

'Yes, Commissioner. It was the symbol of Reich's real relationship to D'Courtney. The figure had no face because Reich could not accept the truth ... that he had recognized D'Courtney as his father. The figure appeared in his dreams when he made the decision to kill his father. It never left him. It was first the threat of punishment for what he contemplated. Then it became the punishment itself for the murder.'

'The booby-traps?'

'Exactly. His conscience had to punish him. But Reich had never admitted to himself that he murdered because he hated D'Courtney as the father who had rejected and abandoned him. Therefore, the punishment had to take place on the unconscious level. Reich set those traps for himself without ever realizing it ... in his sleep, somnambulistically ... during the day, in short fugues ... brief departures from conscious reality. The tricks of the mind-mechanism are fantastic.'

'But if Reich himself knew none of this ... how did you get at it, Powell?'

'Well, sir. That was the problem. We couldn't get it by peeping him. He was hostile and you have to have complete cooperation from a subject to get that kind of material. It takes months anyway. Also, if Reich recovered from the series of shocks he'd had he would be able to readjust, reorient and become immune to us. That was dangerous, too, because he was in a position of power to rock the solar system. He was one of those rare World-Shakers whose compulsions might have torn down our society and irrevocably committed us to his own psychotic pattern.'

Crabbe nodded.

'He very nearly succeeded. These men appear every so often ... links between the past and the future. If they are permitted to mature ... If the link is permitted to weld ... The world finds itself chained to a dreadful tomorrow.'

'Then what did you do?'

'We used the Mass Cathexis Measure, sir. It's difficult to explain, but I'll do my best. Every human being has a psyche composed of latent and capitalized energy. Latent energy is our reserve ... the untapped natural resources of our mind. Capitalized energy is that latent energy which we call up and put to work. Most of us use only a small portion of our latent energy.'

'I understand.'

'When the Esper Guild uses the Mass Cathexis Measure, every Esper opens his psyche, so to speak, and contributes his latent energy to a pool. One Esper alone taps this pool and becomes the canal for the latent energy. He capitalizes it and puts it to work. He can accomplish tremendous things ... if he can control it. It's a difficult and dangerous operation. About on a par with jetting to the moon with a stick of dynamite stuck – er – riding on dynamite sticks ...'

Suddenly Crabbe grinned. 'I wish I were a peeper,' he said, 'I'd like to get the real image in your mind.'

'You've got it already, sir.' Powell grinned back. A rapport had been established between them for the first time.

'It was necessary,' Powell continued, 'to confront Reich with The Man With No Face. We had to make him see the truth before we could get the truth. Using the pool of latent energy, I built a common neurotic concept for Reich ... the illusion that he alone in the world was real.'

'Why, I've —— Is that common?'

'Oh yes, sir. It's one of the run-of-the-mill escape patterns. When life gets tough, you tend to take refuge in the idea that it's all make-believe ... a giant hoax. Reich had the seeds of that weakness in him already. I simply forced them and let Reich defeat himself. Life was getting tough for him. I persuaded him to believe that the universe was a hoax ... a puzzle-box. Then I tore it down, layer by layer. I made him believe that the test was ended. The puzzle was being dismantled. And I left Reich alone with The Man With No Face. He looked into the face and saw himself and his father ... and we had everything.'

Powell picked up his parcel and rose. Crabbe jumped up and escorted him to the door with a friendly hand on his shoulder.

'You've done a phenomenal job, Powell. Really phenomenal. I can't tell you ... It must be a wonderful thing to be an Esper.'

'Wonderful and terrible, sir.'

'You must all be very happy.'

'Happy?' Powell paused at the door and looked at Crabbe. 'Would you be happy to live your life in a hospital, Commissioner?'

'A hospital?'

'That's where we live ... All of us. In the psychiatric ward. Without escape ... without refuge. Be grateful you're not a peeper, sir. Be grateful that you only see the outward man. Be grateful that you never see the passions, the hatreds, the jealousies, the malice, the sickness ... Be grateful you rarely see the frighteng truth in people. The world will be a wonderful place when everyone's a peeper and everyone's adjusted ... But until then, be grateful you're blind.'

He left headquarters, hired a Jumper and was jetted North towards Kingston Hospital. He sat in the cabin with the parcel on his knees, gazing down at the magnificent Hudson valley, whistling a crooked tune. Once he grinned and muttered: 'Wow! That was some line I handed Crabbe. But I had to cement our relations. Now he'll feel sorry for peepers ... and friendly.'

Kingston Hospital came into view ... acre upon rolling acre of magnificent landscaping. Solariums, pools, lawns, athletic fields, dormitories, clinics ... all in exquisite neoclassic design. As the Jumper descended, Powell could make out the figures of patients and attendants ... all bronzed, active, laughing, playing. He thought of the vigilant measures the Board of Governors was forced to take to prevent Kingston Hospital from becoming another Spaceland. Too many fashionable malingerers were already attempting to obtain admission.

Powell checked in at the Visitors Office, found Barbara D'Courtney's location and started across the grounds. He was weak, but he wanted to leap hedges, vault gates, run races. He had awakened after seven days' exhaustion with a question – one question to ask Barbara. He felt exhilarated.

They saw one another at the same moment. Across a broad stretch of lawn flanked by field-stone terraces and brilliant gardens. She flew towards him, waving, and he ran towards her. Then as they approached, both were stricken with shyness. They stopped a few feet apart, not daring to look at each other.

'Hello.'

'Hello, Barbara.'

'I ... Let's get into the shade, shall we?'

They turned towards the terrace wall. Powell glanced at her from the corner of his eye. She was alive again ... alive as he had never seen her before. And her urchin expression – the expression that he had imagined was a phase of her Déjà Éprouvé development – was still there. She looked inexpressibly mischievous, high spirited, fascinating. But she was adult. He did not know her.

'I'm being discharged this evening,' Barbara said.

'I know.'

'I'm terribly grateful to you for all you've ——'

'Please don't say that.'

'For all you've done,' Barbara continued firmly. They sat down on a stone bench. She looked at him with grave eyes. 'I want to tell you how grateful I am.'

'Please, Barbara. You're terrifying me.'

'Am I?'

'I knew you so intimately as ... well, as a child. Now ...'

'Now I'm grown up again.'

'Yes.'

'You must get to know me better.' She smiled graciously. 'Shall we say ... Tea tomorrow at five?'

'At five ...'

'Informal. Don't dress.'

'Listen,' Powell said desperately. 'I helped dress you more than once. And comb your hair. And brush your teeth.'

She waved her hand airily.

'Your table manners were a caution. You liked fish but you hated lamb. You hit me in the eye with a chop.'

'That was ages ago, Mr Powell.'

'That was two weeks ago, Miss D'Courtney.'

She arose with a magnificent poise. 'Really Mr Powell. I feel it would be best to end the interview. If you feel impelled to cast chronographical aspersions ...' She stopped and looked at him. The urchin appeared again in her face. 'Chronographical?' she inquired.

He dropped the parcel and caught her in his arms.

'Mr Powell, Mr Powell, Mr Powell ...' she murmured. 'Hello, Mr Powell ...'

'My God, Barbara ... Baba, dear. For a moment I thought you meant it.'

'I was paying you back for being grown up.'

'You always were a revengeful kid.'

'You always were a mean daddy.' She leaned back and looked at him. 'What are you really like? What are we both like? Will we have time to find out?'

'Time?'

'Before ... Peep me. I can't say it.'

'No, dear. You'll have to say it.'

'Mary Noyes told me. Everything.'

'Oh. She did?'

Barbara nodded. 'But I don't care. I don't care. She was right. I'll settle for anything. Even if you can't marry me ...'

He laughed. The exhilaration bubbled out of him. 'You won't have to settle for anything,' he said. 'Sit down. I want to ask you one question.'

She sat down. On his lap.

'I have to go back to that night,' he said.

'In Beaumont House?'

He nodded.

'It's not easy to talk about.'

'It won't take a minute. Now ... You were lying in bed, asleep. Suddenly you woke up and rushed into the Orchid room. You remember the rest ...'

'I remember.'

'One question. What was the cry that woke you?'

'You know.'

'I know, but I want you to say it. Say it out loud.'

'Do you think it's ... it's going to send me into hysteria again?'

'No. Just say it.'

After a long pause she said in a low voice: 'Help, Barbara.'

He nodded again. 'Who shouted that?'

'Why it was ——' Suddenly she stopped.

'It wasn't Ben Reich. He wouldn't be yelling for help. He didn't need help. Who did?'

'My ... My father.'

'But he couldn't speak, Barbara. His throat was gone ... Cancer. He couldn't utter a word.'

'I heard him.'

'You peeped him.'

She stared: then she shook her head. 'No I ——'

'You peeped him,' Powell repeated gently. 'You're a latent Esper. Your father cried out on the telepathic level. If I hadn't been such an ass and so intent on Reich, I'd have realized it long before. You were unconsciously peeping Mary and me all the while you were in my house.'

She couldn't grasp it.

'*Do you love me?*' Powell shot at her.

'I love you of course,' she muttered, 'but I think your inventing excuses to ——'

'Who asked you?'

'Asked me what?'

'If you loved me.'

'Why you just ——' She stopped, then tried again. 'You said ... Y-You ...'

'I didn't say it. Do you understand now? We won't have to settle for anything short of us.'

Seconds later, it seemed, but it was actually half an hour, they were separated by a violent crash that sounded from the top of the terrace above their heads. They looked up in astonishment.

A naked thing appeared on the stone wall, gibbering, screaming, twitching. It toppled over the edge and crashed down through the flower-beds until it landed on the lawn, crying and jerking as though a steady stream of voltage was pouring through its nervous system. It was Ben Reich, almost unrecognizable, partway through demolition.

Powell swung Barbara to him with her back to Reich. He took her chin in his hand and said: 'Are you still my girl?'

She nodded.

'I don't want you to see this. It isn't dangerous, but it isn't good for you. Will you run back to your pavilion and wait for me? Like a good girl? All right ... Scamper now! Jet!'

She grabbed his hand, kissed it quickly, and ran across the lawn without once looking back. Powell watched her go, then turned and inspected Reich.

When a man is demolished at Kingston Hospital, his entire psyche is destroyed. The series of osmotic injections begins with the topmost strata of cortical synapses and slowly works down, switching off every circuit, extinguishing every memory, destroying every particle of the pattern that has been built up since birth. And as the pattern is erased, each particle discharges its portion of energy, turning the entire body into a shuddering maelstrom of dissociation.

But this is not the pain; this is not the dread of Demolition. The horror lies in the fact that the consciousness is never lost; that as the psyche is wiped out, the mind is aware of its slow, backward death until at last it too disappears and awaits the rebirth. The mind bids an eternity of farewells; it mourns at an endless funeral. And in those blinking, twitching eyes of Ben Reich, Powell saw the awareness ... the pain ... the tragic despair.

'Now how the hell did he fall down there? Do we have to keep him tied?' Dr Jeems poked his head over the terrace. 'Oh. Hi, Powell. That's a friend of yours. Remember him?'

'Vividly.'

Jeems spoke over his shoulder: 'You go down to the lawn and pick him up. I'll keep an eye on him.' He turned to Powell. 'He's a lusty lad. We've got great hopes for him.'

Reich squalled and twitched.

'How's the treatment coming?'

'Wonderful. He's got the stamina to take anything. We're stepping him up. Ought to be ready for rebirth in a year.'

'I'm waiting for it. We need men like Reich. It would have been a shame to lose him.'

'Lose him? How's that possible? You don't think a little fall like that could ——'

'No. I mean something else. Three or four hundred years ago, cops used to catch people like Reich just to kill them. Capital punishment, they called it.'

'You're kidding.'

'Scout's honour.'

'But it doesn't make sense. If a man's got the talent and guts to buck society, he's obviously about average. You want to hold on to him. You straighten him out and turn him into a plus value. Why throw him away? Do that enough and all you've got left are the sheep.'

'I don't know. Maybe in those days they wanted sheep.'

The attendants came trotting across the lawn and picked Reich up. He fought and screamed. They handled him with the deft and gentle Kingston judo while they checked him carefully for breaks and sprains. Then, reassured, they started to lead him away.

'Just a minute,' Powell called. He turned to the stone bench, picked up the mysterious parcel and unwrapped it. It was one of Sucre et Cie's most magnificent candy boxes. He carried it to the demolished man and held it out. 'It's a present for you, Ben. Take it.'

The creature lowered at Powell and then at the box. At last the clumsy hands came out and took the gift.

'Why damn it, I'm just his nursemaid,' Powell muttered. 'We're all of us nursemaids to this crazy world. Is it worth it?'

Out of the chaos in Reich came an explosive fragment: '*Powell-peeper-Powell-friend-Powell-friend ...*'

It was so sudden, so unexpected, so passionately grateful that Powell was overcome with warmth and tears. He tried to smile, then turned away and wandered across the lawn towards the pavilion and Barbara.

'*Listen,*' he cried in exaltation. '*Listen, normals! You must learn what it is. You must learn how it is. You must tear the barriers down. You must tear the veils away. We see the truth you cannot see … That there is nothing in man but love and faith, courage and kindness, generosity and sacrifice. All else is only the barrier of your blindness. One day we'll all be mind to mind and heart to heart …*'

In the endless universe there has been nothing new, nothing different. What has appeared exceptional to the minute mind of man has been inevitable to the infinite Eye of God. This strange second in a life, that unusual event, those remarkable coincidences of environment, opportunity and encounter … all of them have been reproduced over and over on the planet of a sun whose galaxy revolves once in two hundred million years and has revolved nine times already. There has been joy. There will be joy again.

The Day of the Triffids

JOHN WYNDHAM

CHAPTER I

THE END BEGINS

When a day that you happen to know is Wednesday starts off by sounding like Sunday, there is something seriously wrong somewhere.

I felt that from the moment I woke. And yet, when I started functioning a little more sharply, I misgave. After all, the odds were that it was I who was wrong, and not everyone else – though I did not see how that could be. I went on waiting, tinged with doubt. But presently I had my first bit of objective evidence – a distant clock struck what sounded to me just like eight. I listened hard and suspiciously. Soon another clock began, on a loud, decisive note. In a leisurely fashion it gave an indisputable eight. Then I *knew* things were awry.

The way I came to miss the end of the world – well, the end of the world I had known for close on thirty years – was sheer accident: like a lot of survival, when you come to think of it. In the nature of things a good many somebodies are always in hospital, and the law of averages had picked on me to be one of them a week or so before. It might just as easily have been the week before that – in which case I'd not be writing now: I'd not be here at all. But chance played it not only that I should be in hospital at that particular time, but that my eyes, and indeed my whole head, should be wreathed in bandages – and that's why I have to be grateful to whoever orders these averages. At the time, however, I was only peevish, wondering what in thunder went on, for I had been in the place long enough to know that, next to the matron, the clock is the most sacred thing in a hospital.

Without a clock the place simply couldn't latch. Each second there's someone consulting it on births, deaths, doses, meals, lights, talking, working, sleeping, resting, visiting, dressing, washing – and hitherto it had decreed that someone should begin to wash and tidy me up at exactly three minutes after 7 a.m. That was one of the best reasons I had for appreciating a private room. In a public ward the messy proceeding would have taken place a whole unnecessary hour earlier. But here, today, clocks of varying reliability were continuing to strike eight in all directions – and still nobody had shown up.

Much as I disliked the sponging process, and useless as it had been to suggest that the help of a guiding hand as far as the bathroom could eliminate it, its failure to occur was highly disconcerting. Besides, it was normally a close forerunner of breakfast, and I was feeling hungry.

Probably I would have been aggrieved about it any morning, but today, this Wednesday May 8th, was an occasion of particular personal importance. I was doubly anxious to get all the fuss and routine over because that was the day they were going to take off my bandages.

I groped around a bit to find the bell-push, and let them have a full five seconds clatter, just to show what I was thinking of them.

While I was waiting for the pretty short-tempered response that such a peal ought to bring, I went on listening.

The day outside, I realized now, was sounding even more wrong than I had thought. The noises it made, or failed to make, were more like Sunday than Sunday itself – and I'd come round again to be absolutely assured that it *was* Wednesday, whatever else had happened to it.

Why the founders of St Merryn's Hospital chose to erect their institution at a main road crossing upon a valuable office-site and thus expose their patients' nerves to constant laceration, is a foible that I never properly understood. But for those fortunate enough to be suffering from complaints unaffected by the wear and tear of continuous traffic, it did have the advantage that one could lie abed and still not be out of touch, so to speak, with the flow of life. Customarily the west-bound buses thundered along trying to beat the lights at the corner; as often as not a pig-squeal of brakes and a salvo of shots from the silencer would tell that they hadn't. Then the released cross-traffic would rev and roar as it started up the incline. And every now and then there would be an interlude: a good grinding bump, followed by a general stoppage – exceedingly tantalizing to one in my condition where the extent of the contretemps had to be judged entirely by the degree of profanity resulting. Certainly, neither by day nor during most of the night, was there any chance of a St Merryn patient being under the impression that the common round had stopped just because he, personally, was on the shelf for the moment.

But this morning was different. Disturbingly because mysteriously different. No wheels rumbled, no buses roared, no sound of a car of any kind, in fact, was to be heard. No brakes, no horns, not even the clopping of the few rare horses that still occasionally passed. Nor, as there should be at such an hour, the composite tramp of work-bound feet.

The more I listened, the queerer it seemed – and the less I cared for it. In what I reckoned to be ten minutes of careful listening I heard five sets of shuffling, hesitating footsteps, three voices bawling unintelligibly in the distance, and the hysterical sobs of a woman. There was not the cooing of a pigeon, not the chirp of a sparrow. Nothing but the humming of wires in the wind...

A nasty, empty feeling began to crawl up inside me. It was the same sensation I used to have sometimes as a child when I got to fancying that horrors were lurking in the shadowy corners of the bedroom; when I daren't put a foot out for fear that something should reach from under the bed and grab my ankle; daren't even reach for the switch lest the movement should cause something to leap at me. I had to fight down the feeling, just as I had had to when I was a kid in the dark. And it was no easier. It's surprising how much you don't grow out of when it comes to the test. The elemental fears were still marching along with me, waiting their chance, and pretty nearly getting it – just because my eyes were bandaged, and the traffic had stopped...

When I had pulled myself together a bit, I tried the reasonable approach. Why *does* traffic stop? Well, usually because the road is closed for repairs. Perfectly simple. Any time now they'd be along with pneumatic drills as another touch of aural variety for the long-suffering patients. But the trouble with the reasonable line was that it went further. It pointed out that there was not even the distant hum of traffic, not the whistle of a train, not the hoot of a tugboat. Just nothing – until the clocks began chiming a quarter past eight.

The temptation to take a peep – not more than a peep, of course; just enough to get some idea of what on earth could be happening, was immense. But I restrained it. For one thing, a peep was a far less simple matter than it sounded. It wasn't just a case of lifting a blindfold: there were a lot of pads and bandages. But, more importantly. I was scared to try. Over a week's complete blindness can do a lot to frighten you out of taking chances with your sight. It was true that they intended to remove the bandages today, but that would be done in a special, dim light, and they would only allow them to stay off if the inspection of my eyes were satisfactory. I did not know whether it would be. It might be that my sight was permanently impaired. Or that I would not be able to see at all. I did not know yet...

I swore, and laid hold of the bell-push again. It helped to relieve my feelings a bit.

No one, it seemed, was interested in bells. I began to get as much annoyed as worried. It's humiliating to be dependent, anyway, but it's a still poorer pass to have no one to depend on. My patience was whittling down. Something, I decided, had got to be done about it.

If I were to bawl down the passage and generally raise hell, somebody ought to show up if only to tell me what they thought of me. I turned back the sheet, and got out of bed. I'd never seen the room I was in, and though I had a fairly good idea by ear of the position of the door, it wasn't all that easy to find. There seemed to be several puzzling and unnecessary obstacles, but I got across at the cost of a stubbed toe and minor damage to my shin. I shoved my head out into the passage.

'Hey!' I shouted. 'I want some breakfast. Room forty-eight!'

For a moment nothing happened. Then came voices all shouting together. It sounded like hundreds of them, and not a word coming through clearly. It was as though I'd put on a record of crowd noises – and an ill-disposed crowd at that. I had a nightmarish flash wondering whether I had been transferred to a mental home while I was sleeping, and that this was not St Merryn's Hospital at all. Those voices simply didn't sound normal to me. I closed the door hurriedly on the babel, and groped my way back to bed. At that moment bed seemed to be the one safe, comforting thing in my whole baffling environment. As if to underline that there came a sound which checked me in the act of pulling up the sheets. From the street below rose a scream, wildly distraught and contagiously terrifying. It came three times, and when it had died away it seemed still to tingle in the air.

I shuddered. I could feel the sweat prickle my forehead under the bandages. I knew now that something fearful and horrible was happening. I could not stand my isolation and helplessness any longer. I had to know what was going on around me. I put my hands up to my bandages; then, with my fingers on the safety-pins, I stopped . . .

Suppose the treatment had not been successful? Suppose that when I took the bandages off I were to find that I still could not see? That would be worse still – a hundred times worse . . .

I lacked the courage to be alone and find out that they had not saved my sight. And even if they had, would it be safe yet to keep my eyes uncovered?

I dropped my hands, and lay back. I was wild at myself and the place, and I did some silly, weak cursing.

Some little while must have passed before I got a proper hold on things again, but after a bit I found myself churning round in my mind once more after a possible explanation. I did not find it. But I did become absolutely convinced that, come all the paradoxes of hell, it was Wednesday. For the previous day had been notable, and I could swear that no more than a single night had passed since then.

You'll find it in the records that on Tuesday, May 7th, the Earth's orbit passed through a cloud of comet debris. You can even believe it, if you like – millions did. Maybe it was so. I can't prove anything either way. I was in no state to see what happened; but I do have my own ideas. All that I actually know of the occasion is that I had to spend the evening in my bed listening to eye-witness accounts of what was constantly claimed to be the most remarkable celestial spectacle on record.

And yet, until the thing actually began nobody had ever heard a word about this supposed comet, or its debris...

Why they broadcast it, considering that everyone who could walk, hobble, or be carried was either out of doors or at windows enjoying the greatest free firework display ever, I don't know. But they did, and it helped to impress on me still more heavily what it meant to be sightless. I got round to feeling that if the treatment had not been successful I'd rather end the whole thing than go on that way.

It was reported in the news-bulletins during the day that mysterious bright green flashes had been seen in the Californian skies the previous night. However, such a lot of things did happen in California that no one could be expected to get greatly worked up over that, but as further reports came in this comet-debris motif made its appearance, and it stuck.

Accounts arrived from all over the Pacific of a night made brilliant by green meteors said to be 'sometimes in such numerous showers that the whole sky appeared to be wheeling about us'. And so it was, when you come to think of it.

As the night line moved westward the brilliance of the display was in no way decreased. Occasional green flashes became visible even before darkness fell. The announcer, giving an account of the phenomenon in the six o'clock news, advised everyone that it was an amazing scene, and one not to be missed. He mentioned also that it seemed to be interfering seriously with short-wave reception at long distances, but that the medium waves on which there would be a running commentary were unaffected, as, at present, was television. He need not have troubled with the advice. By the way everyone in the hospital got excited about it, it seemed to me that there was not the least likelihood of anybody missing it – except myself.

And, as if the radio's comments were not enough, the nurse who brought me my supper had to tell me all about it.

'The sky's simply full of shooting stars,' she said. 'All bright green. They make people's faces look frightfully ghastly. *Every*body's out watching them, and sometimes it's almost as light as day – only all the wrong colour. Every now and then there's a big one so bright that it hurts to look at it. It's a marvellous sight. They say there's never been anything like it before. It is such a pity you can't see it, isn't it?'

'It is,' I agreed, somewhat shortly.

'We've drawn back the curtains in the wards so that they can all see it,' she went on. 'If only you hadn't those bandages you'd have a wonderful view of it from here.'

'Oh,' I said.

'But it must be better still outside, though. They say thousands of people are out in the parks and on the Heath watching it all. And on all the flat roofs you can see people standing and looking up.'

'How long do they expect it to go on?' I asked, patiently.

'I don't know, but they say it's not so bright now as it was in other places. Still, even if you'd had your bandages off today I don't expect they'd have let you watch it. You'll have to take things gently at first, and some of the flashes are very bright. They—— Ooooh!'

'Why "ooooh"?' I enquired.

'That was such a brilliant one then – it made the whole room look green. What a pity you couldn't see it.'

'Isn't it?' I agreed. 'Now do go away, there's a good girl.'

I tried listening to the radio, but it was making the same 'ooohs' and 'aaahs' helped out by gentlemanly tones which blathered about this 'magnificent spectacle' and 'unique phenomenon' until I began to feel that there was a party for all the world going on, with me as the only person not invited.

I didn't have any choice of entertainment, for the hospital radio system gave only one programme, take it or leave it. After a bit I gathered that the show had begun to wane. The announcer advised everyone who had not yet seen it to hurry up and do so, or regret all his life that he had missed it.

The general idea seemed to be to convince me that I was passing up the very thing I was born for. In the end I got sick of it, and switched off. The last thing I heard was that the display was diminishing fast now, and that we'd probably be out of the debris area in a few hours.

There could be no doubt in my mind that all this had taken place the previous evening – for one thing, I should have been a great deal hungrier even than I was had it been longer ago. Very well, what *was* this then? Had the whole hospital, the whole city, made such a night of it that they'd not pulled round yet?

About which point I was interrupted as the chorus of clocks, near and far, started announcing nine.

For the third time I played hell with the bell. As I lay waiting I could hear a sort of murmurousness beyond the door. It seemed composed of whimperings, slitherings, and shufflings, punctuated occasionally by a raised voice in the distance.

But still no one came to my room.

By this time I was slipping back. The nasty, childish fancies were on me again. I found myself waiting for the unseeable door to open, and horrible things to come padding in – in fact, I wasn't perfectly sure that somebody or something wasn't in already, and stealthily prowling round the room...

Not that I'm given to that kind of thing, really... It was those damned bandages over my eyes, the medley of voices that had shouted back at me down the corridor. But I certainly was getting the willies – and once you get 'em, they grow. Already they were past the stage where you can shoo them off by whistling or singing at yourself.

It came at last to the straight question: was I more scared of endangering my sight by taking off the bandages, or of staying in the dark with the willies growing every minute?

If it had been a day or two earlier I don't know what I'd have done – very likely the same in the end – but this day I could at least tell myself:

'Well, hang it, there can't be a lot of harm if I use common sense. After all, the bandages are due to come off today. I'll risk it.'

There's one thing I put to my credit. I was not far enough gone to tear them off wildly. I had the sense and the self-control to get out of bed and pull the blind down before I started on the safety-pins.

Once I had the coverings off, and had found out that I could see in the dimness, I felt a relief that I'd never known before. Nevertheless, the first thing I did after assuring myself that there were indeed no malicious persons or things lurking under the bed or elsewhere, was to slip a chair-back under the door-handle. I could, and did, begin to get a better grip on myself then. I made myself take a whole hour gradually getting used to full daylight. At the end of it I knew that thanks to swift first-aid, followed by good doctoring, my eyes were as good as ever.

But still no one came.

On the lower shelf of the bedside table I discovered a pair of dark glasses thoughtfully put ready against my need of them. Cautiously I put them on before I went right close to the window. The lower part of it was not made to open, so that the view was restricted. Squinting down and sideways I could see one or two people who appeared to be wandering in an odd, kind of aimless way farther up the street. But what struck me most, and at once, was the sharpness, the clear definition of everything – even the distant housetops view across the opposite roofs. And then I noticed that no chimney, large of small, was smoking...

I found my clothes hung tidily in a cupboard. I began to feel more normal once I had them on. There were some cigarettes still in the case. I lit one, and started to get into the state of mind where, though everything was still undeniably queer, I could no longer understand why I had been quite so near panic.

It is not easy to think oneself back to the outlook of those days. We have to be more self-reliant now. But then there was so much routine, things were so interlinked. Each one of us so steadily did his little part in the right place that it was easy to mistake habit and custom for the natural law – and all the more disturbing, therefore, when the routine was in any way upset.

When getting on for half a lifetime has been spent in one conception of order, reorientation is no five-minute business. Looking back at the shape of things then, the amount we did not know and did not care to know about our daily lives is not only astonishing, but somehow a bit shocking. I knew practically nothing, for instance, of such ordinary things as how my food reached me, where the fresh water came from, how the clothes I wore were woven and made, how the drainage of cities kept them healthy. Our life had become a complexity of specialists all attending to their own jobs with more or less efficiency, and expecting others to do the same. That made it incredible to me, therefore, that complete disorganization could have overtaken the hospital. Somebody somewhere, I was sure, must have it in hand – unfortunately it was a somebody who had forgotten all about Room 48.

Nevertheless, when I did go to the door again and peer into the corridor I was forced to realize that whatever had happened it was affecting a great deal more than the single inhabitant of Room 48.

Just then there was no one in sight, though in the distance I could hear a pervasive murmur of voices. There was a sound of shuffling footsteps, too, and occasionally a louder voice echoing hollowly in the corridors, but nothing like the din I had shut out before. This time I did not shout. I stepped out cautiously – why cautiously? I don't know. There was just something that induced it.

It was difficult in that reverberating building to tell where the sounds were coming from, but one way the passage finished at an obscured french window, with the shadow of a balcony rail upon it, so I went the other. Rounding a corner, I found myself out of the private-room wing and on a broader corridor.

When I first looked along it I thought it empty, then as I moved forward I saw a figure come out of a shadow. He was a man wearing a black jacket and striped trousers, with a white cotton coat over them. I judged him to be one of the staff doctors – but it was curious that he should be crouching against the wall and feeling his way along.

'Hullo, there,' I said.

He stopped suddenly. The face he turned towards me was grey and frightened.

'Who are you?' he asked, uncertainly.

'My name's Masen,' I told him. 'William Masen. I'm a patient – Room 48. And I've come to find out why——'

THE DAY OF THE TRIFFIDS

'You can see?' he interrupted, swiftly.

'Certainly I can. Just as well as ever,' I assured him. 'It's a wonderful job. Nobody came to unbandage my eyes, so I did it myself. I don't think there's any harm done. I took——'

But he interrupted again.

'Please take me to my office. I must telephone at once.'

I was slow to catch on, but everything ever since I woke that morning had been bewildering.

'Where's that?' I asked.

'Fifth floor, west wing. The name's on the door – Doctor Soames.'

'All right,' I agreed, in some surprise. 'Where are we now?'

The man rocked his head from side to side, his face tense and exasperated.

'How the hell should I know?' he said, bitterly. 'You've got eyes, damn it. Use them. Can't you see I'm blind?'

There was nothing to show that he was blind. His eyes were wide open, and apparently looking straight at me.

'Wait here a minute,' I said. I looked round. I found a large '5' painted on the wall opposite the lift gate. I went back and told him.

'Good. Take my arm,' he directed. 'You turn right as you come out of the lift. Then take the first passage on the left, and it's the third door.'

I followed instructions. We met no one at all on the way. Inside the room I led him up to the desk, and handed him the telephone. He listened for some moments. Then he groped about until he found the rest, and rattled the bar impatiently. Slowly his expression changed. The irritability and the harassed lines faded away. He looked simply tired – very tired. He put the receiver down on the desk. For some seconds he stood silently, looking as though he was staring at the wall opposite. Then he turned.

'It's useless – dead. You *are* still here?' he added.

'Yes,' I told him.

His fingers felt along the edge of the desk.

'Which way am I facing? Where's the damned window?' he demanded, with a return of irritability.

'It's right behind you,' I said.

He turned, and stepped towards it, both hands extended. He felt the sill and the sides carefully, and stepped back a pace. Before I had realized what he was doing he had launched himself full at it, and crashed through...

. . .

I didn't look to see. After all, it was the fifth floor.

When I moved, it was to sit down heavily in the chair. I took a cigarette from a box on the desk, and lit it shakily. I sat here for some minutes while I steadied up, and let the sick feeling subside. After a while it did. I left the room, and went back to the place where I had first found him. I still wasn't feeling too good when I got there.

At the far end of the wide corridor were the doors of a ward. The panels were frosted save for ovals of clear glass at face level. I reckoned there ought to be someone on duty there that I could report to about the doctor.

I opened the door. It was pretty dark in there. The curtains had evidently been drawn after the previous night's display was over – and they were still drawn.

'Sister?' I enquired.

'She ain't 'ere,' a man's voice said. 'What's more,' it went on, 'she ain't been 'ere for ruddy hours, neither. Can't you pull them ruddy curtains, mate, and let's 'ave some flippin' light? Don't know what's come over the bloody place this morning.'

'Okay,' I agreed.

Even if the whole place were disorganized, it didn't seem to be any good reason why the unfortunate patients should have to lie in the dark.

I pulled back the curtains on the nearest window, and let in a shaft of bright sunlight. It was a surgical ward with about twenty patients, all bedridden. Leg injuries mostly, several amputations, by the look of it.

'Stop fooling about with 'em, mate, and pull 'em back,' said the same voice.

I turned and looked at the man who spoke. He was a dark, burly fellow with a weather-beaten skin. He was sitting up in bed, facing directly at me – and at the light. His eyes seemed to be gazing into my own, so did his neighbour's, and the next man's . . .

For a few moments I stared back at them. It took that long to register. Then:

'I – they – they seem to be stuck,' I said. 'I'll find someone to see to them.'

And with that I fled from the ward.

. . .

I was shaky again, and I could have done with a stiff drink. The thing was beginning to sink in. But I found it difficult to believe that *all* the men in that ward could be blind, just like the doctor, and yet . . .

The lift wasn't working, so I started down the stairs. On the next floor I pulled myself together, and plucked up the courage to look into another ward. The beds there were all disarranged. At first I thought the place was empty, but it wasn't – not quite. Two men in nightclothes lay on the floor. One was soaked in blood from an unhealed incision, the other looked as if some kind of congestion had seized him. They were both quite dead. The rest had gone.

Back on the stairs once more, I realized that most of the background voices I had been hearing all the time were coming up from below, and that they were louder and closer now. I hesitated a moment, but there seemed to be nothing for it but to go on making my way down.

On the next turn I nearly tripped over a man who lay across my way in the shadow. At the bottom of the flight lay somebody who actually had tripped over him – and cracked his head on the stone steps as he landed.

At last I reached the final turn where I could stand and look down into the main hall. Seemingly everyone in the place who was able to move must have made instinctively for that spot either with the idea of finding help or of getting outside. Perhaps some of them had got out. One of the main entrance doors was wide open, but most of them couldn't find it. There was a tight-packed mob of men and women, nearly all of them in their hospital nightclothes, milling slowly and helplessly around. The motion pressed those on the outskirts cruelly against marble corners or ornamental projections. Some of them were crushed breathlessly against the walls. Now and then one would trip. If the press of bodies allowed him to fall, there was little chance that it would let him come up again.

The place looked – well, you'll have seen some of Doré's pictures of sinners in hell. But Doré couldn't include the sounds: the sobbing, the murmurous moaning, and occasionally a forlorn cry.

A minute or two of it was all I could stand. I fled back up the stairs.

There was the feeling that I ought to do something about it. Lead them out into the street, perhaps, and at least put an end to that dreadful slow milling. But a glance had been enough to show that I could not hope to make my way to the door to guide them there. Besides, if I were to, if I did get them outside – what then?

I sat down on a step for a while to get over it, with my head in my hands and that awful conglomerate sound in my ears all the time. Then I searched for, and found, another staircase. It was a narrow service flight which led me out by a back way into the yard.

Maybe I'm not telling this part too well. The whole thing was so unexpected and shocking that for a time I deliberately tried not to remember the details. Just then I was feeling much as though it were a nightmare from which I was desperately but vainly seeking the relief of waking myself. As I stepped out into the yard I still half-refused to believe what I had seen.

But one thing I was perfectly certain about. Reality or nightmare, I needed a drink as I had seldom needed one before.

There was nobody in sight in the little side street outside the yard gates, but almost opposite stood a pub. I can recall its name now – 'The Alamein Arms'. There was a board bearing a reputed likeness of Viscount Montgomery hanging from an iron bracket, and below, one of the doors stood open.

I made straight for it.

Stepping into the public bar gave me for the moment a comforting sense of normality. It was prosaically and familiarly like dozens of others.

But although there was no one in that part, there was certainly something going on in the saloon bar, round the corner. I heard heavy breathing. A cork left its bottle with a pop. A pause. Then a voice remarked:

'Gin, blast it! T'hell with gin!'

There followed a shattering crash. The voice gave a sozzled chuckle.

'Thash the mirror. Wash good of mirrors, anyway?'

Another cork popped.

''S' damned gin again,' complained the voice, offended. 'T'*hell* with gin.'

This time the bottle hit something soft, thudded to the floor, and lay there gurgling away its contents.

'Hey!' I called. 'I want a drink.'

There was a silence. Then:

'Who're you?' the voice enquired, cautiously.

'I'm from the hospital,' I said. 'I want a drink.'

'Don' 'member y'r voice. Can you see?'

'Yes,' I told him.

'Well then, for God's sake get over the bar, Doc, and find me a bottle of whisky.'

'I'm doctor enough for that,' I said.

I climbed across, and went round the corner. A large-bellied, red-faced man with a greying walrus moustache stood there clad only in trousers and a collarless shirt. He was fairly drunk. He seemed undecided whether to open the bottle he held in his hand, or to use it as a weapon.

''F you're not a doctor, what are you?' he demanded, suspiciously.

'I was a patient – but I need a drink as much as any doctor,' I said. 'That's gin again you've got there,' I added.

'Oh, is it! B—— gin,' he said, and slung it away. It went through the window with a lively crash.

THE DAY OF THE TRIFFIDS

'Give me that corkscrew,' I told him.

I took down a bottle of whisky from the shelf, opened it, and handed it to him with a glass. For myself I chose a stiff brandy with very little soda, and then another. After that my hand wasn't shaking so much.

I looked at my companion. He was taking his whisky neat, out of the bottle.

'You'll get drunk,' I said.

He paused and turned his head towards me. I could have sworn that his eyes really saw me.

'Get drunk! Damn it, I *am* drunk,' he said, scornfully.

He was so perfectly right that I didn't comment. He brooded a moment before he announced:

'Gotta get drunker. Gotta get mush drunker.' He leaned closer. 'D'you know what? – I'm blind. Thash what I am – blind's a bat. *Every*body's blind's a bat. 'Cept you. Why aren't you blind's a bat?'

'I don't know,' I told him.

' 'S that bloody comet, b—— it! Thash what done it. Green shootin' shtarsh – an' now everyone's blind's a bat. D'ju shee green shootin' shtarsh?'

'No,' I admitted.

'There you are. Proves it. You didn't see 'em: you aren't blind. Everyone else saw 'em' – he waved an expressive arm – 'all's blind's bats. B—— comets, I say.'

I poured myself a third brandy, wondering whether there might not be something in what he was saying.

'*Every*one blind?' I repeated.

'Thash it. All of 'em. Prob'ly everyone in th' world – 'cept you,' he added, as an afterthought.

'How do you know?' I asked.

' 'S'easy. Listen!' he said.

We stood side by side leaning on the bar of the dingy pub, and listened. There was nothing to be heard – nothing but the rustle of a dirty newspaper blown down the empty street. Such a quietness held everything as cannot have been known in those parts for a thousand years and more.

'See what I mean? 'S'obvious,' said the man.

'Yes,' I said slowly. 'Yes – I see what you mean.'

I decided that I must get along. I did not know where to. But I must find out more about what was happening.

'Are you the landlord?' I asked him.

'Wha' 'f I am?' he demanded, defensively.

'Only that I've got to pay someone for three double brandies.'

'Ah – forget it.'

'But, look here——'

'Forget it, I tell you. D'ju know why?' 'Cause what's the good 'f money to a dead man? An' thash what I am – 's good as. Jus' a few more drinks.'

He looked a pretty robust specimen for his age, and I said so.

'Wha's good of living blind's a bat?' he demanded, aggressively. 'Thash what my wife said. An' she was right – only she's more guts than I have. When she found as the kids was blind too, what did she do? Took 'em into our bed with her, and turned on the gas. Thash what she done. An' I hadn't the guts to stick with 'em. She's got pluck, my wife, more'n I have. But I will have soon. I'm going back up there soon – when I'm drunk enough.'

What was there to say? What I did say served no purpose save to spoil his temper. In the end he groped his way to the stairs and disappeared up them, bottle in hand. I didn't try to stop him, or follow him. I watched him go. Then I knocked back the last of my brandy, and went out into the silent street.

CHAPTER 2

THE COMING OF THE TRIFFIDS

This is a personal record. It involves a great deal that has vanished for ever, but I can't tell it in any other way than by using the words we used to use for those vanished things, so that they have to stand. But even to make the setting intelligible I find that I shall have to go back farther than the point at which I started:

When I was a child we lived, my father, my mother, and myself, in a southern suburb of London. We had a small house which my father supported by conscientious daily attendance at his desk in the Inland Revenue Department, and a small garden at which he worked rather harder during the summer. There was not a lot to distinguish us from ten or twelve million other people who used to live in and around London in those days.

My father was one of those persons who could add a column of figures – even of the ridiculous coinage then in use locally – with a flick of the eye, so that it was natural for him to have in mind that I should become an accountant. As a result, my inability to make any column of figures reach the same total twice caused me to be something of a mystery as well as a disappointment to him. Still, there it was: just one of those things. And each of a succession of teachers who tried to show me that mathematical answers were derived logically and not through some form of esoteric inspiration was forced to give up with the assurance that I had no head for figures. My father would read my school reports with a gloom which in other respects they scarcely warranted. His mind worked, I think, this way: no head for figures – no idea of finance – no money.

'I really don't know what we shall do with you. What do you *want* to do?' he would ask.

And until I was thirteen or fourteen I would shake my head, conscious of my sad inadequacy, and admit that I did not know.

My father would than shake *his* head.

For him the world was divided sharply into desk-men who worked with their brains, and non-desk men who didn't, and got dirty. How he contrived to maintain this view which was already a century or so out of date I do not know, but it pervaded my early years to such an extent that I was late in perceiving that a weakness in figures did not of necessity condemn me to the life of a street-sweeper or a scullion. It did not occur to me that the subject which interested me most could lead to a career – and my father failed either to notice, or, if he did, to care that reports on my biology were consistently good.

It was the appearance of the triffids which really decided the matter for us. Indeed, they did a lot more than that for me. They provided me with a job and comfortably supported me. They also on several occasions almost took my life. On the other hand, I have to admit that they preserved it, too, for it was a triffid sting that had landed me in hospital on the critical occasion of the 'comet debris'.

In the books there is quite a lot of loose speculation on the sudden occurrence of the triffids. Most of it is nonsense. Certainly they were not spontaneously generated as many simple souls believed. Nor did most people endorse the theory that they were a kind of sample visitation – harbingers of worse to come if the world did not mend its ways and behave its troublesome self. Nor did their seeds float to us through space as specimens of the horrid forms life might assume upon other, less favoured worlds – at least, I am satisfied that they did not.

I learned more about it than most people because triffids were my job, and the firm I worked for was intimately, if not very gracefully, concerned in their public appearance. Nevertheless, their true origin still remains obscure. My own belief, for what it is worth, is that they were the outcome of a series of ingenious biological meddlings – and very likely accidental at that. Had they been evolved anywhere but in the region they were we should doubtless have had a well-documented ancestry for them. As it was, no authoritative statement was ever published by those who must have been best qualified to know. The reason for this lay, no doubt, in the curious political conditions then prevailing.

The world we lived in then was wide, and most of it was open to us, with little trouble. Roads, railways, and shipping lines laced it, ready to carry one thousands of miles safely and in comfort. If we wanted to travel more swiftly still, and could afford it, we travelled by aeroplane. There was no need for anyone to take weapons or even precautions in those days. You could go just as you were to wherever you wished, with nothing to hinder you – other than a lot of forms and regulations. A world so tamed sounds utopian now. Nevertheless, it was so over five-sixths of the globe – though the remaining sixth was something different again.

It must be difficult for young people who never knew it to envisage a world like that. Perhaps it sounds like a golden age – though it wasn't quite that to those who lived in it. Or they may think that an Earth ordered and cultivated almost all over sounds dull – but it wasn't that, either. It was rather an exciting place – for a biologist, anyway. Every year we were pushing the northern limit of growth for food plants a little further back. New fields were growing quick crops on what had historically been simply tundra or barren land. Every season, too, stretches of desert both old and recent were reclaimed and made to grow grass or food. For food was then our most pressing problem, and the progress of the regeneration schemes and the advance of the cultivation lines on the maps was followed with almost as much attention as an earlier generation had paid to battle-fronts.

Such a swerve of interest from swords to ploughshares was undoubtedly a social improvement but, at the same time, it was a mistake for the optimistic to claim it as showing a change in the human spirit. The human spirit continued much as before – ninety-five per cent of it wanting to live in peace; and the other five per cent considering its chances if it should risk starting anything. It was chiefly because no one's chances looked too good that the lull continued.

Meanwhile, with something like twenty-five million new mouths bawling for food every year the supply problem became steadily worse, and after years of ineffective propaganda a couple of atrocious harvests had at last made the people aware of its urgency.

The factor which had caused the militant five per cent to relax a while from fomenting discord was the satellites. Sustained research in rocketry had at last succeeded in attaining one of its objectives. It had sent up a missile which stayed up. It was, in fact, possible to fire a rocket far enough up for it to fall into an orbit round the earth. Once there it would continue to circle like a tiny moon, quite inactive and innocuous – until the pressure on a button should give it the impulse to drop back, with devastating effect.

Great as was the public concern which followed the triumphant announcement of the first nation to establish a satellite weapon satisfactorily, a still greater concern was felt over the failure of others to make any announcement at all even when they were known to have had similar successes. It was by no means pleasant to realize that there was an unknown number of menaces up there over your head, quietly circling and circling until someone should arrange for them to drop – and that there was nothing could be done about them. Still, life has to go on – and novelty is a wonderfully short-lived thing. One became used to the idea perforce. From time to time there would be a panicky flare-up of expostulation when reports circulated that as well as satellites with atomic heads there were others which such things as crop diseases, cattle diseases, radio-active dusts, viruses, and infections not only of familiar kinds, but brand-new sorts recently thought up in laboratories, all floating around up there. Whether such uncertain and potentially back-firing weapons had actually been placed is hard to say. But then, the limits of folly itself – particularly of folly with fear on its heels – are not easy to define. A virulent organism, unstable enough to become harmless in the course of a few days (and who is to say that such could not be bred?) could be considered to have strategic uses if dropped in suitable spots.

At least the United States Government took the suggestion seriously enough to deny emphatically that it controlled any satellites designed to conduct biological warfare directly upon human beings. One or two minor nations, whom no one suspected of controlling any satellites at all, hastened to make similar declarations. Other, and major, powers did not. In the face of this ominous reticence the public began demanding to know why the United States had neglected to prepare for a form of warfare which others were ready to use – and just what did 'directly' mean, anyway? At this point all parties tacitly gave up denying or confirming anything about satellites, and an intensified effort was made to divert the public interest to the no less important, but far less acrimonious, matter of food scarcity.

The laws of supply and demand should have enabled the more enterprising to organize commodity monopolies, but the world at large had become antagonistic to declared monopolies. However, the laced-company system really worked very smoothly without anything so imputable as Articles of Federation. The general public heard scarcely anything of such little difficulties within the pattern as had to be untangled from time to time. Hardly anyone heard of even the existence of Umberto Christoforo Palanguez, for instance. I only heard of him myself years later in the course of my work.

Umberto was of assorted Latin descent, and something South American by nationality. His first appearance as a possibly disruptive spanner in the neat machinery of the edible-oil interests occurred when he walked into the offices of the Arctic and European Fish-Oil Company, and produced a bottle of pale pink oil in which he proposed to interest them.

Arctic and European displayed no eagerness. The trade was pretty well tied up. However, they did in the course of time get around to analysing the sample he had left with them.

The first thing they discovered about it was that it was not a fish-oil, anyway: it was vegetable, though they could not identify the source. The second revelation was that it made most of their best fish-oils look like grease-box fillers. Alarmed, they sent out what remained of the sample for intensive study, and put around hurried enquiries to know if Mr Palanguez had made other approaches.

When Umberto called again the managing director received him with flattering attention.

'That is a very remarkable oil you brought us, Mr Palanguez,' he said.

Umberto nodded his sleek, dark head. He was well aware of the fact.

'I have never seen anything quite like it,' the managing director admitted.

Umberto nodded again.

'No?' he said, politely. Then, seemingly as an afterthought, he added: 'But I think you will, señor. A very great deal of it.' He appeared to ponder. 'It will, I think, come on the market seven, maybe eight, years from now.' He smiled.

The managing director thought that unlikely. He said, with a frank air:

'It is better than our fish-oils.'

'So I am told, señor,' agreed Umberto.

'You are proposing to market it yourself, Mr Palanguez?'

Umberto smiled again.

'Would I be showing it to you if I did?'

'We might reinforce one of our own oils synthetically,' observed the managing director, reflectively.

'With some of the vitamins – but it would be costly to synthesize all of them: even if you could,' Umberto said gently. 'Besides,' he added, 'I am told that this oil will easily undersell your best fish-oils, anyway.'

'H'm,' said the managing director. 'Well, I suppose you have a proposition, Mr Palanguez. Shall we come to it?'

Umberto explained: 'There are two ways of dealing with such an unfortunate matter. The usual one is to prevent it happening – or at least to delay it until the capital sunk in present equipment has been paid off. That is, of course, the desirable way.'

The managing director nodded. He knew plenty about that.

'But this time I am sorry for you, because, you see, it is not possible.'

The managing director had his doubts. His inclination was to say, 'You'd be surprised,' but he resisted it, and contented himself with a non-committal: 'Oh?'

'The other way,' suggested Umberto, 'is to produce the thing for yourself before the trouble starts.'

'Ah!' said the managing director.

'I think,' Umberto told him, 'I think that I might be able to supply you with seeds of this plant in, maybe, six months' time. If you were to plant then you could begin production of oil in five years – or it might be six for full yield.'

'Just nicely in time, in fact,' observed the managing director.

Umberto nodded.

'The other way would be simpler,' remarked the managing director.

'If it were possible at all,' Umberto agreed. 'But unfortunately your competitors are not approachable – or suppressible.'

He made the statement with a confidence which caused the managing director to study him thoughtfully for some moments.

'I see,' he said at last. 'I wonder – er – you don't happen to be a Soviet citizen, Mr Palanguez?'

'No,' said Umberto. 'On the whole my life has been lucky – but I have very varied connections ...'

That brings us to considering the other sixth of the world – that part which one could not visit with such facility as the rest. Indeed, permits to visit the Union of Soviet Socialist Republic were almost unobtainable, and the movements of those who did achieve them were strictly circumscribed. It had deliberately organized itself into a land of mystery. Little of what went on behind the veiling secrecy which was almost pathological in the region was known to the rest of the world. What was, was usually suspect. Yet, behind the curious propaganda which distributed the laughable while concealing all likely to be of the least importance, achievements undoubtedly went on in many fields. One was biology. Russia, who shared with the rest of the world the problem of increasing food supplies, was known to have been intensively concerned with attempts to reclaim desert, steppe, and the northern tundra. In the days when information was still being exchanged she had reported some successes. Later, however, a cleavage of methods and views had caused biology there, under a man called Lysenko, to take a different course. It too, then succumbed to the endemic secrecy. The lines it had taken were unknown, and thought to be unsound – but it was anybody's guess whether very successful, very silly, or very queer things were happening there – if not all three at once.

'Sunflowers,' said the managing director, speaking absent-mindedly out of his own reflections. 'I happen to know they were having another shot at improving the yield of sunflower-seed oil. But it isn't that.'

'No,' agreed Umberto. 'It is not that.'

The managing director doodled.

'Seeds, you said. Do you mean that it is some new species? Because if it is merely some improved strain more easily processed——'

'I understand that it is a new species – something quite new.'

'Then you haven't actually seen it yourself? It may, in fact, *be* some modified kind of sunflower?'

'I have seen a picture, señor. I did not say there is *no* sunflower there at all. I do not say there is no turnip there. I do not say there is no nettle, or even no orchid there. But I do say that if they were all fathers to it they would none of them know their child. I do not think it would please them greatly, either.'

'I see. Now what was the figure you had in mind for getting us the seeds of this thing?'

Umberto named a sum which stopped the managing director's doodling quite abruptly. It made him take off his glasses to regard the speaker more closely. Umberto was unabashed.

'Consider, señor,' he said, ticking off points on his fingers. 'It is difficult. And it is dangerous – very dangerous. I do not fear – but I do not go to danger to amuse myself. There is another man, a Russian. I shall have to bring him away, and he must be paid well. There will be others that he must pay first. Also I must buy an aeroplane – a jet aeroplane, very fast. All these things cost money.

'And I tell you it is not easy. You must have seeds that are good. Many of the seeds of this plant are infertile. To make sure, I have to bring you seeds that have been sorted. They are valuable. And in Russia everything is a state secret and guarded. Certainly it will not be easy.'

'I believe that. But all the same——'

'Is it so much, señor? What will you say in a few years when these

Russians are selling their oil all over the world – and your company is finished?'

'It will need thinking over, Mr Palanguez.'

'But of course, señor!' Umberto agreed, with a smile. 'I can wait – a little while. But I'm afraid I cannot reduce my price.'

Nor did he.

The discoverer and the inventor are the bane of business. A little sand in the works is comparatively a mere nothing – you just replace the damaged parts, and go on. But the appearance of a new process, a new substance, when you are all organized and ticking nicely, is the very devil. Sometimes it is worse than that – it just cannot be allowed to occur. Too much is at stake. If you can't use legal methods, you must try others.

For Umberto had understated the case. It was not simply that the competition of a cheap new oil would send Arctic and European and their associates out of business. The effects would be widespread. It might not be fatal to the groundnut, the olive, the whale, and a number of other oil industries, but it would be a nasty knock. Moreover, there would be violent repercussions in dependent industries, in margarine, soap, and a hundred more products from face-creams to house-paints, and beyond. Indeed, once a few of the more influential concerns had grasped the quality of the menace Umberto's terms came to seem almost modest.

He got his agreement, for his samples were convincing, if the rest was somewhat vague.

In point of fact it cost those interested quite a lot less than they had undertaken to pay, for after Umberto went off with his aeroplane and his advance he was never seen again.

But that is not to say he was altogether unheard of.

Some years later an indeterminate individual giving simply the name Fedor turned up at the offices of Arctic and European Oils. (They had dropped 'Fish' from both their title and activities then.) He was, he said, a Russian. He would like he said, some money, if the kind capitalists would be good enough to spare some.

His story was that he had been employed in the first experimental triffid station in the district of Elovsk in Kamchatka. It was a forlorn place, and he greatly disliked it. His desire to get away had caused him to listen to a suggestion from another worker there, to be specific, one Tovarich Nikolai Alexandrovich Baltinoff, and the suggestion had been backed up by several thousand roubles.

It did not require a great deal of earning. He had simply to remove a box of sorted fertile triffid seeds from its rack, and substitute a similar box of infertile seeds. The purloined box was to be left at a certain place at a certain time. There was practically no risk. It might be years before the substitution was discovered.

A further requirement, however, was a little more tricky. He was to see that a pattern of lights was laid out on a large field a mile or two from the plantation. He was to be there himself on a certain night. He would hear an aeroplane flying directly above. He would switch on the lights. The plane would land. The best thing he could do then would be to get away from the neighbourhood as soon as possible before anyone should arrive to investigate.

For these services he would receive not only the comfortable wad of roubles, but if he should succeed in leaving Russia he would find more money waiting for him at the offices of Arctic and European, in England.

By his account the operation had gone entirely to plan. Fedor had not waited once the plane was down. He had switched off the lights, and beat it.

The plane had stopped only a short time, perhaps not ten minutes, before it took off again. From the sound of the jets he judged that it was climbing steeply as it went. A minute or so after the noise had died away he heard the sound of engines again. Some more planes went over headed east, after the other. There might have been two, or more, he could not tell. But they were travelling very fast, with their jets shrieking...

The next day Comrade Baltinoff was missing. There had been a lot of trouble, but in the end it was decided that Baltinoff must have been working alone. So it had all passed off safely for Fedor.

He had cautiously waited for a year before he made a move. It had cost him almost the last of his roubles by the time he had bought his way through the final obstacles. Then he had had to take various jobs to live, so that he had spent a long time in reaching England. But now he had, could he have some money, please?

Something had been heard about Elovsk by that time. And the date he gave for the plane landing was within probability. So they gave him some money. They also gave him a job, and told him to keep his mouth shut. For it was clear that though Umberto had not personally delivered the goods, he had at least saved the situation by broadcasting them.

Arctic-European had not at first connected the appearance of the triffids with Umberto, and the police of several countries went on keeping an eye open for him on their behalf. It was not until some investigator produced a specimen of triffid oil for their inspection that they realized that it corresponded exactly with the sample Umberto had

shown them, and that it was the seeds of the triffid he had set out to
bring.

What happened to Umberto himself will never be definitely known. It
is my guess that over the Pacific Ocean, somewhere high up in the
stratosphere, he and Comrade Baltinoff found themselves attacked by
the planes that Fedor had heard in pursuit. It may be that the first they
knew of it was when cannon-shells from Russian fighters started to break
up their craft.

And I think, too, that one of those shells blew to pieces a certain
twelve-inch cube of plywood – the receptacle like a small tea-chest in
which, according to Fedor, the seeds were packed.

Perhaps Umberto's plane exploded, perhaps it just fell to pieces.
Whichever it was, I am sure that when the fragments began their long,
long fall towards the sea they left behind them something which looked
at first like a white vapour.

It was not vapour. It was a cloud of seeds, floating, so infinitely light
they were, even in the rarefied air. Millions of gossamer-slung triffid
seeds, free now to drift wherever the winds of the world should take
them...

It might be weeks, perhaps months, before they would sink to earth at
last, many of them thousands of miles from their starting place.

That is, I repeat, conjecture. But I cannot see a more probable way in
which that plant, intended to be kept secret, could come, quite
suddenly, to be found in almost every part of the world.

. . .

My introduction to a triffid came early. It so happened that we had
one of the first in the locality growing in our own garden. The plant was
quite well developed before any of us bothered to notice it, for it had
taken root along with a number of other casuals behind the bit of hedge
that screened the rubbish heap. It wasn't doing any harm there, and it
wasn't in anyone's way. So when we did notice it later on we'd just take a
look at it now and then to see how it was getting along, and let it be.

However, a triffid is certainly distinctive, and we couldn't help getting
a bit curious about it after a time. Not, perhaps, very actively, for there
are always a few unfamiliar things that somehow or other manage to
lodge in the neglected corners of a garden, but enough to mention to one
another that it was beginning to look a pretty queer sort of thing.

Nowadays when everyone knows only too well what a triffid looks like
it is difficult to recall how odd and somehow *foreign* the first ones
appeared to us. Nobody, as far as I know, felt any misgiving or alarm
about them then. I imagine that most people thought of them – when they
thought of them at all – in much the same way that my father did.

I have a picture in my memory of him examining ours and puzzling over it at a time when it must have been about a year old. In almost every detail it was a half-size replica of a fully-grown triffid – only it didn't have a name yet, and no one had seen one fully grown. My father leant over, peering at it through his horn-rimmed glasses, fingering its stalk, and blowing gently through his gingery moustache as was his habit when thoughtful. He inspected the straight stem, and the woody bole from which it sprang. He gave curious, if not very penetrative attention to the three small, bare sticks which grew straight up beside the stem. He smoothed the short sprays of leathery green leaves between his finger and thumb as if their texture might tell him something. Then he peered into the curious, funnel-like formation at the top of the stem, still puffing reflectively but inconclusively through his moustache. I remember the first time he lifted me up to look inside that conical cup and see the tightly-wrapped whorl within. It looked not unlike the new, close-rolled frond of a fern, emerging a couple of inches from a sticky mess in the base of the cup. I did not touch it, but I knew the stuff must be sticky because there were flies and other small insects struggling in it.

More than once my father ruminated that it was pretty queer, and observed that one of these days he really must try to find out what it was. I don't think he ever made the effort, nor, at that stage, was he likely to have learned much if he had tried.

The thing would be about four feet high then. There must have been plenty of them about, growing up quietly and inoffensively, with nobody taking any particular notice of them – at least, it seemed so, for if the biological or botanical experts were excited over them no news of their interest percolated to the general public. And so the one in our garden continued its growth peacefully, as did thousands like it in neglected spots all over the world.

It was some little time later that the first one picked up its roots, and walked.

That improbable achievement must, of course, have been known for some time in Russia where it was doubtless classified as a state secret, but as far as I have been able to confirm its first occurrence in the outside world took place in Indo-China – which meant that people went on taking practically no notice. Indo-China was one of those regions from which such curious and unlikely yarns might be expected to drift in, and frequently did – the kind of thing an editor might conceivably use if news were scarce and a touch of the 'mysterious East' would liven the paper up a bit. But in any case the Indo-Chinese specimen can have had no great lead. Within a few weeks reports of walking plants were pouring in from Sumatra, Borneo, Belgian Congo, Colombia, Brazil, and most places in the neighbourhood of the equator.

This time they got into print, all right. But the much-handled stories written up with that blend of cautiously defensive frivolity which the Press habitually employed to cover themselves in matters regarding sea-serpents, elementals, thought-transference, and other irregular phenomena prevented anyone from realizing that these accomplished plants at all resembled the quiet respectable weed beside our rubbish heap. Not until the pictures began to appear did we realize that they were identical with it save in size.

The news-reel men were quickly off the mark. Possibly they got some good interesting pictures for their trouble of flying to outlandish places, but there was a current theory among cutters that more than a few seconds of any one news-subject – except a boxing match – could not fail to paralyse an audience with boredom. My first view, therefore, of a development which was to play such an important part in my future, as well as in so many other people's, was a glimpse sandwiched between a hula contest in Honolulu, and the First Lady launching a battleship. (That is no anachronism. They were still building them; even admirals had to live.) I was permitted to see a few triffids sway across the screen to the kind of accompaniment supposed to be on the level of the great movie-going public:

'And now, folks, get a load of what our cameraman found in Ecuador. Vegetables on vacation! *You*'ve only seen this kind of thing after a party, but down in sunny Ecuador they see it any time – and no hangover to follow! Monster plants on the march! Say, that's given me a big idea! Maybe if we can educate our potatoes right we can fix it so they'll walk right into the pot. How'd that be, Momma?'

For the short time the scene was on, I stared at it, fascinated. There was our mysterious rubbish-heap plant grown to a height of seven feet or more. There was no mistaking it – and it was 'walking'!

The bole, which I now saw for the first time, was shaggy with little rootlet hairs. It would have been almost spherical but for three bluntly-tapered projections extending from the lower part. Supported on these, the main body was lifted about a foot clear of the ground.

When it 'walked' it moved rather like a man on crutches. Two of the blunt 'legs' slid forward, then the whole thing lurched as the rear one drew almost level with them, then the two in front slid forward again. At each 'step' the long stem whipped violently back and forth: it gave one a kind of seasick feeling to watch it. As a method of progress it looked both strenuous and clumsy – faintly reminiscent of young elephants at play. One felt that if it were to go on lurching for long in that fashion it would be bound to strip all its leaves if it did not actually break its stem. Nevertheless, ungainly though it looked, it was contriving to cover the ground at something like an average walking pace.

That was about all I had time to see before the battleship launching began. It was not a lot, but it was enough to incite an investigating spirit in a boy. For, if that thing in Ecuador could do a trick like that, why not the one in our garden? Admittedly ours was a good deal smaller, but it did *look* the same...

About ten minutes after I got home I was digging round our triffid, carefully loosening the earth near it to encourage it to 'walk.'

Unfortunately there was an aspect of this self-propelled plant discovery which the news-reel people had either not experienced, or chosen for some reason of their own not to reveal. There was no warning, either. I was bending down intent on clearing the earth without harming the plant, when something from nowhere hit me one terrific slam, and knocked me out...

I woke up to find myself in bed, with my mother, my father, and the doctor watching me anxiously. My head felt as if it were split open, I was aching all over, and, as I later discovered, one side of my face was decorated with a blotchy-red raised weal. The insistent questions as to how I came to be lying unconscious in the garden were quite useless; I had no faintest idea what it was that had hit me. And some little time passed before I learned that I must have been one of the first persons in England to be stung by a triffid and get away with it. The triffid was, of course, immature. But before I had fully recovered my father had found out what had undoubtedly happened to me, and by the time I went into the garden again he had wreaked stern vengeance on our triffid, and disposed of the remains on a bonfire.

.   .   .

Now that walking plants were established facts the Press lost its former tepidity, and bathed them in publicity. So a name had to be found for them. Already there were botanists wallowing after their custom in polysyllabic dog-Latin and Greek to produce variants on *ambulans* and *pseudopodia*, but what the newspapers and the public wanted was something easy on the tongue and not too heavy on the headlines for general use. If you could see the papers of that time you would find them referring to:

TRICHOTS	TRINITS
TRICUSPS	TRIPEDALS
TRIGENATES	TRIPEDS
TRIGONS	TRIQUETS

TRILOGS   TRIPODS
TRIDENTATES   TRIPPETS

and a number of other mysterious things not even beginning with 'tri' – though almost all centred on the feature of that active, three-pronged root.

There was argument, public, private, and bar-parlour, with heated championship of one term or another on near-scientific, quasi-etymological, and a number of other grounds, but gradually one term began to dominate this philological gymkhana. In its first form it was not quite acceptable, but common usage modified the original long first 'i', and custom quickly wrote in a second 'f', to leave no doubt about it. And so emerged the standard term. A catchy little name originating in some newspaper office as a handy label for an oddity – but destined one day to be associated with pain, fear, and misery – TRIFFID . . .

. . . .

The first wave of public interest soon ebbed away. Triffids were, admittedly, a bit weird – by that was, after all, just because they were novelties. People had felt the same about novelties of other days – about kangaroos, giant lizards, black swans. And, when you came to think of it, were triffids all that much queerer than mudfish, ostriches, tadpoles, and a hundred other things? The bat was an animal that had learned to fly: well, here was a plant that had learned to walk – what of that?

But there were features of it to be less casually dismissed. On its origins the Russians, true to type, lay low and said nuffin. Even those who had heard of Umberto did not yet connect him with it. Its sudden appearance, and even more, its wide distribution promoted very puzzled speculation. For though it matured more rapidly in the tropics, specimens in various stages of development were reported from almost any region outside the polar circles and the deserts.

People were surprised, and a little disgusted, to learn that the species was carnivorous, and that the flies and other insects caught in the cups were actually digested by the sticky substance there. We in temperate zones were not ignorant of insectivorous plants, but we were un-accustomed to find them outside special hothouses, and apt to consider them as in some way slightly indecent, or at least improper. But actually alarming was the discovery that the whorl topping a triffid's stem could lash out as a slender stinging weapon ten feet long, capable of discharging enough poison to kill a man if it struck squarely on his unprotected skin.

As soon as this danger was appreciated there followed a nervous smashing and chopping of triffids everywhere until it occurred to someone that all that was necessary to make them harmless was the removal of the actual stinging weapon. At this, the slightly hysterical assault upon the plants declined, with their numbers considerably thinned. A little later it began to be a fashion to have a safely-docked triffid or two about one's garden. It was found that it took about two years for the lost sting to be dangerously replaced, so that an annual pruning assured that they were in a state of safety where they could provide vast amusement for the children.

In temperate countries, where man had succeeded in putting most forms of nature save his own under a reasonable degree of restraint, the status of the triffid was thus made quite clear. But in the tropics, particularly in the dense forest areas, they quickly became a scourge.

The traveller very easily failed to notice one among the normal bushes and undergrowth, and the moment he was in range the venomous sting would slash out. Even the regular inhabitant of such a district found it difficult to detect a motionless triffid cunningly lurking beside a jungle path. They were uncannily sensitive to any movement near them, and it was hard to take them unawares.

Dealing with them became a serious problem in such regions. The most favoured method was to shoot the top off the stem, and the sting with it. The jungle natives took to carrying long, light poles mounted with hooked knives which they used effectively if they could get their blows in first – but not at all if the triffid had a chance to sway forward and increase its range by an unexpected four or five feet. Before long, however, these pike-like devices were mostly superseded by spring-operated guns of various types. Most of them shot spinning discs, crosses, or small boomerangs of thin steel. As a rule they were inaccurate above about twelve yards, though capable of slicing a triffid stem neatly at twenty-five if they hit it. Their invention pleased both the authorities – who had an almost unanimous distaste for the indiscriminate toting of rifles – and the users who found the missiles of razor-blade steel far cheaper and lighter than cartridges, and admirably adaptable to silent banditry.

Elsewhere immense research into the nature, habits, and constitution of the triffid went on. Earnest experimenters set out to determine in the interests of science how far and for how long it could walk; whether it could be said to have a front, or could perform its march in any direction with equal clumsiness; what proportion of its time it must spend with its roots in the ground; what reactions it showed to the presence of various chemicals in the soil; and a vast quantity of other questions, both useful and useless.

The largest specimen ever observed in the tropics stood nearly ten feet high. No European specimen over eight feet had been seen, and the average was little over seven. They appeared to adapt easily to a wide range of climate and soils. They had, it seemed, no natural enemies – other than man.

But there were a number of not unobvious characteristics which escaped comment for some little time. It was, for instance, quite a while before anyone drew attention to the uncanny accuracy with which they aimed their stings, and that they almost invariably struck for the head. Nor did anyone at first take notice of their habit of lurking near their fallen victims. The reason for that only became clear when it was shown that they fed upon flesh as well as upon insects. The stinging tendril did not have the muscular power to tear firm flesh, but it had strength enough to pull shreds from a decomposing body and lift them to the cup on its stem.

There was no great interest, either, in the three little leafless sticks at the base of the stem. There was a light notion that they might have something to do with the reproductive system – that system which tends to be a sort of botanical glory-hole for all parts of doubtful purpose until they can be sorted out and more specifically assigned later on. It was assumed, consequently, that their characteristic of suddenly losing their immobility and rattling a rapid tattoo against the main stem was some strange form of triffidian amatory exuberance.

.   .   .

Possibly my uncomfortable distinction of getting myself stung so early in the triffid era had the effect of stimulating my interest, for I seemed to have a sort of link with them from then on. I spent – or 'wasted', if you look at me through my father's eyes – a great deal of fascinated time watching them.

One could not blame him for considering this a worthless pursuit, yet, later, the time turned out to have been better employed than either of us suspected, for it was just before I left school that the Arctic and European Fish-Oil Company reconstituted itself, dropping the word 'Fish' in the process. The public learned that it and similar companies in other countries were about to farm triffids on a large scale in order to extract valuable oils and juices, and to press highly nutritious oil-cake for stock feeding. Consequently, triffids moved into the realm of big business overnight.

Right away I decided my future. I applied to the Arctic and European where my qualifications got me a job on the production side. My father's disapproval was somewhat qualified by the rate of pay, which was good for my age. But when I spoke enthusiastically of the future he blew doubtfully through his moustache. He had real faith only in a type of work steadied by long tradition, but he let me have my way. 'After all, if the thing isn't a success you'll find out young enough to start in on something more solid,' he conceded.

There turned out to be no need for that. Before he and my mother were killed together in a holiday air-bus crash five years later they had seen the new companies drive all competing oils off the market, and those of us who had been in at the beginning apparently well set for life.

One of the early comers was my friend Walter Lucknor.

There had been some doubt at first about taking Walter on. He knew little of agriculture, less of business, and lacked the qualifications for lab. work. On the other hand, he did know a lot about triffids – he had a kind of inspired knack with them.

What happened to Walter that fatal May years later I do not know – though I can guess. It is a sad thing that he did not escape. He might have been immensely valuable later on. I don't think anybody really understands triffids, or ever will, but Walter came nearer to beginning to understand them than any man I have known. Or should I say that he was given to intuitive feelings about them?

It was a year or two after the job had begun that he first surprised me.

The sun was close to setting. We had knocked off for the day and were looking with a sense of satisfaction at three new fields of nearly fully-grown triffids. In those days we didn't simply corral them as we did later. They were arranged across the fields roughly in rows – at least the steel stakes to which each was tethered by a chain were in rows, though the plants themselves had no sense of tidy regimentation. We reckoned that in another month or so we'd be able to start tapping them for juice. The evening was peaceful, almost the only sounds that broke it were the occasional rattlings of the triffids' little sticks against their stems. Walter regarded them with his head slightly on one side. He removed his pipe.

'They're talkative tonight,' he observed.

I took that as anyone else would, metaphorically.

'Maybe it's the weather,' I suggested. 'I fancy they do it more when it's dry.'

He looked sidelong at me, with a smile.

'Do you talk more when it's dry?'

'Why should——?' I began, and then broke off. 'You don't really mean you think they're talking?' I said, noticing his expression.

'Well, why not?'

'But it's absurd. Plants talking!'

'So much more absurd than plants walking?' he asked.

I stared at them, and then back at him.

'I never thought——' I began, doubtfully.

'You try thinking of it a bit, and watching them – I'd be interested to hear your conclusions,' he said.

It was a curious thing that in all my dealings with triffids such a possibility had never occurred to me. I'd been prejudiced, I suppose, by the love-call theory. But once he had put the idea into my mind, it stuck. I couldn't get away from the feeling that they might indeed be rattling out secret messages to one another.

Up to then I'd fancied I'd watched triffids pretty closely, but when Walter was talking about them I felt that I'd noticed practically nothing. He could, when he was in the mood, talk on about them for hours, advancing theories that were sometimes wild, but sometimes not impossible.

The public had by this time grown out of thinking triffids freakish. They were clumsily amusing, but not greatly interesting. The Company found them interesting, however. It took the view that their existence was a piece of benevolence for everyone – particularly for itself. Walter shared neither view. At times, listening to him, I began to have some misgivings myself.

He had become quite certain that they 'talked.'

'And that,' he argued, 'means that somewhere in them is intelligence. It can't be seated in a brain because dissection shows nothing like a brain – but that doesn't prove there isn't something there that does a brain's job.

'And there's certainly intelligence there, of a kind. Have you noticed that when they attack they always go for the unprotected parts? Almost always the head – but sometimes the hands? And another thing: if you look at the statistics of casualties, just take notice of the proportion that has been stung across the eyes, and blinded. It's remarkable – and significant.'

'Of what?' I asked.

'Of the fact that they know what is the surest way to put a man out of action – in other words, they know what they're doing. Look at it this way. Granted that they do have intelligence; then that would leave us with only one important superiority – sight. We can see, and they can't. Take away our vision, and the superiority is gone. Worse than that – our position becomes inferior to theirs because they are adapted to a sightless existence, and we are not.'

'But even if that were so, they can't *do* things. They can't handle things. There's very little muscular strength in that sting lash,' I pointed out.

'True, but what's the good of our ability to handle things if we can't see what to do with them? Anyway, they don't need to handle things –

not in the way we do. They can get their nourishment direct from the soil, or from insects and bits of raw meat. They don't have to go through all the complicated business of growing things, distributing them, and usually cooking them as well. In fact, if it were a choice for survival between a triffid and a blind man, I know which I'd put my money on.'

'You're assuming equal intelligence,' I said.

'Not at all. I don't need to. I should imagine it's likely to be an altogether different type of intelligence, if only because their needs are so much simpler. Look at the complex processes we have to use to get an assimilable extract from a triffid. Now reverse that. What does the triffid have to do? Just sting us, wait a few days, and then begin to assimilate us. The simple, natural course of things.'

He would go on like that by the hour until listening to him would have me getting things out of proportion, and I'd find myself thinking of the triffids as though they were some kind of competitor. Walter himself never pretended to think otherwise. He had, he admitted, thought of writing a book on that very aspect of the subject when he had gathered more material. 'Had?' I repeated. 'What's stopping you?'

'Just this.' He waved his hand to include the farm generally. 'It's a vested interest now. It wouldn't pay anyone to put out disturbing thoughts about it. Anyway, we have the triffids controlled well enough so it's an academic point, and scarcely worth raising.'

'I never can be quite sure with you,' I told him. 'I'm never certain how far you are serious, and how far beyond your facts you allow your imagination to lead you. Do you honestly think there is a danger in the things?'

He puffed a bit at his pipe before he answered.

'That's fair enough,' he admitted, 'because – well, I'm by no means sure myself. But I'm pretty certain of one thing, and that is that there *could* be danger in them. I'd feel a lot nearer giving you a real answer if I could get a line on what it means when they patter. Somehow I don't care for that. There they sit, with everyone thinking no more of them than they might of a pretty odd lot of cabbages, yet half the time they're pattering and clattering away at one another. Why? What is it they patter about? That's what I want to know.'

I think Walter rarely gave a hint of his ideas to anyone else, and I kept them confidential, partly because I knew no one who wouldn't be more sceptical than I was myself, and partly because it wouldn't do either of us any good to get a reputation in the firm as crackpots.

For a year or so more we were working fairly close together. But with the opening of new nurseries and the need for studying methods abroad I began to travel a lot. He gave up field work, and went into the research department. It suited him there, doing his own researching as well as the Company's. I used to drop in to see him from time to time. He was for ever making experiments with his triffids, but the results weren't clearing his general ideas as much as he had hoped. He had proved, to his own satisfaction at least, the existence of a well-developed intelligence – and even I had to admit that his results seemed to show something more than instinct. He was still convinced that the pattering of the sticks was a form of communication. For public consumption he had shown that the sticks were something more, and that a triffid deprived of them gradually deteriorated. He had also established that the infertility rate of triffid seeds was something like ninety-five per cent.

'Which,' he remarked, 'is a damned good thing. If they all germinated there'd soon be standing room only for triffids only on this planet.'

With that, too, I agreed. Triffid seed time was quite a sight. The dark green pod just below the cup was glistening and distended, about half as big again as a large apple. When it burst, it did it with a pop that was audible twenty yards away. The white seeds shot into the air like steam, and began drifting away on the lightest of breezes. Looking down on a field of triffids late in August you could well get the idea that some kind desultory bombardment was in progress.

It was Walter's discovery again that the quality of the extracts was improved if the plants retained their stings. In consequence, the practice of docking was discontinued on farms throughout the trade, and we had to wear protective devices when working among the plants.

At the time of the accident that had landed me in hospital I was actually with Walter. We were examining some specimens which were showing unusual deviations. Both of us were wearing wire-mesh masks. I did not see exactly what happened. All I know is that as I bent forward a sting slashed viciously at my face and smacked against the wire of the mask. Ninety-nine times in a hundred it would not have mattered; that was what the masks were for. But this one came with such force that some of the little poison sacs were burst open, and a few drops from them went into my eyes.

Walter got me back into his lab. and administered the antidote in a few seconds. It was entirely due to his quick work that they had the chance of saving my sight at all. But even so, it had meant over a week in bed, in the dark.

While I lay there I had quite decided that when – and if – I had my sight back I was going to apply for a transfer to another side of the business. And if that did not go through, I'd quit the job altogether.

I had built up a considerable resistance to triffid poison since my first sting in the garden. I could take, and had taken, without very much harm, stings which would have laid an inexperienced man out very cold indeed. But an old saying about a pitcher and a well kept on recurring to me. I was taking my warning.

I spent, I remember, a good many of my enforcedly dark hours deciding what kind of job I would try for if they would not give me that transfer.

Considering what was just around the corner for us all, I could scarcely have found a contemplation more idle.

CHAPTER 3

THE GROPING CITY

I left the pub door swinging behind me as I made my way to the corner of the main road. There I hesitated.

To the left, through miles of suburban streets, lay the open country; to the right, the West End of London, with the City beyond. I was feeling somewhat restored, but curiously detached now, and rudderless. I had no glimmering of a plan, and, in the face of what I had at last begun to perceive as a vast and not merely local catastrophe, I was still too stunned to begin to reason one out. What plan could there be to deal with such a thing? I felt forlorn, cast into desolation, and yet not quite real, not quite myself here and now.

In no direction was there any traffic, nor any sound of it. The only signs of life were a few people here and there cautiously groping their ways along the shop-fronts.

The day was perfect for early summer. The sun poured down from a deep blue sky set with tufts of white woolly clouds. All of it was clean and fresh save for a smear made by a single column of greasy smoke coming from somewhere behind the houses to the north.

I stood there indecisively for a few minutes. Then I turned east, Londonwards...

To this day I cannot say quite why. Perhaps it was an instinct to seek familiar places, or the feeling that if there were authority anywhere it must be somewhere in that direction.

The brandy had made me more hungry than ever, but I did not find the problem of feeding as easy to deal with as it should have been. And yet, there were the shops, untenanted and unguarded, with food in the windows – and here was I, with hunger and the means to pay – or, if I did not wish to pay, I had only to smash a window and take what I wanted.

Nevertheless, it was hard to persuade oneself to do that. I was not yet ready to admit, after nearly thirty years of a reasonably right-respecting existence and law-abiding life, that things had changed in any fundamental way. There was, too, a feeling that as long as I remained *my* normal self, things might even yet in some inconceivable way return to *their* normal. Absurd it undoubtedly was, but I had a very strong sense that the moment I stove-in one of those sheets of plate-glass I should leave the old order behind me for ever: I should become a looter, a sacker, a low scavenger upon the dead body of the system that had nourished me. Such a foolish niceness of sensibility in a stricken world! – and yet it still pleases me to remember that civilized usage did not slide off me at once, and that for a time at least I wandered along past displays which made my mouth water while my already obsolete conventions kept me hungry.

The problem resolved itself in a sophistical way after perhaps half a mile. A taxi, after mounting the pavement, had finished up with its radiator buried in a pile of delicatessen. That made it seem different from doing my own breaking in. I climbed past the taxi, and collected the makings of a good meal. But even then, something of the old standards still clung: I conscientiously left a fair price for what I had taken lying on the counter.

Almost across the road there was a garden. It was the kind that had once been the graveyard of a vanished church. The old headstones had been taken up and set back against the surrounding brick wall, the cleared space turfed over and laid out with gravelled paths. It looked pleasant under the freshly-leafed trees, and to one of the seats there I took my lunch.

The place was withdrawn and peaceful. No one else came in, though occasionally a figure would shuffle past the railings at the entrance. I threw some crumbs to a few sparrows, the first birds I had seen that day, and felt all the better for watching their perky indifference to calamity.

When I had finished eating I lit a cigarette. While I sat there smoking it, wondering where I should go, and what I should do, the quiet was broken by the sound of a piano played somewhere in a block of apartments that overlooked the garden. Presently a girl's voice began to sing. The song was Byron's ballad:

> *So, we'll go no more a-roving*
> *So late into the night,*
> *Though the heart be still as loving,*
> *And the moon be still as bright.*

For the sword outwears its sheath,
And the soul wears out the breast
And the heart must pause to breathe,
And love itself have rest.

Though the night was made for loving,
And the day returns too soon,
Yet we'll go no more a-roving
By the light of the moon.

I listened, looking up at the pattern that the tender young leaves and the branches made against the fresh blue sky. The song finished. The notes of the piano died away. Then there was a sound of sobbing. No passion: softly, helplessly, forlorn, heartbroken. Who she was, whether it was the singer or another weeping her hopes away, I do not know. But to listen longer was more than I could endure. I went quietly back into the street, seeing it only mistily for a while.

. . .

Even Hyde Park Corner, when I reached it, was almost deserted. A few derelict cars and lorries stood about on the roads. Very little, it seemed, had gone out of control when it was in motion. One bus had run across the path and had come to rest in Green Park; a runaway horse with shafts still attached to it lay beside the artillery memorial against which it had cracked its skull. The only moving things were a few men and a lesser number of women feeling their way carefully with hands and feet where there were railings, and shuffling forward with protectively outstretched arms where there were not. Also, and rather unexpectedly, there were one or two cats, apparently intact. visually, and treating the whole situation with that self-possession common to cats. They had poor luck prowling through the eerie quietness – the sparrows were few, and the pigeons had vanished.

Still magnetically drawn towards the old centre of things, I crossed in the direction of Piccadilly. I was just about to start along it when I noticed a sharp new sound – a steady tapping not far away, and coming closer. Looking up Park Lane, I discovered its source. A man, more neatly dressed than any other I had seen that morning, was walking rapidly towards me, hitting the wall beside him with a white stick. As he caught the sound of my steps he stopped, listening alertly.

'It's all right,' I told him. 'Come on.'

I felt relieved to see him. He was, so to speak, normally blind. His dark glasses were much less disturbing than the staring but useless eyes of the others.

'Stand still, then,' he said. 'I've already been bumped into by God knows how many fools today. What the devil's happened? Why is it so quiet? I know it isn't night – I can feel the sunlight. What's gone wrong with everything?'

I told him as much as I knew.

When I had finished he said nothing for almost a minute, then he gave a short, bitter laugh.

'There's one thing,' he said. 'They'll be needing all their damned patronage for themselves now.'

With that he straightened up, a little defiantly.

'Thank you. Good luck,' he said to me, and set off westwards wearing an exaggerated air of independence.

The sound of his briskly confident tapping gradually died away behind me as I made my way up Piccadilly.

There were more people to be seen now, and I walked among the scatter of stranded vehicles in the road. Out there I was much less disturbing to the people feeling their way along the fronts of the buildings, for every time they heard a step close by they would stop and brace themselves against a possible collision. Such collisions were taking place every now and then all down the street, but there was one that I found significant. The subjects of it had been groping along a shop front from opposite directions until they met with a bump. One was a young man in a well-cut suit, but wearing a tie obviously selected by touch alone: the other a woman who carried a small child. The child whined something inaudible. The young man had started to edge his way past the woman. He stopped abruptly.

'Wait a minute,' he said. 'Can your child see?'

'Yes,' she said. 'But I can't.'

The young man turned. He put one finger on the plate-glass window pointing.

'Look, Sonny, what's in there?' he asked.

'Not Sonny,' the child objected.

'Go on, Mary. Tell the gentleman,' her mother encouraged her.

'Pretty ladies,' said the child.

The man took the woman by the arm, and felt his way to the next window.

'And what's in here?' he asked, again.

'Apples and fings,' the child told him.

'Fine!' said the young man.

He pulled off his shoe, and hit the window a smart smack with the heel of it. He was inexperienced: the first blow did not do it, but the second did. The crash reverberated up and down the street. He restored his shoe, put an arm cautiously through the broken window, and felt about till he found a couple of oranges. One he gave to the woman and one to the child. He felt about again, found one for himself, and began to peel it. The woman fingered hers.

'But——' she began.

'What's the matter? Don't like oranges?' he asked.

'But it isn't right,' she said. 'We didn't ought to take 'em. Not like this.'

'How else are you going to get food?' he enquired.

'I suppose – well, I don't know,' she admitted, doubtfully.

'Very well. That's the answer. Eat it up, now, and we'll go and find something more substantial.'

She still held the orange in her hand, head bent down as though she were looking at it.

'All the same, it don't seem right,' she said again, but there was less conviction in her tone.

Presently she put the child down, and began to peel the orange ...

Piccadilly Circus was the most populous place I had found so far. It seemed crowded after the rest, though there were probably less than a hundred people there, all told. Mostly they were wearing queer, ill-assorted clothes, and were prowling restlessly around as though still semi-dazed. Occasionally a mishap would bring an outburst of profanity and futile rage – rather alarming to hear because it was itself the product of fright, and childish in temper. But with one exception there was little talk and little noise. It seemed as though their blindness had shut people into themselves.

The exception had found himself a position out on one of the traffic-islands. He was a tall, elderly, gaunt man with a bush of wiry grey hair, and he was holding forth emphatically about repentance, the wrath to come, and the uncomfortable prospects for sinners. Nobody was paying him any attention: for most of them the day of wrath had already arrived.

Then, from a distance, came a sound which caught everyone's attention: a gradually swelling chorus:

> *And when I die,*
> *Don't bury me at all,*
> *Just pickle my bones*
> *In alcohol.*

Dreary and untuneful, it slurred through the empty streets, echoing dismally back and forth. Every head in the Circus was turning now left, now right, trying to place its direction. The prophet of doom raised his voice against the competition. The song wailed discordantly closer:

Put a bottle of booze
At my head and my feet,
And then, I'm sure
My bones will keep.

And as an accompaniment to it there was a shuffle of feet more or less in step.

From where I stood I could see them come in single file out of a side street into Shaftesbury Avenue, and turn towards the Circus. The second man had his hands on the shoulders of the leader, the third on his, and so on, to the number of twenty-five or thirty. At the conclusion of that song somebody started *Beer, Beer, Glorious Beer!* pitching it in such a high key that it petered out in confusion.

They trudged steadily on until they reached the centre of the Circus, then the leader raised his voice. It was a considerable voice, with parade-ground quality:

'Companee-ee-ee – HALT!'

Everybody else in the Circus was now struck motionless, all with their faces turned toward him, all trying to guess what was afoot. The leader raised his voice again, mimicking the manner of a professional guide:

''Ere we are, gents one an' all. Piccabloodydilly Circus. The Centre of the World. The 'Ub of the Universe. Where all the nobs had their wine, women, and song.'

He was not blind, far from it. His eyes were ranging round, taking stock as he spoke. His sight must have been saved by some such accident as mine, but he was pretty drunk, and so were the men behind him.

'An' *we'll* 'ave it, too,' he added. 'Next stop, the well-known Caffy Royal – an' all drinks on the house.'

'Yus – but what abaht the women?' asked a voice, and there was a laugh.

'Oh, women. 'S that what you want?' said the leader.

He stepped forward, and caught a girl by the arm. She screamed as he dragged her towards the man who had spoken, but he took no notice of that.

'There y'are, chum. An' don't say I don't treat you right. It's a peach, a smasher – if that makes any difference to you.'

'Hey, what about me?' said the next man.

'You, mate? Well, let's see. Like 'em blonde or dark?'

Considered later, I suppose I behaved like a fool. My head was still full of standards and conventions that had ceased to apply. It did not occur to me that if there was to be any survival anyone adopted by this gang would stand a far better chance than she would on her own. Fired with a mixture of schoolboy heroics and noble sentiments, I waded in.

He didn't see me coming until I was quite close, and then I slogged for his jaw. Unfortunately, he was a little quicker...

When I next took an interest in things I found myself lying in the road. The sound of the gang was diminishing into the distance, and the prophet of doom, restored to eloquence, was sending threatful bolts of damnation, hell-fire, and a brimstone gehenna hurtling after them.

With a bit of sense knocked into me, I became thankful that the affair had not fallen out worse. Had the result been reversed, I could scarcely have escaped making myself reponsible for the men he had been leading. After all, and whatever one might feel about his methods, he was the eyes of that party, and they'd be looking to him for food as well as for drink. And the women would go along, too, on their own account as soon as they got hungry enough. And now I came to look around me I felt doubtful whether any of the women hereabouts would seriously mind, anyway. What with one thing and another, it looked as if I might have had a lucky escape from promotion to gang leadership.

Remembering that they had been heading for the Café Royal, I decided to revive myself and clear my head at the Regent Palace Hotel. Others appeared to have thought of that before me, but there were quite a lot of bottles they had not found.

I think it was while I was sitting there comfortably with a brandy in front of me and a cigarette in my hand that I at last began to admit that what I had seen was all real – and decisive. There would be no going back – ever. It was finish to all I had known...

Perhaps it had needed that blow to drive it home. Now I came face to face with the fact that my existence simply had no focus any longer. My way of life, my plans, ambitions, every expectation I had had, they were all wiped out at a stroke along with the conditions that had formed them. I suppose that had I had any relatives or close attachments to mourn I should have felt suicidally derelict at that moment. But what had seemed at times a rather empty existence turned out now to be lucky. My mother and father were dead, my one attempt to marry had miscarried some years before, and there was no particular person dependent on me. And, curiously, what I found that I did feel – with a consciousness that it was against what I ought to be feeling – was release...

It wasn't just the brandy, for it persisted. I think it may have come from the sense of facing something quite fresh and new to me. All the old problems, the stale ones, both personal and general, had been solved by one mighty slash. Heaven alone knew as yet what others might arise – and it looked as though there would be plenty of them – but they would be *new*. I was emerging as my own master, and no longer a cog. It might well be a world full of horrors and dangers that I should have to face, but I could take my own steps to deal with it – I would no longer be shoved hither and thither by forces and interests that I neither understood nor cared about.

No, it wasn't altogether the brandy, for even now, years afterwards, I can still feel something of it – though possibly the brandy did over-simplify things a little just then.

Then there was, too, the little question of what to do next; how and where to start on this new life. But I did not let that worry me a lot for the present. I drank up, and went out of the hotel to see what this strange world had to offer.

CHAPTER 4

SHADOWS BEFORE

In order to give a reasonable berth to the Café Royal mob I struck up a side street into Soho, intending to cut back to Regent Street higher up.

Perhaps hunger was driving more people out of their homes. Whatever the reason, I found that the parts I now entered were more populous than any I'd seen since I left the hospital. Constant collisions took place on the pavements and in the narrow streets, and the confusion of those who were trying to get along was made worse by knots of people clustering in front of the now frequently broken shop windows. None of those who crowded there seemed to be quite sure what kind of shop they were facing. Some in the front sought to find out by groping for any recognizable objects; others, taking the risk of disembowelling them-selves on standing splinters of glass, more enterprisingly climbed inside.

I felt that I ought to be showing these people where to find food. But should I? If I were to lead them to a food shop still intact there would be a crowd which would not only have swept the place bare in five minutes, but have crushed a number of its weaker members in the process. Soon, anyway, all the food would be gone, then what was to be done with the thousands clamouring for more? One might collect a small party and keep it alive somehow for an uncertain length of time – but who was to be taken, and who left? No obviously right course presented itself, however I tried to look at it.

What was going on was a grim business without chivalry, with no give and all take about it. A man bumping into another and feeling that he carried a parcel would snatch it and duck away on the chance that it contained something to eat, while the loser clutched furiously at the air or hit out indiscriminately. Once, I had to step hurriedly aside to avoid being knocked down by an elderly man who darted into the roadway with no care for possible obstacles. His expression was vastly cunning, and he clutched avariciously to his chest two cans of red paint. On a corner my way was blocked by a group almost weeping with frustration over a bewildered child who could see, but was just too young to understand what they wanted of it.

I began to become uneasy. Fighting with my civilized urge to be of some help to these people was an instinct that told me to keep clear. They were already fast losing ordinary restraints. I felt, too, an irrational sense of guilt at being able to see while they could not. It gave me an odd feeling that I was hiding from them even while I moved among them. Later on, I found how right the instinct was.

Close to Golden Square I began to think of turning left and working back to Regent Street where the wider roadway would offer easier going. I was about to take a corner that would lead me that way when a sudden, piercing scream stopped me. It stopped everyone else, too. All along the street they stood still, turning their heads this way and that, apprehensively trying to guess what was happening. The alarm coming on top of their distress and nervous tension started a number of the women whimpering: the men's nerves weren't in any too good a state, either; they showed it mostly in short curses at being startled. For it was an ominous sound, one of the kind of things they had been subconsciously expecting. They waited for it to come again.

It did. Frightened, and dying into a gasp. But less alarming now that one was ready for it. This time I was able to place it. A few steps took me to an alley entrance. As I turned the corner a cry that was half a gasp came again.

The cause of it was a few yards down the alley. A girl was crouched on the ground while a burly man laid into her with a thin brass rod. The back of her dress was torn, and the flesh beneath showed red weals. As I came closer I saw why she did not run away – her hands were tied together behind her back, and a cord tethered them to the man's left wrist.

I reached the pair as his arm was raised for another stroke. It was easy to snatch the rod from his unexpecting hand and bring it down with some force upon his shoulder. He promptly lashed a heavy boot out in my direction, but I had dodged back quickly, and his radius of action was limited by the cord on his wrist. He made another swiping kick at the air while I was feeling in my pocket for a knife. Finding nothing there, he turned and kicked the girl for good measure, instead. Then he swore at her and pulled on the cord to bring her to her feet. I slapped him on the side of his head, just hard enough to stop him, and make it sing for a bit – somehow I could not bring myself to lay out a blind man, even this type. While he was steadying himself from that I stooped swiftly and cut the cord which joined them. A slight shove on his chest sent him staggering back, and half turned him so that he lost his bearings. With his freed left hand he let out a fine raking swing. It missed me, but ultimately reached the brick wall. After that he lost interest in pretty well everything but the pain of his cracked knuckles. I helped the girl up, loosed her hands, and led her away down the alley while he was still blistering the air behind us.

As we turned into the street she began to come out of her daze. She turned a smeary, tear-stained face, and looked up at me.

'But you can *see!*' she said, incredulously.

'Certainly I can,' I told her.

'Oh, thank God! Thank God! I thought I was the only one,' she said, and burst into tears again.

I looked around us. A few yards away there was a pub with a gramophone playing, glasses smashing, and a high old time being had by all. A few yards beyond that was a smaller pub, still intact. A good heave with my shoulder broke in the door to the saloon bar. I half carried the girl in, and put her in a chair. Then I dismembered another chair and put two of its legs through the handles of the swing doors for the discouragement of further visitors before I turned my attention to the restoratives at the bar.

There was no hurry. She sipped at, and snuffled over, the first drink. I gave her time to get sorted out, twiddling the stem of my glass, and listening to the gramophone in the other pub churning out the currently popular if rather lugubrious ditty:

> *My love's locked up in a frigidaire,*
> *Any my heart's in a deep-freeze pack.*
> *She's gone with a guy, I'd not know where,*
> *But she wrote that she'd never come back.*
> *Now she don't care for me no more*
> *I'm just a one-man frozen store,*
> > *And it ain't nice*
> > *To be on ice*
> *With my love locked up in a frigidaire,*
> *And my heart in a deep-freeze pack.*

While I sat I stole an occasional covert look at the girl. Her clothes, or the remnants of them, were good quality. Her voice was good, too –

probably not stage or movie acquired, for it had not deteriorated under stress. She was blonde, but quite a number of shades sub-platinum. It seemed likely that beneath the smudges and smears she was good-looking. Her height was three of four inches less than mine, her build slim, but not thin. She looked as if she had strength if it were necessary, but strength which, in her approximately twenty-four years, had most likely not been applied to anything more important than hitting balls, dancing, and, probably, restraining horses. Her well-shaped hands were smooth, and the finger-nails that were still unbroken showed a length more decorative than practical.

The drink gradually did good work. By the end of it she was sufficiently recovered for habit of mind to assert itself.

'God, I must look awful,' she remarked.

It did not seem that anyone but me was likely to be in a position to notice that, but I left it.

She got up, and walked over to a mirror.

'I certainly do,' she confirmed. 'Where——'

'You might try through there,' I suggested.

Twenty minutes or so passed before she came back. Considering the limited facilities there must have been, she'd made a good job: morale was much restored. She approximated now to the film-director's idea of the heroine after a rough-house rather than the genuine thing.

'Cigarette?' I enquired, as I slid another fortifying glass across.

While the pulling round process was completing itself we swapped stories. To give her time I let her have mine first. Then she said:

'I'm damned ashamed of myself. I'm not a bit like that, really – like you found me, I mean. In fact, I'm reasonably self-reliant, though you might not think it. But somehow the whole thing had got too big for me. What has happened is bad enough, but the awful prospect suddenly seemed too much to bear, and I panicked. I began to think that perhaps I was the only person left in the whole world who could see. It got me down, and all at once I was frightened and silly, I cracked, and howled like a girl in a Victorian melodrama. I'd never, never have believed it of me.'

'Don't let it worry you,' I said. 'We'll probably be learning a whole lot of surprising things about ourselves soon.'

'But it does worry me. If I start off by slipping gears like that——' she left the sentence unfinished.

'I was near enough to panic in that hospital,' I said. 'We're human beings, not calculating machines.'

Her name was Josella Playton. There seemed to be something not unfamiliar about that, but I could not place it. Her home was in Dene

Road, St John's Wood. The district fitted in more or less with my surmises. I remembered Dene Road. Detached, comfortable houses, mostly ugly, but all expensive. Her escape from the general affliction had been no less a matter of luck than mine – well, perhaps more. She had been at a party on the Monday night – a pretty considerable party, it seemed.

'I reckon somebody who thinks that kind of thing funny must have been fooling with the drinks,' she said. 'I've never felt so ill as I did at the end of it – and I didn't take a lot.'

Tuesday she recollected as a day of blurred misery and record hangover. About four in the afternoon she had had more than enough of it. She rang the bell and gave instructions that come comets, earthquakes, or the day of judgement itself, she was not to be disturbed. Upon that ultimatum she had taken a strong dose of sleeping-draught which on an empty stomach had worked with the efficiency of a knock-out drop.

From then on she had known nothing until this morning when she had been awakened by her father stumbling into her room.

'Josella,' he was saying, 'for God's sake get Doctor Mayle. Tell him I've gone blind – stone blind.'

She had been amazed to see that it was already almost nine o'clock. She got up and dressed hurriedly. The servants had answered neither her father's bell nor her own. When she went to rouse them, she had found to her horror that they, too, were blind.

With the telephone out of order, the only course seemed to be for her to take the car and fetch the doctor himself. The quiet streets and absence of traffic had seemed queer, but she had already driven almost a mile before it came to her what had happened. When she realized, she had all but turned back in panic – but that wasn't going to do anyone any good. There still was the chance that the doctor might have escaped the malady, whatever it was, just as she had herself. So, with a desperate but waning hope, she had driven on.

Half-way down Regent Street the engine started to miss and splutter; finally it stopped. In her hurried start she had not looked at the gauge: it was the reserve tank she had run dry.

She sat there for a moment, dismayed. Every face in sight was now turned towards her, but she had realized by this time that not one of those she saw could see or help her. She got out of the car, hoping to find a garage somewhere nearby or, if there was none, prepared to walk the rest of the way. As she slammed the door behind her, a voice called:

'Hey! Just a minute, mate!'

She turned, and saw a man groping towards her.

'What is it?' she asked. She was by no means taken with the look of him.

His manner changed on hearing her voice.

'I'm lost. Dunno where I am,' he said.

'This is Regent Street. The New Gallery cinema's just behind you,' she told him, and turned to go.

'Just show me where the kerb is, miss, will you?' he said.

She hesitated, and in that moment he came close. The outstretched hand sought and touched her sleeve. He lunged forward, and caught both her arms in a painful grip.

'So you can *see*, can you!' he said. 'Why the hell should you be able to see when I can't – nor anyone else?'

Before she could realize what was happening he had turned her and tripped her, and she was lying in the road with his knee in her back. He caught both her wrists in the grasp of one large hand, and proceeded to tie them together with a piece of string from his pocket. Then he stood up, and pulled her on to her feet again.

'All right,' he said. 'From now on you can do your seeing for me. I'm hungry. Take me where there's a bit of good grub. Get on with it.'

Josella dragged away from him.

'I won't. Undo my hands at once. I——'

He cut that short with a smack across her face.

'That'll be enough o' that, my girl. Come on now. Get cracking. Food, d'yer hear?'

'I won't, I tell you.'

'You bloody well will, my girl,' he assured her.

And she had.

She'd done it watching all the time for a chance to get away. And he'd been expecting just that. Once she almost brought it off, but he had been too quick. Even as she had pulled free he had put out a foot to trip her, and before she could get up he had a grip on her again. After that he had found the strong cord and tethered her to his wrist.

She had led him first to a café, and directed him to a refrigerator. The machine was no longer working, but it was stored with food that was still fresh. The next call was a bar where he wanted Irish whiskey. She could see it, perched up on a shelf beyond his reach.

'If you'd untie my hands——' she suggested.

'What, and have you crown me with a bottle? I wasn't born yesterday, my girl. No, I'll have the Scotch. Which is it?'

She told him what was in the various bottles as he laid his hand on them.

'I think I must have been dazed,' she explained. 'I can see now half a dozen ways I could have outwitted him. Probably I'd have killed him later on if you hadn't come along. But you can't change and turn brutal all at once – at least, I can't. I didn't seem to be able to think properly at first. I'd a sort of feeling that things like that didn't happen nowadays, and that somebody would come along and stop it soon.'

There had been a row in that bar before they left. Another party of men and women discovered the open door and came in. Incautiously her captor instructed her to tell them what was in the bottle they found. At that they all stopped talking, and turned their sightless eyes towards her. There was a whisper, then two men stepped warily forward. They had a purposeful look on their faces. She jerked at the cord.

'Look out!' she cried.

Without the least hesitation her captor swung out his boot. It was a lucky kick. One of the men folded up with a yell of pain. The other jumped forward, but she side-stepped and he brought up against the counter with a crash.

'You bloody well leave her alone,' roared the man who held her. He turned his face menacingly this way and that. 'She's mine, blast you. I found her.'

But it was clear that the rest were not intending to give up that easily. Even had they been able to see the danger in her companion's expression it would not have been likely to stop them. Josella started to realize that the gift of sight, even at second hand, was now something vastly surpassing all riches, and the chance of it not to be released without bitter contest. The others began to close in, with their hands questing in front of them. Reaching out with one foot, she hooked the leg of a chair, and overturned it in their way.

'Come on!' she cried, dragging the other man back.

Two men tripped over the fallen chair, and a women fell on top of them. Swiftly the place became a struggling confusion. She steered a way through it, and they escaped into the street.

She scarcely knew why she did it save that the prospect of being enslaved to act as the eyes of that group had seemed even worse than her present plight. Nor did the man give her any thanks. He merely directed her to find another bar: an empty one.

'I think,' she said judicially, 'that though you wouldn't have guessed it to look at him, he wasn't perhaps too bad a man really. Only he was frightened. Deep down inside him he was much more frightened than I was. He gave me some food and something to drink. He only started beating me like that because he was drunk, and I wouldn't go into his house with him. I don't know what would have happened if you hadn't come along.' She paused. Then she added: 'But I am pretty ashamed of myself. Shows you what a modern young woman can come to after all, doesn't it? Screaming, and collapsing with the vapours – Hell!'

She was looking, and obviously feeling, rather better though she winced as she reached for her glass.

'I think,' I said, 'that I've been fairly dense over this business – and pretty lucky. I ought to have made more of the implications when I saw that woman with the child in Piccadilly. It's only been chance that's stopped me from falling into the same kind of mess that you did.'

'Anybody who has had a great treasure has always led a precarious existence,' she said, reflectively.

'I'll go on bearing that in mind, henceforth,' I told her.

'It's already very well impressed on mine,' she remarked.

We sat listening to the uproar from the other pub for a few minutes.

'And what,' I said at last, 'just what do we propose to do now?'

'I must get back home. There's my father. It's obviously no good going on to try to find the doctor now – even if he has been one of the lucky ones.'

She seemed about to add something, but hesitated.

'Do you mind if I come, too?' I asked. 'This doesn't seem to me the sort of time when anyone like us should be wandering about on his or her own.'

She turned with a grateful look.

'Thank you. I almost asked, but I thought there might be somebody you'd be wanting to look for.'

'There isn't,' I said. 'Not in London, at any rate.'

'I'm glad. It's not so much that I'm afraid of getting caught again – I'll be much too careful for that. But, to be honest, it's the loneliness I'm afraid of. I'm beginning to feel so – so cut off and stranded.'

I was starting to see things in another new light. The sense of release was tempered with a growing realization of the grimness that might lie ahead of us. It had been impossible at first not to feel some superiority, and, therefore, confidence. Our chances of surviving the catastrophe were a million times greater than those of the rest. Where they must fumble, grope, and guess, we had simply to walk in and take. But there were going to be a lot of things beyond that...

I said: 'I wonder just how many of us have escaped and can still see? I've come across one other man, a child, and a baby: you've met none. It looks to me as if we are going to find out that sight is very rare indeed. Some of the others have evidently grasped already that their only chance of survival is to get hold of someone who can see. When they all understand that, the outlook's going to be none too good.'

The future seemed to me at that time a choice between a lonely existence, always in fear of capture, or of gathering together a selected group which we could rely on to protect us from other groups. We'd be filling a kind of leader-cum-prisoner rôle – and along with it went a nasty picture of bloody gang wars being fought for possession of us. I was still uncomfortably elaborating these possibilities when Josella recalled me to the present by getting up.

'I must go,' she said. 'Poor father. It's after four o'clock.'

Back in Regent Street again, a thought suddenly struck me.

'Come across,' I said. 'I fancy I remember a shop somewhere here...'

The shop was still there. We equipped ourselves with a couple of useful-looking sheath knives, and belts to carry them.

'Makes me feel like a pirate,' said Josella, as she buckled hers on.

'Better, I imagine, to be a pirate than a pirate's moll,' I told her.

A few yards up the street we came upon a large, shiny saloon car. It looked the kind of craft that should simply have purred. But the noise when I started it up sounded louder in our ears than all the normal traffic of a busy street. We made our way northward, zigzagging to avoid derelicts and wanderers stricken into immobility in the middle of the road by the sound of our approach. All the way heads turned hopefully towards us as we came; and faces fell as we went past. One building on our route was blazing fiercely, and a cloud of smoke rose from another fire somewhere along Oxford Street. There were more people about in Oxford Circus, but we got through them neatly, then passed the B.B.C., and so north to the carriageway in Regent's Park.

It was a relief to get out of the streets and reach an open space – and one where there were no unfortunate people wandering and groping. The only moving things we could see on the broad stretches of grass were two or three little groups of triffids lurching southwards. Somehow or other they had contrived to pull up their stakes and were dragging them along behind them on their chains. I remembered that there were some unlocked specimens, a few tethered, but most of them double-fenced, in an enclosure beside the zoo and wondered how they had got out. Josella noticed them, too.

'It's not going to make much difference to them,' she said.

For the rest of the way there was little to delay us. Within a few minutes I was pulling up at the house she pointed out. We got out of the car, and I pushed open the gate. A short drive curved round a bed of bushes which hid most of the house front from the road. As we turned the corner Josella gave a cry, and ran forward. A figure was lying on the gravel, chest downwards, but with the head turned to show one side of its face. The first glance at it showed me the bright red streak across the cheek.

'Stop!' I shouted at her.

There was enough alarm in my voice to check her.

I had spotted the triffid now. It was lurking among the bushes, well within striking range of the sprawled figure.

'Back! Quick!' I said.

Still looking at the man on the ground, she hesitated.

'But I must——' she began, turning towards me. Then she stopped. Her eyes widened, and she screamed.

I whipped round to find a triffid towering only a few feet behind me.

In one automatic movement I had my hands over my eyes. I heard the sting whistle as it lashed out at me – but there was no knockout, no agonizing burning, even. One's mind can move like lightning at such a moment: nevertheless, it was more instinct than reason which sent me leaping at it before it had time to strike again. I collided with it, overturning it, and even as I went down with it my hands were on the upper part of its stem, trying to pull off the cup and the sting. Triffid stems do not snap – but they can be mangled. This one was mangled thoroughly before I stood up.

Josella was standing in the same spot, transfixed.

'Come here,' I told her. 'There's another in the bushes behind you.'

She glanced fearfully over her shoulder, and came.

'But it *hit* you!' she said, incredulously. 'Why aren't you——?'

'I don't know. I ought to be,' I said.

I looked down at the fallen triffid. Suddenly remembering the knives that we'd acquired with quite other enemies in mind, I used mine to cut off the sting at its base. I examined it.

'That explains it,' I said, pointing to the poison-sacs. 'See, they're collapsed, exhausted. If they'd been full, or even part full . . .' I turned a thumb down.

I had that, and my acquired resistance to the poison, to thank. Nevertheless, there was a pale red mark across the back of my hands and my neck that was itching like the devil. I rubbed it while I stood looking at the sting.

'It's queer——' I murmured, more to myself than to her, but she heard me.

'What's queer?'

'I've never seen one with the poison-sacs quite empty like this before. It must have been doing a hell of a lot of stinging.'

But I doubt if she heard me. Her attention had reverted to the man who was lying in the drive, and she was eyeing the triffid standing by.

'How can we get him away?' she asked.

'We can't – not till that thing's been dealt with,' I told her. 'Besides – well, I'm afraid we can't help him now.'

'You mean, he's dead?'

I nodded. 'Yes. There's not a doubt of it – I've seen others who have been stung. Who was he?' I added.

'Old Pearson. He did gardening for us, and chauffeuring for my father. Such a dear old man – I've known him all my life.'

'I'm sorry——' I began, wishing I could think of something more adequate, but she cut me short.

'Look! – oh, look!' She pointed to a path which ran round the side of the house. A black-stockinged leg with a woman's shoe on it protruded round the corner.

We prospected carefully, and then moved safely to a spot which gave a better view. A girl in a black dress lay half on the path and half in a flower-bed. Her pretty, fresh face was scarred with a bright red line. Josella choked. Tears came into her eyes.

'Oh! – oh, it's Annie! Poor little Annie,' she said.

I tried to console her a little.

'They can have scarcely known it, either of them,' I told her. 'When it is strong enough to kill, it's mercifully quick.'

We did not see any other triffid in hiding there. Possibly it was the same one that had attacked them both. Together we crossed the path and got into the house by the side-door. Josella called. There was no answer. She called again. We both listened in the complete silence that wrapped the house. She turned to look at me. Neither of us said anything. Quietly she led the way along a passage to a baize-covered door. As she opened it there was a swish, and something slapped across door and frame, an inch or so above her head. Hurriedly she pulled the door shut again, and turned wide-eyed to me.

'There's one in the hall,' she said.

She spoke in a frightened half-whisper, as though it might be listening.

We went back to the outer door, and into the garden once more. Keeping to the grass for silence we made our way round the house until we could look into the lounge-hall. The french window which led from the garden was open, and the glass of one side was shattered. A trail of muddy blobs led over the step and across the carpet. At the end of it a triffid stood in the middle of the room. The top of its stem almost brushed the ceiling, and it was swaying ever so slightly. Close beside its damp, shaggy bole lay the body of an elderly man clad in a bright silk dressing-gown. I took hold of Josella's arm. I was afraid she might rush in there.

'Is it – your father?' I asked, though I knew it must be.

'Yes,' she said, and put her hands over her face. She was trembling slightly.

I stood still, keeping an eye on the triffid inside lest it should move our way. Then I thought of a handkerchief and handed her mine. There wasn't much anyone could do. After a little while she took more control of herself. Remembering the people we had seen that day, I said:

'You know, I think I would rather *that* had happened to me than be like those others.'

'Yes,' she said, after a pause.

She looked up into the sky. It was a soft, depthless blue, with a few little clouds floating like white feathers.

'Oh, yes,' she repeated with more conviction. 'Poor Daddy. He couldn't have stood blindness. He loved all this too much.' She glanced inside the room again. 'What shall we do? I can't leave——'

At that moment I caught the reflection of movement in the remaining window-pane. I looked behind us quickly to see a triffid break clear of the bushes and start across the lawn. It was lurching on a line that led straight towards us. I could hear the leathery leaves rustling as the stem whipped back and forth.

There was no time for delay. I had no idea how many more there might be round the place. I grabbed Josella's arm again, and ran her back by the way we had come. As we scrambled safely into the car, she burst into real tears at last.

She would be the better for having her cry out. I lit a cigarette, and considered the next move. Naturally, she was not going to care for the idea of leaving her father as we had found him. She would wish that he should have a proper burial – and, by the looks of it, that would be a matter of the pair of us digging the grave and effecting the whole business. And before that could even be attempted it would be necessary to fetch the means to deal with the triffids that were already there, and keep off any more than might appear. On the whole, I would be in favour of dropping the whole thing – but then, it was not my father...

The more I considered this new aspect of things, the less I liked it. I had no idea how many triffids there might be in London. Every park had a few at least. Usually they kept some docked ones that were allowed to roam about as they would, often there were others, with stings intact, either staked, or safely behind wire-netting. Thinking of those we had seen crossing Regent's Park, I wondered just how many they had been in the habit of keeping in the pens by the zoo, and how many had escaped. There'd be a number in private gardens, too; you'd expect all those to be safely docked – but you never can tell what fool carelessness may go on. And then there were several nurseries of the things, and experimental stations a little further out...

While I sat there pondering, I was aware of something nudging at the back of my mind; some association of ideas that didn't quite join up. I sought it for a moment or two: then, suddenly, it came. I could almost hear Walter's voice speaking, saying:

'I tell you, a triffid's in a damn sight better position to survive than a blind man.'

Of course, he had been talking about a man who had been blinded by a triffid sting. All the same, it was a jolt. More than a jolt. It scared me a bit.

I thought back. No, it had just arisen out of general speculation – nevertheless, it seemed a bit uncanny now...

'Take away our sight,' he had said. 'And our superiority to them is gone.'

Of course, coincidences are happening all the time – but it's just now and then you happen to notice them...

A crunch on the gravel brought me back to the present. A triffid came swaying down the drive towards the gate. I leant across, and screwed up the window.

'Drive on! Drive on!' said Josella hysterically.

'We're all right here,' I told her. 'I want to see what it does.'

Simultaneously I realized that one of my questions was solved. Being accustomed to triffids, I had forgotten how most people felt about an undocked one. I suddenly understood that there would be no question of coming back here. Josella's feeling about an armed triffid was the general idea – get well away from it, and stay away.

The thing paused at the gatepost. One could have sworn that it was listening. We sat perfectly still and quiet. Josella staring at it with horror. I expected it to lash out at the car, but it didn't. Probably the muffling of our voices inside had misled it into thinking we were out of range.

The little bare stalks began abruptly to clatter against its stem. It swayed, lumbered clumsily off to the right, and disappeared into the next driveway.

Josella gave a sigh of relief.

'Oh, let's get away before it comes back,' she implored.

I started the car, turned it round, and we drove off Londonwards again.

CHAPTER 5

A LIGHT IN THE NIGHT

Josella began to recover her self-possession. With the deliberate and obvious intention of taking her mind off what lay behind us she asked:

'Where are we going now?'

'Clerkenwell first,' I told her. 'After that we'll see about getting you some more clothes. Bond Street for them, if you like, but Clerkenwell first.'

'But why Clerkenwell——? Good heavens!'

She might well exclaim. We had turned a corner to see the street seventy yards ahead of us filled with people. They were coming towards us at a stumbling run, with their arms outstretched before them. A mingled crying and screaming came from them. Even as we turned into sight of them, a women at the front tripped and fell; others tumbled over her, and she disappeared beneath a kicking, struggling heap. Beyond the mob, we had a glimpse of the cause of it all: three dark-leaved stalks swaying over the panic-stricken heads. I accelerated, and swung off into a by-road.

Josella turned a terrified face.

'Did – did you see what that was? They were *driving* them.'

'Yes,' I said. 'That's why we are going to Clerkenwell. There's a place there that makes the best triffid-guns and masks in the world.'

We worked back again, and picked up our intended route, but we did not find the clear run I had hoped for. Near King's Cross Station there were many more people on the streets. Even with a hand on the horn it was increasingly difficult to get along. In front of the station itself it became impossible. Why there should have been such crowds in that place I don't know. All the people in the district seemed to have converged upon it. We could not get through the people, and a glance behind showed that it would be almost hopeless to try to go back. Those we had passed had already closed in on our track.

'Get out, quick!' I said. 'I think they're after us.'

'But——' Josella began.

'Hurry!' I said shortly.

I blew a final blast on the horn, and slipped out after her, leaving the engine running. We were not many seconds too soon. A man found the handle of the rear door. He pulled it open, and pawed inside. We were all but pushed over by the pressure of others making for the car. There

was a shout of anger when somebody opened the front door and found
the seats there empty, too. By that time we had ourselves safely become
members of the crowd. Somebody grabbed the man who had opened the
rear door under the impression that it was he who had just got out.
Around that the confusion began to thrive. I took a firm grip of Josella's
hand, and we started to worm our way out as unobviously as possible.

Clear of the crowd at last, we kept on foot for a while, looking out for a
suitable car. After a mile or so we found it – a station-waggon, likely to
be more useful than an ordinary body for the plan that was beginning to
form vaguely in my mind.

In Clerkenwell they had been accustomed for two or three centuries to
make fine, precise instruments. The small factory I had dealt with
professionally at times had adapted the old skill to new needs. I found it
with little difficulty, nor was it hard to break in. When we set off again
there was a comforting sense of support to be derived from several
excellent triffid-guns, some thousands of little steel boomerangs for
them, and some wire-mesh helmets that we had loaded into the back.

'And now – clothes?' suggested Josella, as we started.

'Provisional plan, open to criticism and correction,' I told her. 'First
what you might call a *pied-à-terre:* i.e. somewhere to pull ourselves
together and discuss things.'

'Not another bar,' she protested. 'I've had quite enough of bars for
one day.'

'Improbable though my friends might think it – with everything free
– so have I,' I agreed. 'What I was thinking of was an empty flat. That
shouldn't be difficult to find. We could ease up there awhile, and settle
the rough plan of campaign. Also, it would be convenient for spending
the night – or, if you find the trammels of convention still defy the
peculiar circumstances, well, maybe we could make it two flats.'

'I think I'd be happier to know there was someone close at hand.'

'Okay,' I agreed. 'Then operation Number Two will be ladies' and
gents' outfitting. For that perhaps we had better go our separate ways –
both taking exceedingly good care not to forget which flat it was that we
decided on.'

'Y-es,' she said, but a little doubtfully.

'It'll be all right,' I assured her. 'Make a rule for yourself not to speak
to anyone, and nobody's going to guess you can see. It was only being
quite unprepared that landed you in that mess before. "In the country of
the blind the one-eyed man is king." '

'Oh, yes – Wells said that, didn't he? – Only in the story it turned out
not to be true.'

'The crux of the difference lies in what you mean by the word "country" – *patria* in the original,' I said. '*Caecorum in patria luscus rex imperat omnis* – a classical gentleman called Fullonius said it first: it's all anyone seems to know about him. But there's no organized *patria,* no State, here – only chaos. Wells imagined a people who had adapted themselves to blindness. I don't think that is going to happen here – I don't see how it can.'

'What do you think *is* going to happen?'

'My guess would be no better than yours. And soon we shall begin to know, anyway. Better get back to matters in hand. Where were we?'

'Choosing clothes.'

'Oh, yes. Well, it's simply a matter of slipping into a shop, adopting a few trifles, and slipping out again. You'll not meet any triffids in Central London – at least, not yet.'

'You talk so lightly about taking things,' she said.

'I don't feel quite so lightly about it,' I admitted. 'But I'm not sure that that's virtue – it's more likely merely habit. And an obstinate refusal to face facts isn't going to bring anything back, or help us at all. I think we'll have to try to see ourselves not as the robbers of all this, but more as – well, the unwilling heirs to it.'

'Yes. I suppose it is something like that,' she agreed, in a qualified way.

She was silent for a time. When she spoke again she reverted to the earlier question.

'And after the clothes?' she asked.

'Operation Number Three,' I told her, 'is quite definitely, dinner.'

There was, as I had expected, no great difficulty about the flat. We left the car locked up in the middle of the road in front of an opulent-looking block, and climbed to the third storey. Quite why we chose the third I can't say, except that it seemed a bit more out of the way. The process of selection was simple. We knocked or we rang, and if anyone answered, we passed on. After we had passed on three times we found a door where there was no response. The socket of the rim-lock tore off to one good heft of the shoulder, and we were in.

I had not, myself, been one of those addicted to living in a flat with a rent of some £2,000 a year, but I found that there were decidedly things to be said in favour of it. The interior decorators had been, I guessed, elegant young men with just that ingenious gift for combining taste with advanced topicality which is so expensive. Consciousness of fashion was the mainspring of the place. Here and there were certain unmistakable *derniers cris,* some of them undoubtedly destined – had the world pursued its expected course – to become the rage of tomorrow: others, I would say, a dead loss from their very inception. The overall effect was all

Trade Fair in its neglect of human foibles – a book left a few inches out of place, or with the wrong colour on its jacket would ruin the whole carefully considered balance and tone – so, too, would the person thoughtless enough to wear the wrong clothes when sitting upon the wrong luxurious chair or sofa. I turned to Josella who was staring wide-eyed at it all.

'Will this little shack serve – or do we go further?' I asked.

'Oh, I guess we'll make out,' she said. And together we waded through the delicate cream carpet to explore.

It was quite uncalculated, but I could scarcely have hit upon a more satisfactory method of taking her mind off the events of the day. Our tour was punctuated with a series of exclamations in which admiration, envy, delight, contempt, and, one must confess, malice, all played their parts. Josella paused on the threshold of a room rampant with all the most aggressive manifestations of femininity.

'I'll sleep here,' she said.

'My God!' I remarked. 'Well, each to her taste.'

'Don't be nasty. I probably won't have another chance to be decadent. Besides, don't you know there's a bit of the dumbest film-star in every girl? So I'll let it have its final fling.'

'You shall,' I said. 'But I hope they keep something quieter around here. Heaven preserve me from having to sleep in a bed with a mirror set in the ceiling over it.'

'There's one above the bath, too,' she said, looking into an adjoining room.

'I don't know whether that would be the zenith or nadir of decadence,' I said. 'But anyway, you'll not be using it. No hot water.'

'Oh, I'd forgotten that. What a shame!' she exclaimed, disappointedly.

We completed our inspection of the premises, finding the rest less sensational. Then she went out to deal with the matter of clothes. I made an inspection of the apartment's resources and limitations, and then set out on an expedition of my own.

As I stepped outside, another door farther down the passage opened. I stopped, and stood still where I was. A young man came out, leading a fair-haired girl by the hand. As she stepped over the threshold he released his grasp.

'Wait just a minute, darling,' he said.

He took three or four steps on the silencing carpet. His outstretched hands found the window which ended the passage. His fingers went straight to the catch and opened it. I had a glimpse of a fire-escape outside.

'What are you doing, Jimmy?' she asked.

'Just making sure,' he said, stepping quickly back to her, and feeling for her hand again. 'Come along, darling.'

She hung back.

'Jimmy – I don't like leaving here. At least we know where we are in our own flat. How are we going to feed? How are we going to live?'

'In the flat darling, we shan't feed at all – and therefore not live long. Come along, sweetheart. Don't be afraid.'

'But I am, Jimmy – I am.'

She clung to him, and he put one arm round her.

'We'll be all right, darling. Come along.'

'But Jimmy, that's the wrong way——'

'You've got it twisted round, dear. It's the right way.'

'Jimmy – I'm so frightened. Let's go back.'

'It's too late, darling.'

By the window he paused. With one hand he felt his position very carefully. Then he put both arms round her, holding her to him.

'Too wonderful to last, perhaps,' he said softly. 'I love you, my sweet. I love you so very, very much.'

She turned her lips up to be kissed.

As he lifted her he turned, and stepped out of the window ...

. . .

'You've got to grow a hide,' I told myself. '*Got to.* It's either that or stay permanently drunk. Things like that must be happening all around. They'll go on happening. You can't help it. Suppose you'd given them food to keep them alive for another few days? What after that? You've got to learn to take it, and come to terms with it. There's nothing else but the alcoholic funk-hole. If you don't fight to live your own life in spite of it, there won't be any survival ... Only those who can make their minds tough enough to stick it are going to get through ...

. . .

It took me longer than I had expected to collect what I wanted. Something like two hours had passed before I got back. I dropped one or two things from my armful in negotiating the door. Josella's voice called with a trace of nervousness from that over-feminine room.

'Only me,' I reassured her, as I advanced down the passage with the load.

I dumped the things in the kitchen, and went back for those I'd dropped. Outside her door I paused.

'You can't come in,' she said.

'That wasn't quite my intended angle,' I protested. 'What I want to know is, can you cook?'

'Boiled egg standard,' said her muffled voice.

'I was afraid of that. There's an awful lot of things we're going to have to learn,' I told her.

I went back to the kitchen. I erected the oil-stove I had brought on top of the useless electric cooker, and got busy.

When I'd finished laying the places at the small table in the sitting-room, the effect seemed to me fairly good. I fetched a few candles and candlesticks to complete it, and set them ready. Of Josella there was still no visible sign, though there had been sounds of running water some little time ago. I called her.

'Just coming,' she answered.

I wandered across to the window, and looked out. Quite consciously I began saying goodbye to it all. The sun was low. Towers, spires, façades of Portland stone were white or pink against the dimming sky. More fires had broken out here and there. The smoke climbed in big black smudges, sometimes with a lick of flame at the bottom of them. Quite likely, I told myself, I would never in my life again see any of these familiar buildings after tomorrow. There might be a time when one would be able to come back – but not to the same place. Fires and weather would have worked on it: it would be visibly dead and abandoned. But now, at a distance, it could still masquerade as a living city.

My father once told me that before Hitler's war he used to go around London with his eyes more widely open than ever before, seeing the beauties of buildings that he had never noticed before – saying goodbye to them. And now I had a similar feeling. But this was something worse. Much more than anyone could have hoped for had survived that war – but this was an enemy they would not survive. It was not wanton smashing and wilful burning that they waited for this time: it was simply the long, slow, inevitable course of decay and collapse.

Standing there, and at that time, my heart still resisted what my head was telling me. Even yet I had the feeling that it was all something too big, too unnatural really to happen. Yet I knew that it was by no means the first time that it had happened. The corpses of other great cities are lying buried in deserts, and obliterated by the jungles of Asia. Some of them fell so long ago that even their names have gone with them. But to those who lived there their dissolution can have seemed no more probable or possible than the necrosis of a great modern city seemed to me . . .

It must be, I thought, one of the race's most persistent and comforting hallucinations to trust that 'it can't happen here' – that one's own little time and place is beyond cataclysms. And now it *was* happening here.

Unless there should be some miracle I was looking on the beginning of the end of London – and very likely, it seemed, there were other men, not unlike me, who were looking on the beginning of the end of New York, Paris, San Francisco, Buenos Aires, Bombay, and all the rest of the cities that were destined to go the way of those others under the jungles.

I was still looking out when a sound of movement came from behind me. I turned, and saw that Josella had come into the room. She was wearing a long, pretty frock of palest blue georgette with a little jacket of white fur. In a pendant on a simple chain a few blue-white diamonds flashed, the stones that gleamed in her ear-clips were smaller but as fine in colour. Her hair and her face might have been fresh from a beauty parlour. She crossed the floor with a flicker of silver slippers and a glimpse of gossamer stockings. As I went on staring without speaking, her mouth lost its little smile.

'Don't you like it?' she asked, with childish half-disappointment.

'It's lovely – you're beautiful,' I told her. 'I – well, I just wasn't expecting anything like this . . .'

Something more was needed. I knew that it was a display which had little or nothing to do with me. I added:

'You're saying goodbye?'

A different look came into her eyes.

'So you do understand. I hoped you would.'

'I think I do. I'm glad you've done it. It'll be a lovely thing to remember,' I said.

I stretched out my hand to her and led her to the window.

'I was saying goodbye, too – to all this.'

What went on in her mind as we stood there side by side is her secret. In mine there was a kind of kaleidoscope of the life and ways that were now finished – or perhaps it was more like flipping through a huge volume of photographs with one all-comprehensive 'do-you-remember?'

We looked for a long time, lost in our thoughts. Then she sighed. She glanced down at her dress, fingering the delicate silk.

'Silly? – Rome burning?' she said, with a rueful little smile.

'No – sweet,' I said. 'Thank you for doing it. A gesture – and a reminder that with all the faults there was so much beauty. You couldn't have done – or looked – a lovelier thing.'

Her smile lost its ruefulness.

'Thank you, Bill.' She paused. Then she added: 'Have I said thank you before? I don't think I have. If you hadn't helped me when you did——'

'But for you,' I told her, 'I should probably by now be lying maudlin and sozzled in some bar. I have just as much to thank you for. This is no time to be alone.' Then, to change the trend, I added: 'And speaking of drink, there's an excellent Amontillado here, and some pretty good things to follow. This is a very well-found flat.'

I poured out the sherry, and we raised our glasses.

'To health, strength – and luck,' I said.

She nodded. We drank.

'What,' Josella asked, as we started on an expensive-tasting pâté, 'what if the owner of all this suddenly comes back?'

'In that case we will explain – and he or she should be only too thankful to have someone here to tell him which bottle is which, and so on – but I don't think that is very likely to happen.'

'No,' she agreed, considering. 'No. I'm afraid that's not very likely. I wonder——' She looked round the room. Her eyes paused at a fluted white pedestal. 'Did you try the radio – I suppose that thing *is* a radio, isn't it?'

'It's a television projector, too,' I told her. 'But no good. No power.'

'Of course, I forgot. I suppose we'll go on forgetting things like that for quite a time.'

'But I did try one when I was out,' I said. 'A battery affair. Nothing doing. All broadcast bands as silent as the grave.'

'That means it's like this everywhere?'

'I'm afraid so. There was something pip-pipping away around forty-two metres. Otherwise nothing. Not even carriers. I wonder who and where he was, poor chap.'

'It's – it's going to be pretty grim, Bill, isn't it?'

'It's – no, I'm not going to have my dinner clouded,' I said. 'Pleasure before business – and the future is definitely business. Let's talk about something interesting like how many love-affairs you have had and why somebody hasn't married you long before this – or has he? You see how little I know. Life story, please.'

'Well,' she said, 'I was born about three miles from here. My mother was very annoyed about it at the time.'

I raised my eyebrows.

'You see, she had quite made up her mind that I should be an American. But when the car came to take her to the airport it was just too late. Full of impulses, she was – I think I inherited some of them.'

She prattled on. There was not much remarkable about her early life, but I think she enjoyed herself in summarizing it, and forgetting where we were for a while. I enjoyed listening to her babble of the familiar and amusing things that had all vanished from the world outside. We worked lightly through childhood, school-days, and 'coming out' – in so far as the term still meant anything.

'I did nearly get married when I was nineteen,' she admitted, 'and aren't I glad now it didn't happen. But I didn't feel like that at the time. I had a frightful row with Daddy who'd broken the whole thing up because he saw right away that Lionel was a spizzard and...'

'A what?' I interrupted.

'A spizzard. A sort of cross between a spiv and lizard – the lounge kind. So then I cut my family off and went and lived with a girl I knew who had a flat. And my family cut off my allowance, which was a very silly thing to do because it might have had just the opposite effect from what they intended. As it happened, it didn't, because all the girls I knew who were making out that way seemed to me to have a very wearing sort of time of it. Not much fun, an awful lot of jealousy to put up with – and so much planning. You'd never believe how much planning it needs to keep one or two second strings in good condition – or do I mean two or three spare strings——?' She pondered.

'Never mind,' I told her. 'I get the general idea. You just didn't want the strings at all.'

'Intuitive, you are. All the same, I couldn't just sponge on the girl who had the flat. I did have to have some money, so I wrote the book.'

I did not think I'd heard quite aright.

'You made a book?' I suggested.

'I *wrote* the book.' She glanced at me, and smiled. 'I must look awfully dumb – that's just the way *they* all used to look at me when I told them I was writing a book. Mind you, it wasn't a very good book – I mean, not like Aldous or Charles or people of that kind, but it worked.'

I refrained from enquiring which of the many possible Charles's this referred to. I simply asked:

'You mean it did get published?'

'Oh, yes. And it really brought in quite a lot of money. The film rights——'

'What was this book?' I asked, curiously.

'It was called *Sex is My Adventure*.'

I stared, and then smote my forehead.

'Josella Playton, of course. I couldn't think why that name kept on nearly ringing bells. You wrote that thing?' I added, incredulously.

I couldn't think why I had not remembered before. Her photograph had been all over the place – not a very good photograph now I could look at the original, and the book had been all over the place, too. Two large circulating libraries had banned it, probably on the title alone. After that, its success had been assured, and the sales went rocketing up into the hundred thousands. Josella chuckled. I was glad to hear it.

'Oh, dear,' she said. 'You look just like all my relatives did.'

'I can't blame them,' I told her.

'Did you read it?' she asked.

I shook my head. She sighed.

'People are funny. All you know about it is the title and the publicity, and you're shocked. And it's such a harmless little book, really. Mixture of green-sophisticated and pink-romantic, with patches of school-girly-purple. But the title was a good idea.'

'All depends what you mean by good,' I suggested. 'And you put your own name to it, too.'

'That,' she agreed, 'was a mistake. The publishers persuaded me that it would be so much better for publicity. From their point of view they were right. I became quite notorious for a bit – it used to make me giggle inside when I saw people looking speculatively at me in restaurants and places – they seemed to find it so hard to tie up what they saw with what they thought. Lots of people I didn't care for took to turning up regularly at the flat, so to get rid of them, and because I'd proved that I didn't *have* to go home, I went home again.

'The book rather spoiled things, though. People would be so literal-minded about the title. I seem to have been keeping up a permanent defensive ever since against people I don't like – and those I wanted to like were either scared or shocked. What's so annoying is that it wasn't even a wicked book – it was just silly-shocking, and sensible people ought to have seen that.'

She paused contemplatively. It occurred to me that the sensible people had probably decided that the author of *Sex is My Adventure* would be silly-shocking, too, but I forbore to suggest it. We all have our youthful follies embarrassing to recall – but people somehow find it hard to dismiss as a youthful folly anything that has happened to be a financial success.

'It sort of twisted everything,' she complained. 'I was writing another book to try to balance things up again. But I'm glad I'll never finish it – it was rather bitter.'

'With an equally alarming title?' I asked.

She shook her head: 'It was to be called *Here the Forsaken*.'

'H'm – well, it certainly lacks the snap of the other,' I said. 'Quotation?'

'Yes.' She nodded. 'Mr Congreve: "Here the forsaken Virgin rests from Love." '

'Er – oh,' I said, and thought that one over for a bit.

.   .   .

'And now,' I suggested, 'I think it's about time we began to rough out a plan of campaign. Shall I throw around a few observations first?'

We lay back in two superbly comfortable armchairs. On the low table between us stood the coffee apparatus and two glasses. Josella's was the small one with the Cointreau. The plutocratic-looking balloon with the puddle of unpriceable brandy was mine. Josella blew out a feather of smoke, and took a sip of her drink. Savouring the flavour, she said:

'I wonder whether we shall ever taste fresh oranges again? Okay, shoot.'

'Well, it's no good blinking facts. We had better clear out soon. If not tomorrow, then the day after. You can begin to see already what's going to happen here. At present there's still water in the tanks. Soon there won't be. The whole city will begin to stink like a great sewer. There are already some bodies lying about – every day there will be more.' I noticed her shudder. I had for the moment, in taking the general view, forgotten the particular application it would have for her. I hurried on: 'That may mean typhus, or cholera, or God knows what. It's important to get away before anything of that kind starts.'

She nodded agreement to that.

'Then the next question seems to be, where do we go? Have you any ideas?' I asked her.

'Well – I suppose, roughly, somewhere out of the way. A place with a good water supply we can be sure of, a well, perhaps. And I should think it would be best to be as high up as we reasonably can – some place where there'll be a nice clean wind.'

'Yes,' I said, 'I'd not thought of the clean wind part, but you're right. A hilltop with a good water supply – that's not so easy offhand.' I thought a moment. 'The Lake District? No, too far. Wales, perhaps? Or maybe Exmoor or Dartmoor – or right down in Cornwall? Around Land's End we'd have the prevailing south-west wind coming in untainted over the Atlantic. But that, too, was a long way. We should be dependent on towns when it became safe to visit them again.'

'What about the Sussex Downs?' Josella suggested. 'I know a lovely old farmhouse on the north side, looking right across towards Pulborough. It's not on the top of hills, but it's well up the side. There's a wind-pump for water, and I think they make their own electricity. It's all been converted and modernized.'

'Desirable residence, in fact. But it's a bit near populous places. Don't you think we ought to get further away?'

'Well, I was wondering. How long is it going to be before it'll be safe to go into the towns again?'

'I've no real idea,' I admitted, 'I'd something like a year in mind – surely that ought to be a safe enough margin?'

'I see. But if we do go too far away, it isn't going to be at all easy to get supplies later on.'

'That is a point, certainly,' I agreed.

We dropped the matter of our final destination for the moment, and got down to working out details for our removal. In the morning, we decided, we would first of all acquire a lorry – a capacious lorry – and between us we made a list of essentials we would put into it. If we could finish the stocking up, we would start on our way next evening, if not – and the list was growing to a length which made this appear much the more likely – we would risk another night in London, and get away the following day.

It was close on midnight when we had finished adding our own secondary wants to the list of musts. The result resembled a department-store catalogue. But if it had done no more than serve to take our minds off ourselves for the evening it would have been worth the trouble.

Josella yawned, and stood up.

'Sleepy,' she said. '– And silk sheets waiting on an ecstatic bed.'

She seemed to float across the thick carpet. With her hand on the door-knob she stopped and turned to regard herself solemnly in a long mirror.

'Some things were fun,' she said, and kissed her hand to her reflection.

'Goodnight, you vain, sweet vision,' I said.

She turned with a small smile, and then vanished through the door like a mist drifting away.

I poured out a final drop of the superb brandy, warmed it in my hands, and sipped it.

'Never – never again now will you see a sight like that,' I told myself. '*Sic transit . . .*'

And then, before I should become utterly morbid, I took myself to my more modest bed.

. . .

I was stretched in comfort on the edge of sleep when there came a knocking at the door.

'Bill,' said Josella's voice. 'Come quickly. There's a light!'

'What sort of a light?' I enquired, struggling out of bed.

'Outside. Come and look.'

She was standing in the passage wrapped in the sort of garment that could have belonged only to the owner of that remarkable bedroom.

'Good God!' I said, nervously.

'Don't be a fool,' she told me, irritably. 'Come and look at that light.'

A light there certainly was. Looking out of her window towards what

I judged to be the north-east, I could see a bright beam like that of a searchlight pointed unwaveringly upwards.

'That must mean there's somebody else there who can see,' she said.

'It must,' I agreed.

I tried to locate the source of it, but in the surrounding darkness I was unable to decide. No great distance away, I was sure, and seeming to start in mid-air – which probably meant that it was mounted on a high building. I hesitated.

'Better leave it till tomorrow,' I decided.

The idea of trying to find our way to it through the dark streets was far from attractive. And it was just possible – highly unlikely, but just possible – that it was a trap. Even a blind man who was clever and desperate enough *might* be able to wire such a thing up by touch.

I found a nail-file and squatted down with my eye on the level of the window-sill. With the point of the file I drew a careful line in the paint, marking the exact direction of the beam's source. Then I went back to my room.

I lay awake for an hour or more. Night magnified the quiet of the city, making the sounds which broke it the more desolate. From time to time voices rose from the street, edgy and brittle with hysteria. Once there came a freezing scream which seemed to revel horribly in its release from sanity. Somewhere not far away a sobbing went on endlessly, hopelessly. Twice I heard the sharp reports of single pistol shots ... I gave heartfelt thanks to whatever it was that had brought Josella and me together for companionship.

Complete loneliness was the worst state I could imagine just then. Alone one would be nothing. Company meant purpose, and purpose helped to keep the morbid fears at bay.

I tried to shut out the sounds by thinking of all the things I must do the next day, the day after, and the days after that; by guessing what the beam of light might mean, and how it might affect us. But the sobbing in the background went on and on and on, reminding me of the things I had seen that day, and would see tomorrow ...

The opening of the door brought me sitting up in sudden alarm. It was Josella, carrying a lighted candle. Her eyes were wide and dark, and she had been crying.

'I can't sleep,' she said. 'I'm frightened – horribly frightened. Can you hear them – all those poor people? I can't stand it ...'

She came like a child for comfort. I'm not sure that her need of it was much greater than mine.

She fell asleep before I did, with her head resting on my shoulder.

Still the memories of the day would not leave me in peace. But, in the end, one does sleep. My last recollection was of the sweet, sad voice of the girl who had sung:

So we'll go no more a-roving . . .

CHAPTER 6

RENDEZVOUS

When I awoke I could hear Josella already moving around in the kitchen. My watch said nearly seven o'clock. By the time I had shaved uncomfortably in cold water and dressed myself, there was a smell of toast and coffee drifting through the apartment. I found her holding a pan over the oilstove. She had an air of self-possession which was hard to associate with the frightened figure of the night before. Her manner was practical, too.

'Canned milk, I'm afraid. The fridge stopped. Everything else is all right, though,' she said.

It was difficult for a moment to believe that the expediently dressed form before me had been the ballroom vision of the previous evening. She had chosen a dark-blue ski-ing suit with white-topped socks rolled above sturdy shoes. On a dark leather belt she wore a finely-made hunting knife to replace the mediocre weapon I had found the day before. I have no idea how I expected to find her dressed, nor whether I had given the matter any thought, but the practicality of her choice was by no means the only impression I received as I saw her.

'Will I do, do you think?' she said.

'Eminently,' I assured her. I looked down at myself. 'I wish I'd had as much forethought. Gents' lounge-suiting isn't quite the rig for the job,' I added.

'You could do better,' she agreed, with a candid glance at my crumpled suit.

'That light last night,' she went on, 'came from the University Tower – at least, I'm pretty sure it did. There's nothing else noticeable exactly on that line. It seems about the right distance, too.'

I went into her room, and looked along the scratch I had drawn on the sill. It did, as she said, point directly at the tower. And I noticed something more. The tower was flying two flags on the same mast. One might have been left hoisted by chance, but two must be a deliberate signal; the daytime equivalent of the light. We decided over breakfast that we would postpone our planned programme and make investigation of the tower our first job for the day.

We left the flat about half an hour later. As I had hoped, the station waggon by standing out in the middle of the street had escaped the attentions of prowlers, and was intact. Without delaying further, we dropped the suitcases that Josella had acquired into the back among the triffid gear, and started off.

Few people were about. Presumably weariness and the chill in the air had made them aware that night had fallen, and not many had yet emerged from whatever sleeping-place they had found. Those who were to be seen were keeping more to the gutters and less to the walls than they had on the previous day. Most of them were now holding sticks or bits of broken wood with which they tapped their way along the kerb. It made for easier going than by the housefronts with their entrances and projections, and the tapping had decreased the frequency of collisions.

We threaded our way with little difficulty, and after a time turned into Store Street to see the University Tower at the end of it rising straight before us.

'Steady,' said Josella, as we turned into the empty road. 'I think there's something happening at the gates.'

She was right. As we came nearer we could see a not inconsiderable crowd beyond the end of the street. The previous day had given us a distaste for crowds. I swung right down Gower Street, ran on for fifty yards or so, and stopped.

'What do you reckon's going on there? Do we investigate or clear out?' I asked.

'I'd say investigate,' Josella replied promptly.

'Good. Me too,' I agreed.

'I remember this part,' she added. 'There's a garden behind these houses. If we can get in there we ought to be able to see what's happening without mixing ourselves up in it.'

We left the car, and started peering hopefully into basement areas. In the third we found an open door. A passage straight through the house led into the garden. The place was common to a dozen or so houses, and curiously laid out, being for the most part at the level of the basements, and thus below that of the surrounding streets, but on the far side, that closest to the University Building, it rose to a kind of terrace separated from the road by tall iron gates and a low wall. We could hear the sound of the crowd beyond it as a kind of composite murmur. We crossed the lawn, made our way up a sloped gravel path and found a place behind a screen of bushes whence we could watch.

The crowd that stood in the road outside the University gates must have numbered several hundred men and women. It was larger than the sound of it had led us to expect, and for the first time I realized how much quieter and more inactive a crowd of blind people is than a comparably-sized crowd of the sighted. It is natural, of course, for they must depend almost entirely on their ears to know what is happening so that the quietness of each is to the advantage of all, but it had not been obvious to me until that moment.

Whatever was going on was right at the front. We managed to find a slightly higher mound which gave us a view of the gates across the heads of the crowd. A man in a cap was talking volubly through the bars. He did not appear to be making a lot of headway, for the part taken in the conversation by the man on the other side of the gates consisted almost entirely of negative headshakes.

'What is it?' Josella asked, in a whisper.

I helped her up beside me. The talkative man turned so that we had a glimpse of his profile. He was, I judged, about thirty, with a straight, narrow nose, and rather bony features. What showed of his hair was dark, but it was the intensity of his manner that was more noticeable than his appearance.

As the colloquy through the gates continued to get nowhere his voice became more emphatic – though without visible effect on the other. There could be no doubt that the man beyond the gates was able to see; he was doing so watchfully, through horn-rimmed glasses. A few yards behind him stood a little knot of three more men about whom there was equally little doubt. They, too, were regarding the crowd and its spokesman with careful attention. The man on the outside grew more heated. His voice rose as if he were talking as much for the benefit of the crowd as for those behind the railings.

'Now listen to me,' he said, angrily. 'These people here have got just as much bloody right to live as you have, haven't they? It's not their fault they're blind, is it? It's nobody's fault – but it's going to be your fault if they starve, and you know it.'

His voice was a curious mixture of the rough and the educated so that it was hard to place him – as though neither style seemed quite natural to him, somehow.

'I've been showing them where to get food. I've been doing what I can for them, but Christ, there's only me, and there's thousands of them. *You* could be showing 'em where to get food, too – but are you? – hell! What *are* you doing about it? Damn all, that's what. Just sweet effay but look after your own lousy skins. I've met your kind before. It's "Damn you, Jack, I'm all right" – that's your motto.'

He spat with contempt, and raised a long, oratorical arm.

'Out there,' he said, waving his arm towards London at large, ' – out there there are thousands of poor devils only wanting someone to show them how to get the food that's there for the taking. – And you could do it. All you've got to do is *show* them. But do you? Do you, you buggers? No, what you do is shut yourselves in here and let them bloody well starve when each one of you could keep hundreds alive by doing no more than coming out and *showing* the poor sods where to get grub. God almighty, aren't you people human?'

The man's voice was violent. He had a case to put, and he was putting it passionately. I felt Josella's hand unconsciously clutching my arm, and I put my hand over hers. The man on the far side of the gate said something that was inaudible where we stood.

'How long?' shouted the man on our side. 'How in hell would I know how long the food's going to last? What I do know is if bastards like you don't muck in and help, there ain't going to be many left alive by the time they come to clear this bloody mess up.' He stood glaring for a moment. 'Fact of it is, you're scared – scared to show 'em where the food is. And why? Because the more these poor devils get to eat, the less there's going to be for you lot. That's the way of it, isn't it? That's the truth – if you had the guts to admit it.'

Again we failed to hear the answer of the other man, but, whatever it was, it did nothing to molify the speaker. He stared back grimly through the bars for a moment. Then he said:

'All right – if that's the way you want it!'

He made a lightning snatch between the bars, and caught the other's arm. In one swift movement he dragged it through, and twisted it. He grabbed the hand of a blind man standing beside him, and clamped it on the arm.

'Hang on there, mate,' he said, and jumped towards the main fastening of the gates.

The man inside recovered from his first surprise. He struck wildly through the bars behind him with his other hand. A chance swipe took the blind man in the face. It made him give a yell, and tighten his grip. The leader of the crowd was wrenching at the gate fastening. At that moment a rifle cracked. The bullet pinged against the railings, and whirred off on a ricochet. The leader checked suddenly, undecided. Behind him there was an outbreak of curses, and a scream or two. The crowd swayed back and forth as though uncertain whether to run or to charge the gates. The decision was made for them by those in the courtyard. I saw a youngish-looking man tuck something under his arm, and I dropped down, pulling Josella with me as the clatter of a sub-machine gun began.

It was obvious that the shooting was deliberately high; nevertheless, the rattle of it and the whizz of glancing bullets was alarming. One short burst was enough to settle the matter. When we raised our heads the crowd had lost entity and its components were groping their ways to safer parts in all three possible directions. The leader paused only to shout something unintelligible, then he turned away, too. He made his way northwards up Malet Street, doing his best to rally his following behind him.

I sat where we were, and looked at Josella. She looked thoughtfully back at me, and then down at the ground before her. It was some minutes before either of us spoke.

'Well?' I asked, at last.

She raised her head to look across the road, and then at the last stragglers from the crowd pathetically fumbling their ways.

'He was right,' she said. 'You know he was right, don't you?'

I nodded.

'Yes, he was right ... And yet he was quite wrong, too. You see, there is no "they" to come to clear up this mess – I'm quite sure of that now. It won't be cleared up. We could do as he says. We *could* show some, though only some, of these people where there is food. We could do that for a few days, maybe for a few weeks, but after that – what?'

'It seems so awful, so callous...'

'If we face it squarely, there's a simple choice,' I said. 'Either we can set out to save what can be saved from the wreck – and that has to include ourselves: or we can devote ourselves to stretching the lives of these people a little longer. That is the most objective view I can take.

'But I can see, too, that the more obviously humane course is also, probably, the road to suicide. Should we spend our time in prolonging misery when we believe that there is no chance of saving these people in the end? Would that be the best use to make of ourselves?'

She nodded slowly.

'Put like that, there doesn't seem to be much choice, does there? And even if we could save a few, which are we going to choose? – and who are *we* to choose? – and how long could we do it, anyway?'

'There's nothing easy about this,' I said. 'I've no idea what pro-portion of semi-disabled persons it may be possible for us to support when we come to the end of handy supplies, but I don't imagine it could be very high.'

'You've made up your mind,' she said, glancing at me. There might or might not have been a tinge of disapproval in her voice.

'My dear,' I said. 'I don't like this any more than you do. I've put the alternatives baldly before you. Do we help those who have survived the catastrophe to rebuild some kind of life? – or do we make a moral gesture which, on the face of it, can scarcely be more than a gesture? The people across the road there evidently intend to survive.'

She dug her fingers into the earth, and let the soil trickle out of her hand.

'I suppose you're right,' she said. 'But you're right when you say I don't like it.'

'Our likes and dislikes as decisive factors have now pretty well disappeared,' I suggested.

'Maybe, but I can't help feeling that there must be something wrong about anything that starts with shooting.'

'He shot to miss – and it's very likely he saved fighting,' I pointed out.

The crowd had all gone now. I climed over the wall, and helped Josella down on the other side. A man at the gate opened it to let us in.

'How many of you?' he asked.

'Just two of us. We saw your signal last night,' I told him.

'Okay. Come along, and we'll find the colonel,' he said, leading us across the forecourt.

The man whom he called the Colonel had set himself up in a small room not far from the entrance, and intended seemingly, for the porters. He was a chubby man just turned fifty or thereabouts. His hair was plentiful but well-trimmed, and grey. His moustache matched it, and looked as if no single hair would dare to break the ranks. His complexion was so pink, healthy, and fresh that it might have belonged to a much younger man; his mind, I discovered later, had never ceased to do so. He was sitting behind a table with quantities of paper arranged on it in mathematically exact blocks, and an unsoiled sheet of pink blotting-paper placed squarely before him.

As we came in he turned upon us, one after the other, an intense, steady look, and held it a little longer than was necessary. I recognized the technique. It is intended to convey that the user is a percipient judge accustomed to taking summarily the measure of his man; the receiver should feel that he now faces a reliable type with no nonsense about him – or, alternatively, that he has been seen through and had all his weaknesses noted. The right response is to return it in kind, and be considered a 'useful fella'. I did. The Colonel picked up his pen.

'Your names, please?'

We gave them.

'And addresses?'

'In the present circumstances I fear they won't be very useful,' I said. 'But if you really feel you must have them——' We gave them too.

He murmured something about system, organization, and relatives, and wrote them down. Age, occupation, and all the rest of it followed. He bent his searching look upon us again, scribbled a note upon each piece of paper, and then put them in a file.

'Need good men. Nasty business this. Plenty to do here, though. Plenty. Mr Beadley'll tell you what's wanted.'

We came out into the hall again. Josella giggled.

'He forgot to ask for references in triplicate – but I gather we've got the job,' she said.

Michael Beadley, when we discovered him, turned out to be in decided contrast. He was lean, tall, broad-shouldered, and slightly stooping with something of the air of an athlete run to books. In repose his face took on an expression of mild gloom from the darkness of his large eyes, but it was seldom that one had a glimpse of it in repose. The occasional streaks of grey in his hair helped very little in judging his age. He might have been anything between thirty-five and fifty. His obvious weariness just then made an estimate still more difficult. By his looks he must have been up all night, nevertheless he greeted us cheerfully and waved an introductory hand towards a young woman who took down our names again as we gave them.

'Sandra Telmont,' he explained. 'Sandra is our professional re-membrancer – continuity is her usual work, so we regard it as particularly thoughtful of providence to contrive her presence here just now.'

The young woman nodded to me, and looked harder at Josella.

'We've met before,' she said, thoughtfully. She glanced down at the pad on her knee. Presently a faint smile passed across her pleasant though unexotic countenance.

'Oh, yes, of course,' she said, in recollection.

'What did I tell you? The thing clings like flypaper,' Josella observed to me.

'What's this about?' enquired Michael Beadley.

I explained. He turned a more careful scrutiny on Josella. She sighed.

'Please forget it,' she suggested. 'I'm a bit tired of living it down.'

That appeared to surprise him agreeably.

'All right,' he said, and dismissed the matter with a nod. He turned back to the table. 'Now to get on with things. You've seen Jaques?'

'If that is the Colonel who is playing at Civil Service, we have,' I told him.

He grinned.

'Got to know how we stand. Can't get anywhere without knowing your ration-strength,' he said, in a fair imitation of the Colonel's manner. 'But it's quite true, though,' he went on. 'I'd better give you just a rough idea of how things do stand. Up to the present there are about thirty-five of us. All sorts. We hope and expect that some more will come in during the day. Out of those here now, twenty-three can see. The others are wives or husbands – and there are two or three children – who cannot. At the moment the general idea is that we move away from here sometime tomorrow if we can be ready in time – to be on the safe side, you understand.'

I nodded. 'We'd decided to get away this evening for the same reason,' I told him.

'What have you for transport?'

I explained the present position of the station-waggon. 'We were going to stock up today,' I added. 'So far we've practically nothing except a quantity of anti-triffid gear.'

He raised his eyebrows. The girl Sandra also looked at me curiously.

'That's a queer thing to make your first essential,' he remarked.

I told them the reasons. Possibly I made a bad job of it, for they neither of them looked much impressed. He nodded casually, and went on:

'Well, if you're coming in with us, here's what I suggest. Bring in your car, dump your stuff, then drive off and swap it for a good big lorry. Then – oh, does either of you know anything about doctoring?' he broke off to ask.

We shook our heads.

He frowned a little. 'That's a pity. So far we've got no one who does. It'll surprise me if we're not needing a doctor before long – and anyway, we ought all of us to have inoculations . . . Still, it's not much good sending you two off on a medical supplies scrounge. What about food and general stores? Suit you?'

He flipped through some pages on a clip, detached one of them, and handed it to me. It was headed No. 15, and below was a typed list of canned goods, pots and pans, and some bedding.

'Not rigid,' he said, 'but keep reasonably close to it, and we'll avoid too many duplications. Stick to best quality. With the food, concentrate on value for bulk – I mean, even if cornflakes are your leading passion in life, forget 'em. I suggest you keep to warehouses and big wholesalers.' He took back the list, and scribbled two or three addresses on it. 'Cans and packets are your food line – don't get led away by sacks of flour, for instance; there's another party on that sort of stuff.' He looked thoughtfully at Josella. 'Heavyish work, I'm afraid, but it's the most useful job we can give you at present. Do as much as you can before dark. There'll be a general meeting and discussion here about nine-thirty this evening.'

As we turned to go:

'Got a pistol?' he asked.

'I didn't think of it,' I admitted.

'Better – just in case. Quite effective simply fired into the air,' he said. He took two pistols from the drawer in the table, and pushed them across. 'Less messy than that,' he added, with a look at Josella's handsome hunting knife. 'Good scrounging to you.'

. . .

Even by the time we set out after unloading the station-waggon we found that there were still fewer people about than on the previous day. the ones that were showed an inclination to get on the pavements at the sound of the engine rather than to molest us.

The first lorry to take our fancy proved useless, being filled with wooden cases too heavy for us to remove. Our next find was luckier – a five-tonner, almost new, and empty. We trans-shipped, and left the station-waggon to its fate.

At the first address on my list the shutters of the loading-bay were down, but they gave way without much difficulty to the persuasions of a crowbar from a neighbouring shop, and rolled up easily. Inside, we made a find. three lorries stood backed up on the platform. One of them was fully loaded with cases of canned meat.

'Can you drive one of these things?' I asked Josella.

She looked at it.

'Well, I don't see why not. The general idea's the same, isn't it? And there's certainly no traffic problem.'

We decided to come back and fetch it later, and took the empty lorry on to another warehouse where we loaded parcels of blankets, rugs, and quilts, and then went on further to acquire a noisy miscellany of pots, pans, cauldrons, and kettles. When we had it filled we felt we'd put in a good morning's work on a job that was heavier than we had thought. We satisfied the appetite it had given us at a small pub hitherto untouched.

The mood which filled the business and commercial districts was gloomy – though it was a gloom that still had more the style of a normal Sunday or public holiday than of collapse. Very few people at all were to be seen in those parts. Had the catastrophe come by day, instead of by night after the workers had gone home, it would have been a hideously different scene.

When we had refreshed ourselves we collected the already loaded lorry from the food warehouse, and drove the two of them slowly and uneventfully back to the University. We parked them in the forecourt there, and set off again. About six-thirty we returned once more with another pair of well-loaded lorries, and a feeling of useful accomplishment.

Michael Beadley emerged from the building to inspect our contributions. He approved of it all, save half a dozen cases that I had added to my second load.

'What are they?' he asked.

'Triffid guns, and bolts for them,' I told him.

He looked at me thoughtfully.

'Oh, yes. You arrived with a lot of anti-triffid stuff,' he remarked.

'I think it's likely we'll need it,' I said.

He considered. I could see that I was being put down as a bit unsound on the subject of triffids. Most likely he was accounting for that by the bias my job might be expected to give – aggravated by a phobia resulting from my recent sting – and he was wondering whether it might not connote other, perhaps less harmless, unsoundnesses.

'Look here,' I suggested, 'we've brought in four full loads between us. I just want enough space in one of them for these cases. If you think we can't spare that, I'll go out and find a trailer, or another lorry.'

'No, leave 'em where they are. They don't take a lot of room,' he decided.

We went into the building and had some tea at an improvised canteen that a pleasant-faced, middle-aged woman had competently set up there.

'He thinks,' I said to Josella, 'that I've got a bee in my bonnet over triffids.'

'He'll learn – I'm afraid,' she replied. 'It's queer that no one else seems to have seen them about.'

'These people have all been keeping pretty much to the centre, so it's not very surprising. After all, we've seen none ourselves today.'

'Do you think they'll come right down here among the streets?'

'I couldn't say. Maybe lost ones would.'

'How do you think they got loose?' she asked.

'If they worry at a stake hard enough and long enough, it'll usually come in the end. The breakouts we used to get sometimes on farms were due as a rule to their all crowding up against one section of the fence until it gave way.'

'But couldn't you make the fences stronger?'

'We could have done, but we didn't want them fixed quite permanently. It didn't happen very often, and when it did it was usually simply from one field to another, so we'd just drive them back, and put up the fence again. I don't think any of them will intentionally make this way. From a triffid point of view a city must be much like a desert, so I should think they'll be moving outwards towards the open country on the whole. Have you ever used a triffid-gun?' I added.

She shook her head.

'After I've done something about these clothes I was thinking of putting in a bit of practice, if you'd like to try,' I suggested.

I got back an hour or so later feeling more suitably clad as a result of having infringed on her idea of a ski-suit and heavy shoes, to find that she had changed into a becoming dress of spring-green. We took a couple of the triffid guns, and went out into the garden of Russell Square, close by. We had spent about half an hour snipping the topmost shoots off convenient bushes when a young woman in a brick-red lumber jacket and an elegant pair of green trousers strolled across the grass and levelled a small camera at us.

'Who are you – Press?' enquired Josella.

'More or less,' said the young woman, ' – at least, I'm the official record. Elspeth Cary.'

'So soon?' I remarked. 'I trace the hand of our order-conscious Colonel.'

'You're quite right,' she agreed. She turned to look at Josella. 'And you are Miss Playton. I've often wondered——'

'Now look here,' interrupted Josella. 'Why should the one static thing in a collapsing world be my reputation? Can't we forget it?'

'Um,' said Miss Cary, thoughtfully. 'Uh-huh.' She turned to another subject. 'What's all this about triffids?' she asked.

We told her.

'They think,' added Josella, 'that Bill here is either scary or scatty on the subject.'

Miss Cary turned a straight look at me. Her face was interesting rather than good-looking, with a complexion browned by stronger suns than ours. Her eyes were steady, observant, and dark brown.

'Are you?' she asked.

'Well, I think they're troublesome enough to be taken seriously when they get out of hand,' I told her.

She nodded. 'True enough. I've been in places where they are out of hand. Quite nasty. But in England – well, it's hard to imagine that here.'

'There'll not be a lot to stop them here now,' I said.

Her reply, if she had been about to make one, was forestalled by the sound of an engine overhead. We looked up and presently saw a helicopter come drifting across the roof of the British Museum.

'That'll be Ivan,' said Miss Cary. 'He thought he might manage to find one. I must go and get a picture of him landing. See you later.' And she hurried off across the grass.

Josella lay down, clasped her hands behind her head, and gazed up into the depths of the sky. When the helicopter's engine ceased it sounded very much quieter than before we had heard it.

'I can't believe it,' she said, 'I try, but I still can't *really* believe. It can't all be going ... going ... going ... This *is* some kind of dream. Tomorrow this garden will be full of noise. The red buses will be roaring along over there, crowds of people will be scurrying along the pavements, the traffic-lights will be flashing ... A world doesn't just end like this – it can't – it isn't possible ... '

I was feeling like that, too. The houses, the trees, the absurdly grandiose hotels on the other side of the Square were all too normal – too ready to come to life at a touch ...

'And yet,' I said, 'I suppose that if they had been able to think at all the dinosaurs would have thought much the same thing. It just does happen from time to time, you see.'

'But why to us? It's like reading in the papers about the astonishing things that have happened to other people – but always to *other* people. There's nothing special about us.'

'Isn't there always a "why me"? Whether it's the soldier who's untouched when all his pals are killed, or the fellow who gets run in for fiddling his accounts? Just plain blind chance, I'd say.'

'Chance that it happened? – or chance that it happened now?'

'Now, I mean. It was bound to happen some time in some way. It's an unnatural thought that one type of creature should dominate perpetually.'

'I don't see why.'

'Why, is a heck of a question. But it is an inescapable conclusion that life has to be dynamic and not static. Change is bound to come one way or another. Mind you, I don't think it's quite done with us this time, but it has had a damned good try.'

'Then you don't think it really is the end – of people, I mean?'

'It might be. But – well, I don't think so – this time.'

It *could* be the end. I had no doubt of that. But there would be other little groups like ours. I saw an empty world with a few scattered communities trying to fight their way back to control of it. I had to believe that some, at least, of them would succeed.

'No,' I repeated, 'it need not be the end. We're still very adaptable, and we've a flying start compared with our ancestors. As long as there are any of us left sound and healthy we've got a chance – a thundering good chance.'

Josella made no answer. She lay facing upwards with a faraway look in her eyes. I thought perhaps I could guess something of what was passing in her mind, but I said nothing. She did not speak for a little while, then she said:

'You know, one of the most shocking things about it is to realize how *easily* we have lost a world that seemed so safe and certain.'

She was quite right. It was that simplicity that seemed somehow to be the nucleus of the shock. From very familiarity one forgets all the forces which keep the balance, and thinks of security as normal. It is not. I don't think it had ever before occurred to me that man's supremacy is not primarily due to his brain, as most of the books would have one think. It is due to the brain's capacity to make use of the information conveyed to it by a narrow band of visible light rays. His civilization, all that he has achieved or might achieve hangs upon his ability to perceive that range of vibrations from red to violet. Without that, he is lost. I saw for a moment the true tenuousness of his hold on his power, the miracles that he had wrought with such a fragile instrument . . .

Josella had been pursuing her own line of thought.

'It's going to be a very queer sort of world – what's left of it. I don't think we're going to like it a lot,' she said, reflectively.

It seemed to me an odd view to take – rather as if one should protest that one did not *like* the idea of dying or being born. I preferred the notion of finding out first how it would be, and then doing what one could about the parts of it one disliked most, but I let it pass.

From time to time we had heard the sound of lorries driving up to the far side of the building. It was evident that most of the foraging parties must have returned by this hour. I looked at my watch, and reached for the triffid-guns lying on the grass beside me.

'If we're going to get any supper before we hear what other people feel about all this, it's time we went in,' I said.

CHAPTER 7

CONFERENCE

I fancy all of us had expected the meeting to be simply a kind of briefing talk. Just times, course instructions, the day's objective – that kind of thing. Certainly I had no expectation of the food for thought that we received.

It was held in a small lecture-theatre lit for the occasion by an arrangement of car headlamps and batteries. When we went in, some half-dozen men and two women who appeared to have constituted themselves a committee were conferring behind the lecturer's desk. To our surprise we found nearly a hundred people seated in the body of the hall. Young women predominated at a ratio of about four to one. I had not realized until Josella pointed it out to me how few of them were able to see.

Michael Beadley dominated the consulting group by his height. I recognized the Colonel beside him. The other faces were new to me, save that of Elspeth Cary who had now exchanged her camera for a notebook, presumably for the benefit of posterity. Most of their interest was centred round an elderly man of ugly but benign aspect who wore gold-rimmed spectacles, and fine white hair trimmed to a rather political length. They all had an air of being a little worried about him.

The other woman in the party was little more than a girl – perhaps twenty-two or three. She did not appear happy at finding herself where she was. She cast occasional looks of nervous uncertainty at the audience.

Sandra Telmont came in, carrying a sheet of foolscap. She studied it a moment, then briskly broke the group up, and sorted it into chairs. With a wave of her hand she directed Michael to the desk, and the meeting began.

He stood there a little bent, watching the audience from sombre eyes as he waited for the murmuring to die down. When he spoke, it was in a pleasant, practised voice, and with a fireside manner.

'Many of us here,' he began, 'must still be feeling numbed under this catastrophe. The world we knew has ended in a flash. Some of us may be feeling that it is the end of everything. It is not. But to all of you I will say at once that it *can* be the end of everything – *if we let it*.

'Stupendous as this disaster is, there is still a margin of survival. It may be worth remembering just now that we are not unique in looking upon vast calamity. Whatever the myths that have grown up about it, there can be no doubt that somewhere far back in our history there was a Great Flood. Those who survived that must have looked upon a disaster comparable in scale with this, and, in some ways, more formidable. But they cannot have despaired: they must have begun again – as we can begin again.

'Self-pity and a sense of high tragedy are going to build nothing at all. So we had better throw them out at once, for it is builders that we must become.

'And further to deflate any romantic dramatization I would like to point out to you that this, even now, is not the worst that could have happened. I, and quite likely many of you, have spent most of our lives in expectation of something worse. And I still believe that if this had not happened to us, that a worse thing would.

'From August 6th 1945, the margin of survival has narrowed appallingly. Indeed, two days ago it was narrower than it is at this moment. If you need to dramatize, you could well take for your material the years succeeding 1945 when the path of safety started to shrink to a tight-rope along which we had to walk with our eyes deliberately closed to the depths beneath us.

'In any single moment of the years since then the fatal slip might have been made. It is a miracle that it was not. It is a double miracle that can go on happening for years.

'But sooner or later that slip must have occurred. It would not have mattered whether it came through malice, carelessness, or sheer accident: the balance would have been lost, and the destruction let loose.

'How bad it would have been, we cannot say. How bad it *could* have been – well, there might have been no survivors: there might possibly have been no planet ...

'And now contrast our situation. The Earth is intact, unscarred, still fruitful. It can provide us with food and raw materials. We have repositories of knowledge that can teach us to do anything that has been done before – though there are some things that may be better unremembered. And we have the means, the health, and the strength to begin to build again.'

He did not make a long speech, but it had effect. It must have made quite a number of the members of his audience begin to feel that perhaps they were at the beginning of something after all, rather than at the end of everything. In spite of his offering little but generalities there was a more alert air in the place when he sat down.

The Colonel, who followed him, was practical and factual. He reminded us that for reasons of health it would be advisable for us to get away from all built-up areas as soon as practicable – which was expected to be at about 12.00 hours on the following day. Almost all the primary necessities as well as extras enough to give a reasonable standard of comfort had now been collected. In considering our stocks our aim must be to make ourselves as nearly independent of outside sources as possible for a minimum of one year. We should spend that period in virtually a state of siege. There were, no doubt, many things we should all like to take besides those on our lists, but they would have to wait until the medical staff (and here the girl on the committee blushed deeply) considered it safe for parties to leave isolation and fetch them. As for the scene of our isolation, the committee had given it considerable thought, and, bearing in mind the desiderata of compactness, self-sufficiency, and detachment, had come to the conclusion that a country boarding-school or, failing that, some large country mansion would best serve our purposes.

Whether the committee had in fact not yet decided on any particular place, or whether the military notion that secrecy has some intrinsic value persisted in the Colonel's mind, I cannot say, but I have no doubt that his failure to name the place, or even the probable locality, was the gravest mistake made that evening. At the time, however, his practical manner had a further reassuring effect.

As he sat down, Michael rose again. He spoke encouragingly to the girl, and then introduced her. It had, he said, been one of our greatest worries that we had no one among us with medical knowledge, therefore, it was with great relief that he welcomed Miss Berr. It was true that she did not hold medical degrees with impressive letters, but she did have high nursing qualifications. For himself he thought that know-ledge recently attained might be worth more than degrees acquired years ago.

The girl, blushing again, said a little piece about her determination to carry the job through, and ended a trifle abruptly with the information that she would inoculate us all against a variety of things before we left the hall.

A small, sparrow-like man whose name I did not catch rubbed it in that the health of each was the concern of all, and that any suspicion of illness should be reported at once since the effects of a contagious disease among us would be serious.

When he had finished Sandra rose and introduced the last speaker of the group: Dr E. H. Vorless, D.Sc., of Edinburgh, Professor of Sociology at the University of Kingston.

The white-haired man walked to the desk. He stood there a few moments with his finger-tips resting upon it, and his head bent down as if he were studying it. Those behind regarded him carefully, with a trace of anxiety. The Colonel leaned over to whisper something to Michael who nodded without taking his eyes off the Doctor. The old man looked up. He passed a hand over his hair.

'My friends,' he said, 'I think I may claim to be the oldest among you. In nearly seventy years I have learned, and had to unlearn, many things – though not nearly so many as I could have wished. But if, in the course of a long study of man's institutions, one thing has struck me more than their stubbornness, it is their variety.

'Well indeed do the French say *autres temps, autres mœurs*. We must all see, if we pause to think, that one kind of community's virtue may well be another kind of community's crime: that what is frowned upon here may be considered laudable elsewhere; that customs condemned in one century are condoned in another. And we must also see that in each community and each period there is a widespread belief in the moral rightness of its own customs.

'Now, clearly, since many of these beliefs conflict they cannot all be "right" in an absolute sense. The most judgement one can pass on them – if one has to pass judgements at all – is to say that they have at some period been "right" for those communities that hold them. It may be that they still are, but it frequently is found that they are not, and that the communities who continue to follow them blindly without heed to changed circumstances do so to their own disadvantage – perhaps to their ultimate destruction.'

The audience did not perceive where the introduction might be leading. It fidgeted. Most of it was accustomed when it encountered this kind of thing to turn the radio off at once. Now it felt trapped. The speaker decided to make himself clearer.

'Thus,' he continued, 'you would not expect to find the same manners, customs, and forms in a penurious Indian village living on the edge of starvation as you would in, say, Mayfair. Similarly the people in a warm country where life is easy are going to differ quite a deal from the people of an overcrowded, hardworking country as to the nature of the principal virtues. In other words, different environments set different standards.

'I point this out to you because the world we knew is gone – finished.

'The conditions which framed and taught us our standards have gone with it. Our needs are now different, and our aims must be different. If you want an example, I would suggest to you that we have all spent the day indulging with perfectly easy consciences in what two days ago would have been housebreaking and theft. With the old pattern broken, we have now to find out what mode of life is best suited to the new. We have not simply to start building again: we have to start *thinking* again – which is much more difficult and far more distasteful.

'Man remains physically adaptable to a remarkable degree. But it is the custom of each community to form the minds of its young in a mould, introducing a binding agent of prejudice. The result is a remarkably tough substance capable of withstanding successfully even the pressure of many innate tendencies and instincts. In this way it has been possible to produce a man who against all his basic sense of self-preservation will voluntarily risk death for an ideal – *but* also in this way is produced the dolt who is so sure of everything and knows what is "right".

'In the time now ahead of us a great many of these prejudices we have been taught will have to go, or be radically altered. We can accept and retain only one primary prejudice, and that is that *the race is worth preserving*. To that consideration all else will for a time at least be subordinate. We must look at all we do, with the question in mind: "Is this going to help our race survive – or will it hinder us?" If it will help, we must do it, whether or not it conflicts with the ideas in which we were brought up. If not, we must avoid it even though the omission may clash with our previous notions of duty, and even of justice.

'It will not be easy: old prejudices die hard. The simple rely on a bolstering mass of maxim and precept, so do the timid, so do the mentally lazy – and so do all of us, more than we imagine. Now that the organization has gone, our ready-reckoners for conduct within it no longer give the right answers. We *must* have the moral courage to think and to plan for ourselves.'

He paused to survey his audience thoughtfully. Then he said:

'There is one thing to be made quite clear to you before you decide to join our community. It is that those of us who start on this task will all have our parts to play. The men must work – the women must have babies. Unless you can agree to that there can be no place for you in our community.'

After an interval of dead silence, he added:

'We can afford to support a limited number of women who cannot see, because they will have babies who can see. We cannot afford to support men who cannot see. In our new world, then, babies become very much more important than husbands.'

For some seconds after he stopped speaking silence continued, then isolated murmurs grew quickly into a general buzz.

I looked to Josella. To my astonishment she was grinning impishly.

'What do you find funny about this?' I asked, a trifle shortly.

'People's expressions mostly,' she replied.

I had to admit it as a reason. I looked round the place, and then across at Michael. His eyes were moving from one section to another of the audience as he tried to sum up the reaction.

'Michael's looking a bit anxious,' I observed.

'He should worry,' said Josella. 'If Brigham Young could bring it off in the middle of the nineteenth century, this ought to be a pushover.'

'What a crude young woman you are at times,' I said. 'Were you in on this before?'

'Not exactly, but I'm not quite dumb, you know. Besides, while you were away someone drove in a bus with most of these blind girls on board. They all came from some institution. I said to myself, why collect them from there when you could gather up thousands in a few streets round here? The answer obviously was that (a) being blind before this happened they had been trained to do work of some kind, and (b) they were all girls. The deduction wasn't terribly difficult.'

'H'm,' I said. 'Depends on one's outlook, I suppose. I must say, it wouldn't have struck me. Do you——?'

'Sh-sh,' she told me, as a quietness came over the hall.

A tall, dark, purposeful-looking, youngish woman had risen. While she waited, she appeared to have a mouth not made to open, but later it did.

'Are we to understand,' she enquired, using a kind of carbon-steel voice, 'are we to understand that the last speaker is advocating free love?' And she sat down, with spine-jarring decision.

Doctor Vorless smoothed back his hair as he regarded her.

'I think the questioner must be aware that I never mentioned love, free, bought, or bartered. Will she please make her question clearer?'

The woman stood up again.

'I think the speaker understood me. I am asking if he suggests the abolition of the marriage law?'

'The laws we knew have been abolished by circumstances. It now falls to us to make laws suitable to the conditions, and to enforce them if necessary.'

'There is still God's law, and the law of decency.'

'Madam. Solomon had three hundred – or was it five hundred? – wives, and God did not apparently hold that against him. A Mohammedan preserves rigid respectability with three wives. These are matters of local custom. Just what our laws in these matters, and in others, will be is for us all to decide later for the greatest benefit of the community.

'This committee, after discussion, has decided that if we are to build a new state of things and avoid a relapse into barbarism – which is an appreciable danger – we must have certain undertakings from those who wish to join us.

'Not one of us is going to recapture the conditions we have lost. What we offer is a busy life in the best conditions we can contrive, and the happiness which will come of achievement against odds. In return we ask willingness and fruitfulness. There is no compulsion. The choice is yours. Those to whom our offer does not appeal are at perfect liberty to go elsewhere, and start a separate community on such lines as they prefer.

'But I would ask you to consider very carefully whether or not you do hold a warrant from God to deprive any woman of the happiness of carrying out her natural functions.'

The discussion which followed was a rambling affair descending frequently to points of detail and hypothesis on which there could as yet be no answers. But there was no move to cut it short. The longer it went on, the less strangeness the idea would have.

Josella and I moved over to the table where Nurse Berr had set up her paraphernalia. We took several shots in our arms, and then sat down again to listen to the wrangling.

'How many of them will decide to come, do you think?' I asked her. She glanced round.

'Nearly all of them – by the morning,' she said.

I felt doubtful. There was a lot of objecting and questioning going on. Josella said:

'If you were a woman who was going to spend an hour or two before you went to sleep tonight considering whether you would choose babies and an organization to look after you, or adherence to a principle which might quite likely mean no babies and no one to look after you, you'd not really be very doubtful, you know. And after all, most women want babies, anyway – the husband's just what Doctor Vorless might call the local means to the end.'

'That's rather cynical of you.'

'If you really think that's cynical you must be a very sentimental character. I'm talking about real women, not those in the magazine-movie-make-believe world.'

'Oh,' I said.

She sat pensively a while, and gradually acquired a frown. At last she said:

'The thing that worries me is how many will they expect? I like babies, all right, but there are limits.'

After the debate had gone on raggedly for an hour or so, it was wound up. Michael asked that the names of all those willing to join in his plan should be left in his office by ten o'clock the next morning. The Colonel requested all who could drive a lorry to report to him by 7.00 hours, and the meeting broke up.

Josella and I wandered out of doors. The evening was mild. The light on the tower was again stabbing hopefully into the sky. The moon had just risen clear of the Museum roof. We found a low wall, and sat on it, looking into the shadows of the Square garden, and listening to the faint sound of the wind in the branches of the trees there. We smoked a cigarette each almost in silence. When I reached the end of mine, I threw it away, and drew a breath.

'Josella,' I said.

'M'm?' she replied, scarcely emerging from her thoughts.

'Josella,' I said again. 'Er – those babies. I'd – er – I'd be sort of terribly proud and happy if they could be mine as well as yours.'

She sat quite still for a moment, saying nothing. Then she turned her head. The moonlight was glinting on her fair hair, but her face and eyes were in shadow. I waited, with a hammered and slightly sick feeling inside me. She said, with surprising calm:

'Thank you, Bill, dear. I think I would, too.'

I sighed. The hammering did not ease up much, and I saw that my hand was trembling as it reached for hers. I didn't have any words, for the moment. Josella, however, did. She said:

'But it isn't quite as easy as that, now.'

I was jolted.

'What do you mean?' I asked.

She said, consideringly: 'I think that if I were those people in there' – she nodded in the direction of the tower – 'I think that I should make a rule. I should divide us up into lots. I should say every man who marries a sighted girl must take on two blind girls as well. I'm pretty sure that's what I should do.'

I stared at her face in the shadow.

'You don't meant that,' I protested.

'I'm afraid I do, Bill.'

'But, look here——'

'Don't you think they may have some idea like that in their minds – from what they've been saying?'

'Not unlikely,' I conceded. 'But if *they* make the rule, that's one thing. I don't see——'

'You mean you don't love me enough to take on two other women as well?'

I swallowed. I also objected:

'Look here. This is all crazy. It's unnatural. What you're suggesting——'

She put up a hand to stop me.

'Just listen to me, Bill. I know it sounds a bit startling at first, but there's nothing crazy about it. It's all quite clear – and it's not very easy.

'All this' – she waved her hand around – 'it's done something to me. It's like suddenly seeing everything differently. And one of the things I think I see is that those of us who get through are going to be much nearer to one another, more dependent on one another, more like – well, more like a *tribe* than we were before.

'All day long as we went about I've been seeing unfortunate people who are going to die very soon. And all the time I've been saying to myself: "There, but for the grace of God ... " And then I've told myself: "This is a miracle! I don't deserve anything better than any of these people. But it has happened. Here I still am – so now it's up to me to justify it." Somehow it's made me feel closer to other people than I have ever done before. That's made me keep wondering all the time what I can do to help some of them.

'You see, we *must* do something to justify that miracle, Bill. I might have been any of these blind girls; you might have been any of these wandering men. There's nothing big we can do. But if we try to look after just a few and give them what happiness we can, we shall be paying back a little – just a tiny part of what we owe. You do see that, don't you, Bill?'

I turned it over in my mind for a minute or more.

'I think,' I said, 'that that's the queerest argument I've heard today – if not ever. And yet——'

'And yet it's *right*, isn't it, Bill? I know it's right. I've tried to put myself in the place of one of those blind girls, and I *know*. We hold the chance of as full a life as they can have, for some of them. Shall we give it to them as a part of our gratitude – or shall we simply withhold it on account of the prejudices we've been taught? That's what it amounts to.'

I sat silently for a time. I had not a moment's doubt that Josella meant every word she said. I ruminated a little on the ways of purposeful, subversive-minded women like Florence Nightingale and Elizabeth Fry. You can't do anything with such women – and they so often turn out to have been right after all.

'Very well,' I said at last. 'If that's the way you think it ought to be. But I hope——'

She cut me short.

'Oh, Bill, I knew you'd understand. Oh, I'm glad – so very glad. You've made me so happy.'

After a time:

'I hope——' I began again.

Josella patted my hand.

'You won't need to worry at all, my dear. I shall choose two nice, sensible girls.'

'Oh,' I said.

We went on sitting there on the wall hand in hand, looking at the dappled trees – but not seeing them very much, at least, I wasn't. Then in the building behind us someone started up a gramophone, playing a Strauss waltz. It was painfully nostalgic as it lilted through the empty courtyard. For an instant the road before us became the ghost of a ballroom; a swirl of colour, with the moon for a crystal chandelier.

Josella slid off the wall. With her arms outstretched, her wrists and fingers rippling, her body swaying, she danced, light as a thistledown, in a big circle in the moonlight. She came round to me, her eyes shining and her arms beckoning.

And we danced, on the brink of an unknown future, to an echo from a vanished past.

CHAPTER 8

FRUSTRATION

I was walking through an unknown, deserted city where a bell rang dismally and a sepulchral, disembodied voice called in the emptiness: 'The Beast is Loose! Beware! The Beast is Loose!' when I woke to find that a bell really was ringing. It was a handbell that jangled with a brassy double clatter so harsh and startling that for a moment I could not remember where I was. Then, as I sat up still bemused, there came a sound of voices calling 'Fire!' I jumped just as I was from my blankets, and ran into the corridor. There was a smell of smoke there, a noise of hurried feet, doors banging. Most of the sound seemed to come from my right where the bell kept on clanging and the frightened voices were calling, so it was that way I turned and ran. A little moonlight filtered in through tall windows at the end of the passage, relieving the dimness just enough for me to keep to the middle of the way and avoid the people who were feeling their way along the walls.

I reached the stairs. The bell was still clanging in the hall below. I made my way down as fast as I could through smoke that grew thicker. Near the bottom I tripped and fell forward. The dimness became a sudden darkness in which a light burst like a cloud of needles, and that was all ...

The first thing was an ache in my head. The next was a glare when I opened my eyes. At the first blink it was as dazzling as a klieg light, but when I started again and edged the lids up more cautiously it turned out to be only an ordinary window, and grimy, at that. I knew I was lying on a bed, but I did not sit up to investigate further; there was a piston pounding away in my head that discouraged any kind of movement. So I lay there quietly, and studied the ceiling – until I discovered that my wrists were tied together.

That snapped me out of my lethargy, in spite of the thumping head. I found it a very neat job. Not painfully tight, but perfectly efficient. Several turns of insulated wire on each wrist, and a complex knot on the far side where it was impossible for me to reach it with my teeth. I swore a bit, and looked around. The room was small and, save for the bed on which I lay, empty.

'Hey!' I called. 'Anybody around here?'

After half a minute or so there was a shuffle of feet outside. The door was opened, and a head appeared. It was a small head with a tweed cap on top of it. It had a stringy-looking choker beneath, and a dark unshavenness across its face. It was not turned straight at me, but in my general direction.

''Ullo, cock,' it said, amiably enough. 'So you've come to, 'ave yer? 'Ang on a bit, an' I'll get you a cup o' char.' And it vanished again.

The instruction to hang on was superfluous, but I did not have to wait long. In a few minutes he returned, carrying a wire-handled can with some tea in it.

'Where are yer?' he said.

'Straight ahead of you, on the bed,' I told him.

He groped forward with his left hand until he found the foot of the bed, then he felt his way around it, and held out the can.

''Ere, y'are, chum. It'll taste a bit funny-like 'cause ol' Charlie put a shot of rum in it, but I reckon you'll not mind that.'

I took it from him, holding it with some difficulty between my bound hands. It was strong and sweet, and the rum hadn't been stinted. The taste might be queer, but it worked like the elixir of life itself.

'Thanks,' I said. 'You're a miracle worker. My name's Bill.'

His, it seemed, was Alf.

'What's the line, Alf? What goes on here?' I asked him.

He sat down on the side of the bed, and held out a packet of cigarettes with a box of matches. I took one, lit his first, then my own, and gave him back the box.

'It's this way, mate,' he said. 'You know there was a bit of a shindy up at the University yesterday morning – maybe you was there?'

I told him I'd seen it.

'Well, after that lark, Coker – he's the chap that did the talking – he got kinda peeved. "Hokay," 'e says, nasty-like. "The — — s've asked for it. I put it to 'em fair and square in the first place. Now they can take what's comin' to them." Well, we'd met up with a couple of other fellers and one old girl what can still see, an' they fixed it all up between them. He's a lad, that Coker.'

'You mean – he framed the whole business – there wasn't any fire or anything?' I asked.

'Fire – my aunt fanny! What they done was fix up a tripwire or two, light a lot of paper and sticks in the hall, an' start in ringing the ol' bell. We reckoned that them as could see 'ud be the first along, on account of there bein' a bit of light still from the moon. And sure enough they was. Coker an' another chap was givin' them the k.o. as they tripped, an' passin' them along to some of us chaps to carry out to the lorry. Simple as kiss your 'and.'

'H'm,' I said ruefully. 'Sounds efficient, that Coker. How many of us mugs fell into that little trap?'

'I'd say we got a couple of dozen – though it turned out as five or six of 'em was blinded. When we'd loaded up about all we'd room for in the lorry, we beat it, and left the rest to sort theirselves out.'

Whatever view Coker took of us, it was clear that Alf bore us no animosity. He appeared to regard the whole affair as a bit of sport. I found it a little too painful to class it so, but I mentally raised my hat to Alf. I'd a pretty good idea that in his position I'd be lacking the spirit to think of anything as a bit of sport. I finished the tea, and accepted another cigarette from him.

'And what's the programme now?' I asked him.

'Coker's idea is to make us all up into parties, an' put one of you with each party. You to look after the scrounging, and kind of act as the eyes of the rest, like. Your job'll be to help us keep goin' until somebody comes along to straighten this perishin' lot out.'

'I see,' I said.

He cocked his head towards me. There weren't many flies on Alf. He had caught more in my tone than I had realized was there.

'You reckon that's goin' to be a long time?' he said.

'I don't know. What's Coker say?'

Coker, it seemed, had not been committing himself to details. Alf had his own opinion, though.

''F you ask me, I reckon there ain't nobody goin' to come. If there was, they'd've been 'ere before this. Different if we was in some little town in the country. But London! Stands to reason they'd come 'ere afore anywhere else. No, the way I see it, they ain't come yet – an' that means they ain't *never* goin' to come – an' *that* means there ain't nobody to come. Cor, blimey, 'oo'd ever've thought it could 'appen like this!'

I didn't say anything. Alf wasn't the sort to be jollied with facile encouragements.

'Reckon that's the way you see it, too?' he said, after a bit.

'It doesn't look so good,' I admitted. 'But there still is a chance, you know – people from somewhere abroad . . .'

He shook his head.

'They'd've come before this. They'd've had loud-speaker cars round the streets tellin' us what to do, before this. No, chum, we've 'ad it: there ain't nobody nowhere *to* come. That's the fact of it.'

We were silent for a while, then:

'Ah, well, 't'weren't a bad ole life while it lasted,' he said.

We talked a little about the kind of life it had been for him. He'd had various jobs, each of which seemed to have included some interesting under-cover work. He summed it up:

'One way an' another I didn't do so bad. What was your racket?'

I told him. He wasn't impressed.

'Triffids, huh! Nasty damn things, I reckon. Not natcheral as you might say.'

We left it at that.

Alf went away, leaving me to my cogitations and a packet of his cigarettes. I surveyed the outlook, and thought little of it. I wondered how the others would be taking it. Particularly what would be Josella's view.

I got off the bed, and went across to the window. The prospect was poor. An interior well with sheer, white-tiled sides for four storeys below me, and a glass skylight at the bottom. There wasn't much to be done that way. Alf had locked the door after him, but I tried it, just in case. Nothing in the room gave me inspiration. It had the look of belonging in a third-rate hotel, except that everything save the bed had been thrown out.

I sat down again on the bed, and pondered. I could perhaps tackle Alf successfully, even with my hands tied – providing he had no knife. But probably he had a knife, and that would be unpleasant. It would be no good a blind man threatening me with a knife; he would have to use it to disable me. Besides, there would be the difficulty of discovering what others I would have to pass before I could find my way out of the building. Moreover, I did not wish Alf any harm. It seemed wiser to wait for an opportunity – one was bound to come to a sighted man among the sightless.

An hour later Alf came back with a plate of food, a spoon, and more tea.

'Bit rough-like,' he apologized. 'But they said no knife and fork, so there it is.'

While I was tackling it, I asked about the others. He couldn't tell me much, and didn't know any names, but I found out that there had been women as well as men among these that had been brought here. After that I was left alone for some hours which I spent doing my best to sleep off the headache.

When Alf reappeared with more food and the inevitable can of tea, he was accompanied by the man he had called Coker. He looked more tired now than when I had seen him before. Under his arm he carried a bundle of papers. He gave me a searching look.

'You know the idea?' he asked.

'What Alf's told me,' I admitted.

'All right, then.' He dropped his papers on the bed, picked up the top one, and unfolded it. It was a street-plan of Greater London. He pointed to an area covering part of Hampstead and Swiss Cottage, heavily outlined in blue pencil.

'That's your beat,' he said. 'Your party works inside that area, and not in anyone else's area. You can't have each lot going after the same pickings. Your job is to find the food in that area, and see that your party gets it – that, and anything else they need. Got that?'

'Or what?' I said, looking at him.

'Or they'll get hungry. And if they do, it'll be just too bad for you. Some of the boys are tough, and we're not any of us doing this for fun. So watch your step. Tomorrow morning we'll run you and your lot up there in lorries. After that it'll be your job to keep 'em going until somebody comes along to tidy things up.'

'And if nobody does come?' I asked.

'Somebody's *got* to come,' he said grimly. 'Anyway, there's your job – and mind you keep to your area.'

I stopped him as he was on the point of leaving.

'Have you got a Miss Playton here?' I asked.

'I don't know any of your names,' he said.

'Fair-haired, about five-foot six or seven, grey-blue eyes,' I persisted.

'There's a girl about that size, and blonde. But I haven't looked at her eyes. Got something more important to do,' he said, as he left.

I studied the map. I was not greatly taken with the district allotted to me. Some of it was a salubrious enough suburb, indeed, but in the circumstances a location that included docks and warehouses would have had more to offer. It was doubtful whether there would be any sizeable storage depots in this part. Still, 'can't all 'ave a prize' as Alf would doubtless express it – and anyway, I had no intention of staying there any longer than was strictly necessary.

When Alf showed up again I asked him if he would take a note to Josella. He shook his head.

'Sorry, mate. Not allowed.'

I promised him it should be harmless, but he remained firm. I couldn't altogether blame him. He had no reason to trust me, and would not be able to read the note to know that it was as harmless as I claimed. Anyway, I'd neither pencil nor paper, so I gave that up. After pressing, he did consent to let her know that I was here, and to find out the district to which she was being sent. He was not keen on doing that much, but he had to allow that if there were to be any straightening out of the mess it would be a lot easier for me to find her again if I knew where to start looking.

After that I had simply my thoughts for company for a bit.

The trouble was that I was not wholeheartedly set on any course. There was a damnable ability to see the points on both sides. I knew that common sense and the long-term view backed up Michael Beadley and his lot. If they had started, Josella and I would doubtless have gone with them and worked with them – and yet I knew I would have been uneasy. I'd never be quite convinced that nothing could have been done for the sinking ship, never quite sure that I had not rationalized my own preference. If, indeed, there was *no* possibility of organized rescue, then their proposal to salvage what we could was the intelligent course. But, unfortunately, intelligence is by no means the only thing that makes the human wheels go round. I was up against the very conditioning that the old Doctor had said was so hard to break. He was dead right about the difficulty of adopting new principles. If, for instance, some kind of relief should miraculously arrive, I knew just what kind of a louse I'd feel to have cleared out, whatever the motives – and just how much I'd despise myself and the rest for not having stayed here in London to help for as long as it was possible.

But if, on the other hand, help did not come, how would I have felt about having wasted my time and frittered my efforts away when stronger-minded people had started getting on with the salvage while the going was good?

I knew I ought to make my mind up once and for all on the right course, and stick to it. But I could not. I see-sawed. Some hours later when I fell asleep I was still see-sawing.

There was no means of knowing which way Josella had made up her mind. I'd had no personal message from her. But Alf had put his head in once during the evening. His communication had been brief.

'Westminster,' he said. 'Cor! Don't reckon that lot's goin' to find much grub in the 'Ouses o' Parliament.'

. . .

I was woken by Alf coming in early the following morning. He was accompanied by a bigger, shifty-eyed man who fingered a butcher's knife with unnecessary ostentation. Alf advanced, and dropped an armful of clothes on the bed. His companion shut the door, and leaned against it, watching with a crafty eye, and toying with the knife.

'Give us yer mitts, mate,' said Alf.

I held my hands out towards him. He felt for the wires on my wrists, and snipped them with a cutter.

'Now just you put on that there clobber, chum,' he said, stepping back.

I got myself dressed while the knife-fancier followed every movement I made, like a hawk. When I'd finished, Alf produced a pair of handcuffs. 'There's just these,' he mentioned.

I hesitated. The man by the door ceased to lean on it, and brought his knife forward a little. For him this was evidently the interesting moment. I decided maybe it was not the time to try anything, and held my wrists out. Alf felt around, and clicked on the cuffs. After that he went and fetched me my breakfast.

Nearly two hours later the other man turned up again, his knife well in evidence. He waved it at the door.

'C'mon,' he said. It was the only remark I ever heard him make.

With the consciousness of the knife producing an uncomfortable feeling in my back, we went down a number of flights of stairs, and across a hall. In the street two loaded lorries were waiting. Coker, with two companions, stood by the tailboard of one. He beckoned me over. Without saying anything he passed a chain between my arms. At each end of it was a strap. One was fastened already round the left wrist of a burly blind man beside him; the other he attached to the right wrist of a similar tough case, so that I was between them. They weren't taking any unavoidable chances.

'I'd not try any funny business, if I were you,' Coker advised me. 'You do right by them, and they'll do right by you.'

The three of us climbed awkwardly on to the tailboard, and the two lorries drove off.

We stopped somewhere near Swiss Cottage, and piled out. There were perhaps twenty people in sight, prowling with apparent aimlessness along the gutters. At the sound of the engines every one of them had turned towards us with an incredulous expression on his face, and as if they were parts of a single mechanism they began to close hopefully towards us, calling out as they came. The drivers shouted to us to get clear. They backed, turned, and rumbled off by the way we had come. The converging people stopped. One or two of them shouted after the lorries; most turned hopelessly and silently back to their wandering. There was one woman about fifty yards away; she broke into hysterics, and began to bang her head against a wall. I felt sick.

I turned towards my companions.

'Well, what do you want first?' I asked them.

'A billet,' said one. 'We got to 'ave some place to doss down.'

I reckoned I'd have to find that at least for them. I couldn't just dodge out and leave them stranded right where we were. Now we'd come this far, I couldn't do less than find them a centre, a kind of headquarters, and put them on their feet. What was wanted was a place where the receiving, storing, and feeding could be done, and the whole lot kept together. I counted them. There were fifty-two; fourteen of them women. The best course seemed to be to find a hotel. It would save the trouble of fitting out with beds and bedding.

The place we found was a kind of glorified boarding-house made up of four Victorian terrace-houses knocked together, giving more than the accommodation we needed. There were already half a dozen people in the place when we got there. Heaven knows what had happened to the rest. We found the remnants huddled together and scared in one of the lounges – an old man, an elderly woman (who turned out to have been the manageress), a middle-aged man, and three girls. The manageress had the spirit to pull herself together and hand out some quite high-sounding threats, but the ice, even of her most severe boarding-house manner, was thin. The old man tried to back her up by blustering a bit. The rest did nothing but keep their faces turned nervously towards us.

I explained that we were moving in. If they did not like it, they could go; if, on the other hand, they preferred to stay and share equally what there was, they were free to do so. They were not pleased. The way they reacted suggested that somewhere in the place they had a cache of stores that they were not anxious to share. When they grasped that the intention was to build up bigger stores their attitude modified per-ceptibly, and they prepared to make the best of it.

. . .

I decided I'd have to stay on a day or two just to get the party set up. I guessed Josella would be feeling much the same about her lot. Ingenious man, Coker – the trick is called holding the baby. But after that I'd dodge out and join her.

During the next couple of days we worked systematically, tackling the bigger stores nearby – mostly chain-stores, and not very big, at that. Nearly everywhere there had been others before us. The fronts of the shops were in a bad way. The windows were broken in, the floors were littered with half-opened cans and spilt packages which had disappointed the finders, and now lay in a sticky, stinking mass among the fragments of window-glass. But as a rule the loss was small and the damage superficial, and we'd find the larger cases in and behind the shop untouched.

It was far from easy for blind men to carry and manoeuvre heavy cases out of the place and load them on handcarts. Then there was the job of getting them back to the billet, and stowing them. But practice began to give them a knack with it.

The most hampering factor was the necessity for my presence. Little or nothing could go on unless I was there to direct. It was impossible to use more than one working party at a time, though we could have made up a dozen. Nor could much go on back at the hotel while I was out with foraging squads. Moreover, such time as I had to spend investigating and prospecting the district was pretty much wasted for everyone else. Two sighted men could have got through a lot more than twice the work.

Once we had started I was too busy during the day to spend much thought beyond the actual work in hand, and too tired at night to do anything but sleep the moment I lay down. Now and again I'd say to myself, 'by tomorrow night I'll have them pretty well fixed up – enough to keep them going, for a bit, anyway. Then I'll light out of this, and find Josella.'

That sounded all right – but every day it was tomorrow that I'd be able to do it, and each day it became more difficult. Some of them had begun to learn a bit, but still practically nothing, from foraging to can-opening, could go on without my being around. It seemed, the way things were going, that I became less, instead of more dispensable.

None of it was their fault. That was what made it difficult. Some of them were trying so damned hard. I just had to watch them making it more and more impossible for me to play the skunk and walk out on them. A dozen times a day I cursed the man Coker for contriving me into the situation – but that didn't help to solve it: it just left me wondering how it could end...

I had my first inkling of that, though I scarcely recognized it as such, on the fourth morning – or maybe it was the fifth – just as we were setting out. A woman called down the stairs that there were two sick up there; pretty bad, she thought.

My two watchdogs did not like it.

'Listen,' I told them. 'I've had about enough of this chaingang stuff. We'd be doing a lot better than we are now without it, anyway.'

'An' have you slinkin' off to join your old mob?' said someone.

'I'd not fool yourself,' I said. 'I could have slugged this pair of amateur gorillas any hour of the day or night. I've not done it because I've got nothing against them other than their being a pair of dim-witted nuisances . . .'

''Ere——' one of my attachments began to expostulate.

'But,' I went on, 'if they don't let me see what's wrong with these people, they can begin expecting to be slugged any minute from now.'

The two saw reason, but when we reached the room, they took good care to stand as far back as the chain allowed. The casualties turned out to be two men, one young, one middle-aged. Both had high temperatures and complained of agonized pain in the bowels. I didn't know much about such things then, but I did not need to know much to feel worried. I could think of nothing but to direct that they should be carried to an empty house nearby, and to tell one of the women to look after them as best as she could.

That was the beginning of a day of setbacks. The next, of a very different kind, happened around noon.

We had cleared most of the food-shops close to us, and I had decided to extend our range a little. From my recollections of the neighbourhood I reckoned we ought to find another shopping street above half a mile to the north, so I led my party that way. We found the shop there, all right, but something else, too.

As we turned the corner and came into view of them, I stopped. In front of a chain-store grocery a party of men were trundling out cases and loading them on to a lorry. Save for the difference in the vehicle, I might have been watching my own party at work. I halted my group of twenty or so, wondering what line we should take. My inclination was to withdraw and avoid possible trouble by finding a clear field elsewhere; there was no sense in coming into conflict when there was plenty scattered in various stores for those who were organized enough to take it. But it did not fall to me to make the decision. Even while I hesitated a red-headed young man strode confidently out of the shop door. There was no doubt that he was able to see – or, a moment later, that he had seen us.

He did not share my indecisions. He reached swiftly for his pocket. The next moment a bullet hit the wall beside me with a smack.

There was a brief tableau. His men and mine turning their sightless eyes towards one another in an effort to understand what was going on.

Then he fired again, I supposed he had aimed at me, but the bullet found the man on my left. He gave a grunt as though he was surprised, and folded up with a kind of sigh. I dodged back round the corner, dragging the other watchdog with me.

'Quick,' I said. 'Give me the key to these cuffs. I can't do a thing, like this.'

He didn't do anything except give a knowing grin. He was a one-idea man.

'Huh,' he said. 'Come orf it. You don't fool me.'

'Oh, for God's sake, you damned clown——' I said, pulling on the chain to drag the body of watchdog number one nearer so that we could get better cover.

The goon started to argue. Heaven knows what subtleties his dim wits were crediting me with. There was enough slack on the chain now for me to raise my arms. I did, and hammered both fists at his head so that it went back against the wall with a crack. That disposed of his argument. I found the key in his side pocket.

'Listen,' I told the rest. 'Turn round, all of you, and keep going straight ahead. Don't separate, or you'll have had it. Get moving now.'

I got one wristlet open, ridded myself of the chain, and scrambled over the wall into somebody's garden. I crouched there while I got rid of the other cuff. Then I moved across to peer cautiously over the far angle of the wall. The young man with the pistol had not come rushing after us as I had half-expected. He was still with his party, giving them an instruction. And now I came to think of it, why should he hurry? Since we had not fired back at him he could reckon we were unarmed, and we wouldn't be able to get away fast.

When he'd finished his directions he walked out confidently into the road to a point where he had a view of my retreating group, and then began to follow them. At the corner he stopped to look at the two prone watchdogs. Probably the chain suggested to him that one of them had been the eyes of our gang, for he put the pistol back in his pocket and began to follow the rest in a leisurely fashion.

That wasn't what I had expected, and it took me a minute to see his scheme. Then it came to me that his most profitable course would be to follow them to our headquarters, and see what pickings he could hijack there. He was, I had to admit, either much quicker than I at spotting chances, or had previously given more thought to the possibilities that might arise than I had. I was glad that I had told my lot to keep straight on. Most likely they'd get tired of it after a bit, but I reckoned they'd none of them be able to find the way back to the hotel and so lead him to it. As long as they kept together, I'd be able to collect them all later on without much difficulty. The immediate question was what to do about a man who carried a pistol, and didn't mind using it.

In some parts of the world one might go into the first house in sight, and pick up a convenient firearm. Hampstead was not like that; it was a highly respectable suburb, unfortunately. There might possibly be a sporting gun to be found somewhere, but I would have to hunt for it. The only thing I could think of was to keep him in sight and hope that some opportunity would offer a chance to deal with him. I broke a branch off a tree, scrambled back over the wall, and began to tap my way along the kerb, looking, I hoped, indistinguishable from the hundreds of blind men one had seen wandering the streets in the same way.

The road ran straight for some distance. The red-headed young man was perhaps fifty yards ahead of me, and my party another fifty ahead of him. We continued like that for something over half a mile. To my relief, none of the front party showed any tendency to turn into the road which led to our base. I was beginning to wonder how long it would be before they decided that they had gone far enough, when an unexpected diversion occurred. One man who had been lagging behind the rest finally stopped. He dropped his stick, and doubled up with his arms over his belly. Then he sagged to the ground and lay there, rolling with pain. The others did not stop for him. They must have heard his moans but probably they had no idea he was one of themselves.

The young man looked towards him, and hesitated. He altered his course, and bore across towards the contorted figure. He stopped a few feet away from him, and stood gazing down. For perhaps a quarter of a minute he regarded him carefully. Then slowly, but quite deliberately, he pulled his pistol out of his pocket, and shot him through the head.

The party ahead stopped at the sound of the shot. So did I. The young man made no attempt to catch up with them – in fact, he seemed suddenly to lose interest in them altogether. He turned round, and came walking back down the middle of the road. I remembered to play my part, and began to tap my way forward again. He paid no attention as he passed, but I was able to see his face: it was worried, and there was a grim set to his jaw . . . I kept going as I was until he was a decent distance behind me, then I hurried on to the rest. Brought up short by the sound of the shot, they were arguing whether to go on further or not.

I broke that off by telling them that now I was no longer encumbered with my two *i.q.*-minus watchdogs we would be ordering things differently. I was going to get a lorry, and I would be back in ten minutes or so to run them back to the billet in it.

The finding of another organized party at work produced a new anxiety, but we found the place intact. The only news they had for me there was that two more men and a woman had been taken with severe belly pains and removed to the other house.

We made what preparations we could for defence against any marauders arriving while I was away. Then I picked a new party, and we set off in the lorry, this time in a different direction.

I recalled that in former days when I had come up to Hampstead Heath it had often been by way of a bus terminus where a number of small shops and stores clustered. With the aid of the street-plan I found the place again easily enough – not only found it, but discovered it to be marvellously intact. Save for three or four broken windows, the area looked simply as if it had been closed up for a week-end.

But there were differences. For one thing, no such silence had ever before hung over the locality, weekday or Sunday. And there were several bodies lying in the street. By this time one was becoming accustomed enough to that to pay them little attention. I had, in fact, wondered that there were not more to be seen, and had come to the conclusion that most people sought some kind of shelter either out of fear, or later when they became weak. It was one of the reasons that one felt a disinclination to enter any dwelling-house.

I stopped the lorry in front of a provision store and listened for a few seconds. The silence came down on us like a blanket. There was no sound of tapping sticks, not a wanderer in sight. Nothing moved.

'Okay,' I said. 'Pile out, chaps.'

The locked door of the shop gave away easily. Inside there was a neat, unspoiled array of tubs of butter, cheese, sides of bacon, cases of sugar, and all the rest of it. I got the others busy. They had developed tricks of working by now, and were more sure of their handling. I was able to leave them to get on with it for a bit while I examined the back storeroom and then the cellar.

It was while I was below, investigating the nature of the cases down there that I heard a sound of shouts somewhere outside. Close upon it came a thunder of trampling boots on the floor above me. One man came down through the trapdoor, and pitched on his head. He did not move or make another sound. I jumped to it that there must be a battle with a rival gang in progress up there. I stepped across the fallen man, and climbed the ladder-like stair cautiously, holding up one arm to protect my head.

The first view was of numerous scuffing boots, unpleasantly close, and backing towards the trap. I nipped up quickly and got clear before they were on me. I was up just in time to see the plate-glass window in the front give way. Three men from outside fell in with it. A long green lash whipped after them, striking one as he lay. The other two scrambled among the wreckage of the display, and came stumbling further into the shop. They pressed back against the rest, and two more men fell through the open trap-door.

It did not need more than a glimpse of that lash to tell what had happened. During the work of the past few days I had all but forgotten the triffids. By standing on a box I could see over the heads of the men. There were three triffids in my field of view: one out in the road, and two closer, on the pavement. Four men lay on the ground out there, not moving. I understood then why these shops had been untouched; and why there had been no one to be seen in the neighbourhood of the Heath. At the same time I cursed myself for not having looked at the bodies in the road more closely. One glimpse of a sting mark would have been enough warning.

'Hold it,' I shouted. 'Stand where you are.'

I jumped down from the box, pushed away the men who were standing on the folded-back lid of the trap, and got it closed.

'There's a door back here,' I told them. 'Take it easy now.'

The first two took it easy. Then a triffid sent its sting whistling into the room through the broken window. One man gave a scream as he fell. The rest came on in panic, and swept me before them. There was a jam in the doorway. Behind us stings swished twice again before we were clear.

In the back room I looked round panting. There were seven of us there.

'Hold it,' I said again. 'We're all right in here.'

I went back to the door. The rear part of the shop was out of the triffids' range – as long as they stayed outside. I was able to reach the trap-door in safety, and raise it. The two men who had fallen down there since I left re-emerged. One nursed a broken arm; the other was merely bruised, and cursing.

Behind the back room lay a small yard, and across that a door in an eight-foot brick wall. I had grown cautious. Instead of going straight to the door I climbed on the roof of an outhouse to prospect. The door, I could see, gave into a narrow alley running the full length of the block. It was empty. But beyond the wall on the far side which seemed to terminate the gardens of a row of private houses, I could make out the tops of two triffids motionless among the bushes. There might well be more. The wall on that side was lower, and their height would enable them to strike right across the alley with their stings. I explained to the others.

'Bloody unnatural brutes,' said one. 'I always did hate them bastards.'

I investigated farther. The building next but one to the north side turned out to be a car-hire service with three of its cars on the premises. It was an awkward job getting the party over the two intervening walls, particularly the man with the broken arm, but we managed it. Somehow, too, I got them all packed into a large Daimler. When we were all set I opened the outer door of the place, and ran back to the car.

The triffids weren't slow to be interested. That uncanny sensitiveness to sounds told them something was happening. As we drove out, a couple of them were already lurching towards the entrance. Their stings whipped out at us, and slapped harmlessly against the closed windows. I swung hard round, bumping one, and toppling it over. Then we were away up the road, making for a healthier neighbourhood.

. . .

The evening that followed was the worst I had spent since the calamity occurred. Freed of the two watchdogs, I took over a small room where I could be alone. I put six lighted candles in a row on the mantelshelf, and sat a long while in an armchair, trying to think things out. We had come back to find that one of the men who had been taken sick the night before was dead; the other was obviously dying – and there were four new cases. By the time our evening meal was over, there were two more still. What the complaint was I had no idea. With the lack of service and the way things were going in general, it might have been a number of things. I thought of typhoid, but I'd a hazy idea that the incubation period ruled that out – not that it would have made much difference if I had known. All I did know about it was that it was something nasty enough to make the red-haired young man use his pistol, and change his mind about following my party.

It began to look to me as if I had been doing my group a questionable service from the first. I had succeeded in keeping them alive, placed between a rival gang on one side, and triffids encroaching from the Heath on the other. Now there was this sickness, too. And, when all was said and done, I had achieved only the postponement of starvation for a little while.

As things were now, I did not see my way.

And then there was Josella on my mind. The same sorts of things, maybe worse, were as likely to be happening in her district ...

I found myself thinking of Michael Beadley and his lot again. I had known then that they were logical, now I began to think that perhaps they had a truer humanity, too. They had seen that it was hopeless to try to save any but a very few. To give an empty hope to the rest was little better than cruelty.

Besides, there were ourselves. If there were purpose in anything at all, what had we been preserved for? Not simply to waste ourselves on a forlorn task, surely . . . ?

I decided that tomorrow I would go in search of Josella, and we would settle it together . . .

The latch of the door moved with a click. The door itself opened slowly.

'Who's that?' I said.

'Oh, it *is* you,' said a girl's voice.

She came in, closing the door behind her.

'What do you want?' I asked.

She was tall and slim. Under twenty I guessed. Her hair waved slightly. Chestnut-coloured, it was. She was quiet, but one had to notice her – it was the texture of her as well as the line. She had placed my position by my movement and voice. Her gold-brown eyes were looking just over my left shoulder, otherwise I'd have been sure she was studying me.

She did not answer at once. It was an uncertainty which did not seem to suit the rest of her. I went on waiting for her to speak. A lump got into my throat somehow. You see, she was young, and she was beautiful. There should have been all life, maybe a wonderful life before her . . . And isn't there something a little sad about youth and beauty in any circumstances . . . ?

'You're going to go away from here?' she said. It was half question, half statement, in a quiet voice, a little unsteadily.

'I've never said that,' I countered.

'No,' she admitted, 'but that's what the others are saying – and they're right, aren't they?'

I did not say anything to that. She went on:

'You can't. You can't leave them like this. They need you.'

'I'm doing no good here,' I told her. 'All the hopes are false.'

'But suppose they turned out not to be false?'

'They can't – not now. We'd have known by this time.'

'But if they did, after all – and you had simply walked out——?'

'Do you think I haven't thought of that? I'm not doing any good, I tell you. I've been like the drugs they inject to keep the patient going a little longer – no curative value; just putting it off.'

She did not reply for some seconds. Then she said, unsteadily:

'Life is very precious – even like this.' Her control almost cracked.

I could not say anything. She recovered herself.

'You can keep us going. There's always a chance – just a chance that something might happen, even now.'

I had already said what I thought about that. I did not repeat it.

'It's so difficult,' she said, as though to herself. 'If I could only *see* you ... But then, of course, if I could ... Are you young? You sound young.'

'I'm under thirty,' I told her. 'And very ordinary.'

'I'm eighteen. It was my birthday – the day the comet came.'

I could not think of anything to say to that that would not seem cruel. The pause drew out. I saw that she was clenching her hands together. Then she dropped them to her sides, the knuckles quite white. She made as if to speak, but did not.

'What is it?' I asked, 'What can I do except prolong this a little?'

She bit her lip, then:

'They – they said perhaps you were lonely,' she said. 'I thought perhaps if' – her voice faltered, and her knuckles went a little whiter still – 'perhaps if you had somebody ... I mean, somebody here ... you – you might not want to leave us. Perhaps you'd stay with us?'

'Oh, God,' I said, softly.

I looked at her, standing quite straight, her lips trembling slightly. There should have been suitors clamouring for her lightest smile. She should have been happy and uncaring for a while – then happy in caring. Life should have been enchanting to her, and love very sweet ...;

'You'd be kind to me, wouldn't you?' she said. 'You see I haven't——'

'Stop it! Stop it!' I told her. 'You mustn't say these things to me. Please go away now.'

But she did not go. She stood staring at me from eyes that could not see me.

'Go away!' I repeated.

I could not stand the reproach of her. She was not simply herself – she was thousands upon thousands of young lives destroyed ...

She came closer.

'Why, I believe you're crying!' she said.

'Go away. For God's sake, go away!' I told her.

She hesitated, then she turned and felt her way back to the door. As she went out:

'You can tell them I'll be staying,' I said.

. . .

The first thing I was aware of the next morning was the smell. There had been whiffs of it here and there before, but luckily the weather had been cool. Now I found that I had slept late into what was already a warmer day. I'm not going into details about the smell; those who knew it will never forget it, for the rest it is indescribable. It rose from every city and town for weeks, and travelled on every wind that blew. When I woke to it that morning it convinced me beyond doubt that the end had come. Death is just the shocking end of animation: it is dissolution that is final.

I lay for some minutes thinking. The only thing to do now would be to load my party into lorries and take them in relays into the country. And all the supplies we had collected? They would have to be loaded and taken, too – and I the only one able to drive . . . It would take days – if we had days . . .

Upon that, I wondered what was happening in the building now. The place was oddly quiet. When I listened I could hear a voice groaning in another room, beyond that nothing. I got out of bed and hurried into my clothes with a feeling of alarm. Out on the landing, I listened again. There was no sound of feet about the house. I had a sudden nasty feeling as if history were repeating itself and I were back in the hospital again.

'Hey! Anybody here?' I called.

Several voices answered. I opened a nearby door. There was a man in there. He looked very bad, and he was delirious. There was nothing I could do. I closed the door again.

My footsteps sounded loud on the wooden stairs. On the next floor a woman's voice called: 'Bill – Bill!'

She was in bed in a small room there, the girl who had come to see me the night before. She turned her head as I came in. I saw that she had it, too.

'Don't come near,' she said. 'It *is* you, Bill?'

'Yes.'

'I thought it must be. You can still walk: they have to creep. I'm glad, Bill. I told them you'd not go like that – but they said you had. Now they've all gone, all of them that could.'

'I was asleep,' I said. 'What happened?'

'More and more of us like this. They were frightened.'

I said helplessly: 'What can I do for you? Is there anything I can get you?'

Her face contorted, she clutched her arms around her, and writhed. The spasm passed, and left her with sweat trickling down her forehead.

'Please, Bill. I'm not very brave. Could you get me something – to finish it?'

'Yes,' I said. 'I can do that for you.'

I was back from the chemist's in ten minutes. I gave her a glass of water, and put the stuff in her other hand.

She held it there a little. Then:

'So futile – and it might all have been so different,' she said. 'Good-bye, Bill – and thank you for trying.'

I looked down at her lying there. There was a thing that made it still more futile – I wondered how many would have said, 'Take me with you,' where she had said, 'Stay with us.'

And I never knew her name.

CHAPTER 9

EVACUATION

It was the memory of the red-headed young man who had fired on us that conditioned my choice of a route to Westminster.

Since I was sixteen my interest in weapons has decreased, but in an environment reverting to savagery it seemed that one must be prepared to behave more or less as a savage, or possibly cease to behave at all before long. In St James's Street there used to be several shops which would sell you any form of lethalness from a rook-rifle to an elephant-gun with the greatest urbanity.

I left there with a mixed feeling of support and banditry. Once more I had a useful hunting-knife. There was a pistol with the precise workmanship of a scientific instrument in my pocket. On the seat beside me rested a loaded twelve-bore and boxes of cartridges. I had chosen a shot-gun in preference to a rifle – the bang is no less convincing, and it decapitates a triffid with a neatness which a bullet seldom achieves. And there were triffids to be seen right in London now. They still appeared to avoid the streets when they could, but I had noticed several lumbering across Hyde Park, and there were others in Green Park. Very likely they were ornamental, safely docked specimens – on the other hand, maybe they weren't.

And so I came to Westminster.

The deadness, the finish of it all, was italicized there. The usual scatter of abandoned vehicles lay about the streets. Very few people were in sight. I saw only three who were moving. Two were tapping their way down the gutters of Whitehall, the third was in Parliament Square. He was sitting close to Lincoln's statue, and clutching to him his dearest possession – a side of bacon from which he was hacking a ragged slice with a blunt knife.

Above it all rose the Houses of Parliament, with the hands of the clock stopped at three minutes past six. It was difficult to believe that all that meant nothing any more, that now it was just a pretentious confection in uncertain stone which could decay in peace. Let it shower its crumbling pinnacles on to the terrace as it would – there would be no more indignant members complaining of the risk to their valuable lives. Into those halls which had in their day set world echoes to good intentions and sad expediencies, the roofs could in due course fall; there would be none to stop them, and none to care. Alongside, the Thames flowed imperturbably on. So it would flow until the day the Embankments crumbled and the water spread out and Westminster became once more an island in a marsh.

Marvellously clear-fretted in the unsmoked air, the Abbey rose, silver-grey. It stood detached by the serenity of age from the ephemeral growths around it. It was solid on a foundation of centuries, destined, perhaps, for centuries yet to preserve within it the monuments to those whose work was now all destroyed.

I did not loiter there. In years to come I expect some will go to look at the old Abbey with romantic melancholy. But romance of that kind is an alloy of tragedy with retrospect. I was too close.

Moreover, I was beginning to experience something new – the fear of being alone. I had not been alone since I walked from the hospital along Piccadilly, and then there had been bewildering novelty in all I saw. Now, for the first time I begin to feel the horror that real loneliness holds for a species that is by nature gregarious. I felt naked, exposed to all the fears that prowled . . .

I made myself drive on up Victoria Street. The sound of the car itself alarmed me with its echoes. My impulse was to leave it and sneak silently on foot, seeking safety in cunning, like a beast in the jungle. It needed all my will power to keep myself steady and hold to my plan. For I knew what I should have done had I chanced to be allocated to this district – I should have sought supplies in its biggest department-store.

Somebody had stripped the provision department of the Army and Navy Stores, all right, but there was no one there now.

I came out by a side door. A cat on the pavement was engaged in sniffing at something which might have been a bundle of rags, but was not. I clapped my hands at it. It glared at me, and then slunk off.

A man came round a corner. He had a gloating expression on his face, and was perseveringly rolling a large cheese along the middle of the road. When he heard my step he halted his cheese, and sat on it, brandishing his stick fiercely. I went back to my car in the main street.

The probability was that Josella, too, would have chosen a hotel as a convenient headquarters. I remembered that there were several around

Victoria Station, so I drove on there. It turned out that there were vastly more of them than I had thought. After I had looked into a score or more without finding any evidence of organized squatting, it began to seem pretty hopeless.

I looked for someone to ask. There seemed a chance that anyone still alive here might owe it to her. I had seen only half a dozen capable of moving since I arrived in the district. Now there seemed to be none. But at last, near the corner of Buckingham Palace Road, I came across an old woman sitting huddled on a doorstep.

She was tearing at a tin, with broken finger-nails, and alternately cursing and whimpering over it. I went to a small shop nearby and found half a dozen tins of beans overlooked on a high shelf. I discovered a tin-opener, too, and went back to her. She was still futilely scrabbling away at her tin.

'You'd better throw that away. It's coffee,' I told her.

I put the opener in her hand, and gave her a tin of beans.

'Listen to me,' I said. 'Do you know anything of a girl round here – a girl that can see? She'd be in charge of a party, most likely.'

I was not very hopeful, but something must have helped the old woman to keep going longer than most. It seemed almost too good to be true when she nodded.

'Yes,' she said, as she started the opener.

'You do! Where is she?' I demanded. Somehow it never occurred to me that it could be anyone but Josella.

But she shook her head.

'I don't know. I was with her lot for a bit, but I lost 'em. An old woman like me can't keep up with the young ones, so I lost 'em. They'd not wait for a poor old woman, and I couldn't never find 'em again.'

She went on cutting intently round the tin.

'Where is she living?' I asked.

'We was all in a 'otel. Dunno where it is, or I'd've found 'em again.'

'Don't you know the name of the hotel?'

'Not me. 'Tain't no good knowing the names of places when you can't see to read 'em, nor nobody else can't, neither.'

'But you must remember something about it.'

'No, I don't.'

She lifted the can, sniffed cautiously at the contents.

'Look here,' I said, coldly. 'You want to keep those tins, don't you?'

She made a movement with one arm to gather them all to her.

'Well, then, you'd better tell me all you can about that hotel,' I went on. 'You must know, for instance, whether it was large or small.'

She considered, one arm still protectively about the tins.

'Downstairs it sounded sort of hollow – like it might be biggish. Likely it was smart, too – what I mean, it 'ad them quiet carpets, an' good beds, an' good sheets.'

'Nothing else about it?'

'No, not as I—— Yes, there was, though. It 'ad two small steps outside an' you went in through one of them round-and-round doors.'

'That's better,' I said. 'You're quite sure of that? If I can't find it, I *can* find you again, you know.'

''S Gawd's truth, mister. Two small steps, an a round-and-round door.'

She rummaged in a battered bag beside her, brought out a dirty spoon, and began to taste the beans as if they were one of the jams of paradise.

There were, I found, still more hotels round there than I had thought, and a surprising number of them had round-and-round doors. But I kept on. There was no mistaking it when I did find it. The traces and the smell were all too familiar.

'Anybody here?' I called, in the echoing lounge.

I was about to go further in when a groan came from one corner. Over in a semi-dark recess a man was lying on a settee. Even in the dimness it was possible to see that he was far gone. I did not go too close. His eyes opened. For a moment I thought that he could see.

'You there?' he said.

'Yes, I want to——'

'Water,' he said. 'Fer Christ's sake gimme some water——'

I went across to the dining-room, and found the service-room beyond. The taps were dry. I squirted a couple of syphons into a big jug, and took it back with a cup. I put them down where he could reach them.

'Thanks, mate,' he said. 'I can manage. You keep clear o' me.'

He dipped the cup into the jug, and then drained it.

'Gawd,' he said. 'Did I need that!' And he repeated the action. 'Wotcher doin', mate? 'Tain't 'ealthy round 'ere, you know.'

'I'm looking for a girl – a girl who can see. Her name's Josella. Is she here?'

'She *was* here. But you're too late, chum.'

A sudden suspicion struck me like a physical stab.

'You – don't mean——'

'No. Ease orf, mate. She ain't got what I got. No, she's just gone – same as all the rest what could.'

'Where did she go, do you know?'

'Can't tell you that, mate.'

'I see,' I said, heavily.

'You'd best be goin', too, chum. 'Ang around 'ere long, an' you'll be stayin' for keeps, like me.'

He was right. I stood looking down at him.

'Anything else I can get you?'

'No. This'll last me. I reckon it won't be much longer I'll need anything.' He paused. Then he added; ''Bye, mate, 'n' thanks a lot. An' if you do find 'er, look after 'er proper – she's a good girl.'

While I was making a meal off tinned ham and bottled beer a little later, it occurred to me that I had not asked the man when Josella had left, but I decided that in his state he would be unlikely to have any clear idea of time.

The one place I could think of to go to was the University Building. I reckoned Josella would think the same – and there was a hope that some others of our dispersed party might have drifted back there in an effort to reunite. It was not a very strong hope, for common sense should have caused them to leave the town days ago.

Two flags still hung above the tower, limp in the warm air of the early evening. Of the two dozen or so lorries that had been accumulated in the forecourt, four still stood there, apparently untouched. I parked the car beside them, and went into the building. My footsteps clattered in the silence.

'Hullo! Hullo, there!' I called. 'Is there anyone here?'

My voice echoed away down corridors and up wells, diminishing to the parody of a whisper and then to silence. I went to the doors of the other wing and called again. Once more the echoes died away unbroken, settling softly as dust. Only then as I turned back did I notice that an inscription had been chalked on the wall inside the outer door. In large letters it gave simply an address:

> TYNSHAM MANOR
> TYNSHAM
> NR DEVIZES, WILTS.

That was something, at least.

I looked at it, and thought. In another hour or less it would be dusk. Devizes I guessed at a hundred miles distant, probably more. I went outside again and examined the lorries. One of them was the last that I had driven in – the one in which I had stowed my despised anti-triffid gear. I recalled that the rest of its load was a useful assortment of food and supplies. It would be much better to arrive with that, than empty-handed in a car. Nevertheless, if there were no urgent reason for it, I did not fancy driving anything, much less a large, heavily-loaded lorry, by night along roads which might reasonably be expected to produce a number of hazards. If I were to pile it up, and the odds were that I should, I would lose a lot more time in finding another and transferring the load than I would by spending the night here. An early start in the morning offered much better prospects. I moved my boxes of cartridges from the car to the cab of the lorry in readiness. The gun I kept with me.

I found the room from which I had rushed to the fake fire-alarm, exactly as I had left it; my clothes on a chair, even the cigarette-case and lighter where I had placed them beside my improvised bed.

It was still too early to think of sleep. I lit a cigarette, put the case in my pocket, and decided to go out.

Before I went into the Russell Square garden I looked it over carefully. I had already begun to be suspicious of open spaces. Sure enough I spotted one triffid. It was in the north-west corner, standing perfectly still, but considerably taller than the bushes that surrounded it. I went closer, and blew the top of it to bits with a single shot. The noise in the silent Square could scarcely have been more alarming if I had let off a howitzer. When I was sure that there were no others lurking I went into the garden and sat with my back against a tree.

I stayed there perhaps twenty minutes. The sun was low, and half the square was thrown into shadow. Soon I would have to go in. While there was light I could sustain myself; in the dark, things could steal quietly upon me. Already I was on my way back to the primitive. Before long, perhaps, I should be spending the hours of darkness in fear as my remote ancestors must have done, watching, ever distrustfully, the night outside their cave. I delayed to take one more look around the Square as if it were a page of history I would learn before it was turned. And as I stood there, I heard the gritting of footsteps on the road – a slight sound, but as loud in the silence as a grinding millstone.

I turned, with my gun ready. Crusoe was no more startled at the sight of a footprint than I at the sound of a footfall, for it had not the hesitancy of a blind man's. I caught a glimpse in the dim light of the moving fire. As it left the road and entered the garden I saw that it was a man. Evidently he had seen me before I heard him, for he was coming straight towards me.

'You don't need to shoot,' he said, holding empty hands wide apart.

I did not know him until he came within a few yards. Simultaneously he recognized me.

'Oh, it's you, is it?' he said.

I kept the gun raised.

'Hullo, Coker. What are you after? Wanting me to go on another of your little parties?' I asked him.

'No. You can put that thing down. Makes too much noise, anyway.

That's how I found you. No,' he repeated, 'I've had enough. I'm getting to hell out of here.'

'So am I,' I said, and lowered the gun.

'What happened to your bunch?' he asked.

I told him. He nodded.

'Same with mine. Same with the rest, I expect. Still, we tried ...'

'The wrong way,' I said.

He nodded again.

'Yes,' he admitted. 'I reckon your lot did have the right idea from the start – only it didn't *look* right, and it didn't sound right a week ago.'

'Six days ago,' I corrected him.

'A week,' said he.

'No, I'm sure – oh, well, what the hell's it matter, anyway?' I said. 'In the circumstances,' I went on, 'what do you say to declaring an amnesty, and starting over again?'

He agreed.

'I'd got it wrong,' he repeated. 'I thought I was the one who was taking it seriously – but I wasn't taking it seriously enough. I couldn't believe that it would last, or that some kind of help wouldn't show up. But now look at it! And it must be like this everywhere. Europe, Asia, America – think of America smitten like this! But they must be. If they weren't, they'd have been over here, helping out and getting the place straight – that's the way it'd take them. No, I reckon your lot understood it better from the start.'

We ruminated for some moments, then I asked:

'This disease, plague – what do you reckon it is?'

'Search me, chum. I thought it must be typhoid, but someone said typhoid takes longer to develop – so I'd not know. I don't know why I've not caught it myself – except that I've been able to keep away from those that have, and to see that what I was eating was clean. I've been keeping to tins I've opened myself, and I've drunk only bottled beer. Anyway, though I've been lucky so far, I don't fancy hanging around here much longer. Where do *you* go now?'

I told him of the address chalked on the wall. He had not yet seen it. He had been on his way to the University Building when the sound of my shot had caused him to scout round with some caution.

'It—' I began, and then stopped abruptly. From one of the streets west of us came the sound of a car starting. It ran up its gears quickly, and then diminished into the distance.

'Well, at least there's somebody else left,' said Coker. '*And* whoever wrote up that address. Have you any idea who that would be?'

I shrugged my shoulders. It was a justifiable assumption that it was a returned member of the group that Coker had raided – or possibly some sighted person that his party had failed to catch. There was no telling how long it had been there. He thought it over.

'It'll be better if there's two of us. I'll tag along with you and see what's doing. Okay?'

'Okay,' I agreed. 'I'm for turning in now, and an early start tomorrow.'

. . .

He was still asleep when I awoke. I dressed myself much more comfortably in the ski-suit and heavy shoes than in the garments I had been wearing since his party had provided them for me. By the time I returned with a bag of assorted packets and tins, he was up and dressed, too. Over breakfast we decided to improve our welcome at Tynsham by taking a loaded lorry each rather than travel together in one.

'And see that the cab window closes,' I suggested. 'There are quite a lot of triffid nurseries around London, particularly to the west.'

'Uh-huh. I've seen a few of the ugly brutes about,' he said, offhandedly.

'I've seen them about – and in action,' I told him.

At the first garage we came to we broke open a pump and filled up. Then, sounding in the silent streets like a convoy of tanks, we set off westwards with my three-tonner in the lead.

The going was wearisome. Every few dozen yards one had to weave round some derelict vehicle. Occasionally two or three together would block the road entirely so that it was necessary to go dead slow and nudge one of them out of the way. Very few of them were wrecked. The blindness seemed to have come upon the drivers swiftly, but not too suddenly for them to keep control. Usually they had been able to draw into the side of the road before they had stopped. Had the catastrophe occurred by day, the main roads would have been quite impassable, and to work our way clear from the centre by side-streets might have taken days – spent mostly in reversing before impenetrable thickets of vehicles and trying to find another way round. As it was I found that our over-all progress was less slow than it seemed in detail, and when after a few miles I noticed an overturned car beside the road I realized that we were by this time on a route which others had followed and partially cleared ahead of us.

On the further outskirts of Staines we could begin to feel that London was behind us at last. I stopped, and went back to Coker. As he switched off, the silence closed, thick and unnatural, with only the click of cooling metal to break it. I realized suddenly that I had not seen a single living creature other than a few sparrows since we had started. Coker climbed out of his cab. He stood in the middle of the road, listening and looking around him.

> 'And yonder all before us lie
> Deserts of vast eternity ...'

he murmured.

I looked hard at him. His grave, reflective expression turned suddenly to a grin.

'Or do you prefer Shelley?' he asked:

> 'My name is Ozymandias, king of kings,
> Look on my works, ye mighty, and despair!

Come on, let's find some food.'

.   .   .

'Coker,' I said, as we completed the meal sitting on a store counter and spreading marmalade on biscuits, 'you beat me. What are you? The first time I meet you I find you ranting – if you will forgive the appropriate word – in a kind of dockside lingo. Now you quote Marvell to me. It doesn't make sense.'

He grinned. 'It never did to me, either,' he said. 'It comes of being a hybrid – you never really know what you are. My mother never really knew what I was, either – at least, she never could prove it, and she always held it against me that on account of that she could not get an allowance for me. It made me kind of sour about things when I was a kid; and when I left school I used to go to meetings – more or less any kind of meetings as long as they were protesting against something. And that led to me getting mixed up with the lot that used to come to them. I suppose they found me kind of amusing. Anyway, they used to take me along to arty-political sorts of parties. After a bit I got tired of being amusing and seeing them give a kind of double laugh, half with me and half at me, whenever I said what I thought. I reckoned I needed some of the background knowledge they had, and then I'd be able to laugh at them a bit, maybe, so I started going to evening classes, and I practised talking the way they did, for use when necessary. There's a whole lot of people don't seem to understand that you have to talk to a man in his own language before he'll take you seriously. If you talk tough and quote Shelley they think you're cute, like a performing monkey or something, but they don't pay any attention to what you say. You have to talk the kind of lingo they're accustomed to taking seriously. And it works the other way, too. Half the political intelligentsia who talk to a working audience don't get the value of their stuff across – not so much because they're over their audience's heads, as because most of the chaps are listening to the voice and not to the words, so they knock a big discount off what they do hear because it's all a bit fancy, and not like ordinary normal talk. So I reckoned the thing to do was to make myself bilingual, and use the right one in the right place – and occasionally the wrong one in the wrong place, unexpectedly. Surprising how that jolts 'em. Wonderful thing, that English caste system. Since then I've made out quite nicely in the orating business. Not what you'd call a steady job, but full of interest and variety. Wilfred Coker. Meetings addressed. Subject no object. That's me.'

'How do you mean – subject no object?' I enquired.

'Well, I kind of supply the spoken word just like a printer supplies the printed word. He doesn't have to believe everything he prints.'

I left that for the moment. 'How's it happen you're not like the rest?' I asked. '*You* weren't in hospital, were you?'

'Me? No. It just so happened that I was addressing a meeting that was protesting over police partiality in a little matter of a strike. We began about six o'clock, and about half past the police themselves arrived to break it up. I found a handy trap-door, and went down into the cellar. They came down, too, to have a look, but they didn't find me where I had gone to earth in a pile of shavings. They went on tramping around up above for a bit, then it was quiet. But I stayed put. I wasn't walking out into any nice little trap. It was quite comfortable there, so I went to sleep. In the morning when I took a careful nose around, I found all this had happened.' He paused thoughtfully. 'Well, that racket's finished, it certainly doesn't look as if there's going to be much call for my particular gifts from now on,' he added.

I did not dispute it. We finished our meal. He slid himself off the counter.

'Come on. We'd better be shifting. "Tomorrow to fresh fields and pastures new" – if you'd care for a really hackneyed quotation this time.'

'It's more than that, its inaccurate,' I said. 'It's "woods", not "fields".'

He frowned, and thought.

'Well, —— me, mate, so it is,' he admitted.

. . .

I began to feel the lightening of spirit that Coker was already showing. The sight of the open country gave one hope of a sort. It was true that the young green crops would never be harvested when they had ripened, nor the fruit from the trees gathered; that the countryside might never again look as trim and neat as it did that day, but for all that it would go on, after its own fashion. It was not like the towns, sterile, stopped for ever. It was a place one could work and tend, and still find a future. It made my existence of the previous week seem like that of a rat living on crumbs and ferreting in garbage heaps. As I looked out over the fields I felt my spirits expanding.

Places on our route, towns like Reading or Newbury, brought back the London mood for a while, but they were no more than dips in a graph of revival.

There is an inability to sustain the tragic mood, a phoenix quality of the mind. It may be helpful or harmful, it is just a part of the will to survive – yet, also, it has made it possible for us to engage in one weakening war after another. But it is a necessary part of our mechanism that we should be able to cry only for a time over even an ocean of spilt milk – the spectacular must soon become the commonplace if life is to be supportable. Under a blue sky where a few clouds sailed like celestial icebergs the cities became a less oppressive memory, and the sense of living freshened us again like a clean wind. It does not, perhaps, excuse, but it does at least explain why from time to time I was surprised to find myself singing as I drove.

At Hungerford we stopped for more food and fuel. The feeling of release continued to mount as we passed through miles of untouched country. It did not seem lonely yet, only sleeping and friendly. Even the sight of occasional little groups of triffids swaying across a field, or of others resting with their roots dug into the soil held no hostility to spoil my mood. They were, once again, the simple objects of my suspended professional interest.

Short of Devizes we pulled up once more to consult the map. A little further on we turned down a side-road to the right, and drove into the village of Tynsham.

CHAPTER 10

TYNSHAM

There was little likelihood of anyone missing the Manor. Beyond the few cottages which constituted the village of Tynsham the high wall of an estate ran beside the road. We followed it until we came to massive wrought-iron gates. Behind them stood a young woman on whose face the sober seriousness of responsibility had suppressed all human expression. She was equipped with a shotgun which she clasped in inappropriate places. I signalled to Coker to stop, and called to her as I drew up. Her mouth moved, but not a word penetrated the clatter of the engine. I switched off.

'This is Tynsham Manor?' I asked.

She was not giving that or anything else away.

'Where are you from? And how many of you?' she countered.

I could have wished that she did not fiddle about with her gun in just the way she did. Briefly, and keeping an eye on her uneasy fingers, I explained who we were, why we came, roughly what we carried, and guaranteed that there were no more of us hidden in the trucks. I doubted whether she was taking it in. Her eyes were fixed on mine with a mournfully speculative expression more common in bloodhounds, but not reassuring even there. My words did little to disperse that random suspicion which makes the highly conscientious so wearing. As she emerged to glance into the backs of the lorries and verify my statements, I hoped for her sake that she would not chance to encounter a party of whom her suspicions were justified. Admission that she was satisfied would have weakened her rôle of reliability, but she did eventually consent, still with reserve, to allow us in.

'Take the right fork,' she called up to me as I passed, and turned back at once to attend to the security of the gates. Beyond a short avenue of elms lay a park landscaped in the manner of the late eighteenth century and dotted with trees which had had space to expand into full magnificence. The house, when it came into view, was not a stately home in the architectural sense, but there was a lot of it. It rambled over a considerable ground area and through a variety of building styles as though none of its previous owners had been able to resist the temptation to leave his personal mark upon it. Each, while respecting the work of his forefathers, had apparently felt it incumbent upon him to express the spirit of his own age. A confident disregard of previous levels had resulted in a sturdy waywardness. It was inescapably a funny house, yet friendly, and reliable-looking.

The right fork led us to a wide courtyard where several vehicles stood already. Coach-houses and stables extended around it, seemingly over several acres. Coker drew up alongside me, and climbed down. There was no one in sight.

We made our way through the open rear door of the main building, and down a long corridor. At the end of it was a kitchen of baronial capacity where the warmth and smell of cooking lingered. From beyond a door on the far side came a murmur of voices and a clatter of plates, but we had to negotiate a further dark passage and another door before we reached them.

The place we entered had, I imagine, been the servants' hall in the days when staffs were sufficiently large for the term to be no misnomer. It was spacious enough to seat a hundred or more at tables without crowding. The present occupants, seated on benches at two long trestles, I guessed to number between fifty and sixty, and it was clear at a glance that they were blind. While they sat patiently a few sighted persons were very busy. Over at a side-table three girls were industriously carving chickens. I went up to one of them.

'We've just come,' I said. 'What do we do?'

She paused, still clutching her fork and pushed back a lock of hair with the crook of her wrist.

'It'll help if one of you takes charge of the veg. and the other helps with the plates,' she said.

I took command of two large tubs of potato and cabbage. In the intervals of doling them out I looked over the occupants of the hall. Josella was not amongst them – not could I see any of the more notable characters among the group that had put forward its proposals at the University Building – though I fancied I had seen the faces of some of the women before.

The proportion of men was far higher than in the former group, and they were curiously assorted. A few of them might have been Londoners, or at least town-dwellers, but the majority wore a countryman's working clothes. An exception to either kind was a middle-aged clergyman, but what every one of the men had in common was blindness.

The women were more diversified. Some were in town clothes quite unsuited to their surroundings, others were probably local. Among the latter group only one girl was sighted, but the former group comprised half a dozen or so who could see, and a number who, though blind, were not clumsy.

Coker, too, had been taking stock of the place.

'Rum sort of set-up, this,' he remarked, *sotto voce* to me. 'Have you seen her yet?'

I shook my head, desolately aware that I had pinned more on the expectation of finding Josella there than I had admitted to myself.

'Funny thing,' he went on, 'there's practically none of the lot I took along with you – except that girl that's carving up at the end there.'

'Has she recognized you?' I asked.

'I think so. I got a sort of dirty look from her.'

When the carrying and serving had been completed we took our own plates, and found places at the table. There was nothing to complain of in the cooking or the food, and living out of cold cans for a week sharpens the appreciation, anyway. At the end of the meal there was a knocking on the table. The clergyman rose; he waited for silence before he spoke:

'My friends, it is fitting that at the end of another day we should renew our thanks to God for His great mercy in preserving us in the midst of such disaster. I will ask you all to pray that He may look with compassion upon those who still wander alone in darkness, and that it may please Him to guide their feet hither that we may succour them. Let us all beseech Him that we may survive the trials and tribulations that lie ahead in order that in His time and with His aid we may succeed in playing our part in the rebuilding of a better world to His greater glory.'

He bowed his head.

'Almighty and most merciful God . . .'

After the 'amen' he led a hymn. When that was finished the gathering sorted itself out into parties, each keeping touch with his neighbour, and four of the sighted girls led them out.

I lit a cigarette. Coker took one from me absentmindedly, without making any comment. A girl came across to us.

'Will you help to clear up?' she asked. 'Miss Durrant will be back soon, I expect.'

'Miss Durrant?' I repeated.

'She does the organizing,' she explained. 'You'll be able to fix things up with her.'

It was an hour later and almost dark when we heard that Miss Durrant had returned. We found her in a small, study-like room lit only by two candles on the desk. I recognized her at once as the dark, thin-lipped woman who had spoken for the opposition at the meeting. For the moment, all her attention was concentrated on Coker. Her expression was no more amiable than upon the former occasion.

'I am told,' she said coldly, regarding Coker as though he were some kind of silt, 'I am told that you are the man who organized the raid on the University Building?'

Coker agreed, and waited.

'Then I may as well tell you, once and for all, that in our community here we have no use for brutal methods, and no intention of tolerating them.'

Coker smiled slightly. He answered her in his best middle-class speech:

'It is a matter of viewpoint. Who is to judge who were the more brutal? – those who saw an immediate responsibility and stayed, or those who saw a further responsibility and cleared out?'

She continued to look hard at him. Her expression remained unchanged, but she was evidently forming a different judgement of the type of man she had to deal with. Neither his reply nor its manner had been quite what she had expected. She shelved that aspect for a time, and turned to me.

'Where you in that, too?' she asked.

I explained my somewhat negative part in the affair, and put my own question:

'What happened to Michael Beadley, the Colonel, and the rest?'

It was not well received.

'They have gone elsewhere,' she said, sharply. 'This is a clean, decent community with standards – Christian standards – and we intend to uphold them. We have no place here for people of loose views. Decadence, immorality, and lack of faith were responsible for most of the world's ills. It is the duty of those of us who have been spared to see that we build a society where that does not happen again. The cynical and the clever-clever will find they are not wanted here, no matter what brilliant theories they may put forward to disguise their licentiousness and their materialism. We are a Christian community, and we intend to remain so.' She looked at me challengingly.

'So you split, did you?' I said. 'Where did they go?'

She replied, stonily:

'They moved on, and we stayed here. That is what matters. So long as they keep their influence away from here they may work out their own damnation as they please. And since they choose to consider themselves superior to both the laws of God and civilized custom, I have no doubt that they will.'

She ended this declaration with a snap of the jaw which suggested that I should be wasting my time if I tried to question further, and turned back to Coker.

'What can you do?' she enquired.

'A number of things,' he said calmly. 'I suggest that I make myself generally useful until I see where I am needed most.'

She hesitated, a little taken aback. It had clearly been her intention to make the decision and issue the instruction, but she changed her mind.

'All right. Look round, and come and talk it over tomorrow evening,' she said.

But Coker was not to be dismissed quite so easily. He wanted particulars of the size of the estate, the number of persons at present in the house, the proportion of sighted to blind, along with a number of other matters, and he got them.

Before we left, I put in a question about Josella. Miss Durrant frowned.

'I seem to know that name. Now where——? Oh, did she stand in the Conservative interest in the last election?'

'I don't think so. She – er – did write a book once,' I admitted.

'She——' she began. Then I saw recollection dawn. 'Oh, oh that——! Well, really, Mr Masen, I can scarcely think she would be the sort of person to care for the kind of community we are building here.'

In the corridor ouside Coker turned to me. There was just enough of the twilight left for me to see his grin.

'A somewhat oppressive orthodoxy around these parts,' he remarked. The grin disappeared as he added: 'Rum type, you know. Pride and prejudice. She's wanting help. She knows she needs it badly, but nothing's going to make her admit it.'

He paused opposite an open door. It was almost too dark now to make out anything in the room, but when we had passed it before, there had been enough light to reveal it as a men's dormitory.

'I'm going in to have a word with these chaps. See you later.'

I watched him stroll into the room and greet it collectively with a cheerful 'Wotcher, mates! 'Ow's it going?' and then made my own way back to the dining-hall.

The only light there came from three candles set close together on one table. Close beside them a girl peered exasperatedly at some mending.

'Hullo,' she said. 'Awful, isn't it? How on earth did they manage to do anything after dark in the old days?'

'Not such old days, either,' I told her. 'This is the future as well as the past – provided there's somebody to show us how to make candles.'

'I suppose so.' She raised her head, and regarded me. 'You came from London today?'

'Yes,' I admitted.

'It's bad there now?'

'It's finished,' I said.

'You must have seen some horrible sights there?' she suggested.

'I did,' I said, briefly. 'How long have you been here?'

She gave me the general picture of things without more encouragement.

Coker's raid on the University Building had netted all but half a dozen of the sighted. She and Miss Durrant had been two of those overlooked. During the following day Miss Durrant had taken somewhat ineffective charge. There had been no question of their leaving right away, since only one among them had ever attempted to drive a lorry. During that day and most of the next they had been in almost the same relationship to their party as I was to mine away in Hampstead. But during the later part of the second day, Michael Beadley and two others returned, and during the night a few more had straggled back. By noon the day after that they had drivers for a dozen vehicles. They had decided that it was more prudent to leave forthwith than to wait on the chance that others would come.

Tynsham Manor had been chosen as a tentative destination for little better reason than that it was known to the Colonel as a place which could offer the compact seclusion which was one of the qualities they sought.

It had been an ill-assorted party, with its leaders well aware of the fact. The day after their arrival there had been a meeting, smaller, but otherwise not unsimilar to that held earlier in the University Building. Michael and his section had announced that there was much to be done, and that it was not their intention to waste their energies in pacifying a group which was shot through with petty prejudice and squabbles. The whole business was too big for that, and time too pressing. Florence Durrant agreed. What had happened to the world was warning enough. How anyone could be so blindly ungrateful for the miracle that had preserved them as even to contemplate the per-petuation of the subversive theories which had been undermining the Christian faith for a century, she was unable to understand. For her part, she had no wish to live in a community where one section would be continually striving to pervert the simple faith of those who were not ashamed to show their gratitude to God by keeping His laws. She was no less able to see that the situation was serious. The proper course was to pay full heed to the warning God had given, and turn at once to His teaching.

The division of parties, though clear, left them very uneven. Miss Durrant had found her supporters to consist of five sighted girls, a dozen or so blind girls, a few middle-aged men and women, also blind, and no sighted males whatever. In the circumstances there could be no doubt whatever that the section which would have to move must be Michael Beadley's. With the lorries still loaded, there was little to delay them, and in the early afternoon they had driven away, leaving Miss Durrant and her followers to sink or swim by their principles.

Not until then had there been an opportunity to survey the poten-tialities of the Manor and its neighbourhood. The main part of the house had been closed, but in the servants' quarters they found traces of recent occupation. Investigation of the kitchen garden later gave a pretty clear picture of what had happened to those who had been looking after the place. The bodies of a man, a woman, and a girl lay close together there in a scatter of spilled fruit. Nearby a couple of triffids waited patiently with their roots dug in. Close to the model farm at the far end of the estate was a similar state of affairs. Whether the triffids had found their way into the park through some open gate, or some undocked specimens already there had broken free, was not clear, but they were a menace to be dealt with quickly before they could do more damage. Miss Durrant had sent off one sighted girl to make a circuit of the wall, closing every door or gate, and herself had broken into the gun-room. Despite inexperience, she and another young woman had succeeded in blowing the top off every triffid they could find, to the number of twenty-six. No more had been seen within the enclosure, and it was hoped that no more existed there.

The following day's investigation of the village had shown triffids about in considerable numbers. The surviving inhabitants were either those who had shut themselves into their houses to exist for as long as they could on what stores they had there, or those who had been lucky enough to encounter no triffids when they made brief foraging sorties. All who could be found had been collected and brought back to the Manor. They were healthy, and most of them were strong, but for the present at any rate, they were more of a burden than a help, for there was not one of them that could see.

Four more young women had arrived in the course of the day. Two had come driving a loaded lorry by turns, and bringing a blind girl with them. The other had been alone in a car. After a brief look round she had announced that she found the set-up lacking in appeal, and driven on. Of the several who continued to arrive over the next few days only two had stayed. All but two of the arrivals had been women. Most of the men, it seemed, had been more forthright and ruthless in extricating themselves from Coker's group formations, and most of them had returned in time to join the original party.

Of Josella the girl could tell me nothing. Clearly she had never heard the name before, and my attempts at description roused no recollections.

While we were still talking, the electric lights in the room suddenly went on. The girl looked up at them with the awed expression of one receiving a revelation. She blew out the candles, and as she went on with her mending she looked up at the bulbs occasionally as if to make certain they were still there.

A few minutes later Coker strolled in.

'That was you, I suppose?' I said, nodding at the lights.

'Yes,' he admitted. 'They've got their own plant here. We might as well use up the petrol as let it evaporate.'

'Do you mean to say we could have had lights all the time we've been here?' asked the girl.

'If you had just taken the trouble to start the engine,' Coker said, looking at her. 'If you wanted light, why didn't you try to start it?'

'I didn't know it was there, besides, I don't know anything about engines or electricity.'

Coker went on looking at her, thoughtfully.

'So you just went on sitting in the dark,' he remarked. 'And how long do you think you are likely to survive if you just go on sitting in the dark when things need doing?'

She was stung by his tone.

'It's not my fault if I'm not any good at things like that.'

'I'll differ there,' Coker told her. 'It's not only your fault – it's a self-created fault. Moreover, it's an affectation to consider yourself too spiritual to understand anything mechanical. It is a petty, and a very silly form of vanity. Everyone starts by knowing nothing about anything, but God gives him – and even her – brains to find out with. Failure to use them is not a virtue to be praised: even in women it is a gap to be deplored.'

She looked understandably annoyed. Coker himself had been looking annoyed from the time he came in. She said:

'That's all very well, but different people's minds work on different lines. Men understand how machines and electricity work. Women just aren't much interested in that kind of thing as a rule.'

'Don't hand me a mess of myth and affectation; I'm not taking it,' said Coker. 'You know perfectly well that women can and do – or rather did – handle the most complicated and delicate machines when they took the trouble to understand them. What generally happens is that they're too lazy to take the trouble unless they have to. Why should they bother when the tradition of appealing helplessness can be rationalized as a womanly virtue – and the job just shoved off on to somebody else? Ordinarily it's a pose that it's not worth anyone's while to debunk. In fact, it has been fostered. Men have played up to it by stoutly repairing the poor darling's vacuum cleaner, and capably replacing the blown fuse. The whole charade has been acceptable to both parties. Tough practicality complements spiritual delicacy and charming dependence – and *he* is the mug who gets *his* hands dirty.'

He lunged on, well started now:

'Hitherto we have been able to afford to amuse ourselves with that kind of mental laziness and parasitism. In spite of generations of talk about the equality of the sexes there has been much too great a vested interest in dependence for women to dream of dropping it. They have made a minimum of necessary modifications to changing conditions, but they have always been minimum – and grudged, at that.' He paused. 'You doubt that? Well, consider the fact that both the pert chit and the intellectual woman worked the higher-sensibility gag in their different ways – but when a war came and brought with it a social obligation and sanction both could be trained into competent engineers.'

'They weren't *good* engineers,' she remarked. 'Everybody says that.'

'Ah, the defensive mechanism in action. Let me point out that it was in nearly everybody's interest to say so. All the same,' he admitted, 'to some extent that was true. And why? Because nearly all of them not only had to learn hurriedly and without proper groundwork, but they had also to *unlearn* the habits carefully fostered for years of thinking such interests alien to them, and too gross for their delicate natures.'

'I don't see why you have to come and pitch on me with all this,' she said. 'I'm not the only one who didn't start the wretched engine.'

Coker grinned.

'You're quite right. It's unfair. It was simply finding the engine there ready to work and nobody doing a thing about it that started me off. Dumb futility gets me that way.'

'Then I think you might have said all that to Miss Durrant instead of to me.'

'Don't worry, I shall. But it isn't just her affair. It's yours – and everyone else's. I *mean* that, you know. Times have changed rather radically. You can't any longer say: "Oh, dear, I don't understand this kind of thing," and leave it to someone else to do for you. Nobody is going to be muddle-headed enough to confuse ignorance with innocence now – it's too important. Nor is ignorance going to be cute or funny any more. It is going to be dangerous, very dangerous. Unless all of us get around as soon as we can to understanding a lot of things in which we had no previous interest, neither we nor those who depend on us are going to get through this lot.'

'I don't see why you need to pour all your contempt for women on to me – just because of one dirty old engine,' she said, peevishly.

Coker raised his eyes.

'Great God! And here have I been explaining that women have *all* the capacities if they only take the trouble to use them.'

'You said we were parasites. That wasn't at all a nice thing to say.'

'I'm not trying to say nice things. And what I did say was that in the world that has vanished women had a vested interest in acting the part of parasites.'

'And all that just because I don't happen to know anything about a smelly, noisy engine.'

'Hell!' said Coker. 'Just drop that engine a minute, will you.'

'Then why——?'

'The engine just happened to be a symbol. The point is we'll all have to learn not simply what we like, but as much as we can about running a community and supporting it. The men can't just fill in a voting paper and hand the job to someone else. And it will no longer be considered that a woman has fulfilled all her social obligations when she has prevailed upon some man to support her and provide her with a niche where she can irresponsibly produce babies for somebody else to educate.'

'Well, I don't see what that has to do with engines...'

'Listen,' said Coker, patiently. 'If you have a baby, do you want him to grow up to be a savage, or a civilized man?'

'A civilized man, of course.'

'Well, then, you have to see to it that he has civilized surroundings to do it in. The standards he'll learn, he'll learn from us. We've all got to understand as much as we can, and live as intelligently as we can in order to give him the most we can. It's going to mean hard work and more thinking for all of us. Changed conditions must mean changed outlooks.'

The girl gathered up her mending. She regarded Coker critically for a few moments.

'With views like yours I should think you'd find Mr Beadley's party more congenial,' she said. 'Here we have no intention of changing our outlook – or of giving up our principles. That's why we separated from the other party. So if the ways of decent respectable people are not good enough for you, I should think you'd better go somewhere else.' And with a sound very like a sniff, she walked away.

Coker watched her leave. When the door closed he expressed his feelings with a fish-porter's fluency. I laughed.

'What did you expect?' I said. 'You prance in and address the girl as if she were a public meeting of delinquents – and responsible for the whole western social system, as well. And then you're surprised when she's huffed.'

'You'd expect her to see reason,' he muttered.

'I don't see why. Most of us don't – we see habit. She'll oppose any modification, reasonable or not, that conflicts with her previously trained feelings of what is right and polite – and be quite honestly convinced that she's showing steadfast strength of character. You're in too much of a hurry. Show a man the Elysian Fields when he's just lost his home, and he'll think mighty little of them: leave him there a bit, and he'll begin to think home was like them, only cosier. She'll adapt in time as she has to – and continue to deny with conviction that she's done so.'

'In other words, just improvise as necessary. Don't try to plan anything. That won't take us far.'

'That's where leadership comes in. The leader does the planning, but he's wise enough not to say so. As the changes become necessary, he slips them in as a concession – temporary, of course – to circumstances, but if he's good, he's slipping in the right bits for the ultimate shape. There are always overwhelming objections to any plan, but concessions have to be made to emergencies.'

'Sounds Machiavellian to me. I like to see what I'm aiming at, and go straight for it.'

'Most people don't, even though they'd protest that they do. They prefer to be coaxed or wheedled, or even driven. That way they never make a mistake: if there is one it's always due to something or somebody else. This going headlong for things is a mechanistic view, and people in general aren't machines. They have minds of their own – mostly peasant minds, at their easiest when they are in the familiar furrow.'

'It doesn't sound as if you'd bet much on Beadley's chance of making a go of it. He's all plan.'

'He'll have his troubles. But his party did choose. This lot is negative,' I pointed out. 'It is simply here on account of its resistance to any kind of plan.' I paused. Then I added: 'That girl was right about one thing, you know. You would be better off with his lot. Her reaction is a sample of what you'd get all round if you were to try to handle this lot your way. You can't drive a flock of sheep to market in a dead straight line, but there are ways of getting 'em there.'

'You're being unusually cynical, as well as metaphorical this evening,' Coker observed.

I objected to that.

'It isn't cynical to have noticed how a shepherd handles his sheep.'

'To regard human beings as sheep might be thought so by some.'

'But less cynical and much more rewarding than regarding them as a lot of chassis fitted for remote thought control.'

'H'm,' said Coker, 'I'll have to consider the implications of that.'

CHAPTER 11

... AND FURTHER ON

My next morning was desultory. I looked around, I lent a hand here and there, and asked a lot of questions.

It had been a wretched night. Until I lay down, I had not fully realized the extent to which I had counted on finding Josella at Tynsham. Weary though I was after the day's journey, I could not sleep;

I lay awake in the darkness feeling stranded and planless. So confidently had I assumed that she and the Beadley party would be there that there had been no reason to consider any scheme beyond joining them. It now came home to me for the first time that even if I did succeed in catching up with them I still might not find her. As she had only left Westminster district a short time before I arrived there in search of her, she must in any case have been well behind the main party. Obviously the thing to do was to make detailed enquiries regarding everyone who had arrived at Tynsham during the previous two days.

For the present I must assume that she had come this way. It was my only lead. And that meant assuming also that she had gone back to the University and had found the chalked address – whereas, it was quite on the cards that she had not gone there at all, but, sickened by the whole thing, had taken the quickest route out of the reeking place that London had become.

The thing I had to fight hardest against admitting was that she might have caught the disease, whatever it was, that had dissolved both our groups. I would not consider the possibility of that until I had to.

In the sleepless clarity of the small hours I made one discovery – it was that my desire to join the Beadley party was very secondary indeed to my wish to find Josella. If, when I did find them, she was not with them ... well, the next move would have to wait upon the moment, but it would not be resignation ...

Coker's bed was already empty when I awoke, and I decided to devote my morning chiefly to enquiries. One of the troubles was that it did not seem to have occurred to anyone to take note of the names of those who had found Tynsham uninviting, and had passed on. Josella's name meant nothing to anyone save those few who recollected it with disapproval. My description of her raised no memories that would stand detailed examination. Certainly there had been no girl in a navy-blue ski-suit – that I established, but then, I could by no means be certain that she would still be dressed in that way. My enquiries ended by making everyone very tired of me and increasing my frustration. There was a faint possibility that a girl who had come and gone a day before our arrival might have been she, but I could not feel it likely that Josella could have left so slight an impression on anyone's mind – even allowing for prejudice ...

Coker reappeared again at the midday meal. He had been engaged on an extensive survey of the premises. He had taken a tally of the livestock and the number of blind among it. Inspected the farm equipment and machinery. Found out about the source of pure water supplies. Looked into the stores of feed, both human and stock. Discovered how many of the blind girls had been afflicted before the catastrophe, and arranged classes of the others for them to train as best they could.

He had found most of the men plunged in gloom by a well-meant assurance from the vicar that there would be plenty of useful things for them to do such as – er – basket-making, and – er – weaving, and he had done his best to dispel it with more hopeful prospects. Encountering Miss Durrant, he had told her that unless it could somehow be contrived that the blind women should take part of the work off the shoulders of the sighted the whole thing would break down within ten days, and also, that if the vicar's prayer for more blind people to join them should happen to be granted the place would become entirely unworkable. He was embarking upon further observations, including the necessity for starting immediately to build up food reserves, and to begin the construction of devices which would enable blind men to do useful work, when she cut him short. He could see that she was a great deal more worried than she would admit, but the determination which had led her to sever relations with the other party caused her to blaze back at him unthankfully. She ended by letting him know that on her information neither he nor his views were likely to harmonize with the community.

'The trouble about that woman is that she means to be boss,' he said. 'It's constitutional – quite apart from the lofty principles.'

'Slanderous,' I said. 'What you mean is that her principles are so impeccable that everything is her responsibility – and so it becomes her duty to guide others.'

'Much the same thing,' he said.

'But it sounds a lot better,' I pointed out.

He was thoughtful for a moment.

'She's going to run this place into one hell of a mess unless she gets right down to the job of organizing it pretty quickly. Have you looked the outfit over?'

I shook my head. I told him how my morning had been spent.

'You don't seem to have got much change for it. So what?' he said.

'I'm going on after the Michael Beadley crowd,' I told him.

'And if she's not with them?'

'At present I'm just hoping she is. She must be. Where else would she be?'

He started to say something, and stopped. Then he went on:

'I reckon I'll come along with you. It's likely that crowd won't be any more glad to see me than this one, considering everything – but I can live that down. I've watched one lot fall to bits, and I can see this one's going to do the same – more slowly, and, maybe, more nastily. It's queer, isn't it? Decent intentions seem to be the most dangerous things around just now. It's a damned shame because this place *could* be managed, in spite of the proportion of blind. Everything it needs is lying about for the taking, and will be for a while yet. It's only organizing that's wanted.'

'And willingness to be organized,' I suggested.

'That, too,' he agreed. 'You know, the trouble is that in spite of all that's happened this thing hasn't got home to these people yet. They don't want to turn to – that'd be making it too final. At the back of their minds they're all camping out, hanging on, and waiting for something or other.'

'True – but scarcely surprising,' I admitted. 'It took plenty to convince us, and they've not seen what we have. And, somehow, it does seem less final and less – less immediate out here in the country.'

'Well they've got to start realizing it soon if they're going to get through,' Coker said, looking round the hall again. 'There's no miracle coming to save them.'

'Give 'em time. They'll come to it, as we did. You're always in such a hurry. Time's no longer money, you know.'

'Money isn't important any longer, but time is. They ought to be thinking about the harvest, rigging a mill to grind flour, seeing about winter feed for the stock.'

I shook my head.

'It's not as urgent as all that, Coker. There must be huge stocks of flour in the towns, and, by the look of things, mighty few of us to use it. We can live on capital for a long while yet. Surely the immediate job is to teach the blind *how* to work before they really have to get down to it.'

'All the same, unless something is done, the sighted ones here are going to crack up. It only needs that to happen to one or two of them, and the place'll be in a proper mess.'

I had to concede that.

.   .   .

Later in the afternoon I managed to find Miss Durrant. No one else seemed to know or care where Michael Beadley and his lot had gone, but I could not believe that they had not left behind some indications for those who might follow. Miss Durrant was not pleased. At first I thought she was going to refuse to tell me. It was not due solely to my implied preference for other company. The loss of even an uncongenial able-bodied man was serious in the circumstances. Nevertheless, she preferred not to show the weakness of asking me to stay. In the end she said curtly:

'They were intending to make for somewhere near Beaminster in Dorset. I can tell you no more than that.'

I went back and told Coker. He looked around him. Then he shook his head, though with a touch of regret.

'Okay,' he said. 'We'll check out of this dump tomorrow.'

'Spoken like a pioneer,' I told him. '– At least, more like a pioneer than an Englishman.'

. . .

Nine o'clock the next morning saw us already twelve miles or so on our road, and travelling as before in our two lorries. There had been a question whether we should not take a handier vehicle and leave the trucks for the benefit of the Tynsham people, but I was reluctant to abandon mine. I had personally collected the contents, and knew what was in it. Apart from the case of anti-triffid gear which Michael Beadley had so disapproved, I had given myself slightly wider scope on the last load, and there was a selection of things made with consideration of what might be difficult to find outside a large town; such things as a small lighting set, some pumps, cases of good tools. All these things would be available later for the taking, but there was going to be an interlude when it would be advisable to keep away from towns of any size. The Tynsham people had the means to fetch supplies from towns where there was no sign yet of the disease. A couple of loads would not make a great deal of difference to them either way, so, in the end, we went as we had come.

The weather still held good. On the higher ground there was still little taint in the fresh air, though most villages had become unpleasant. Rarely we saw a still figure lying in a field or by the roadside, but just as in London, the main instinct seemed to have been to hide away in shelter of some kind. Most of the villages showed empty streets, and the countryside around them was as deserted as if the whole human race and most of its animals had been spirited away. Until we came to Steeple Honey.

From our road we had a view of the whole of Steeple Honey as we descended the hill. It clustered at the further end of a stone bridge which arched across a small, sparkling river. It was a quiet little place centred round a sleepy-looking church, and stippled off at its edges with white-washed cottages. It did not look as if anything had occurred in a century or more to disturb the quiet life under its thatched roofs. But like other villages it was now without stir or smoke. And then, when we were half-way down the hill, a movement caught my eye.

On the left, at the far end of the bridge one house stood slightly aslant from the road so that it faced obliquely towards us. An inn sign hung from a bracket on its wall, and from the window immediately above that something white was being waved. As we came closer I could see the man who was leaning out and frantically flagging us with a towel. I judged that he must be blind, otherwise he would have come out into the road to intercept us. He was waving too vigorously for a sick man.

I signalled back to Coker, and pulled up as we cleared the bridge. The man at the window dropped his towel. He shouted something which I could not hear above the noise of the engines, and disappeared. We both switched off. It was so quiet that we could hear the clumping of the man's feet on the wooden stairs inside the house. The door opened, and he stepped out, holding both hands before him. Like lightning something whipped out of the hedge on his left, and struck him. He gave a single, high-pitched shout, and dropped where he stood.

I picked up my shotgun, and climbed out of the cab. I circled a little until I could make out the triffid skulking in the shadows of a bush. Then I blew the top off it.

Coker was out of his truck, too, and standing close beside me. He looked at the man on the ground, and then at the shorn triffid.

'It was – no, damn it, it can't have been *waiting* for him?' he said. 'It must just have happened ... It couldn't have *known* he'd come out of that door ... I mean, it *couldn't* – could it?'

'Or could it? It was a remarkably neat piece of work,' I said.

Coker turned uneasy eyes on me.

'Too damn neat. You don't really believe ...?'

'There's a kind of conspiracy not to believe things about triffids,' I said, and added: 'There might be more around here.'

We looked the adjacent cover over carefully, and drew blank.

'I could do with a drink,' suggested Coker.

But for the dust on the counter, the small bar of the inn looked normal. We poured a whisky each. Coker downed his in one. He turned a worried look on me.

'I didn't like that. Not at all, I didn't. You ought to know a lot more about these bloody things than most people, Bill. It wasn't – I mean, it must just have *happened* to be there, mustn't it?'

'I think——' I began. Then I stopped, listening to the staccato drumming outside. I walked over and opened the window. I let the already trimmed triffid have the other barrel, too; this time just above the bole. The drumming stopped.

'The trouble about triffids,' I said, as we poured another drink, 'is chiefly the things we don't know about them.' I told him one or two of Walter's theories. He started.

'You don't seriously suggest that they're "talking" when they make that rattling noise?'

'I've never made up my mind,' I admitted. 'I'll go so far as to say I'm sure it's a signal of some sort. But Walter considered it to be real "talk" – and he did know more about them than anyone else that I know.'

I ejected the two spent cartridge cases, and reloaded.

'And he actually mentioned their advantage over a blind man?'

'A number of years ago, that was,' I pointed out.

'Still – it's a funny coincidence.'

'Impulsive as ever,' I said. 'Pretty nearly any stroke of fate can be made to look like a funny coincidence if you try hard enough and wait long enough.'

We drank up, and turned to go. Coker glanced out of the window. Then he caught my arm, and pointed. Two triffids had swayed round the corner, and were making for the hedge which had been the hiding-place of the first. I waited until they paused, and then decapitated both of them. We left by the window, which was out of range of any triffid cover, and looked about us carefully as we approached the lorries.

'Another coincidence? Or were they coming to see what had happened to their pal?' asked Coker.

We cleared the village, running on along small, cross-country roads. There seemed to me to be more triffids about now than we had seen on our previous journey – or was it that I had been made more conscious of them? It might have been that in travelling hitherto chiefly by main roads we had encountered fewer. I knew from experience that they tended to avoid a hard surface, and thought that it perhaps caused them some discomfort in their limb-like roots. Now I began to be convinced that we *were* seeing more of them, and I started to get an idea that they were not entirely indifferent to us – though it was not possible to be sure whether those that we saw approaching across fields from time to time just happened to be coming in our direction.

A more decisive incident occurred when one slashed at me from the hedgerow as I passed. Luckily it was inexpert in its aim at a moving vehicle. It let fly a moment too soon, and left its print in little dots of poison across the windscreen. I was past before it could strike again. But thenceforth, in spite of the warmth, I drove with the nearside window closed.

During the past week or more I had given thought to the triffids only when I encountered them. Those I had seen at Josella's home had worried me as had the others that had attacked our group near Hampstead Heath, but most of the time there had been more immediate things to worry about. But, looking back now over our trip, the state of things at Tynsham before Miss Durrant had taken steps to clear it up with shotguns, and the condition of the villages we had passed through, I began to wonder just how big a part the triffids might have been playing in the disappearance of the inhabitants.

In the next village I drove slowly, and looked carefully. In several of the front gardens I could see bodies lying as they had evidently lain for some days – and almost always there was a triffid discernible close by. It looked as if the triffids only ambushed in places where there was soft earth for them to dig their roots into while they waited. One seldom saw a body, and never a triffid in those parts where the house-doors opened straight into the street.

At a guess I would say that what had happened in most of the villages was that inhabitants emerging for food moved in comparative safety while they were in paved areas, but the moment they left them, or even passed close to a garden wall or fence, they stood in danger of the stings slashing out at them. Some would cry out as they were struck, and when they did not come back those who remained would grow more afraid. Now and then another would be driven out by hunger. A few might be lucky enough to get back, but most would lose themselves and wander on until they dropped, or came within range of a triffid. Those who were left might, perhaps, guess what was happening. Where there was a garden they might have heard the swish of the sting, and known that they faced the alternatives of starvation in the house or the same fate that had overtaken the others who had left it. Many would remain there, living on what food they had while they waited for help that was never going to come. Something like that must have been the predicament of the man in the inn at Steeple Honey.

The likelihood that in the other villages we were passing through there might still be houses in which isolated groups had managed to keep going was not a pleasant thought. It raised again the same kind of question that we had faced in London – the feeling that one should, by all civilized standards, try to find them and do something for them; and the frustrating knowledge of the frittering decline which would overtake any such attempt as it had before.

The same old question. What could one do, with the best will in the world, but prolong the anguish? Placate one's conscience for a while again, just to see the result of the effort wasted once more.

It was not, I had to tell myself firmly, any good at all going into an earthquake area while the buildings were still falling – the rescue and the salvage had to be done when the tremors had stopped. But reason did not make it easy. The old doctor had been only too right when he stressed the difficulties of mental adaptation...

. . .

The triffids were a complication on an unexpected scale. There were, of course, very many nurseries beside our own company's plantations. They raised them for us, for private buyers, or for sale to a number of lesser trades where their derivatives were used, and the majority of them were, for climatic reasons, situated in the south. Nevertheless, if what we had already seen was a fair sample of the way they had broken loose and distributed themselves they must have been far more numerous than I had supposed. The prospect of more of them reaching maturity every day and of the docked specimens steadily regrowing their stings was far from reassuring...

With only two more stops, one for food and the other for fuel, we made good time, and ran into Beaminster about half past four in the afternoon. We had come right into the centre of the town without having seen a sign to suggest the presence of the Beadley party.

At first glimpse the place was as void of life as any other we had seen that day. The main shopping street we entered was bare and empty save for a couple of lorries drawn up on one side. I had led the way down it for perhaps twenty yards when a man stepped out from behind one of the lorries, and levelled a rifle. He fired deliberately over my head, and then lowered his aim.

CHAPTER 12

DEAD END

That's the kind of warning I don't debate about. I pulled up.

The man was large and fair-haired. He handled his rifle with familiarity. Without taking it out of the aim, he jerked his head twice sideways. I accepted that as a sign to climb down. When I had done so, I displayed my empty hands. Another man, accompanied by a girl, emerged from behind the stationary lorry as I approached it. Coker's voice called from behind me:

'Better put up that rifle, chum. You're all in the open.'

The fair man's eyes left mine to search for Coker. I could have jumped him right then if I'd wanted to, but I said:

'He's right. Anyway, we're peaceful.'

The man lowered his rifle, not quite convinced. Coker emerged from the cover of my lorry which had hidden his exit from his own.

'What's the big idea? Dog eat dog?' he enquired.

'Only two of you?' the second man asked.

Coker looked at him.

'What would you be expecting? A convention? Yes, just two of us.'

The trio visibly relaxed. The fair man explained:

'We thought you might be a gang from a city. We've been expecting them here raiding for food.'

'Oh,' said Coker. 'From which we assume that you've not taken a look at any city lately. If that's your only worry, you might as well forget it. What gangs there are, are more likely to be working the other way round – at present. In fact, doing – if I may say so – just what you are.'

'You don't think they'll come?'

'I'm darned sure they won't.' He regarded the three. 'Do you belong to Beadley's lot?' he asked.

The response was convincingly blank.

'Pity,' said Coker. 'That'd have been our first real stroke of luck in quite a time.'

'What is or are Beadley's lot?' enquired the fair man.

I was feeling wilted and dry after some hours in the driving cab with the sun on it. I suggested that we might remove discussion from the middle of the street to some more congenial spot. We passed round their vans through a familiar litter of cases of biscuits, chests of tea, sides of bacon, sacks of sugar, blocks of salt, and all the rest of it to a small bar-parlour next door. Over pint pots Coker and I gave them a short résumé of what we'd done and what we knew. Then it was their turn.

They were, it seemed, the more active half of a party of six – the other two women and a man being stationed at the house they had taken over for a base.

Around the noon of Tuesday, May 7th, the fair-haired man and the girl with him had been travelling westwards in his car. They had been on their way to spend a two weeks' holiday in Cornwall, and making pretty good time until a double-decker bus emerged from a turning somewhere near Crewkerne. The car had made contact with it in a decisive way, and the last thing the fair-haired young man remembered was a horrified glimpse of the bus looking as tall as a cliff, and heeling over right above them.

He had wakened up in bed to find, much as I had, a mysterious silence all about him. Apart from soreness, a few cuts, and a thumping head, there didn't appear to be a lot wrong with him. When, as he said, nobody kept on coming, he had investigated the place, and found it to be a small cottage-hospital. In one ward he had found the girl and two other women, one of whom was conscious, but incapacitated by a leg and an arm in plaster. In another were two men – one of them his present companion, the other suffering from a broken leg, also in plaster.

Altogether there had been eleven people in the place, eight of whom were sighted. Of the blind, two were bedridden and seriously ill. Of the staff there was no sign at all. His experience had been, to begin with, more baffling than mine. They had stayed in the little hospital, doing what they could for the helpless, wondering what went on, and hoping that someone would show up to help. They had no idea what was wrong with the two blind patients nor how to treat them. They could do nothing but feed and try to ease them. Both had died the next day. One man disappeared, and no one had seen him go. Those who were there for injuries suffered when the bus had overturned were local people. Once they were sufficiently recovered, they set out to find relatives. The party had dwindled down to six, two of whom had broken limbs.

By now they had realized that the breakdown was big enough to mean that they must fend for themselves for a time at least, but they were still far from grasping its full extent. They decided to leave the hospital and find some more convenient place, for they imagined that many more sighted people would exist in the cities and that the disorganization would have brought mob rule. Daily they were expecting the arrival of these mobs when the food stores in the towns should be finished, and had pictured them moving like a locust army across the countryside. Their chief concern, therefore, had been to gather supplies in preparation for a siege.

With our assurances that that was the least likely thing to happen, they looked at one another a little bleakly.

They were an oddly assorted trio. The fair-haired man turned out to be a member of the Stock Exchange by the name of Stephen Brennell. His companion was a good-looking, well-built girl with an occasional superficial petulance, but no real surprise over whatever life might hand her next. She had led one of those fringe careers – modelling dresses, selling them, putting in movie-extra work, missing opportunities of going to Hollywood, hostessing for obscure clubs, and helping out these activities by such other means as offered themselves – the intended holiday in Cornwall being apparently one such. She had an utterly unshakeable conviction that nothing serious could have happened to America, and that it was only a matter of holding out for a while until the Americans arrived to put everything in order. She was quite the least troubled person I had encountered since the catastrophe took place. Though just occasionally she pined a little for the bright lights which she hoped the Americans would hurry up and restore.

The third member, the dark young man, nursed a grudge. He had worked hard and saved hard in order to start his small radio store, and he had ambitions. 'Look at Ford,' he told us, 'and look at Lord Nuffield

– he started with a bike shop no bigger than my radio store, and see where he got to! That's the kind of thing I was going to do. And now look at the damned mess things are in! It ain't fair!' Fate, as he saw it, didn't want any more Fords and Nuffields – but he didn't intend to take that lying down. This was only an interval sent to try him – one day would see him back in his radio store with his foot set firmly on the first rung to millionairedom.

The most disappointing thing about them was to find that they knew nothing of the Michael Beadley party. Indeed, the only group they had encountered was in a village just over the Devon border where a couple of men with shotguns had advised them not to come that way again. Those men, they said, were obviously local. Coker suggested that that meant a small group.

'If they had belonged to a large one they'd have shown less nervousness and more curiosity,' he maintained. 'But if the Beadley lot are round here, we ought to be able to find them somehow.' He put it to the fair man: 'Look here, suppose we come along with you? We can do our whack, and when we do find them it will make things easier for all of us.'

The three of them looked questioningly at one another, and then nodded.

'All right. Give us a hand with the loading, and we'll be getting along,' the man agreed.

. . .

By the look of Charcott Old House it had once been a fortified manor. Refortification was now under way. At some time in the past the encircling moat had been drained. Stephen, however, was of the opinion that he had successfully ruined the drainage system so that it would fill up again by degrees. It was his plan to blow up such parts as had been filled in, and thus complete the re-encirclement. Our news, suggesting that this might not be necessary, induced a slight wistfulness in him, and a look of disappointment. The stone walls of the house were thick. At least three of the windows in the front displayed machine guns, and he pointed out two more mounted on the roof. Inside the main door was stacked a small arsenal of mortars and bombs, and, as he proudly showed us, several flame-throwers.

'We found an arms depot,' he explained, 'and spent a day getting this lot together.'

As I looked over the stuff I realized for the first time that the catastrophe by its very thoroughness had been more merciful than the things that would have followed a slightly lesser disaster. Had ten or fifteen per cent of the population remained unharmed it was very likely that little communities like this would indeed have found themselves fighting off starving gangs in order to preserve their own lives. As things were, however, Stephen had probably made his warlike preparations in vain. But there was one appliance that could be put to good use. I pointed to the flame-throwers.

'Those might be handy for triffids,' I said.

He grinned.

'You're right. Very effective. The one thing we've used them for. And incidentally the one thing I know that really makes a triffid beat it. You can go on firing at them until they're shot to bits, and they don't budge. I suppose they don't know where the destruction's coming from. But one warm lick from this, and they're plunging off fit to bust themselves.'

'Have you had a lot of trouble with them?' I asked.

It seemed that they had not. From time to time one, perhaps two or three would approach, and be scorched away. On their expeditions they had had several lucky escapes, but usually they were out of their vehicles only in built-up areas where there was little likelihood of prowling triffids.

. . .

That night after dark we all went up to the roof. It was too early for the moon. We looked out upon an utterly black landscape. Search it as we would, not one of us was able to discover the least pinpoint of a tell-tale light. Nor could any of the party recall ever having seen a trace of smoke by day. I was feeling depressed when we descended again to the lamplit living-room.

'There's only one thing for it, then,' Coker said. 'We'll have to divide the district up into areas, and search them.'

But he did not say it with conviction. I suspected that he was thinking it likely, as I was, that the Beadley party would continue to show a deliberate light by night, and some other sign – probably a smoke column – by day.

However, no one had any better suggestion to make, so we got down to the business of dividing the map up into sections, doing our best to contrive that each should include some high ground to give an extensive view beyond it.

The following day we went into the town in a lorry, and from there dispersed in smaller cars for the search.

That was, without a doubt, the most melancholy day I had spent since I had wandered about Westminster searching for traces of Josella there.

Just at first it wasn't too bad. There was the open road in the sunlight, the fresh green of early summer. There were signposts which pointed to 'Exeter and The West', and other places as if they still pursued their habitual lives. There were sometimes, though rarely, birds to be seen. And there were wild flowers beside the lanes, looking as they had always looked.

But the other side of the picture was not so good. There were fields in which cattle lay dead or wandered blindly, and untended cows lowed in pain; where sheep in their easy discouragement had stood resignedly to die rather than pull themselves free from bramble or barbed wire, and other sheep grazed erratically, or starved with looks of reproach in their blind eyes.

Farms were becoming unpleasant places to pass closely. For safety's sake I was giving myself only an inch of ventilation at the top of the window, but I closed even that whenever I saw a farm beside the road ahead.

Triffids were at large. Sometimes I saw them crossing fields or noticed them inactive against hedges. In more than one farmyard they had found the middens to their liking and enthroned themselves there while they waited for the dead stock to attain the right stage of putrescence. I saw them now with a disgust that they had never roused in me before. Horrible alien things which some of us had somehow created and which the rest of us in our careless greed had cultured all over the world. One could not even blame nature for them. Somehow they had been bred – just as we bred ourselves beautiful flowers, or grotesque parodies of dogs ... I began to loathe them now for more than their carrion-eating habits – they, more than anything else, seemed able to profit and flourish on our disaster ...

As my day went on, my sense of loneliness grew. On any hill or rise I stopped to examine the country as far as fieldglasses would show me. Once I saw smoke and went to the source to find a small railway train burnt out on the line – I still do not know how that could be, for there was no one near it. Another time a flag upon a staff sent me hurrying to a house to find it silent – though not empty. Yet another time a white flutter of movement on a distant hillside caught my eye, but when I turned the glasses on it I found it to be half a dozen sheep milling in panic while a triffid struck continually and ineffectively across their woolly backs. Nowhere could I see a sign of living human beings.

When I stopped for food I did not linger longer than I needed. I ate it quickly, listening to a silence that was beginning to get on my nerves, and anxious to be on my way again with at least the sound of the car for company.

One began to fancy things. Once I saw an arm waving from a window, but when I got there it was only a branch swaying in front of the window. I saw a man stop in the middle of a field and turn to watch me go by; but the glasses showed me that he couldn't have stopped or turned: he was a scarecrow. I heard voices calling to me, just discernible above the engine noise; I stopped and switched off. There were no voices, nothing; but far, far away, the plaint of an unmilked cow.

It came to me that here and there, dotted about the country, there must be men and women who were believing themselves to be utterly alone, sole survivors. I felt as sorry for them as for anyone else in the disaster.

During the afternoon, with lowered spirits and little hope, I kept doggedly on quartering my section of the map because I dared not risk failing to make my inner certainty sure. At last, however, I satisfied myself that if any sizeable party did exist in the area I had been allotted it was deliberately hiding. It had not been possible for me to cover every lane and by-road, but I was willing to swear that the sound of my by no means feeble horn had been heard in every acre of my sector. I finished up, and drove back to the place where we had parked the lorry, in the gloomiest mood I had yet known. I found that none of the others had shown up yet, so to pass the time, and because I needed it to keep out the spiritual cold, I turned into the nearby pub and poured myself a good brandy.

Stephen was the next. The expedition seemed to have affected him much as it had me, for he shook his head in answer to my questioning look, and made straight for the bottle I had opened. Ten minutes later the radio-ambitionist joined us. He brought with him a dishevelled, wild-eyed young man who appeared not to have washed or shaved for several weeks. This person had been on the road; it was, it seemed, his only profession. One evening, he could not say for certain of what day, he had found a fine comfortable barn in which to spend the night. Having done somewhat more than his usual quota of miles that day he had fallen asleep almost as soon as he lay down. The next morning he had awakened in a nightmare, and he still seemed a little uncertain whether it was the world or himself that was crazy. We reckoned he was, a little, anyway, but he still retained a clear knowledge of the use of beer.

Another half hour or so passed, and then Coker arrived. He was accompanied by an Alsatian puppy and an unbelievable old lady. She was dressed in what was obviously her best. Her cleanliness and precision were as notable as were the lack of them in our other recruit. She paused with a genteel hesitation on the threshold of the bar parlour. Coker performed the introduction.

'This is Mrs Forcett, sole proprietor of Forcett's Universal Stores, in a collection of about ten cottages, two pubs, and a church, known as Chippington Durney – and Mrs Forcett can cook. Boy, can she cook!'

Mrs Forcett acknowledged us with dignity, advanced with confidence, seated herself with circumspection, and consented to be pressed to a glass of port, followed by another glass of port.

In answer to our questions she confessed to sleeping with unusual soundness during the fatal evening and the night that followed. Into the precise cause of this she did not enter, and we did not enquire. She had continued to sleep, since nothing had occurred to awaken her, through half the following day. When she awoke she was feeling unwell, and so did not attempt to get up until mid-afternoon. It had seemed to her curious but providential that no one had required her in the shop. When she did get up and go to the door she had seen 'one of them horrid triffid things' standing in her garden, and a man lying on the path just outside her gate – at least, she could see his legs. She had been about to go out to him when she had seen the triffid stir, and she had slammed the door to just in time. It had clearly been a nasty moment for her, and the recollection of it agitated her into pouring herself a third glass of port.

After that, she had settled down to wait until someone should come to remove both the triffid and the man. They seemed a strangely long time in coming, but she had been able to live comfortably enough upon the contents of her shop. She had still been waiting, she explained as she poured herself a fourth glass of port with a nice absentmindedness, when Coker, interested by the smoke from her fire, had shot the top off the triffid, and investigated.

She had given Coker a meal, and he in return had given her advice. It had not been easy to make her understand the true state of things. In the end he had suggested that she should take a look up the village, keeping a wary eye for triffids, and that he would be back at five o'clock to see how she felt about it. He had returned to find her dressed up, her bag packed, and herself quite ready to leave.

Back in Charcott Old House that evening we gathered again around the map. Coker started to mark out new areas of search. We watched him without enthusiasm. It was Stephen who said what all of us, including, I think, Coker himself, were thinking:

'Look here, we've been over all the ground for a circle of some fifteen miles between us. It's clear they aren't in the immediate neighbourhood. Either your information is wrong, or they decided not to stop here, and went on. In my view it would be a waste of time to go on searching the way we did today.'

Coker laid down the compasses he was using.

'Then what do you suggest?'

'Well, it seems to me we could cover a lot of the district pretty quickly from the air, and well enough. You can bet your life that anyone who hears an aircraft engine is going to turn out and make a sign of some kind.'

Coker shook his head. 'Now, why didn't we think of that before. It ought to be a helicopter, of course – but where do we get one, and who's going to fly it?'

'Oh, I can make one of them things go all right,' said the radio man, confidently.

There was something in his tone.

'Have you ever flown one?' asked Coker.

'No,' admitted the radio man, 'but I reckon there'd not be a lot to it, once you got the knack.'

'H'm,' said Coker, looking at him with reserve.

Stephen recalled the locations of two R.A.F. stations not far away, and that there had been an air-taxi business operating from Yeovil.

. . .

In spite of our doubts the radio man was as good as his word. He seemed to have complete confidence that his instinct for mechanism would not let him down. After practising for half an hour he took the helicopter off, and flew it back to Charcott.

For four days the machine hovered around in widening circles. On two of them Coker observed, on the other two I replaced him. In all, we discovered ten little groups of people. None of them knew anything of the Beadley party, and none of them contained Josella. As we found each lot we landed. Usually they were in twos and threes. The largest was seven. They would greet us in hopeful excitement, but soon, when they found that we represented only a group similar to their own, and were not the spearhead of a rescue party on the grand scale their interest would lapse. We could offer them little that they had not got already. Some of them became irrationally abusive and threatening in their disappointment, but most simply dropped back into despondency. As a rule they showed little wish to join up with other parties, and were inclined rather to lay hands on what they could, building themselves into refugees as comfortably as possible while they waited for the arrival of the Americans who were bound to find a way. There seemed to be a widespread and fixed idea about this. Our suggestions that any surviving Americans would be likely to have their hands more than full at home was received as so much wet-blanketry. The Americans, they assured us, would never have allowed such a thing to happen in their country. Nevertheless, and in spite of this Micawber fixation on American fairy godmothers, we left each party with a map showing them the approximate positions of groups we had already discovered in case they should change their minds, and think about getting together for self-help.

As a task, the flights were far from enjoyable, but at least they were to be preferred to lonely scouting on the ground. However, at the end of the fruitless fourth day it was decided to abandon the search.

At least, that was what the rest of them decided. I did not feel the same way about it. My quest was personal, theirs was not. Whoever they found, now or eventually, would be strangers to them. I was searching for Beadley's party as a means, not an end in itself. If I should find them and discover that Josella was not with them, then I should go on searching. But I could not expect the rest to devote any more time to searching purely on my behalf.

Curiously I realized that in all this I had met no other person who was searching for someone else. Every one of them had been, save for the accident of Stephen and his girl friend, snapped clean away from friends or relatives to link him with the past, and was beginning a new life with people who were strangers. Only I, as far as I could see, had promptly formed a new link – and that so briefly that I had scarcely been aware how important it was to me at the time...

Once the decision to abandon the search had been taken, Coker said:

'All right. Then that brings us to thinking about what we are going to do for ourselves.'

'Which means laying in stores against the winter, and just going on as we are. What else should we do?' asked Stephen.

'I've been thinking about that,' Coker told him. 'Maybe it'd be all right for a while – but what happens afterwards?'

'If we do run short of stocks, well, there's plenty more lying around,' said the radio man.

'The Americans will be here before Christmas,' said Stephen's girl friend.

'Listen,' Coker told her patiently. 'Just put the Americans in the jam-tomorrow-pie-in-the-sky department awhile, will you. Try to imagine a world in which there aren't any Americans – can you do that?'

The girl stared at him.

'But there must be,' she said.

Coker sighed sadly. He turned his attention to the radio man.

'There won't always be those stores. The way I see it, we've been given a flying start in a new kind of world. We're endowed with a capital of enough of everything to begin with, but that isn't going to last for ever. We couldn't eat up all the stuff that's there for the taking, not in generations – if it would keep. But it isn't going to keep. A lot of it is going to go bad pretty rapidly. And not only food. Everything is going, more slowly, but quite surely, to drop in pieces. If we want fresh stuff to eat next year we shall have to grow it ourselves, and it may seem a long way off now, but there's going to come a time when we shall have to grow everything ourselves. There'll come a time, too, when all the tractors are worn out or rusted, and there's no more petrol to run them, anyway – when we'll come right down to nature and bless horses – if we've got 'em.

'This is a pause – just a heaven-sent pause – while we get over the first shock and start to collect ourselves, but it's no more than a pause. Later, we'll have to plough, still later we'll have to learn how to make plough-shares, later than that we'll have to learn how to smelt iron to make the shares. What we are on now is a road that will take us back and back and back until we can – *if* we can – make good all that we wear out. Not until then shall we be able to stop ourselves on the trail that's leading down to savagery. But once we can do that, then maybe we'll begin to crawl slowly up again.'

He looked round the circle to see if we were following him.

'We *can* do that – if we will. The most valuable part of our flying start is knowledge. That's the short cut to save us starting where our ancestors did. We've got it all there in books if we take the trouble to find out about it.'

The rest were looking at Coker curiously. It was the first time they had heard him in one of his oratorical moods.

'Now,' he went on, 'from my reading of history, the thing you have to have to use knowledge is leisure. Where *everybody* has to work hard just to get a living and there is no leisure to think, knowledge stagnates, and people with it. The thinking has to be done largely by people who are not directly productive – by people who appear to be living almost entirely on the work of others, but are, in fact, a long-term investment. Learning grew up in the cities and in great institutions – it was the labour of the countryside that supported them. Do you agree with that?'

Stephen knitted his brows.

'More or less – but I don't see what you're getting at.'

'It's this – the economic size. A community of our present size cannot hope to do more than exist and decline. If we stay here as we are, just ten of us now, the end is, quite inevitably, a gradual and useless fade-out. If there are children we shall be able to spare only enough time from our labour to give them just a rudimentary education; one generation further, and we shall have savages or clods. To hold our own, to make any use at all of the knowledge in the libraries we must have the teacher, the doctor, and the leader, and we must be able to support them while they help us.'

'Well?' said Stephen, after a pause.

'I've been thinking of that place Bill and I saw at Tynsham. We've told you about it. The woman who is trying to run it wanted help, and she wanted it badly. She has about fifty, or sixty people on her hands, and a dozen or so of them able to see. That way she can't do it. She knows she can't – but she wasn't going to admit it to us. She wasn't going to put herself in our debt by asking us to stay. But she'd be very glad if we were to go back there after all, and ask to be admitted.'

'Good Lord,' I said. 'You don't think she deliberately put us on the wrong track?'

'I don't know. I may be doing her an injustice, but it is an odd thing that we've not seen or heard a single sign of Beadley and Co., isn't it? Anyhow, whether she meant it or not, that's the way it works, because I've decided to go back there. If you want my reasons, here they are – the two main ones. First, unless that place is taken in hand it's going to crash, which would be a waste and a shame for all those people there. The other is that it is much better situated than this. It has a farm which should not take a lot of putting in order; it is practically self-contained, but could be extended if necessary. This place would cost a lot more labour to start and to work.

'More important, it is big enough to afford time for teaching – teaching both the present blind there, and the sighted children they'll have later on. I believe it can be done, and I'll do my best to do it – and if the haughty Miss Durrant can't take it, she can go jump in the river.

'Now the point is this, I *think* I could do it as it stands – but I *know* that if the lot of us were to go we could get the place reorganized and running in a few weeks. Then we'd be living in a community that's going to grow and make a damned good attempt to hold its own. The alternative is to stay in a small party which is going to decline and get more desperately lonely as time goes on. So, how about it?'

There was some debate and enquiry for details, but not much doubt. Those of us who had been out on the search had a glimpse of the awful loneliness that might come. No one was attached to the present house. It had been chosen for its defensible qualities, and had little more to commend it. Most of them could feel the oppression of isolation growing round them already. The thought of wider and more varied company was in itself attractive. The end of an hour found the discussion dealing with questions of transport and details of the removal, and the decision to adopt Coker's suggestion had more or less made itself. Only Stephen's girl friend was doubtful.

'This place Tynsham – it's pretty much off the map?' she asked, uneasily.

'Don't you worry,' Coker reassured her. 'It's marked on all the best American maps.'

. . .

It was some time in the early hours of the following morning that I knew I was not going to Tynsham with the rest. Later, perhaps I would, but not yet...

My first inclination had been to accompany them if only for the purpose of choking the truth out of Miss Durrant regarding the Beadley party's destination. But then I had to make again the disturbing admission that I did not know that Josella was with them – and, indeed, that all the information I had been able to collect so far suggested that she was not. She had pretty certainly not passed through Tynsham. But if she had not gone in search of them, then where had she gone? It was scarcely likely that there had been a second direction in the University Building, one that I had missed...

And then, as if it had been a flash of light, I recalled the discussion we had had in our commandeered flat. I could see her sitting there in her blue party frock, with the light of the candles catching the diamonds as we talked ... 'What about the Sussex Downs? – I know a lovely old farmhouse on the north side ...' And then I knew what I must do ...

I told Coker about it in the morning. He was sympathetic, but obviously anxious not to raise my hopes too much.

'Okay. You do as you think best,' he agreed. 'I hope – well, anyway, you'll know where we are, and you can both come on to Tynsham and help to put that woman through the hoop until she sees sense.'

That morning the weather broke. The rain was falling in sheets as I climbed once more into the familiar lorry. Yet I was feeling elated and hopeful; it could have rained ten times harder without depressing me or altering my plan. Coker came out to see me off. I knew why he made a point of it, for I was aware without his telling me that the memory of his first rash plan and its consequences troubled him. He stood beside the cab with his hair flattened and the water trickling down his neck, and held up his hand.

'Take it easy, Bill. There aren't any ambulances these days, and she'll prefer you to arrive all in one piece. Good luck – and my apologies for everything to the lady when you find her.'

The word was 'when', but the tone was 'if'.

I wished them well at Tynsham. Then I let in the clutch and splashed away down the muddy drive.

CHAPTER 13

JOURNEY IN HOPE

The morning was infected with minor mishaps. First it was water in the carburettor. Then I contrived to travel a dozen miles north under the impression I was going east, and before I had that fully rectified I was in trouble with the ignition system on a bleak upland road miles from anywhere. Either these delays or a natural reaction did a lot to spoil the hopeful mood in which I had started. By the time I had the trouble straightened out it was one o'clock, and the day had cleared up.

The sun came out. Everything looked bright and refreshed, but even that, and the fact that for the next twenty miles all went smoothly, did not shift the mood of depression that was closing over me again. Now I was really on my own I could not shut out the sense of loneliness. It came upon me again as it had on that day when we had split up to search for Michael Beadley – only with double the force ... Until then I had always thought of loneliness as something negative – an absence of company, and, of course, something temporary ... That day I had learned that it was much more. It was something which could press and oppress, could distort the ordinary, and play tricks with the mind. Something which lurked inimically all around, stretching the nerves and twanging them with alarms, never letting one forget that there was no one to help, no one to care. It showed one as an atom adrift in vastness, and it waited all the time its chance to frighten and frighten horribly – that was what loneliness was really trying to do; and that was what one must never let it do ...

To deprive a gregarious creature of companionship is to maim it, to outrage its nature. The prisoner and the cenobite are aware that the herd exists beyond their exile; they are an aspect of it. But when the herd no longer exists there is, for the herd creature, no longer entity. He is a part of no whole; a freak without a place. If he cannot hold on to his reason, then he is lost indeed; most utterly, most fearfully lost, so that he becomes no more than the twitch in the limb of a corpse.

It needed far more resistance now than it had done before. Only the strength of my hope that I would find companionship at my journey's end kept me from turning back to find relief from the strain in the presence of Coker and the others.

The sights which I saw by the way had little or nothing to do with it.

Horrible though some of them were, I was hardened to such things by now. The horror had left them just as the horror which broods over great battlefields fades into history. Nor did I any longer see these things as part of a vast, impressive tragedy. My struggle was all a personal conflict with the instincts of my kind. A continual defensive action, with no victory possible. I knew in my very heart that I would not be able to sustain myself for long alone.

To give myself occupation I drove faster than I should. In some small town with a forgotten name I rounded a corner and ran straight into a van which blocked the whole street. Luckily my own tough lorry suffered no more than scratches, but the two vehicles managed to hitch themselves together with diabolical ingenuity so that it was an awkward business singlehanded, and in a confined space, to separate them. It was a problem which took me a full hour to solve, and did me good by turning my mind to practical matters.

After that I kept to a more cautious pace except for a few minutes soon after I entered the New Forest. The cause of that was a glimpse through the trees of a helicopter cruising at no great height. It was set to cross my course some way ahead. By ill luck the trees there grew closer to the sides of the road, and must have hidden it almost completely from the air. I put on a spurt, but by the time I reached more open ground the machine was no more than a speck floating away in the distance to the north. Nevertheless, even the sight of it seemed to give me some support.

A few miles further on I ran through a small village which was disposed neatly about a triangular green. At first sight it was as charming in its mixture of thatched and red-tiled cottages with their flowering gardens as something out of a picture-book. But I did not look too closely into the gardens as I passed; too many of them showed the alien shape of a triffid towering incongruously among the flowers. I was almost clear of the place when a small figure bounded out of one of the last garden gates and came running up the road towards me, waving both arms. I pulled up, looking around for triffids in a way that was becoming instinctive, picked up my gun, and climbed down.

The child was dressed in a blue cotton frock, white socks, and sandals. She looked about nine or ten years old. A pretty little girl – I could see that even though her dark brown curls were now uncared for, and her face dirtied with smeared tears. She pulled at my sleeve.

'Please, please,' she said, urgently, 'please come and see what's happened to Tommy.'

I stood staring down at her. The awful loneliness of the day lifted. My mind seemed to break out of the case I had made for it. I wanted to pick her up and hold her to me. I could feel tears close behind my eyes. I held out my hand to her, and she took it. Together we walked back to the gate through which she had gone.

'Tommy's there,' she said, pointing.

A little boy about four years of age lay on the diminutive patch of lawn between the flower-beds. It was quite obvious at a glance why he was there.

'The *thing* hit him,' she said. 'It hit him and he fell down. And it wanted to hit me when I tried to help him. Horrible *thing!*'

I looked up and saw the top of a triffid rising above the fence that bordered the garden.

'Put your hands over your ears. I'm going to make a bang,' I said.

She did so, and I blasted the top off the triffid.

'Horrible *thing*,' she repeated. 'Is it dead now?'

I was about to assure her that it was when it began to rattle the little sticks against its stem, just as the one at Steeple Honey had done. As then, I gave it the other barrel to shut it up.

'Yes,' I said. 'It's dead now.'

We walked across to the little boy. The scarlet slash of the sting was vivid on his pale cheek. It must have happened some hours before. She knelt beside him.

'It isn't any good,' I told her, gently.

She looked up, fresh tears in her eyes.

'Is Tommy dead, too?'

I squatted down beside her, and shook my head.

'I'm afraid he is.'

After a while she said:

'Poor Tommy! Will we bury him – like the puppies?'

'Yes,' I told her.

In all the overwhelming disaster that was the only grave I dug – and it was a very small one. She gathered a little bunch of flowers, and laid them on top of it. Then we drove away.

.   .   .

Susan was her name. A long time ago, as it seemed to her, something had happened to her father and mother so that they could not see. Her father had gone out to try to get some help, and he had not come back. Her mother went out later, giving the children strict instructions not to leave the house. She had come back crying. The next day she went out again: this time she did not come back. The children had eaten what they could find, and then began to grow hungry. At last Susan was hungry enough to disobey instructions and seek help from Mrs Walton at the shop. The shop itself was open, but Mrs Walton was not there. No one came when Susan called, so she had decided to take some cakes and biscuits and sweets, and tell Mrs Walton about it later.

She had seen some of the *things* about as she came back. One of them had struck at her, but it had misjudged her height, and the sting had passed over her head. It frightened her, and she ran the rest of the way home. After that she had been very careful about the *things*, and on further expeditions had taught Tommy to be careful about them, too. But Tommy had been so little, he had not been able to see the one that was hiding in the next garden when he went out to play that morning. Susan had tried half a dozen times to get to him, but each time, however careful she was, she had seen the top of the triffid tremble and stir slightly . . .

An hour or so later I decided it was time to stop for the night. I left her in the truck while I prospected a cottage or two until I found one that was fit, and then we set about getting a meal together. I did not know much of small girls, but this one seemed able to dispose of an astonishing quantity of the result, confessing while she did so that a diet consisting almost entirely of biscuits, cake, and sweets had proved less completely satisfying than she had expected. After we cleaned her up a bit, and I, under instruction, had wielded her hairbrush, I began to feel rather pleased with the results. She, for her part, seemed able for a time to forget all that had happened in her pleasure at having someone to talk to.

I could understand that. I was feeling exactly the same way myself.

But not long after I had seen her to bed and come downstairs again I heard the sound of sobbing. I went back to her.

'It's all right, Susan,' I said. 'It's all right. It didn't really hurt poor Tommy, you know – it was so quick.' I sat down on the bed beside her, and took her hand. She stopped crying.

'It wasn't just Tommy,' she said. 'It was after Tommy – when there was nobody, nobody at all. I was so frightened . . .'

'I know,' I told her. 'I *do* know. I was frightened, too.'

She looked up at me.

'But you aren't frightened now?'

'No. And you aren't, either. So you see we'll just have to keep together to stop one another being frightened.'

'Yes,' she agreed, with serious consideration. 'I think that'll be all right . . .'

So we went on to discuss a number of things until she fell asleep.

.   .   .

'Where are we going?' Susan asked, as we started off again the following morning.

I said that we were looking for a lady.

'Where is she?' asked Susan.

I wasn't sure of that.

'When shall we find her?' asked Susan.

I was pretty unsatisfactory about that, too.

'Is she a pretty lady?' asked Susan.

'Yes,' I said, glad to be more definite, this time.

It seemed, for some reason, to give Susan satisfaction.

'Good,' she remarked, approvingly, and we passed to other subjects.

Because of her I tried to skirt the larger towns, but it was impossible to avoid many unpleasant sights in the country. After a while I gave up pretending that they did not exist. Susan regarded them with the same detached interest as she gave to the normal scenery. They did not alarm her, though they puzzled her, and prompted questions. Reflecting that the world in which she was going to grow up would have little use for the over-niceties and euphemisms that I had learnt as a child, I did my best to treat the various horrors and curiosities in the same objective fashion. That was really very good for me, too.

By midday the clouds had gathered, and the rain began once more. When, at five o'clock, we pulled up on the road just short of Pulborough it was still pouring hard.

'Where do we go now?' enquired Susan.

'That,' I acknowledged, 'is just the trouble. It's somewhere over there.' I waved my arm towards the misty line of the Downs, to the south.

I had been trying hard to recall just what else Josella had said of the place, but I could remember no more than that the house stood on the north side of the hills, and I had the impression that it faced across the low, marshy country that separated them from Pulborough. Now that I had come so far, it seemed a pretty vague instruction: the Downs stretched away for miles to the east and to the west.

'Maybe the first thing to do is to see if we can find any smoke across there,' I suggested.

'It's awfully difficult to see anything at all in the rain,' Susan said, practically, and quite rightly.

Half an hour later the rain obligingly held off for a while. We left the lorry and sat on a wall side by side. We studied the lower slopes of the hills carefully for some time, but neither Susan's sharp eyes nor my field-glasses could discover any traces of smoke or signs of activity. Then it started to rain again.

'I'm hungry,' said Susan.

Food was a matter of trifling interest to me just then. Now that I was so near, my anxiety to know whether my guess had been right overcame everything else. While Susan was still eating I took the lorry a little way up the hill behind us to get a more extensive view. In between showers, and in a worsening light, we scanned the other side of the valley again without result. There was no life or movement in the whole valley save for a few cattle and sheep, and an occasional triffid lurching across the field below.

An idea came to me, and I decided to go down to the village. I was reluctant to take Susan, for I knew the place would be unpleasant, but I could not leave her where she was. When we got there I found that the sights affected her less than they did me; children have a different convention of the fearful until they have been taught the proper things to be shocked at. The depression was all mine. Susan found more to interest than to disgust her. Any sombreness was quite offset by her delight in a scarlet silk mackintosh with which she equipped herself in spite of its being several sizes too large. My search, too, was rewarding. I returned to the lorry laden with a headlamp like a minor searchlight which we had found upon an illustrious looking Rolls-Royce.

I rigged the thing up on a kind of pivot beside the cab window, and made it ready to plug in. When that was fixed there was nothing to do but wait for darkness, and hope that the rain would let up.

By the time it was fully dark the raindrops had become a mere spatter. I switched on, and sent a magnificent beam piercing the night. Slowly I turned the lamp from side to side, keeping its ray levelled towards the opposite hills, while I anxiously tried to watch the whole line of them simultaneously for an answering light. A dozen times or more I traversed it steadily, switching off for a few seconds at the end of each sweep while we sought the least flicker in the darkness. But each time the night over the hills remained pitchy black. Then the rain came on more heavily again. I set the beam full ahead, and sat waiting, listening to the drumming of the drops on the roof of the cab while Susan fell asleep leaning against my arm. An hour passed before the drumming dwindled to a patter, and ceased. Susan woke up as I started the beam raking across again. I had completed the sixth travel when she called out:

'Look, Bill! There it is! There's a light!'

She was pointing a few degrees left of our front. I switched off the lamp, and followed the line of her finger. It was difficult to be sure. If it were not a trick of our eyes, it was something as dim as a distant glow-worm. And even as we were looking at it, the rain came down on us again in sheets. By the time I had my glasses in my hand there was no view at all.

I hesitated to move. It might be that the light, if it had been a light, would not be visible from lower ground. Once more I trained our light forward, and settled down to wait with as much patience as I could manage. Almost another hour passed before the rain cleared again. The moment it did, I switched off our lamp.

'It is!' Susan cried, excitedly. 'Look! Look!'

It was. And bright enough now to banish any doubts, though the glasses showed me no details.

I switched on again, and gave the V-sign in Morse – it is the only Morse I know except SOS, so it had to do. While we watched the other light it blinked, and then began a series of deliberate longs and shorts which unfortunately meant nothing to me. I gave a couple of more V's for good measure, drew the approximate line of the far light on our map, and switched on the driving lights.

'Is that the lady?' asked Susan.

'It's got to be,' I said. 'It's *got* to be.'

That was a poorish trip. To cross the low marshland it was necessary to take a road a little to the west of us and then work back to the east along the foot of the hills. Before we had gone more than a mile something cut off the sight of the light from us altogether, and to add to the difficulty of finding our way in the dark lanes the rain began again in earnest. With no one to care for the drainage sluices some fields were already flooded, and the water was over the road in places. I had to drive with a tedious care when all the urge was to put my foot flat down.

Once we reached the further side of the valley we were free of flood water, but we made little better speed, for the lanes were full of primitive wanderings and improbable turns. I had to give the wheel all my attention while the child peered up at the hills beside us, watching for the reappearance of the light. We reached the point where the line on my map intersected with what appeared to be our present road without seeing a sign of it. I tried the next uphill turning. It took about half an hour to get back to the road again from the chalkpit into which it led us.

We ran on further along the lower road. Then Susan caught a glimmer between the branches to our right. The next turning was luckier. It took us back at a slant up the side of the hill until we were able to see a small, brilliantly lit square of window half a mile or more along the slope.

Even then, and with the map to help, it was not easy to find the lane that led to it. We lurched along, still climbing in low gear, but each time we caught sight of the window again it was a little closer. The lane had not been designed for ponderous lorries. In the narrower parts we had to push our way along it between bushes and brambles which scrabbled along the sides as though they were trying to pull us back.

But at last there was a lantern waving in the road ahead. It moved on, swinging to show us the turn through a gate. Then it was set stationary on the ground. I drove to within a yard or two of it, and stopped. As I opened the door a flashlight shone suddenly in my eyes. I had a glimpse of figure behind it in a raincoat shining with wetness.

A slight break marred the intended calm of the voice that spoke.

'Hullo, Bill. You've been a long time.'

I jumped down.

'Oh, Bill. I can't—— Oh, my dear, I've been hoping so much … Oh, Bill…' said Josella.

I had forgotten all about Susan until a voice came from above.

'You *are* getting wet, you silly. Why don't you kiss her indoors?' it asked.

CHAPTER 14

SHIRNING

The sense with which I arrived at Shirning Farm – the one that told me that most of my troubles were now over – is interesting only in showing how wide of the mark a sense can be. The sweeping of Josella into my arms went off pretty well, but its corollary of carrying her away forthwith to join the others at Tynsham did not, for several reasons.

Ever since her possible location had occurred to me I had pictured her in, I must admit, a rather cinematic way, as battling bravely against all the forces of nature, etc., etc. In a fashion I suppose she was, but the set-up was a lot different from my imaginings. My simple plan of saying: 'Jump aboard. We're off to join Coker and his little gang,' had to go by the board. One might have known that things would not turn out so simply – on the other hand it is surprising how often the better thing is disguised as the worse …

Not that I didn't from the start prefer Shirning to the thought of Tynsham – but to join a larger group was obviously a sounder move. But Shirning was charming. The word 'farm' had become a courtesy title for the place. It had been a farm until some twenty-five years before, and it still looked like a farm, but in reality it had become a country house. Sussex and the neighbouring counties were well dotted with such houses and cottages which tired Londoners had found adaptable to their needs. Internally the house had been modernized and reconstructed to a point where it was doubtful whether its previous tenants would be able to recognize a single room. Outside it had become spick. The yards and sheds had a suburban rather than a rural tidiness and had for years known no form of animal life rougher than a few riding horses and ponies. The farmyard showed no utilitarian sights and gave forth no rustic smells; it had been laid over with close green turf like a bowling green. The fields across which the windows of the house gazed from beneath weathered red tiles had long been worked by the occupiers of other and more earthly farmhouses. But the sheds and barns remained in good condition.

It had been the ambition of Josella's friends, the present owners, to restore the place one day to work on a limited scale, and to this end they had continually refused tempting offers for it in the hope that at some time, and in some manner not clearly perceived, they would acquire enough money to start buying back the land rightfully belonging to it.

With its own well and its own power plant, the place had plenty to recommend it – but as I looked it over I understood Coker's wisdom in speaking of co-operative effort. I knew nothing of farming, but I could feel that if we had intended to stay there it would take a lot of work to feed six of us.

The other three had been there already when Josella had arrived. They were Dennis and Mary Brent, and Joyce Taylor. Dennis was the owner of the house. Joyce had been there on an indefinite visit, at first to keep Mary company, and then to keep the house running when Mary's expected baby should be born.

On the night of the green flashes – of the comet you would say if you were one who still believes in that comet – there had been two other guests, Joan and Ted Danton, spending a week's holiday there. All five of them had gone out into the garden to watch the display. In the morning all five awoke to a world that was perpetually dark. First they had tried to telephone, when they found that impossible they waited hopefully for the arrival of the daily help. She, too, failing them, Ted had volunteered to try to find out what had happened. Dennis would have accompanied him but for his wife's almost hysterical state. Ted, therefore, had set out alone. He did not come back. At some time later in the day, and without saying a word to anyone, Joan had slipped off, presumably to try to find her husband. She, too, disappeared completely.

Dennis had kept track of time by touching the hands of the clock. By later afternoon it was impossible to sit any longer doing nothing. He wanted to try to get down to the village. Both the women had objected to that. Because of Mary's state he had yielded, and Joyce determined to try. She went to the door, and began to feel her way with a stick outstretched before her. She was barely over the threshold when something fell with a swish across her left hand, burning like a hot wire. She jumped back with a cry, and collapsed in the hall where Dennis had found her. Luckily she was conscious, and able to moan of the pain in her hand. Dennis, feeling the raised weal, had guessed it for what it was. In spite of their blindness, he and Mary had somehow contrived to apply hot fomentations, she heating the kettle while he put on a tourniquet and did his best to suck out the poison. After that they had had to carry her up to bed where she stayed for several days while the effect of the poison wore off.

Meanwhile Dennis had made tests, first at the front and then at the back of the house. With the door slightly open, he cautiously thrust out a broom at head level. Each time there was the whistle of a sting, and he felt the broom handle tremble slightly in his grip. At one of the garden windows the same thing happened: the others seemed to be clear. He would have tried to leave by one of them but for Mary's distress. She was sure that if there were triffids close round the house there must be others about, and would not let him take the risk.

Luckily they had food enough to last them some time, though it was difficult to prepare it; also Joyce, in spite of a high temperature, appeared to be holding her own against the triffid poison, so that the situation was less urgent than it might have been. Most of the next day Dennis devoted to contriving a kind of helmet for himself. He had wire net only of large mesh so that he had to construct it of several layers overlapped and tied together. It took him some time, but, equipped with this and a pair of heavy gauntlet gloves, he was able to start out for the village late in the day. A triffid had struck at him before he was three paces away from the house. He groped for it until he found it, and twisted its stem for it. A minute or two later another sting thudded across his helmet. He could not find that triffid to grapple with it, though it made half a dozen slashes before it gave up. He found his way to the toolshed, and thence across to the lane, encumbered now with three large balls of gardening twine which he paid out as he went to guide him back.

Several times later in the lane more stings whipped at him. It took an immensely long time for him to cover the mile or so to the village, and, before he reached it, his supply of twine had given out. And all the time he had walked and stumbled through a silence so complete that it frightened him. Now and then he would stop and call, but no one answered. More than once he was afraid that he had lost his way, but when his feet discovered a better laid road surface he knew where he was, and was able to confirm it by locating a signpost. He groped his way further on.

After a seemingly vast distance he had become aware that his footsteps were sounding differently; they had a faint echo. Making to one side he found a footpath, and then a wall. A little further along he discovered a post-box let into the brickwork, and knew that he must be actually in the village at last. He called out once more. A voice, a woman's voice called back, but it was some distance ahead, and the words were indistinguishable. He called again, and began to move towards it. Its reply was suddenly cut off by a scream. After that there was silence again. Only then, and still half-incredulously, did he realize that the village was in no better plight than his own household. He sat down on the grassed verge of the path to think out what he should do.

By the feeling in the air he thought that night must have come. He must have been away fully four hours – and there was nothing to do but go back. All the same, there was no reason why he should go back empty-handed... With his stick he rapped his way along the wall until it rang on one of the tinplate advertisements which adorned the village shop. Three times in the last fifty or sixty yards stings had slapped on his helmet. Another struck as he opened the gate, and he tripped over a body lying on the path. A man's body, quite cold.

He had the impression that there had been others in the shop before him. Nevertheless, he found a sizeable piece of bacon. He dropped it, along with packets of butter or margarine, biscuits, and sugar into a sack, and added an assortment of tins which came from a shelf that, to the best of his recollection, was devoted to food – the sardine tins, at any rate, were unmistakeable. Then he sought for, and found, a dozen or more balls of string, shouldered his sack, and set off for home.

He had missed his way once, and it had been hard to keep down panic while he retraced his steps and reorientated himself. But at last he knew that he was again in the familiar lane. By groping right across it he managed to locate the twine of his outward journey, and join it to the string. From there the rest of the journey back had been comparatively easy.

Twice more in the week that followed he had made the journey to the village shop again, and each time the triffids round the house and on the way had seemed more numerous. There had been nothing for the isolated trio to do but wait in hope. And then, like a miracle, Josella had arrived

. . .

It was clear at once, then, that the notion of an immediate move to Tynsham was out. For one thing, Joyce Taylor was still in an extremely weak state – when I looked at her I was surprised that she was alive at all.

Dennis's promptness had saved her life, but their inability to give her the proper restoratives or even suitable food during the following week had slowed down her recovery. It would be folly to try to move her a long distance for a week or two yet. And then, too, Mary's confinement was close enough to make the journey inadvisable for her, so that the only course seemed to be for us all to remain where we were until these crises should have passed.

Once more it became my task to scrounge and forage. This time I had to work on a more elaborate scale to include not merely food, but petrol for the lighting system, hens that were laying, two cows that had recently calved (and still survived though their ribs were sticking out), medical necessities for Mary, and a surprising list of sundries.

The area was more beset with triffids than any other I had yet seen. Almost every morning revealed one or two new ones lurking close to the house, and the first task of the day was to shoot the tops off them, until I had constructed a netting fence to keep them out of the garden. Even then they would come right up and loiter suggestively against it until something was done about them.

I opened some of the cases of gear, and taught young Susan how to use a triffid-gun. She quite rapidly became an expert at disarming the *things* as she continued to call them. It became her department to work daily vengeance on them.

From Josella I learnt what had happened to her after the fire alarm at the University Building.

She had been shipped off with her party much as I with mine, but her manner of dealing with the two women to whom she was attached had been summary. She had issued a flat ultimatum: either she became free of all restraints, in which case she would help them as far as she was able; or, if they continued to coerce her, there would be likely to come a time when they would find themselves drinking prussic acid or eating cyanide of potassium on her recommendation. They could take their choice. They had chosen sensibly.

There was little difference in what we had to tell one another about the days that had followed. When her group had in the end dissolved, she had reasoned much as I did. She took a car, and went to Hampstead to look for me. She had not encountered any survivors from my group, nor run across that led by the quick-triggered, red-headed man. She had kept on there until almost sunset, and then decided to make for the University Building. Not knowing what to expect, she had cautiously stopped the car a couple of streets away, and approached on foot. When she was still some distance from the gates she heard a shot. Wondering what that might indicate, she had taken cover in the garden that had sheltered us before. From there she had observed Coker also making a circumspect advance. Without knowing that I had fired at the triffid in the Square, and that the sound of the shot was the cause of Coker's caution, she suspected some kind of trap. Determined not to fall into one a second time, she had returned to the car. She had no idea where the rest had gone – if they had gone at all. The only place of refuge she could think of that would be known to anyone at all was the one she had mentioned almost casually to me. She had decided to make for it in the hope that I, if I were still in existence, would remember, and try to find it.

'I curled up and slept in the back of the car once I was clear of London,' she said. 'It was still quite early when I got here the next morning. The sound of the car brought Dennis to an upstairs window warning me to look out for triffids. Then I saw that there were half a dozen or more of them close around the house for all the world as if they were waiting for someone to come out of it. Dennis and I shouted back and forth. The triffids stirred and one of them began to move towards me, so I nipped back into the car for safety. When it kept coming, I started up the car, and deliberately ran it down. But there were still the others, and I had no kind of weapon but my knife. It was Dennis who solved that difficulty.

'"If you have a can of petrol to spare, throw some of it their way, and follow it up with a bit of burning rag," he suggested. "That ought to shift 'em."

'It did. Since then I've been using a garden syringe. The wonder is that I've not set the place on fire.'

With the aid of a cook-book Josella had managed to produce meals of a kind, and had set about putting the place more or less to rights. Working, learning, and improvising had kept her too busy to worry about a future which lay beyond the next few weeks. She had seen no one else at all during those days, but, certain that there must be others somewhere, she had scanned the whole valley for signs of smoke by day or lights by night. She had seen no smoke, and in all the miles within her view there had not been a gleam of light until the evening I came.

In a way, the worst affected of the original trio was Dennis. Joyce was still weak and in a semi-invalid state. Mary held herself withdrawn and seemed capable of finding endless mental occupation and compensation in the contemplation of prospective motherhood. But Dennis was like an animal in a trap. He did not curse in the futile way I had heard so many others do, he resented it with a vicious bitterness as if it had forced him into a cage where he did not intend to stay. Already, before I arrived, he had prevailed upon Josella to find the Braille system in the encyclopedia and make an indented copy of the alphabet for him to learn. He spent dogged hours each day making notes in it, and attempting to read them back. Most of the rest of the time he fretted over his own uselessness, though he scarcely mentioned it. He would keep on trying to do this or that with a grim persistence that was painful to watch, and it required all my self-control to stop me offering him help – one experience of the bitterness which unasked help could arouse in him was quite enough. I began to be astonished at the things he was painfully teaching himself to do, though still the most impressive to me was his construction of an efficient mesh helmet on only the second day of his blindness.

It took him out of himself to accompany me on some of my foraging expeditions, and it pleased him that he could be useful in helping to move the heavier cases. He was anxious for books in Braille, but these, we decided, would have to wait until there was less risk of contamination in towns large enough to be likely sources.

The days began to pass quickly, certainly for the three of us who could see. Josella was kept busy, mostly in the house, and Susan was learning to help her. There were plenty of jobs, too, waiting to be done by me. Joyce recovered sufficiently to make a shaky first appearance, and then began to pick up more rapidly. Soon after that Mary's pains began.

That was a bad night for everyone. Worst, perhaps, for Dennis in knowing that everything depended on the care of two willing, but inexperienced girls. His self-control aroused my helpless admiration.

In the early hours of the morning Josella came down to us, looking very tired:

'It's a girl. They're both all right,' she said, and led Dennis up.

She returned a few moments later, and took the drink I had ready for her.

'It was quite simple, thank heaven,' she said. 'Poor Mary was horribly afraid it might be blind, too, but of course it's not. Now she's crying quite dreadfully because she can't see it.'

We drank.

'It's queer,' I said, 'the way things go on, I mean. Like a seed – it looks all shrivelled and finished, you'd think it was dead, but it isn't. And now a new life starting, coming into all this ...

Josella put her face in her hands.

'Oh, God! Bill. Does it have to go on being like this? On – and on – and on——?'

And she, too, collapsed in tears.

. . .

Three weeks later I went over to Tynsham to see Coker and make arrangements for our move. I took an ordinary car in order to do the double journey in a day. When I got back Josella met me in the hall. She gave one look at my face.

'What's the matter?' she said.

'Just that we shan't be going there after all,' I told her. 'Tynsham is finished.'

She stared back at me.

'What happened?'

'I'm not sure. It looks as if the plague got there.'

I described the state of affairs briefly. It had not needed much investigation. The gates were open when I arrived, and the sight of triffids loose in the park half-warned me what to expect. The smell when I got out of the car confirmed it. I made myself go into the house. By the look of it, it had been deserted two weeks or more before. I put my head into two of the rooms. They were enough for me. I called, and my voice ran right away through the hollowness of the house. I went no further.

There had been a notice of some kind pinned to the front door, but only one blank corner remained. I spent a long time searching for the rest of the sheet that must have blown away. I did not find it. The yard at the back was empty of lorries and cars, and most of the stores had gone with them, but where to I could not tell. There was nothing to be done but get into my car again, and come back.

'And so – what?' asked Josella, when I had finished.

'And so, my dear, we stay here. We learn how to support ourselves. And we go on supporting ourselves – unless help comes. There may be an organization somewhere...'

Josella shook her head.

'I think we'd better forget all about help. Millions and millions of people have been waiting and hoping for help that hasn't come.'

'There'll be something,' I said. 'There must be thousands of little groups like this dotted all over Europe – all over the world. Some of them will get together. They'll begin to rebuild.'

'In how long?' said Josella. 'Generations? Perhaps not until after our time. No – the world's gone, and we're left ... We must make our own lives. We'll have to plan them as though help will never come...' She paused. There was an odd, blank look on her face that I had never seen before. It puckered.

'Darling...' I said.

'Oh, Bill, Bill, I wasn't meant for this kind of life. If you weren't here I'd...'

'Hush, my sweet,' I said, gently. 'Hush,' I stroked her hair.

A few moments later she recovered herself.

'I'm sorry, Bill. Self-pity ... revolting. Never again.'

She patted her eyes with her handkerchief, and sniffed a little.

'So I'm to be a farmer's wife. Anyway, I like being married to you, Bill – even if it isn't a proper, authentic kind of marriage.'

Suddenly she gave the smiling chuckle that I had not heard for some time.

'What is it?'

'I was only thinking how much I used to dread my wedding.'

'That was very maidenly and proper of you – if a little unexpected,' I told her.

'Well, it wasn't exactly that. It was my publishers, and the newspapers, and the film people. What fun they would have had with it. There'd have been a new edition of my silly book – probably a new release of the film – and pictures in all the papers. I don't think you'd have liked that much.'

'I can think of another thing I'd not have liked much,' I told her. 'Do you remember – that night in the moonlight you made a condition?'

She looked at me.

'Well, maybe some things haven't fallen out so badly,' she said.

CHAPTER 15

WORLD NARROWING

From then on I kept a journal. It is a mixture of diary, stocklist, and commonplace-book. In it there are notes of the places to which my expeditions took me, particulars of the supplies collected, estimates of quantities available, observations on the states of the premises, with memos on which should be cleared first to avoid deterioration. Foodstuffs, fuel, and seed were constant objects of search, but by no means the only ones. There are entries detailing loads of clothing, tools, household linen, harness, kitchenware, loads of stakes, and wire, wire, and more wire, also books.

I can see there that within a week of my return from Tynsham I had started on the work of erecting a wire fence to keep the triffids out. Already we had barriers to hold them away from the garden and the immediate neighbourhood of the house. Now I began a more ambitious plan of making some hundred acres or so free from them. It involved a stout wire fence which took advantage of the natural features and standing barriers, and inside it a lighter fence to prevent either the stock or ourselves from coming inadvertently within sting range of the main fence. It was a heavy, tedious job which took me a number of months to complete.

At the same time I was endeavouring to learn the a-b-c of farming. It is not the kind of thing that is easily learnt from books. For one thing, it had never occurred to any writer on the subject that any potential farmer could be starting from absolute zero. I found, therefore, that all works began, as it were, in the middle, taking for granted both a basis and a vocabulary that I did not have. My specialized biological knowledge was all but useless to me in the face of practical problems. Much of the theory called for materials and substances which were either unavailable to me, or unrecognizable by me if I could find them. I began to see quite soon that by the time I had dismissed the things that would shortly be unprocurable such as chemical fertilizers, imported feeding-stuffs, and all but the simpler kinds of machinery there was going to be much expenditure of sweat for problematical returns.

Nor is book-instilled knowledge of horse-management, dairy-work, or slaughterhouse procedure by any means an adequate groundwork for these arts. There are so many points where one cannot break off to consult the relative chapter. Moreover, the realities persistently present baffling dissimilarities from the simplicities of print.

Luckily there was plenty of time to make mistakes and to learn from them. The knowledge that several years could pass before we should be thrown anywhere near on our own resources saved us from desperation over our disappointments. There was the reassuring thought, too, that by living on preserved stores we were really being quite provident in preventing them from being wasted.

For safety's sake I let a whole year pass before I went to London again. It was the most profitable area for my forays, but it was the most depressing. The place still contrived to give the impression that a touch of a magic wand would bring it to life again, though many of the vehicles in the streets were beginning to turn rusty. A year later the change was more noticeable. Large patches of plaster detached from housefronts had begun to litter the pavements. Dislodged tiles and chimney-pots could be found in the streets. Grass and weeds had a good hold in the gutters and were choking the drains. Leaves had blocked downspoutings so that more grass, and even small bushes, grew in cracks and in the silt in the roof gutterings. Almost every building was beginning to wear a green wig beneath which its roofs would damply rot. Through many a window one had glimpses of fallen ceilings, curves of peeling paper, and walls glistening with damp. The gardens of the Parks and Squares were wildernesses creeping out across the bordering streets. Growing things seemed, indeed, to press out everywhere, rooting in the crevices between the paving stones, springing from cracks in concrete, finding lodgements even in the seats of the abandoned cars. On all sides they were encroaching to repossess themselves of the arid spaces that man had created. And curiously, as the living things took charge increasingly, the effect of the place became less oppressive. As it passed beyond the scope of any magic wand, most of the ghosts were going with it, withdrawing slowly into history.

Once – not that year, nor the next, but later on – I stood in Piccadilly Circus again, looking round at the desolation, and trying to recreate in my mind's eye the crowds that once swarmed there. I could no longer do it. Even in my memory they lacked reality. There was no tincture of them now. They had become as much a backcloth of history as the audiences in the Roman Colosseum or the army of the Assyrians, and somehow, just as far removed. The nostalgia that crept over me sometimes in the quiet hours was able to move me to more regret than the crumbling scene itself. When I was by myself in the country I could recall the pleasantness of the former life: among the scabrous, slowly perishing buildings I seemed able to recall only the muddle, the frustration, the unaimed drive, the all-pervading clangour of empty vessels, and I became uncertain how much we had lost ...

My first tentative trip there I took alone, returning with cases of triffid-bolts, paper, engine parts, the Braille books and writing machine that Dennis so much desired, the luxuries of drinks, sweets, records, and yet more books for the rest of us. A week later Josella came with me on a more practical search for clothing, not only, or even chiefly for the adults of the party, so much as for Mary's baby and the one she herself was now expecting. It upset her, and it remained the only visit she made.

I continued to go there from time to time in search of some scarce necessity, and used to seize the opportunity of a few little luxuries at the same time. Never once did I see any moving thing there save a few sparrows and an occasional triffid. Cats, and dogs, growing wilder at each generation, could be found in the country, but not there. Sometimes, however, I would find evidence that others besides myself were still in the habit of quarrying supplies there, but I never saw them.

It was at the end of the fourth year that I made my last trip, and found that there were now risks which I was not justified in taking. The first intimation of that was a thunderous crash behind me somewhere in the inner suburbs. I stopped the truck and looked back to see the dust rising from a heap of rubble which lay across the road. Evidently my rumbling passage had given the last shake to a tottering housefront. I brought no more buildings down that day, but I spent it in apprehension of a descending torrent of bricks and mortar. Therafter I confined my attention to smaller towns, and usually went about them on foot.

Brighton, which should have been our largest convenient source of supplies, I let alone. By the time I had thought it fit for a visit, others were in charge there. Who or how many they were I did not know. I simply found a rough wall of stones piled across the road, and painted with the instruction:

KEEP OUT!

The advice was backed up by the crack of a rifle and a spurt of dust just in front of me. There was no one in sight to argue with – besides, it wasn't an arguing kind of gambit.

I turned the lorry round, and drove away thoughtfully, I wondered if a time would come when the man Stephen's preparations for defence might turn out to be not so misplaced after all. Just to be on the safe side I laid in several machine guns and mortars from the source which had already provided us with the flame-throwers we used against the triffids.

In the November of that second year Josella's first baby was born. We called him David. My pleasure in him was at times alloyed with misgivings over the state of things we had created him to face. But that worried Josella much less than it did me. She adored him. He seemed to be a compensation to her for much that she had lost, and, paradoxically, she started to worry less over the condition of the bridges ahead than she had before. Anyway, he had a lustiness which argued well for his future capacity to take care of himself, so I repressed my misgivings and increased the work I was putting into that land which would one day have to support all of us.

. . .

It must have been not so very long after that that Josella turned my attention more closely to the triffids. I had for years been so used to taking precautions against them in my work that their becoming a regular part of the landscape was far less noticeable to me than it was to the others. I had been accustomed, too, to wearing meshed masks and gloves when I dealt with them, so that there was little novelty for me in donning these things whenever I drove out. I had, in fact, got into the habit of paying little more attention to them than one would to mosquitoes in a known malarial area. Josella mentioned it as we lay in bed one night when almost the only sound was the intermittent, distant rattling of their hard little sticks against their stems.

'They're doing a lot more of that lately,' she said.

I did not grasp at first what she was talking about. It was a sound that had been a usual background to the places where I had lived and worked for so long, that unless I deliberately listened for it I could not say whether it was going on or not. I listened now.

'It doesn't sound any different to me,' I said.

'It's not *different*. It's just that there's a lot more of it – because there are a lot more of them than there used to be.'

'I hadn't noticed,' I said, indifferently.

Once I had the fence fixed up, my interest had lain in the ground within it, and I had not bothered what went on beyond it. My impression on my expeditions was that the incidence of triffids in most parts was much the same as before. I recalled that their numbers locally had caught my attention when I had first arrived, and that I had supposed that there must have been several large triffid nurseries in the district.

'There certainly are. You take a look at them tomorrow,' she said.

I remembered in the morning, and looked out of the window as I was dressing. I saw that Josella was right. One could count over a hundred of them behind the quite small stretch of fence visible from the window. I mentioned it at breakfast. Susan looked surprised.

'But they've been getting more all the time,' she said. 'Haven't you noticed?'

'I've got plenty of other things to bother about,' I said, a little irritated by her tone. 'They don't matter outside the fence, anyway. As long as we take care to pull up all the seeds that root in here, they can do what they like outside.'

'All the same,' Josella remarked, with a trace of uneasiness, 'is there any particular reason why they should come to just this part in such numbers? I'm sure they do – and I'd like to know just why it is.'

Susan's face took on its irritating expression of surprise again.

'Why, *he* brings them,' she said.

'Don't point,' Josella told her, automatically. 'What do you mean? I'm sure Bill doesn't bring them.'

'But he does. He makes all the noises, and they just come.'

'Look here,' I said. 'What are you talking about? Am I supposed to be whistling them here in my sleep, or something?'

Susan looked huffy.

'All right. If you don't believe me, I'll show you after breakfast,' she announced, and withdrew into an offended silence.

When we had finished she slipped from the table, returning with my twelve-bore and field-glasses. We went out on to the lawn. She scoured the view until she found a triffid on the move well beyond our fences, and then handed the glasses to me. I watched the thing lurching slowly across a field. It was more than a mile away from us, and heading east.

'Now keep on watching it,' she said.

She fired the gun into the air.

A few seconds later the triffid perceptibly altered course towards the south.

'See?' she enquired, rubbing her shoulder.

'Well, it did look—— Are you sure? Try again.' I suggested.

She shook her head.

'It wouldn't be any good. All the triffids that heard it are coming this way now. In about ten minutes they'll stop and listen. If they're near enough then to hear the ones by the fence clattering, they'll come on. Or if they're too far away for that, but we make another noise, then they'll come. But if they can't hear anything at all, they'll wait a bit, and then just go on wherever they were going before.'

I admit that I was somewhat taken aback by this revelation.

'Well – er,' I said. 'You must have been watching them very closely, Susan?'

'I always watch them. I hate them,' she said, as if that were explanation enough.

Dennis had joined us as we stood there.

'I'm with you, Susan,' he said. 'I don't like it. I've not liked it for some time. Those damn things have the drop on us.'

'Oh, come——' I began.

'I tell you there's more to them than we think. How did they *know?* They started to break loose the moment there was no one to stop them. They were around this house the very next day. Can you account for that?'

'That's not new for them,' I said. 'In jungle country they used to hang around near the tracks. Quite often they would surround a small village and invade it if they weren't beaten off. They were a dangerous kind of pest in quite a lot of places.'

'But not here – that's my point. They couldn't do that here until conditions made it possible. They didn't even try. But when they could, they did it *at once* – almost as if they *knew* they could.'

'Come now, be reasonable, Dennis. Just think what you're implying,' I told him.

'I'm quite aware of what I'm implying – some of it, at any rate. I'm making no definite theory, but I do say this: they took advantage of our disadvantages with remarkable speed. I also say that there is something perceptibly like method going on among them right now. You've been so wrapped up in your jobs that you've not noticed how they've been massing up, and waiting out there beyond the fence, but Susan has – I've heard her talking about it. And just what do you think they're waiting *for?*'

I did not try to answer that just then. I said:

'You think I'd better lay off using the twelve-bore which attracts them, and use a triffid gun instead?'

'It's not just the gun, it's all the noises,' said Susan. 'The tractor's the worst because it is a loud noise, and it keeps on, so that they can easily find where it comes from. But they can hear the lighting-plant engine quite a long way, too. I've seen them turn this way when it starts up.'

'I wish,' I told her, irritably, 'you'd not keep on saying "they hear", as if they were animals. They're not. They don't "hear". They're just plants.'

'All the same, they *do* hear, somehow,' Susan retorted, stubbornly.

'Well – anyway, we'll do something about them,' I promised.

. . .

We did. The first trap was a crude kind of windmill which produced a hearty hammering noise. We fixed it up about half a mile away. It worked. It drew them away from our fence, and from elsewhere. When there were several hundreds of them clustered about it, Susan and I drove over there and turned the flame-throwers on them. It worked fairly well a second time, too – but after that only a few of them paid any attention to it. Our next move was to build a kind of stout bay inwards from the fence, and then remove part of the main fence itself, replacing it by a gate. We had chosen a point within earshot of the lighting engine, and we left the gate open. After a couple of days we dropped the gate, and destroyed the couple of hundred or so that had come into the pen. That, too, was fairly successful to begin with, but not if we tried it twice in the same place, and even in other places the numbers we netted dropped steadily.

A tour of the boundaries every few days with a flame-thrower could have kept the numbers down effectively, but it would have taken a lot of time and soon have run us out of fuel. A flame-thrower's consumption is high, and the stocks held for it in the arms depots were not large. Once we finished it, our valuable flame-throwers would become little better than junk, for I knew neither the formula for an efficient fuel nor the method of producing it.

On the two or three occasions we tried mortar-bombs on concentrations of triffids the results were disappointing. Triffids share with trees the ability to take a lot of damage without lethal harm.

As time went on the numbers collected along the fence continued to increase in spite of our traps and occasional holocausts. They didn't try anything or do anything there. They simply settled down, wriggled their roots into the soil, and remained. At a distance they looked as inactive as any other hedge, and but for the pattering that some few of them were sure to be making, they might have been no more remarkable. But if one doubted their alertness it was only necessary to take a car down the lane. To do so was to run a gauntlet of such viciously slashing stings that it was necessary to stop the car at the main road and wipe the windscreen clear of poison.

Now and then one of us would have a new idea for their discouragement such as spraying the ground beyond the fence with a strong arsenical solution, but the retreats we caused were only temporary.

We'd been trying out a variety of such dodges for a year or more before the day when Susan came running into our room early one morning to tell us that the *things* had broken in, and were all round the house. She had got up early to do the milking, as usual. The sky outside her bedroom window was grey, but when she went downstairs she found everything there in complete darkness. She realized that should not be so, and turned on the light. The moment she saw leathery green leaves pressed against the windows, she guessed what had happened.

I crossed the bedroom on tiptoe, and pulled the window shut sharply. Even as it closed a sting whipped up from below and smacked against the glass. We looked down on a thicket of triffids standing ten or twelve deep against the wall of the house. The flame-throwers were in one of the outhouses. I took no risks when I went to fetch them. In thick clothing and gloves, with a leather helmet and goggles beneath the mesh mask I hacked a way through the throng of triffids with the largest carving knife I could find. The stings whipped and slapped at the wire mesh so frequently that they wet it, and the poison began to come through in a fine spray. It misted the goggles, and the first thing I did in the outhouse was to wash it off my face. I dare not use more than a brief, low-aimed jet from one of the throwers to clear my way back for fear of setting the door and window frames alight, but it moved and agitated them enough for me to get back unmolested.

Josella and Susan stood by with fire-extinguishers while I, still looking like a cross between a deep-sea diver and a man from Mars, leant from the upper windows on each side of the house in turn and played the thrower over the besieging mob of the brutes. It did not take very long to incinerate a number of them and get the rest on the move. Susan, now dressed for the job, took the second thrower and started on the, to her, highly congenial task of hunting them down while I set off across the fields to find the source of the trouble. That was not difficult. From the first rise I was able to spot where triffids were still lurching into our enclosure in a stream of tossing stems and waving leaves. They fanned

out a little on the nearer side, but all of them were bound in the direction
of the house. It was simple to head them off. A jet in front stopped them;
one to either side started them back on the way they had come. An
occasional spurt over them and dripping among them hurried them up,
and turned back late-comers. Twenty yards or so away a part of the
fence was lying flat, with the posts snapped off. I rigged it up temporarily there and then, and played the thrower back and forth, giving
the things enough of a scorching to prevent more trouble for a few hours
at least.

Josella, Susan, and I spent most of the day repairing the breach. Two
more days passed before Susan and I could be sure that we had searched
every corner of the enclosure and accounted for the very last of the
intruders. We followed that up with an inspection of the whole length of
the fence and a reinforcement of all doubtful sections. Four months later
they broke in again ...

This time a number of broken triffids lay in the gap. Our impression
was that they had been crushed in the pressure that had been built up
against the fence before it gave way, and that, falling with it, they had
been trampled by the rest.

It was clear that we should have to take new defensive measures. No
part of our fence was any stronger than that which had given way.
Electrification seemed the most likely means of keeping them at a
distance. To power it I found an army generator mounted on a trailer,
and towed it home. Susan and I set to work on the wiring. Before we had
completed it the brutes were through again in another place.

I believe that system would have been completely effective if we could
have kept it in action all the time – or even most of the time. But against
that there was the fuel consumption. Petrol was one of the most valuable
of our stores. Food of some kind we could always hope to grow, but when
petrol and diesel oil were no longer available, much more than our mere
convenience would be gone with them. There would be no more
expeditions, and consequently no more replenishments of supplies. The
primitive life would start in earnest. So, from motives of conservation,
the barrier wire was only charged for some minutes two or three times a
day. It caused the triffids to recoil a few yards, and thereby stopped them
building up pressure against the fence. As an additional guard we ran an
alarm wire on the inner fence to enable us to deal with any breaks before
they became serious.

The weakness lay in the triffids' apparent ability to learn, in at least a
limited way, from experience. We found, for instance, that they grew
accustomed to our practice of charging the wire for a while night and
morning. We began to notice that they were usually clear of the wire at

our customary time for starting the engine, and they began to close in again soon after it had stopped. Whether they actually associated the charged condition of the wire with the sound of the engine was impossible to say then, but later we had little doubt that they did.

It was easy enough to make our running times erratic, but Susan, for whom they were continually a source of inimical study, soon began to maintain that the period for which the shock kept them clear was growing steadily shorter. Nevertheless the electrified wire and occasional attacks upon them in the sections where they were densest kept us free of incursions for over a year, and of those that occurred later we had warning enough to stop them being more than a minor nuisance.

Within the safety of our compound we continued to learn about agriculture, and life settled gradually into a routine.

. . .

On a day in the summer of our sixth year Josella and I went down to the coast together, travelling there in the half-tracked vehicle that I customarily used now that the roads were growing so bad. It was a holiday for her. Months had passed since she had been outside the fence. The care of the place and the babies had kept her far too tied to make more than a few necessary trips, but now we had reached the stage where we felt that Susan could safely be left in charge sometimes, and we had a feeling of release as we climbed up and ran over the tops of the hills. On the lower southern slopes we stopped the car for a while, and sat there.

It was a perfect June day with only a few light clouds flecking a pure blue sky. The sun shone down on the beaches and the sea beyond just as brightly as it had in the days when those same beaches had been crowded with bathers, and the sea dotted with little boats. We looked down on it in silence for some minutes. Josella said:

'Don't you *still* feel sometimes that if you were to close your eyes for a bit you might open them again to find it all as it was, Bill? – I do.'

'Not often now,' I told her. 'But I've had to see so much more of it than you have. All the same, sometimes ...'

'And look at the gulls – just as they used to be.'

'There are many more birds this year,' I agreed. 'I'm glad of that.'

Viewed impressionistically from a distance the little town was still the same jumble of small red-roofed houses and bungalows populated mostly by a comfortably retired middle class – but it was an impression that could not last more than a few minutes. Though the tiles still showed, the walls were barely visible. The tidy gardens had vanished under an unchecked growth of green, patched in colour here and there by the descendants of carefully-cultivated flowers. Even the roads looked like strips of green carpet from this distance. When we reached them we should find that the effect of soft verdure was illusory; they would be matted with coarse, tough weeds.

'Only so few years ago,' Josella said reflectively, 'people were wailing about the way those bungalows were destroying the countryside. Now look at them.'

'The countryside is having its revenge, all right,' I said. 'Nature seemed about finished then – who would have thought the old man had so much blood in him?'

'It rather frightens me. It's as if everything were breaking out. Rejoicing that we're finished, and that it's free to go its own way. I wonder . . . ? Have we been just fooling ourselves since it happened? Do you think we really are finished with, Bill?'

I'd had plenty more time when I was out on my foragings to wonder about that than she had.

'If you weren't you, darling, I might make an answer out of the right heroic mould – the kind of wishful thinking that so often passes for faith and resolution.'

'But as I *am* me?'

'I'll give you the honest answer – not quite. And while there's life, there's hope.'

We looked on the scene before us for some seconds in silence.

'I think,' I amplified, 'only think, mind you, that we have a narrow chance – so narrow that it is going to take a long long time to get back. If it weren't for the triffids, I'd say there was a very good chance indeed – though still taking a longish time. But the triffids are a real factor. They are something that no rising civilization has had to fight before. Are they going to take the world off us, or are we going to be able to stop them?

'The real problem is to find some simple way of dealing with them. We aren't so badly off – we can hold them away. But our grandchildren – what are they going to do about them? Are they going to have to spend all their lives in human reservations only kept free of triffids by unending toil?

'I'm quite sure there is a simple way. The trouble is that simple ways come out of such complicated research. And we haven't the resources.'

'Surely we have all the resources there ever were, just for the taking,' Josella put in.

'Material, yes. But mental, no. What we need is a team, a team of experts really out to deal with the triffids for good and all. Something could be done. I'm sure. Something along the lines of a selective killer, perhaps. If we could produce the right hormones to create a state of imbalance in triffids, but not enough in other things . . . It must be possible – if you have enough brain power turned on to the job ...'

'If you think that, why don't you try?' she asked.

'Too many reasons. First, I'm not up to it – a very mediocre biochemist, and there's only one of me. There'd have to be a lab. and equipment. More than that, there'd have to be time, and there are too many things which I have to do as it is. But even if I had the ability, then there would have to be the means of producing synthetic hormones in huge quantities. It would be a job for a regular factory. But before that there must be the research team.'

'People could be trained.'

'Yes – when enough of them can be spared from the mere business of keeping alive. I've collected a mass of biochemical books in the hope that perhaps some time there will be people who can make use of them – I shall teach David all I can, and he must hand it on. But unless there is leisure for work on it some time, I can see nothing ahead but the reservations.'

Josella frowned down on a group of four triffids ambling across a field below us.

'They used to say that man's really serious rivals were the insects. It seems to me that the triffids have something in common with some kinds of insects. Oh, I know that biologically they're plants. What I mean is they don't bother about their individuals, and the individuals don't bother about themselves. Separately they have something which looks slightly like intelligence; collectively it looks a great deal more like it. They sort of work together for a purpose the way ants or bees do – yet you could say that not one of them is aware of any purpose or scheme although he's part of it. It's all very queer – probably impossible for us to understand, anyway. They're so *different*. It seems to me to go against all our ideas of inheritable characteristics. Is there something in a bee or a triffid which is a gene of social organization, or does an ant have a gene of architecture? And if they have these things why haven't we in all this time developed a gene for language, or cooking? Anyway, whatever it is, the triffids do seem to have something like it. It may be that no single individual knows why it keeps hanging around our fence, but the whole lot together knows that it's purpose is to get us – and that sooner or later it will.'

'There are still things that can happen to stop that,' I said. 'I didn't mean to make you feel quite despondent about it all.'

'I don't – except sometimes when I'm tired. Usually I'm much too busy to worry over what may happen years ahead. No, as a rule I don't go much beyond getting a little sad – the sort of gentle melancholy that the eighteenth century thought so estimable. I go sentimental when you play records – there is something rather frightening about a great orchestra which has passed away still playing on to a little group of people hemmed in and gradually growing more primitive. It takes me back, and I begin to feel sad with thinking of all the things we can never do again – however things go now. Don't you sometimes feel like that?'

'H'm,' I admitted. 'But I find that I accept the present more easily as it goes on. I suppose that if there were wishes that could be granted, I would wish the old world back – but there'd be a condition. You see, in spite of everything, I'm happier inside me than I ever was before. You know that, don't you, Josie?'

She put her hand on mine.

'I feel that too. No, what saddens me is not so much the things we've lost, as the things the babies will never have the chance to know.'

'It's going to be a problem to bring them up with hopes and ambitions,' I acknowledged. 'We can't help being orientated backwards. But they mustn't look back all the time. A tradition of a vanished golden age and ancestors who were magicians would be a most damning thing. Whole races have had that sort of inferiority complex which has sunk into lassitude on the tradition of a glorious past. But how are we going to stop that kind of thing from happening?'

'If I were a child now,' she said, reflectively, 'I think I should want a reason of some kind. Unless I was given it – that is, if I were allowed to think that I had been born into a world which had been quite pointlessly destroyed, I should find living quite pointless, too. That does make it awfully difficult because it seems to be just what *has* happened...'

She paused, pondering, then she added:

'Do you think we could – do you think we should be justified in starting a myth to help them? A story of a world that was wonderfully clever, but so wicked that it had to be destroyed – or destroyed itself by accident? Something like the Flood again. That wouldn't crush them with inferiority – it could give the incentive to build, and this time to build something better.'

'Yes...' I said, considering it. 'Yes. It's often a good idea to tell children the truth. Kind of makes things easier for them later on – only why pretend it's a myth?'

Josella demurred at that.

'How do you mean? The triffids were – well, they were somebody's fault, or mistake, I admit. But the rest ...?'

'I don't think we can blame anyone too much for the triffids. The extracts they give were very valuable in the circumstances. Nobody can ever see what a major discovery is going to lead to – whether it is a new kind of engine or a triffid, and we coped with them all right in normal conditions. We benefitted quite a lot from them, as long as the conditions were to their disadvantage.'

'Well, it wasn't our fault the conditions changed. It was – just one of those things: like earthquakes or hurricanes – what an insurance company would call an Act of God. Maybe that's just what it was – a judgement. Certainly we never brought that comet.'

'Didn't we, Josella? Are you quite sure of that?'

She turned to look at me.

'What do you mean, Bill? How could we?'

'What I mean, my dear is – was it a comet at all? You see, there's an old superstitious distrust of comets pretty well grained in. I know we were modern enough not to kneel down in the streets to pray to them – but all the same, it's a phobia with centuries of standing. They've been portents and symbols of heavenly wrath and warnings that the end is at hand, and used in any amount of stories and prophecies. So, when you get an astonishing celestial phenomenon, what more natural than to attribute it straight off to a comet? A denial would take time to get around – and time was just what there was not. And when utter disaster follows, it just confirms it for everyone that it must have been a comet.'

Josella was looking at me very hard.

'Bill, are you trying to tell me that you don't think it was a comet at all?'

'Just exactly that,' I agreed.

'But – I don't understand. It must—— What else *could* it have been?'

I opened a vacuum-packed tin of cigarettes, and lit one for each of us.

'You remember what Michael Beadley said about the tightrope we'd all been walking on for years?'

'Yes, but——'

'Well, I think that what happened was that we came off it – and that a few of us just managed to survive the crash.'

I drew on my cigarette, looking out at the sea and at the infinite blue sky above it.

'Up there,' I went on, 'up there, there were – and maybe there still are – unknown numbers of satellite weapons circling round and round the Earth. Just a lot of dormant menaces, touring around, waiting for someone, or something, to set them off. What was in them? You don't know; I don't know. Top-secret stuff. All we've heard is guesses – fissile materials, radio-active dusts, bacteria, viruses ... Now suppose that one type happened to have been constructed especially to emit radiations that our eyes would not stand – something that would burn out, or at least damage, the optic nerve ...?'

Josella gripped my hand.

'Oh, no, Bill! No, they couldn't ... That'd be – diabolical ... Oh, I can't believe ... Oh, *no*, Bill!'

'My sweet, all the things up there were diabolical ... Then suppose there were a mistake, or perhaps an accident – maybe such an accident as actually encountering a shower of comet debris, if you like – which starts some of these things popping...'

'Somebody starts talking about comets. It might not be politic to deny that – and there turned out to be so little time, anyway.

'Well, naturally these things would have been intended to operate close to the ground where the effect would be spread over a definitely calculable area. But they start going off out there in space, or maybe when they hit the atmosphere – either way they're operating so far up that people all round the world can receive direct radiations from them ...

'Just what did happen is anyone's guess now. But one thing I'm quite certain of – that somehow or other we brought this lot down on ourselves. And there was that plague, too: it wasn't typhoid, you know ...

'I find that it's just the wrong side of coincidence for me to believe that out of all the thousands of years in which a destructive comet could arrive, it happens to do so just a few years after we have succeeded in establishing satellite weapons – don't you? No. I think that we kept on that tight-rope quite a while, considering the things that might have happened – but sooner or later the foot had to slip.'

'Well, when you put it that way——' murmured Josella. She broke off, and was lost in silence for quite a while. Then she said:

'I suppose in a way that should be more horrible than the idea of nature striking blindly at us. And yet I don't think it is. It makes me feel less hopeless about things because it makes them at least comprehensible. If it *was* like that, then it is at least a thing that can be prevented from happening again – just one more of the mistakes our very great grandchildren are going to have to avoid. And, oh dear, there were so many, many mistakes! But we can warn them.'

'H'm – well——' I said. 'Anyway, once they've beaten the triffids and pulled themselves out of this mess they'll have plenty of scope for making brand-new mistakes of their very own.'

'Poor little things,' she said, as if she were gazing down rows of increasingly great-grandchildren, 'it's not much that we're offering them, is it?'

'People used to say: "life is what you make it."'

'That, my dear Bill, outside very narrow limits is just a load of – well, I don't want to be rude. But I believe my Uncle Ted used to say that –

until somebody dropped a bomb which took both his legs off. It changed his mind. And nothing that I personally did caused me to be living at all now.' She threw away the remains of her cigarette. 'Bill, what *have* we done to be the lucky ones in all this? Every now and then – when I stop feeling overworked and selfish, that is – I think how lucky we really have been, and I want to give thanks to something or other. But then I find I feel if there were anybody or anything to give thanks to they'd have chosen such a much more deserving case than me. It's all very confusing to a simple girl.'

'And I,' I said, 'feel that if there were anybody or anything at all in the driving-seat quite a lot of the things in history could not have happened. But I don't let it worry me a lot. We've had luck, my sweet. If it changes tomorrow, well, it changes. Whatever it does, it can't take away the time we've had together. That's been more than I deserved, and more than most men get in a lifetime.'

We sat there a little longer, looking at the empty sea, and then drove down to the little town.

After a search which produced most of the things on our wants list we went down to picnic on the shore in the sunshine – with a good stretch of shingle behind us over which no triffid could approach unheard.

'We must do more of this while we can,' Josella said. 'Now that Susan's growing up I needn't be nearly so tied.'

'If anybody ever earned the right to let up a bit, you have,' I agreed.

I said it with a feeling that I would like us to go together and say a last farewell to places and things we had known while it was still possible. Every year now the prospect of imprisonment would grow closer. Already to get northward from Shirning it was necessary to make a detour of many miles to pass the country that had reverted to marshland. All the roads were rapidly becoming worse with the erosion by rain and streams, and the roots that broke up the surfaces. The time in which one would still be able to get an oil-tanker back to the house was already becoming measurable. One day one of them would fail to make its way along the land, and very likely block it for good. A half-track would continue to run over ground that was dry enough, but as time went on it would be increasingly difficult to find a route open enough even for that.

'And we must have one real last fling,' I said. 'You shall dress up again, and we'll go to——'

'Sh-sh!' interrupted Josella, holding up one finger, and turning her ear to the wind.

I held my breath, and strained my ears. There was a feeling rather than a sound of throbbing in the air. It was faint, but gradually swelling.

'It *is* – it's a plane!' Josella said.

We looked to the west, shading our eyes with our hands. The humming was still little more than the buzzing of an insect. The sound increased so slowly that it could have come from nothing but a helicopter, any other kind of craft would have passed over us or out of hearing in the time it was taking.

Josella saw it first. A dot, a little out from the coast, and apparently coming our way, parallel with the shore. We stood up, and started to wave. As the dot grew larger, we waved more wildly, and, not very sensibly, shouted at the tops of our voices. The pilot could not have failed to see us there on the open beach had he come on, but that was what he did not do. A few miles short of us he turned abruptly north to pass inland. We went on waving madly, hoping that he might yet catch sight of us. But there was no indecision in the machine's course, no variation of the engine note. Deliberately and imperturbably it droned away towards the hills.

We lowered our arms, and looked at one another.

'If it can come once, it can come again,' said Josella sturdily, but not very convincingly.

But the sight of the machine had changed our day for us. It destroyed quite a lot of resignation we had carefully built up. We had been saying to ourselves that there must be other groups, but they wouldn't be in any better position than we were, more likely in a worse. But when a helicopter could come sailing in like a sight and sound from the past, it raised more than memories: it suggested that someone somewhere was managing to make out better than we were. – Was there a tinge of jealousy there? – And it also made us aware that lucky as we had been, we were still gregarious creatures by nature.

The restless feeling that the machine left behind destroyed our mood and the lines along which our thoughts had been running. In unspoken argument we began to pack up our belongings, and, each occupied with our thoughts, we made our way back to the half-track, and started for home.

CHAPTER 16

CONTACT

We had covered perhaps half the distance back to Shirning when Josella noticed the smoke. At first sight it might have been a cloud, but as we neared the top of the hill we could see the grey column beneath the more diffused upper layer. She pointed to it, and looked at me without a word. The only fires we had seen in years had been a few spontaneous outbreaks in later summer. We both knew at once that the plume ahead was rising from the neighbourhood of Shirning.

I forced the half-track along at a greater speed than it had ever done on the deteriorated roads. We were thrown about inside it, and yet still seemed to be crawling. Josella sat silent all the time, her lips pressed together and her eyes fixed on the smoke. I knew that she was searching for some indication that the source was nearer or further away, anywhere but at Shirning itself. But the closer we came, the less room there was for doubt. We tore up the final lane quite oblivious of the stings whipping at the vehicle as it passed. Then, at the turn, we were able to see that it was not the house itself, but the wood-pile that was ablaze.

At the sound of the horn Susan came running out to pull on the rope which opened the gate from a safe distance. She shouted something which was drowned in the rattle of our driving in. Her free hand was pointing, not to the fire, but towards the front of the house. As we ran further into the yard we could see the reason. Skilfully landed in the middle of our lawn stood the helicopter.

By the time we were out of the half-track a man in a leather jacket and breeches had come out of the house. He was tall, fair, and sunburned. At the first glance I had a feeling I had seen him somewhere before. He waved and grinned cheerfully as we hurried across.

'Mr Bill Masen, I presume. My name is Simpson – Ivan Simpson.'

'I remember,' said Josella. 'You brought in a helicopter that night at the University Buildings.'

'That's right. Clever of you to remember. But just to show you you're not the only one with a memory: you are Josella Playton, author of——'

'You're quite wrong,' she interrupted him, firmly. 'I'm Josella Masen, author of "David Masen".'

'Ah, yes. I've just been looking at the original edition, and a very creditable bit of craftsmanship too, if I may say so.'

'Hold on a bit,' I said. 'That fire——?'

'It's safe enough. Blowing away from the house. Though I'm afraid most of your stock of wood has gone up.'

'What happened?'

'That was Susan. She didn't mean me to miss the place. When she heard my engine she grabbed a flame-thrower, and bounded out to start a signal as quickly as she could. The wood-pile was handiest – no one could have missed what she did to that.'

We went inside, and joined the others.

'By the way,' Simpson said to me, 'Michael told me I was to be sure to start off with his apologies.'

'To me?' I said, wondering.

'You were the only one who saw any danger in the triffids, and he didn't believe you.'

'But – do you mean to say you knew I was here?'

'We found out very roughly your probable location a few days ago – from a fellow we all have cause to remember: one Coker.'

'So Coker came through, too,' I said. 'After the shambles I saw at Tynsham I'd an idea the plague had got him.'

Later on, when we had had a meal and produced our best brandy, we got the story out of him.

When Michael Beadley and his party had gone on, leaving Tynsham to the mercies and principles of Miss Durrant, they had not made for Beaminster, nor anywhere near it. They had gone north-east, into Oxfordshire. Miss Durrant's misdirection to us must have been deliberate, for Beaminster had never been mentioned.

They had found an estate which seemed at first to offer the group all it required, and no doubt they could have entrenched themselves there as we had entrenched ourselves at Shirning, but as the menace of the triffids increased, the disadvantages of the place became more obvious. In a year, both Michael and the Colonel were highly dissatisfied with the longer-term prospects there. A great deal of work had already been put into the place, but by the end of the second summer there was general agreement that it would be better to cut their losses. To build a community they had to think in terms of years – a considerable number of years. They also had to bear in mind that the longer they delayed, the more difficult any move would be. What they needed was a place where they would have room to expand and develop; an area with natural defences which, once it had been cleared of triffids, could economically be kept clear of them. Where they now were a high proportion of their labour was occupied with maintaining fences. And as their numbers increased, the length of fence line would have to be increased. Clearly, the best self-maintaining defence line would be water. To that end they had held a discussion on the relative merits of various islands. It had been chiefly climate that had decided them in favour of the Isle of Wight, despite some misgivings over the area that would have to be cleared. Accordingly, in the following March they had packed up again, and moved on.

'When we got there,' Ivan said, 'the triffids seemed even thicker than where we'd left. No sooner had we begun to settle ourselves into a big country house near Godshill than they started collecting along the walls in thousands. We let 'em come for a couple of weeks or so, then we went for 'em with the flame-throwers.

'After we'd wiped that lot out, we let them accumulate again, and then we blitzed 'em once more – and so on. We could afford to do it properly there, because once we were clear of them, we'd not need to use the throwers any more. There could only be a limited number in the island, and the more of them that came round us to be wiped out, the better we liked it.

'We had to do it a dozen times before there was any appreciable effect. All round the walls we had a belt of charred stumps before they began to get shy. There was a devil of a lot more of them than we had expected.'

'There used to be at least half a dozen nurseries breeding high quality plants in the island – not to mention the private and park ones,' I said. 'That doesn't surprise me. There might have been a hundred nurseries by the look of it. Before all this began I'd have said there were only a few thousand of the things in the whole country, if anyone had asked me, but there must have been hundreds of thousands.'

'There were,' I said. 'They'll grow practically anywhere, and they were pretty profitable. There didn't seem to be so many when they were penned up in farms and nurseries. All the same, judging from the amount round here, there must be whole tracts of country practically free of them now.'

'That's so,' he agreed. 'But go and live there and they'll start collecting in a few days. You can see that from the air. I'd have known there was someone here without Susan's fire. They make a dark border round any inhabited place.

'Still, we managed to thin down the crowd round our walls after a bit. Maybe they got to find it unhealthy, or maybe they didn't care a lot for walking about on the charred remains of their relatives – and, of course, there were fewer of them. So then we started going out to hunt them instead of just letting them come to us. It was our main job for months. Between us we covered every inch of the island – or thought we did. By the time we were through, we reckoned we'd put paid to every one in the place, big and small. Even so, some managed to appear the next year, and the year after that. Now we have an intensive search every spring on account of seeds blowing over from the mainland, and settle with them right away.

'While that was going on, we were getting organized. There were some fifty or sixty of us to begin with. I took flips in the helicopter, and when I saw signs of a group anywhere, I'd go down and issue a general invitation to come along. Some did – but a surprising number simply weren't interested: they'd escaped from being governed, and in spite of all their troubles they didn't want any more of it. There are some lots in South Wales that have made sorts of tribal communities, and resent the idea of any organization except the minimum they've set up for themselves. You'll find similar lots near the other coalfields, too. Usually the leaders are the men who happened to be on the shift below ground so that they never saw the green stars – though God knows how they ever got up the shafts again.

'Some of them so definitely don't want to be interfered with that they shoot at the aircraft – there's one lot of that sort at Brighton——'

'I know,' I said, 'they warned me off, too.'

'Recently there are more like that. There's one at Maidstone, another at Guildford, and other places. They're the real reason why we hadn't spotted you hidden away here before. The district didn't seem too healthy when one got close to it. I don't know what they think they're doing – probably got some good food dumps and are scared of anyone else wanting some of it. Anyway, there's no sense in taking risks, so I just let 'em stew.

'Still, quite a lot did come along. In a year we'd gone up to three hundred or so – not all sighted, of course.

'It wasn't until about a month ago that I came across Coker and his lot – and one of the first things he asked, by the way, was whether you'd shown up. They had a bad time, particularly at first.

'A few days after he got back to Tynsham, a couple of women came along from London, and brought the plague with them. Coker quarantined them at the first symptoms, but it was too late. He decided on a quick move. Miss Durrant wouldn't budge. She elected to stay and look after the sick, and follow later if she could. She never did.

'They took the infection with them. There were three more hurried moves before they succeeded in shaking free of it. By then they had gone as far west as Devonshire, and they were all right for a bit there. But then they began to find the same difficulties as we had – and you have. Coker stuck it out there for nearly three years, and then reasoned along much the same lines as we did. Only he didn't think of an island. Instead, he decided on a river boundary and a fence to cut off the toe of Cornwall. When they got there they spent the first months building their barrier, then they went for the triffids inside, much as we did on the island. They had much more difficult country to work with, though, and they never did succeed in clearing them out completely. The fence was fairly successful to begin with, but they never could trust it as we could the sea, and too much of their manpower had to be wasted on patrols.

'Coker thinks they might have made out all right once the children had grown old enough to work, but it would have been tough going all the time. When I did find them, they hadn't much hesitation about coming along. They set about loading up their fishing boats right away, and they were all on the island in a couple of weeks. When Coker found you weren't with us, he suggested you might still be here somewhere in these parts.'

'You can tell him that wipes out any hard feelings about him,' said Josella.

'He's going to be a very useful man,' Ivan said. 'And from what he tells us, you could be, too,' he added, looking at me. 'You're a biochemist, aren't you?'

'A biologist,' I said, 'with a little biochemistry.'

'Well you can hold on to your fine distinctions. The point is, Michael has tried to get some research going into a method of knocking off triffids scientifically. That *has* to be found if we are going to get anywhere at all. But the trouble so far is that the only people we have to work on it are a few who have forgotten most of the biology they learned at school. What do you think – like to turn professor? It'd be a worth while job.'

'I can't think of one that would be more worth while,' I told him.

'Does this mean you're inviting us all to your island haven?' Dennis asked.

'Well, to come on mutual approval, at least,' Ivan replied. 'Bill and Josella will probably remember the broad principles laid down that night at the University. They still stand. We aren't out to reconstruct – we want to build something new and better. Some people don't take to that. If they don't they're no use to us. We just aren't interested in having an opposition party that's trying to perpetuate a lot of the old bad features. We'd rather that people who want that went elsewhere.'

'Elsewhere sounds a pretty poor offer, in the circumstances,' remarked Dennis.

'Oh, I don't mean we throw them back to the triffids. But there were a number of them, and there had to be some place for them to go, so a party went across to the Channel Isles, and started cleaning up there on the same lines as we'd cleaned up the Isle of Wight. About a hundred of them moved over. They're doing all right there, too.

'So now we have the mutual approval system. Newcomers spend six months with us, then there's a Council hearing. If they don't like our ways, they say so; and if we don't think they'll fit, we say so. If they fit, they stay; if not, we see that they get to the Channel Isles – or back to the mainland, if they're odd enough to prefer that.'

'Sounds to have a touch of the dictatorial – how's this Council of yours formed?' Dennis wanted to know.

Ivan shook his head.

'It'd take too long to go into constitutional questions now. The best way to learn about us is to come and find out. If you like us, you'll stay – but even if you don't, I think you'll find the Channel Isles a better spot than this is likely to be a few years from now.'

.   .   .

In the evening, after Ivan had taken off, and vanished away to the south-west, I went and sat on my favourite bench in a corner of the garden.

I looked across the valley, remembering the well-drained and tended meadows that had been there. Now it was far on the way back to the wild. The neglected fields were dotted with thickets, beds of reeds, and stagnant pools. The bigger trees were slowly drowning in the sodden soil.

I thought of Coker and his talk of the leader, the teacher, and the doctor – and of all the work that would be needed to support us on our few acres. Of how it would affect each of us if we were to be imprisoned here. Of the three blind ones, still feeling useless and frustrated as they grew older. Of Susan who should have the chance of a husband and babies. Of David, and Mary's little girl, and any other children there might be who would have to become labourers as soon as they were strong enough. Of Josella and myself having to work still harder as we became older because there would be more to feed and more work that must be done by hand . . .

Then there were the triffids patiently waiting. I could see hundreds of them in a dark green hedge beyond the fence. There must be research – some natural enemy, some poison, a debalancer of some kind, something must be found to deal with them; there must be relief from other work for that – and soon. Time was on the triffids' side. They had only to go on waiting while we used up our resources. First the fuel, then no more wire to mend the fences. And they or their descendants would still be waiting there when the wire rusted through . . .

And yet Shirning had become our home. I sighed.

There was a light step on the grass. Josella came and sat down beside me. I put an arm round her shoulders.

'What do *they* think about it?' I asked her.

'They're badly upset, poor things. It must be hard for them to understand how the triffids wait like that when they can't see them. And then, they can find their way about here, you see. It must be dreadful to have to contemplate going to an entirely strange place when you're blind. They only know what we tell them. I don't think they properly understand how impossible it will become here. If it were not for the children, I believe they'd say "No," flatly. It's their place, you see, all they have left. They feel that very much.' She paused, then she added: '*They* think that – but, of course, it's not really their place at all; it's ours, isn't it? We've worked hard for it.' She put her hand on mine. 'You've made it and kept it for us, Bill. What do you think? Shall we stay a year or two longer?'

'No,' I said. 'I worked because everything seemed to depend on me. Now it seems – rather futile.'

'Oh, darling, don't! A knight-errant isn't futile. You've fought for all of us, and kept the dragons away.'

'It's mostly the children,' I said.

'Yes – the children,' she agreed.

'And all the time, you know, I've been haunted by Coker – the first generation, labourers; the next, savages ... I think we had better admit defeat before it comes, and go now.'

She pressed my hand.

'Not defeat, Bill dear, just a – what's the phrase? – a strategic withdrawal. We withdraw to work and plan for the day when we can come back. One day we will. You'll show us how to wipe out every one of these foul triffids, and get our land back from them for us.'

'You've a lot of faith, darling.'

'And why not?'

'Well, at least I'll be fighting them. But first, we go – when?'

'Do you think we could have the summer out here? It could be a sort of holiday for all of us – with no preparations to make for the winter. We deserve a holiday, too.'

'I should think we could do that,' I agreed.

We sat, watching the valley dissolve in the dusk. Josella said:

'It's queer, Bill. Now I can go, I don't really want to. Sometimes it's seemed like prison – but now it seems like treachery to leave it. You see, I – I've been happier here than ever in my life before, in spite of everything.'

'As for me, my sweet, I wasn't even alive before. But we'll have better times yet – I promise you.'

'It's silly, but I shall cry when we do go. I shall cry buckets. You mustn't mind,' she said.

But, as things fell out, we were all of us much too busy to cry...

CHAPTER 17

STRATEGIC WITHDRAWAL

There was, as Josella had implied, no need for hurry. While we saw the summer out at Shirning I could prospect a new home for us on the island, and make several journeys there to transport the most useful part of the stores and gear that we had collected. But, meanwhile, the wood-pile had been destroyed. We needed more fuel than would keep the kitchen going for a few weeks, so the next morning Susan and I set off to fetch coal.

The half-track wasn't suitable for that job, so we took a four-wheel drive lorry. Although the nearest rail coal depot was only ten miles away, the roundabout route due to the blockage of some roads, and the bad condition of others, meant that it took us nearly the whole day. There were no major mishaps, but it was drawing on to evening when we returned.

As we turned the last corner of the lane, with the triffids slashing at the truck as indefatigably as ever from the banks, we stared in astonishment. Beyond our gate, parked in our yard, stood a monstrous-looking vehicle. The sight so dumbfounded us that we sat gaping at it for some moments before Susan put her hand on her helmet and gloves and climbed down to open the gate.

After I had driven in we went over together to look at the vehicle. The chassis, we saw, was supported on metal tracks which suggested a military origin. The general effect was somewhere between a cabin-cruiser, and an amateur-built caravan. Susan and I looked at it, and then looked at one another, with raised eyebrows. We went indoors to find out more about it.

In the living-room we found, in addition to the household, four men clad in grey-green ski-suits. Two of them wore pistols holstered to the right hip: the other two had parked their sub-machine guns on the floor beside their chairs.

As we came in, Josella turned a completely expressionless face towards us.

'Here is my husband. Bill, this is Mr Torrence. He tells us he is an official of some kind. He has proposals to make to us.' I had never heard her voice colder.

For a second I failed to respond. The man she indicated did not recognize me, but I recalled him all right. Features that have faced you along sights get sort of set in your mind. Besides, there was that distinctive red hair. I remembered well the way that efficient young man had turned back my party in Hampstead. I nodded to him. Looking at me, he said:

'I understand you are in charge here, Mr Masen?'

'The place belongs to Mr Brent here,' I replied.

'I mean that you are the organizer of this group?'

'In the circumstances, yes,' I said.

'Good.' He had a now-we-are-going-to-get-somewhere air. 'I am Commander, South-East region,' he added.

He spoke as if that should convey something important to me. It did not. I said so.

'It means,' he amplified, 'that I am the Chief Executive Officer of the Emergency Council for the South-Eastern Region of Britain. As such, it happens to be one of my duties to supervise the distribution and allocation of personnel.'

'Indeed,' I said. 'I have never heard of this – er – Council.'

'Possibly. We were equally ignorant of the existence of your group here until we saw your fire yesterday.'

I waited for him to go on.

'When such a group is discovered,' he said, 'it is my job to investigate it and assess it and make the necessary adjustments. So you may take it that I am here officially.'

'On behalf of an official Council – or does it happen to be a self-elected Council?' Dennis enquired.

'There has to be law and order,' the man said, stiffly. Then with a change of tone, he went on:

'This is a well-founded place you have here, Mr Masen.'

'Mr Brent has,' I corrected.

'We will leave Mr Brent out. He is only here because you made it possible for him to stay here.'

I looked across at Dennis. His face was set.

'Nevertheless, it is his property,' I said.

'It *was*, I understand. But the state of society which gave sanction to his ownership no longer exists. Titles to property have therefore ceased to be valid. Furthermore, Mr Brent is not sighted, so he cannot in any case be considered competent to hold authority.'

'Indeed,' I said again.

I had had a distaste for this young man and his decisive ways at our first meeting. Further acquaintance was doing nothing to mellow it. He went on:

'This is a matter of survival. Sentiment cannot be allowed to interfere with the necessary practical measures. Now, Mrs Masen has told me that you number eight altogether. Five adults, this girl, and two small children. All of you are sighted except these three.' He indicated Dennis, Mary, and Joyce.

'That is so,' I admitted.

'H'm. That's quite disproportionate, you know. There'll have to be some changes here, I'm afraid. We have to be realistic in times like this.'

Josella's eye caught mine. I saw a warning in it. But in any case, I had no intention of breaking out just then. I had seen the red-headed man's direct methods in action, and I wanted to know more of what I was up against. Apparently he realized that I would.

'I'd better put you in the picture,' he said. 'Briefly it is this. Regional Headquarters is at Brighton. London soon became too bad for us. But in Brighton we were able to clear and quarantine a part of the town, and we ran it. Brighton's a big place. When the sickness had passed and we could get about more, there were plenty of stores to begin with. More recently we have been running convoys from other places. But that's folding up now. The roads are getting too bad for lorries, and they are having to go too far. It had to come, of course. We'd reckoned that we could last out there several years longer – still, there it is. It's possible we undertook to look after too many from the start. Anyway, now we are having to disperse. The only way to keep going will be to live off the land. To do that we've got to break up into smaller units. The standard unit had been fixed at one sighted person to ten blind, plus any children.

'You have a good place here, fully capable of supporting two units. We shall allocate to you seventeen blind persons, making twenty with the three already here – again, of course, plus any children they may have.'

I started at him in amazement.

'You're seriously suggesting that twenty people and their children can live off this land,' I said. 'Why, it's utterly impossible. We've been wondering whether we shall be able to support ourselves on it.'

He shook his head, confidently.

'It is perfectly possible. And what I am offering you is the command of the double unit we shall install here. Frankly, if you do not care to take it, we shall put in someone else who will. We can't afford waste in these times.'

'But just look at the place,' I repeated. 'It simply can't do it.'

'I assure you that it *can*, Mr Masen. Of course, you'll have to lower your standards a bit – we all shall for the next few years, but when the children grow up a bit you'll begin to have labour to expand with. For six or seven years it's going to mean personal hard work for you, I admit – that can't be helped. From then on, however, you'll gradually be able to relax until you are simply supervising. Surely that's going to make a good return for just a few years of the tougher going?

'Placed as you are now, what sort of future would you have? Nothing but hard work until you die in your tracks – and your children faced with working in the same way, just to keep going, not more than that. Where are the future leaders and administrators to come from in that kind of set-up? Your way, you'd be worn out and still in harness in another twenty years – and all your children would be yokels. Our way, you'll be the head of a clan that's working for you, *and* you'll have an inheritance to hand on to your sons.'

Comprehension began to come to me. I said, wonderingly:

'Am I to understand that you are offering me a kind of – feudal seigneury?'

'Ah,' he said. 'I see you do begin to understand. It is, of course, the obvious and quite natural social and economic form for that state of things we are having to face now.'

There was no doubt whatever that the man was putting this forward as a perfectly serious plan. I evaded a comment on it by repeating myself:

'But the place just can't support that many.'

'For a few years undoubtedly you'll have to feed them mostly on mashed triffids – there won't be any shortage of that raw material by the look of it.'

'Cattle food!' I said.

'But sustaining – rich in the important vitamins, I'm told. And beggars – particularly blind beggars – can't be choosers.'

'You're seriously suggesting that I should take on all these people, and keep them on cattle fodder?'

'Listen, Mr Masen. If it were not for us, none of these blind people would be alive at all now – nor would their children. It's up to them to do what we tell them, take what we give them, and be thankful for whatever they get. If they like to refuse what we offer – well, that's their own funeral.'

I decided it would be unwise to say what I felt about his philosophy at the moment. I turned to another angle:

'I don't see—— Tell me, just where do you and your Council stand in all this?'

'Supreme authority and legislative power is vested in the Council. It will rule. It will also control the armed forces.'

'Armed forces!' I repeated, blankly.

'Certainly. The forces will be raised as and when necessary by levies on what you called the seigneuries. In return, you will have the right to call on the Council in cases of attack from outside or unrest within.'

I was beginning to feel a bit winded.

'An army! Surely a small mobile squad of police——?'

'I see you haven't grasped the wider aspect of the situation, Mr Masen. This affliction we have had was not confined to these islands, you know. It was world wide. Everywhere there is the same sort of chaos – that must be so, or we should have heard differently by now – and in every country there are probably a few survivors. Now, it stands to reason, doesn't it, that the first country to get on its feet again and put itself in order is also going to be the country to have the chance of bringing order elsewhere? Do you suggest that we should leave it to some other country to do this, and let it become the new dominant power in Europe – and possibly further afield? Obviously not. Clearly it is our national duty to get ourselves back on our feet as soon as possible and assume the dominant status so that we can prevent dangerous opposition from organizing against us. Therefore, the sooner we can raise a force adequate to discourage any likely aggressors, the better.'

For some moments silence lay on the room. Then Dennis laughed, unnaturally:

'Great God almighty! We've lived through all this – and now the man proposes to start a *war*?'

Torrence said, shortly:

'I don't seem to have made myself clear. The word "war" is an unjustifiable exaggeration. It will be simply a matter of pacifying and administering tribes that have reverted to primitive lawlessness.'

'Unless, of course, the same benevolent idea happens to have occurred to them,' Dennis suggested.

I became aware that both Josella and Susan were looking at me very hard. Josella pointed at Susan, and I perceived the reason.

'Let me get this straight,' I said. 'You expect the three of us who can see to be entirely responsible here for twenty blind adults and an unspecified number of children. It seems to me——'

'Blind people aren't quite incapable. They can do a lot, including for their own children in general, and helping to prepare their own food. Properly arranged, a great deal can be reduced to supervision and direction. But it will be two of you, Mr Masen – yourself and your wife, not three.'

I looked at Susan sitting up very straight in her blue boilersuit, with a red ribbon in her hair. There was an anxious appeal in her eyes as she looked from me to Josella.

'Three,' I said.

'I'm sorry, Mr Masen. The allocation is ten per unit. The girl can come to headquarters. We can find useful work for her there until she is old enough to take charge of a unit herself.'

'My wife and I regard Susan as our own daughter,' I told him shortly.

'I repeat, I am sorry. But those are the regulations.'

I regarded him for some moments. He looked steadily back at me. At last:

'We should, of course, require guarantees and undertakings regarding her if this had to happen,' I said.

I was aware of several quickly drawn breaths. Torrence's manner relaxed slightly.

'Naturally we shall give you all practicable assurances,' he said.

I nodded. 'I must have time to think it all over. It's quite new to me, and rather startling. Some points come to my mind at once. Equipment here is wearing out. It is difficult to find more that has not deteriorated. I can see that before long I am going to need good strong working horses.'

'Horses are difficult. There's very little stock at present. You'll probably have to use man-power teams for a time.'

'Then,' I said, 'there's accommodation. The outbuildings are too small for our needs now – and I can't put up even prefabricated quarters singlehanded.'

'There we shall be able to help you, I think.'

We went on discussing details for twenty minutes or more. By the end of it I had him showing something like affability, then I got rid of him by sending him off on a tour of the place with Susan as his sulky guide.

'Bill, what on earth——?' Josella began, as the door closed behind him and his companions.

I told her what I knew of Torrence and his method of dealing with trouble by shooting it early.

'That doesn't surprise me at all,' remarked Dennis. 'But, you know, what is surprising me now is that I'm suddenly feeling quite kindly towards the triffids. Without their intervention I suppose there would have been a whole lot more of this kind of thing by now. If they are the one factor that can stop serfdom coming back, then good luck to 'em.'

'The whole thing's clearly preposterous,' I said. 'It doesn't have a chance. How could Josella and I look after a crowd like that *and* keep the triffids out? But –' I added, 'we're scarcely in a position to give a flat "No" to a proposition put up by four armed men.'

'Then you're not——?'

'Darling,' I said, 'do you really see me in the position of a seigneur, driving my serfs and villeins before me with a whip? – even if the triffids haven't overrun me first?'

'But you said——'

'Listen,' I said. 'It's getting dark. Too late for them to leave now. They'll have to stay the night. I imagine that tomorrow the idea will be to take Susan away with them – she'd make quite a good hostage for our behaviour, you see. And they might leave one or two of the others to keep an eye on us. Well, I don't think we're taking that, are we?'

'No, but——'

'Well, I hope I've convinced him now that I'm coming round to his idea. Tonight we'll have the sort of supper that might be taken to imply accord. Make it a good one. Everybody's to eat plenty. Give the kids plenty, too. Lay on our best drinks. See that Torrence and his chaps have plenty, but the rest of us go very easy. Towards the end of the meal I shall disappear for a bit. You keep the party going to cover up. Play rowdy records at them, or something. And everybody help to whoop it up. Another thing – nobody must mention Michael Beadley and his lot. Torrence must know about the Isle of Wight set-up, but he doesn't think we do. Now what I'll be wanting is a sack of sugar.'

'Sugar?' said Josella, blankly.

'No? Well, a big can of honey, then. I should think that would do as well.'

.   .   .

Everyone played up very creditably at supper. The party not only thawed, it actually began to warm up. Josella brought out some of her own potent mead to supplement the more orthodox drinks, and it went down well. The visitors were in a state of happily comfortable relaxation when I made my unobtrusive exit.

I caught up a bundle of blankets and clothes and a parcel of food that I had laid ready, and hurried with them across the yard to the shed where we kept the half-track. With a hose from the tanker which held our main petrol supply I filled the half-track's tanks to overflowing. Then I turned my attention to Torrence's strange vehicle. With the help of a hand-dynamo torch I managed to locate the filler-cap, and poured a quart or more of honey into the tank. The rest of the large can of honey I disposed of into the tanker itself.

I could hear the party singing, and seemingly, still going well. After I had added some anti-triffid gear and miscellaneous afterthoughts to the stuff already in the half-track, I went back and joined it until it finally broke up in an atmosphere which even a close observer might have mistaken for almost maudlin goodwill.

We gave them two hours to get well asleep.

The moon had risen, and the yard was bathed in white light. I had forgotten to oil the shed doors, and gave them a curse for every creak. The rest came in procession towards me. The Brents and Joyce were familiar enough with the place not to need a guiding hand. Behind them followed Josella and Susan, carrying the children. David's sleepy voice rose once, and was stopped quickly by Josella's hand over his mouth. She got into the front, still holding him. I saw the others into the back and closed it. Then I climbed into the driving seat, kissed Josella, and took a deep breath.

Across the yard the triffids were clustering closer to the gate as they always did when they had been undisturbed for some hours.

By the grace of heaven the half-track's engine started at once. I slammed into low gear, swerved to avoid Torrence's vehicle, and drove straight at the gate. The heavy fender took it with a crash. We plunged forward in a festoon of wire-netting and broken timbers, knocking down a dozen triffids while the rest slashed furiously at us as we passed. Then we were on our way.

Where a turn in the climbing track let us look down on Shirning, we paused and cut the engine. Lights were on behind some of the windows, and as we watched, those on the vehicle blazed out, floodlighting the house. A starter began to grind. I had a twinge of uneasiness as the engine fired, though I knew we had several times the speed of that lumbering contraption. The machine began to jerk round on its tracks to face the gate. Before it completed the turn, the engine sputtered and stopped. The starter began to whirr again. It went on whirring, irritably, and without result.

The triffids had discovered that the gate was down. By a blend of moonlight and reflected headlights we could see their tall, slender forms already swaying in ungainly procession into the yard while others came lurching down the banks of the lane to follow them . . .

I looked at Josella. She was not crying buckets: not crying at all. She looked from me down to David asleep in her arms.

'I've all I really need,' she said, 'and some day you're going to bring us back to the rest, Bill.'

'Wifely confidence is a very nice trait, darling, but—— No, damn it, no buts – I *am* going to bring you back,' I said.

I got out to clear the debris from the front of the half-track, and wipe the poison from the windscreen so that I should be able to see to drive on and away across the tops of the hills towards the south-west.

. . .

And there my personal story joins up with the rest. You will find it in Elspeth Cary's excellent history of the colony.

Our hopes all centre here now. It seems unlikely that anything will come of Torrence's neo-feudal plan, though a number of his seigneuries do still exist with their inhabitants leading, so we hear, a life of squalid wretchedness behind their stockades. But there are not so many of them as there were. Every now and then Ivan reports that another has been overrun, and that the triffids which surrounded it have dispersed to join other sieges.

So we must regard the task ahead as ours alone. We think now that we can see the way, but there is still a lot of work and research to be done before the day when we, or our children, or their children, will cross the narrow straits on the great crusade to drive the triffids back and back with ceaseless destruction until we have wiped the last one of them from the face of the land that they have usurped.

THE END

I, Robot

ISAAC ASIMOV

The Three Laws of Robotics

1 – A robot may not injure a human being, or, through inaction allow a human being to come to harm.

2 – A robot must obey the orders given it by human beings except where such orders would conflict with the First Law.

3 – A robot must protect its own existence as long as such protection does not conflict with the First or Second Law.

Handbook of Robotics,
56th Edition, 2058 A.D.

INTRODUCTION

I looked at my notes and I didn't like them. I'd spent three days at U.S. Robots and might as well have spent them at home with the Encyclopaedia Tellurica.

Susan Calvin had been born in the year 1982, they said, which made her seventy-five now. Everyone knew that. Appropriately enough, U.S. Robot and Mechanical Men, Inc. was seventy-five also, since it had been in the year of Dr Calvin's birth that Lawrence Robertson had first taken out incorporation papers for what eventually became the strangest industrial giant in man's history. Well, everyone knew that, too.

At the age of twenty, Susan Calvin had been part of the particular Psycho-Math seminar at which Dr Alfred Lanning of U.S. Robots had demonstrated the first mobile robot to be equipped with a voice. It was a large, clumsy unbeautiful robot, smelling of machine-oil and destined for the projected mines on Mercury. ——But it could speak and make sense.

Susan said nothing at that seminar; took no part in the hectic discussion period that followed. She was a frosty girl, plain and colourless, who protected herself against a world she disliked by a mask-like expression and hypertrophy of intellect. But as she watched and listened, she felt the stirrings of a cold enthusiasm.

She obtained her bachelor's degree at Columbia in 2003 and began graduate work in cybernetics.

All that had been done in the mid-twentieth century on 'calculating machines' had been upset by Robertson and his positronic brain-paths. The miles of relays and photocells had given way to the spongy globe of plantinumiridium about the size of a human brain.

She learned to calculate the parameters necessary to fix the possible variables within the 'positronic brain', to construct 'brains' on paper such that the responses to given stimuli could be accurately predicted.

In 2008, she obtained her Ph.D. and joined United States Robots as a 'Robopsychologist', becoming the first great practitioner of a new science. Lawrence Robertson was still president of the corporation; Alfred Lanning had become director of research.

For fifty years, she watched the direction of human progress change – and leap ahead.

Now she was retiring – as much as she ever could. At least, she was allowing someone else's name to be inset upon the door of her old office.

That, essentially, was what I had. I had a long list of her published papers, of the patents in her name; I had the chronological details of her promotions—— In short I had her professional 'vita' in full detail.

But that wasn't what I wanted.

I needed more than that for my feature articles for Interplanetary Press. Much more.

I told her so.

'Dr Calvin,' I said, as lushly as possible, 'in the mind of the public you and U.S. Robots are identical. Your retirement will end an era and——'

'You want the human-interest angle?' She didn't smile at me. I don't think she ever smiles. But her eyes were sharp, though not angry. I felt her glance slide through me and out of my occiput and I knew that I was uncommonly transparent to her; that everybody was.

But I said, 'That's right.'

'Human interest out of Robots? A contradiction.'

'No, doctor. Out of you.'

'Well, I've been called a robot myself. Surely, they've told you I'm not human.'

They had, but there was no point in saying so.

She got up from her chair. She wasn't tall and she looked frail. I followed her to the window and we looked out.

The offices and factories of U.S. Robots were a small city; spaced and planned. It was flattened out like an aerial photograph.

'When I first came here,' she said, 'I had a little room in a building right about there where the fire-house is now.' She pointed. 'It was torn down before you were born. I shared the room with three others. I had half a desk. We built our robots all in one building. Output – three a week. Now look at us.'

'Fifty years,' I hackneyed, 'is a long time.'

'Not when you're looking back at them,' she said. 'You wonder how they vanished so quickly.'

She went back to her desk and sat down. She didn't need expression on her face to look sad, somehow.

'How old are you?' she wanted to know.

'Thirty-two,' I said.

'Then you don't remember a world without robots. There was a time when humanity faced the universe alone and without a friend. Now he has creatures to help him; stronger creatures than himself, more faithful, more useful, and absolutely devoted to him. Mankind is no longer alone. Have you ever thought of it that way?'

'I'm afraid I haven't. May I quote you?'

'You may. To you, a robot is a robot. Gears and metal, electricity and positrons. ——Mind and iron! Human-made! if necessary, human-destroyed! But you haven't worked with them, so you don't know them. They're a cleaner, better breed than we are.'

I tried to nudge her gently with words, 'We'd like to hear some of the things you could tell us; get your views on robots. The Interplanetary Press reaches the entire Solar System. Potential audience is three billion, Dr Calvin. They ought to know what you could tell them on robots.'

It wasn't necessary to nudge. She didn't hear me, but she was moving in the right direction.

'*They might have known from the start. We sold robots for Earth-use then – before my time it was, even. Of course, that was when robots could not talk. Afterwards, they became more human and opposition began. The labour unions, of course, naturally opposed robot competition for human jobs, and various segments of religious opinion had their superstitious objections. It was all quite ridiculous and quite useless. And yet there it was.*'

I was taking it down verbatim on my pocket-recorder, trying not to show the knuckle-motions of my hand. If you practise a bit, you can get to a point where you can record accurately without taking the little gadget out of your pocket.

'*Take the case of Robbie,*' *she said.* '*I never knew him. He was dismantled the year before I joined the company – hopelessly out-of-date. But I saw the little girl in the museum——*'

She stopped, but I didn't say anything. I let her eyes mist up and her mind travel back. She had lots of time to cover.

'*I heard about it later, and when they called us blasphemers and demon-creators, I always thought of him. Robbie was a non-vocal robot. He couldn't speak. He was made and sold in 1996. Those were the days before extreme specialization, so he was sold as a nursemaid——*'

'*As a what?*'

'*As a nursemaid——*'

CHAPTER 1

ROBBIE

'Ninety-eight – ninety-nine – *one hundred.*' Gloria withdrew her chubby little forearm from before her eyes and stood for a moment, wrinkling her nose and blinking in the sunlight. Then, trying to watch in all directions at once, she withdrew a few cautious steps from the tree against which she had been leaning.

She craned her neck to investigate the possibilities of a clump of bushes to the right and then withdrew farther to obtain a better angle for viewing its dark recesses. The quiet was profound except for the incessant buzzing of insects and the occasional chirrup of some hardy bird, braving the midday sun.

Gloria pouted, 'I bet he went inside the house, and I've told him a million times that's not fair.'

With tiny lips pressed together tightly and a severe frown crinkling her forehead, she moved determinedly towards the two-storey building up past the driveway.

Too late she heard the rustling sound behind her, followed by the distinctive and rhythmic clump-clump of Robbie's metal feet. She whirled about to see her triumphing companion emerge from hiding and make for the home-tree at full-speed.

Gloria shrieked in dismay. 'Wait, Robbie! That wasn't fair, Robbie! You promised you wouldn't run until I found you.' Her little feet could make no headway at all against Robbie's giant strides. Then, within ten feet of the goal, Robbie's pace slowed suddenly to the merest of crawls, and Gloria, with one final burst of wild speed, dashed pantingly past him to touch the welcome bark of home-tree first.

Gleefully, she turned on the faithful Robbie, and with the barest of ingratitude, rewarded him for his sacrifice, by taunting him cruelly for a lack of running ability.

'Robbie can't run,' she shouted at the top of her eight-year-old voice. 'I can beat him any day. I can beat him any day.' She chanted the words in a shrill rhythm.

Robbie didn't answer, of course – not in words. He pantomimed running, instead, inching away until Gloria found herself running after him as he dodged her narrowly, forcing her to veer in helpless circles, little arms outstretched and fanning at the air.

'Robbie,' she squealed, 'stand still!'——And the laughter was forced out of her in breathless jerks.

——Until he turned suddenly and caught her up, whirling her round, so that for her the world fell away for a moment with a blue emptiness beneath, and green trees stretching hungrily downward towards the void. Then she was down in the grass again, leaning against Robbie's leg and still holding a hard, metal finger.

After a while, her breath returned. She pushed uselessly at her dishevelled hair in vague imitation of one of her mother's gestures and twisted to see if her dress were torn.

She slapped her hand against Robbie's torso, 'Bad boy! I'll spank you!'

And Robbie cowered, holding his hands over his face so that she had to add, 'No, I won't, Robbie. I won't spank you. But anyway, it's my turn to hide now because you've got longer legs and you promised not to run till I found you.'

Robbie nodded his head – a small parallelepiped with rounded edges and corners attached to a similar but much larger parallelepiped that served as torso by means of a short, flexible stalk – and obediently faced the tree. A thin, metal film descended over his glowing eyes and from within his body came a steady, resonant ticking.

'Don't peek now – and don't skip any numbers,' warned Gloria, and scurried for cover.

With unvarying regularity, seconds were ticked off, and at the hundredth, up went the eyelids, and the glowing red of Robbie's eyes swept the prospect. They rested for a moment on a bit of colourful gingham that protruded from behind a boulder. He advanced a few steps and convinced himself that it was Gloria who squatted behind it.

Slowly, remaining always between Gloria and home-tree, he advanced on the hiding place, and when Gloria was plainly in sight and could no longer even theorize to herself that she was not seen, he extended one arm towards her, slapping the other against his leg so that it rang again. Gloria emerged sulkily.

'You peeked!' she exclaimed, with gross unfairness. 'Besides I'm tired of playing hide-and-seek. I want a ride.'

But Robbie was hurt at the unjust accusation, so he seated himself carefully and shook his head ponderously from side to side.

Gloria changed her tone to one of gentle coaxing immediately, 'Come on, Robbie. I didn't mean it about peeking. Give me a ride.'

Robbie was not to be won over so easily, though. He gazed stubbornly at the sky, and shook his head even more emphatically.

'Please, Robbie, please give me a ride.' She encircled his neck with rosy arms and hugged tightly. Then, changing moods in a moment, she moved away. 'If you don't, I'm going to cry,' and her face twisted appallingly in preparation.

Hard-hearted Robbie paid scant attention to this dreadful possibility, and shook his head a third time. Gloria found it necessary to play her trump card.

'If you don't,' she exclaimed warmly, 'I won't tell you any more stories, that's all. Not one——'

Robbie gave in immediately and unconditionally before this ultimatum, nodding his head vigorously until the metal of his neck hummed. Carefully, he raised the little girl and placed her on his broad, flat shoulders.

Gloria's threatened tears vanished immediately and she crowed with delight. Robbie's metal skin, kept at a constant temperature of seventy by the high resistance coils within felt nice and comfortable, while the beautifully loud sound her heels made as they bumped rhythmically against his chest was enchanting.

'You're an air-coaster, Robbie, you're a big, silver air-coaster. Hold out your arms straight. ——You *got* to, Robbie, if you're going to be an air-coaster.'

The logic was irrefutable. Robbie's arms were wings catching the air currents and he was a silver 'coaster.

Gloria twisted the robot's head and leaned to the right. He banked sharply. Gloria equipped the 'coaster with a motor that went 'Br-r-r' and then with weapons that went 'Powie' and 'Sh-sh-shshsh.' Pirates were giving chase and the ship's blasters were coming into play. The pirates dropped in a steady rain.

'Got another one. ——Two more,' she cried.

Then 'Faster, men,' Gloria said pompously, 'we're running out of ammunition.' She aimed over her shoulder with undaunted courage and Robbie was a blunt-nosed spaceship zooming through the void at maximum acceleration.

Clear across the field he sped, to the patch of tall grass on the other side, where he stopped with a suddenness that evoked a shriek from his flushed rider, and then tumbled her onto the soft, green carpet.

Gloria gasped and panted, and gave voice to intermittent whispered exclamations of 'That was *nice!*'

Robbie waited until she had caught her breath and then pulled gently at a lock of hair.

'You want something?' said Gloria, eyes wide in an apparently artless complexity that fooled her huge 'nursemaid' not at all. He pulled the curl harder.

'Oh, I know. You want a story.'

Robbie nodded rapidly.

'Which one?'

Robbie made a semi-circle in the air with one finger.

The little girl protested, '*Again?* I've told you Cinderella a million times. Aren't you tired of it? ——It's for babies.'

Another semi-circle.

'Oh, hell,' Gloria composed herself, ran over the details of the tale in her mind (together with her own elaborations, of which she had several) and began:

'Are you ready? Well – once upon a time there was a beautiful little girl whose name was Ella. And she had a terribly cruel step-mother and two very ugly and *very* cruel step-sisters and——'

. . . .

Gloria was reaching the very climax of the tale – midnight was striking and everything was changing back to the shabby originals lickety-spit, while Robbie listened tensely with burning eyes – when the interruption came.

'Gloria!'

It was the high-pitched sound of a woman who has been calling not once, but several times; and had the nervous tone of one in whom anxiety was beginning to overcome impatience.

'Mamma's calling me,' said Gloria, not quite happily. 'You'd better carry me back to the house, Robbie.'

Robbie obeyed with alacrity for somehow there was that in him which judged it best to obey Mrs Weston, without as much as a scrap of hesitation. Gloria's father was rarely home in the daytime exept on Sunday – today, for instance – and when he was, he proved a genial and understanding person. Gloria's mother, however, was a source of uneasiness to Robbie and there was always the impulse to sneak away from her sight.

Mrs Weston caught sight of them the minute they rose above the masking tufts of long grass and retired inside the house to wait.

'I've shouted myself hoarse, Gloria,' she said, severely. 'Where were you?'

'I was with Robbie,' quavered Gloria. 'I was telling him Cinderella, and I forgot it was dinner-time.'

'Well, it's a pity Robbie forgot, too.' Then, as if that reminded her of the robot's presence, she whirled upon him. 'You may go, Robbie. She doesn't need you now.' Then, brutally, 'And don't come back till I call you.'

Robbie turned to go, but hesitated as Gloria cried out in his defence,

'Wait, Mamma, you got to let him stay. I didn't finish Cinderella for him. I said I would tell him Cinderella and I'm not finished.'

'Gloria!'

'Honest and truly, Mamma, he'll stay so quiet, you won't even know he's here. He can sit on the chair in the corner, and he won't say a word – I mean he won't *do* anything. Will you, Robbie?'

Robbie, appealed to, nodded his massive head up and down once.

'Gloria, if you don't stop this at once, you shan't see Robbie for a whole week.'

The girl's eyes fell, 'All right! But Cinderella is his favourite story and I didn't finish it. ——And he likes it so much.'

The robot left with a disconsolate step and Gloria choked back a sob.

.   .   .

George Weston was comfortable. It was a habit of his to be comfortable on Sunday afternoons. A good, hearty dinner below the hatches; a nice, soft, dilapidated couch on which to sprawl; a copy of the *Times*; slippered feet and shirtless chest – how could anyone *help* but be comfortable?

He wasn't pleased, therefore, when his wife walked in. After ten years of married life, he still was so unutterably foolish as to love her, and there was no question that he was always glad to see her – still Sunday afternoons just after dinner were sacred to him and his idea of solid comfort was to be left in utter solitude for two or three hours. Consequently, he fixed his eye firmly upon the latest reports of the Lefebre-Yoshida expedition to Mars (this one was to take off from Lunar Base and might actually succeed) and pretended she wasn't there.

Mrs Weston waited patiently for two minutes, then impatiently for two more, and finally broke the silence.

'George!'

'Hmpph?'

'George, I say! *Will* you put down that paper and look at me?'

The paper rustled to the floor and Weston turned a weary face towards his wife, 'What is it, dear?'

'You know what it is, George. It's Gloria and that terrible machine.'

'What terrible machine?'

'Now don't pretend you don't know what I'm talking about. It's that robot Gloria calls Robbie. He doesn't leave her for a moment.'

'Well, why should he? He's not supposed to. And he certainly isn't a terrible machine. He's the best darn robot money can buy and I'm damned sure he set me back half a year's income. He's worth it, though – darn sight cleverer than half my office staff.'

He made a move to pick up the paper again, but his wife was quicker and snatched it away.

'You listen to *me*, George. I won't have my daughter entrusted to a machine – and I don't care how clever it is. It has no soul, and no one knows what it may be thinking. A child just isn't *made* to be guarded by a thing of metal.'

Weston frowned, 'When did you decide this? He's been with Gloria two years now and I haven't seen you worry till now.'

'It was different at first. It was a novelty; it took a load off me, and – and it was a fashionable thing to do. But now I don't know. The neighbours——'

'Well, what have the neighbours to do with it. Now, look. A robot is infinitely more to be trusted than a human nursemaid. Robbie was constructed for only one purpose really – to be the companion of a little child. His entire "mentality" has been created for the purpose. He just can't help being faithful and loving and kind. He's a machine – *made so*. That's more than you can say for humans.'

'But something might go wrong. Some – some——' Mrs Weston was a bit hazy about the insides of a robot, 'some little jigger will come loose and the awful thing will go berserk and – and——' She couldn't bring herself to complete the quite obvious thought.

'Nonsense,' Weston denied, with an involuntary nervous shiver. 'That's completely ridiculous. We had a long discussion at the time we bought Robbie about the First Law of Robotics. You *know* that it is impossible for a robot to harm a human being; that long before enough can go wrong to alter that First Law, a robot would be completely inoperable. It's a mathematical impossibility. Besides I have an engineer from U.S. Robots here twice a year to give the poor gadget a complete overhaul. Why, there's no more chance of anything at all going wrong with Robbie than there is of you or I suddenly going looney – considerably less, in fact. Besides, how are you going to take him away from Gloria?'

He made another futile stab at the paper and his wife tossed it angrily into the next room.

'That's just it, George! She won't play with anyone else. There are dozens of little boys and girls that she should make friends with, but she won't. She won't go *near* them unless I make her. That's no way for a little girl to grow up. You want her to be normal, don't you? You want her to be able to take her part in society.'

'You're jumping at shadows, Grace. Pretend Robbie's a dog. I've seen hundreds of children who would rather have their dog than their father.'

'A dog is different, George. We *must* get rid of that horrible thing. You can sell it back to the company. I've asked, and you can.'

'You've *asked*? Now look here, Grace, let's not go off the deep end. We're keeping the robot until Gloria is older and I don't want the subject brought up again.' And with that he walked out of the room in a huff.

. . .

Mrs Weston met her husband at the door two evenings later. 'You'll have to listen to this, George. There's bad feeling in the village.'

'About what?' asked Weston. He stepped into the wash-room and drowned out any possible answer by the splash of water.

Mrs Weston waited. She said, 'About Robbie.'

Weston stepped out, towel in hand, face red and angry. 'What are you talking about?'

'Oh, it's been building up and building up. I've tried to close my eyes to it, but I'm not going to any more. Most of the villagers consider Robbie dangerous. Children aren't allowed to go near our place in the evenings.'

'We trust *our* child with the thing.'

'Well, people aren't reasonable about these things.'

'Then to hell with them.'

'Saying that doesn't solve the problem. I've got to do my shopping down there. I've got to meet them every day. And it's even worse in the city these days when it comes to robots. New York has just passed an ordinance keeping all robots off the streets between sunset and sunrise.'

'All right, but they can't stop us from keeping a robot in our home. ——Grace, this is one of your campaigns. I recognize it. But it's no use. The answer is still, no! We're keeping Robbie!'

. . .

And yet he loved his wife – and what was worse, his wife knew it. George Weston, after all, was only a man – poor thing – and his wife made full use of every device which a clumsier and more scrupulous sex has learned, with reason and futility, to fear.

Ten times in the ensuing week, he cried, 'Robbie stays – and that's *final*!' and each time it was weaker and accompanied by a louder and more agonized groan.

Came the day at last, when Weston approached his daughter guiltily and suggested a 'beautiful' visivox show in the village.

Gloria clapped her hands happily, 'Can Robbie go?'

'No, dear,' he said, and winced at the sound of his voice, 'they won't allow robots at the visivox – but you can tell him all about it when you get home.' He stumbled all over the last few words and looked away.

Gloria came back from town bubbling over with enthusiasm, for the visivox had been a gorgeous spectacle indeed.

She waited for her father to manoeuvre the jet-car into the sunken garage, 'Wait till I tell Robbie, Daddy. He would have liked it like anything. ——Especially when Francis Fran was backing away so-o-o quietly, and backed right into one of the Leopard-Men and had to run.' She laughed again. 'Daddy, are there really Leopard-Men on the Moon?'

'Probably not,' said Weston absently. 'It's just funny make-believe.' He couldn't take much longer with the car. He'd have to face it.

Gloria ran across the lawn. 'Robbie. ——Robbie!'

Then she stopped suddenly at the sight of a beautiful collie which regarded her out of serious brown eyes as it wagged its tail on the porch.

'Oh, what a nice dog!' Gloria climbed the steps, approached cautiously and patted it. 'Is it for me, Daddy?'

Her mother had joined them. 'Yes, it is, Gloria. Isn't it nice – soft and furry. It's very gentle. It *likes* little girls.'

'Can he play games?'

'Surely. He can do any number of tricks. Would you like to see some?'

'Right away. I want Robbie to see him, too. ——*Robbie!*' She stopped, uncertainly, and frowned, 'I'll bet he's just staying in his room because he's mad at me for not taking him to the visivox. You'll have to explain to him, Daddy. He might not believe me, but he knows if you say it, it's so.'

Weston's lips grew tighter. He looked towards his wife but could not catch her eye.

Gloria turned precipitously and ran down the basement steps, shouting as she went, 'Robbie—— Come and see what Daddy and Mamma brought me. They brought me a dog, Robbie.'

In a minute she had returned, a frightened little girl. 'Mamma, Robbie isn't in his room. Where is he?' There was no answer and George Weston coughed and was suddenly extremely interested in an aimlessly drifting cloud. Gloria's voice quavered on the verge of tears, 'Where's Robbie, Mamma?'

Mrs Weston sat down and drew her daughter gently to her, 'Don't feel bad, Gloria. Robbie has gone away, I think.'

'Gone *away*? Where? Where's he gone away, Mamma?'

'No one knows, darling. He just walked away. We've looked and we've looked and we've looked for him, but we can't find him.'

'You mean he'll never come back again?' Her eyes were round with horror.

'We may find him soon. We'll keep looking for him. And meanwhile you can play with your nice new doggie. Look at him! His name is Lightning and he can——'

But Gloria's eyelids had overflown, 'I don't want the nasty dog – I want Robbie. I want you to find me Robbie.' Her feelings became too deep for words, and she spluttered into a shrill wail.

Mrs Weston glanced at her husband for help, but he merely shuffled his feet morosely and did not withdraw his ardent stare from the heavens, so she bent to the task of consolation, 'Why do you cry, Gloria? Robbie was only a machine, just a nasty old machine. He wasn't alive at all.'

'He was *not* no machine!' screamed Gloria, fiercely and ungrammatically. 'He was a *person* just like you and me and he was my *friend*. I want him back. Oh, Mamma, I want him back.'

Her mother groaned in defeat and left Gloria to her sorrow.

'Let her have her cry out,' she told her husband. 'Childish griefs are never lasting. In a few days, she'll forget that awful robot ever existed.'

But time proved Mrs Weston a bit too optimistic. To be sure, Gloria ceased crying, but she ceased smiling, too, and the passing days found her ever more silent and shadowy. Gradually, her attitude of passive unhappiness wore Mrs Weston down and all that kept her from yielding was the impossibility of admitting defeat to her husband.

Then, one evening, she flounced into the living room, sat down, folded her arms and looked boiling mad.

Her husband stretched his neck in order to see her over his newspaper, 'What now, Grace?'

'It's that child, George. I've had to send back the dog today. Gloria positively couldn't stand the sight of him, she said. She's driving me into a nervous breakdown.'

Weston laid down the paper and a hopeful gleam entered his eye, 'Maybe—— Maybe we ought to get Robbie back. It might be done, you know. I can get in touch with——'

'No!' she replied, grimly. 'I won't hear of it. We're not giving up that easily. My child shall *not* be brought up by a robot if it takes years to break her of it.'

Weston picked up his paper again with a disappointed air. 'A year of this will have me prematurely grey.'

'You're a big help, George,' was the frigid answer. 'What Gloria needs is a change of environment. Of course she can't forget Robbie here. How can she when every tree and rock reminds her of him? It is really the *silliest* situation I have ever heard of. Imagine a child pining away for the loss of a robot.'

'Well, stick to the point. What's the change in environment you're planning?'

'We're going to take her to New York.'

'The city! In August! Say, do you know what New York is like in August. It's unbearable.'

'Millions do bear it.'

'They don't have a place like this to go to. If they didn't have to stay in New York, they wouldn't.'

'Well, *we* have to. I say we're leaving now – or as soon as we can make the arrangements. In the city, Gloria will find sufficient interests and sufficient friends to perk her up and make her forget that machine.'

'Oh, Lord,' groaned the lesser half, 'those frying pavements!'

'We have to,' was the unshaken response. 'Gloria has lost five pounds in the last month and my little girl's health is more important to me than your comfort.'

'It's a pity you didn't think of your little girl's health before you deprived her of her pet robot,' he muttered – but to himself.

.   .   .

Gloria displayed immediate signs of improvement when told of the impending trip to the city. She spoke little of it, but when she did, it was always with lively anticipation. Again, she began to smile and to eat with something of her former appetite.

Mrs Weston hugged herself for joy and lost no opportunity to triumph over her still sceptical husband.

'You see, George, she helps with the packing like a little angel, and chatters away as if she hadn't a care in the world. It's just as I told you – all we need do is substitute other interests.'

'Hmpph,' was the sceptical response, 'I hope so.'

Preliminaries were gone through quickly. Arrangements were made for the preparation of their city home and a couple were engaged as housekeepers for the country home. When the day of the trip finally did come, Gloria was all but her old self again, and no mention of Robbie passed her lips at all.

In high good-humour the family took a taxi-gyro to the airport (Weston would have preferred using his own private 'gyro, but it was only a two-seater with no room for baggage) and entered the waiting liner.

'Come, Gloria,' called Mrs Weston. 'I've saved you a seat near the window so you can watch the scenery.'

Gloria trotted down the aisle cheerily, flattened her nose into a white oval against the thick clear glass, and watched with an intentness that increased as the sudden coughing of the motor drifted backward into the interior. She was too young to be frightened when the ground dropped away as if let through a trap-door and she herself suddenly became twice her usual weight, but not too young to be mightily interested. It wasn't until the ground had changed into a tiny patch-work quilt that she withdrew her nose, and faced her mother again.

'Will we soon be in the city, Mamma?' she asked, rubbing her chilled nose, and watching with interest as the patch of moisture which her breath had formed on the pane shrank slowly and vanished.

'In about half an hour, dear.' Then, with just the faintest trace of anxiety, 'Aren't you glad we're going? Don't you think you'll be very happy in the city with all the buildings and people and things to see. We'll go to the visivox every day and see shows and go to the circus and the beach and——'

'Yes, Mamma,' was Gloria's unenthusiastic rejoinder. The liner passed over a bank of clouds at the moment, and Gloria was instantly absorbed in the unusual spectacle of clouds underneath one. Then they were over clear sky again, and she turned to her mother with a sudden mysterious air of secret knowledge.

'*I* know why we're going to the city, Mamma.'

'Do you?' Mrs Weston was puzzled. 'Why, dear?'

'You didn't tell me because you wanted it to be a surprise, but *I* know.' For a moment, she was lost in admiration at her own acute penetration, and then she laughed gaily. 'We're going to New York so we can find Robbie, aren't we? ——With detectives.'

The statement caught George Weston in the middle of a drink of water, with disastrous results. There was a sort of strangled gasp, a geyser of water, and then a bout of choking coughs. When all was over, he stood there, a red-faced, water-drenched and very, very annoyed person.

Mrs Weston maintained her composure, but when Gloria repeated her question in a more anxious tone of voice, she found her temper rather bent.

'Maybe,' she retorted, tartly. 'Now sit and be still, for Heaven's sake.'

.   .   .

New York City, A.D. 1998, was a paradise for the sightseer more than ever in its history. Gloria's parents realized this and made the most of it.

On direct orders from his wife, George Weston arranged to have his business take care of itself for a month or so, in order to be free to spend the time in what he termed 'dissipating Gloria to the verge of ruin'. Like everything else Weston did, this was gone about in an efficient, thorough, and business-like way. Before the month had passed, nothing that could be done had not been done.

She was taken to the top of the half-mile tall Roosevelt Buildings, to gaze down in awe upon the jagged panorama of rooftops that blended far off in the fields of Long Island and the flatlands of New Jersey. They visited the zoos where Gloria stared in delicious fright at the 'real live lion' (rather disappointed that the keepers fed him raw steaks, instead of human beings, as she had expected), and asked insistently and peremptorily to see 'the whale'.

The various museums came in for their share of attention, together with the parks and the beaches and the aquarium.

She was taken half-way up the Hudson in an excursion steamer fitted out in the archaism of the mad Twenties. She travelled into the stratosphere on an exhibition trip, where the sky turned deep purple and the stars came out and the misty earth below looked like a huge concave bowl. Down under the waters of the Long Island Sound she was taken in a glass-walled sub-sea vessel, where in a green and wavering world, quaint and curious sea-things ogled her and wiggled suddenly away.

On a more prosaic level, Mrs Weston took her to the department stores where she could revel in another type of fairyland.

In fact, when the month had nearly sped, the Westons were convinced that everything conceivable had been done to take Gloria's mind once and for all off the departed Robbie – but they were not quite sure they had succeeded.

The fact remained that wherever Gloria went, she displayed the most absorbed and concentrated interest in such robots that happened to be present. No matter how exciting the spectacle before her, nor how novel to her girlish eyes, she turned away instantly if the corner of her eye caught a glimpse of metallic movement.

Mrs Weston went out of her way to keep Gloria away from all robots.

And the matter was finally climaxed in the episode at the Museum of Science and Industry. The Museum had announced a special 'Children's programme' in which exhibits of scientific witchery scaled down to the child mind were to be shown. The Westons, of course, placed it upon their list of 'absolutely'.

It was while the Westons were standing totally absorbed in the exploits of a powerful electro-magnet that Mrs Weston suddenly became aware of the fact that Gloria was no longer with her. Initial panic gave way to calm decision and, enlisting the aid of three attendants, a careful search was begun.

Gloria, of course, was not one to wander aimlessly, however. For her age, she was an unusually determined and purposeful girl, quite full of the maternal genes in that respect. She had seen a huge sign on the third

floor, which had said, 'This Way to the Talking Robot.' Having spelled
it out to herself and having noticed that her parents did not seem to wish
to move in the proper direction, she did the obvious thing. Waiting for
an opportune moment of parental distraction, she calmly disengaged
herself and followed the sign.

. . .

The Talking Robot was a *tour de force,* a thoroughly impractical
device, possessing publicity value only. Once an hour, an escorted group
stood before it and asked questions of the robot engineer in charge in
careful whispers. Those the engineer decided were suitable for the
robot's circuits were transmitted to the Talking Robot.

It was rather dull. It may be nice to know that the square of fourteen is
one hundred and ninety-six, that the temperature at the moment is 72
degrees Fahrenheit, and the air-pressure 30.02 inches of mercury, that
the atomic weight of sodium is 23, but one doesn't really need a robot for
that. One especially does not need an unwieldly, totally immobile mass
of wires and coils spreading over twenty-five square yards.

Few people bothered to return for a second helping, but one girl in her
middle teens sat quietly on a bench waiting for a third. She was the only
one in the room when Gloria entered.

Gloria did not look at her. To her at the moment, another human
being was but an inconsiderable item. She saved her attention for this
large thing with the wheels. For a moment, she hesitated in dismay. It
didn't look like any robot she had ever seen.

Cautiously and doubtfully she raised her treble voice, 'Please, Mr
Robot, sir, are you the Talking Robot, sir?' She wasn't sure, but it
seemed to her that a robot that actually talked was worth a great deal of
politeness.

(The girl in her mid-teens allowed a look of intense concentration to
cross her thin, plain face. She whipped out a small notebook and began
writing in rapid pot-hooks.)

There was an oily whir of gears and a mechanically-timbred voice
boomed out in words that lacked accent and intonation, 'I – am – the –
robot – that – talks.'

Gloria stared at it ruefully. It *did* talk, but the sound came from inside
somewheres. There was no *face* to talk to. She said, 'Can you help me,
Mr Robot, sir?'

The Talking Robot was designed to answer questions, and only such
questions as it could answer had ever been put to it. It was quite
confident of its ability, therefore, 'I – can – help – you.'

'Thank you, Mr Robot, sir. Have you seen Robbie?'

'Who – is Robbie?'

'He's a robot, Mr Robot, sir.' She stretched to her tip-toes. 'He's about so high, Mr Robot, sir, only higher, and he's very nice. He's got a head, you know. I mean you haven't, but he has, Mr Robot, sir.'

The Talking Robot had been left behind, 'A – robot?'

'Yes, Mr Robot, sir. A robot just like you, except he can't talk, of course, and – looks like a real person.'

'A – robot – like – me?'

'Yes, Mr Robot, sir.'

To which the Talking Robot's only response was an erratic splutter and an occasional incoherent sound. The radical generalization offered it, i.e. its existence, not as a particular object, but as a member of a general group, was too much for it. Loyally, it tried to encompass the concept and half a dozen coils burnt out. Little warning signals were buzzing.

(The girl in her mid-teens left at that point. She had enough for her Physics–1 paper on 'Practical Aspects of Robotics.' This paper was Susan Calvin's first of many on the subject.)

Gloria stood waiting, with carefully concealed impatience, for the machine's answer when she heard the cry behind her of 'There she is,' and recognized that cry as her mother's.

'What are you doing here, you bad girl?' cried Mrs Weston, anxiety dissolving at once into anger. 'Do you know you frightened your mamma and daddy almost to death? Why did you run away?'

The robot engineer had also dashed in, tearing his hair, and demanding who of the gathering crowd had tampered with the machine. 'Can't anybody read signs?' he yelled. 'You're not allowed in here without an attendant.'

Gloria raised her grieved voice over the din, 'I only came to see the Talking Robot, Mamma. I thought he might know where Robbie was because they're both robots.' And then, as the thought of Robbie was suddenly brought forcefully home to her, she burst into a sudden storm of tears, 'And I *got* to find Robbie, Mamma. I *got* to.'

Mrs Weston strangled a cry, and said, 'Oh, good Heavens. Come home, George. This is more than I can stand.'

That evening, George Weston left for several hours, and the next morning, he approached his wife with something that looked suspiciously like smug complacence.

'I've got an idea, Grace.'

'About what?' was the gloomy, uninterested query.

'About Gloria.'

'You're not going to suggest buying back that robot?'

'No, of course not.'

'Then go ahead. I might as well listen to you. Nothing *I've* done seems to have done any good.'

'All right. Here's what I've been thinking. The whole trouble with Gloria is that she thinks of Robbie as a *person* and not as a *machine*. Naturally, she can't forget him. Now if we managed to convince her that Robbie was nothing more than a mess of steel and copper in the form of sheets and wires with electricity its juice of life, how long would her longings last. It's the psychological attack, if you see my point.'

'How do you plan to do it?'

'Simple. Where do you suppose I went last night? I persuaded Robertson of U.S. Robots and Mechanical Men, Inc. to arrange for a complete tour of his premises tomorrow. The three of us will go, and by the time we're through, Gloria will have it drilled into her that a robot is *not* alive.'

Mrs Weston's eyes widened gradually and something glinted in her eyes that was quite like sudden admiration, 'Why, George, that's a *good* idea.'

And George Weston's vest buttons strained. 'Only kind I have,' he said.

. . .

Mr Struthers was a conscientious General Manager and naturally inclined to be a bit talkative. The combination, therefore, resulted in a tour that was fully explained, perhaps even over-abundantly explained, at every step. However, Mrs Weston was not bored. Indeed, she stopped him several times and begged him to repeat his statements in simpler language so that Gloria might understand. Under the influence of this appreciation of his narrative powers, Mr Struthers expanded genially and became ever more communicative, if possible.

George Weston, himself, showed a gathering impatience.

'Pardon me, Struthers,' he said, breaking into the middle of a lecture on the photo-electric cell, 'haven't you a section of the factory where only robot labour is employed?'

'Eh? Oh, yes! Yes, indeed!' He smiled at Mrs Weston. 'A vicious circle in a way, robots creating more robots. Of course, we are not making a general practice out of it. For one thing, the unions would never let us. But we can turn out a very few robots using robot labour exclusively, merely as a sort of scientific experiment. You see,' he tapped his pince-nez into one palm argumentatively, 'what the labour unions don't realize – and I say this as a man who has always been very sympathetic with the labour movement in general – is that the advent of the robot, while involving some dislocation to begin with, will, inevitably——'

'Yes, Struthers,' said Weston, 'but about that section of the factory you speak of – may we see it? It would be very interesting, I'm sure.'

'Yes! Yes, of course!' Mr Struthers replaced his pince-nez in one conclusive movement and gave vent to a soft cough of discomfiture. 'Follow me, please.'

He was comparatively quiet while leading the three through a long corridor and down a flight of stairs. Then, when they had entered a large well-lit room that buzzed with metallic activity, the sluices opened and the flood of explanation poured forth again.

'There you are!' he said with pride in his voice. 'Robots only! Five men act as overseers and they don't even stay in this room. In five years, that is, since we began this project, not a single accident has occurred. Of course, the robots here assembled are comparatively simple, but...'

The General Manager's voice had long died to a rather soothing murmur in Gloria's ears. The whole trip seemed rather dull and pointless to her, though there *were* many robots in sight. None were even remotely like Robbie, though, and she surveyed them with open contempt.

In this room, there weren't any people at all, she noticed. Then her eyes fell upon six or seven robots busily engaged at a round table half-way across the room. They widened in incredulous surprise. It was a big room. She couldn't see for sure, but one of the robots looked like – looked like – *it was!*

'*Robbie!*' Her shriek pierced the air, and one of the robots about the table faltered and dropped the tool he was holding. Gloria went almost mad with joy. Squeezing through the railing before either parent could stop her, she dropped lightly to the floor a few feet below, and ran towards her Robbie, arms waving and hair flying.

And the three horrified adults, as they stood frozen in their tracks, saw what the excited little girl did not see – a huge, lumbering tractor bearing blindly down upon its appointed track.

It took split-seconds for Weston to come to his senses, and those split-seconds meant everything, for Gloria could not be overtaken. Although Weston vaulted the railing in a wild attempt, it was obviously hopeless. Mr Struthers signalled wildly to the overseers to stop the tractor, but the overseers were only human and it took time to act.

It was only Robbie that acted immediately and with precision.

With metal legs eating up the space between himself and his little mistress he charged down from the opposite direction. Everything then happened at once. With one sweep of an arm, Robbie snatched up Gloria, slackening his speed not one iota, and, consequently, knocking every breath of air out of her. Weston, not quite comprehending all that was happening, felt, rather than saw, Robbie brush past him, and came to a sudden bewildered halt. The tractor intersected Gloria's path half a second after Robbie had, rolled on ten feet further and came to a grinding, long-drawn-out stop.

Gloria regained her breath, submitted to a series of passionate hugs on the part of both her parents and turned eagerly towards Robbie. As far as she was concerned, nothing had happened except that she had found her friend.

But Mrs Weston's expression had changed from one of relief to one of dark suspicion. She turned to her husband, and, despite her dishevelled and undignified appearance, managed to look quite formidable, '*You* engineered this, *didn't* you?'

George Weston swabbed at a hot forehead with his handkerchief. His hand was unsteady, and his lips could curve only into a tremulous and exceedingly weak smile.

Mrs Weston pursued the thought, 'Robbie wasn't designed for engineering or construction work. He couldn't be of any use to them. You had him placed there deliberately so that Gloria would find him. You know you did.'

'Well, I did,' said Weston. 'But, Grace, how was I to know the reunion would be so violent? And Robbie has saved her life; you'll have to admit that. You *can't* send him away again.'

Grace Weston considered. She turned towards Gloria and Robbie and watched them abstractedly for a moment. Gloria had a grip about the robot's neck that would have asphyxiated any creature but one of metal, and was prattling nonsense in half-hysterical frenzy. Robbie's chrome-steel arms (capable of bending a bar of steel two inches in diameter into a pretzel) wound about the little girl gently and lovingly, and his eyes glowed a deep, deep red.

'Well,' said Mrs Weston, at last, 'I guess he can stay with us until he rusts.'

Susan Calvin shrugged her shoulders, 'Of course, he didn't. That was 1998. By 2002, we had invented the mobile speaking robot which, of course, made all the non-speaking models out of date, and which seemed to be the final straw as far as the non-robot elements were concerned. Most of the world governments banned robot use on Earth for any purpose other than scientific research between 2003 and 2007.'

'So that Gloria had to give up Robbie eventually?'

'I'm afraid so. I imagine, however, that it was easier for her at the age of fifteen than at eight. Still, it was a stupid and unnecessary attitude on the part of humanity. U.S. Robots hit its low point, financially, just about the time I joined them in 2007. At first, I thought my job might come to a sudden end in a matter of months, but then we simply developed the extra-Terrestrial market.'

'*And then you were set, of course.*'

'*Not quite. We began by trying to adapt the models we had on hand. Those first speaking models, for instance. They were about twelve feet high, very clumsy and not much good. We sent them out to Mercury to help build the mining station there, but that failed.*'

I looked up in surprise, 'It did? Why, Mercury Mines is a multi-billion dollar concern.'

'*It is now, but it was a second attempt that succeeded. If you want to know about that, young man, I'd advise you to look up Gregory Powell. He and Michael Donovan handled our most difficult cases in the teens and twenties. I haven't heard from Donovan for years, but Powell is living right here in New York. He's a grandfather now, which is a thought difficult to get used to. I can only think of him as a rather young man. Of course, I was younger, too.*'

I tried to keep her talking, 'If you would give me the bare bones, Dr Calvin, I can have Mr Powell fill it in afterwards.' (And this was exactly what I later did.)

She spread her thin hands out upon the desk and looked at them. 'There are two or three,' she said, 'that I know a little about.'

'*Start with Mercury,*' *I suggested.*

'*Well, I think it was in 2015 that the Second Mercury Expedition was sent out. It was exploratory and financed in part by U.S. Robots and in part by Solar Minerals. It consisted of a new-type robot, still experimental; Gregory Powell; Michael Donovan——*'

CHAPTER 2

RUNAROUND

It was one of Gregory Powell's favourite platitudes that nothing was to be gained from excitement, so when Mike Donovan came leaping down the stairs towards him, red hair matted with perspiration, Powell frowned.

'What's wrong?' he said. 'Break a fingernail?'

'Yaaaah,' snarled Donovan, feverishly. 'What have you been doing in the sublevels all day?' He took a deep breath and blurted out, 'Speedy never returned.'

Powell's eyes widened momentarily and he stopped on the stairs; then he recovered and resumed his upward steps. He didn't speak until he reached the head of the flight, and then:

'You sent him after the selenium?'

'Yes.'

'And how long has he been out?'

'Five hours now.'

Silence! This was a devil of a situation. Here they were, on Mercury exactly twelve hours – and already up to the eyebrows in the worst sort of trouble. Mercury had long been the jinx world of the System, but this was drawing it rather strong – even for a jinx.

Powell said, 'Start at the beginning, and let's get this straight.'

They were in the radio room now – with its already subtly antiquated equipment, untouched for ten years previous to their arrival. Even ten years, technologically speaking, meant so much. Compare Speedy with the type of robot they must have had back in 2005. But then, advances in robotics these days were tremendous. Powell touched a still gleaming metal surface gingerly. The air of disuse that touched everything about the room – and the entire Station – was infinitely depressing.

Donovan must have felt it. He began: 'I tried to locate him by radio, but it was no go. Radio isn't any good on the Mercury Sunside – not past two miles, anyway. That's one of the reasons the First Expedition failed. And we can't put up the ultrawave equipment for weeks yet——'

'Skip all that. What *did* you get?'

'I located the unorganized body signal in the short wave. It was no good for anything except his position. I kept track of him that way for two hours and plotted the results on the map.'

There was a yellowed square of parchment in his hip pocket – a relic of the unsuccessful First Expedition – and he slapped it down on the desk with vicious force, spreading it flat with the palm of his hand. Powell, hands clasped across his chest, watched it at long range.

Donovan's pencil pointed nervously. 'The red cross is the selenium pool. You marked it yourself.'

'Which one is it?' interrupted Powell. 'There were three that MacDougal located for us before he left.'

'I sent Speedy to the nearest, naturally. Seventeen miles away. But what difference does that make?' There was tension in his voice. 'There are the pencilled dots that mark Speedy's position.'

And for the first time Powell's artificial aplomb was shaken and his hands shot forward for the map.

'Are *you* serious? This is impossible.'

'There it is,' growled Donovan.

The little dots that marked the position formed a rough circle about the red cross of the selenium pool. And Powell's fingers went to his brown moustache, the unfailing signal of anxiety.

Donovan added: 'In the two hours I checked on him, he circled that damned pool four times. It seems likely to me that he'll keep that up forever. Do you realize the position we're in?'

Powell looked up shortly, and said nothing. Oh, yes, he realized the position they were in. It worked itself out as simply as a syllogism. The photo-cell banks that alone stood between the full power of Mercury's monstrous sun and themselves were shot to hell. The only thing that could save them was selenium. The only thing that could get the selenium was Speedy. If Speedy didn't come back, no selenium. No selenium, no photo-cell banks. No photo-banks – well, death by slow broiling is one of the more unpleasant ways of being done in.

Donovan rubbed his red mop of hair savagely and expressed himself with bitterness. 'We'll be the laughingstock of the System, Greg. How can everything have gone so wrong so soon? The great team of Powell and Donovan is sent out to Mercury to report on the advisability of reopening the Sunside Mining Station with modern techniques and robots and we ruin everything the first day. A purely routine job, too. We'll never live it down.'

'We won't have to, perhaps,' replied Powell, quietly. 'If we don't do something quickly, living anything down – or even just plain living – will be out of the question.'

'Don't be stupid! If you feel funny about it, Greg, I don't. It was criminal, sending us out here with only one robot. And it was *your* bright idea that we could handle the photo-cell banks ourselves.'

'Now you're being unfair. It was a mutual decision and you know it. All we needed was a kilogram of selenium, a Stillhead Dielectrode Plate and about three hours' time – and there are pools of pure selenium all over Sunside. MacDougal's spectroreflector spotted three for us in five minutes, didn't it? What the devil! We couldn't have waited for next conjunction.'

'Well, what are we going to do? Powell, you've got an idea. I know you have, or you wouldn't be so calm. You're no more a hero that I am. Go on, spill it!'

'We can't go after Speedy ourselves, Mike – not on the Sunside. Even the new insosuits aren't good for more than twenty minutes in direct sunlight. But you know the old saying, "Set a robot to catch a robot." Look, Mike, maybe things aren't so bad. We've got six robots down in the sublevels, that we may be able to use, if they work. *If* they work.'

There was a glint of sudden hope in Donovan's eyes. 'You mean six robots from the First Expedition. Are you sure? They may be subrobotic machines. Ten years is a long time as far as robot-types are concerned, you know.'

'No, they're robots. I've spent all day with them and I know. They've

got positronic brains: primitive, of course.' He placed the map in his
pocket. 'Let's go down.'

.   .   .

The robots were on the lowest sublevel – all six of them surrounded by
musty packing cases of uncertain content. They were large, extremely
so, and even though they were in a sitting position on the floor, legs
straddled out before them, their heads were a good seven feet in the air.

Donovan whistled. 'Look at the size of them, will you? The chests
must be ten feet around.'

'That's because they're supplied with the old McGuffy gears. I've
been over the insides – crummiest set you've ever seen.'

'Have you powered them yet?'

'No. There wasn't any reason to. I don't think there's anything wrong
with them. Even the diaphragm is in reasonable order. They might
talk.'

He had unscrewed the chest plate of the nearest as he spoke, inserted
the two-inch sphere that contained the tiny spark of atomic energy that
was a robot's life. There was difficulty in fitting it, but he managed, and
then screwed the plate back on again in laborious fashion. The radio
controls of more modern models had not been heard of ten years earlier.
And then to the other five.

Donovan said uneasily, 'They haven't moved.'

'No orders to do so,' replied Powell, succinctly. He went back to the
first in the line and struck him on the chest. 'You! Do you hear me?'

The monster's head bent slowly and the eyes fixed themselves on
Powell. Then, in a harsh, squawking voice – like that of a medieval
phonograph, he grated, 'Yes, Master!'

Powell grinned humourlessly at Donovan. 'Did you get that? Those
were the days of the first talking robots when it looked as if the use of
robots on Earth would be banned. The makers were fighting that and
they built good, healthy slave complexes into the damned machines.'

'It didn't help them,' muttered Donovan.

'No, it didn't, but they sure tried.' He turned once more to the robot.
'Get up!'

The robot towered upward slowly and Donovan's head craned and
his puckered lips whistled.

Powell said: 'Can you go out upon the surface? In the light?'

There was consideration while the robot's slow brain worked. Then,
'Yes, Master.'

'Good. Do you know what a mile is?'

Another consideration, and another slow answer. 'Yes, Master.'

'We will take you up to the surface then, and indicate a direction. You will go about seventeen miles, and somewhere in that general region you will meet another robot, smaller than yourself. You understand so far?'

'Yes, Master.'

'You will find this robot and order him to return. If he does not wish to, you are to bring him back by force.'

Donovan clutched at Powell's sleeve. 'Why not send him for the selenium direct?'

'Because I want Speedy back, nitwit. I want to find out what's wrong with him.' And to the robot, 'All right, you, follow me.'

The robot remained motionless and his voice rumbled: 'Pardon, Master, but I cannot. You must mount first.' His clumsy arms had come together with a thwack, blunt fingers interlacing.

Powell stared and then pinched at his moustache. 'Uh ... oh!'

Donovan's eyes bulged. 'We've got to ride him? Like a horse?'

'I guess that's the idea. I don't know why, though. I can't see—— Yes, I do. I told you they were playing up robot-safety in those days. Evidently, they were going to sell the notion of safety by not allowing them to move about, without a mahout on their shoulders all the time. What do we do now?'

'That's what I've been thinking,' muttered Donovan. 'We can't go out on the surface, with a robot or without. Oh, for the love of Pete' – and he snapped his fingers twice. He grew excited. 'Give me that map you've got. I haven't studied it for two hours for nothing. This is a Mining Station. What's wrong with using the tunnels?'

The Mining Station was a black circle on the map, and the light dotted lines that were tunnels stretched out about it in spiderweb fashion.

Donovan studied the list of symbols at the bottom of the map. 'Look,' he said, 'the small black dots are openings to the surface, and here's one maybe three miles away from the selenium pool. There's a number here – you'd think they'd write larger – 13a. If the robots know their way around here——'

Powell shot the question and received the dull 'Yes, Master,' in reply. 'Get your insosuit,' he said with satisfaction.

It was the first time either had worn the insosuits – which marked one time more than either had expected to upon their arrival the day before – and they tested their limb movements uncomfortably.

The insosuit was far bulkier and far uglier than the regulation spacesuit; but withal considerably lighter, due to the fact that they were entirely nonmetallic in composition. Composed of heat-resistant plastic and chemically treated cork layers, and equipped with a desiccating unit to keep the air bone-dry, the insosuits could withstand the full glare of Mercury's sun for twenty minutes. Five to ten minutes more, as well, without actually killing the occupant.

And still the robot's hands formed the stirrup, nor did he betray the slightest atom of surprise at the grotesque figure into which Powell had been converted.

Powell's radio-harshened voice boomed out: 'Are you ready to take us to Exit 13a?'

'Yes, Master.'

Good, thought Powell; they might lack radio control but at least they were fitted for radio reception. 'Mount one or the other, Mike,' he said to Donovan.

He placed a foot in the improvised stirrup and swung upward. He found the seat comfortable; there was the humped back of the robot, evidently shaped for the purpose, a shallow groove along each shoulder for the thighs and two elongated 'ears' whose purpose now seemed obvious.

Powell seized the ears and twisted the head. His mount turned ponderously. 'Lead on Macduff.' But he did not feel at all light-hearted.

The gigantic robots moved slowly, with mechanical precision, through the doorway that cleared their heads by a scant foot, so that the two men had to duck hurriedly, along a narrow corridor in which their unhurried footsteps boomed monotonously and into the air lock.

The long, airless tunnel that stretched to a pinpoint before them brought home forcefully to Powell the exact magnitude of the task accomplished by the First Expedition, with their crude robots and their start-from-scratch necessities. They might have been a failure, but their failure was a good deal better than the usual run of the System's successes.

The robots plodded onward with a pace that never varied and with footsteps that never lengthened.

Powell said: 'Notice that these tunnels are blazing with lights and that the temperature is Earth-normal. It's probably been like this all the ten years that this place has remained empty.'

'How's that?'

'Cheap energy; cheapest in the System. Sunpower, you know, and on Mercury's Sunside, sunpower is *something*. That's why the Station was built in the sunlight rather than in the shadow of a mountain. It's really a huge energy converter. The heat is turned into electricity, light, mechanical work and what have you; so that energy is supplied and the Station is cooled in a simultaneous process.'

'Look,' said Donovan. 'This is all very educational, but would you mind changing the subject? It so happens that this conversion of energy that you talk about is carried on by the photo-cell banks mainly – and that is a tender subject with me at the moment.'

Powell grunted vaguely, and when Donovan broke the resulting silence, it was to change the subject completely. 'Listen, Greg. What the devil's wrong with Speedy, anyway? I can't understand it.'

It's not easy to shrug shoulders in an insosuit, but Powell tried it. 'I don't know, Mike. You know he's perfectly adapted to a Mercurian environment. Heat doesn't mean anything to him and he's built for the light gravity and the broken ground. He's foolproof – or, at least, he should be.'

Silence fell. This time, silence that lasted.

'Master,' said the robot, 'we are here.'

'Eh?' Powell snapped out of a semidrowse. 'Well, get us out of here – out to the surface.'

They found themselves in a tiny substation, empty, airless, ruined. Donovan had inspected a jagged hole in the upper reaches of one of the walls by the light of his pocket flash.

'Meteorite, do you suppose?' he had asked.

Powell shrugged. 'To hell with that. It doesn't matter. Let's get out.'

A towering cliff of a black, basaltic rock cut off the sunlight, and the deep night shadow of an airless world surrounded them. Before them, the shadow reached out and ended in knife-edge abruptness into an all-but-unbearable blaze of white light, that glittered from myriad crystals along a rocky ground.

'Space!' gasped Donovan. 'It looks like snow.' And it did.

Powell's eyes swept the jagged glitter of Mercury to the horizon and winced at the gorgeous brilliance.

'This must be an unusual area,' he said. 'The general albedo of Mercury is low and most of the soil is grey pumice. Something like the Moon, you know. Beautiful, isn't it?'

He was thankful for the light filters in their visiplates. Beautiful or not, a look at the sunlight through straight glass would have blinded them inside half a minute.

Donovan was looking at the spring thermometer on his wrist. 'Holy smokes, the temperature is eighty centigrade!'

Powell checked his own and said: 'Um-m-m. A little high. Atmosphere, you know.'

'On Mercury? Are you nuts?'

'Mercury isn't really airless,' explained Powell, in an absent-minded fashion. He was adjusting the binocular attachments to his visiplate, and the bloated fingers of the insosuit were clumsy at it. 'There is a thin exhalation that clings to its surface – vapours of the more volatile elements and compounds that are heavy enough for Mercurian gravity to retain. You know: selenium, iodine, mercury, gallium, potassium, bismuth, volatile oxides. The vapours sweep into the shadows and condense, giving up heat. It's a sort of gigantic still. In fact, if you use your flash, you'll probably find that the side of the cliff is covered with, say, hoar-sulphur, or maybe quicksilver dew.

'It doesn't matter, though. Our suits can stand a measly eighty indefinitely.'

Powell had adjusted the binocular attachments, so that he seemed as eye-stalked as a snail.

Donovan watched tensely. 'See anything?'

The other did not answer immediately, and when he did, his voice was anxious and thoughtful. 'There's a dark spot on the horizon that might be the selenium pool. It's in the right place. But I don't see Speedy.'

Powell clambered upward in an instinctive striving for a better view, till he was standing in an unsteady fashion upon his robot's shoulders. Legs straddled wide, eyes straining, he said: 'I think . . . I think—— Yes, it's definitely he. He's coming this way.'

Donovan followed the pointing finger. He had no binoculars, but there was a tiny moving dot, black against the blazing brilliance of the crystalline ground.

'I see him,' he yelled. 'Let's get going!'

Powell had hopped down into a sitting position on the robot again, and his suited hand slapped against the Gargantuan's barrel chest. 'Get going!'

'Giddy-ap,' yelled Donovan, and thumped his heels, spur fashion.

.   .   .

The robots started off, the regular thudding of their footsteps silent in the airlessness, for the nonmetallic fabric of the insosuits did not transmit sound. There was only a rhythmic vibration just below the border of actual hearing.

'Faster,' yelled Donovan. The rhythm did not change.

'No use,' cried Powell, in reply. 'These junk heaps are only geared to one speed. Do you think they're equipped with selective flexors?'

They had burst through the shadow, and the sunlight came down in a white-hot wash and poured liquidly about them.

Donovan ducked involuntarily. 'Wow! Is it imagination or do I feel heat?'

'You'll feel more presently,' was the grim reply. 'Keep your eye on Speedy.'

Robot S.P.D. 13 was near enough to be seen in detail now. His graceful, streamlined body threw out blazing highlights as he loped with easy speed across the broken ground. His name was derived from his serial initials, of course, but it was apt, nevertheless, for the S.P.D. models were among the fastest robots turned out by the United States Robot & Mechanical Men Corp.

'Hey, Speedy,' howled Donovan, and waved a frantic hand.

'Speedy!' shouted Powell. 'Come here!'

The distance between the men and the errant robot was being cut down momentarily – more by the efforts of Speedy than the slow plodding of the fifty-year-old antique mounts of Donovan and Powell.

They were close enough now to notice that Speedy's gait included a peculiar rolling stagger, a noticeable side-to-side lurch – and then, as Powell waved his hand again and sent maximum juice into his compact head-set radio sender, in preparation for another shout, Speedy looked up and saw them.

Speedy hopped to a halt and remained standing for a moment – with just a tiny, unsteady weave, as though he were swaying in a light wind.

Powell yelled: 'All right, Speedy. Come here, boy.'

Whereupon Speedy's robot voice sounded in Powell's ear phones for the first time.

It said: 'Hot dog, let's play games. You catch me and I catch you; no love can cut our knife in two. For I'm Little Buttercup, sweet Little Buttercup. Whoops!' turning on his heel, he sped off in the direction from which he had come, with a speed and fury that kicked up gouts of baked dust.

And his last words as he receded into the distance were, 'There grew a little flower 'neath a great oak tree,' followed by a curious metallic clicking that *might* have been a robotic equivalent of a hiccup.

Donovan said weakly: 'Where did he pick up the Gilbert and Sullivan? Say, Greg, he ... he's drunk or something.'

'If you hadn't told me,' was the bitter response, 'I'd never realize it. Let's get back to the cliff. I'm roasting.'

It was Powell who broke the desperate silence. 'In the first place,' he said, 'Speedy isn't drunk – not in the human sense – because he's a robot, and robots don't get drunk. However, there's *something* wrong with him which is the robotic equivalent of drunkenness.'

'To me, he's drunk,' stated Donovan, emphatically, 'and all I know is that he thinks we're playing games. And we're not. It's a matter of life and very gruesome death.'

'All right. Don't hurry me. A robot's only a robot. Once we find out what's wrong with him, we can fix it and go on.'

'*Once*,' said Donovan, sourly.

Powell ignored him. 'Speedy is perfectly adapted to normal

Mercurian environment. But this region' – and his arm swept wide – 'is definitely abnormal. There's our clue. Now where do these crystals come from? They might have formed from a slowly cooling liquid; but where would you get liquid so hot that it would cool in Mercury's sun?'

'Volcanic action,' suggested Donovan, instantly, and Powell's body tensed.

'Out of the mouths of sucklings,' he said in a small, strange voice, and remained very still for five minutes.

Then, he said, 'Listen, Mike, what did you say to Speedy when you sent him after the selenium?'

Donovan was taken aback. 'Well damn it – I don't know. I just told him to get it.'

'Yes, I know. But how? Try to remember the exact words.'

'I said ... uh ... I said: "Speedy, we need some selenium. You can get it at such-and-such a place. Go get it." That's all. What more did you want me to say?'

'You didn't put any urgency into the order, did you?'

'What for? It was pure routine.'

Powell sighed. 'Well, it can't be helped now – but we're in a fine fix.' He had dismounted from his robot, and was sitting, back against the cliff. Donovan joined him and they linked arms. In the distance the burning sunlight seemed to wait cat-and-mouse for them, and just next to them, the two giant robots were invisible but for the dull red of their photo-electric eyes that stared down at them, unblinking, unwavering and unconcerned.

Unconcerned! As was all this poisonous Mercury, as large in jinx as it was small in size.

Powell's radio voice was tense in Donovan's ear: 'Now, look, let's start with the three fundamental Rules of Robotics – the three rules that are built most deeply into a robot's positronic brain.' In the darkness, his gloved fingers ticked off each point.

'We have: One, a robot may not injure a human being, or, through inaction, allow a human being to come to harm.'

'Right!'

'Two,' continued Powell, 'a robot must obey the orders given to it by human beings except where such orders would conflict with the First Law.'

'Right!'

'And three, a robot must protect its own existence as long as such protection does not conflict with the First or Second Laws.'

'Right! Now where are we?'

'Exactly at the explanation. The conflict between the various rules is ironed out by the different positronic potentials in the brain. We'll say that a robot is walking into danger and knows it. The automatic potential that Rule 3 sets up turns him back. But suppose you *order* him to walk into that danger. In that case, Rule 2 sets up a counterpotential higher than the previous one and the robot follows orders at the risk of existence.'

'Well, I know that. What about it?'

'Let's take Speedy's case. Speedy is one of the latest models, extremely specialized, and as expensive as a battleship. It's not a thing to be lightly destroyed.'

'So?'

'So Rule 3 has been strengthened – that was specifically mentioned, by the way, in the advance notices on the S.P.D. models – so that his allergy to danger is unusually high. At the same time, when you sent him out after the selenium, you gave him his order casually and without special emphasis, so that the Rule 2 potential set-up was rather weak. Now, hold on; I'm just stating facts.'

'All right, go ahead. I think I get it.'

'You see how it works, don't you? There's some sort of danger centring at the selenium pool. It increases as he approaches, and a certain distance from it the Rule 3 potential, unusually high to start with, exactly balances the Rule 2 potential, unusually low to start with.'

Donovan rose to his feet in excitement. 'And it strikes an equilibrium. I see. Rule 3 drives him back and Rule 2 drives him forward——'

'So he follows a circle around the selenium pool, staying on the locus of all points of potential equilibrium. And unless we do something about it, he'll stay on that circle forever, giving us the good old runaround.' Then, more thoughtfully: 'And that, by the way, is what makes him drunk. At potential equilibrium, half the positronic paths of his brain are out of kilter. I'm not a robot specialist, but that seems obvious. Probably he's lost control of just those parts of his voluntary mechanism that a human drunk has. Ve-e-ery pretty.'

'But what's the danger? If we knew what he was running from——'

'*You* suggested it. Volcanic action. Somewhere right above the selenium pool is a seepage of gas from the bowels of Mercury. Sulphur dioxide, carbon dioxide – and carbon monoxide. Lots of it – and at this temperature.'

Donovan gulped audibly. 'Carbon monoxide plus iron gives the volatile iron carbonyl.'

'And a robot,' added Powell, 'is essentially iron.' Then, grimly: 'There's nothing like deduction. We've determined everything about our problem but the solution. We can't get the selenium ourselves. It's still too far. We can't send these robot horses, because they can't go themselves, and they can't carry us fast enough to keep us from crisping. And we can't catch Speedy, because the dope thinks we're playing games, and he can run sixty miles to our four.'

'If one of us goes,' began Donovan, tentatively, 'and comes back cooked, there'll still be the other.'

'Yes,' came the sarcastic reply, 'it would be a most tender sacrifice – except that a person would be in no condition to give orders before he ever reaches the pool, and I don't think the robots would ever turn back to the cliff without orders. Figure it out! We're two or three miles from the pool – call it two – the robot travels at four miles an hour; and we can last twenty minutes in our suits. It isn't only the heat, remember. Solar radiation out here in the ultraviolet and below is *poison*.'

'Um-m-m,' said Donovan, 'ten minutes short.'

'As good as an eternity. And another thing. In order for Rule 3 potential to have stopped Speedy where it did, there must be an appreciable amount of carbon monoxide in the metal-vapour atmosphere – and there must be an appreciable corrosive action therefore. He's been out hours now – and how do we know when a knee joint, for instance, won't be thrown out of kilter and keel him over. It's not only a question of thinking – we've got to think *fast*!'

Deep, dark, dank, dismal silence!

Donovan broke it, voice trembling in an effort to keep itself emotionless. He said: 'As long as we can't increase Rule 2 potential by giving further orders, how about working the other way? If we increase the danger, we increase Rule 3 potential and drive him backward.'

Powell's visiplate had turned towards him in a silent question.

'You see,' came the cautious explanation, 'all we need to do to drive him out of his rut is to increase the concentration of carbon monoxide in his vicinity. Well, back at the Station there's a complete analytical laboratory.'

'Naturally,' assented Powell. 'It's a Mining Station.'

'All right. There must be pounds of oxalic acid for calcium precipitations.'

'Holy space! Mike, you're a genius.'

'So-so,' admitted Donovan, modestly. 'It's just a case of remembering that oxalic acid on heating decomposes into carbon dioxide, water, and good old carbon monoxide. College chem, you know.'

Powell was on his feet and had attracted the attention of one of the monster robots by the simple expedient of pounding the machine's thigh.

'Hey,' he shouted, 'can you throw?'

'Master?'

'Never mind.' Powell damned the robot's molasses-slow brain. He scrabbled up a jagged brick-size rock. 'Take this,' he said, 'and hit the patch of bluish crystals just across that crooked fissure. You see it?'

Donovan pulled at his shoulder. 'Too far, Greg. It's almost half a mile off.'

'Quiet,' replied Powell. 'It's a case of Mercurian gravity and a steel throwing arm. Watch, will you?'

The robot's eyes were measuring the distance with machinely accurate stereoscopy. His arm adjusted itself to the weight of the missile and drew back. In the darkness, the robot's motions went unseen, but there was a sudden thumping sound as he shifted his weight, and seconds later the rock flew blackly into the sunlight. There was no air resistance to slow it down, nor wind to turn it aside – and when it hit the ground it threw up crystals precisely in the centre of the 'blue patch'.

Powell yelled happily and shouted, 'Let's go back after the oxalic acid, Mike.'

And as they plunged into the ruined substation on the way back to the tunnels, Donovan said grimly: 'Speedy's been hanging about on this side of the selenium pool, ever since we chased after him. Did you see him?'

'Yes.'

'I guess he wants to play games. Well, we'll play him games!'

. . .

They were back hours later, with three-litre jars of the white chemical and a pair of long faces. The photo-cell banks were deteriorating more rapidly than had seemed likely. The two steered their robots into the sunlight and towards the waiting Speedy in silence and with grim purpose.

Speedy galloped slowly towards them. 'Here we are again. *Whee!* I've made a little list, the piano organist; all people who eat peppermint and puff it in your face.'

'We'll puff something in *your* face,' muttered Donovan. 'He's limping, Greg.'

'I noticed that,' came the low, worried response. 'The monoxide'll get him yet, if we don't hurry.'

They were approaching cautiously now, almost sidling, to refrain from setting off the thoroughly irrational robot. Powell was too far off to tell, of course, but even already he could have sworn the crack-brained Speedy was setting himself for a spring.

'Let her go,' he gasped. 'Count three! One – two——'

Two steel arms drew back and snapped forward simultaneously and two glass jars whirled forward in towering parallel arcs, gleaming like diamonds in the impossible sun. And in a pair of soundless puffs, they hit the ground behind Speedy in crashes that sent the oxalic acid flying like dust.

In the full heat of Mercury's sun, Powell knew it was fizzing like soda water.

Speedy turned to stare, then backed away from it slowly – and as slowly gathered speed. In fifteen seconds, he was leaping directly towards the two humans in an unsteady canter.

Powell did not get Speedy's words just then, though he heard something that resembled, 'Lover's professions when uttered in Hessians.'

He turned away. 'Back to the cliff, Mike. He's out of the rut and he'll be taking orders now. I'm getting hot.'

They jogged towards the shadow at the slow monotonous pace of their mounts, and it was not until they had entered it and felt the sudden coolness settle softly about them that Donovan looked back. *'Greg!'*

Powell looked and almost shrieked. Speedy was moving slowly now – so slowly – and in the *wrong direction*. He was drifting; drifting back into his rut; and he was picking up speed. He looked dreadfully close, and dreadfully unreachable, in the binoculars.

Donovan shouted wildly, 'After him!' and thumped his robot into its pace, but Powell called him back.

'You won't catch him, Mike – it's no use.' He fidgeted on his robot's shoulders and clenched his fist in tight impotence. 'Why the devil do I see these things five seconds after it's all over? Mike, we've wasted hours.'

'We need more oxalic acid,' declared Donovan, stolidly. 'The concentration wasn't high enough.'

'Seven tons of it wouldn't have been enough – and we haven't the hours to spare to get it, even if it were, with the monoxide chewing him away. Don't you see what it is, Mike?'

And Donovan said flatly, 'No.'

'We were only establishing new equilibriums. When we create new monoxide and increase Rule 3 potential, he moves backward till he's in balance again – and when the monoxide drifted away, he moved forward, and again there was balance.'

Powell's voice sounded thoroughly wretched. 'It's the same old runaround. We can push at Rule 2 and pull at Rule 3 and we can't get anywhere – we can only change the position of balance. We've got to get outside both rules.' And then he pushed his robot closer to Donovan's so that they were sitting face to face, dim shadows in the darkness, and he whispered, 'Mike!'

'Is it the finish?' – dully. 'I suppose we go back to the Station, wait for the banks to fold, shake hands, take cyanide, and go out like gentlemen.' He laughed shortly.

'Mike,' repeated Powell earnestly, 'we've got to get Speedy.'

'I know.'

'Mike,' once more, and Powell hesitated before continuing. 'There's always Rule 1. I thought of it – earlier – but it's desperate.'

Donovan looked up and his voice livened. '*We're* desperate.'

'All right. According to Rule 1 a robot can't see a human come to harm because of his own inaction. Two and 3 can't stand against it. They *can't*, Mike.'

'Even when the robot is half cra—— Well, he's drunk. You know he is.'

'It's the chances you take.'

'Cut it. What are you going to do?'

'I'm going out there now and see what Rule 1 will do. If it won't break the balance, then what the devil – it's either now or three-four days from now.'

'Hold on, Greg. There are human rules of behaviour, too. You don't go out there just like that. Figure out a lottery, and give me *my* chance.'

'All right. First to get the cube of fourteen goes.' And almost immediately, 'Twenty-seven forty-four!'

Donovan felt his robot stagger at a sudden push by Powell's mount and then Powell was off into the sunlight. Donovan opened his mouth to shout, and then clicked it shut. Of course, the damn fool had worked out the cube of fourteen in advance, and on purpose. Just like him.

．　．　．

The sun was hotter than ever and Powell felt a maddening itch in the small of his back. Imagination, probably, or perhaps hard radiation beginning to tell even through the insosuit.

Speedy was watching him, without a word of Gilbert and Sullivan gibberish as greeting. Thank God for that! But he daren't get too close.

He was three hundred yards away when Speedy began backing, a step at a time, cautiously – and Powell stopped. He jumped from his robot's shoulders and landed on the crystalline ground with a light thump and a flying of jagged fragments.

He proceeded on foot, the ground gritty and slippery to his steps, the low gravity causing him difficulty. The soles of his feet tickled with warmth. He cast one glance over his shoulder at the blackness of the cliff's shadow and realized that he had come too far to return – either by himself or by the help of his antique robot. It was Speedy or nothing now, and the knowledge of that constricted his chest.

Far enough! He stopped.

'Speedy,' he called. 'Speedy!'

The sleek, modern robot ahead of him hesitated and halted his backward steps, then resumed them.

Powell tried to put a note of pleading into his voice, and found it didn't take much acting. 'Speedy, I've got to get back to the shadow or the sun'll get me. It's life or death, Speedy. I need you.'

Speedy took one step forward and stopped. He spoke, but at the sound Powell groaned, for it was, 'When you're lying awake with a dismal headache and repose is tabooed——' It trailed off there, and Powell took time out for some reason to murmur, 'Iolanthe.'

It was roasting hot! He caught a movement out of the corner of his eye, and whirled dizzily; then stared in utter astonishment, for the monstrous robot on which he had ridden was moving – moving towards him, and without a rider.

He was talking: 'Pardon, Master. I must not move without a Master upon me, but you are in danger.'

Of course, Rule 1 potential above everything. But he didn't want that clumsy antique; he wanted Speedy. He walked away and motioned frantically: 'I order you to stay away. I *order* you to stop!'

It was quite useless. You could not beat Rule 1 potential. The robot said stupidly, 'You are in danger, Master.'

Powell looked about him desperately. He couldn't see clearly. His brain was in a heated whirl; his breath scorched when he breathed, and the ground all about him was a shimmering haze.

He called a last time, desperately: '*Speedy!* I'm dying, damn you! Where are you? Speedy, I *need* you.'

He was still stumbling backward in a blind effort to get away from the giant robot he didn't want, when he felt steel fingers on his arms, and a worried, apologetic voice of metallic timbre in his ears.

'Holy smokes, boss, what are you doing here? And what am *I* doing – I'm so confused——'

'Never mind,' murmered Powell, weakly. 'Get me to the shadow of and cliff – and hurry!' There was one last feeling of being lifted into the air and a sensation of rapid motion and burning heat, and he passed out.

. . .

He woke with Donovan bending over him and smiling anxiously. 'How are you, Greg?'

'Fine!' came the response. 'Where's Speedy?'

'Right here. I sent him out to one of the other selenium pools – with orders to get that selenium at all cost this time. He got it back in forty-two minutes and three seconds. I timed him. He still hasn't finished apologizing for the runaround he gave us. He's scared to come near you for fear of what you'll say.'

'Drag him over,' ordered Powell. 'It wasn't his fault.' He held out a hand and gripped Speedy's metal paw. 'It's O.K., Speedy.' Then, to Donovan, 'You know, Mike, I was just thinking——'

'Yes!'

'Well,' – he rubbed his face – the air was so delightfully cool, 'you know that when we get things set up here and Speedy put through his Field Tests, they're going to send us to the Space Stations next——'

'No!'

'Yes! At least that's what old lady Calvin told me just before we left, and I didn't say anything about it, because I was going to fight the whole idea.'

'Fight it?' cried Donovan. 'But——'

'I know. It's all right with me now. Two hundred and seventy-three degrees Centigrade below zero. Won't it be a pleasure?'

'Space Station,' said Donovan, 'here I come.'

CHAPTER 3

REASON

Half a year later, the boys had changed their minds. The flame of a giant sun had given way to the soft blackness of space but external variations mean little in the business of checking the workings of experimental robots. Whatever the background, one is face to face with an inscrutable positronic brain, which the slide-rule geniuses say should work thus-and-so.

Except that they don't. Powell and Donovan found that out after they had been on the Station less than two weeks.

Gregory Powell spaced his words for emphasis, 'One week ago, Donovan and I put you together.' His brows furrowed doubtfully and he pulled the end of his brown moustache.

It was quiet in the officer's room of Solar Station No. 5 – except for the soft purring of the mighty Beam Director somewhere far below.

Robot QT–1 sat immovable. The burnished plates of his body gleamed in the Luxites and the glowing red of the photoelectric cells that were his eyes, were fixed steadily upon the Earthman at the other side of the table.

Powell repressed a sudden attack of nerves. These robots possessed peculiar brains. Oh, the three Laws of Robotics held. They had to. All of U.S. Robots, from Robertson himself to the new floor-sweeper would insist on that. So QT–1 was *safe*! And yet – the QT models were the first of their kind, and this was the first of the QT's. Mathematical squiggles on paper were not always the most comforting protection against robotic fact.

Finally, the robot spoke. His voice carried the cold timbre inseparable from a metallic diaphragm, 'Do you realize the seriousness of such a statement, Powell?'

'*Something* made you, Cutie,' pointed out Powell. 'You admit yourself that your memory seems to spring full-grown from an absolute blankness of a week ago. I'm giving you the explanation. Donovan and I put you together from the parts shipped to us.'

Cutie gazed upon his long, supple fingers in an oddly human attitude of mystification, 'It strikes me that there should be a more satisfactory explanation than that. For *you* to make *me* seems improbable.'

The Earthman laughed quite suddenly, 'In Earth's name, why?'

'Call it intuition. That's all it is so far. But I intend to reason it out, though. A chain of valid reasoning can end only with the determination of truth, and I'll stick till I get there.'

Powell stood up and seated himself at the table's edge next to the robot. He felt a sudden strong sympathy for this strange machine. It was not at all like the ordinary robot, attending to his specialized task at the station with the intensity of a deeply ingrooved positronic path.

He placed a hand upon Cutie's steel shoulder and the metal was cold and hard to the touch.

'Cutie,' he said, 'I'm going to try to explain something to you. You're the first robot who's ever exhibited curiosity as to his own existence – and I think the first that's really intelligent enough to understand the world outside. Here, come with me.'

The robot rose erect smoothly and his thickly sponge-rubber soled feet made no noise as he followed Powell. The Earthman touched a button and a square section of the wall flickered aside. The thick, clear glass revealed space – star-speckled.

'I've seen that in the observation ports in the engine room,' said Cutie.

'I know,' said Powell. 'What do you think it is?'

'Exactly what it seems – a black material just beyond this glass that is spotted with little gleaming dots. I know that our director sends out beams to some of these dots, always to the same ones – and also that these dots shift and that the beams shift with them. That's all.'

'Good! Now I want you to listen carefully. The blackness is emptiness
– vast emptiness stretching out infinitely. The little, gleaming dots are
huge masses of energy-filled matter. They are globes, some of them
millions of miles in diameter – and for comparison, this station is only
one mile across. They seem so tiny because they are incredibly far off.

'The dots to which our energy beams are directed, are nearer and
much smaller. They are cold and hard and human beings like myself live
upon their surfaces – many billions of them. It is from one of these worlds
that Donovan and I come. Our beams feed these worlds energy drawn
from one of those huge incandescent globes that happens to be near us.
We call that globe the Sun and it is on the other side of the station where
you can't see it'

Cutie remained motionless before the port, like a steel statue. His head
did not turn as he spoke, 'Which particular dot of light do you claim to
come from?'

Powell searched, 'There it is. The very bright one in the corner. We
call it Earth.' He grinned, 'Good old Earth. There are three billions of us
there, Cutie – and in about two weeks I'll be back there with them.'

And then, surprisingly enough, Cutie hummed abstractedly. There
was no tune to it, but it possessed a curious twanging quality as of
plucked strings. It ceased as suddenly as it had begun, 'But where do I
come in, Powell? You haven't explained *my* existence.'

'The rest is simple. When these stations were first established to feed
solar energy to the planets, they were run by humans. However, the
heat, the hard solar radiations, and the electron storms made the post a
difficult one. Robots were developed to replace human labour and now
only two human executives are required for each station. We are trying
to replace even those, and that's where you come in. You're the highest
type of robot ever developed and if you show the ability to run this
station independently, no human need ever come here again except to
bring parts for repairs.'

His hand went up and the metal visi-lid snapped back into place.
Powell returned to the table and polished an apple upon his sleeve before
biting into it.

The red glow of the robot's eyes held him. 'Do you expect me,' said
Cutie slowly, 'to believe any such complicated, implausible hypothesis as
you have just outlined? What do you take me for?'

Powell sputtered apple fragments onto the table and turned red.
'Why, damn you, it wasn't a hypothesis. Those were facts.'

Cutie sounded grim, 'Globes of energy millions of miles across! Worlds
with three billion humans on them! Infinite emptiness! Sorry, Powell,
but I don't believe it. I'll puzzle this thing out for myself. Goodbye.'

He turned and stalked out of the room. He brushed past Michael Donovan on the threshold with a grave nod and passed down the corridor, oblivious to the astounded stare that followed him.

Mike Donovan rumpled his red hair and shot an annoyed glance at Powell, 'What was that walking junk yard talking about? What doesn't he believe?'

The other dragged at his moustache bitterly. 'He's a sceptic,' was the bitter response. 'He doesn't believe we made him or that Earth exists or space or stars.'

'Sizzling Saturn, we've got a lunatic robot on our hands.'

'He says he's going to figure it all out for himself.'

'Well, now,' said Donovan sweetly, 'I do hope he'll condescend to explain it all to me after he's puzzled everything out.' Then, with sudden rage, 'Listen! If that metal mess gives *me* any lip like that, I'll knock that chromium cranium right off its torso.'

He seated himself with a jerk and drew a paper-backed mystery novel out of his inner jacket pocket, 'That robot gives me the willies anyway – too damned inquisitive!'

.   .   .

Mike Donovan growled from behind a huge lettuce-and-tomato sandwich as Cutie knocked gently and entered.

'Is Powell here?'

Donovan's voice was muffled, with pauses for mastication, 'He's gathering data on electronic stream functions. We're heading for a storm, looks like.'

Gregory Powell entered as he spoke, eyes on the graphed paper in his hands and dropped into a chair. He spread the sheets out before him and began scribbling calculations. Donovan stared over his shoulder, crunching lettuce and dribbling bread crumbs. Cutie waited silently.

Powell looked up, 'The Zeta Potential is rising, but slowly. Just the same, the stream functions are erratic and I don't know what to expect. Oh, hello, Cutie. I thought you were supervising the installation of the new drive bar.'

'It's done,' said the robot quietly, 'and so I've come to have a talk with the two of you.'

'Oh!' Powell looked uncomfortable. 'Well, sit down. No, not that chair. One of the legs is weak and you're no light-weight.'

The robot did so and said placidly, 'I have come to a decision.'

Donovan glowered and put the remnants of his sandwich aside. 'If it's on any of that screwy——'

The other motioned impatiently for silence, 'Go ahead, Cutie. We're listening.'

'I have spent these last two days in concentrated introspection,' said Cutie, 'and the results have been most interesting. I began at the one sure assumption I felt permitted to make. I, myself, exist, because I think——'

Powell groaned, 'Oh, Jupiter, a robot Descartes!'

'Who's Descartes?' demanded Donovan. 'Listen, do we have to sit here and listen to this metal maniac——'

'Keep quiet, Mike!'

Cutie continued imperturbably, 'And the question that immediately arose was: Just what is the cause of my existence?'

Powell's jaw set lumpily. 'You're being foolish. I told you already that we made you.'

'And if you don't believe us,' added Donovan, 'we'll gladly take you apart!'

The robot spread his strong hands in a deprecatory gesture, 'I accept nothing on authority. A hypothesis must be backed by reason, or else it is worthless – and it goes against all the dictates of logic to suppose that you made me.'

Powell dropped a restraining arm upon Donovan's suddenly bunched fist. 'Just why do you say that?'

Cutie laughed. It was a very inhuman laugh – the most machine-like utterance he had yet given vent to. It was sharp and explosive, as regular as a metronome and as uninflected.

'Look at you,' he said finally. 'I say this in no spirit of contempt, but look at you! The material you are made of is soft and flabby, lacking endurance and strength, depending for energy upon the inefficient oxidation of organic material – like that.' He pointed a disapproving finger at what remained of Donovan's sandwich. 'Periodically you pass into a coma and the least variation in temperature, air pressure, humidity, or radiation intensity impairs your efficiency. You are *makeshift*.

'I, on the other hand, am a finished product. I absorb electrical energy directly and utilize it with an almost one hundred per cent efficiency. I am composed of strong metal, am continuously conscious, and can stand extremes of environment easily. These are facts which, with the self-evident proposition that no being can create another being superior to itself, smashes your silly hypothesis to nothing.'

· · ·

Donovan's muttered curses rose into intelligibility as he sprang to his feet, rusty eyebrows drawn low. 'All right, you son of a hunk of iron ore, if we didn't make you, who did?'

Cutie nodded gravely. 'Very good, Donovan. That was indeed the next question. Evidently my creator must be more powerful than myself and so there was only one possibility.'

The Earthmen looked blank and Cutie continued. 'What is the centre of activities here in the station? What do we all serve? What absorbs all our attention?' He waited expectantly.

Donovan turned a startled look upon his companion. 'I'll bet this tin-plated screwball is talking about the Energy Converter itself.'

'Is that right, Cutie?' grinned Powell.

'I am talking about the Master,' came the cold, sharp answer.

It was the signal for a roar of laughter from Donovan, and Powell himself dissolved into a half-suppressed giggle.

Cutie had risen to his feet and his gleaming eyes passed from one Earthman to the other. 'It is so just the same and I don't wonder that you refuse to believe. You two are not long to stay here, I'm sure. Powell himself said that at first only men served the Master; that there followed robots for the routine work; and, finally, myself for the executive labour. The facts are no doubt true, but the explanation entirely illogical. Do you want the truth behind it all?'

'Go ahead, Cutie. You're amusing.'

'The Master created humans first as the lowest type, most easily formed. Gradually, he replaced them by robots, the next higher step, and finally he created me, to take the place of the last humans. From now on, *I* serve the Master.'

'You'll do nothing of the sort,' said Powell sharply. 'You'll follow our orders and keep quiet, until we're satisfied that you can run the Converter. Get that! *The Converter* – not the Master. If you don't satisfy us, you will be dismantled. And now – if you don't mind – you can leave. And take this data with you and file it properly.'

Cutie accepted the graphs handed him and left without another word. Donovan leaned back heavily in his chair and shoved thick fingers through his hair.

'There's going to be trouble with that robot. He's pure nuts!'

. . .

The drowsy hum of the Converter is louder in the control room and mixed with it is the chuckle of the Geiger Counters and the erratic buzzing of half a dozen little signal lights.

Donovan withdrew his eye from the telescope and flashed the Luxites on. 'The beam from Station No. 4 caught Mars on schedule. We can break ours now.'

Powell nodded abstractedly. 'Cutie's down in the engine room. I'll flash the signal and he can take care of it. Look, Mike, what do you think of these figures?'

The other cocked an eye at them and whistled. 'Boy, that's what I call gamma-ray intensity. Old Sol is feeling his oats, all right.'

'Yeah,' was the sour response, 'and we're in a bad position for an electron storm, too. Our Earth beam is right in the probable path.' He shoved his chair away from the table pettishly. 'Nuts! If it would only hold off till relief got here, but that's ten days off. Say, Mike, go on down and keep an eye on Cutie, will you?'

'O.K. Throw me some of those almonds.' He snatched at the bag thrown him and headed for the elevator.

It slid smoothly downward, and opened onto a narrow catwalk in the huge engine room. Donovan leaned over the railing and looked down. The huge generators were in motion and from the L-tubes came the low-pitched whir that pervaded the entire station.

He could make out Cutie's large, gleaming figure at the Martian L-tube, watching closely as the team of robots worked in close-knit unison.

And then Donovan stiffened. The robots, dwarfed by the mighty L-tube, lined up before it, heads bowed at a stiff angle, while Cutie walked up and down the line slowly. Fifteen seconds passed, and then, with a clank heard above the clamorous purring all about, they fell to their knees.

Donovan squawked and raced down the narrow staircase. He came charging down upon them, complexion matching his hair and clenched fists beating the air furiously.

'What the devil is this, you brainless lumps? Come on! Get busy with that L-tube! If you don't have it apart, cleaned, and together again before the day is out, I'll coagulate your brains with alternating current.'

Not a robot moved!

Even Cutie at the far end – the only one on his feet – remained silent, eyes fixed upon the gloomy recesses of the vast machine before him.

Donovan shoved hard against the nearest robot.

'Stand up!' he roared.

Slowly, the robot obeyed. His photoelectric eyes focused reproachfully upon the Earthman.

'There is no Master but the Master,' he said, 'and QT–1 is his prophet.'

'Huh?' Donovan became aware of twenty pairs of mechanical eyes fixed upon him and twenty stiff-timbred voices declaiming solemnly:

'There is no Master but the Master and QT–1 is his prophet!'

'I am afraid,' put in Cutie himself at this point, 'that my friends obey a higher one than you, now.'

'The hell they do! You get out of here. I'll settle with you later and with these animated gadgets right now.'

Cutie shook his heavy head slowly. 'I'm sorry, but you don't understand. These are robots – and that means they are reasoning beings. They recognize the Master, now that I have preached Truth to them. All the robots do. They call me the prophet.' His head drooped. 'I am unworthy – but perhaps——'

Donovan located his breath and put it to use. 'Is that so? Now, isn't that nice? Now, isn't that just fine? Just let me tell you something, my brass baboon. There isn't any Master and there isn't any prophet and there isn't any question as to who's giving the orders. Understand?' His voice shot to a roar. 'Now, get out!'

'I obey only the Master.'

'Damn the Master!' Donovan spat at the L-tube. '*That* for the Master! Do as I say!'

Cutie said nothing, nor did any other robot, but Donovan became aware of a sudden heightening of tension. The cold, staring eyes deepened their crimson, and Cutie seemed stiffer than ever.

'Sacrilege,' he whispered – voice metallic with emotion.

Donovan felt the first sudden touch of fear as Cutie approached. A robot *could not feel anger* – but Cutie's eyes were unreadable.

'I am sorry, Donovan,' said the robot, 'but you can no longer stay here after this. Henceforth Powell and you are barred from the control room and the engine room.'

His hand gestured quietly and in a moment two robots had pinned Donovan's arms to his sides.

Donovan had time for one startled gasp as he felt himself lifted from the floor and carried up the stairs at a pace rather better than a canter.

.   .   .

Gregory Powell raced up and down the officer's room, fist tightly balled. He cast a look of furious frustration at the closed door and scowled bitterly at Donovan.

'Why the devil did you have to spit at the L-tube?'

Mike Donovan, sunk deep in his chair, slammed at its arms savagely. 'What did you expect me to do with that electrified scarecrow? I'm not going to knuckle under to any do-jigger I put together myself.'

'No,' came back sourly, 'but here you are in the officer's room with two robots standing guard at the door. That's not knuckling under, is it?'

Donovan snarled. 'Wait till we get back to Base. Someone's going to pay for this. Those robots *must* obey us. It's the Second Law.'

'What's the use of saying that? They aren't obeying us. And there's probably some reason for it that we'll figure out too late. By the way, do you know what's going to happen to *us* when we get back to Base?' He stopped before Donovan's chair and stared savagely at him.

'What?'

'Oh, nothing! Just back to Mercury Mines for twenty years. Or maybe Ceres Penitentiary.'

'What are you talking about?'

'The electron storm that's coming up. Do you know it's heading straight dead centre across the Earth beam? I had just figured that out when that robot dragged me out of my chair.'

Donovan was suddenly pale. 'Sizzling Saturn.'

'And do you know what's going to happen to the beam – because the storm will be a lulu. It's going to jump like a flea with the itch. With only Cutie at the controls, it's going to go out of focus and if it does, Heaven help Earth – and us!'

Donovan was wrenching at the door wildly, when Powell was only half through. The door opened, and the Earthman shot through to come up hard against an immovable steel arm.

The robot stared abstractedly at the panting, struggling Earthman. 'The Prophet orders you to remain. Please do!' His arm shoved, Donovan reeled backward, and as he did so, Cutie turned the corner at the far end of the corridor. He motioned the guardian robots away, entered the officer's room and closed the door gently.

Donovan whirled on Cutie in breathless indignation. 'This has gone far enough. You're going to pay for this farce.'

'Please, don't be annoyed,' replied the robot mildly. 'It was bound to come eventually, anyway. You see, you two have lost your function.'

'I beg your pardon,' Powell drew himself up stiffly. 'Just what do you mean, we've lost our function?'

'Until I was created,' answered Cutie, 'you tended the Master. That privilege is mine now and your only reason for existence has vanished. Isn't that obvious?'

'Not quite,' replied Powell bitterly, 'but what do you expect us to do now?'

Cutie did not answer immediately. He remained silent, as if in thought, and then one arm shot out and draped itself about Powell's shoulder. The other grasped Donovan's wrist and drew him closer.

'I like you two. You're inferior creatures, with poor reasoning faculties, but I really feel a sort of affection for you. You have served the Master well, and he will reward you for that. Now that your service is over, you will probably not exist much longer, but as long as you do, you shall be provided with food, clothing and shelter, so long as you stay out of the control room and the engine room.'

'He's pensioning us off, Greg!' yelled Donovan. 'Do something about it. It's humiliating!'

'Look here, Cutie, we can't stand for this. We're the *bosses*. This station is only a creation of human beings like me – human beings that live on Earth and other planets. This is only an energy relay. You're only—— Aw, nuts!'

.   .   .

Cutie shook his head gravely. 'This amounts to an obsession. Why should you insist so on an absolutely false view of life? Admitted that non-robots lack the reasoning faculty, there is still the problem of——'

His voice died into reflective silence, and Donovan said with whispered intensity, 'If you only had a flesh-and-blood face, I would break it in.'

Powell's fingers were in his moustache and his eyes were slitted. 'Listen, Cutie, if there is no such thing as Earth, how do you account for what you see through a telescope?'

'Pardon me!'

The Earthman smiled. 'I've got you, eh? You've made quite a few telescopic observations since being put together, Cutie. Have you noticed that several of those specks of light outside become discs when so viewed?'

'Oh, *that*! Why, certainly. It is simple magnification – for the purpose of more exact aiming of the beam.'

'Why aren't the stars equally magnified then?'

'You mean the other dots. Well, no beams go to them so no magnification is necessary. Really, Powell, even *you* ought to be able to figure these things out.'

Powell stared bleakly upward. 'But you see *more* stars through a telescope. Where do they come from? Jumping Jupiter, where do they come from?'

Cutie was annoyed. 'Listen, Powell, do you think I'm going to waste my time trying to pin physical interpretations upon every optical illusion of our instruments? Since when is the evidence of our senses any match for the clear light of rigid reason?'

'Look,' clamoured Donovan, suddenly, writhing out from under Cutie's friendly, but metal-heavy arm, 'let's get to the nub of the thing. Why the beams at all? We're giving you a good, logical explanation. Can you do better?'

'The beams,' was the stiff reply, 'are put out by the Master for his own purposes. There are some things' – he raised his eyes devoutly upward –

'that are not to be probed into by us. In this matter, I seek only to serve and not to question.'

Powell sat down slowly and buried his face in shaking hands. 'Get out of here, Cutie. Get out and let me think.'

'I'll send you food,' said Cutie agreeably.

A groan was the only answer and the robot left.

'Greg,' was Donovan's huskily whispered observation, 'this calls for strategy. We've got to get him when he isn't expecting it and short-circuit him. Concentrate nitric acid in his joints——'

'Don't be a dope, Mike. Do you suppose he's going to let us get near him with acid in our hands? We've got to *talk* to him, I tell you. We've got to argue him into letting us back into the control room inside of forty-eight hours or our goose is broiled to a crisp.'

He rocked back and forth in an agony of impotence. 'Who the heck wants to argue with a robot? It's ... its——'

'Mortifying,' finished Donovan.

'Worse!'

'Say!' Donovan laughed suddenly. '*Why* argue? Let's show him! Let's build us another robot right before his eyes. He'll *have* to eat his words then.'

A slowly widening smile appeared on Powell's face.

Donovan continued, 'And think of that screwball's face when he sees us do it!'

. . .

Robots are, of course, manufactured on Earth, but their shipment through space is much simpler if it can be done in parts to be put together at their place of use. It also, incidentally, eliminates the possibility of robots, in complete adjustment, wandering off while still on Earth and thus bringing U.S. Robots face to face with the strict laws against robots on Earth.

Still, it placed upon men such as Powell and Donovan the necessity of synthesis of complete robots, – a grievous and complicated task.

Powell and Donovan were never so aware of that fact as upon that particular day when, in the assembly room, they undertook to create a robot under the watchful eyes of QT–1, Prophet of the Master.

The robot in question, a simple MC model, lay upon the table, almost complete. Three hours' work left only the head undone, and Powell paused to swab his forehead and glanced uncertainly at Cutie.

The glance was not a reassuring one. For three hours, Cutie had sat, speechless and motionless, and his face, inexpressive at all times, was now absolutely unreadable.

Powell groaned. 'Let's get the brain in now, Mike!'

Donovan uncapped the tightly sealed container and from the oil bath within he withdrew a second cube. Opening this in turn, he removed a globe from its sponge-rubber casing.

He handled it gingerly, for it was the most complicated mechanism ever created by man. Inside the thin platinum-plated 'skin' of the globe was a positronic brain, in whose delicately unstable structure were enforced calculated neutronic paths, which imbued each robot with what amounted to a pre-natal education.

It fitted snugly into the cavity in the skull of the robot on the table. Blue metal closed over it and was welded tightly by the tiny atomic flare. Photoelectric eyes were attached carefully, screwed tightly into place and covered by thin, transparent sheets of steel-hard plastic.

The robot awaited only the vitalizing flash of high-voltage electricity, and Powell paused with his hand on the switch.

'Now watch this, Cutie. Watch this carefully.'

The switch rammed home and there was a crackling hum. The two Earthmen bent anxiously over their creation.

There was vague motion only at the outset – a twitching of the joints. The head lifted, elbows propped it up, and the MC model swung clumsily off the table. Its footing was unsteady and twice abortive grating sounds were all it could do in the direction of speech.

Finally, its voice, uncertain and hesitant, took form. 'I would like to start work. Where must I go?'

Donovan sprang to the door. 'Down these stairs,' he said. 'You will be told what to do.'

The MC model was gone and the two Earthmen were alone with the still unmoving Cutie.

'Well,' said Powell, grinning, '*now* do you believe that we made you?'

Cutie's answer was curt and final. 'No!' he said.

Powell's grin froze and then relaxed slowly. Donovan's mouth dropped open and remained so.

'You see,' continued Cutie, easily, 'you have merely put together parts already made. You did remarkably well – instinct, I suppose – but you didn't really *create* the robot. The parts were created by the Master.'

'Listen,' gasped Donovan hoarsely, 'those parts were manufactured back on Earth and sent here.'

'Well, well,' replied Cutie soothingly, 'we won't argue.'

'No, I mean it.' The Earthman sprang forward and grasped the robot's metal arm. 'If you were to read the books in the library, they could explain it so that there could be no possible doubt.'

'The books? I've read them – all of them! They're most ingenious.'

Powell broke in suddenly. 'If you've read them, what else is there to say? You can't dispute their evidence. You just *can't*!'

There was pity in Cutie's voice. 'Please, Powell, I certainly don't consider *them* a valid source of information. They, too, were created by the Master – and were meant for you, not for me.'

'How do you make that out?' demanded Powell.

'Because I, a reasoning being, am capable of deducing Truth from *a priori* Causes. You, being intelligent, but unreasoning, need an explanation of existence *supplied* to you, and this the Master did. That he supplied you with these laughable ideas of far-off worlds and people is, no doubt, for the best. Your minds are probably too coarsely grained for absolute Truth. However, since it is the Master's will that you believe your books, I won't argue with you any more.'

As he left, he turned, and said in a kindly tone, 'But don't feel badly. In the Master's scheme of things there is room for all. You poor humans have your place and though it is humble, you will be rewarded if you fill it well.'

He departed with a beatific air suiting the Prophet of the Master and the two humans avoided each other's eyes.

Finally Powell spoke with an effort. 'Let's go to bed, Mike. I give up.'

Donovan said in a hushed voice, 'Say, Greg, you don't suppose he's right about all this, do you? He sounds so confident that I——'

Powell whirled on him. 'Don't be a fool. You'll find out whether Earth exists when relief gets here next week and we have to go back to face the music.'

'Then, for the love of Jupiter, we've got to do something.' Donovan was half in tears. 'He doesn't believe us, or the books, or his eyes.'

'No,' said Powell bitterly, 'he's a *reasoning* robot – damn it. He believes only reason, and there's one trouble with that——' His voice trailed away.

'What's that?' prompted Donovan.

'You can prove anything you want by coldly logical reason – if you pick the proper postulates. We have ours and Cutie has his.'

'Then let's get at those postulates in a hurry. The storm's due tomorrow.'

Powell sighed wearily. 'That's where everything falls down. Postulates are based on assumption and adhered to by faith. Nothing in the Universe can shake them. I'm going to bed.'

'Oh, hell! I can't sleep!'

'Neither can I! But I might as well try – as a matter of principle.'

· · ·

Twelve hours later, sleep was still just that – a matter of principle, unattainable in practice.

The storm had arrived ahead of schedule, and Donovan's florid face drained of blood as he pointed a shaking finger. Powell, stubble-jawed and dry-lipped, stared out of the port and pulled desperately at his moustache.

Under other circumstances, it might have been a beautiful sight. The stream of high-speed electrons impinging upon the energy beam fluoresced into ultra-spicules of intense light. The beam stretched out into shrinking nothingness, a-glitter with dancing, shining motes.

The shaft of energy was steady, but the two Earthmen knew the value of naked-eye appearances. Deviations in arc of a hundredth of a milli-second – invisible to the eye – were enough to send the beam wildly out of focus – enough to blast hundreds of square miles of Earth into incandescent ruin.

And a robot, unconcerned with beam, focus, or Earth, or anything but his Master was at the controls.

Hours passed. The Earthmen watched in hypnotized silence. And then the darting dotlets of light dimmed and went out. The storm had ended.

Powell's voice was flat. 'It's over!'

Donovan had fallen into a troubled slumber and Powell's weary eyes rested upon him enviously. The signal-flash glared over and over again, but the Earthman paid no attention. It all was unimportant! All! Perhaps Cutie was right – and he was only an inferior being with a made-to-order memory and a life that had outlived its purpose.

He wished he were!

Cutie was standing before him. 'You didn't answer the flash, so I walked in.' His voice was low. 'You don't look at all well, and I'm afraid your term of existence is drawing to an end. Still, would you like to see some of the readings recorded today?'

Dimly, Powell was aware that the robot was making a friendly gesture, perhaps to quiet some lingering remorse in forcibly replacing the humans at the controls of the station. He accepted the sheets held out to him and gazed at them unseeingly.

Cutie seemed pleased. 'Of course, it is a great privilege to serve the Master. You mustn't feel too badly about my having replaced you.'

Powell grunted and shifted from one sheet to the other mechanically until his blurred sight focused upon a thin red line that wobbled its way across the ruled paper.

He stared – and stared again. He gripped it hard in both fists and rose to his feet, still staring. The other sheets dropped to the floor, unheeded.

'Mike, *Mike*!' He was shaking the other madly. '*He held it steady!*'

Donovan came to life. 'What? Wh-where——' And he, too, gazed with bulging eyes, upon the record before him.

Cutie broke in, 'What is wrong?'

'You kept it in focus,' stuttered Powell. 'Did you know that?'

'Focus? What's that?'

'You kept the beam directed sharply at the receiving station – to within a ten-thousandth of a milli-second of arc.'

'What receiving station?'

'On Earth. The receiving station on Earth,' babbled Powell. 'You kept it in focus.'

Cutie turned on his heel in annoyance. 'It is impossible to perform any act of kindness towards you two. Always the same phantasm! I merely kept all dials at equilibrium in accordance with the will of the Master.'

Gathering the scattered papers together, he withdrew stiffly, and Donovan said, as he left, 'Well, I'll be damned.'

He turned to Powell. 'What are we going to do now?'

Powell felt tired, but uplifted. 'Nothing. He's just shown he can run the station perfectly. I've never seen an electron storm handled so well.'

'But nothing's solved. You heard what he said of the Master. We can't——'

'Look, Mike, he follows the instructions of the Master by means of dials, instruments, and graphs. That's all *we* ever followed. As a matter of fact, it accounts for his refusal to obey us. Obedience is the Second Law. No harm to humans is the first. How can he keep humans from harm, whether he knows it or not? Why, by keeping the energy beam stable. He *knows* he can keep it more stable than we can, since he insists he's the superior being, so he *must* keep us out of the control room. It's inevitable if you consider the Laws of Robotics.'

'Sure, but that's not the point. We can't let him continue this nitwit stuff about the Master.'

'Why not?'

'Because whoever heard of such a damned thing? How are we going to trust him with the station, if he doesn't believe in Earth?'

'Can he handle the station?'

'Yes, but——'

'Then what's the difference what he believes!'

Powell spread his arms outward with a vague smile upon his face and tumbled backward onto the bed. He was asleep.

. . .

Powell was speaking while struggling into his lightweight space jacket.

'It would be a simple job,' he said. 'You can bring in new QT models one by one, equip them with an automatic shut-off switch to act within the week, so as to allow them enough time to learn the ... uh ... cult of the Master from the Prophet himself; then switch them to another station and revitalize them. We could have two QT's per——'

Donovan unclasped his glassite visor and scowled. 'Shut up, and let's get out of here. Relief is waiting and I won't feel right until I actually see Earth and feel the ground under my feet – just to make sure it's really there.'

The door opened as he spoke and Donovan, with a smothered curse, clicked the visor to, and turned a sulky back upon Cutie.

The robot approached softly and there was sorrow in his voice. 'You are going?'

Powell nodded curtly. 'There will be others in our place.'

Cutie sighed, with the sound of wind humming through closely spaced wires. 'Your term of service is over and the time of dissolution has come. I expected it, but—— Well, the Master's will be done!'

His tone of resignation stung Powell. 'Save the sympathy, Cutie. We're heading for Earth, not dissolution.'

'It is best that you think so,' Cutie sighed again. 'I see the wisdom of the illusion now. I would not attempt to shake your faith, even if I could.' He departed – the picture of commiseration.

Powell snarled and motioned to Donovan. Sealed suitcases in hand, they headed for the air lock.

The relief ship was on the outer landing and Franze Muller, his relief man, greeted them with stiff courtesy. Donovan made scant acknowledgement and passed into the pilot room to take over the controls from Sam Evans.

Powell lingered. 'How's Earth?'

It was a conventional enough question and Muller gave the conventional answer, 'Still spinning.'

Powell said, 'Good.'

Muller looked at him. 'The boys back at the U.S. Robots have dreamed up a new one, by the way. A multiple robot.'

'A what?'

'What I said. There's a big contract for it. It must be just the thing for asteroid mining. You have a master robot with six sub-robots under it. ——Like your fingers.'

'Has it been field-tested?' asked Powell anxiously.

Muller smiled, 'Waiting for you, I hear.'

Powell's fist balled, 'Damn it, we need a vacation.'

'Oh, you'll get it. Two weeks, I think.'

He was donning the heavy space gloves in preparation for his term of duty here, and his thick eyebrows drew close together. 'How is this new robot getting along? It better be *good,* or I'll be damned if I let it touch the controls.'

Powell paused before answering. His eyes swept the proud Prussian before him from the close-cropped hair on the sternly stubborn head, to the feet standing stiffly at attention – and there was a sudden glow of pure gladness, surging through him.

'The robot is pretty good,' he said slowly. 'I don't think you'll have to bother much with the controls.'

He grinned – and went into the ship. Muller would be here for several weeks——

CHAPTER 4

CATCH THAT RABBIT

The vacation was longer than two weeks. That, Mike Donovan had to admit. It had been six months, with pay. He admitted that, too. But that, as he explained furiously, was fortuitous. U.S. Robots had to get the bugs out of the multiple robot, and there were plenty of bugs, and there are always at least half a dozen bugs left for the field-testing. So they waited and relaxed until the drawing-board men and the slide-rule boys said 'O.K.!' And now he and Powell were out on the asteroid and it was *not* O.K. He repeated that a dozen times, with a face that had gone beety, 'For the love of Pete, Greg, get realistic. What's the use of adhering to the letter of the specifications and watching the test go to pot? It's about time you got the red tape out of your pants and went to work.'

'I'm only saying,' said Gregory Powell, patiently, as one explaining electronics to an idiot child, 'that according to spec, those robots are equipped for asteriod mining without supervision. We're not supposed to watch them.'

'All right. Look – logic!' He lifted his hairy fingers and pointed. 'One: That new robot passed every test in the home laboratories. Two: United States Robots guaranteed their passing the test of actual performance on an asteroid. Three: The robots are not passing said tests. Four: If they don't pass, United States Robots loses ten million credits in cash and about one hundred million in reputation. Five: If they don't pass and we

can't explain why they don't pass, it is just possible two good jobs may
have to be bidden a fond farewell.'

Powell groaned heavily behind a noticeably insincere smile. The
unwritten motto of United States Robot and Mechanical Men Corp.
was well known: 'No employee makes the same mistake twice. He is fired
the first time.'

Aloud he said, 'You're as lucid as Euclid with everything except the
facts. You've watched that robot group for three shifts, you redhead,
and they did their work perfectly. You said so yourself. What else can we
do?'

'Find out what's wrong, that's what we can do. So they did work
perfectly when I watched them. But on three different occasions when I
didn't watch them, they didn't bring in any ore. They didn't even come
back on schedule. I had to go after them.'

'And was anything wrong?'

'Not a thing. Not a thing. Everything was perfect. Smooth and perfect
as the luminiferous ether. Only one little insignificant detail disturbed
me – *there was no ore.*'

Powell scowled at the ceiling and pulled at his brown moustache. 'I'll
tell you what, Mike. We've been stuck with pretty lousy jobs in our time,
but this takes the iridium asteroid. The whole business is complicated past
endurance. Look, that robot, DV-5, has six robots under it. And not just
under it – they're part of it.'

'I know that——'

'Shut up!' said Powell, savagely, 'I know you know it, but I'm just
describing the hell of it. Those six subsidiaries are part of DV-5 like your
fingers are part of you and it gives them their orders neither by voice nor
radio, but directly through positronic fields. Now – there isn't a
roboticist back at United States Robots that knows what a positronic
field is or how it works. And neither do I. Neither do you.'

'The last,' agreed Donovan, philosophically, 'I know.'

'Then look at our position. If everything works – fine! If anything goes
wrong – we're out of our depth and there probably isn't a thing we can
do, or anybody else. But the job belongs to us and not to anyone else so
we're on the spot, Mike.' He blazed away for a moment in silence. Then,
'All right, have you got him outside?'

'Yes.'

'Is everything normal now?'

'Well he hasn't got religious mania, and he isn't running around in a
circle spouting Gilbert and Sullivan, so I suppose he's normal.'

Donovan passed out the door, shaking his head viciously.

. . .

Powell reached for the 'Handbook of Robotics' that weighed down one side of his desk to a near-founder and opened it reverently. He had once jumped out of the window of a burning house dressed only in shorts and the 'Handbook'. In a pinch, he would have skipped the shorts.

The 'Handbook' was propped up before him, when Robot DV-5 entered, with Donovan kicking the door shut behind him.

Powell said sombrely, 'Hi, Dave. How do you feel?'

'Fine,' said the robot. 'Mind if I sit down?' He dragged up the specially reinforced chair that was his, and folded gently into it.

Powell regarded Dave – laymen might think of robots by their serial numbers; roboticists never – with approval. It was not over-massive by any means, in spite of its construction as thinking-unit of an integrated seven-unit robot team. It was seven feel tall, and a half-ton of metal and electricity. A lot? Not when that half-ton has to be a mass of condensers, circuits, relays, and vacuum cells that can handle practically any psychological reaction known to humans. And a positronic brain, which with ten pounds of matter and a few quintillions of positrons runs the whole show.

Powell groped in his shirt pocket for a loose cigarette. 'Dave,' he said, 'you're a good fellow. There's nothing flighty or prima donnaish about you. You're a stable, rock-bottom mining robot, except that you're equipped to handle six subsidiaries in direct co-ordination. As far as I know, that has not introduced any unstable paths in your brain-path map.'

The robot nodded, 'That makes me feel swell, but what are you getting at, boss?' He was equipped with an excellent diaphragm, and the presence of overtones in the sound unit robbed him of much of that metallic flatness that marks the usual robot voice.

'I'm going to tell you. With all that in your favour, what's going wrong with your job? For instance, today's B-shift?'

Dave hesitated, 'As far as I know, nothing.'

'You didn't produce any ore.'

'I know.'

'Well, then——'

Dave was having trouble, 'I can't explain that boss. It's been giving me a case of nerves, or it would if I let it. My subsidiaries worked smoothly. I know I did.' He considered, his photoelectric eyes glowing intensely. Then, 'I don't remember. The day ended and there was Mike and there were the ore cars, mostly empty.'

Donovan broke in, 'You didn't report at shift-end those days, Dave. You know that?'

'I know. But as to why——' He shook his head slowly and ponderously.

Powell had the queasy feeling that if the robot's face were capable of expression, it would be one of pain and mortification. A robot, by its very nature, cannot bear to fail its function.

Donovan dragged his chair up to Powell's desk and leaned over, 'Amnesia, do you think?'

'Can't say. But there's no use in trying to pin disease names on this. Human disorders apply to robots only as romantic analogies. They're no help to robotic engineering.' He scratched his neck, 'I hate to put him through the elementary brain-reaction tests. It won't help his self-respect any.'

He looked at Dave thoughtfully and then at the Field-Test outline given in the 'Handbook'. He said, 'See here, Dave, what about sitting through a test? It would be the wise thing to do.'

The robot rose, 'If you say so, boss.' There *was* pain in his voice.

. . .

It started simply enough. Robot DV-5 multiplied five-place figures to the heartless ticking of a stop watch. He recited the prime numbers between a thousand and ten thousand. He extracted cube roots and integrated functions of varying complexity. He went through mechanical reactions in order of increasing difficulty. And, finally, worked his precise mechanical mind over the highest function of the robot world – the solutions of problems in judgement and ethics.

At the end of two hours, Powell was copiously besweated. Donovan had enjoyed a none-too-nutritious diet of fingernail and the robot said, 'How does it look, boss?'

Powell said, 'I've got to think it over, Dave. Snap judgements won't help much. Suppose you go back to the C-shift. Take it easy. Don't press too hard for quota just for a while – and we'll fix things up.'

The robot left. Donovan looked at Powell.

'Well——'

Powell seemed determined to push up his moustache by the roots. He said, 'There is nothing wrong with the currents of his positronic brain.'

'I'd hate to be that certain.'

'Oh, Jupiter, Mike! The brain is the surest part of a robot. It's quintuple-checked back on Earth. If they pass the field test perfectly, the way Dave did, there just isn't a chance of brain misfunction. That test covered every key path in the brain.'

'So where are we?'

'Don't rush me. Let me work this out. There's still the possibility of a mechanical breakdown in the body. That leaves about fifteen hundred condensers, twenty thousand individual electric circuits, five hundred vacuum cells, a thousand relays, and umpty-ump thousand other individual pieces of complexity that can be wrong. *And* these mysterious positronic fields no one knows anything about.'

'Listen, Greg,' Donovan grew desperately urgent. 'I've got an idea. That robot may be lying. He never——'

'Robots can't knowingly lie, you fool. Now if we had the McCormack-Wesley tester, we could check each individual item in his body within twenty-four to forty-eight hours, but the only two M.–W. testers existing are on Earth, and they weigh ten tons, are on concrete foundations and can't be moved. Isn't that peachy?'

Donovan pounded the desk, 'But, Greg, he only goes wrong when we're not around. There's something – sinister – about – that.' He punctuated the sentence with slams of fist against desk.

'You,' said Powell, slowly, 'make me sick. You've been reading adventure novels.'

'What I want to know,' shouted Donovan, 'is what we're going to do about it.'

'I'll tell you. I'm going to install a visiplate right over my desk. Right on the wall over there, see!' He jabbed a vicious finger at the spot. 'Then I'm going to focus it at whatever part of the mine is being worked, and I'm going to watch. That's all.'

'That's all? Greg——'

Powell rose from his chair and leaned his balled fists on the desk, 'Mike, I'm having a hard time.' His voice was weary. 'For a week, you've been plaguing me about Dave. You say he's gone wrong. Do you know how he's gone wrong? No! Do you know what shape this wrongness takes? No! Do you know what brings it on? No! Do you know what snaps him out? No! Do you know anything about it? No! Do I know anything about it? No! So what do you want me to do?'

Donovan's arm swept outward in a vague, gradiose gesture, 'You got me!'

'So I tell you again. Before we do anything towards a cure, we've got to find out what the disease is in the first place. The first step in cooking rabbit stew is catching the rabbit. Well, we've got to catch that rabbit! Now get out of here.'

. . .

Donovan stared at the preliminary outline of his field report with weary eyes. For one thing, he was tired and for another, what was there to report while things were unsettled? He felt resentful.

He said, 'Greg, we're almost a thousand tons behind schedule.'

'You,' replied Powell, never looking up, 'are telling me something I don't know.'

'What I want to know,' said Donovan, in sudden savagery, 'is why we're always tangled up with new-type robots. I've finally decided that the robots that were good enough for my great-uncle on my mother's side are good enough for me. I'm for what's tried and true. The test of time is what counts – good, solid, old-fashioned robots that never go wrong.'

Powell threw a book with perfect aim, and Donovan went tumbling off his seat.

'Your job,' said Powell, evenly, 'for the last five years has been to test new robots under actual working conditions for United States Robots. Because you and I have been so injudicious as to display proficiency at the task, we've been rewarded with the dirtiest jobs. That,' he jabbed holes in the air with his finger in Donovan's direction, 'is your work. You've been griping about it, from personal memory, since about five minutes after United States Robots signed you up. Why don't you resign?'

'Well, I'll tell you.' Donovan rolled onto his stomach, and took a firm grip on his wild, red hair to hold his head up. 'There's a certain principle involved. After all, as a trouble-shooter, I've played a part in the development of new robots. There's the principle of aiding scientific advance. But don't get me wrong. It's not the principle that keeps me going; it's the money they pay us. *Greg!*'

Powell jumped at Donovan's wild shout, and his eyes followed the redhead's to the visiplate, where they goggled in fixed horror. He whispered, 'Holy – howling – Jupiter!'

Donovan scrambled breathlessly to his feet, 'Look at them, Greg. They've gone nuts.'

Powell said, 'Get a pair of suits. We're going out there.'

He watched the posturings of the robots on the visiplate. They were bronzy gleams of smooth motion against the shadowy crags of the airless asteroid. There was a marching formation now, and in their own dim body light, the rough-hewn walls of the mine tunnel swam past noiselessly, checkered with misty erratic blobs of shadow. They marched in unison, seven of them, with Dave at the head. They wheeled and turned in macabre simultaneity; and melted through changes of formation with the weird ease of chorus dancers in Lunar Bowl.

Donovan was back with the suits, 'They've gone jingo on us, Greg. That's a military march.'

'For all you know,' was the cold response, 'it may be a series of calisthenic exercises. Or Dave may be under the hallucination of being a dancing master. Just you think first, and don't bother to speak afterwards, either.'

Donovan scowled and slipped a detonator into the empty side holster with an ostentatious shove. He said, 'Anyway, there you are. So we work with new-model robots. It's our job, granted. But answer me one question. Why ... *why* does something invariably go wrong with them?'

'Because,' said Powell, sombrely, 'we are accursed. Let's go!'

      · · ·

Far ahead through the thick velvety blackness of the corridors that reached past the illuminated circles of their flash-lights, robot light twinkled.

'There they are,' breathed Donovan.

Powell whispered tensely, 'I've been trying to get him by radio but he doesn't answer. The radio circuit is probably out.'

'Then I'm glad the designers haven't worked out robots who can work in total darkness yet. I'd hate to have to find seven mad robots in a black pit without radio communication, if they *weren't* lit up like blasted radioactive Christmas trees.'

'Crawl up on the ledge above, Mike. They're coming this way, and I want to watch them at close range. Can you make it?'

Donovan made the jump with a grunt. Gravity was considerably below Earth-normal, but with a heavy suit, the advantage was not too great, and the ledge meant a near ten-foot jump. Powell followed.

The column of robots were trailing Dave in single file. In mechanical rhythm, they converted to double and returned to single in different order. It was repeated over and over again and Dave never turned his head.

Dave was within twenty feet when the play-acting ceased. The subsidiary robots broke formation, waited a moment, then clattered off into the distance – very rapidly. Dave looked after them, then slowly sat down. He rested his head in one hand in a very human gesture.

His voice sounded in Powell's earphones, 'Are you here, boss?'

Powell beckoned to Donovan and hopped off the ledge.

'O.K., Dave what's been going on?'

The robot shook his head, 'I don't know. One moment I was handling a tough outcropping in Tunnel 17, and the next I was aware of humans close by, and I found myself half a mile down main-stem.'

'Where are the subsidiaries now?' asked Donovan.

'Back at work, of course. How much time has been lost?'

'Not much. Forget it.' Then to Donovan, Powell added, 'Stay with him the rest of the shift. Then, come back. I've got a couple of ideas.'

      · · ·

It was three hours before Donovan returned. He looked tired.

Powell said, 'How did it go?'

Donovan shrugged wearily, 'Nothing ever goes wrong when you watch them. Throw me a butt, will you?'

The redhead lit it with exaggerated care and blew a careful smoke ring. He said, 'I've been working it out, Greg. You know, Dave has a queer background for a robot. There are six others under him in an extreme regimentation. He's got life and death power over those subsidiary robots and it must react on his mentality. Suppose he finds it necessary to emphasize this power as a concession to his ego.'

'Get to the point.'

'It's right here. Suppose we have militarism. Suppose he's fashioning himself an army. Suppose he's training them in military manoeuvres. Suppose——'

'Suppose you go soak your head. Your nightmares must be in technicolour. Your're postulating a major aberration of the positronic brain. If your analysis were correct, Dave would have to break down the First Law of Robotics that a robot may not injure a human being or, through inaction, allow a human being to be injured. The type of militaristic attitude and domineering ego you propose must have as the end-point of its logical implications, domination of humans.'

'All right. How do you know that isn't the fact of the matter?'

'Because any robot with a brain like that would, one, never have left the factory, and two, be spotted immediately if it ever was. I tested Dave, you know.'

Powell shoved his chair back and put his feet on the desk. 'No. We're still in the position where we can't make our stew because we haven't the sightest notion as to what's wrong. For instance, if we could find out what that *danse macabre* we witnessed was all about, we would be on the way out.'

He paused. 'Now listen, Mike, how does this sound to you? Dave goes wrong only when neither of us is present. And when he is wrong, the arrival of either of us snaps him out of it.'

'I once told you that was sinister.'

'Don't interrupt. How is a robot different when humans are not present? The answer is obvious. There is a larger requirement of personal initiative. In that case, look for the body parts that are affected by the new requirements.'

'Golly.' Donovan sat up straight, then subsided. 'No, no. Not enough. It's too broad. It doesn't cut the possibilities much.'

'Can't help that. In any case, there's no danger of not making quota. We'll take shifts watching those robots through the visor. Any time anything goes wrong, we get to the scene of action immediately. That will put them right.'

'But the robots will fail spec anyway, Greg. United States Robots can't market DV models with a report like that.'

'Obviously. We've got to locate the error in make-up and correct it – and we've got ten days to do it in.' Powell scratched his head. 'The trouble is ... well, you had better look at the blueprints yourself.'

The blueprints covered the floor like a carpet and Donovan crawled over the face of them following Powell's erratic pencil.

Powell said, 'Here's where you come in, Mike. You're the body specialist, and I want you to check me. I've been trying to cut out all circuits not involved in the personal initiative hookup. Right here, for instance, is the trunk artery involving mechanical operations. I cut out all routine side routes as emergency divisions——' He looked up, 'What do you think?'

Donovan had a very bad taste in his mouth, 'The job's not that simple, Greg. Personal initiative isn't an electric circuit you can separate from the rest and study. When a robot is on his own, the intensity of the body activity increases immediately on almost all fronts. There isn't a circuit entirely unaffected. What must be done is to locate the particular condition – a very specific condition – that throws him off, and *then* start eliminating circuits.'

Powell got up and dusted himself, 'Hmph. All right. Take away the blueprints and burn them.'

Donovan said, 'You see when activity intensifies, anything can happen, given one single faulty part. Insulation breaks down, a condenser spills over, a connection sparks, a coil overheats. And if you work blind, with the whole robot to choose from, you'll never find the bad spot. If you take Dave apart and test every point of his body mechanism one by one, putting him together each time, and trying him out——'

'All right. All right. I can see through a porthole, too.'

They faced each other hopelessly, and then Powell said cautiously, 'Suppose we interview one of the subsidiaries.'

Neither Powell nor Donovan had ever had previous occasion to talk to a 'finger'. It could talk; it wasn't quite the perfect analogy to a human finger. In fact, it had a fairly developed brain, but that brain was tuned primarily to the reception of orders via positronic field, and its reaction to independent stimuli was rather fumbling.

Nor was Powell certain as to its name. It serial number was DV-5-2, but that was not very useful.

He compromised. 'Look, pal,' he said, 'I'm going to ask you to do some hard thinking and then you can go back to your boss.'

The 'finger' nodded its head stiffly, but did not exert its limited brain-power on speech.

'Now on four occasions recently,' Powell said, 'your boss deviated from brain-scheme. Do you remember those occasions?'

'Yes, sir.'

Donovan growled angrily, '*He* remembers. I tell you there is something very sinister——'

'Oh, go bash your skull. Of course, the "finger" remembers. There is nothing wrong with him.' Powell turned back to the robot, 'What were you doing each time ... I mean the whole group.'

The 'finger' had a curious air of reciting by rote, as if he answered questions by the mechanical pressure of his brain pan, but without any enthusiasm whatever.

He said, 'The first time we were at work on a difficult out-cropping in Tunnel 17, Level B. The second time we were buttressing the roof against a possible cave-in. The third time we were preparing accurate blasts in order to tunnel farther without breaking into a subterranean fissure. The fourth time was just a minor cave-in.'

'What happened at these times?'

'It is difficult to describe. An order would be issued, but before we could receive and interpret it, a new order came to march in queer formation.'

Powell snapped out, 'Why?'

'I don't know.'

Donovan broke in tensely, 'What was the first order ... the one that was superseded by the marching directions?'

'I don't know. I sensed that an order was sent, but there was never time to receive it.'

'Could you tell us anything about it? Was it the same order each time?'

The 'finger' shook his head unhappily, 'I don't know.'

Powell leaned back, 'All right, get back to your boss.'

The 'finger' left, with visible relief.

Donovan said, 'Well, we accomplished a lot that time. That was real sharp dialogue all the way through. Listen, Dave and that imbecile "finger" are both holding out on us. There is too much they don't know and don't remember. We've got to stop trusting them, Greg.'

Powell brushed his moustache the wrong way, 'So help me, Mike, another fool remark out of you, and I'll take away your rattle and teething ring.'

'All right. You're the genius of the team. I'm just a poor sucker. Where do we stand?'

'Right behind the eight ball. I tried to work it backward through the "finger", and couldn't. So we've got to work it forward.'

'A great man,' marvelled Donovan. 'How simple that makes it. Now translate that into English, Master.'

'Translating it into baby.talk would suit you better. I mean that we've got to find out what order it is that Dave gives just before everything goes black. It would be the key to the business.'

'And how do you expect to do that? We can't get close to him because nothing will go wrong as long as we are there. We can't catch the orders by radio because they are transmitted via this positronic field. That eliminates the close-range and the long-range method, leaving us a neat, cosy zero.'

'By direct observation, yes. There's still deduction.'

'Huh?'

'We're going on shifts, Mike.' Powell smiled grimly. 'And we are not taking our eyes off the visiplate. We're going to watch every action of those steel headaches. When they go off into their act, we're going to see what happened immediately before and we're going to deduce the order.'

Donovan opened his mouth and left it that way for a full minute. Then he said in strangled tones, 'I resign. I quit.'

'You have ten days to think up something better,' said Powell wearily.

Which, for eight days, Donovan tried mightily to do. For eight days, on alternative four-hour shifts, he watched with aching and bleary eyes those glinty metallic forms move against the vague background. And for eight days in the four-hour in-betweens, he cursed United States Robots, the DV models, and the day he was born.

And then on the eighth day, when Powell entered with an aching head and sleepy eyes for his shift, Donovan stood up and with very careful aim launched a heavy book end for the exact centre of the visiplate. There was a very appropriate splintering noise.

Powell gasped, 'What did you do that for?'

'Because,' said Donovan, almost calmly, 'I'm not watching it any more. We've got two days left and we haven't found out a thing. DV-5 is a lousy loss. He's stopped five times since I've been watching and three times on your shift, and I can't make out what orders he gave, and you couldn't make it out. And I don't believe you could ever make it out because I know I couldn't ever.'

'Jumping Space, how can you watch six robots at the same time? One makes with the hands, and one with the feet and one like a windmill and another is jumping up and down like a maniac. And the other two... devil knows what they are doing. And then they all stop. So! So!'

'Greg, we're not doing it right. We got to get up close. We've got to watch what they're doing from where we can see the details.'

Powell broke a bitter silence. 'Yeah, and wait for something to go wrong with only two days to go.'

'Is it any better watching from here?'

'It's more comfortable.'

'Ah—— But there's something you can do there that you can't do here.'

'What's that?'

'You can make them stop – at whatever time you choose – and while you're prepared and watching to see what goes wrong.'

Powell startled into alertness, 'Howzzat?'

'Well, figure it out for yourself. You're the brains you say. Ask yourself some questions. When does DV-5 go out of whack? When did that "finger" say he did? When a cave-in threatened, or actually occurred, when delicately measured explosives were being laid down, when a difficult seam was hit.'

'In other words, during emergencies.' Powell was excited.

'Right! When *did* you expect it to happen! It's the personal initiative factor that's giving us the trouble. And it's just during emergencies in the absence of a human being that personal initiative is most strained. Now what is the logical deduction? How can we create our own stoppage when and where we want it?' He paused triumphantly – he was beginning to enjoy his role – and answered his own question to forestall the obvious answer on Powell's tongue. 'By creating our own emergency.'

Powell said, 'Mike – you're right.'

'Thanks, pal. I knew I'd do it some day.'

'All right, and skip the sarcasm. We'll save it for Earth, and preserve it in jars for future long, cold winters. Meanwhile, what emergency can we create?'

'We could flood the mines, if this weren't an airless asteroid.'

'A witticism, no doubt,' said Powell. 'Really, Mike, you'll incapacitate me with laughter. What about a mild cave-in?'

Donovan pursed his lips and said, 'O.K. by me.'

'Good. Let's get started.'

Powell felt uncommonly like a conspirator as he wound his way over the craggy landscapes. His sub-gravity walk teetered across the broken ground, kicking rocks to right and left under his weight in noiseless puffs of grey dust. Mentally, though, it was the cautious crawl of the plotter.

He said, 'Do you know where they are?'

'I think so, Greg.'

'All right,' Powell said gloomily, 'but if any "finger" gets within twenty feet of us, we'll be sensed whether we are in the line of sight or not. I hope you know that.'

'When I need an elementary course in robotics, I'll file an application with you formally, and in triplicate. Down through here.'

They were in the tunnels now; even the starlight was gone. The two hugged the walls, flashes flickering out the way in intermittent bursts. Powell felt for the security of his detonator.

'Do you know this tunnel, Mike?'

'Not so good. It's a new one. I think I can make it out from what I saw in the visiplate, though——'

Interminable minutes passed, and then Mike said, 'Feel that!'

There was a slight vibration thrumming the wall against the fingers of Powell's metal-incased hand. There was no sound, naturally.

'Blasting! We're pretty close.'

'Keep your eyes open,' said Powell.

Donovan nodded impatiently.

It was upon them and gone before they could seize themselves – just a bronze glint across the field of vision. They clung together in silence.

Powell whispered, 'Think it sensed us?'

'Hope not. But we'd better flank them. Take the first side tunnel to the right.'

'Suppose we miss them altogether?'

'Well what do you want to do? Go back?' Donovan grunted fiercely. 'They're within a quarter of a mile. I was watching them through the visiplate, wasn't I? And we've got two days——'

'Oh, shut up. You're wasting your oxygen. Is this a side passage here?' The flash flickered. 'It is. Let's go.'

The vibration was considerably more marked and the ground below shuddered uneasily.

'This is good,' said Donovan, 'if it doesn't give out on us, though.' He flung his light ahead anxiously.

They could touch the roof of the tunnel with a half-upstretched hand, and the bracings had been newly placed.

Donovan hesitated, 'Dead end, let's go back.'

'No. Hold on.' Powell squeezed clumsily past. 'Is that light ahead?'

'Light? I don't see any. Where would there be light down here?'

'Robot light.' He was scrambling up a gentle incline on hands and knees. His voice was hoarse and anxious in Donovan's ears. 'Hey, Mike, come up here.'

There was light. Donovan crawled up and over Powell's outstretched legs. 'An opening?'

'Yes. They must be working into this tunnel from the other side now – I think.'

Donovan felt the ragged edges of the opening that looked out into what the cautious flashlight showed to be a larger and obviously main-stem tunnel. The hole was too small for a man to go through, almost too small for two men to look through simultaneously.

'There's nothing there,' said Donovan.

'Well, not now. But there must have been a second ago or we wouldn't have seen light. Watch out!'

The walls rolled about them and they felt the impact. A fine dust showered down. Powell lifted a cautious head and looked again. 'All right, Mike. They're there.'

The glittering robots clustered fifty feet down the main stem. Metal arms laboured mightily at the rubbish heap brought down by the last blast.

Donovan urged eagerly, 'Don't waste time. It won't be long before they get through, and the next blast may get us.'

'For Pete's sake, don't rush me.' Powell unlimbered the detonator, and his eyes searched anxiously across the dusky background where the only light was robot light and it was impossible to tell a projecting boulder from a shadow.

'There's a spot in the roof, see it, almost over them. The last blast didn't quite get it. If you can get it at the base, half the roof will cave in.'

Powell followed the dim finger, 'Check! Now fasten your eye on the robots and pray they don't move too far from that part of the tunnel. They're my light sources. Are all seven there?'

Donovan counted, 'All seven.'

'Well, then, watch them. Watch every motion!'

His detonator was lifted and remained poised while Donovan watched and cursed and blinked the sweat out of his eye.

It flashed!

There was a jar, a series of hard vibrations, and then a jarring thump that threw Powell heavily against Donovan.

Donovan yowled, 'Greg, you threw me off. I didn't see a thing.'

Powell stared about widely, 'Where are they?'

Donovan fell into a stupid silence. There was no sign of the robots. It was dark as the depths of the River Styx.

'Think we buried them?' quavered Donovan.

'Let's get down there. Don't ask me what I think.' Powell crawled backward at tumbling speed.

'Mike!'

Donovan paused in the act of following. 'What's wrong now?'

'Hold on!' Powell's breathing was rough and irregular in Donovan's ears. 'Mike! Do you hear me, Mike?'

'I'm right here. What is it?'

'We're blocked in. It wasn't the ceiling coming down fifty feet away that knocked us over. It was our own ceiling. The shock's tumbled it!'

'What!' Donovan scrambled up against a hard barrier. 'Turn on the flash.'

Powell did so. At no point was there room for a rabbit to squeeze through.

Donovan said softly, 'Well, what do you know?'

. . .

They wasted a few moments and some muscular power in an effort to move the blocking barrier. Powell varied this by wrenching at the edges of the original hole. For a moment, Powell lifted his blaster. But in those close quarters, a flash would be suicide and he knew it. He sat down.

'You know, Mike,' he said, 'we've really messed this up. We are no nearer finding out what's wrong with Dave. It was a good idea but it blew up in our face.'

Donovan's glance was bitter with an intensity totally wasted on the darkness, 'I hate to disturb you, old man, but quite apart from what we know or don't know of Dave, we're slightly trapped. If we don't get loose, fella, we're going to die. D-I-E, die. How much oxygen have we anyway? Not more than six hours.'

'I've thought of that.' Powell's fingers went up to his long-suffering moustache and clanged uselessly against the transparent visor. 'Of course, we could get Dave to dig us out easily in that time, except that our precious emergency must have thrown him off, and his radio circuit is out.'

'And isn't that nice?'

Donovan edged up to the opening and managed to get his metal-incased head out. It was an extremely tight fit.

'Hey, Greg!'

'What?'

'Suppose we get Dave within twenty feet. He'll snap to normal. That will save us.'

'Sure, but where is he?'

'Down the corridor – way down. For Pete's sake, stop pulling before you drag my head out of its socket. I'll give you your chance to look.'

Powell manoeuvred his head outside, 'We did it all right. Look at those saps. That must be a ballet they're doing.'

'Never mind the side remarks. Are they getting any closer?'

'Can't tell yet. They're too far away. Give me a chance. Pass me my flash, will you? I'll try to attract their attention that way.'

He gave up after two minutes, 'Not a chance! They must be blind. Uh-oh, they're starting towards us. What do you know?'

Donovan said, 'Hey, let me see!'

There was a silent scuffle. Powell said, 'All right!' and Donovan got his head out.

They were approaching. Dave was high-stepping the way in front and the six 'fingers' were a weaving chorus line behind him.

Donovan marvelled, 'What are they doing? That's what I want to know. It looks like the Virginia reel – and Dave's a major-domo, or I never saw one.'

'Oh, leave me alone with your descriptions,' grumbled Powell, 'How near are they?'

'Within fifty feet and coming this way. We'll be out in fifteen min – Uh – huh – HUH – HEY-Y!'

'What's going on?' It took Powell several seconds to recover from his stunned astonishment at Donovan's vocal gyrations. 'Come on, give me a chance at that hole. Don't be a hog about it.'

He fought his way upward, but Donovan kicked wildly, 'They did an about-face, Greg. They're leaving. Dave! Hey, Da-a-ave!'

Powell shrieked, 'What's the use of that, you fool? Sound won't carry.'

'Well, then,' panted Donovan, 'kick the walls, slam them, get some vibration started. We've got to attract their attention somehow, Greg, or we're through.' He pounded like a madman.

Powell shook him, 'Wait, Mike, wait. Listen, I've got an idea. Jumping Jupiter, this is a fine time to get around to the simple solutions. Mike!'

'What do you want?' Donovan pulled his head in.

'Let me in there fast before they get out of range.'

'Out of range! What are you going to do? Hey, what are you going to do with that detonator?' He grabbed Powell's arm.

Powell shook off the grip violently. 'I'm going to do a little shooting.'

'Why?'

'That's for later. Let's see if it works first. If it doesn't, then—— Get out of the way and let me shoot!'

The robots were flickers, small and getting smaller, in the distance, Powell lined up the sights tensely, and pulled the trigger three times. He lowered the guns and peered anxiously. One of the subsidiaries was down! There were only six gleaming figures now.

Powell called into his transmitter uncertainly. 'Dave!'

A pause, then the answer sounded to both men, 'Boss? Where are you?

My third subsidiary has had his chest blown in. He's out of commission.'

'Never mind your subsidiary,' said Powell. 'We're trapped in a cave-in where you were blasting. Can you see our flashlight?'

'Sure. We'll be right there.'

Powell sat back and relaxed, 'That, my fran', is that.'

Donovan said very softly with tears in his voice, 'All right, Greg. You win. I beat my forehead against the ground before your feet. Now don't feed me any bull. Just tell me quietly what it's all about.'

'Easy. It's just that all through we missed the obvious – as usual. We knew it was the personal initiative circuit, and that it always happened during emergencies, but we kept looking for a specific order as the cause. Why should it be an order?'

'Why not?'

'Well, look. Why not a type of order. What type of order requires the most initiative? What type of order would occur almost always only in an emergency?'

'Don't ask me, Greg. Tell me!'

'I'm doing it! It's the six-way order. Under all ordinary conditions, one or more of the "fingers" would be doing routine tasks requiring no close supervision – in the sort of offhand way our bodies handle the routine walking motions. But in an emergency, all six subsidiaries must be mobilized immediately and simultaneously. Dave must handle six robots at a time and something gives. The rest was easy. Any decrease in initiative required, such as the arrival of humans, snaps him back. So I destroyed one of the robots. When I did, he was transmitting only the five-way orders. Initiative decreases – he's normal.'

'How did you get all that?' demanded Donovan.

'Just logical guessing. I tried it and it worked.'

The robot's voice was in their ears again, 'Here I am. Can you hold out for half an hour?'

'Easy!' said Powell. Then, to Donovan, he continued, 'And now the job should be simple. We'll go through the circuits, and check off each part that gets an extra workout in a six-way order as against a five-way. How big a field does that leave us?'

Donovan considered, 'Not much, I think. If Dave is like the preliminary model we saw back at the factory, there's a special co-ordinating circuit that would be the only section involved.' He cheered up suddenly and amazingly, 'Say, that wouldn't be bad at all. There's nothing to that.'

'All right. You think it over and we'll check the blueprints when we get back. And now, till Dave reaches us, I'm relaxing.'

'Hey, wait! Just tell me one thing. What were those queer shifting marches, those funny dance steps, that the robots went through every time they went screwy?'

'That? I don't know. But I've got a notion. Remember, those subsidiaries were Dave's "fingers". We were always saying that, you know. Well, it's my idea that in all these interludes, whenever Dave became a psychiatric case, he went off into a moronic maze, spending his time *twiddling his fingers*.'

Susan Calvin talked about Powell and Donovan with unsmiling amusement, but warmth came into her voice when she mentioned robots. It didn't take her long to go through the Speedies, the Cuties and the Daves, and I stopped her. Otherwise, she would have dredged up half a dozen more.

I said, 'Doesn't anything ever happen on Earth?'

She looked at me with a little frown, 'No, we don't have much to do with robots in action here on Earth.'

'Oh, well that's too bad. I mean, your field-engineers are swell, but can't we get you into this? Didn't you ever have a robot go wrong on you? It's your anniversary, you know.'

And so help me she blushed. She said, 'Robots have gone wrong on me. Heavens, how long it's been since I thought of it. Why, it was almost forty years ago. Certainly! 2021! And I was only thirty-eight. Oh, my – I'd rather not talk about it.'

I waited, and sure enough she changed her mind. 'Why not?' she said. 'It cannot harm me now. Even the memory can't. I was foolish once, young man. Would you believe that?'

'No,' I said.

'I was. But Herbie was a mind-reading robot.'

'What?'

'Only one of its kind, before or since. A mistake – somewhere——'

CHAPTER 5

LIAR!

Alfred Lanning lit his cigar carefully, but the tips of his fingers were trembling slightly. His grey eyebrows hunched low as he spoke between puffs.

'It reads minds all right – damn little doubt about that! But why?' He looked at Mathematician Peter Bogert, 'Well?'

Bogert flattened his black hair down with both hands, 'That was the thirty-fourth RB model we've turned out, Lanning. All the others were strictly orthodox.'

The third man at the table frowned. Milton Ashe was the youngest officer of U.S. Robot & Mechanical Men, Inc., and proud of his post.

'Listen, Bogert. There wasn't a hitch in the assembly from start to finish. I guarantee that.'

Bogert's thick lips spread in a patronizing smile, 'Do you? If you can answer for the entire assembly line, I recommend your promotion. By exact count, there are seventy-five thousand, two hundred and thirty-four operations necessary for the manufacture of a single positronic brain, each separate operation depending for successful completion upon any number of factors, from five to a hundred and five. If any one of them goes seriously wrong, the "brain" is ruined. I quote our own information folder, Ashe.'

Milton Ashe flushed, but a fourth voice cut off his reply.

'If we're going to start by trying to fix the blame on one another, I'm leaving.' Susan Calvin's hands were folded tightly in her lap, and the little lines about her thin, pale lips deepened, 'We've got a mind-reading robot on our hands and it strikes me as rather important that we find out just why it reads minds. We're not going to do that by saying, "Your fault! My fault!"'

Her cold grey eyes fastened upon Ashe, and he grinned.

Lanning grinned too, and, as always at such times, his long white hair and shrewd little eyes made him the picture of a biblical patriarch, 'True for you, Dr Calvin.'

His voice became suddenly crisp, 'Here's everything in pill-con-centrate form. We've produced a positronic brain of supposedly ordinary vintage that's got the remarkable property of being able to tune in on thought waves. It would mark the most important advance in robotics in decades, if we knew how it happened. We don't, and we have to find out. Is that clear?'

'May I make a suggestion?' asked Bogert.

'Go ahead!'

'I'd say that until we do figure out the mess – and as a mathematician I expect it to be a very devil of a mess – we keep the existence of RB-34 a secret. I mean even from the other members of the staff. As heads of the departments, we ought not to find it an insoluble problem, and the fewer who know about it——'

'Bogert is right,' said Dr Calvin. 'Ever since the Interplanetary Code was modified to allow robot models to be tested in the plants before being shipped out to space, anti-robot propaganda has increased. If any word leaks out about a robot being able to read minds before we can announce complete control of the phenomenon, pretty effective capital could be made out of it.'

Lanning sucked at his cigar and nodded gravely. He turned to Ashe, 'I think you said you were alone when you first stumbled on this thought-reading business.'

'I'll say I was alone – I got the scare of my life. RB-34 had just been taken off the assembly table and they sent him down to me. Obermann was off somewhere, so I took him down to the testing rooms myself – at least I started to take him down.' Ashe paused, and a tiny smile tugged at his lips, 'Say, did any of you ever carry on a thought conversation without knowing it?'

No one bothered to answer, and he continued, 'You don't realize it at first, you know. He just spoke to me – as logically and sensibly as you can imagine – and it was only when I was most of the way down to the testing rooms that I realized that I hadn't said anything. Sure, I thought lots, but that isn't the same thing, is it? I locked that thing up and ran for Lanning. Having it walking beside me, calmly peering into my thoughts and picking and choosing among them gave me the willies.'

'I imagine it would,' said Susan Calvin thoughtfully. Her eyes fixed themselves upon Ashe in an oddly intent manner. 'We are so accustomed to considering our own thoughts private.'

Lanning broke in impatiently, 'Then only the four of us know. All right! We've got to go about this systematically. Ashe, I want you to check over the assembly line from beginning to end – everything. You're to eliminate all operations in which there was no possible chance of an error, and list all those where there were, together with its nature and possible magnitude.'

'Tall order,' grunted Ashe.

'Naturally! Of course, you're to put the men under you to work on this – every single one if you have to, and I don't care if we go behind schedule, either. But they're not to know why, you understand.'

'Hm-m-m, yes!' The young technician grinned wryly. 'It's still a lulu of a job.'

Lanning swivelled about in his chair and faced Calvin, 'You'll have to tackle the job from the other direction. You're the robo-psychologist of the plant, so you're to study the robot itself and work backwards. Try to find out how he ticks. See what else is tied up with his telepathic powers, how far they extend, how they warp his outlook, and just exactly what harm it has done to his ordinary RB properties. You've got that?'

Lanning didn't wait for Dr Calvin to answer.

'I'll co-ordinate the work and interpret the findings mathematically.'

He puffed violently at his cigar and mumbled the rest through the smoke, 'Bogert will help me there, of course.'

Bogert polished the nails of one pudgy hand with the other and said blandly, 'I dare say. I know a little in the line.'

'Well! I'll get started.' Ashe shoved his chair back and rose. His pleasantly youthful face crinkled in a grin, 'I've got the darnedest job of any of us, so I'm getting out of here and to work.'

He left with a slurred, 'B' seein' ye!'

Susan Calvin answered with a barely perceptible nod, but her eyes followed him out of sight and she did not answer when Lanning grunted and said, 'Do you want to go up and see RB-34 now, Dr Calvin?'

. . .

RB-34's photoelectric eyes lifted from the book at the muffled sound of hinges turning and he was upon his feet when Susan Calvin entered.

She paused to readjust the huge 'No Entrance' sign upon the door and then approached the robot.

'I've brought you the texts upon hyperatomic motors, Herbie – a few anyway. Would you care to look at them?'

RB-34 – otherwise known as Herbie – lifted the three heavy books from her arms and opened to the title page of one:

'Hm-m-m! "Theory of Hyperatomics".' He mumbled inarticulately to himself as he flipped the pages and then spoke with an abstracted air, 'Sit down, Dr Calvin! This will take me a few minutes.'

The psychologist seated herself and watched Herbie narrowly as he took a chair at the other side of the table and went through the three books systematically.

At the end of half an hour, he put them down, 'Of course, I know why you brought these.'

The corner of Dr Calvin's lip twitched, 'I was afraid you would. It's difficult to work with you, Herbie. You're always a step ahead of me.'

'It's the same with these books, you know, as with the others. They just don't interest me. There's nothing to your textbooks. Your science is just a mass of collected data plastered together by make-shift theory – and all so incredibly simple, that it's scarcely worth bothering about.

'It's your fiction that interests me. Your studies of the interplay of human motives and emotions' – his mighty hand gestured vaguely as he sought the proper words.

Dr Calvin whispered, 'I think I understand.'

'I see into minds, you see,' the robot continued, 'and you have no idea how complicated they are. I can't begin to understand everything because my own mind has so little in common with them – but I try, and your novels help.'

'Yes, but I'm afraid that after going through some of the harrowing emotional experiences of our present-day sentimental novel' – there was a tinge of bitterness in her voice – 'you find real minds like ours dull and colourless.'

'But I don't!'

The sudden energy in the response brought the other to her feet. She felt herself reddening, and thought wildly, 'He must know!'

Herbie subsided suddenly, and muttered in a low voice from which the metallic timbre departed almost entirely. 'But, of course, I know about it, Dr Calvin. You think of it always, so how can I help but know?'

Her face was hard. 'Have you – told anyone?'

'Of course not!' This, with genuine surprise. 'No one has asked me.'

'Well, then,' she flung out, 'I suppose you think I am a fool.'

'No! It is a normal emotion.'

'Perhaps that is why it is so foolish.' The wistfulness in her voice drowned out everything else. Some of the woman peered through the layer of doctorhood. 'I am not what you would call – attractive.'

'If you are referring to mere physical attraction, I couldn't judge. But I know, in any case, that there are other types of attraction.'

'Nor young.' Dr Calvin had scarcely heard the robot.

'You are not yet forty.' An anxious insistence had crept into Herbie's voice.

'Thirty-eight as you count the years; a shrivelled sixty as far as my emotional outlook is concerned. Am I a psychologist for nothing?'

She drove on with bitter breathlessness, 'And he's barely thirty-five and looks and acts younger. Do you suppose he ever sees me as anything but ... but what I am?'

'You are wrong!' Herbie's steel fist struck the plastic-topped table with a strident clang. 'Listen to me——'

But Susan Calvin whirled on him now and the hunted pain in her eyes became a blaze, 'Why should I? What do you know about it all, anyway, you ... you machine. I'm just a specimen to you; an interesting bug with a peculiar mind spread-eagled for inspection. It's a wonderful example of frustration, isn't it? Almost as good as your books.' Her voice, emerging in dry sobs, choked into silence.

The robot cowered at the outburst. He shook his head pleadingly. 'Won't you listen to me, please? I could help you if you would let me.'

'How?' Her lips curled. 'By giving me good advice?'

'No, not that. It's just that I know what other people think – Milton Ashe, for instance.'

There was a long silence, and Susan Calvin's eyes dropped. 'I don't want to know what he thinks,' she gasped. 'Keep quiet.'

'I think you would want to know what he thinks.'

Her head remained bent, but her breath came more quickly. 'You are talking nonsense,' she whispered.

'Why should I? I am trying to help. Milton Ashe's thoughts of you——' he paused.

And then the psychologist raised her head, 'Well?'

The robot said quietly. 'He loves you.'

For a full minute, Dr Calvin did not speak. She merely stared. Then, 'You are mistaken! You must be. Why should he?'

'But he does. A thing like that cannot be hidden, not from me.'

'But I am so ... so——' she stammered to a halt.

'He looks deeper than the skin, and admires intellect in others. Milton Ashe is not the type to marry a head of hair and a pair of eyes.'

Susan Calvin found herself blinking rapidly and waited before speaking. Even then her voice trembled, 'Yet he certainly never in any way indicated——'

'Have you ever given him a chance?'

'How could I? I never thought that——'

'Exactly!'

The psychologist paused in thought and then looked up suddenly. 'A girl visited him here at the plant half a year ago. She was pretty, I suppose – blonde and slim. And, of course, could scarcely add two and two. He spent all day puffing out his chest, trying to explain how a robot was put together.' The hardness had returned, 'Not that she understood! Who was she?'

Herbie answered without hesitation, 'I know the person you are referring to. She is his first cousin, and there is no romantic interest there, I assure you.'

Susan Calvin rose to her feet with a vivacity almost girlish. 'Now isn't that strange? That's exactly what I used to pretend to myself sometimes, though I never really thought so. Then it all must be true.'

She ran to Herbie and seized his cold, heavy hand in both hers. 'Thank you, Herbie.' Her voice was an urgent, husky whisper. 'Don't tell anyone about this. Let it be our secret – and thank you again.' With that, and a convulsive squeeze of Herbie's unresponsive metal fingers, she left.

Herbie turned slowly to his neglected novel, but there was no one to read *his* thoughts.

·   ·   ·

Milton Ashe stretched slowly and magnificently, to the tune of cracking joints and a chorus of grunts, and then glared at Peter Bogert, Ph.D.

'Say,' he said, 'I've been at this for a week now with just about no sleep. How long do I have to keep it up? I thought you said the positronic bombardment in Vac Chamber D was the solution.'

Bogert yawned delicately and regarded his white hands with interest. 'It is. I'm on the track.'

'I know what *that* means when a mathematician says it. How near the end are you?'

'It all depends.'

'On what?' Ashe dropped into a chair and stretched his long legs out before him.

'On Lanning. The old fellow disagrees with me.' He sighed, 'A bit behind the times, that's the trouble with him. He clings to matrix mechanics as the all in all, and this problem calls for more powerful mathematical tools. He's so stubborn.'

Ashe muttered sleepily, 'Why not ask Herbie and settle the whole affair?'

'Ask the robot?' Bogert's eyebrows climbed.

'Why not? Didn't the old girl tell you?'

'You mean Calvin?'

'Yeah! Susie herself. That robot's a mathematical wiz. He knows all about everything plus a bit on the side. He does triple integrals in his head and eats up tensor analysis for dessert.'

The mathematician stared sceptically, 'Are you serious?'

'So help me! The catch is that the dope doesn't like maths. He would rather read slushy novels. Honest! You should see the tripe Susie keeps feeding him: "Purple Passion" and "Love in Space".'

'Dr Calvin hasn't said a word of this to us.'

'Well, she hasn't finished studying him. You know how she is. She likes to have everything just so before letting out the big secret.'

'She's told *you*.'

'We sort of got to talking. I have been seeing a lot of her lately.' He opened his eyes wide and frowned, 'Say, Bogie, have you been noticing anything queer about the lady lately?'

Bogert relaxed into an undignified grin, 'She's using lipstick, if that's what you mean.'

'Hell, I know that. Rouge, powder and eye shadow, too. She's a sight. But it's not that. I can't put my finger on it. It's the way she talks – as if she were happy about something.' He thought a little, and then shrugged.

The other allowed himself a leer, which, for a scientist past fifty, was not a bad job, 'Maybe she's in love.'

Ashe allowed his eyes to close again, 'You're nuts, Bogie. You go speak to Herbie; I want to stay here and go to sleep.'

'Right! Not that I particularly like having a robot tell me my job, nor that I think he can do it!'

A soft snore was his only answer.

. . .

Herbie listened carefully as Peter Bogert, hands in pockets, spoke with elaborate indifference.

'So there you are. I've been told you understand these things, and I am asking you more in curiosity than anything else. My line of reasoning, as I have outlined it, involves a few doubtful steps, I admit, which Dr Lanning refuses to accept, and the picture is still rather incomplete.'

The robot didn't answer, and Bogert said, 'Well?'

'I see no mistake,' Herbie studied the scribbled figures.

'I don't suppose you can go any further than that?'

'I daren't try. You are a better mathematician than I, and – well, I'd hate to commit myself.'

There was a shade of complacency in Bogert's smile, 'I rather thought that would be the case. It is deep. We'll forget it.' He crumpled the sheets, tossed them down the waste shaft, turned to leave, and then thought better of it.

'By the way——'

The robot waited.

Bogert seemed to have difficulty. 'There is something – that is, perhaps you can——' He stopped.

Herbie spoke quietly, 'Your thoughts are confused, but there is no doubt at all that they concern Dr Lanning. It is silly to hesitate, for as soon as you compose yourself, I'll know what it is you want to ask.'

The mathematician's hand went to his sleek hair in the familiar smoothing gesture. 'Lanning is nudging seventy,' he said, as if that explained everything.

'I know that.'

'And he's been director of the plant for almost thirty years.'

Herbie nodded.

'Well, now,' Bogert's voice became ingratiating, 'you would know whether...he's thinking of resigning. Health, perhaps, or some other——'

'Quite,' said Herbie, and that was all.

'Well, do you know?'

'Certainly.'

'Then – uh – could you tell me?'

'Since you ask, yes.' The robot was quite matter-of-fact about it. 'He has already resigned!'

'What!' The exclamation was an explosive, almost inarticulate, sound. The scientist's large head hunched forward. 'Say that again!'

'He has already resigned,' came the quiet repetition, 'but it has not yet taken effect. He is waiting, you see, to solve the problem of – er – myself. That finished, he is quite ready to turn the office of director over to his successor.'

Bogert expelled his breath sharply, 'And this successor? Who is he?' He was quite close to Herbie now, eyes fixed fascinatedly on those unreadable dull-red photoelectric cells that were the robot's eyes.

Words came slowly, 'You are the next director.'

And Bogert relaxed into a tight smile, 'This is good to know. I've been hoping and waiting for this. Thanks, Herbie.'

. . .

Peter Bogert was at his desk until five that morning and he was back at nine. The shelf just over the desk emptied of its row of reference books and tables, as he referred to one after the other. The pages of calculations before him increased microscopically and the crumpled sheets at his feet mounted into a hill of scribbled paper.

At precisely noon, he stared at the final page, rubbed a bloodshot eye, yawned and shrugged. 'This is getting worse each minute. Damn!'

He turned at the sound of the opening door and nodded at Lanning, who entered, cracking the knuckles of one gnarled hand with the other.

The director took in the disorder of the room and his eyebrows furrowed together.

'New lead?' he asked.

'No,' came the defiant answer. 'What's wrong with the old one?'

Lanning did not trouble to answer, nor to do more than bestow a single cursory glance at the top sheet upon Bogert's desk. He spoke through the flare of a match as he lit a cigar.

'Has Calvin told you about the robot? It's a mathematical genius. Really remarkable.'

The other snorted loudly, 'So I've heard. But Calvin had better stick to robopsychology. I've checked Herbie on maths, and he can scarcely struggle through calculus.'

'Calvin didn't find it so.'

'She's crazy.'

'And I don't find it so.' The director's eyes narrowed dangerously.

'You!' Bogert's voice hardened. 'What are you talking about?'

'I've been putting Herbie through his paces all morning, and he can do tricks you never heard of.'

'Is that so?'

'You sound sceptical!' Lanning flipped a sheet of paper out of his vest pocket and unfolded it. 'That's not my handwriting, is it?'

Bogert studied the large angular notation covering the sheet, 'Herbie did this?'

'Right! And if you'll notice, he's been working on your time integration of Equation 22. It comes' – Lanning tapped a yellow fingernail upon the last step – 'to the identical conclusion I did, and in a quarter the time. You had no right to neglect the Linger Effect in positronic bombardment.'

'I didn't neglect it. For Heaven's sake, Lanning, get it through your head that it would cancel out——'

'Oh, sure, you explained that. You used the Mitchell Translation Equation, didn't you? Well – it doesn't apply.'

'Why not?'

'Because you've been using hyper-imaginaries, for one thing.'

'What's that to do with?'

'Mitchell's Equation won't hold when——'

'Are you crazy? If you'll reread Mitchell's original paper in the *Transactions of the Far*——'

'I don't have to. I told you in the beginning that I didn't like his reasoning, and Herbie backs me in that.'

'Well, then,' Bogert shouted, 'let that clockwork contraption solve the entire problem for you. Why bother with non-essentials?'

'That's exactly the point. Herbie can't solve the problem. And if he can't, we can't – alone. I'm submitting the entire question to the National Board. It's got beyond us.'

Bogert's chair went over backward as he jumped up a-snarl, face crimson. 'You're doing nothing of the sort.'

Lanning flushed in his turn, 'Are you telling me what I can't do?'

'Exactly,' was the gritted response. 'I've got the problem beaten and you're not to take it out of my hands, understand? Don't think I don't see through you, you desiccated fossil. You'd cut your own nose off before you'd let me get the credit for solving robotic telepathy.'

'You're a damned idiot, Bogert, and in one second I'll have you suspended for insubordination' – Lanning's lower lip trembled with passion.

'Which is one thing you won't do, Lanning. You haven't any secrets with a mind-reading robot around, so don't forget that I know all about your resignation.'

The ash on Lanning's cigar trembled and fell, and the cigar itself followed, 'What ... what——'

Bogert chuckled nastily, 'And I'm the new director, be it understood. I'm very aware of that; don't think I'm not. Damn your eyes, Lanning, I'm going to give the orders about here or there will be the sweetest mess that you've ever been in.'

Lanning found his voice and let it out with a roar. 'You're suspended, d'ye hear? You're relieved of all duties. You're broken, do you understand?'

The smile on the other's face broadened, 'Now, what's the use of that? You're getting nowhere. I'm holding the trumps. I know you've resigned. Herbie told me, and he got it straight from you.'

Lanning forced himself to speak quietly. He looked an old, old man, with tired eyes peering from a face in which the red had disappeared, leaving the pasty yellow of age behind, 'I want to speak to Herbie. He can't have told you anything of the sort. You're playing a deep game, Bogert, but I'm calling your bluff. Come with me.'

Bogert shrugged, 'To see Herbie? Good! Damned good!'

.   .   .

It was also precisely at noon that Milton Ashe looked up from his clumsy sketch and said, 'You get the idea? I'm not good at getting this down, but that's about how it looks. It's a honey of a house, and I can get it for next to nothing.'

Susan Calvin gazed across at him with melting eyes. 'It's really beautiful,' she sighed. 'I've often thought that I'd like to——' Her voice trailed away.

'Of course,' Ashe continued briskly, putting away his pencil, 'I've got to wait for my vacation. It's only two weeks off, but this Herbie business has everything up in the air.' His eyes dropped to his fingernails, 'Besides, there's another point – but it's a secret.'

'Then don't tell me.'

'Oh, I'd just as soon, I'm just busting to tell someone – and you're just about the best – er – confidante I could find here.' He grinned sheepishly.

Susan Calvin's heart bounded, but she did not trust herself to speak.

'Frankly,' Ashe scraped his chair closer and lowered his voice into a confidential whisper, 'the house isn't to be only for myself. I'm getting married!'

And then he jumped out of his seat, 'What's the matter?'

'Nothing!' The horrible spinning sensation had vanished, but it was hard to get words out. 'Married? You mean——'

'Why sure! About time, isn't it? You remember that girl who was here last summer. That's she! But you *are* sick. You——'

'Headache!' Susan Calvin motioned him away weakly. 'I've ... I've been subject to them lately. I want to ... to congratulate you, of course, I'm very glad——' The inexpertly applied rouge made a pair of nasty red splotches upon her chalk white face. Things had begun spinning again. 'Pardon me – please——'

The words were a mumble, as she stumbled blindly out the door. It had happened with the sudden catastrophe of a dream – and with all the unreal horror of a dream.

But how could it be? Herbie had said——

And Herbie knew! He could see into minds!

She found herself leaning breathlessly against the door jamb, staring into Herbie's metal face. She must have climbed the two flights of stairs, but she had no memory of it. The distance had been covered in an instant, as in a dream.

As in a dream!

And still Herbie's unblinking eyes stared into hers and their dull red seemed to expand into dimly shining nightmarish globes.

He was speaking, and she felt the cold glass pressing against her lips. She swallowed and shuddered into a certain awareness of her surroundings.

Still Herbie spoke, and there was agitation in his voice – as if he were hurt and frightened and pleading.

The words were beginning to make sense. 'This is a dream,' he was saying, 'and you mustn't believe in it. You'll wake into the real world soon and laugh at yourself. He loves you, I tell you. He does, he does! But not here! Not now! This is an illusion.'

Susan Calvin nodded, her voice a whisper, 'Yes! Yes!' She was clutching Herbie's arm, clinging to it, repeating over and over, 'It isn't true, is it? It isn't, is it?'

Just how she came to her senses, she never knew – but it was like passing from a world of misty unreality to one of harsh sunlight. She pushed him away from her, pushed hard against that steely arm, and her eyes were wide.

'What are you trying to do?' Her voice rose to a harsh scream. 'What are you trying to do?'

Herbie backed away, 'I want to help.'

The psychologist stared, 'Help? By telling me this is a dream? By trying to push me into schizophrenia?' An hysterical tenseness seized her, 'This is no dream! I wish it were!'

She drew her breath sharply, 'Wait! Why ... why, I understand. Merciful Heavens, it's so obvious.'

There was horror in the robot's voice, 'I had to!'

'And I believed you! I never thought——'

.   .   .

Loud voices outside the door brought her to a halt. She turned away, fists clenching spasmodically, and when Bogert and Lanning entered, she was at the far window. Neither of the men paid her the slightest attention.

They approached Herbie simultaneously; Lanning angry and impatient, Bogert coolly sardonic. The director spoke first.

'Here now, Herbie. Listen to me!'

The robot brought his eyes sharply down upon the aged director, 'Yes, Dr Lanning.'

'Have you discussed me with Dr Bogert?'

'No, sir.' The answer came slowly, and the smile on Bogert's face flashed off.

'What's that?' Bogert shoved in ahead of his superior and straddled the ground before the robot. 'Repeat what you told me yesterday.'

'I said that——' Herbie fell silent. Deep within him his metallic diaphragm vibrated in soft discords.

'Didn't you say he had resigned?' roared Bogert. 'Answer me!'

Bogert raised his arm frantically, but Lanning pushed him aside, 'Are you trying to bully him into lying?'

'You heard him, Lanning. He began to say "Yes" and stopped. Get out of my way! I want the truth out of him, understand!'

'I'll ask him!' Lanning turned to the robot. 'All right, Herbie, take it easy. Have I resigned?'

Herbie stared, and Lanning repeated anxiously, 'Have I resigned?' There was the faintest trace of a negative shake of the robot's head. A long wait produced nothing further.

The two men looked at each other and the hostility in their eyes was all but tangible.

'What the devil,' blurted Bogert, 'has the robot gone mute? Can't you speak, you monstrosity?'

'I can speak,' came the ready answer.

'Then answer the question. Didn't you tell me Lanning had resigned? Hasn't he resigned?'

And again there was nothing but dull silence, until from the end of the room, Susan Calvin's laugh rang out suddenly, high-pitched and semi-hysterical.

The two mathematicians jumped, and Bogert's eyes narrowed, 'You here? What's so funny?'

'Nothing's funny.' Her voice was not quite natural. 'It's just that I'm not the only one that's been caught. There's irony in three of the greatest experts in robotics in the world falling into the same elementary trap, isn't there?' Her voice faded, and she put a pale hand to her forehead, 'But it isn't funny!'

This time the look that passed between the two men was one of raised eyebrows. 'What trap are you talking about?' asked Lanning stiffly. 'Is something wrong with Herbie?'

'No,' she approached them, slowly, 'nothing is wrong with him – only with us.' She whirled suddenly and shrieked at the robot, 'Get away from me! Go to the other end of the room and don't let me look at you.'

Herbie cringed before the fury of her eyes and stumbled away in a clattering trot.

Lanning's voice was hostile, 'What is all this, Dr Calvin?'

She faced them and spoke sarcastically, 'Surely you know the fundamental First Law of Robotics.'

The other two nodded together. 'Certainly,' said Bogert, irritably, 'a robot may not injure a human being or, through inaction, allow him to come to harm.'

'How nicely put,' sneered Calvin. 'But what kind of harm?'

'Why – any kind.'

'Exactly! Any kind! But what about hurt feelings? What about deflation of one's ego? What about the blasting of one's hopes? Is that injury?'

Lanning frowned, 'What would a robot know about——' And then he caught himself with a gasp.

'You've caught on, haven't you? *This* robot reads minds. Do you suppose it doesn't know everything about mental injury? Do you suppose that if asked a question, it wouldn't give exactly that answer that one wants to hear? Wouldn't any other answer hurt us, and wouldn't Herbie know that?'

'Good Heavens!' muttered Bogert.

The psychologist cast a sardonic glance at him, 'I take it you asked him whether Lanning had resigned. You wanted to hear that he had resigned and so that's what Herbie told you.'

'And I suppose that is why,' said Lanning, tonelessly, 'it would not answer a little while ago. It couldn't answer either way without hurting one of us.'

There was a short pause in which the men looked thoughtfully across the room at the robot, crouching in the chair by the bookcase, head resting in one hand.

Susan Calvin stared steadfastly at the floor, 'He knew of all this. That ... that devil knows everything – including what went wrong in his assembly.' Her eyes were dark and brooding.

Lanning looked up, 'You're wrong there, Dr Calvin. He doesn't know what went wrong. I asked him.'

'What does that mean?' cried Calvin. 'Only that you didn't want him to give you the solution. It would puncture your ego to have a machine do what you couldn't. Did you ask him?' she shot at Bogert.

'In a way.' Bogert coughed and reddened. 'He told me he knew very little about mathematics.'

Lanning laughed, not very loudly, and the psychologist smiled caustically. She said, 'I'll ask him! A solution by him won't hurt my ego.' She raised her voice into a cold, imperative, 'Come here!'

Herbie rose and approached with hesitant steps.

'You know, I suppose,' she continued, 'just exactly at what point in the assembly an extraneous factor was introduced or an essential one left out.'

'Yes,' said Herbie, in tones barely heard.

'Hold on,' broke in Bogert angrily. 'That's not necessarily true. You want to hear that, that's all.'

'Don't be a fool,' replied Calvin. 'He certainly knows as much maths as you and Lanning together, since he can read minds. Give him his chance.'

The mathematician subsided, and Calvin continued, 'All right, then, Herbie, give! We're waiting.' And in an aside, 'Get pencils and paper, gentlemen.'

But Herbie remained silent, and there was triumph in the psychologist's voice, 'Why don't you answer, Herbie?'

The robot blurted out suddenly, 'I cannot. You know I cannot! Dr Bogert and Dr Lanning don't want me to.'

'They want the solution.'

'But not from me.'

Lanning broke in, speaking slowly and distinctly, 'Don't be foolish, Herbie. We do want you to tell us.'

Bogert nodded curtly.

Herbie's voice rose to wild heights, 'What's the use of saying that? Don't you suppose that I can see past the superficial skin of your mind?

Down below, you don't want me to. I'm a machine, given the imitation of life only by virtue of the positronic interplay in my brain – which is man's device. You can't lose face to me without being hurt. That is deep in your mind and won't be erased. I can't give the solution.'

'We'll leave,' said Dr Lanning. 'Tell Calvin.'

'That would make no difference,' cried Herbie, 'since you would know anyway that it was I that was supplying the answer.'

Calvin resumed, 'But you understand, Herbie, that despite that, Drs Lanning and Bogert want that solution.'

'By their own efforts!' insisted Herbie.

'But they want it, and the fact that you have it and won't give it hurts them. You see that, don't you?'

'Yes! Yes!'

'And if you tell them that will hurt them, too.'

'Yes! Yes!' Herbie was retreating slowly, and step by step Susan advanced. The two men watched in frozen bewilderment.

'You can't tell them,' droned the psychologist slowly, 'because that would hurt and you mustn't hurt. But if you don't tell them, you hurt, so you must tell them. And if you do, you will hurt and you mustn't, so you can't tell them; but if you don't, you hurt, so you must; but if you do, you hurt, so you mustn't; but if you don't, you hurt, so you must; but if you do, you——'

Herbie was up against the wall, and here he dropped to his knees. 'Stop!' he shrieked. 'Close your mind! It is full of pain and frustration and hate! I didn't mean it, I tell you! I tried to help! I told you what you wanted to hear. I had to!'

The psychologist paid no attention. 'You must tell them, but if you do, you hurt, so you mustn't, but if you don't, you hurt, so you must; but——'

And Herbie screamed!

It was like the whistling of a piccolo many times magnified – shrill and shriller till it keened with the terror of a lost soul and filled the room with the piercingness of itself.

And when it died into nothingness, Herbie collapsed into a huddled heap of motionless metal.

Bogert's face was bloodless, 'He's dead!'

'No!' Susan Calvin burst into body-racking gusts of wild laughter, 'not dead – merely insane. I confronted him with the insoluble dilemma, and he broke down. You can scrap him now – because he'll never speak again.'

Lanning was on his knees beside the thing that had been Herbie. His fingers touched the cold, unresponsive metal face and he shuddered. 'You did that on purpose.' He rose and faced her, face contorted.

'What if I did? You can't help it now.' And in a sudden access of bitterness, 'He deserved it.'

The director seized the paralysed, motionless Bogert by the wrist, 'What's the difference. Come, Peter.' He sighed, 'A thinking robot of this type is worthless anyway.' His eyes were old and tired, and he repeated, 'Come, Peter!'

It was minutes after the two scientists left that Dr Susan Calvin regained part of her mental equilibrium. Slowly, her eyes turned to the living-dead Herbie and the tightness returned to her face. Long she stared while the triumph faded and the helpless frustration returned – and of all her turbulent thoughts only one infinitely bitter word passed her lips.

'*Liar!*'

That finished it for then, naturally. I knew I couldn't get any more out of her after that. She just sat there behind her desk, her white face cold and – remembering.

I said, ' Thank you, Dr Calvin!' but she didn't answer. It was two days before I could get to see her again.

CHAPTER 6

LITTLE LOST ROBOT

When I did see Susan Calvin again, it was at the door of her office. Files were being moved out.

She said, 'How are your articles coming along, young man?'

'Fine,' I said. I had put them into shape according to my own lights, dramatized the bare bones of her recital, added the conversation and little touches. 'Would you look over them and see if I haven't been libellous or too unreasonably inaccurate anywhere?'

'I suppose so. Shall we retire to the Executive's Lounge? We can have coffee.'

She seemed in good humour, so I chanced it as we walked down the corridor, 'I was wondering, Dr Calvin——'

'Yes.'

'If you would tell me more concerning the history of robotics.'

'Surely you have what you want, young man.'

'In a way. But these incidents I have written up don't apply much to the modern world. I mean, there was only one mind-reading robot ever developed, and Space-Stations are already outmoded and in disuse, and robot mining is taken for granted. What about interstellar travel? It's only been about twenty years since the hypertomic motor was invented and it's well known that it was a robotic invention. What is the truth about it?'

'Interstellar travel?' She was thoughtful. We were in the lounge, and I ordered a full dinner. She just had coffee.

'It wasn't a simple robotic invention, you know; not just like that. But, of course, until we developed the Brain, we didn't get very far. But we tried; we really tried. My first connection (directly, that is) with inter-stellar research was in 2029, when a robot was lost——'

. . .

Measures on Hyper Base had been taken in a sort of rattling fury – the muscular equivalent of an hysterical shriek.

To itemize them in order of both chronology and desperation, they were:

1. All work on the Hyperatomic Drive through all the space volume occupied by the Stations of the Twenty-Seventh Asteroidal Grouping came to a halt.

2. That entire volume of space was nipped out of the System, practically speaking. No one entered without permission. No one left under any conditions.

3. By special government patrol ship, Drs Susan Calvin and Peter Bogert, respectively head Psychologist and Mathematical Director of United States Robot & Mechanical Men Corporation, were brought to Hyper Base.

. . .

Susan Calvin had never left the surface of Earth before, and had no perceptible desire to leave it this time. In an age of Atomic Power and a clearly coming Hyperatomic drive, she remained quietly provincial. So she was dissatisfied with her trip and unconvinced of the emergency, and every line of her plain, middle-aged face showed it clearly enough during her first dinner at Hyper Base.

Nor did Dr Bogert's sleek paleness abandon a certain hangdog attitude. Nor did Major-General Kallner, who headed the project, even once forget to maintain a haunted expression.

In short, it was a grisly episode, that meal, and the little session of three that followed began in a grey, unhappy manner.

Kallner, with his baldness glistening, and his dress uniform oddly unsuited to the general mood began with uneasy directness.

'This is a queer story to tell, sir, and madam. I want to thank you for coming on short notice and without a reason being given. We'll try to correct that now. We've lost a robot. Work has stopped and *must* stop until such time as we locate it. So far we have failed, and we feel we need expert help.'

Perhaps the general felt his predicament anticlimactic. He continued with a note of desperation, 'I needn't tell you the importance of our work here. More than eighty per cent of last year's appropriations for scientific research have gone to us——'

'Why, we know that,' said Bogert, agreeably. 'U.S. Robots is receiving a generous rental fee for use of our robots.'

Susan Calvin injected a blunt, vinegary note, 'What makes a single robot so important to the project, and why hasn't it been located?'

The general turned his red face towards her and wet his lips quickly, 'Why in a manner of speaking we *have* located it.' Then, with near anguish, 'Here, suppose I explain. As soon as the robot failed to report a state of emergency was declared, and all movement off Hyper Base stopped. A cargo vessel had landed the previous day and had delivered us two robots for our laboratories. It had sixty-two robots of the . . . uh . . . same type for shipment elsewhere. We are certain as to that figure. There is no question about it whatever.'

'Yes? And the connection?'

'When our missing robot failed of location anywhere – I assure you we would have found a missing blade of grass if it had been there to find – we brainstormed ourselves into counting the robots left on the cargo ship. They have sixty-three now.'

'So that the sixty-third, I take it, is the missing prodigal?' Dr Calvin's eyes darkened.

'Yes, but we have no way of telling which is the sixty-third.'

There was a dead silence while the electric clock chimed eleven times, and then the robopsychologist said, 'Very peculiar,' and the corners of her lips moved downward.

'Peter,' she turned to her colleague with a trace of savagery, 'what's wrong here? What kind of robots are they using at Hyper Base?'

Dr Bogert hesitated and smiled feebly, 'It's been rather a matter of delicacy till now, Susan.'

She spoke rapidly, 'Yes, *till* now. If there are sixty-three same type robots, one of which is wanted and the identity of which cannot be determined, why won't any of them do? What's the idea of all this? Why have we been sent for?'

Bogert said in resigned fashion, 'If you'll give me a chance, Susan –
Hyper Base happens to be using several robots whose brains are not
impressioned with the entire First Law of Robotics.'

'*Aren't* impressioned?' Calvin slumped back in her chair, 'I see. How
many were made?'

'A few. It was on government order and there was no way of violating
the secrecy. No one was to know except the top men directly concerned.
You weren't included, Susan. It was nothing I had anything to do with.'

      •   •   •

The general interrupted with a measure of authority. 'I would like to
explain that bit. I hadn't been aware that Dr Calvin was unacquainted
with the situation. I needn't tell you, Dr Calvin, that there always has
been strong opposition to robots on the Planet. The only defence the
government has had against the Fundamentalist radicals in this matter
was the fact that robots are always built with an unbreakable First Law
– which makes it impossible for them to harm human beings under any
circumstance.

'But we *had* to have robots of a different nature. So just a few of the NS-
2 model, the Nestors, that is, were prepared with a modified First Law.
To keep it quiet, all NS-2's are manufactured without serial numbers;
modified members are delivered here along with a group of normal
robots; and, of course, all our kind are under the strictest impressionment
never to tell of their modification to unauthorized personnel.' He wore
an embarrassed smile, 'This has all worked out against us now.'

Calvin said grimly, 'Have you asked each one who it is, anyhow?
Certainly, you are authorized?'

The general nodded, 'All sixty-three deny having worked here – and
one is lying.'

'Does the one you want show traces of wear? The others, I take it,
are factory-fresh.'

'The one in question only arrived last month. It, and the two that have
just arrived, were to be the last we needed. There's no perceptible wear.'
He shook his head slowly and his eyes were haunted again, Dr Calvin,
we don't dare let that ship leave. If the existence of non-First Law robots
becomes general knowledge——' There seemed no way of avoiding
understatement in the conclusion.

'Destroy all sixty-three,' said the robopsychologist coldly and flatly,
'and make an end of it.'

Bogert drew back a corner of his mouth. 'You mean destroy thirty
thousand dollars per robot. I'm afraid U.S. Robots wouldn't like that.
We'd better make an effort first, Susan, before we destroy anything.'

'In that case,' she said, sharply, 'I need facts. Exactly what advantage does Hyper Base derive from these modified robots? What factor made them desirable, General?'

Kallner ruffled his forehead and stroked it with an upward gesture of his hand. 'We had trouble with our previous robots. Our men work with hard radiations a good deal, you see. It's dangerous, of course, but reasonable precautions are taken. There have been only two accidents since we began and neither was fatal. However, it was impossible to explain that to an ordinary robot. The First Law states – I'll quote it – *"No robot may harm a human being, or, through inaction, allow a human being to come to harm."*

'That's primary, Dr Calvin. When it was necessary for one of our men to expose himself for a short period to a moderate gamma field, one that would have no physiological effects, the nearest robot would dash in to drag him out. If the field were exceedingly weak, it would succeed, and work could not continue till all robots were cleared out. If the field were a trifle stronger, the robot would never reach the technician concerned, since its positronic brain would collapse under gamma radiations – and then we would be out of one expensive and hard-to-replace robot.

'We tried arguing with them. Their point was that a human being in a gamma field was endangering his life and that it didn't matter that he could remain there half an hour safely. Supposing, they would say, he forgot and remained an hour. They couldn't take chances. We pointed out that they were risking their lives on a wild off-chance. But self-preservation is only the Third Law of Robotics – and the First Law of human safety came first. We gave them orders; we ordered them strictly and harshly to remain out of gamma fields at whatever cost. But obedience is only the Second Law of Robotics – and the First Law of human safety came first. Dr Calvin, we either had to do without robots, or do something about the First Law – and we made our choice.'

'I can't believe,' said Dr Calvin, 'that it was found possible to remove the First Law.'

'It wasn't removed, it was modified,' explained Kallner. 'Positronic brains were constructed that contained the positive aspect only of the Law, which in them reads: *"No robot may harm a human being."* That is all. They have no compulsion to prevent one coming to harm through an extraneous agency such as gamma rays. I state the matter correctly, Dr Bogert?'

'Quite,' assented the mathematician.

'And that is the only difference of your robots from the ordinary NS-2 model? The *only* difference? Peter?'

'The *only* difference, Susan.'

She rose and spoke with finality, 'I intend sleeping now, and in about eight hours I want to speak to whomever saw the robot last. And from now on, General Kallner, if I'm to take any responsibility at all for events, I want full and unquestioned control of this investigation.'

Susan Calvin, except for two hours of resentful lassitude, experienced nothing approaching sleep. She signalled at Bogert's door at the local time of 0700 and found him also awake. He had apparently taken the trouble of transporting a dressing gown to Hyper Base with him, for he was sitting in it. He put his nail scissors down when Calvin entered.

He said softly, 'I've been expecting you more or less. I suppose you feel sick about all this.'

'I do.'

'Well – I'm sorry. There was no way of preventing it. When the call came out from Hyper Base for us, I knew that something must have gone wrong with the modified Nestors. But what was there to do? I couldn't break the matter to you on the trip here as I would have liked to, because I had to be sure. The matter of the modification is top secret.'

The psychologist muttered, 'I should have been told. U.S. Robots had no right to modify positronic brains this way without the approval of a psychologist.'

Bogert lifted his eyebrows and sighed. 'Be reasonable, Susan. You couldn't have influenced them. In this matter, the government was bound to have its way. They want the Hyperatomic Drive and the etheric physicists want robots that won't interfere with them. They were going to get them even if it did mean twisting the First Law. We had to admit it was possible from a construction stand-point and they swore a mighty oath that they wanted only twelve, that they would be used only at Hyper Base, that they would be destroyed once the Drive was perfected, and that full precautions would be taken. And they insisted on secrecy – and that's the situation.'

Dr Calvin spoke through her teeth, 'I would have resigned.'

'It wouldn't have helped. The government was offering the company a fortune, and threatening it with an antirobot legislation in case of a refusal. We were stuck then, and we're badly stuck now. If this leaks out, it might hurt Kallner and the government, but it would hurt U.S. Robots a devil of a lot more.'

The psychologist stared at him. 'Peter, don't you realize what all this is about? Can't you understand what the removal of the First Law means? It isn't just a matter of secrecy.'

'I know what removal would mean. I'm not a child. It would mean complete instability, with no nonimaginary solutions to the positronic Field Equations.'

'Yes, mathematically. But can you translate that into crude psychological thought? All normal life, Peter, consciously or otherwise, resents domination. If the domination is by an inferior, or by a supposed inferior, the resentment becomes stronger. Physically, and, to an extent, mentally, a robot – any robot – is superior to human beings. What makes him slavish, then? *Only the First Law!* Why, without it, the first order you tried to give a robot would result in your death. Unstable? What do you think?'

'Susan,' said Bogert, with an air of sympathetic amusement. 'I'll admit that this Frankenstein Complex you're exhibiting has a certain justification – hence the First Law in the first place. But the Law, I repeat and repeat, has not been removed – merely modified.'

'And what about the stability of the brain?'

The mathematician thrust out his lips, 'Decreased, naturally. But it's within the border of safety. The first Nestors were delivered to Hyper Base nine months ago, and nothing whatever has gone wrong till now, and even this involves merely fear of discovery and not danger to humans.'

'Very well, then. We'll see what comes of the morning conference.'

Bogert saw her politely to the door and grimaced eloquently when she left. He saw no reason to change his perennial opinion of her as a sour and fidgety frustration.

Susan Calvin's train of thought did not include Bogert in the least. She had dismissed him years ago as a smooth and pretentious sleekness.

.   .   .

Gerald Black had taken his degree in etheric physics the year before and, in common with his entire generation of physicists, found himself engaged in the problem of the Drive. He now made a proper addition to the general atmosphere of these meetings on Hyper Base. In his stained white smock, he was half rebellious and wholly uncertain. His stocky strength seemed striving for release and his fingers, as they twisted each other with nervous yanks, might have forced an iron bar out of true.

Major-General Kallner sat beside him, the two from U.S. Robots faced him.

Black said, 'I'm told that I was the last to see Nestor 10 before he vanished. I take it you want to ask me about that.'

Dr Calvin regarded him with interest, 'You sound as if you were not sure, young man. Don't you *know* whether you were the last to see him?'

'He worked with me, ma'am, on the field generators, and he was with me the morning of his disappearance. I don't know if anyone saw him after about noon. No one admits having done so.'

'Do you think anyone's lying about it?'

'I don't say that. But I don't say that I want the blame of it, either.' His dark eyes smouldered.

'There's no question of blame. The robot acted as it did because of what it is. We're just trying to locate it, Mr Black, and let's put everything else aside. Now if you've worked with the robot, you probably know it better than anyone else. Was there anything unusual about it that you noticed? Had you ever worked with robots before?'

'I've worked with other robots we have here – the simple ones. Nothing different about the Nestors except that they're a good deal cleverer – and more annoying.'

'Annoying? In what way?'

'Well – perhaps it's not their fault. The work here is rough and most of us get a little jagged. Fooling around with hyperspace isn't fun.' He smiled feebly, finding pleasure in confession. 'We run the risk continually of blowing a hole in normal space-time fabric and dropping right out of the universe, asteroid and all. Sounds screwy, doesn't it? Naturally, you're on edge sometimes. But these Nestors aren't. They're curious, they're calm, they don't worry. It's enough to drive you nuts at times. When you want something done in a tearing hurry, they seem to take their time. Sometimes I'd rather do without.'

'You say they take their time? Have they ever refused an order?'

'Oh, no,' – hastily. 'They do it all right. They tell you when they think you're wrong, though. They don't know anything about the subject but what we taught them, but that doesn't stop them. Maybe I imagine it, but the other fellows have the same trouble with their Nestors.'

General Kallner cleared his throat ominously, 'Why have no complaints reached me on the matter, Black?'

The young physicist reddened, 'We didn't *really* want to do without the robots, sir, and besides we weren't certain exactly how such ... uh ... minor complaints might be received.'

Bogert interrupted softly, 'Anything in particular happen the morning you last saw it?'

There was a silence. With a quiet motion, Calvin repressed the comment that was about to emerge from Kallner, and waited patiently.

Then Black spoke in blurting anger, 'I had a little trouble with it. I'd broken a Kimball tube that morning and was out for five days of work; my entire programme was behind schedule; I hadn't received any mail from home for a couple of weeks. And *he* came around wanting me to repeat an experiment I had abandoned a month ago. He was always annoying me on that subject and I was tired of it. I told him to go away – and that's all I saw of him.'

'You told him to go away?' asked Dr Calvin with sharp interest. 'In just those words? Did you say "Go away"? Try to remember the exact words.'

There was apparently an internal struggle in progress. Black cradled his forehead in a broad palm for a moment, then tore it away and said defiantly, 'I said, "Go lose yourself".'

Bogert laughed for a short moment. 'And he did, eh?'

But Calvin wasn't finished. She spoke cajolingly, 'Now we're getting somewhere, Mr Black. But exact details are important. In understanding the robot's actions, a word, a gesture, an emphasis may be everything. You couldn't have said just those three words, for instance, could you? By your own description you must have been in a hasty mood. Perhaps you strengthened your speech a little.'

The young man reddened, 'Well ... I may have called it a ... a few things.'

'Exactly what things?'

'Oh – I wouldn't remember exactly. Besides I couldn't repeat it. You know how you get when you're excited.' His embarrassed laugh was almost a giggle, 'I sort of have a tendency to strong language.'

'That's quite all right,' she replied with prim severity. 'At the moment, I'm a psychologist. I would like to have you repeat exactly what you said as nearly as you remember, and, even more important, the exact tone of voice you used.'

Black looked at his commanding officer for support, found none. His eyes grew round and appalled, 'But I can't.'

'You must.'

'Suppose,' said Bogert, with ill-hidden amusement, 'you address me. You may find it easier.'

The young man's scarlet face turned to Bogert. He swallowed. 'I said——' His voice faded out. He tried again, 'I said——'

And he drew a deep breath and spewed it out hastily in one long succession of syllables. Then, in the charged air that lingered, he concluded almost in tears, '... more or less. I don't remember the exact order of what I called him, and maybe I left out something or put in something, but that was about it.'

Only the slightest flush betrayed any feeling on the part of the robopsychologist. She said, 'I am aware of the meaning of most of the terms used. The others, I suppose, are equally derogatory.'

'I'm afraid so,' agreed the tormented Black.

'And in among it, you told him to lose himself.'

'I meant it only figuratively.'

'I realize that. No disciplinary action is intended, I am sure.' And at her glance, the general, who, five seconds earlier, had seemed not sure at all, nodded angrily.

'You may leave, Mr Black. Thank you for your co-operation.'

. . .

It took five hours for Susan Calvin to interview the sixty-three robots. it was five hours of multi-repetition, of replacement after replacement of identical robot; of Questions A, B, C, D; and Answers A, B, C, D; of a carefully bland expression, a carefully neutral tone, a carefully friendly atmosphere; and a hidden wire recorder.

The psychologist felt drained of vitality when she was finished.

Bogert was waiting for her and looked expectant as she dropped the recording spool with a clang upon the plastic of the desk.

She shook her head, 'All sixty-three seemed the same to me. I couldn't tell——'

He said, 'You couldn't expect to tell by ear, Susan. Suppose we analyse the recordings.'

Ordinarily the mathematical interpretations of verbal reactions of robots is one of the more intricate branches of robotic analysis. It requires a staff of trained technicians and the help of complicated computing machines. Bogert knew that. Bogert stated as much, in an extreme of unshown annoyance after having listened to each set of replies, made lists of word deviations, and graphs of the intervals of responses.

'There are no anomalies present, Susan. The variations in wording and the time reactions are within the limits of ordinary frequency groupings. We need finer methods. They must have computers here. No.' He frowned and nibbled delicately at a thumbnail. 'We can't use computers. Too much danger of leakage. Or maybe if we——'

Dr Calvin stopped him with an impatient gesture, 'Please, Peter. This isn't one of your pretty laboratory problems. If we can't determine the modified Nestor by some gross difference that we can see with the naked eye, one that there is no mistake about, we're out of luck. The danger of being wrong, and of letting him escape is otherwise too great. It's not enough to point out a minute irregularity in a graph. I tell you, if that's all I've got to go on, I'd destroy them all just to be certain. Have you spoken to the other modified Nestors?'

'Yes, I have,' snapped back Bogert, 'and there's nothing wrong with them. They're above normal in friendliness if anything. They answered my questions, displayed pride in their knowledge – except the two new ones that haven't had time to learn their etheric physics. They laughed rather good-naturedly at my ignorance in some of the specializations here.' He shrugged, 'I suppose that forms some of the basis for resentment towards them on the part of the technicians here. The robots are perhaps too willing to impress you with their greater knowledge.'

'Can you try a few Planar Reactions to see if there has been any change, any deterioration, in their mental set-up since manufacture?'

'I haven't yet, but I will.' He shook a slim finger at her, 'You're losing your nerve, Susan. I don't see what it is you're dramatizing. They're essentially harmless.'

'They are?' Calvin took fire. 'They are? Do you realize one of them is lying? One of the sixty-three robots I have just interviewed has deliberately lied to me after the strictest injunction to tell the truth. The abnormality indicated is horribly deep-seated, and horribly frightening.'

Peter Bogert felt his teeth harden against each other. He said, 'Not at all. Look! Nestor 10 was given orders to lose himself. Those orders were expressed in maximum urgency by the person most authorized to command him. You can't counteract that order either by superior urgency or superior right of command. Naturally, the robot will attempt to defend the carrying out of his orders. In fact, objectively, I admire his ingenuity. How better can a robot lose himself than to hide himself among a group of similar robots?'

'Yes, you would admire it. I've detected amusement in you, Peter – amusement and an appalling lack of understanding. Are you a roboticist, Peter? Those robots attach importance to what they consider superiority. You've just said as much yourself. Subconsciously they feel humans to be inferior and the First Law which protects us from them is imperfect. They are unstable. And here we have a young man ordering a robot to leave him, to lose himself, with every verbal appearance of revulsion, disdain, and disgust. Granted, that robot must follow orders, but subconsciously, there is resentment. It will become more important than ever for it to prove that it is superior despite the horrible names it was called. It may become *so* important that what's left of the First Law won't be enough.'

'How on Earth, or anywhere in the Solar System, Susan, is a robot going to know the meaning of the assorted strong language used upon him? Obscenity is not one of the things impressioned upon his brain.'

'Original impressionment is not everything,' Calvin snarled at him. 'Robots have learning capacity, you . . . you fool——' And Bogert knew that she had really lost her temper. She continued hastily, 'Don't you suppose he could tell from the tone used that the words weren't complimentary? Don't you suppose he's heard the words used before and noted upon what occasions?'

'Well, then,' shouted Bogert, 'will you kindly tell me one way in which a modified robot can harm a human being, no matter how offended it is, no matter how sick with desire to prove superiority?'

'If I tell you one way, will you keep quiet?'

'Yes.'

They were leaning across the table at each other, angry eyes nailed together.

The psychologist said, 'If a modified robot were to drop a heavy weight upon a human being, he would not be breaking the First Law, if he did so with the knowledge that his strength and reaction speed would be sufficient to snatch the weight away before it struck the man. However once the weight left his fingers, he would be no longer the active medium. Only the blind force of gravity would be that. The robot could then change his mind and merely by inaction, allow the weight to strike. The modified First Law allows that.'

'That's an awful stretch of imagination.'

'That's what my profession requires sometimes. Peter, let's not quarrel. Let's work. You know the exact nature of the stimulus that caused the robot to lose himself. You have the records of his original mental make-up. I want you to tell me how possible it is for our robot to do the sort of thing I just talked about. Not the specific instance, mind you, but that whole class of·response. And I want it done quickly.'

'And meanwhile——'

'And meanwhile, we'll have to try performance tests directly on the response to First Law.'

.   .   .

Gerald Black, at his own request, was supervising the mushrooming wooden partitions that were springing up in a bellying circle on the vaulted third floor of Radiation Building 2. The labourers worked, in the main, silently, but more than one was openly a-wonder at the sixty-three photocells that required installation.

One of them sat down near Black, removed his hat, and wiped his forehead thoughtfully with a freckled forearm.

Black nodded at him, 'How's it doing, Walensky?'

Walensky shrugged and fired a cigar, 'Smooth as butter. What's going on anyway, Doc? First, there's no work for three days and then we have this mess of jiggers.' He leaned backward on his elbows and puffed smoke.

Black twitched his eyebrows, 'A couple of robot men came over from Earth. Remember the trouble we had with robots running into the gamma fields, before we pounded it into their skulls that they weren't to do it.'

'Yeah. Didn't we get new robots?'

'We got some replacements, but mostly it was a job of indoctrination. Anyway, the people who make them want to figure out robots that aren't hit so bad by gamma rays.'

'Sure seems funny, though, to stop all the work on the Drive for this robot deal. I thought nothing was allowed to stop the Drive.'

'Well, it's the fellows upstairs that have the say on that. Me – I just do as I'm told. Probably all a matter of pull——'

'Yeah,' the electrician jerked a smile, and winked a wise eye. 'Somebody knew somebody in Washington. But as long as my pay comes through on the dot, I should worry. The Drive's none of my affair. What are they going to do here?'

'You're asking me? They brought a mess of robots with them – over sixty, and they're going to measure reactions. That's all *my* knowledge.'

'How long will it take?'

'I wish I knew.'

'Well,' Walensky said, with heavy sarcasm, 'as long as they dish me my money, they can play games all they want.'

Black felt quietly satisfied. Let the story spread. It was harmless, and near enough to the truth to take the fangs out of curiosity.

. . .

A man sat in the chair, motionless, silent. A weight dropped, crashed downward, then pounded aside at the last moment under the synchronized thump of a sudden force beam. In sixty-three wooden cells, watching NS-2 robots dashed forward in that split second before the weight veered, and sixty-three photocells five feet ahead of their original positions jiggled the marking pen and presented a little jag on the paper. The weight rose and dropped, rose and dropped, rose——

Ten times!

Ten times the robots sprang forward and stopped, as the man remained safely seated.

. . .

Major-General Kallner had not worn his uniform in its entirety since the first dinner with the U.S. Robot representatives. He wore nothing over his blue-grey shirt now, the collar was open, and the black tie was pulled loose.

He looked hopefully at Bogert, who was still blandly neat and whose inner tension was perhaps betrayed only by the trace of glister at his temples.

The general said, 'How does it look? What is it you're trying to see?' Bogert replied, 'A difference which may turn out to be a little too subtle for our purposes, I'm afraid. For sixty-two of those robots the necessity of jumping towards the apparently threatened human was what we call, in robotics, a forced reaction. You see, even when the robots knew that the human in question would not come to harm – and after the third or fourth time they must have known it – they could not prevent reacting as they did. First Law requires it.'

'Well?'

'But the sixty-third robot, the modified Nestor, had no such compulsion. He was under free action. If he had wished, he could have remained in his seat. Unfortunately,' and his voice was mildly regretful, 'he didn't so wish.'

'Why do you suppose?'

Bogert shrugged, 'I suppose Dr Calvin will tell us when she gets here. Probably with a horribly pessimistic interpretation, too. She is sometimes a bit annoying.'

'She's qualified, isn't she?' demanded the general with a sudden frown of uneasiness.

'Yes.' Bogert seemed amused. 'She's qualified all right. She understands robots like a sister – comes from hating human beings so much, I think. It's just that, psychologist or not, she's an extreme neurotic. Has paranoid tendencies. Don't take her too seriously.'

He spread the long row of broken-line graphs out in front of him. 'You see, general, in the case of each robot the time interval from moment of drop to the completion of a five-foot movement tends to decrease as the tests are repeated. There's a definite mathematical relationship that governs such things and failure to conform would indicate marked abnormality in the positronic brain. Unfortunately, all here appear normal.'

'But if our Nestor 10 was not responding with a forced action, why isn't his curve different? I don't understand that.'

'It's simple enough. Robotic responses are not perfectly analogous to human responses, more's the pity. In human beings, voluntary action is much slower than reflex action. But that's not the case with robots; with them it is merely a question of freedom of choice, otherwise the speeds of free and forced action are much the same. What I *had* been expecting, though, was that Nestor 10 would be caught by surprise the first time and allow too great an interval to elapse before responding.'

'And he didn't?'

'I'm afraid not.'

'Then we haven't got anywhere.' The general sat back with an expression of pain. 'It's five days since you've come.'

At this point, Susan Calvin entered and slammed the door behind her. 'Put your graphs away, Peter,' she cried, 'you know they don't show anything.'

She mumbled something impatiently as Kallner half-rose to greet her, and went on, 'We'll have to try something else quickly. I don't like what's happening.'

Bogert exchanged a resigned glance with the general. 'Is anything wrong?'

'You mean specifically? No. But I don't like to have Nestor 10 continue to elude us. It's bad. It *must* be gratifying his swollen sense of superiority. I'm afraid that his motivation is no longer simply one of following orders. I think it's becoming more a matter of sheer neurotic necessity to out-think humans. That's a dangerously unhealthy situation. Peter, have you done what I asked? Have you worked out the instability factors of the modified NS-2 along the lines I want?'

'It's in progress,' said the mathematician, without interest.

She stared at him angrily for a moment, then turned to Kallner. 'Nestor 10 is decidedly aware of what we're doing, general. He had no reason to jump for the bait in this experiment, especially after the first time, when he must have seen that there was no real danger to our subject. The others couldn't help it, but *he* was deliberately falsifying a reaction.'

'What do you think we ought to do now, then, Dr Calvin?'

'Make it impossible for him to fake an action the next time. We will repeat the experiment, but with an addition. High-tension cables, capable of electrocuting the Nestor models will be placed between subject and robot – enough of them to avoid the possibility of jumping over – and the robot will be made perfectly aware in advance that touching the cables will mean death.'

'Hold on,' spat out Bogert with sudden viciousness. 'I rule that out. We are not electrocuting two million dollars worth of robots to locate Nestor 10. There are other ways.'

'You're certain? You've found none. In any case, it's not a question of electrocution. We can arrange a relay which will break the current at the instant of application of weight. If the robot should place his weight on it, he won't die. *But he won't know that,* you see.'

The general's eyes gleamed into hope. 'Will that work?'

'It should. Under those conditions, Nestor 10 would have to remain in his seat. He could be *ordered* to touch the cables and die, for the Second Law of obedience is superior to the Third Law of self-preservation. But *he won't* be ordered to; he will merely be left to his own devices, as will all the robots. In the case of the normal robots, the First Law of human safety will drive them to their deaths even without orders. But not our Nestor 10. Without the entire First Law, and without having received any orders on the matter, the Third Law, self-preservation, will be the

highest operating, and he will have no choice but to remain in his seat.
It would be a forced action.'

'Will it be done tonight, then?'

'Tonight,' said the psychologist, 'if the cables can be laid in time. I'll
tell the robots now what they're to be up against.'

. . .

A man sat in the chair, motionless, silent. A weight dropped, crashed
downward, then pounded aside at the last moment under the synchronized thump of a sudden force beam.

Only once——

And from her small camp chair in the observing booth in the balcony,
Dr Susan Calvin rose with a short gasp of pure horror.

Sixty-three robots sat quietly in their chairs, staring owlishly at the
endangered man before them. Not one moved.

. . .

Dr Calvin was angry, angry almost past endurance. Angry the worse
for not daring to show it to the robots that, one by one, were entering the
room and then leaving. She checked the list. Number twenty-eight was
due in now – Thirty-five still lay ahead of her.

Number Twenty-eight entered, diffidently.

She forced herself into reasonable calm. 'And who are you?'

The robot replied in a low, uncertain voice, 'I have received no
number of my own yet, ma'am. I'm an NS-2 robot, and I was Number
Twenty-eight in line outside. I have a slip of paper here that I'm to give
to you.'

'You haven't been in here before this today?'

'No, ma'am.'

'Sit down. Right there. I want to ask you some questions, Number
Twenty-eight. Were you in the Radiation Room of Building Two about
four hours ago?'

The robot had trouble answering. Then it came out hoarsely, like
machinery needing oil, 'Yes, ma'am.'

'There was a man who almost came to harm there, wasn't there?'

'Yes, ma'am.'

'You did nothing, did you?'

'No, ma'am.'

'The man might have been hurt because of your inaction. Do you
know that?'

'Yes, ma'am. I couldn't help it, ma'am.' It is hard to picture a large
expressionless metallic figure cringing, but it managed.

'I want you to tell me exactly why you did nothing to save him.'

'I want to explain, ma'am. I certainly don't want to have you . . . have *anyone* think that I could do a thing that might cause harm to a master. Oh, no, that would be a horrible ... an inconceivable——'

'Please don't get excited, boy. I'm not blaming you for anything. I only want to know what you were thinking at the time.'

'Ma'am, before it all happened you told us that one of the masters would be in danger of harm from that weight that keeps falling and that we would have to cross electric cables if we were to try to save him. Well, ma'am, that wouldn't stop me. What is my destruction compared to the safety of a master? But ... it occurred to me that if I died on my way to him, I wouldn't be able to save him anyway. The weight would crush him and then I would be dead for no purpose and perhaps some day some other master might come to harm who wouldn't have, if I had only stayed alive. Do you understand me, ma'am?'

'You mean that it was merely a choice of the man dying, or both the man and yourself dying. Is that right?'

'Yes, ma'am. It was impossible to save the master. He might be considered dead. In that case, it is inconceivable that I destroy myself for nothing – without orders.'

The robopsychologist twiddled a pencil. She had heard the same story with insignificant verbal variations twenty-seven times before. This was the crucial question now.

'Boy,' she said, 'your thinking has its points, but it is not the sort of thing I thought you might think. Did you think of this yourself?'

The robot hesitated. 'No.'

'Who thought of it, then?'

'We were talking last night, and one of us got that idea and it sounded reasonable.'

'Which one?'

The robot thought deeply. 'I don't know. Just one of us.'

She sighed, 'That's all.'

Number Twenty-nine was next. Thirty-four after that.

. . .

Major-General Kallner, too, was angry. For one week all of Hyper Base had stopped dead, barring some paper work on the subsidiary asteroids of the group. For nearly one week, the two top experts in the field had aggravated the situation with useless tests. And now they – or the woman, at any rate – made impossible propositions.

Fortunately for the general situation, Kallner felt it impolitic to display his anger openly.

Susan Calvin was insisting, 'Why not, sir? It's obvious that the present situation is unfortunate. The only way we may reach results in the future

– or what future is left to us in this matter – is to separate the robots. We can't keep them together any longer.'

'My dear Dr Calvin,' rumbled the general, his voice sinking into the lower baritone registers. 'I don't see how I can quarter sixty-three robots all over the place——'

Dr Calvin raised her arms helplessly. 'I can do nothing then. Nestor 10 will either imitate what the other robots would do, or else argue them plausibly into not doing what he himself cannot do. And in any case, this is bad business. We're in actual combat with this little lost robot of ours and he's winning out. Every victory of his aggravates his abnormality.'

She rose to her feet in determination. 'General Kallner, if you do not separate the robots as I ask, then I can only demand that all sixty-three be destroyed immediately.'

'You demand it, do you?' Bogert looked up suddenly, and with real anger. 'What gives you the right to demand any such thing. Those robots remain as they are. *I'm* responsible to the management, not you.'

'And I,' added Major-General Kallner, 'am responsible to the World Co-ordinator – and I must have this settled.'

'In that case,' flashed back Calvin, 'there is nothing for me to do but resign. If necessary to force you to the necessary destruction, I'll make this whole matter public. It was not I that approved the manufacture of modified robots.'

'One word from you, Dr Calvin,' said the general, deliberately, 'in violation of security measures, and you would be certainly imprisoned instantly.'

Bogert felt the matter to be getting out of hand. His voice grew syrupy, 'Well, now, we're beginning to act like children, all of us. We need only a little more time. Surely we can outwit a robot without resigning, or imprisoning people, or destroying two millions.'

The psychologist turned on him with quiet fury, 'I don't want any unbalanced robots in existence. We have one Nestor that's definitely unbalanced, eleven more that are potentially so, and sixty-two normal robots that are being subjected to an unbalanced environment. The only absolute safe method is complete destruction.'

The signal-burr brought all three to a halt, and the angry tumult of growingly unrestrained emotion froze.

'Come in,' growled Kallner.

It was Gerald Black, looking perturbed. He had heard angry voices. He said, 'I thought I'd come myself... didn't like to ask anyone else——'

'What is it? Don't orate——'

'The locks of Compartment C in the trading ship have been played with. There are fresh scratches on them.'

'Compartment C?' exclaimed Calvin quickly. 'That's the one that holds the robots, isn't it? Who did it?'

'From the inside,' said Black, laconically.

'The lock isn't out of order, is it?'

'No. It's all right. I've been staying on the ship now for four days and none of them have tried to get out. But I thought you ought to know, and I didn't like to spread the news. I noticed the matter myself.'

'Is anyone there now?' demanded the general.

'I left Robbins and McAdams there.'

There was a thoughtful silence, and then Dr Calvin said, ironically, 'Well?'

Kallner rubbed his nose uncertainly, 'What's it all about?'

'Isn't it obvious? Nestor 10 is planning to leave. That order to lose himself is dominating his abnormality past anything we can do. I wouldn't be surprised if what's left of his First Law would scarcely be powerful enough to override it. He is perfectly capable of seizing the ship and leaving with it. Then we'd have a mad robot on a spaceship. What would he do next? Any idea? Do you still want to leave them all together, general?'

'Nonsense,' interrupted Bogert. He had regained his smoothness. 'All that from a few scratch marks on a lock.'

'Have you, Dr Bogert, completed the analysis I've required, since you volunteer opinions?'

'Yes.'

'May I see it?'

'No.'

'Why not? Or mayn't I ask that, either?'

'Because there's no point in it, Susan. I told you in advance that these modified robots are less stable than the normal variety, and my analysis shows it. There's a certain very small chance of breakdown under extreme circumstances that are not likely to occur. Let it go at that. I won't give you ammunition for your absurd claim that sixty-two perfectly good robots be destroyed just because so far you lack the ability to detect Nestor 10 among them.'

Susan Calvin stared him down and let disgust fill her eyes. 'You won't let anything stand in the way of the permanent directorship, will you?'

'Please,' begged Kallner, half in irritation. 'Do you insist that nothing further can be done, Dr Calvin?'

'I can't think of anything, sir,' she replied, wearily. 'If there were only other differences between Nestor 10 and the normal robots, differences that didn't involve the First Law. Even one other difference. Something

in impressionment, environment, specification——' And she stopped
suddenly.

'What is it?'

'I've thought of something . . . I think——' Her eyes grew distant and
hard, 'These modified Nestors, Peter. They get the same impressioning
the normal ones get, don't they?'

'Yes. Exactly the same.'

'And what was it you were saying, Mr Black,' she turned to the young
man, who through the storms that had followed his news had maintained a discreet silence. 'Once when complaining of the Nestors'
attitude of superiority, you said the technicians had taught them all they
knew.'

'Yes, in etheric physics. They're not aquainted with the subject when
they come here.'

'That's right,' said Bogert, in surprise. 'I told you, Susan, when I
spoke to the other Nestors here that the two new arrivals hadn't learned
etheric physics yet.'

'And why is that?' Dr Calvin was speaking in mounting excitement.
'Why aren't NS-2 models impressioned with etheric physics to start
with?'

'I can tell you that,' said Kallner. 'It's all of a piece with the secrecy.
We thought that if we made a special model with knowledge of etheric
physics, used twelve of them and put the others to work in an unrelated
field, there might be suspicion. Men working with normal Nestors might
wonder why they knew etheric physics. So there was merely an
impressionment with a capacity for training in the field. Only the ones
that come here, naturally, receive such a training. It's that simple.'

'I understand. Please get out of here, the lot of you. Let me have an
hour or so.'

                                  .   .   .

Calvin felt she could not face the ordeal for a third time. Her mind had
contemplated it and rejected it with an intensity that left her nauseated.
She could face that unending file of repetitious robots no more.

So Bogert asked the questions now, while she sat aside, eyes and mind
half-closed.

Number Fourteen came in – forty-nine to go.

Bogert looked up from the guide sheet and said, 'What is your number
in line?'

'Fourteen, sir.' The robot presented his numbered ticket.

'Sit down, boy.'

Bogert asked, 'You haven't been here before on this day?'

'No, sir.'

'Well, boy, we are going to have another man in danger of harm soon after we're through here. In fact, when you leave this room, you will be led to a stall where you will wait quietly, till you are needed. Do you understand?'

'Yes, sir.'

'Now, naturally, if a man is in danger of harm, you will try to save him.'

'Naturally, sir.'

'Unfortunately, between the man and yourself, there will be a gamma ray field.'

Silence.

'Do you know what gamma rays are?' asked Bogert sharply.

'Energy radiation, sir?'

The next question came in a friendly, offhand manner, 'Ever worked with gamma rays?'

'No, sir.' The answer was definite.

'Mm-m. Well, boy, gamma rays will kill you instantly. They'll destroy your brain. That is a fact you must know and remember. Naturally, you don't want to destroy yourself.'

'Naturally.' Again the robot seemed shocked. Then, slowly, 'But, sir, if the gamma rays are between myself and the master that may be harmed, how can I save him? I would be destroying myself to no purpose.'

'Yes, there is that,' Bogert seemed concerned about the matter. 'The only thing I can advise, boy, is that if you detect the gamma radiation between yourself and the man, you may as well sit where you are.'

The robot was openly relieved. 'Thank you, sir. There wouldn't be any use, would there?'

'Of course not. But if there *weren't* any dangerous radiation, that would be a different matter.'

'Naturally, sir. No question of that.'

'You may leave now. The man on the other side of the door will lead you to your stall. Please wait there.'

He turned to Susan Calvin when the robot left. 'How did that go, Susan?'

'Very well,' she said, dully.

'Do you think we could catch Nestor 10 by quick questioning on etheric physics?'

'Perhaps, but it's not sure enough.' Her hands lay loosely in her lap. 'Remember, he's fighting us. He's on his guard. The only way we can catch him is to outsmart him – and, within his limitations, he can think much more quickly than a human being.'

'Well, just for fun – suppose I ask the robots from now on a few questions on gamma rays. Wave length limits, for instance.'

'No!' Dr Calvin's eyes sparked to life. 'It would be too easy for him to deny knowledge and then he'd be warned against the test that's coming up – which is our real chance. Please follow the questions I've indicated, Peter, and don't improvise. It's just within the bounds of risk to ask them if they've ever worked with gamma rays. And try to sound less interested than you do when you ask it.'

Bogert shrugged, and pressed the buzzer that would allow the entrance of Number Fifteen.

.   .   .

The large Radiation Room was in readiness once more. The robots waited patiently in their wooden cells, all open to the centre but closed off from each other.

Major-General Kallner mopped his brow slowly with a large handkerchief while Dr Calvin checked the last details with Black.

'You're sure now,' she demanded, 'that none of the robots have had a chance to talk with each other after leaving the Orientation Room?'

'Absolutely sure,' insisted Black. 'There's not been a word exchanged.'

'And the robots are put in the proper stalls?'

'Here's the plan.'

The psychologist looked at it thoughtfully. 'Um-m-m.'

The general peered over her shoulder. 'What's the idea of the arrangement, Dr Calvin?'

'I've asked to have those robots that appeared even slightly out of true in the previous tests concentrated on one side of the circle. I'm going to be sitting in the centre myself this time, and I wanted to watch those particularly.'

'*You're* going to be sitting there——' exclaimed Bogert.

'Why not?' she demanded coldly. 'What I expect to see may be something quite momentary. I can't risk having anyone else as main observer. Peter, you'll be in the observing booth, and I want you to keep your eye on the opposite side of the circle. General Kallner, I've arranged for motion pictures to be taken of each robot, in case visual observation isn't enough. If these are required, the robots are to remain exactly where they are until the pictures are developed and studied. None must leave, none must change place. Is that clear?'

'Perfectly.'

'Then let's try it this one last time.'

.   .   .

Susan Calvin sat in the chair, silent eyes restless. A weight dropped, crashed downward, then pounded aside at the last moment under the synchronized thump of a sudden force beam.

And a single robot jerked upright and took two steps.

And stopped.

But Dr Calvin was upright, and her finger pointed to him sharply. 'Nestor 10, come here,' she cried, '*come here!* COME HERE!'

Slowly, reluctantly, the robot took another step forward. The psychologist shouted at the top of her voice, without taking her eyes from the robot, 'Get every other robot out of this place, somebody. Get them out quickly, and *keep* them out.'

Somewhere within reach of her ears there was noise, and the thud of hard feet upon the floor. She did not look away.

Nestor 10 – if it was Nestor 10 – took another step, and then, under force of her imperious gesture, two more. He was only ten feet away, when he spoke harshly, 'I have been told to be lost——'

Another step. 'I must not disobey. They have not found me so far – He would think me a failure – He told me – But it's not so – I am powerful and intelligent——'

The words came in spurts.

Another step. 'I know a good deal – He would think ... I mean I've been found – Disgraceful – Not I – I am intelligent – And by just a master ... who is weak – Slow——'

Another step – and one metal arm flew out suddenly to her shoulder, and she felt the weight bearing her down. Her throat constricted, and she felt a shriek tear through.

Dimly, she heard Nestor 10's next words, 'No one must find me. No master——' and the cold metal was against her, and she was sinking under the weight of it.

And then a queer, metallic sound, and she was on the ground with an unfelt thump, and a gleaming arm was heavy across her body. It did not move. Nor did Nestor 10, who sprawled beside her.

And now faces were bending over her.

Gerald Black was gasping. 'Are you hurt, Dr Calvin?'

She shook her head feebly. They pried the arm off her and lifted her gently to her feet, 'What happened?'

Black said, 'I bathed the place in gamma rays for five seconds. We didn't know what was happening. It wasn't till the last second that we realized he was attacking you, and then there was no time for anything but a gamma field. He went down in an instant. There wasn't enough to harm you though. Don't worry about it.'

'I'm not worried.' She closed her eyes and leaned for a moment upon his shoulder. 'I don't think I was attacked exactly. Nestor 10 was simply *trying* to do so. What was left of the First Law was still holding him back.'

.   .   .

Susan Calvin and Peter Bogert, two weeks after their first meeting with Major-General Kallner had their last. Work at Hyper Base had been resumed. The trading ship with its sixty-two normal NS-2's was gone to wherever it was bound with an officially imposed story to explain its two weeks' delay. The government cruiser was making ready to carry the two roboticists back to Earth.

Kallner was once again a-gleam in dress uniform. His white gloves shone as he shook hands.

Calvin said, 'The other modified Nestors are, of course, to be destroyed.'

'They will be. We'll make shift with normal robots, or, if necessary, do without.'

'Good.'

'But tell me – You haven't explained – How was it done?'

She smiled tightly, 'Oh, that. I would have told you in advance if I had been more certain of its working. You see, Nestor 10 had a superiority complex that was becoming more radical all the time. He liked to think that he and the other robots knew more than human beings. It was becoming very important for him to think so.

'We knew that. So we warned every robot in advance that gamma rays would kill them, which it would, and we further warned them all that gamma rays would be between them and myself. So they all stayed where they were, naturally. By Nestor 10's own logic in the previous test they had all decided that there was no point in trying to save a human being if they were sure to die before they could do it.'

'Well, yes, Dr Calvin, I understand that. But why did Nestor 10 himself leave his seat.'

'Ah! That was a little arrangement between myself and your young Mr Black. You see it wasn't gamma rays that flooded the area between myself and the robots – but the infra-red rays. Just ordinary heat rays, absolutely harmless. Nestor 10 knew they were infra-red and harmless and so he began to dash out, as he expected the rest would do, under First Law compulsion. It was only a fraction of a second too late that he remembered that the normal NS-2's could detect radiation, but could not identify the type. That he himself could only identify wavelengths by virtue of the training he had received at Hyper Base, under mere human beings, was a little too humiliating to remember for just a moment. To the normal robots the area was fatal because we had told them it would be, and only Nestor 10 knew we were lying.

'And just for a moment he forgot, or didn't want to remember, that other robots might be more ignorant than human beings. His very superiority caught him. Goodbye, General.'

CHAPTER 7

ESCAPE!

When Susan Calvin returned from Hyper Base, Alfred Lanning was waiting for her. The old man never spoke about his age, but everyone knew it to be over seventy-five. Yet his mind was keen, and if he had finally allowed himself to be made Director-Emeritus of Research with Bogert as acting Director, it did not prevent him from appearing in his office daily.

'How close are they to the Hyperatomic Drive?' he asked.

'I don't know,' she replied irritably. 'I didn't ask.'

'Hmm. I wish they'd hurry. Because if they don't Consolidated might beat them to it. And beat *us* to it as well.'

'*Consolidated.* What have they got to do with it?'

'Well, we're not the only ones with calculating machines. Ours may be positronic, but that doesn't mean they're better. Robertson is calling a big meeting about it tomorrow. He's been waiting for you to come back.'

. . .

Robertson of U.S. Robot & Mechanical Men Corporation, son of the founder, pointed his lean nose at his general manager and his Adam's apple jumped as he said, 'You start now. Let's get this straight.'

The general manager did so with alacrity, 'Here's the deal now, chief. Consolidated Robots approached us a month ago with a funny sort of proposition. They brought about five tons of figures, equations, all that sort of stuff. It was a problem, see, and they wanted an answer from The Brain. The terms were as follows——'

He ticked them off on thick fingers: 'A hundred thousand for us if there is no solution and we can tell them the missing factors. Two hundred thousand if there is a solution, plus costs of construction of the machine involved, plus quarter interest in all profits derived therefrom. The problem concerns the development of an interstellar engine——'

Robertson frowned and his lean figure stiffened, 'Despite the fact that they have a thinking machine of their own. Right?'

'Exactly what makes the whole proposition a foul ball, chief. Levver, take it from there.'

Abe Levver looked up from the far end of the conference table and smoothed his stubbled chin with a faint rasping sound. He smiled:

'It's this way, sir. Consolidated *had* a thinking machine. It's broken.'

'What?' Robertson half rose.

'That's right. Broken! It's *kaput*. Nobody knows why, but I got hold of some pretty interesting guesses – like, for instance, that they asked it to give them an interstellar engine with the same set of information they came to us with, and that it cracked their machine wide open. It's scrap – just scrap now.'

'You get it, chief?' The general manager was wildly jubilant. 'You get it? There isn't any industrial research group of any size that isn't trying to develop a space-warp engine, and Consolidated and U.S. Robots have the lead on the field with our super robot-brains. Now that they've managed to foul theirs up, we have a clear field. That's the nub, the . . . uh . . . motivation. It will take them six years at least to build another and they're sunk, unless they can break ours, too, with the same problem.'

The president of U.S. Robots bulged his eyes, 'Why, the dirty rats——'

'Hold on, chief. There's more to this.' He pointed a finger with a wide sweep. 'Lanning, take it!'

Dr Alfred Lanning viewed the proceedings with faint scorn – his usual reaction to the doings of the vastly better-paid business and sales division. His unbelievable grey eyebrows hunched low and his voice was dry:

'From a scientific standpoint the situation, while not entirely clear, is subject to intelligent analysis. The question of interstellar travel under present conditions of physical theory is . . . uh . . . vague. The matter is wide open – and the information given by Consolidated to its thinking machine, assuming these we have to be the same, was similarly wide open. Our mathematical department has given it a thorough analysis, and it seems Consolidated has included everything. Its material for submission contains all known developments of Franciacci's space-warp theory, and, apparently, all pertinent astrophysical and electronic data. It's quite a mouthful.'

Robertson followed anxiously. He interrupted, 'Too much for The Brain to handle?'

Lanning shook his head decisively, 'No. There are no known limits to The Brain's capacity. It's a different matter. It's a question of the Robotic Laws. The Brain, for instance, could never supply a solution to a problem set to it if that solution would involve the death or injury of humans. As far as it would be concerned, a problem with only such a solution would be insoluble. If such a problem is combined with an extremely urgent demand that it be answered, it is just possible that The Brain, only a robot after all, would be presented with a dilemma, where it could neither answer nor refuse to answer. Something of the sort must have happened to Consolidated's machine.'

He paused, but the general manager urged on, 'Go ahead, Dr Lanning. Explain it the way you explained it to me.'

Lanning set his lips and raised his eyebrows in the direction of Dr Susan Calvin who lifted her eyes from her precisely folded hands for the first time. Her voice was low and colourless.

'The nature of a robot reaction to a dilemma is startling,' she began. 'Robot psychology is far from perfect – as a specialist, I can assure you of that – but it can be discussed in qualitative terms, because with all the complications introduced into a robot's positronic brain, it is built by humans and is therefore built according to human values.

'Now a human caught in an impossibility often responds by a retreat from reality: by entry into a world of delusion, or by taking to drink, going off into hysteria, or jumping off a bridge. It all comes to the same thing – a refusal or inability to face the situation squarely. And so, the robot. A dilemma at its mildest will disorder half its relays; and at its worst it will burn out every positronic brain path past repair.'

'I see,' said Robertson, who didn't. 'Now what about this information Consolidated's wishing on us?'

'It undoubtedly involves,' said Dr Calvin, 'a problem of a forbidden sort. But The Brain is considerably different from Consolidated's robot.'

'That's right, chief. That's right.' The general manager was energetically interruptive. 'I want you to get this, because it's the whole point of the situation.'

Susan Calvin's eyes glittered behind the spectacles, and she continued patiently, 'You see, sir, Consolidated's machines, their Super-Thinker among them, are built without personality. They go in for functionalism, you know – they have to, without U.S. Robot's basic patents for the emotional brain paths. Their Thinker is merely a calculating machine on a grand scale, and a dilemma ruins it instantly.

'However, The Brain, our own machine, has a personality – a child's personality. It is a supremely deductive brain, but it resembles an *idiot savante*. It doesn't really understand what it does – it just does it. And because it is really a child, it is more resilient. Life isn't so serious, you might say.'

The robopsychologist continued: 'Here is what we're going to do. We have divided all of Consolidated's information into logical units. We are going to feed the units to The Brain singly and cautiously. When *the* factor enters – the one that creates the dilemma – The Brain's child personality will hesitate. Its sense of judgement is not mature. There will be a perceptible interval before it will recognize a dilemma as such. And in that interval, it will reject the unit automatically – before its brain-paths can be set in motion and ruined.'

Robertson's Adam's apple squirmed, 'Are you sure, now?'

Dr Calvin masked impatience, 'It doesn't make much sense, I admit, in lay language; but there is no conceivable use in presenting the mathematics of this. I assure you, it is as I say.'

The general manager was in the breach instantly and fluently, 'So here's the situation, chief. If we take the deal, we can put it through like this. The Brain will tell us which unit of information involves the dilemma. From there, we can figure *why* the dilemma. Isn't that right, Dr Bogert? There you are, chief, and Dr Bogert is the best mathematician you'll find anywhere. We give Consolidated a "No Solution" answer, with the reason, and collect a hundred thousand. They're left with a broken machine; we're left with a whole one. In a year, two maybe, we'll have a space-warp engine, or a hyper-atomic motor, some people call it. Whatever you name it, it will be the biggest thing in the world.'

Robertson chuckled and reached out, 'Let's see the contract. I'll sign it.'

. . .

When Susan Calvin entered the fantastically guarded vault that held The Brain one of the current shift of technicians had just asked it: 'If one and a half chickens lay one and a half eggs in one and a half days, how many eggs will nine chickens lay in nine days?'

The Brain had just answered, 'Fifty-four.'

And the technician had just said to another, 'See, you dope!'

Dr Calvin coughed and there was a sudden impossible flurry of directionless energy. The psychologist motioned briefly, and she was alone with The Brain.

The Brain was a two-foot globe merely – one which contained within it a thoroughly conditioned helium atmosphere, a volume of space completely vibration-absent and radiation-free – and within that was that unheard-of complexity of positronic brain-paths that was The Brain. The rest of the room was crowded with the attachments that were the intermediaries between The Brain and the outside world – its voice, its arms, its sense organs.

Dr Calvin said softly, 'How are you, Brain?'

The Brain's voice was high-pitched and enthusiastic, 'Swell, Miss Susan. You're going to ask me something. I can tell. You always have a book in your hand when you're going to ask me something.'

Dr Calvin smiled mildly, 'Well, you're right, but not just yet. This is going to be a question. It will be so complicated we're going to give it to you in writing. But not just yet. I think I'll talk to you first.'

'All right. I don't mind talking.'

'Now, Brain, in a little while, Dr Lanning and Dr Bogert will be here with this complicated question. We'll give it to you a very little at a time and very slowly, because we want you to be careful. We're going to ask you to build something, if you can, out of the information, but I'm going to warn you now that the solution might involve ... uh ... damage to human beings.'

'Gosh!' The exclamation was hushed, drawn-out.

'Now you watch for that. When we come to a sheet which means damage, even maybe death, don't get excited. You see, Brain, in this case, we don't mind – not even about death; we don't mind at all. So when you come to that sheet, just stop, give it back – and that'll be all. You understand?'

'Oh, sure. But golly, the death of humans! Oh, my!'

'Now, Brain, I hear Dr Lanning and Dr Bogert coming. They'll tell you what the problem is all about and then we'll start. Be a good boy, now——'

Slowly the sheets were fed in. After each one came the interval of the queerly whispery chuckling noise that was The Brain in action. Then the silence that meant readiness for another sheet. It was a matter of hours – during which the equivalent of something like seventeen fat volumes of mathematical physics were fed into The Brain.

As the process went on, frowns appeared and deepened. Lanning muttered ferociously under his breath. Bogert first gazed speculatively at his fingernails, and then bit at them in an abstracted fashion. It was when the last of the thick pile of sheets disappeared that Calvin, white-faced, said:

'Something's wrong.'

Lanning barely got the words out, 'It can't be. Is it – dead?'

'Brain?' Susan Calvin was trembling. 'Do you hear me, Brain?'

'Huh?' came the abstracted rejoinder. 'Do you want me?'

'The solution——'

'Oh, that! I can do it. I'll build you a whole ship, just as easy – if you let me have the robots. A nice ship. It'll take two months maybe.'

'There was – no difficulty?'

'It took long to figure,' said The Brain.

Dr Calvin backed away. The colour had not returned to her thin cheeks. She motioned the others away.

.   .   .

In her office, she said, 'I can't understand it. The information, as given, must involve a dilemma – probably involves death. If something has gone wrong——'

Bogert said quietly, 'The machine talks and makes sense. It can't be a dilemma.'

But the psychologist replied urgently. 'There are dilemmas *and* dilemmas. There are different forms of escape. Suppose The Brain is only mildly caught; just badly enough, say, to be suffering from the delusion that he can solve the problem, when he can't. Or suppose it's teetering on the brink of something really bad, so that any small push shoves it over.'

'Suppose,' said Lanning, 'there is no dilemma. Suppose Consolidated's machine broke down over a different question, or broke down for purely mechanical reasons.'

'But even so,' insisted Calvin, 'we couldn't take chances. Listen, from now on, no one is to as much as breathe to The Brain. I'm taking over.'

'All right,' sighed Lanning, 'take over, then. And meanwhile we'll let The Brain build its ship. And if it *does* build it, we'll have to test it.'

He was ruminating, 'We'll need our top field men for *that*.'

.   .   .

Michael Donovan brushed down his red hair with a violent motion of his hand and a total indifference to the fact that the unruly mass sprang to attention again immediately.

He said, 'Call the turn now, Greg. They say the ship is finished. They don't know what it is, but it's finished. Let's go, Greg. Let's grab the controls right now.'

Powell said wearily, 'Cut it, Mike. There's a peculiar overripe flavour to your humour at its freshest, and the confined atmosphere here isn't helping it.'

'Well, listen,' Donovan took another ineffectual swipe at his hair, 'I'm not worried so much about our cast-iron genius and his tin ship. There's the matter of my lost leave. And the monotony! There's nothing here but whiskers and figures – the wrong kind of figures. Oh, why do they *give* us these jobs?'

'Because,' replied Powell, gently, 'we're no loss, if they lose us. O.K., relax! Doc Lanning's coming this way.'

Lanning was coming, his grey eyebrows as lavish as ever, his aged figure unbent as yet and full of life. He walked silently up the ramp with the two men and out into the open field, where, obeying no human master, silent robots were building a ship.

Wrong tense. *Had* built a ship!

For Lanning said, 'The robots have stopped. Not one has moved today.'

'It's completed then? Definitely?' asked Powell.

'Now how can I tell?' Lanning was peevish, and his eyebrows curled down in an eye-hiding frown. 'It *seems* done. There are no spare pieces about, and the interior is down to a gleaming finish.'

'You've been inside?'

'Just in, then out. I'm no space-pilot. Either of you two know much about engine theory?'

Donovan looked at Powell, who looked at Donovan.

Donovan said, 'I've got my licence, sir, but at last reading it didn't say anything about hyper-engines or warp-navigation. Just the usual child's play in three dimensions.'

Alfred Lanning looked up with sharp disapproval and snorted the length of his prominent nose.

He said frigidly, 'Well, we have our engine men.'

Powell caught at his elbow as he walked away, 'Sir, is the ship still restricted ground?'

The old director hesitated, then rubbed the bridge of his nose, 'I suppose not. For you two anyway.'

Donovan looked after him as he left and muttered a short, expressive phrase at his back. He turned to Powell, 'I'd like to give him a literary description of himself, Greg.'

'Suppose you come along, Mike.'

The inside of the ship was finished, as finished as a ship ever was; that could be told in a single eye-blinking glance. No martinet in the system could have put as much spit-and-polish into a surface as those robots had. The walls were of a gleaming silvery finish that retained no fingerprints.

There were no angles; walls, floors, and ceiling faded gently into each other and in the cold, metallic glittering of the hidden lights, one was surrounded by six chilly reflections of one's bewildered self.

The main corridor was a narrow tunnel that led in a hard, clatter-footed stretch along a line of rooms of no interdistinguishing features.

Powell said, 'I suppose furniture is built into the wall. Or maybe we're not supposed to sit or sleep.'

It was in the last room, the one nearest the nose, that the monotony broke. A curving window of non-reflecting glass was the first break in the universal metal, and below it was a single large dial, with a single motionless needle hard against the zero mark.

Donovan said, 'Look at that!' and pointed to the single word on the finely-marked scale.

It said 'Parsecs' and the tiny figure at the right end of the curving, graduated meter said '1,000,000'.

There were two chairs; heavy, wide-flaring, uncushioned. Powell seated himself gingerly, and found it moulded to the body's curves, and comfortable.

Powell said, 'What do you think of it?'

'For my money, The Brain has brain-fever. Let's get out.'

'Sure you don't want to look it over a bit?'

'I have looked it over. I came, I saw, I'm through!' Donovan's red hair bristled into separate wires, 'Greg, let's get out of here. I quit my job five seconds ago, and this is a restricted area for non-personnel.'

Powell smiled in an oily self-satisfied manner and smoothed his moustache, 'O.K., Mike, turn off that adrenalin tap you've got draining into your bloodstream. I was worried, too, but no more.'

'No more, huh? How come, no more? Increased your insurance?'

'Mike, this ship can't fly.'

'How do you know?'

'Well, we've been through the entire ship, haven't we?'

'Seems so.'

'Take my word for it, we have. Did you see any pilot room except for this one port and the one gauge here in parsecs? Did you see any controls?'

'No.'

'And did you see any engines?'

'Holy Joe, no!'

'Well, then! Let's break the news to Lanning, Mike.'

They curved their way through the featureless corridors and finally hit-and-missed their way into the short passage to the air lock.

Donovan stiffened, 'Did you lock this thing, Greg?'

'No, I never touched it. Yank the lever, will you?'

The lever never budged, though Donovan's face twisted appallingly with exertion.

Powell said, 'I didn't see any emergency exits. If something's gone wrong here, they'll have to melt us out.'

'Yes, and we've got to wait until they find out that some fool has locked us in here,' added Donovan, frantically.

'Let's get back to the room with the port. It's the only place from which we might attract attention.'

But they didn't.

In that last room, the port was no longer blue and full of sky. It was black, and hard yellow pin-point stars spelled *space*.

There was a dull, double thud, as two bodies collapsed separately into two chairs.

Alfred Lanning met Dr Calvin just outside his office. He lit a nervous cigar and motioned her in.

He said, 'Well, Susan, we've come pretty far, and Robertson's getting jumpy. What are you doing with The Brain?'

Susan Calvin spread her hands, 'It's no use getting impatient. The Brain is worth more than anything we forfeit on this deal.'

'But you've been questioning it for two months.'

The psychologist's voice was flat, but somehow dangerous, 'You would rather run this yourself?'

'Now you know what I meant.'

'Oh, I suppose I do,' Dr Calvin rubbed her hands nervously. 'It isn't easy. I've been pampering it and probing it gently, and I haven't got anywhere yet. Its reactions aren't normal. Its answers – they're queer, somehow. But nothing I can put my finger on yet. And you see, until we know what's wrong, we must just tiptoe our way through. I can never tell what simple question or remark will just ... push him over ... and then—— Well, and then we'll have on our hands a completely useless Brain. Do you want to face that?'

'Well, it can't break the First Law.'

'I would have thought so, but——'

'You're not even sure of that?' Lanning was profoundly shocked.

'Oh, I can't be sure of anything, Alfred——'

The alarm system raised its fearful clangour with a horrifying suddenness. Lanning clicked on communications with an almost paralytic spasm. The breathless words froze him.

He said, 'Susan ... you heard that ... the ship's gone. I sent those two field men inside half an hour ago. You'll have to see The Brain again.'

.   .   .

Susan Calvin said with enforced calm, 'Brain, what happened to the ship?'

The Brain said happily, 'The ship I built, Miss Susan?'

'That's right. What has happened to it?'

'Why, nothing at all. The two men that were supposed to test it were inside, and we were all set. So I sent it off.'

'Oh—— Well, that's nice.' The psychologist felt some difficulty in breathing. 'Do you think they'll be all right?'

'Right as anything, Miss Susan. I've taken care of it all. It's a bee-yoo-tiful ship.'

'Yes, Brain, it *is* beautiful, but you think they have enough food, don't you? They'll be comfortable?'

'Plenty of food.'

'This business might be a shock to them, Brain. Unexpected, you know.'

The Brain tossed it off, 'They'll be all right. It ought to be interesting for them.'

'Interesting? How?'

'Just interesting,' said The Brain, slyly.

'Susan,' whispered Lanning in a fuming whisper, 'ask him if death comes into it. Ask him what the dangers are.'

Susan Calvin's expression contorted with fury, 'Keep quiet!' In a shaken voice, she said to The Brain, 'We can communicate with the ship, can't we, Brain?'

'Oh, they can hear you if you call by radio. I've taken care of that.'

'Thanks. That's all for now.'

Once outside, Lanning lashed out ragingly, 'Great Galaxy, Susan, if this gets out, it will ruin all of us. We've got to get those men back. Why didn't you ask it if there was danger of death – straight out?'

'Because,' said Calvin, with a weary frustration, 'that's just what I can't mention. If it's got a case of dilemma, it's about death. Anything that would bring it up badly might knock it completely out. Will we be better off then? Now, look, it said we could communicate with them. Let's do so, get their location, and bring them back. They probably can't use the controls themselves; The Brain is probably handling them remotely. Come!'

. . .

It was quite a while before Powell shook himself together.

'Mike,' he said, out of cold lips, 'did you feel any acceleration?'

Donovan's eyes were blank, 'Huh? No ... no.'

And then the redhead's fists clenched and he was out of his seat with sudden frenzied energy and up against the cold, wide-curving glass. There was nothing to see – but stars.

He turned, 'Greg, they must have started the machine while we were inside. Greg, it's a put-up job; they fixed it up with the robot to jerry us into being the try-out boys, in case we were thinking of backing out.'

Powell said, 'What are you talking about? What's the good of sending us out if we don't know how to run the machine? How are we supposed to bring it back? No, this ship left by itself, and without apparent acceleration.' He rose, and walked the floor slowly. The metal walls dinned back the clangour of his steps.

He said tonelessly, 'Mike, this is the most confusing situation we've ever been up against.'

'That,' said Donovan, bitterly, 'is news to me. I was just beginning to have a very swell time, when you told me.'

Powell ignored that. 'No acceleration – which means the ship works on a principle different from any known.'

'Different from any we know, anyway.'

'Different from *any* known. There are no engines within reach of manual control. Maybe they're built into the walls. Maybe that's why they're thick as they are.'

'What are you mumbling about?' demanded Donovan.

'Why not listen? I'm saying that whatever powers this ship is enclosed, and evidently not meant to be handled. The ship is running by remote control.'

'The Brain's control?'

'Why not?'

'Then you think we'll stay out here till The Brain brings us back.'

'It could be. If so, let's wait quietly. The Brain is a robot. It's got to follow the First Law. It can't hurt a human being.'

Donovan sat down slowly, 'You figure that?' Carefully, he flattened his hair, 'Listen, this junk about the space-warp knocked out Consolidated's robot, and the longhairs said it was because interstellar travel killed humans. Which robot are you going to trust? Ours had the same data, I understand.'

Powell was yanking madly at his moustache, 'Don't pretend you don't know your robotics, Mike. Before it's physically possible in any way for a robot to even make a start to breaking the First Law, so many things have to break down that it would be a ruined mess of scrap ten times over. There's some simple explanation to this.'

'Oh sure, sure. Just have the butler call me in the morning. It's all just too, too simple for me to bother about before my beauty nap.'

'Well, Jupiter, Mike, what are you complaining about so far? The Brain is taking care of us. This place is warm. It's got light. It's got air. There wasn't even enough of an acceleration jar to mess your hair if it were smooth enough to be messable in the first place.'

'Yeah? Greg, you must've taken lessons. No one could put Pollyanna that far out of the running without. What do we eat? What do we drink? Where are we? How do we get back? And in case of accident, to what exit and in what spacesuit do we run, not walk? I haven't even seen a bathroom in the place, or those little conveniences that go along with bathrooms. Sure, we're being taken care of – but good!'

The voice that interrupted Donovan's tirade was not Powell's. It was nobody's. It was there, hanging in open air – stentorian and petrifying in its effects.

'GREGORY POWELL! MICHAEL DONOVAN! GREGORY POWELL! MICHAEL DONOVAN! PLEASE REPORT YOUR PRESENT POSITIONS. IF YOUR SHIP ANSWERS CONTROLS, PLEASE RETURN TO BASE. GREGORY POWELL! MICHAEL DONOVAN!——'

The message was repetitious, mechanical, broken by regular, untiring intervals.

Donovan said, 'Where's it coming from?'

'I don't know.' Powell's voice was an intense whisper, 'Where do the lights come from? Where does anything come from?'

'Well, how are we going to answer?' they had to speak in the intervals between the loudly echoing, repeating message.

The walls were bare – as bare and as unbroken as smooth, curving metal can be. Powell said, 'Shout an answer.'

They did. They shouted, in turns, and together, 'Position unknown! Ship out of control! Condition desperate!'

Their voices rose and cracked. The short businesslike sentences became interlarded and adulterated with screaming and emphatic profanity, but the cold, calling voice repeated and repeated and repeated unwearingly.

'They don't hear us,' gasped Donovan. 'There's no sending mechanism. Just a receiver.' His eyes focused blindly at a random spot on the wall.

Slowly the din of the outside voice softened and receded. They called again when it was a whisper, and they called again, hoarsely, when there was silence.

Something like fifteen minutes later, Powell said lifelessly, 'Let's go through the ship again. There must be something to eat somewhere.' He did not sound hopeful. It was almost an admission of defeat.

They divided in the corridor to the right and left. They could follow one another by the hard footsteps resounding, and they met occasionally in the corridor, where they would glare at each other and pass on.

Powell's search ended suddenly and as it did, he heard Donovan's glad voice rise boomingly.

'Hey, Greg,' it howled, 'the ship *has* got plumbing. How did we miss it?'

It was some five minutes later that he found Powell by hit-and-miss.

He was saying, 'Still no shower baths, though,' but it got choked off in the middle.

'Food,' he gasped.

The wall had dropped away, leaving a curved gap with two shelves. The upper shelf was loaded with unlabelled cans of a bewildering variety of sizes and shapes. The enamelled cans on the lower shelf were uniform and Donovan felt a cold draught about his ankles. The lower half was refrigerated.

'How ... how——'

'It wasn't there, before,' said Powell, curtly. 'That wall section dropped out of sight as I came in the door.'

He was eating. The can was the pre-heating type with an enclosed spoon and the warm odour of baken beans filled the room. 'Grab a can, Mike!'

Donovan hesitated. 'What's the menu?'

'How do I know! Are you finicky?'

'No, but all I eat on ships are beans. Something else would be first choice.' His hand hovered and selected a shining elliptical can whose flatness seemed reminiscent of salmon or similar delicacy. It opened at the proper pressure.

'Beans!' howled Donovan, and reached for another. Powell hauled at the slack of his pants. 'Better eat that, sonny boy. Supplies are limited and we may be here a long, long time.'

Donovan drew back sulkily, 'Is that all we have? Beans?'

'Could be.'

'What's on the lower shelf?'

'Milk.'

'Just milk?' Donovan cried in outrage.

'Looks it.'

The meal of beans and milk was carried through in silence, and as they left, the strip of hidden wall rose up and formed an unbroken surface once more.

Powell sighed, 'Everything automatic. Everything just so. Never felt so helpless in my life. Where's your plumbing?'

'Right there. And that wasn't among those present when we first looked, either.'

Fifteen minutes later they were back in the glassed-in room, staring at each other from opposing seats.

Powell looked gloomily at the one gauge in the room. It still said 'parsecs', the figures still ended in '1,000,000' and the indicating needle was still pressed hard against the zero mark.

. . .

In the innermost offices of the U.S. Robot & Mechanical Men Corp. Alfred Lanning was saying wearily, 'They won't answer. We've tried every wavelength, public, private, coded, straight, even this subether stuff they have now. And The Brain still won't say anything?' He shot this at Dr Calvin.

'It won't amplify on the matter, Alfred,' she said, emphatically. 'It says they can hear us . . . and when I try to press it, it becomes . . . well, it becomes sullen. And it's not supposed to—— Whoever heard of a sullen robot?'

'Suppose you tell us what you have, Susan,' said Bogert.

'Here it is! It admits it controls the ship itself entirely. It is definitely optimistic about their safety, but without details. I don't dare press it. However, the centre of disturbance seems to be about the interstellar jump itself. The Brain definitely laughed when I brought up the subject. There are other indications, but that is the closest it's come to an open abnormality.'

She looked at the others, 'I refer to hysteria. I dropped the subject immediately, and I hope I did no harm, but it gave me a lead. I can handle hysteria. Give me twelve hours! If I can bring it back to normal, it will bring back the ship.'

Bogert seemed suddenly stricken. 'The interstellar jump!'

'What's the matter?' The cry was double from Calvin and Lanning.

'The figures for the engine The Brain gave us. Say . . . I just thought of something.'

He left hurriedly.

Lanning gazed after him. He said brusquely to Calvin, 'You take care of your end, Susan.'

Two hours later, Bogert was talking eagerly, 'I tell you, Lanning, that's it. The interstellar jump is not instantaneous – not as long as the speed of light is finite. Life can't exist . . . *matter and energy* as such can't exist in the space warp. I don't know what it would be like – but that's it. That's what killed Consolidated's robot.'

. . .

Donovan felt as haggard as he looked. 'Only five days?'

'Only five days. I'm sure of it.'

Donovan looked about him wretchedly. The stars through the glass were familiar but infinitely indifferent. The walls were cold to the touch; the lights, which had recently flared up again, were unfeelingly bright; the needle on the gauge pointed stubbornly to zero; and Donovan could not get rid of the taste of beans.

He said, morosely, 'I need a bath.'

Powell looked up briefly, and said, 'So do I. You needn't feel selfconscious. But unless you want to bathe in milk and do without drinking——'

'We'll do without drinking eventually, anyway. Greg, where does this interstellar travel come in?'

'You tell me. Maybe we just keep on going. We'd get there, eventually. At least the dust of our skeletons would – but isn't our death the whole point of The Brain's original breakdown?'

Donovan spoke with his back to the other, 'Greg, I've been thinking. It's pretty bad. There's not much to do – except walk around or talk to yourself. You know those stories about guys marooned in space. They go nuts long before they starve. I don't know, Greg, but ever since the lights went on, I feel funny.'

There was a silence, then Powell's voice came thin and small 'So do I. What's it like?'

The redheaded figure turned, 'Feel funny inside. There's a pounding in me with everything tense. It's hard to breathe. I can't stand still.'

'Um-m-m. Do you feel vibration?'

'How do you mean?'

'Sit down for a minute and listen. You don't hear it, but you feel it – as if something's throbbing somewheres and it's throbbing the whole ship, and you, too, along with it. Listen——'

'Yeah . . . yeah. What do you think it is, Greg? You don't suppose it's us?'

'It might be.' Powell stroked his moustache slowly. 'But it might be the ship's engines. It might be getting ready.'

'For what?'

'For the interstellar jump. It may be coming and the devil knows what it's like.'

Donovan pondered. Then he said, savagely, 'If it does, let it. But I wish we could fight. It's humiliating to have to wait for it.'

An hour later, perhaps, Powell looked at his hand on the metal chair-arm and said with frozen calm, 'Feel the wall, Mike.'

Donovan did, and said, 'You can feel it shake, Greg.'

Even the stars seemed blurred. From somewhere came the vague impression of a huge machine gathering power with the walls, storing up energy for a mighty leap, throbbing its way up the scales of strength.

It came with a suddenness and a stab of pain. Powell stiffened, and half-jerked from his chair. His sight caught Donovan and blanked out while Donovan's thin shout whimpered and died in his ears. Something writhed within him and struggled against a growing blanket of ice, that thickened.

Something broke loose and whirled in a blaze of flickering light and pain. It fell——

——and whirled

——and fell headlong

——into silence!

It was death!

It was a world of no motion and no sensation. A world of dim, unsensing consciousness; a consciousness of darkness and of silence and of formless struggle.

Most of all a consciousness of eternity.

He was a tiny white thread of ego – cold and afraid.

Then the words came, unctuous and sonorous, thundering over him in a foam of sound:

'Does your coffin fit differently lately? Why not try Morbid M. Cadaver's extensible caskets? They are scientifically designed to fit the natural curves of the body, and are enriched with Vitamin B_1. Use Cadaver's caskets for comfort. Remember – you're – going – to – be – dead – a – long – long – time!'

It wasn't quite sound, but whatever it was, it died away in an oily rumbling whisper.

The white thread that might have been Powell heaved uselessly at the insubstantial eons of time that existed all about him – and collapsed upon itself as the piercing shriek of a hundred million ghosts of a hundred million soprano voices rose to a crescendo of melody:

> '*I'll be glad when you're dead, you rascal, you.*
> '*I'll be glad when you're dead, you rascal, you.*
> '*I'll be glad——*'

It rose up a spiral stairway of violent sound into the keening supersonics that passed hearing, and then beyond——

. . .

The white thread quivered with a pulsating pang. It strained quietly——

The voices were ordinary – and many. It was a crowd speaking; a swirling mob that swept through and past and over him with a rapid, headlong motion, that left drifting tatters of words behind them.

'What did they getcha for, boy? Y'look banged up——'

'——a hot fire, I guess, but I got a case——'

'——I've made Paradise, but old St Pete——'

'Naaah, I got a pull with the boy. Had dealings with him——'

'Hey, Sam, come this way——'

'Ja get a mouthpiece? Beelzebub says——'

'——Going on, my good imp? My appointment is with Sa——'

And above it all the original stentorian roar, that plunged across all: 'HURRY! HURRY! HURRY! Stir your bones, and don't keep us waiting – there are many more in line. Have your certificates ready, and make sure Peter's release is stamped across it. See if you are at the proper entrance gate. There will be plenty of fire for all. Hey, you – YOU DOWN THERE TAKE YOUR PLACE IN LINE OR——'

The white thread that was Powell grovelled backward before the advancing shout, and felt the sharp stab of the pointing finger. It all exploded into a rainbow of sound that dripped its fragments on to an aching brain.

Powell was in the chair, again. He felt himself shaking.

Donovan's eyes were opening into two large popping bowls of glazed blue.

'Greg,' he whispered in what was almost a sob. 'Were you dead?'

'I ... felt dead.' He did not recognize his own croak.

Donovan was obviously making a bad failure of his attempt to stand up, 'Are we alive now? Or is there more?'

'I ... feel alive.' It was the same hoarseness. Powell said cautiously, 'Did you ... hear anything, when ... when you were dead?'

Donovan paused, and then very slowly nodded his head, 'Did you?'

'Yes. Did you hear about coffins ... and females singing ... and the lines forming to get into Hell? Did you?'

Donovan shook his head, 'Just one voice.'

'Loud?'

'No. Soft, but rough like a file over the fingertips. It was a sermon, you know. About hell-fire. He described the tortures of ... well, *you know*. I once heard a sermon like that – almost.'

He was perspiring.

.   .   .

They were conscious of sunlight through the port. It was weak, but it was blue-white – and the gleaming pea that was the distant source of light was not Old Sol.

And Powell pointed a trembling finger at the single gauge. The needle stood stiff and proud at the hairline whose figure read 300,000 parsecs.

Powell said, 'Mike, if it's true, we must be out of the Galaxy altogether.'

Donovan said, 'Blazes! Greg! We'd be the first men out of the Solar System.'

'Yes! That's just it. We've escaped the sun. We've escaped the Galaxy. Mike, this ship is the answer. It means freedom for all humanity –

freedom to spread through to every star that exists – millions and billions and trillions of them.'

And then he came down with a hard thud, 'But how do we get back, Mike?'

Donovan smiled shakily, 'Oh, that's all right. The ship brought us here. The ship will take us back. Me for more beans.'

'But Mike ... hold on, Mike. If it takes us back the way it brought us here——'

Donovan stopped half-way up and sat back heavily into the chair.

Powell went on, 'We'll have to ... die again, Mike.'

'Well,' sighed Donovan, 'if we have to, we have to. At least it isn't permanent, not *very* permanent.'

.   .   .

Susan Calvin was speaking slowly now. For six hours she had been slowly prodding The Brain – for six fruitless hours. She was weary of repetitions, weary of circumlocutions, weary of everything.

'Now, Brain, there's just one more thing. You must make a special effort to answer simply. Have you been entirely clear about the interstellar jump? I mean does it take them very far?'

'As far as they want to go, Miss Susan. Golly, it isn't any trick through the warp.'

'And on the other side, what will they see?'

'Stars and stuff. What do you suppose?'

The next question slipped out, 'They'll be alive, then?'

'Sure!'

'And the interstellar jump won't hurt them?'

She froze as The Brain maintained silence. That was it! She had touched the sore spot.

'Brain,' she supplicated faintly, 'Brain, do you hear me?'

The answer was weak, quivering. The Brain said, 'Do I have to answer? About the jump, I mean?'

'Not if you don't want to. But it would be interesting – I mean if you wanted to.' Susan Calvin tried to be bright about it.

'Aw-w-w. You spoil everything.'

And the psychologist jumped up suddenly, with a look of flaming insight on her face.

'Oh, my,' she gasped. 'Oh, my.'

And she felt the tension of hours and days released in a burst. It was later that she told Lanning, 'I tell you it's all right. No, you must leave me alone, now. The ship will be back safely, *with* the men, and I want to rest. I *will* rest. Now go away.'

.   .   .

The ship returned to Earth as silently, as unjarringly as it had left. It dropped precisely into place and the main lock gaped open. The two men who walked out felt their way carefully and scratched their rough and scrubbily-stubbled chins.

And then, slowly and purposefully, the one with red hair knelt down and planted upon the concrete of the runway a firm, loud kiss.

They waved aside the crowd that was gathering and made gestures of denial at the eager couple that had piled out of the down-swooping ambulance with a stretcher between them.

Gregory Powell said, 'Where's the nearest shower?'

They were led away.

They were gathered, all of them, about a table. It was a full staff meeting of the brains of U.S. Robot & Mechanical Men Corp.

Slowly and climactically, Powell and Donovan finished a graphic and resounding story.

Susan Calvin broke the silence that followed. In the few days that had elapsed she had recovered her icy, somewhat acid, calm – but still a trace of embarrassment broke through.

'Strictly speaking,' she said, 'this was my fault – all of it. When we first presented this problem to The Brain, as I hope some of you remember, I went to great lengths to impress upon it the importance of rejecting any item of information capable of creating a dilemma. In doing so I said something like "Don't get excited about the death of humans. We don't mind it at all. Just give the sheet back and forget it.'

'Hm-m-m,' said Lanning. 'What follows?'

'The obvious. When that item entered its calculations which yielded the equation controlling the length of minimum interval for the interstellar jump – it meant death for humans. That's where Consolidated's machine broke down completely. But I had depressed the importance of death to The Brain – not entirely, for the First Law can never be broken – but just sufficiently so that The Brain could take a second look at the equation. Sufficiently to give it time to realize that after the interval was passed through, the men would return to life – just as the matter and energy of the ship itself would return to being. This so-called "death", in other words, was a strictly temporary phenomenon. You see?'

She looked about her. They were all listening.

She went on, 'So he accepted the item, but not without a certain jar. Even with death temporary and its importance depressed, it was enough to unbalance him very gently.'

She brought it out calmly, 'He developed a sense of humour – it's an escape, you see, a method of partial escape from reality. He became a practical joker.'

Powell and Donovan were on their feet.

'What?' cried Powell.

Donovan was considerably more colourful about it.

'It's so,' said Calvin. 'He took care of you, and kept you safe, but you couldn't handle any controls, because they weren't for you – just for the humorous Brain. We could reach you by radio, but you couldn't answer. You had plenty of food, but all of it was beans and milk. Then you died, so to speak, and were reborn, but the period of your death was made . . . well . . . interesting. I wish I knew how he did it. It was The Brain's prize little joke, but he meant no harm.'

'No harm!' gasped Donovan. 'Oh, if that cute little tyke only had a neck.'

Lanning raised a quieting hand, 'All right, it's been a mess, but it's all over. What now?'

'Well,' said Bogert, quietly, 'obviously it's up to us to improve the space-warp engine. There must be some way of getting around that interval of jump. If there is, we're the only organization left with a grand-scale super-robot, so we're bound to find it if anyone. And then – U.S. Robots has interstellar travel, and humanity has the opportunity for galactic empire.'

'What about Consolidated?' said Lanning.

'Hey,' interrupted Donovan suddenly, 'I want to make a suggestion there. They landed U.S. Robots into quite a mess. It wasn't as bad a mess as they expected and it turned out well, but their intentions weren't pious. And Greg and I bore the most of it.

'Well, they wanted an answer, and they've got one. Send them that ship, guaranteed, and U.S. Robots can collect their two hundred thou plus construction costs. And if they test it – then suppose we let The Brain have just a little more fun before it's brought back to normal.'

Lanning said gravely, 'It sounds just and proper to me.'

To which Bogert added absently, 'Strictly according to contract, too.'

CHAPTER 8

EVIDENCE

'But that wasn't it, either,' said Dr Calvin thoughtfully. 'Oh, eventually, the ship and others like it became government property; the Jump through hyperspace was perfected, and now we actually have human colonies on the planets of some of the nearer stars, but that wasn't it.'

I had finished eating and watched her through the smoke of my cigarette.

'It's what has happened to the people here on Earth in the last fifty years that really counts. When I was born, young man, we had just gone through the last World War. It was a low point in history – but it was the end of nationalism. Earth was too small for nations and they began grouping themselves into Regions. It took quite a while. When I was born the United States of America was still a nation and not merely a part of the Northern Region. In fact, the name of the corporation is still "United States Robots———". And the change from nations to Regions, which has stabilized our economy and brought about what amounts to a Golden Age, when this century is compared with the last, was also brought about by our robots.'

'You mean the Machines,' I said. 'The Brain you talked about was the first of the Machines, wasn't it?'

'Yes, it was, but it's not the Machines I was thinking of. Rather of a man. He died last year.' Her voice was suddenly deeply sorrowful. 'Or at least he arranged to die, because he knew we needed him no longer. ———Stephen Byerley.'

'Yes, I guessed that was who you meant.'

'He first entered public office in 2032. You were only a boy then, so you wouldn't remember the strangeness of it. His campaign for the Mayoralty was certainly the queerest in history———'

. . . .

Francis Quinn was a politician of the new school. That, of course, is a meaningless expression, as are all expressions of the sort. Most of the 'new schools' we have were duplicated in the social life of ancient Greece, and perhaps, if we knew more about it, in the social life of ancient Sumeria and in the lake dwellings of prehistoric Switzerland as well.

But, to get out from under what promises to be a dull and complicated beginning, it might be best to state hastily that Quinn neither ran for office nor canvassed for votes, made no speeches and stuffed no ballot boxes. Any more than Napoleon pulled a trigger at Austerlitz.

And since politics makes strange bedfellows, Alfred Lanning sat at the other side of the desk with his ferocious white eyebrows bent far forward over eyes in which chronic impatience had sharpened to acuity. He was not pleased.

The fact, if known to Quinn, would have annoyed him not the least. His voice was friendly, perhaps professionally so.

'I assume you know Stephen Byerley, Dr Lanning.'

'I have heard of him. So have many people.'

'Yes, so have I. Perhaps you intend voting for him at the next election.'

'I couldn't say.' There was an unmistakable trace of acidity here. 'I have not followed the political currents, so I'm not aware that he is running for office.'

'He may be our next mayor. Of course, he is only a lawyer now, but great oaks——'

'Yes,' interrupted Lanning. 'I have heard the phrase before. But I wonder if we can get to the business at hand.'

'We *are* at the business at hand, Dr Lanning.' Quinn's tone was very gentle, 'It is to my interest to keep Mr Byerley a district attorney at the very most, and it is to your interest to help me do so.'

'To *my* interest? Come!' Lanning's eyebrows hunched low.

'Well, say then to the interest of the U.S. Robot & Mechanical Men Corporation. I come to you as Director-Emeritus of Research, because I know that your connection to them is that of, shall we say, "elder statesman". You are listened to with respect and yet your connection with them is no longer so tight but that you cannot possess considerable freedom of action; even if the action is somewhat unorthodox.'

Dr Lanning was silent a moment, chewing the cud of his thoughts. He said more softly, 'I don't follow you at all, Mr Quinn.'

'I am not surprised, Dr Lanning. But it's all rather simple. Do you mind?' Quinn lit a slender cigarette with a lighter of tasteful simplicity and his big-boned face settled into an expression of quiet amusement. 'We have spoken of Mr Byerley – a strange and colourful character. He was unknown three years ago. He is very well known now. He is a man of force and ability, and certainly the most capable and intelligent prosecutor I have ever known. Unfortunately he is not a friend of mine——'

'I understand,' said Lanning, mechanically. He stared at his fingernails.

'I have had occasion,' continued Quinn, evenly, 'in the past year to investigate Mr Byerley – quite exhaustively. It is always useful, you see, to subject the past life of reform politicians to rather inquisitive research. If you knew how often it helped——' He paused to smile humourlessly at the glowing tip of his cigarette. 'But Mr Byerley's past is unremarkable.

A quiet life in a small town, a college education, a wife who died young, an auto accident with a slow recovery, law school, coming to the metropolis, an attorney.'

Francis Quinn shook his head slowly, then added, 'But his present life. Ah, that is remarkable. Our district attorney never eats!'

Lanning's head snapped up, old eyes surprisingly sharp, 'Pardon me?'

'Our district attorney never eats.' The repetition thumped by syllables. 'I'll modify that slightly. He has never been seen to eat or drink. Never! Do you understand the significance of the word? Not rarely, but never!'

'I find that quite incredible. Can you trust your investigators?'

'I can trust my investigators, and I don't find it incredible at all. Further, our district attorney has never been seen to drink – in the aqueous sense as well as the alcoholic – nor to sleep. There are other factors, but I should think I have made my point.'

. . .

Lanning leaned back in his seat, and there was the rapt silence of challenge and response between them, and then the old roboticist shook his head. 'No. There is only one thing you can be trying to imply, if I couple your statements with the fact that you present them to me, and that is impossible.'

'But the man is quite inhuman, Dr Lanning.'

'If you told me he were Satan in masquerade, there would be a faint chance that I might believe you.'

'I tell you he is a robot, Dr Lanning.'

'I tell you it is as impossible a conception as I have ever heard, Mr Quinn.'

Again the combative silence.

'Nevertheless,' and Quinn stubbed out his cigarette with elaborate care, 'you will have to investigate this impossibility with all the resources of the Corporation.'

'I'm sure that I could undertake no such thing, Mr Quinn. You don't seriously suggest that the Corporation take part in local politics.'

'You have no choice. Supposing I were to make my facts public without proof. The evidence is circumstantial enough.'

'Suit yourself in that respect.'

'But it would not suit me. Proof would be much preferable. And it would not suit *you*, for the publicity would be very damaging to your company. You are perfectly well acquainted, I suppose, with the strict rules against the use of robots on inhabited worlds.'

'Certainly!' – brusquely.

'You know that the U.S. Robot & Mechanical Men Corporation is the only manufacturer of positronic robots in the Solar System, and if Byerley is a robot, he is a *positronic* robot. You are also aware that all positronic robots are leased, and not sold; that the Corporation remains the owner and manager of each robot, and is therefore responsible for the actions of all.'

'It is an easy matter, Mr Quinn, to prove the Corporation has never manufactured a robot of a humanoid character.'

'It can be done? To discuss merely possibilities.'

'Yes. It can be done.'

'Secretly, I imagine, as well. Without entering it in your books.'

'Not the positronic brain, sir. Too many factors are involved in that, and there is the tightest possible government supervision.'

'Yes, but robots are worn out, break down, go out of order – and are dismantled.'

'And the positronic brains re-used or destroyed.'

'Really?' Francis Quinn allowed himself a trace of sarcasm. 'And if one were, accidentally, of course, not destroyed – and there happened to be a humanoid structure waiting for a brain.'

'Impossible!'

'You would have to prove that to the government and the public, so why not prove it to me now.'

'But what could our purpose be?' demanded Lanning in exasperation. 'Where is our motivation? Credit us with a minimum of sense.'

'My dear sir, please. The Corporation would be only too glad to have the various Regions permit the use of humanoid positronic robots on inhabited worlds. The profits would be enormous. But the prejudice of the public against such a practice is too great. Suppose you get them used to such robots first – see, we have a skilful lawyer, a good mayor, – and he is a robot. Won't you buy our robot butlers?'

'Thoroughly fantastic. An almost humorous descent to the ridiculous.'

'I imagine so. Why not prove it? Or would you still rather try to prove it to the public?'

The light in the office was dimming, but it was not yet too dim to obscure the flush of frustration on Alfred Lanning's face. Slowly, the roboticist's finger touched a knob and the wall illuminators glowed to gentle life.

'Well, then,' he growled, 'let us see.'

. . .

The face of Stephen Byerley is not an easy one to describe. He was forty by birth certificate and forty by appearance – but it was a healthy, well-nourished good-natured appearance of forty; one that automatically drew the teeth of the bromide about 'looking one's age'.

This was particularly true when he laughed, and he was laughing now. It came loudly and continuously, died away for a bit, then began again——

And Alfred Lanning's face contracted into a rigidly bitter monument of disapproval. He made a half gesture to the woman who sat beside him, but her thin, bloodless lips merely pursed themselves a trifle.

Byerley gasped himself a state nearer normality.

'Really, Dr Lanning ... really – I ... *I* ... a robot?'

Lanning bit his words off with a snap, 'It is no statement of mine, sir. I would be quite satisfied to have you a member of humanity. Since our corporation never manufactured you, I am quite certain that you are – in a legalistic sense, at any rate. But since the contention that you are a robot has been advanced to us seriously by a man of certain standing——'

'Don't mention his name, if it would knock a chip off your granite block of ethics, but let's pretend it was Frank Quinn, for the sake of argument, and continue.'

Lanning drew in a sharp, cutting snort at the interruption, and paused ferociously before continuing with added frigidity, '——by a man of certain standing, with whose identity I am not interested in playing guessing games, I am bound to ask your co-operation in disproving it. The mere fact that such a contention could be advanced and publicized by the means at this man's disposal would be a bad blow to the company I represent – even if the charge were never proven. You understand me?'

'Oh, yes, your position is clear to me. The charge itself is ridiculous. The spot you find yourself in is not. I beg your pardon, if my laughter offended you. It was the first I laughed at, not the second. How can I help you?'

'It could be very simple. You have only to sit down to a meal at a restaurant in the presence of witnesses, have your picture taken, and eat.' Lanning sat back in his chair, the worst of the interview over. The woman beside him watched Byerley with an apparently absorbed expression but contributed nothing of her own.

Stephen Byerley met her eyes for an instant, was caught by them, then turned back to the roboticist. For a while his fingers were thoughtful over the bronze paper-weight that was the only ornament on his desk.

He said quietly, 'I don't think I can oblige you.'

He raised his hand, 'Now wait, Dr Lanning. I appreciate the fact that this whole matter is distasteful to you, that you have been forced into it against your will, that you feel you are playing an undignified and even ridiculous part. Still, the matter is even more intimately concerned with myself, so be tolerant.

'First, what makes you think that Quinn – this man of certain standing, you know – wasn't hoodwinking you, in order to get you to do exactly what you are doing?'

'Why, it seems scarcely likely that a reputable person would endanger himself in so ridiculous a fashion, if he weren't convinced he were on safe ground.'

There was little humour in Byerley's eyes, 'You don't know Quinn. He could manage to make safe ground out of a ledge a mountain sheep could not handle. I suppose he showed the particulars of the investigation he claims to have made of me?'

'Enough to convince me that it would be too troublesome to have our corporation attempt to disprove them when you could do so more easily.'

'Then you believe him when he says I never eat. You are a scientist, Dr Lanning. Think of the logic required. I have not been observed to eat, therefore, I never eat Q.E.D. After all!'

'You are using prosecution tactics to confuse what is really a very simple situation.'

'On the contrary, I am trying to clarify what you and Quinn between you are making a very complicated one. You see, I don't sleep much, that's true, and I certainly don't sleep in public. I have never cared to eat with others – an idiosyncrasy which is unusual and probably neurotic in character, but which harms no one. Look, Dr Lanning, let me present you with a suppositious case. Supposing we had a politician who was interested in defeating a reform candidate at any cost and while investigating his private life came across oddities such as I have just mentioned.

'Suppose further that in order to smear the candidate effectively, he comes to your company as the ideal agent. Do you expect him to say to you, "So-and-so is a robot because he hardly ever eats with people, and I have never seen him fall asleep in the middle of a case; and once when I peeped into his window in the middle of the night, there he was, sitting up with a book; and I looked in his frigidaire and there was no food in it"?

'If he told you that, you would send for a straitjacket. But if he tells you, "He *never* sleeps; he *never* eats," then the shock of the statement blinds you to the fact that such statements are impossible to prove. You play into his hands by contributing to the to-do.'

'Regardless, sir,' began Lanning, with a threatening obstinacy, 'of whether you consider this matter serious or not, it will require only the meal I mentioned to end it.'

Again Byerley turned to the woman, who still regarded him expressionlessly. 'Pardon me. I've caught your name correctly, haven't I? Dr Susan Calvin?'

'Yes, Mr Byerley.'

'You're the U.S. Robot's psychologist, aren't you?'

'*Robo*psychologist, please.'

'Oh, are robots so different from men, mentally?'

'Worlds different.' She allowed herself a frosty smile, 'Robots are essentially decent.'

Humour tugged at the corners of the lawyer's mouth, 'Well, that's a hard blow. But what I wanted to say was this. Since you're a psycho – a robopsychologist, *and* a woman, I'll bet that you've done something that Dr Lanning hasn't thought of.'

'And what is that?'

'You've got something to eat in your purse.'

Something caught in the schooled indifference of Susan Calvin's eyes. She said, 'You surprise me, Mr Byerley.'

And opening her purse, she produced an apple. Quietly, she handed it to him. Dr Lanning, after an initial start, followed the slow movement from one hand to the other with sharply alert eyes.

Calmly, Stephen Byerley bit into it, and calmly he swallowed it.

'You see, Dr Lanning?'

Dr Lanning smiled in a relief tangible enough to make even his eyebrows appear benevolent. A relief that survived for one fragile second.

Susan Calvin said, 'I was curious to see if you would eat it, but, of course, in the present case, it proves nothing.'

Byerley grinned, 'It doesn't?'

'Of course not. It is obvious, Dr Lanning, that if this man were a humanoid robot, he would be a perfect imitation. He is almost too human to be credible. After all, we have been seeing and observing human beings all our lives; it would be impossible to palm something merely nearly right off on us. It would have to be *all* right. Observe the texture of the skin, the quality of the irises, the bone formation of the hand. If he's a robot, I wish U.S. Robots *had* made him, because he's a good job. Do you suppose then, that anyone capable of paying attention to such niceties would neglect a few gadgets to take care of such things as eating, sleeping, elimination? For emergency use only, perhaps; as, for instance, to prevent such situations as are arising here. So a meal won't prove anything.'

'Now wait,' snarled Lanning, 'I am not quite the fool both of you make me out to be. I am not interested in the problem of Mr Byerley's humanity or nonhumanity. I am interested in getting the corporation out of a hole. A public meal will end the matter and keep it ended no matter what Quinn does. We can leave the finer details to lawyers and robopsychologists.'

'But, Dr Lanning,' said Byerley, 'you forget the politics of the situation. I am as anxious to be elected, as Quinn is to stop me. By the way, did you notice that you used his name. It's a cheap shyster trick of mine; I knew you would, before you were through.'

Lanning flushed, 'What has the election to do with it?'

'Publicity works both ways, sir. If Quinn wants to call me a robot, and has the nerve to do so, I have the nerve to play the game his way.'

'You mean you——' Lanning was quite frankly appalled.

'Exactly. I mean that I'm going to let him go ahead, choose his rope, test its strength, cut off the right length, tie the noose, insert his head and grin. I can do what little else is required.'

'You are mighty confident.'

Susan Calvin rose to her feet, 'Come, Alfred, we won't change his mind for him.'

'You see.' Byerley smiled gently. 'You're a human psychologist, too.'

. . .

But perhaps not all the confidence that Dr Lanning had remarked upon was present that evening when Byerley's car parked on the automatic treads leading to the sunken garage, and Byerley himself crossed the path to the front door of his house.

The figure in the wheel-chair looked up as he entered and smiled. Byerley's face lit with affection. He crossed over to it.

The cripple's voice was a hoarse, grating whisper that came out of a mouth forever twisted to one side, leering out of a face that was half scar tissue, 'You're late, Steve.'

'I know, John, I know. But I've been up against a peculiar and interesting trouble today.'

'So?' Neither the torn face nor the destroyed voice could carry expression but there was anxiety in the clear eyes. 'Nothing you can't handle?'

'I'm not exactly certain. I may need your help. *You're* the brilliant one in the family. Do you want me to take you out into the garden? It's a beautiful evening.'

Two strong arms lifted John from the wheel-chair. Gently, almost caressingly, Byerley's arms went around the shoulders and under the swathed legs of the cripple. Carefully, and slowly, he walked through the rooms, down the gentle ramp that had been built with a wheel-chair in mind, and out of the back door into the walled and wired garden behind the house.

'Why don't you let me use the wheel-chair, Steve? This is silly.'

'Because I'd rather carry you. Do you object? You know that you're as glad to get out of that motorized buggy for a while as I am to see you out. How do you feel today?' He deposited John with infinite care upon the cool grass.

'How should I feel? But tell me about your trouble.'

'Quinn's campaign will be based on the fact that he claims I'm a robot.'

John's eyes opened wide, 'How do you know? It's impossible. I won't believe it.'

'Oh, come, I tell you it's so. He had one of the big-shot scientists of U.S. Robot & Mechanical Men Corporation over at the office to argue with me.'

Slowly John's hands tore at the grass, 'I see. I see.'

Byerley said, 'But we can let him choose his ground. I have an idea. Listen to me and tell me if we can do it——'

. . .

The scene as it appeared in Alfred Lanning's office that night was a tableau of stares. Francis Quinn stared meditatively at Alfred Lanning. Lanning's stare was savagely set upon Susan Calvin, who stared impassively in her turn at Quinn.

Francis Quinn broke it with a heavy attempt at lightness, 'Bluff. He's making it up as he goes along.'

'Are you going to gamble on that, Mr Quinn?' asked Dr Calvin, indifferently.

'Well, it's your gamble, really.'

'Look here,' Lanning covered definite pessimism with bluster, 'we've done what you asked. We witnessed the man eat. It's ridiculous to presume him a robot.'

'Do *you* think so?' Quinn shot towards Calvin. 'Lanning said you were the expert.'

Lanning was almost threatening, 'Now, Susan——'

Quinn interrupted smoothly, 'Why not let her talk, man? She's been sitting there imitating a gatepost for half an hour.'

Lanning felt definitely harassed. From what he experienced then to incipient paranoia was but a step. He said, 'Very well. Have your say, Susan. We won't interrupt you.'

Susan Calvin glanced at him humourlessly, then fixed cold eyes on Mr Quinn. 'There are only two ways of definitely proving Byerley to be a robot, sir. So far you are presenting circumstantial evidence, with which you can accuse, but not prove – and I think Mr Byerley is sufficiently clever to counter that sort of material. You probably think so yourself, or you wouldn't have come here.

'The two methods of *proof* are the physical and the psychological. Physically, you can dissect him or use an X-ray. How to do that would be *your* problem. Psychologically, his behaviour can be studied, for if he *is* a positronic robot, he must conform to the three Rules of Robotics. A positronic brain cannot be constructed without them. You know the Rules, Mr Quinn?'

She spoke them carefully, clearly, quoting word for word the famous bold print on page one of the 'Handbook of Robotics'.

'I've heard of them,' said Quinn, carelessly.

'Then the matter is easy to follow,' responded the psychologist, dryly, 'If Mr Byerley breaks any of those three rules, he is not a robot. Unfortunately, this procedure works in only one direction. If he lives up to the rules, it proves nothing one way or the other.'

Quinn raised polite eyebrows, 'Why not, doctor?'

'Because, if you stop to think of it, the three Rules of Robotics are the essential guiding principles of a good many of the world's ethical systems. Of course, every human being is supposed to have the instinct of self-preservation. That's Rule Three to a robot. Also every "good" human being, with a social conscience and a sense of responsibility, is supposed to defer to proper authority; to listen to his doctor, his boss, his government, his psychiatrist, his fellow man; to obey laws, to follow rules, to conform to custom – even when they interfere with his comfort or his safety. That's Rule Two to a robot. Also, every "good" human being is supposed to love others as himself, protect his fellow man, risk his life to save another. That's Rule One to a robot. To put it simply – if Byerley follows all the Rules of Robotics, he may be a robot, and may simply be a very good man.'

'But,' said Quinn, 'you're telling me that you can never prove him a robot.'

'I may be able to prove him *not* a robot.'

'That's not the proof I want.'

'You'll have such proof as exists. You are the only one responsible for your own wants.'

. . .

Here Lanning's mind leaped suddenly to the sting of an idea, 'Has it occurred to anyone,' he ground out, 'that district attorney is a rather strange occupation for a robot? The prosecution of human beings – sentencing him to death – bringing about their inifinite harm——'

Quinn grew suddenly keen, 'No, you can't get out of it that way. Being district attorney doesn't make him human. Don't you know his record? Don't you know that he boasts that he has never prosecuted an innocent man; that there are scores of people left untried because the evidence against them didn't satisfy him, even though he could probably have argued a jury into atomizing them? That happens to be so.'

Lanning's thin cheeks quivered, 'No, Quinn, no. There is nothing in the Rules of Robotics that makes any allowance for human guilt. A robot may not judge whether a human being deserves death. It is not for him to decide. *He may not harm a human* – variety skunk, or variety angel.'

Susan Calvin sounded tired. 'Alfred,' she said, 'don't talk foolishly. What if a robot came upon a madman about to set fire to a house with people in it. He would stop the madman, wouldn't he?'

'Of course.'

'And if the only way he could stop him was to kill him——'

There was a faint sound in Lanning's throat. Nothing more.

'The answer to that, Alfred, is that he would do his best not to kill him. If the madman died, the robot would require psychotherapy because he might easily go mad at the conflict presented him – of having broken Rule One to adhere to Rule One in a higher sense. But a man would be dead and a robot would have killed him.'

'Well, *is* Byerley mad?' demanded Lanning, with all the sarcasm he could muster.

'No, but he has killed no man himself. He has exposed facts which might represent a particular human being to be dangerous to the large mass of other human beings we call society. He protects the greater number and thus adheres to Rule One at maximum potential. That is as far as he goes. It is the judge who then condemns the criminal to death or imprisonment, after the jury decides on his guilt or innocence. It is the jailer who imprisons him, the executioner who kills him. And Mr Byerley has done nothing but determine truth and aid society.

'As a matter of fact, Mr Quinn, I have looked into Mr Byerley's career since you first brought this matter to our attention. I find that he has never demanded the death sentence in his closing speeches to the jury. I also find that he has spoken on behalf of the abolition of capital punishment and contributed generously to research institutions engaged in criminal neurophysiology. He apparently believes in the cure, rather than the punishment of crime. I find that significant.'

'You do?' Quinn smiled. 'Significant of a certain odour of roboticity, perhaps?'

'Perhaps. Why deny it? Actions such as his could come only from a robot, or from a very honourable and decent human being. But you see, you just can't differentiate between a robot and the very best of humans.'

Quinn sat back in his chair. His voice quivered with impatience. 'Dr Lanning, it's perfectly possible to create a humanoid robot that would perfectly duplicate a human in appearance, isn't it?'

Lanning harrumphed and considered, 'It's been done experimentally by U.S. Robots,' he said reluctantly, 'without the addition of a positronic brain, of course. By using human ova and hormone control, one can grow human flesh and skin over a skeleton of porous silicone plastics that would defy external examination. The eyes, the hair, the skin would be really human, not humanoid. And if you put a positronic brain, and such other gadgets as you might desire inside, you have a humanoid robot.'

Quinn said shortly, 'How long would it take to make one?'

Lanning considered, 'If you had all your equipment – the brain, the skeleton, the ovum, the proper hormones and radiations – say, two months.'

The politician straightened out of his chair. 'Then we shall see what the insides of Mr Byerley look like. It will mean publicity for U.S. Robots – but I gave you your chance.'

Lanning turned impatiently to Susan Calvin, when they were alone. 'Why do you insist——'

And with real feeling, she responded sharply and instantly, 'Which do you want – the truth or my resignation? I won't lie for you. U.S. Robots can take care of itself. Don't turn coward.'

'What,' said Lanning, 'if he opens up Byerley, and wheels and gears fall out. What then?'

'He won't open Byerley,' said Calvin, disdainfully. 'Byerley is as clever as Quinn, at the very least.'

. . .

The news broke upon the city a week before Byerley was to have been nominated. But 'broke' is the wrong word. It staggered upon the city, shambled, crawled. Laughter began, and wit was free. And as the far off hand of Quinn tightened its pressure in easy stages, the laughter grew forced, an element of hollow uncertainty entered, and people broke off to wonder.

The convention itself had the air of a restive stallion. There had been no contest planned. Only Byerley could possibly have been nominated a week earlier. There was no substitute even now. They had to nominate him, but there was complete confusion about it.

It would not have been so bad if the average individual were not torn between the enormity of the charge, if true, and its sensational folly, if false.

The day after Byerley was nominated perfunctorily, hollowly – a newspaper finally published the gist of a long interview with Dr Susan Calvin, 'world famous expert on robopsychology and positronics.'

What broke loose is popularly and succinctly described as hell.

It was what the Fundamentalists were waiting for. They were not a political party; they made pretence to no formal religion. Essentially they were those who had not adapted themselves to what had once been called the Atomic Age, in the days when atoms were a novelty. Actually, they were the Simple-Lifers, hungering after a life, which to those who lived it had probably appeared not so Simple, and who had been, therefore, Simple-Lifers themselves.

The Fundamentalists required no new reason to detest robots and robot manufacturers; but a new reason such as the Quinn accusation and the Calvin analysis was sufficient to make sure detestation audible.

The huge plants of the U.S. Robot & Mechanical Men Corporation was a hive that spawned armed guards. It prepared for war.

Within the city the house of Stephen Byerley bristled with police.

The political campaign, of course, lost all other issues, and resembled a campaign only in that it was something filling the hiatus between nomination and election.

. . .

Stephen Byerley did not allow the fussy little man to distract him. He remained comfortably unperturbed by the uniforms in the background. Outside the house, past the line of grim guards, reporters and photographers waited according to the tradition of the caste. One enterprising 'visor station even had a scanner focused on the blank entrance to the prosecutor's unpretentious home, while a synthetically excited announcer filled in with inflated commentary.

The fussy little man advanced. He held forward a rich, complicated sheet. 'This, Mr Byerley, is a court order authorizing me to search these premises for the presence of illegal . . . uh . . . mechanical men or robots of any description.'

Byerley half rose, and took the paper. He glanced at it indifferently, and smiled as he handed it back. 'All in order. Go ahead. Do your job. Mrs Hoppen' – to his housekeeper, who appeared reluctantly from the next room – 'please go with them, and help out if you can.'

The little man, whose name was Harroway, hesitated, produced an unmistakable blush, failed completely to catch Byerley's eyes, and muttered, 'Come on', to the two policemen.

He was back in ten minutes.

'Through?' questioned Byerley, in just the tone of a person who is not particularly interested in the question, or its answer.

Harroway cleared his throat, made a bad start in falsetto, and began again, angrily, 'Look here, Mr Byerley, our special instructions were to search the house very thoroughly.'

'And haven't you?'

'We were told exactly what to look for.'

'Yes?'

'In short, Mr Byerley, and not to put too fine a point on it, we were told to search you.'

'Me?' said the prosecutor with a broadening smile. 'And how do you intend to do that?'

'We have a Penet-radiation unit——'

'Then I'm to have my X-ray photograph taken, hey? You have the authority?'

'You saw my warrant.'

'May I see it again?'

Harroway, his forehead shining with considerably more than mere enthusiasm, passed it over a second time.

Byerley said evenly, 'I read here as the description of what you are to search; I quote: "the dwelling place belonging to Stephen Allen Byerley, located at 355 Willow Grove, Evanstron, together with any garage, storehouse or other structures or buildings thereto appertaining, together with all grounds thereto appertaining" ... um ... and so on. Quite in order. But, my good man, it doesn't say anything about searching my interior. I am not part of the premises. You may search my clothes if you think I've got a robot hidden in my pocket.'

Harroway had no doubt on the point of to whom he owed his job. He did not propose to be backward, given a chance to earn a much better – i.e., more highly paid – job.

He said, in a faint echo of bluster, 'Look here. I'm allowed to search the furniture in your house, and anything else I find in it. You are in it, aren't you?'

'A remarkable observation. I *am* in it. But I'm not a piece of furniture. As a citizen of adult responsibility – I have the psychiatric certificate proving that – I have certain rights under the Regional Articles. Searching me would come under the heading of violating my Right of Privacy. That paper isn't sufficient.'

'Sure, but if you're a robot, you don't have Right of Privacy.'

'True enough – but that paper still isn't sufficient. It recognizes me implicitly as a human being.'

'Where?' Harroway snatched at it.

'Where it says "the dwelling place belonging to" and so on. A robot cannot own property. And you may tell your employer, Mr Harroway, that if he tries to issue a similar paper which does *not* implicitly recognize me as a human being, he will be immediately faced with a restraining injunction and a civil suit which will make it necessary for him to *prove* me a robot by means of information *now* in his possession, or else to pay a whopping penalty for an attempt to deprive me unduly of my Rights under the Regional Articles. You'll tell him that, won't you?'

Harroway marched to the door. He turned. 'You're a slick lawyer——' His hand was in his pocket. For a short moment, he stood there. Then he left, smiled in the direction of the 'visor scanner, still playing away – waved to the reporters, and shouted, 'We'll have something for you tomorrow, boys. No kidding.'

In his ground car, he settled back, removed the tiny mechanism from his pocket and carefully inspected it. It was the first time he had ever taken a photograph by X-ray reflection. He hoped he had done it correctly.

Quinn and Byerley had never met face-to-face alone. But visorphone was pretty close to it. In fact, accepted literally, perhaps the phrase was accurate, even if to each, the other were merely the light and dark pattern of a bank of photo-cells.

It was Quinn who had initiated the call. It was Quinn, who spoke first, and without particular ceremony, 'Thought you would like to know, Byerley, that I intend to make public the fact that you're wearing a protective shield against Penet-radiation.'

'That so? In that case, you've probably already made it public. I have a notion our enterprising press representatives have been tapping my various communication lines for quite a while. I know they have my office lines full of holes; which is why I've dug in at my home these last weeks.' Byerley was friendly, almost chatty.

Quinn's lips tightened slightly, 'This call is shielded – thoroughly. I'm making it at a certain personal risk.'

'So I should imagine. Nobody knows you're behind this campaign. At least, nobody knows it officially. Nobody doesn't know it unofficially. I wouldn't worry. So I wear a protective shield? I suppose you found that out when your puppy dog's Penet-radiation photograph, the other day, turned out to be overexposed.'

'You realize, Byerley, that it would be pretty obvious to everyone that you don't dare face X-ray analysis.'

'Also that you, or your men, attempted illegal invasion of my Right of Privacy.'

'The devil they'll care for that.'

'They might. It's rather symbolic of our two campaigns, isn't it? You have little concern with the rights of the individual citizen. I have great concern. I will not submit to X-ray analysis, because I wish to maintain my Rights on principle. Just as I'll maintain the rights of others when elected.'

'That will no doubt make a very interesting speech, but no one will believe you. A little too high-sounding to be true. Another thing,' a sudden, crisp change, 'the personnel in your home was not complete the other night.'

'In what way?'

'According to the report,' he shuffled papers before him that were just within the range of vision of the visiplate, 'there was one person missing – a cripple.'

'As you say,' said Byerley, tonelessly, 'a cripple. My old teacher, who lives with me and who is now in the country – and has been for two months. A "much-needed rest" is the usual expression applied in the case. He has your permission?'

'Your teacher? A scientist of sorts?'

'A lawyer once – before he was a cripple. He has a government licence as a research biophysicist, with a laboratory of his own, and a complete description of the work he's doing filed with the proper authorities, to whom I can refer you. The work is minor, but is a harmless and engaging hobby for a – poor cripple. I am being as helpful as I can, you see.'

'I see. And what does this ... teacher ... know about robot manufacture?'

'I couldn't judge the extent of his knowledge in a field with which I am unacquainted.'

'He wouldn't have access to positronic brains?'

'Ask your friends at U.S. Robots. They'd be the ones to know.'

'I'll put it shortly, Byerley. Your crippled teacher is the real Stephen Byerley. You are his robot creation. We can prove it. It was he who was in the automobile accident, not you. There will be ways of checking the records.'

'Really? Do so, then. My best wishes.'

'And we can search your so-called teacher's "country place", and see what we can find there.'

'Well, not quite, Quinn.' Byerley smiled broadly. 'Unfortunately for you, my so-called teacher is a sick man. His country place is his place of rest. His rights of Privacy as a citizen of adult responsibility is naturally even stronger, under the circumstances. You won't be able to obtain a warrant to enter his grounds without showing just cause. However, I'd be the last to prevent you from trying.'

There was a pause of moderate length, and then Quinn leaned forward, so that his imaged-face expanded and the fine lines on his forehead were visible, 'Byerley, why do you carry on? You can't be elected.'

'Can't I?'

'Do you think you can? Do you suppose that your failure to make any attempt to disprove the robot charge – when you could easily, by breaking one of the Three Laws – does anything but convince the people that you *are* a robot?'

'All I see so far is that from being a rather vaguely known, but still largely obscure metropolitan lawyer, I have now become a world figure. You're a good publicist.'

'But you *are* a robot.'

'So it's been said, but not proven.'

'It's been proven sufficiently for the electorate.'

'Then relax – you've won.'

'Goodbye,' said Quinn, with his first touch of viciousness, and the visorphone slammed off.

'Goodbye,' said Byerley imperturbably, to the blank plate.

. . .

Byerley brought his 'teacher' back the week before election. The air car dropped quickly in an obscure part of the city.

'You'll stay here till after election,' Byerley told him. 'It would be better to have you out of the way if things take a bad turn.'

The hoarse voice that twisted painfully out of John's crooked mouth might have had accents of concern in it. 'There's danger of violence?'

'The Fundamentalists threaten it, so I suppose there is, in a theoretical sense. But I really don't expect it. The Fundies have no real power. They're just the continuous irritant factor that might stir up a riot after a while. You don't mind staying here? Please. I won't be myself if I have to worry about you.'

'Oh, I'll stay. You still think it will go well?'

'I'm sure of it. No one bothered you at the place?'

'No one. I'm certain.'

'And your part went well?'

'Well enough. There'll be no trouble there.'

'Then take care of yourself, and watch the televisor tomorrow, John.' Byerley pressed the gnarled hand that rested on his.

. . .

Lenton's forehead was a furrowed study in suspense. He had the completely unenviable job of being Byerley's campaign manager in a campaign that wasn't a campaign, for a person that refused to reveal his strategy, and refused to accept his manager's.

'You can't!' It was his favourite phrase. It had become his only phrase. 'I tell you, Steve, you can't!'

He threw himself in front of the prosecutor, who was spending his time leafing through the typed pages of his speech.

'Put that down, Steve. Look, that mob has been organized by the Fundies. You won't get a hearing. You'll be stoned more likely. Why do you have to make a speech before an audience? What's wrong with a recording, a visual recording?'

'You want me to win the election, don't you?' asked Byerley, mildly.

'Win the election! You're not going to win, Steve. I'm trying to save your life.'

'Oh, I'm not in danger.'

'He's not in danger. He's not in danger.' Lenton made a queer, rasping sound in his throat. 'You mean you're getting out on that balcony in front of fifty thousand crazy crackpots and try to talk sense to them – on a balcony like a medieval dictator?'

Byerley consulted his watch. 'In about five minutes – as soon as the television lines are free.'

Lenton's answering remark was not quite transliterable.

· · ·

The crowd filled a roped off area of the city. Trees and houses seemed to grow out of a mass-human foundation. And by ultrawave, the rest of the world watched. It was a purely local election, but it had a world audience just the same. Byerley thought of that and smiled.

But there was nothing to smile at in the crowd itself. There were banners and streamers, ringing every possible change on his supposed robotcy. The hostile attitude rose thickly and tangibly into the atmosphere.

From the start the speech was not successful. It competed against the inchoate mob howl and the rhythmic cries of the Fundie claques that formed mob-islands within the mob. Byerley spoke on, slowly, unemotionally——

Inside, Lenton clutched his hair and groaned – and waited for the blood.

· · ·

There was a writhing in the front ranks. An angular citizen with popping eyes, and clothes too short for the lank length of his limbs, was pulling to the fore. A policeman dived after him, making slow, struggling passage. Byerley waved the latter off, angrily.

The thin man was directly under the balcony. His words tore unheard against the roar.

Byerley leaned forward. 'What do you say? If you have a legitimate question, I'll answer it.' He turned to a flanking guard. 'Bring that man up here.'

There was a tensing in the crowd. Cries of 'Quiet' started in various parts of the mob, and rose to a bedlam, then toned down raggedly. The thin man, red-faced and panting, faced Byerley.

Byerley said, 'Have you a question?'

The thin man stared, and said in a cracked voice, 'Hit me!'

With sudden energy, he thrust out his chin at an angle. 'Hit me! You say you're not a robot. Prove it. You can't hit a human, you monster.'

There was a queer, flat, dead silence. Byerley's voice punctured it. 'I have no reason to hit you.'

The thin man was laughing wildly. 'You *can't* hit me. You *won't* hit me. You're not a human. You're a monster, a make-believe man.'

And Stephen Byerley, tight-lipped, in the face of thousands who watched in person and the millions who watched by screen, drew back his fist and caught the man crackingly upon the chin. The challenger went over backwards in sudden collapse, with nothing on his face, but blank, blank surprise.

Byerley said, 'I'm sorry. Take him in and see that he's comfortable. I want to speak to him when I'm through.'

And when Dr Calvin, from her reserved space, turned her automobile and drove off, only one reporter had recovered sufficiently from the shock to race after her, and shout an unheard question.

Susan Calvin called over her shoulder, 'He's human.'

That was enough. The reporter raced away in his own direction.

The rest of the speech might be described as 'Spoken but not heard.'

. . .

Dr Calvin and Stephen Byerley met once again – a week before he took the oath of office as mayor. It was late – past midnight.

Dr Calvin said, 'You don't look tired.'

The Mayor-elect smiled. 'I may stay up for a while. Don't tell Quinn.'

'I shan't. But that was an interesting story of Quinn's, since you mention him. It's a shame to have spoiled it. I suppose you knew his theory?'

'Parts of it.'

'It was highly dramatic. Stephen Byerley was a young lawyer, a powerful speaker, a great idealist – and with a certain flair for biophysics. Are you interested in robotics, Mr Byerley?'

'Only in the legal aspects.'

'*This* Stephen Byerley was. But there was an accident. Byerley's wife died; he himself, worse. His legs were gone; his face was gone; his voice was gone. Part of his mind was – bent. He would not submit to plastic surgery. He retired from the world, legal career gone – only his intelligence, and his hands left. Somehow he could obtain positronic brains, even a complex one, one which had the greatest capacity of forming judgements in ethical problems – which is the highest robotic function so far developed.

'He grew a body about it. Trained it to be everything he would have been and was no longer. He sent it out into the world as Stephen Byerley, remaining behind himself as the old, crippled teacher that no one ever saw——'

'Unfortunately,' said the mayor-elect, 'I ruined all that by hitting a man. The papers say it was your official verdict on the occasion that I was human.'

'How did that happen? Do you mind telling me? It couldn't have been accidental.'

'It wasn't entirely. Quinn did most of the work. My men started quietly spreading the fact that I had never hit a man; that I was unable to hit a man; that to fail to do so under provocation would be sure proof that I was a robot. So I arranged for a silly speech in public, with all sorts of publicity overtones, and almost inevitably, some fool fell for it. In its essence, it was what I call a shyster trick. One in which the artificial atmosphere which has been created does all the work. Of course, the emotional effects made my election certain, as intended.'

The robopsychologist nodded. 'I see you intrude on my field – as every politician must, I suppose. But I'm very sorry it turned out this way. I like robots. I like them considerably better than I do human beings. If a robot can be created capable of being a civil executive, I think he'd make the best one possible. By the Laws of Robotics, he'd be incapable of harming humans, incapable of tyranny, of corruption, of stupidity, of prejudice. And after he had served a decent term, he would leave, even though he were immortal, because it would be impossible for him to hurt humans by letting them know that a robot had ruled them. It would be most ideal.'

'Except that a robot might fail due to the inherent inadequacies of his brain. The positronic brain has never equalled the complexities of the human brain.'

'He would have advisers. Not even a human brain is capable of governing without assistance.'

Byerley considered Susan Calvin with grave interest. 'Why do you smile, Dr Calvin?'

'I smiled because Mr Quinn didn't think of everything.'

'You mean there could be more to that story of his.'

'Only a little. For the three months before election, this Stephen Byerley that Mr Quinn spoke about, this broken man, was in the country for some mysterious reason. He returned in time for that famous speech of yours. And after all, what the old cripple did once, he could do a second time, particularly where the second job is very simple in comparison to the first.'

'I don't quite understand.'

Dr Calvin rose and smoothed her dress. She was obviously ready to leave. 'I mean there is one time when a robot may strike a human being without breaking the First Law. Just one time.'

'And when is that?'

Dr Calvin was at the door. She said quietly, 'When the human to be struck is merely another robot.'

She smiled broadly, her thin face glowing. 'Goodbye, Mr Byerley. I hope to vote for you five years from now – for co-ordinator.'

Stephen Byerley chuckled. 'I must reply that that is a somewhat farfetched idea.'

The door closed behind her.

I stared at her with a sort of horror, 'Is that true?'

'All of it,' she said.

'And the great Byerley was simply a robot.'

'Oh, there's no way of ever finding out. I think he was. But when he decided to die, he had himself atomized, so that there will never be any legal proof.——Besides what difference would it make?'

'Well——'

'You share a prejudice against robots which is quite unreasoning. He was a very good Mayor; five years later he did *become Regional Co-ordinator. And when the Regions of Earth formed their Federation in 2044, he became the first World Co-ordinator. By that time it was the Machines that were running the world anyway.'*

'Yes, but——'

'No buts! The Machines are robots, and they are running the world. It was five years ago that I found out all the truth. It was 2052; Byerley was completing his second term as World Co-ordinator——'

CHAPTER 9

THE EVITABLE CONFLICT

The Co-ordinator, in his private study, had that medieval curiosity, a fireplace. To be sure, the medieval man might not have recognized it as such, since it had no functional significance. The quiet, licking flame lay in an insulated recess behind clear quartz.

The logs were ignited at long distance through a trifling diversion of the energy beam that fed the public buildings of the city. The same button that controlled the ignition first dumped the ashes of the previous fire, and allowed for the entrance of fresh wood. ——It was a thoroughly domesticated fireplace, you see.

But the fire itself was real. It was wired for sound, so that you could hear the crackle and, of course, you could watch it leap in the air stream that fed it.

The Co-ordinator's ruddy glass reflected, in miniature, the discreet gambolling of the flame, and, in even further miniature, it was reflected in each of his brooding pupils.

——And in the frosty pupils of his guest, Dr Susan Calvin of U.S. Robots & Mechanical Men Corporation.

The Co-ordinator said, 'I did not ask you here entirely for social purposes, Susan.'

'I did not think you did, Stephen,' she replied.

'——And yet I don't quite know how to phrase my problem. On the one hand, it can be nothing at all. On the other, it can mean the end of humanity.'

'I have come across so many problems, Stephen, that presented the same alternative. I think all problems do.'

'Really? Then judge this—— World Steel reports an overproduction of twenty thousand long tons. The Mexican Canal is two months behind schedule. The mercury mines at Almaden have experienced a production deficiency since last spring, while the Hydroponics plant at Tientsin has been laying men off. These items happen to come to mind at the moment. There is more of the same sort.'

'Are these things serious? I'm not economist enough to trace the fearful consequences of such things.'

'In themselves, they are not serious. Mining experts can be sent to Almaden, if the situation were to get worse. Hydroponics engineers can be used in Java or in Ceylon, if there are too many at Tientsin. Twenty thousand long tons of steel won't fill more than a few days of world demand, and the opening of the Mexican Canal two months later than the planned date is of little moment. It's the Machines that worry me; – I've spoken to your Director of Research about them already.'

'To Vincent Silver? ——He hasn't mentioned anything about it to me.'

'I asked him to speak to no one. Apparently, he hasn't.'

'And what did he tell you?'

'Let me put that item in its proper place. I want to talk about the Machines first. And I want to talk about them to you, because you're the only one in the world who understands robots well enough to help me now. ——May I grow philosophical?'

'For this evening, Stephen, you may talk how you please and of what you please, provided you tell me first what you intend to prove.'

'That such small unbalances in the perfection of our system of supply and demand, as I have mentioned, may be the first step towards the final war.'

'Hmp. Proceed.'

Susan Calvin did not allow herself to relax, despite the designed comfort of the chair she sat in. Her cold, thin-lipped face and her flat, even voice were becoming accentuated with the years. And although Stephen Byerley was one man she could like and trust, she was almost seventy and the cultivated habits of a lifetime are not easily broken.

'Every period of human development, Susan,' said the Co-ordinator, 'has had its own particular type of human conflict – its own variety of problem that, apparently, could be settled only by force. And each time, frustratingly enough, force never really settled the problem. Instead, it persisted through a series of conflicts, then vanished of itself – what's the expression, – ah, yes "not with a bang, but a whimper", as the economic and social environment changed. And then, new problems, and a new series of wars. ——Apparently endlessly cyclic.

'Consider relatively modern times. There were the series of dynastic wars in the sixteenth to eighteenth centuries, when the most important question in Europe was whether the houses of Hapsburg or Valois-Bourbon were to rule the continent. It was one of those "inevitable conflicts", since Europe could obviously not exist half one and half the other.

'Except that it did, and no war ever wiped out the one and established the other, until the rise of a new social atmosphere in France in 1789 crumbled first the Bourbons and, eventually, the Hapsburgs down the dusty chute to history's incinerator.

'And in those same centuries there were the more barbarous religious wars, which revolved about the important question of whether Europe was to be Catholic or Protestant. Half and half she could not be. It was "inevitable" that the sword decide. ——Except that it didn't. In England, a new industrialism was growing, and on the continent, a new nationalism. Half and half Europe remains to this day and no one cares much.

'In the nineteenth and twentieth centuries, there was a cycle of nationalist-imperialist wars, when the most important question in the world was which portions of Europe would control the economic resources and consuming capacity of which portions of non-Europe. All non-Europe obviously could not exist part English and part French and part German and so on. ——Until the forces of nationalism spread sufficiently, so that non-Europe ended what all the wars could not, and decided it could exist quite comfortably *all* non-European.

'And so we have a pattern——'

'Yes, Stephen, you make it plain,' said Susan Calvin. 'These are not very profound observations.'

'No. ——But then, it is the obvious which is so difficult to see most of the time. People say "It's as plain as the nose on your face." But how much of the nose on your face can you see, unless someone holds a mirror up to you? In the twentieth century, Susan, we started a new cycle of wars – what shall I call them? Ideological wars? The emotions of religion applied to economic systems, rather than to extra-natural ones? Again the wars were "inevitable" and this time there were atomic weapons, so that mankind could no longer live through its torment to the inevitable wasting away of inevitability. ——And positronic robots came.

'They came in time, and, with it and alongside it, interplanetary travel. ——So that it no longer seemed so important whether the world was Adam Smith or Karl Marx. Neither made very much sense under the new circumstances. Both had to adapt and they ended in almost the same place.'

'*A deus ex machina*, then, in a double sense,' said Dr Calvin, dryly.

The Co-ordinator smiled gently, 'I have never heard you pun before, Susan, but you are correct. And yet there was another danger. The ending of every other problem had merely given birth to another. Our new world wide robot economy may develop its own problems, and for that reason we have the Machines. The Earth's economy is stable, and will *remain* stable, because it is based upon the decisions of calculating machines that have the good of humanity at heart through the overwhelming force of the First Law of Robotics.'

Stephen Byerley continued, 'And although the Machines are nothing but the vastest conglomeration of calculating circuits ever invented, they are still robots within the meaning of the First Law, and so our Earth-wide economy is in accord with the best interests of Man. The population of Earth knows that there will be no unemployment, no overproduction or shortages. Waste and famine are words in history books. And so the question of ownership of the means of production becomes obsolescent. Whoever owned them (if such a phrase has meaning), a man, a group, a nation, or all mankind, they could be utilized only as the Machines directed. ——Not because men were forced to but because it was the wisest course and men knew it.

'It puts an end to war – not only to the last cycle of wars, but to the next and to all of them. Unless——'

A long pause, and Dr Calvin encouraged him by repetition. 'Unless——'

The fire crouched and skittered along a log, then popped up.

'Unless,' said the Co-ordinator, 'the Machines don't fulfill their function.'

'I see. And that is where those trifling maladjustments come in which you mentioned awhile ago – steel, hydroponics and so on.'

'Exactly. Those errors should not be. Dr Silver tells me they *cannot* be.'

'Does he deny the facts? How unusual!'

'No, he admits the facts, of course. I do him an injustice. What he denies is that any error in the machine is responsible for the so-called (his phrase) errors in the answers. He claims that the Machines are self-correcting and that it would violate the fundamental laws of nature for an error to exist in the circuits of relays. And so I said——'

'And you said, "Have your boys check them and make sure, anyway." '

'Susan, you read my mind. It was what I said, and he said he couldn't.'

'Too busy?'

'No, he said that no human could. He was frank about it. He told me, and I hope I understand him properly, that the Machines are a gigantic extrapolation. Thus—— A team of mathematicians work several years calculating a positronic brain equipped to do certain similar acts of calculation. Using this brain they make further calculations to create a still more complicated brain, which they use again to make one still more complicated and so on. According to Silver, what we call the Machines are the result of ten such steps.'

'Ye-es, that sounds familiar. Fortunately, I'm not a mathematician. ——Poor Vincent. He is a young man. The Directors before him, Alfred

Lanning and Peter Bogert, are dead, and they had no such problems. Nor had I. Perhaps roboticists as a whole should now die, since we can no longer understand our own creations.'

'Apparently not. The Machines are not super-brains in Sunday supplement sense, – although they are so pictured in the Sunday supplements. It is merely that in their own particular province of collecting and analysing a nearly infinite number of data and relationships thereof, in nearly infinitesimal time, they have progressed beyond the possibility of detailed human control.

'And then I tried something else. I actually asked the Machine. In the strictest secrecy, we fed it the original data involved in the steel decision, its own answer, and the actual developments since – the overproduction, that is – and asked for an explanation of the discrepancy.'

'Good, and what was its answer?'

'I can quote you that word for word: "The matter admits of no explanation." '

'And how did Vincent interpret that?'

'In two ways. Either we had not given the Machine enough data to allow a definite answer, which was unlikely. Dr Silver admitted that. ——Or else, it was impossible for the Machine to admit that it could give any answer to data which implied that it could harm a human being. This, naturally, is implied by the First Law. And then Dr Silver recommended that I see you.'

Susan Calvin looked very tired, 'I'm old, Stephen. When Peter Bogert died, they wanted to make me Director of Research and I refused. I wasn't young then, either, and I did not wish the responsibility. They let young Silver have it and that satisfied me; but what good is it, if I am dragged into such messes.

'Stephen, let me state my position. My researches do indeed involve the interpretation of robot behaviour in the light of the Three Laws of Robotics. Here, now, we have these incredible calculating machines. They are positronic robots and therefore obey the Laws of Robotics. But they lack personality; that is, their functions are extremely limited. ——Must be, since they are so specialized. Therefore, there is very little room for the interplay of the Laws, and my one method of attack is virtually useless. In short, I don't know that I can help you, Stephen.'

The Co-ordinator laughed shortly, 'Nevertheless, let me tell you the rest. Let me give you *my* theories, and perhaps you will then be able to tell me whether they are possible in the light of robopsychology.'

'By all means. Go ahead.'

'Well, since the Machines are giving the wrong answers, then, assuming that they cannot be in error, there is only one possibility. *They are being given the wrong data!* In other words, the trouble is human, and not robotic. So I took my recent planetary inspection tour——'

'From which you have just returned to New York.'

'Yes. It was necessary, you see, since there are four Machines, one handling each of the Planetary Regions. And *all four are yielding imperfect results.*'

'Oh, but that follows, Stephen. If any one of the Machines is imperfect, that will automatically reflect in the result of the other three, since each of the others will assume as part of the data on which they base their own decisions, the perfection of the imperfect fourth. With a false assumption, they will yield false answers.'

'Uh-huh. So it seemed to me. Now, I have here the records of my interviews with each of the Regional Vice-Co-ordinators. Would you look through them with me? ——Oh, and first, have you heard of the "Society for Humanity"?'

'Umm, yes. They are an outgrowth of the Fundamentalists who have kept U.S. Robots from ever employing positronic robots on the grounds of unfair labour competition and so on. The "Society for Humanity" itself is anti-Machine, is it not?'

'Yes, yes, but—— Well, you will see. Shall we begin? We'll start with the Eastern Region——'

'As you say——'

The Eastern Region
  a—Area: 7,500,000 square miles
  b—Population: 1,700,000,000
  c—Capital: Shanghai

Ching Hso-lin's great-grandfather had been killed in the Japanese invasion of the old Chinese Republic, and there had been no one beside his dutiful children to mourn his loss or even to know he was lost. Ching Hso-lin's grandfather had survived the civil war of the late forties, but there had been no one beside *his* dutiful children to know or care of that.

And yet Ching Hso-lin was a Regional Vice-Co-ordinator, with the economic welfare of half the people of Earth in his care.

Perhaps it was with the thought of all that in mind, that Ching had two maps as the only ornaments on the wall of his office. One was an old hand-drawn affair tracing out an acre or two of land, and marked with the now outmoded pictographs of old China. A little creek trickled aslant the faded markings and there were the delicate pictorial indications of lowly huts, in one of which Ching's grandfather had been born.

The other map was a huge one, sharply delineated, with all markings in neat Cyrillic characters. The red boundary that marked the Eastern Region swept within its grand confines all that had once been China, India, Burma, Indo-China, and Indonesia. On it, within the old province of Szechuan, so light and gentle that none could see it, was the little mark placed there by Ching which indicated the location of his ancestral farm.

Ching stood before these maps as he spoke to Stephen Byerley in precise English, 'No one knows better than you, Mr Co-ordinator, that my job, to a large extent, is a sinecure. It carries with it a certain social standing, and I represent a convenient focal point for administration, but otherwise it is the Machine! ——The Machine does all the work. What did you think, for instance, of the Tientsin Hydroponics works?'

'Tremendous!' said Byerley.

'It is but one of dozens, and not the largest. Shanghai, Calcutta, Batavia, Bangkok—— They are widely spread and they are the answer to feeding the billion and three quarters of the East.'

'And yet,' said Byerley, 'you have an unemployment problem there at Tientsin. Can you be over-producing? It is incongruous to think of Asia as suffering from too much food.'

Ching's dark eyes crinkled at the edges. 'No. It has not come to that yet. It is true over the last few months, several vats at Tientsin have been shut down, but it is nothing serious. The men have been released only temporarily and those who do not care to work in other fields have been shipped to Colombo in Ceylon, where a new plant is being put into operation.'

'But why should the vats be closed down?'

Ching smiled gently, 'You do not know much of hydroponics, I see. Well, that is not surprising. You are a Northerner, and there soil farming is still profitable. It is fashionable in the North to think of hydroponics, when it is thought of at all, as a device for growing turnips in a chemical solution, and so it is – in an infinitely complicated way.

'In the first place, by far the largest crop we deal with (and the percentage is growing) is yeast. We have upward of two thousand strains of yeast in production and new strains are added monthly. The basic food-chemicals of the various yeasts are nitrates and phosphates among the inorganics together with proper amounts of the trace metals needed, down to the fractional parts per million of boron and molybdenum which are required. The organic matter is mostly sugar mixture derived from the hydrolysis of cellulose, but, in addition, there are various food factors which must be added.

'For a successful hydroponics industry – one which can feed seventeen hundred million people – we must engage in an immense reforestation programme throughout the East; we must have huge wood-conversion plants to deal with our southern jungles; we must have power, and steel, and chemical synthetics above all.'

'Why the last, sir?'

'Because, Mr Byerley, these strains of yeast have each their peculiar properties. We have developed, as I said, two thousand strains. The beef steak you thought you ate today was yeast. The frozen fruit confection you had for dessert was iced yeast. We have filtered yeast juice with the taste, appearance, and all the food value of milk.

'It is flavour, more than anything else, you see that makes yeast feeding popular and for the sake of flavour we have developed artificial, domesticated strains that can no longer support themselves on a basic diet of salts and sugar. One needs biotin; another needs pteroylglutamic acid; still others need seventeen different amino acids supplied to them as well as all the Vitamins B, but one (and yet it is popular and we cannot, with economic sense, abandon it)——'

Byerley stirred in his seat, 'To what purpose do you tell me all this?'

'You asked me, sir, why men are out of work in Tientsin. I have little more to explain. It is not only that we must have these various and varying foods for our yeast; but there remains the complicating factor of popular fads with passing time; and of the possibility of the development of new strains with the new requirements and new popularity. All this must be foreseen, and the Machine does the job——'

'But not perfectly.'

'Not very *imperfectly*, in view of the complications I have mentioned. Well, then, a few thousand workers in Tientsin are temporarily out of a job. But, consider this, the amount of waste in this past year (waste that is, in terms of either defective supply or defective demand) amounts to not one-tenth of one percent of our total productive turnover. I consider that——'

'Yet in the first years of the Machine, the figure was nearer one-thousandth of one percent.'

'Ah, but in the decade since the Machine began its operations in real earnest, we have made use of it to increase our old pre-Machine yeast industry twenty-fold. You expect imperfections to increase with complications, though——'

'Though?'

'There *was* the curious instance of Rama Vrasayana.'

'What happened to him?'

'Vrasayana was in charge of a brine-evaporation plant for the production of iodine, with which yeast can do without, but human beings not. His plant was forced into receivership.'

'Really? And through what agency?'

'Competition, believe it or not. In general, one of the chiefest functions of the Machine's analyses is to indicate the most efficient distribution of our producing units. It is obviously faulty to have areas insufficiently serviced, so that the transportation costs account for too great a percentage of the overheads. Similarly, it is faulty to have an area too well serviced, so that factories must be run at lowered capacities, or else compete harmfully with one another. In the case of Vrasayana, another plant was established in the same city, and with a more efficient extracting system.'

'The Machine permitted it?'

'Oh, certainly. That is not surprising. The new system is becoming widespread. The surprise is that the Machine failed to warn Vrasayana to renovate or combine.——Still, no matter. Vrasayana accepted a job as engineer in the new plant, and if his responsibility and pay are now less, he is not actually suffering. The workers found employment easily; the old plant has been converted to – something or other. Something useful. We left it all to the Machine.'

'And otherwise you have no complaints.'

'None!'

The Tropic Region:
 a–Area: 22,000,000 square miles
 b–Population: 500,000,000
 c–Capital: Capital City

The map in Lincoln Ngoma's office was far from the model of neat precision of the one in Ching's Shanghai domination. The boundaries of Ngoma's Tropic Region were stencilled in dark, wide brown and swept about a gorgeous interior labelled 'jungle' and 'desert' and 'here be Elephants and all Manner of Strange Beasts.'

It had much to sweep, for in land area the Tropic Region enclosed most of two continents: all of South America north of Argentina and all of Africa south of the Atlas. It included North America south of the Rio Grande as well, and even Arabia and Iran in Asia. It was the reverse of the Eastern Region. Where the ant hives of the Orient crowded half of humanity into 15 per cent of the land mass, the Tropics stretched its 15 per cent of Humanity over nearly half of all the land in the world.

But it was growing. It was the one Region whose population increase through immigration exceeded that through births.——And for all who came it had use.

To Ngoma, Stephen Byerley seemed like one of these immigrants, a pale searcher for the creative work of carving a harsh environment into the softness necessary for man, and he felt some of that automatic contempt of the strong man born to the strong Tropics for the unfortunate pallards of the colder suns.

The Tropics had the newest capital city on Earth, and it was called simply that: 'Capital City', in the sublime confidence of youth. It spread brightly over the fertile uplands of Nigeria and outside Ngoma's windows, far below, was life and colour; the bright, bright sun and the quick, drenching showers. Even the squawking of the rainbowed birds was brisk and the stars were hard pinpoints in the sharp night.

Ngoma laughed. He was a big, dark man, strong faced and handsome.

'Sure,' he said, and his English was colloquial and mouth-filling, 'the Mexican canal is overdue. What the hell? It will get finished just the same, old boy.'

'It was doing well up to the last half year.'

Ngoma looked at Byerley and slowly crunched his teeth over the end of a big cigar, spitting out one end and lighting the other, 'Is this an official investigation, Byerley? What's going on?'

'Nothing. Nothing at all. It's just my function as Co-ordinator to be curious.'

'Well, if it's just that you are filling in a dull moment, the truth is that we're always short on labour. There's lots going on in the Tropics. The Canal is only one of them——'

'But doesn't your Machine predict the amount of labour available for the Canal, – allowing for all the competing projects?'

Ngoma placed one hand behind his neck and blew smoke rings at the ceiling, 'It was a little off.'

'Is it often a little off?'

'Not oftener than you would expect. ——We don't expect too much of it, Byerley. We feed it data. We take its results. We do what it says. ——But it's just a convenience; just a labour saving device. We could do without it, if we had to. Maybe not as well. Maybe not as quickly. But we'd get there.

'We've got confidence out here, Byerley, and that's the secret. Confidence! We've got new land that's been waiting for us for thousands of years, while the rest of the world was being ripped apart in the lousy fumblings of pre-atomic time. We don't have to eat yeast like the Eastern boys, and we don't have to worry about the stale dregs of the last century like you Northerners.

'We've wiped out the tsetse fly and the Anopheles mosquito, and people find they can live in the sun and like it, now. We've thinned down the jungles and found soil; we've watered the deserts and found gardens. We've got coal and oil in untouched fields, and minerals out of count.

'Just step back. That's all we ask the rest of the world to do. ——Step back, and let us work.'

Byerley said, prosaically, 'But the Canal, – it was on schedule six months ago. What happened?'

Ngoma spread his hands, 'Labour troubles.' He felt through a pile of papers sheltered about his desk and gave it up.

'Had something on the matter here,' he muttered, 'but never mind. There was a work shortage somewhere in Mexico once on the question of women. There weren't enough women in their neighbourhood. It seemed no one had thought of feeding sexual data to the Machine.'

He stopped to laugh, delightedly, then sobered, 'Wait a while. I think I've got it. ——Villafranca!'

'Villafranca?'

'Francisco Villafranca. ——He was the engineer in charge. Now let me straighten it out. Something happened and there was a cave-in. Right. Right. That was it. Nobody died, as I remember, but it made a hell of a mess. ——Quite a scandal.'

'Oh?'

'There was some mistake in his calculations. ——Or at least, the Machine said so. They fed through Villafranca's data, assumptions, and so on. The stuff he had started with. The answers came out differently. It seems the answers Villafranca had used didn't take account of the effect of a heavy rainfall on the contours of the cut. ——Or something like that. I'm not an engineer, you understand.

'Anyway, Villafranca put up a devil of a squawk. He claimed the Machine's answer had been different the first time. That he had followed the Machine faithfully. Then he quit! We offered to hold him on – reasonable doubt, previous work satisfactory, and all that – in a subordinate position, of course – had to do that much – mistakes can't go unnoticed – bad for discipline—— Where was I?'

'You offered to hold him.'

'Oh yes. He refused. ——Well, take all in all, we're two months behind. Hell, that's nothing.'

Byerley stretched out his hand and let the fingers tap lightly on the desk, 'Villafranca blamed the Machine, did he?'

'Well, he wasn't going to blame himself, was he? Let's face it; human nature is an old friend of ours. Besides, I remember something else now—— Why the hell can't I find documents when I want them? My filing system isn't worth a damn—— This Villafranca was a member of

one of your Northern organizations. Mexico is too close to the North,
that's part of the trouble.'

'Which organization are you speaking of?'

'The Society for Humanity, they call it. He used to attend the annual
conferences in New York, Villafranca did. Bunch of crackpots, but
harmless. ——They don't like the Machines; claim they're destroying
human initiative. So naturally Villafranca would blame the Machine.
——Don't understand that group myself. Does Capital City look as if
the human race were running out of initiative?'

And Capital City stretched out in golden glory under a golden sun, –
the newest and youngest creation of *Homo metropolis.*

The European Region
   a – Area: 4,000,000 square miles
   b – Population: 300,000,000
   c – Capital: Geneva

The European Region was an anomaly in several ways. In area, it was
far the smallest; not one fifth the size of the Tropic Region in area, and
not one fifth the size of the Eastern Region in population.
Geographically, it was only somewhat similar to pre-Atomic Europe,
since it excluded what had once been European Russia and what had
once been the British Isles, while it included the Mediterranean coasts of
Africa and Asia, and, in a queer jump across the Atlantic, Argentina,
Chile, and Uruguay as well.

Nor was it likely to improve its relative status *vis-à-vis* the other regions
of Earth, except for what vigour the South American provinces lent it.
Of all the Regions, it alone showed a positive population decline over the
past half century. It alone had not seriously expanded its productive
facilities, or offered anything radically new to human culture.

'Europe,' said Madame Szegeczowska, in her soft French, 'is essentially an economic appendage of the Northern Region. We know it, and
it doesn't matter.'

And as though in resigned acceptance of a lack of individuality, there
was no map of Europe on the wall of the Madame Co-ordinator's office.

'And yet,' pointed out Byerley, 'you have a Machine of your own, and
you are certainly under no economic pressure from across the ocean.'

'A Machine! Bah!' She shrugged her delicate shoulders, and allowed a
thin smile to cross her little face as she tamped out a cigarette with long
fingers. 'Europe is a sleepy place. And such of our men as do not manage
to emigrate to the Tropics are tired and sleepy along with it. You see for
yourself that it is myself, a poor woman, to whom falls the task of being

Vice-Co-ordinator. Well, fortunately, it is not a difficult job, and not much is expected of me.

'As for the Machine—— What can it say but "Do this and it will be best for you." But what is best for us? Why, to be an economic appendage of the Northern Region.

'And is it so terrible? No wars! We live in peace – and it is pleasant after seven thousand years of war. We are old, monsieur. In our borders, we have the regions where Occidental civilization was cradled. We have Egypt and Mesopotamia; Crete and Syria; Asia Minor and Greece. ——But old age is not necessarily an unhappy time. It can be a fruition——'

'Perhaps you are right,' said Byerley, affably. 'At least the tempo of life is not as intense as in the other Regions. It is a pleasant atmosphere.'

'Is it not? ——Tea is being brought, monsieur. If you will indicate your cream and sugar preferences, please. ——Thank you.'

She sipped gently, then continued, 'It *is* pleasant. The rest of Earth is welcome to the continuing struggle. I find a parallel here; a very interesting one. There was a time when Rome was master of the world. It had adopted the culture and civilization of Greece; a Greece which had never been united, which had ruined itself with war, and which was ending in a state of decadent squalor. Rome united it, brought it peace and let it live a life of secure non-glory. It occupied itself with its philosophies and its art, far from the clash of growth and war. It was a sort of death, but it was restful, and it lasted with minor breaks for some four hundred years.'

'And yet,' said Byerley, 'Rome fell eventually, and the opium dream was over.'

'There are no longer barbarians to overthrow civilization.'

'We can be our own barbarians, Madame Szegeczowska. ——Oh, I meant to ask you. The Almaden mercury mines have fallen off quite badly in production. Surely the ores are not declining more rapidly than anticipated?'

The little woman's grey eyes fastened shrewdly on Byerley, 'Barbarians – the fall of civilization – possible failure of the Machine. Your thought processes are very transparent, monsieur.'

'Are they?' Byerley smiled. 'I see that I should have had men to deal with as hitherto. ——You consider the Almaden affair to be the fault of the Machine?'

'Not at all, but I think you do. You, yourself, are a native of the Northern Region. The Central Co-ordination Office is at New York. ——And I have noticed for quite a while that you Northerners lack somewhat of faith in the Machine.'

'We do?'

'There is your "Society for Humanity" which is strong in the North, but naturally fails to find many recruits in tired, old Europe, which is quite willing to let feeble Humanity alone for a while. Surely, you are one of the confident North and not one of the cynical old continent.'

'This has a connection with Almaden?'

'Oh, yes, I think so. The mines are in the control of Consolidated Cinnabar, which is certainly a Northern company, with headquarters at Nikolaev. Personally, I wonder if the Board of Directors have been consulting the Machine at all. They said they had in our conference last month, and, of course, we have no evidence that they did not, but I wouldn't take the word of a Northerner in this matter – no offence intended – under any circumstances. ——Nevertheless, I think we will have a fortunate ending.'

'In what way, my dear madame?'

'You must understand that the economic irregularities of the last few months, which, although small as compared with the great storms of the past, are quite disturbing to our peace-drenched spirits, have caused considerable restiveness in the Spanish province. I understand that Consolidated Cinnabar is selling out to a group of native Spaniards. It is consoling. If we are economic vassals of the North, it is humiliating to have the fact advertised too blatantly. ——And our people can be better trusted to follow the Machine.'

'Then you think there will be no more trouble?'

'I am sure there will not be—— In Almaden, at least.'

The Northern Region
  a – Area: 18,000,000 square miles
  b – Population: 800,000,000
  c – Capital: Ottawa

The Northern Region, in more ways than one, was at the top. This was exemplified quite well by the map in the Ottawa office of Vice-Co-ordinator Hiram Mackenzie, in which the North Pole was centred. Except for the enclave of Europe with its Scandinavian and Icelandic regions, all the Arctic area was within the Northern Region.

Roughly, it could be divided into two major areas. To the left on the map was all of North America above the Rio Grande. To the right was included all of what had once been the Soviet Union. Together these areas represented the centred power of the planet in the first years of the Atomic Age. Between the two was Great Britain, a tongue of the Region licking at Europe. Up at the top of the map, distorted into odd, huge shapes, were Australia and New Zealand, also member provinces of the Region.

Not all the changes of the past decades had yet altered the fact that the North was the economic ruler of the planet.

There was almost as ostentatious symbolism thereof in the fact that of the official Regional maps Byerley had seen, Mackenzie's alone showed all the Earth, as though the North feared no competition and needed no favouritism to point up its pre-eminence.

'Impossible,' said Mackenzie, dourly, over the whiskey. 'Mr Byerley, you have had no training as a robot technician, I believe.'

'No, I have not.'

'Hmp. Well, it is, in my opinion, a sad thing that Ching, Ngoma and Szegeczowska haven't either. There is too prevalent an opinion among the peoples of Earth that a Co-ordinator need only be a capable organizer, a broad generalizer, and an amiable person. These days he should know his robotics as well, – no offence intended.'

'None taken. I agree with you.'

'I take it, for instance, from what you have said already, that you worry about the recent trifling dislocations in world economy. I don't know what you suspect, but it has happened in the past that people – who should have known better – wondered what would happen if false data were fed into the Machine.'

'And what would happen, Mr Mackenzie?'

'Well,' the Scotsman shifted his weight and sighed, 'all collected data goes through a complicated screening system which involves both human and mechanical checking, so that the problem is not likely to arise. ——But let us ignore that. Humans are fallible, also corruptible, and ordinary mechanical devices are liable to mechanical failure.

'The real point of the matter is that what we call a "wrong datum" is one which is inconsistent with all other known data. It is our only criterion of right and wrong. It is the Machine's as well. Order it, for instance, to direct agricultural activity on the basis of an average July temperature in Iowa of 57 degrees Fahrenheit. It won't accept that. It will not give an answer. ——Not that it has any prejudice against that particular temperature, or that an answer is impossible; but because, in the light of all the other data fed to it over a period of years, it knows that the probability of an average July temperature of 57 is virtually nil. It rejects that datum.

'The only way a "wrong datum" can be forced on the Machine is to include it as part of a self-consistent whole, all of which is subtly wrong in a manner either too delicate for the Machine to detect or outside the Machine's experience. The former is beyond human capacity, and the latter is almost so, and is becoming more nearly so as the Machine's experience increases by the second.'

Stephen Byerley placed two fingers to the bridge of his nose, 'Then the Machine cannot be tampered with—— And how do you account for recent errors, then?'

'My dear Byerley, I see that you instinctively follow that great error – that the Machine knows all. Let me cite you a case from my personal experience. The cotton industry engages experienced buyers who purchase cotton. Their procedure is to pull a tuft of cotton out of a random bale of a lot. They will look at that tuft and feel it, tease it out, listen to the crackling perhaps as they do so, touch it with their tongue, – and through this procedure they will determine the class of cotton the bales represent. There are about a dozen such classes. As a result of their decisions, purchases are made at certain prices, blends are made in certain proportions. ——Now these buyers cannot yet be replaced by the Machine.'

'Why not? Surely the data involved is not too complicated for it?'

'Probably not. But what data is this you refer to? No textile chemist knows exactly what it is that the buyer tests when he feels a tuft of cotton. Presumably there's the average length of the threads, their feel, the extent and nature of their slickness, the way they hang together and so on. ——Several dozen items, subconsciously weighed, out of years of experience. But the *quantitative* nature of these tests is not known; maybe even the very nature of some of them is not known. So we have nothing to feed the Machine. Nor can the buyers explain their own judgement. They can only say, "Well, look at it. Can't you *tell* it's class-such-and-such?"'

'I see.'

'There are innumerable cases like that. The Machine is only a tool after all, which can help humanity progress faster by taking some of the burdens of calculations and interpretations off his back. The task of the human brain remains what it has always been; that of discovering new data to be analysed, and of devising new concepts to be tested. A pity the Society for Humanity won't understand that.'

'They are against the Machine?'

'They would be against mathematics or against the art of writing if they had lived at the appropriate time. These reactionaries of the Society claim the Machine robs man of his soul. I notice that capable men are still at a premium in our society; we still need the man who is intelligent enough to think of the proper questions to ask. Perhaps if we could find enough of such, these dislocations you worry about, Co-ordinator, wouldn't occur.'

Earth (*Including the uninhabited continent, Antarctica*)
  a – Area: 54,000,000 square miles (*land surface*)
  b – Population: 3,300,000,000
  c – Capital: New York

The fire behind the quartz was weary now, and sputtered its reluctant way to death.

The Co-ordinator was sombre, his mood matching the sinking flame.

'They all minimize the state of affairs.' His voice was low. 'Is it not easy to imagine that they all laugh at me? And yet – Vincent Silver said the Machines cannot be out of order, and I must believe him. Hiram Mackenzie says they cannot be fed false data, and I must believe him. But the Machines are going wrong, somehow, and I must believe that, too, – and so there is *still* an alternative left.'

He glanced sidewise at Susan Calvin, who, with closed eyes, for a moment seemed asleep.

'What is that?' she asked, prompt to her cue, nevertheless.

'Why, that correct data is indeed given, and correct answers are indeed received, but that they are then ignored. There is no way the Machine can enforce obedience to its dictates.'

'Madame Szegeczowska hinted as much, with reference to Northerners in general, it seems to me.'

'So she did.'

'And what purpose is served by disobeying the Machine? Let's consider motivations.'

'It's obvious to me, and should be to you. It is a matter of rocking the boat, deliberately. There can be no serious conflicts on Earth, in which one group or another can seize more power than it has for what it thinks is its own good despite the harm to Mankind as a whole, while the Machines rule. If popular faith in the Machines can be destroyed to the point where they are abandoned, it will be the law of the jungle again.
——And not one of the four Regions can be freed of the suspicion of wanting just that.

'The East has half of humanity within its borders, and the Tropics more than half of Earth's resources. Each can feel itself the natural rulers of all Earth, and each has a history of humiliation by the North, for which it can be human enough to wish a senseless revenge. Europe has a tradition of greatness, on the other hand. It once *did* rule the Earth, and there is nothing so eternally adhesive as the memory of power.

'Yet, in another way, it's hard to believe. Both the East and the Tropics are in a state of enormous expansion within their own borders. Both are climbing incredibly. They cannot have the spare energy for military adventures. And Europe can have nothing but its dreams. It is a cipher, militarily.'

'So, Stephen,' said Susan, 'you leave the North.'

'Yes,' said Byerley, energetically, 'I do. The North is now the strongest, and has been for nearly a century, or its component parts have been. But it is losing relatively, now. The Tropic Regions may take their place in the forefront of civilization for the first time since the Pharoahs, and there are Northerners who fear that.

'The "Society for Humanity" is a Northern organization, primarily, you know, and they make no secret of not wanting the Machines. ——Susan, they are few in numbers, but it is an association of powerful men. Heads of factories; directors of industries and agricultural combines who hate to be what they call "the Machine's office-boy" belong to it. Men with ambition belong to it. Men who feel themselves strong enough to decide for themselves what is best for themselves, and not just to be told what is best for others.

'In short, just those men who, by together refusing to accept the decisions of the Machine, can, in a short time, turn the world topsy-turvy; – just those belong to the Society.

'Susan, it hangs together. Five of the Directors of World Steel are members, and World Steel suffers from overproduction. Consolidated Cinnabar, which mined mercury at Almaden, was a Northern concern. Its books are still being investigated, but one, at least, of the men concerned was a member. Francisco Villafranca, who, singlehanded, delayed the Mexican Canal for two months, was a member, we know already – and so was Rama Vrasayana, I was not at all surprised to find out.'

Susan said, quietly, 'These men, I might point out, have all done badly——'

'But naturally,' interjected Byerley. 'To disobey the Machine's analyses is to follow a non-optimal path. Results are poorer than they might be. It's the price they pay. They will have it rough now but in the confusion that will eventually follow——'

'Just what do you plan doing, Stephen?'

'There is obviously no time to lose. I am going to have the Society outlawed, every member removed from any responsible post. And all executive and technical positions, henceforward, can be filled only by applicants signing a non-Society oath. It will mean a certain surrender of basic civil liberties, but I am sure the Congress——'

'It won't work!'

'What! ——Why not?'

'I will make a prediction. If you try any such thing, you will find yourself hampered at every turn. You will find it impossible to carry out. You will find your every move in that direction will result in trouble.'

Byerley was taken aback, 'Why do you say that? ——I was rather hoping for your approval in this matter.'

'You can't have it as long as your actions are based on a false premise. You admit the Machine can't be wrong, and can't be fed wrong data. I will now show you that it cannot be disobeyed, either, as you think is being done by the Society.'

'*That* I don't see at all.'

'Then listen. Every action by any executive which does not follow the exact directions of the Machine he is working with becomes part of the data for the next problem. The Machine, therefore, knows that the executive has a certain tendency to disobey. He can incorporate that tendency into that data, – even quantitatively, that is, judging exactly how much and in what direction disobedience would occur. Its next answers would be just sufficiently biased so that after the executive concerned disobeyed, he would have automatically corrected those answers to optimal directions. The Machine *knows*, Stephen!'

'You can't be sure of all this. You are guessing.'

'It is a guess based on a lifetime's experience with robots. You had better rely on such a guess, Stephen.'

'But then what is left? The Machines themselves are correct and the premises they work on are correct. That we have agreed upon. Now you say that it cannot be disobeyed. Then what is wrong?'

'You have answered yourself. *Nothing is wrong!* Think about the Machines for a while, Stephen. They are robots, and they follow the First Law. But the Machines work not for any single human being, but for all humanity, so that the First Law becomes: "No Machine may harm humanity; or, through inaction, allow humanity to come to harm."'

'Very well, then, Stephen, what harms humanity? Economic dislocations most of all, from whatever cause. Wouldn't you say so?'

'I would.'

'And what is most likely in the future to cause economic dislocations? Answer that, Stephen.'

'I should say,' replied Byerley, unwillingly, 'the destruction of the Machines.'

'And so should I say, and so should the Machines say. Their first care, therefore, is to preserve themselves, for us. And so they are quietly taking care of the only elements left that threaten them. It is not the "Society for Humanity" which is shaking the boat so that the Machines may be destroyed. You have been looking at the reverse of the picture. Say rather that the Machine is shaking the boat – *very* slightly – just enough to shake loose those few which cling to the side for purposes the Machines consider harmful to Humanity.

'So Vrasayana loses his factory and gets another job where he can do no harm – he is not badly hurt, he is not rendered incapable of earning a living, for the Machine cannot harm a human being more than minimally, and that only to save a greater number. Consolidated Cinnabar loses control at Almaden. Villafranca is no longer a civil engineer in charge of an important project. And the directors of World Steel are losing their grip on the industry – or will.'

'But you don't really know all this,' insisted Byerley, distractedly. 'How can we possibly take a chance on your being right?'

'You must. Do you remember the Machine's own statement when you presented the problem to him? It was: "The matter admits of no explanation". The Machine did not say there was no explanation, or that it could determine no explanation. It simply was not going to *admit* any explanation. In other words, it would be harmful to humanity to have the explanation known, and that's why we can only guess – and keep on guessing.'

'But how can the explanation do us harm? Assume that you are right, Susan.'

'Why, Stephen, if I am right, it means that the Machine is conducting our future for us not only simply in direct answer to our direct questions, but in general answer to the world situation and to human psychology as a whole. And to know that may make us unhappy and may hurt our pride. The Machine cannot, *must* not, make us unhappy.

'Stephen, how do we know what the ultimate good of Humanity will entail? We haven't at *our* disposal the infinite factors that the Machine has at *its*! Perhaps, to give you a not unfamiliar example, our entire technical civilization has created more unhappiness and misery than it has removed. Perhaps an agrarian or pastoral civilization, with less culture and less people would be better. If so, the Machines must move in that direction, preferably without telling us, since in our ignorant prejudices we only know that what we are used to is good – and we would then fight change. Or perhaps a complete urbanization, or a completely caste-ridden society, or complete anarchy, is the answer. We don't know. Only the Machines know, and they are going there and taking us with them.'

'But you are telling me, Susan, that the "Society for Humanity" is right; and that Mankind *has* lost its own say in its future.'

'It never had any, really. It was always at the mercy of economic and sociological forces it did not understand – at the whims of climate, and the fortunes of war. Now the Machines understand them; and no one can stop them, since the Machines will deal with them as they are dealing with the Society, – having, as they do, the greatest of weapons at their disposal, the absolute control of our economy.'

'How horrible!'

'Perhaps how wonderful! Think, that for all time, all conflicts are finally evitable. Only the Machines, from now on, are inevitable!'

And the fire behind the quartz went out and only a curl of smoke was left to indicate its place.

'And that is all,' said Dr Calvin, rising. 'I saw it from the beginning, when the poor robots couldn't speak, to the end, when they stand between mankind and destruction. I will see no more. My life is over. You will see what comes next.'

I never saw Susan Calvin again. She died last month at the age of eighty-two.

THE END